"You have slaves here?" the Dragon asked, his voice a deadly hiss. "Here? Aboard the ship?"

The captain must have sensed the danger, but it seemed as though the atherian's spell of fear was failing as Omara glanced around, realizing just how many men he had left compared to Arro alone. With another nod, he took a second step forward, and this time the entirety of the crew began to press in around the beast.

"Aye," he said with another cruel smile, bringing his scimitar and axe up in preparation. "You should have heard them, as we set sail. Whispering amongst themselves and praying to every god of the world. Apparently you're something of a hero to their kind. Let's see what happens when we—!"

Shlunk.

The Dragon moved so fast, Ykero thought he had blinked and missed it. There was a moment in which the atherian had been standing before the gangplank, still as stone, listening to the captain speak. Then in a blur, he was suddenly in front of Omara, materializing like some great dark shadow in the smoke before the man. No one saw the spear move. No one saw it arc back, then rip around with all the force of a sharpened battering ram.

All they saw was their captain falling to the deck, his body severed in half, cleaved in two from hip to armpit.

There was a space of two heartbeats in which all was silent. The world itself seemed to still, the sounds of the battle echoing over them as though from far, far away. Every eye was on the body of Omara, his chest, arms, and head convulsing as his legs kicked weakly some three feet away. Terror, unlike anything he had ever felt or *thought* he could ever feel, washed over Ykero.

"I'm sorry," Arro said, lowering the spear slowly and bending down over the corpse to tug the sagaris free of Omara's twitching fingers. "I had intended to challenge the man. I'd hoped to end this without more bloodshed."

He hefted the axe experimentally as he stood up again, slashing it through the air as he tested its weight. Apparently satisfied, he brought it to his face, studying the narrow steel head with interest.

"You've made that impossible."

And then the Dragon was moving again, a black blur streaked with silver and gold, and all the world was blood.

"As Iron Falls

Book Four of The Wings of War series
Bryce O'Connor
Copyright © 2018 Bryce O'Connor

ISBN: 978-0-9988106-6-9

Edited by Laura Hughes
Map by Bryce O'Connor
Cover Art by Andreas Zafiratos
Cover Design by Bryce O'Connor & Andreas Zafiratos"

As Iron Falls

Bryce O'Connor

For Laura and David.
To the wonderful life you have led so far,
and to the beautiful one that now extends before you.
On your own, each of you is nothing short of incredible…

…Together, though, you put to shame the magnificence of even the greatest magic.

ACKNOWLEDGMENTS

Never will I start an acknowledgements section of my books without thanking my family first for all they have done. My mother and father, Vince and Isaure, who continue to this day to push and support me, and my sister Sabine, whose pations and interests make me feel like a wimp.

To Nick and Alex, who are recent but wonderful additions to my life. At the time of writing this, Nick is up 11 chess games on me… I swear by Laor that as of the next release, I'll be in the lead.

To Dan and Steph, for all the wonderful influence you have had on my life and writing. STOP RAISING THE BAR OF MY RELATIONSHIP GOALS, DAMMIT!

Once more to my unbelievable cover artist Andreas Zafiratos, who has *yet again* managed to blow the lid on every expectation. See more of his work at www.facebook.com/artofalbinoz or contact him with business inquiries directly at andreaszafeiratos@gmail.com. Yes, the last name is different. Take it up with him, ha!

Again to the myriad of authors and writers who continue to inspired me as a creator, whose worlds I borrow and steal from without hesitation or remorse. Thank you all.

A new influence! To the incredible creators of my recent anime favorites, which are too many to name. Just a few: *Is It Wrong to Pick Up Girls In a Dungeon?, Black Clover, Maid Sama!,* and especially *Toradora!* and *Sword Art Online,*

To my alpha and beta readers, as well as my review team! Without you, NONE of the books I have published thus far would be half as good as they ended up:

Adam Siefertson, Adarsh Venkatesh, His Lordship Jervis Funglehold, Amy Lizette Davalos, Ronni Adams, Her Majesty Ashley Klimek, Bruce L Hevener, Cat Zablocki, Chris G, Colby Stanley, Daniel Crain, Daniel A. Shay, David Lubkin, David Nott, Mr. Derek E. Larson, MMus, Med, Devin Fuoco, Drake Vato, Elise Woodfolk, Emi-Jo Smith, Master Seamen Walsh, Emily-Ann, Emma Ellen Clor, Erin "shammy" Lindstrom, Professor Ethan L. Alderman, Fuchsia Aurelius, H. Skipper, Harley Strutton queen of literature, Jacques Smit, Jennifer, Jeremy Freeman, Jerri-Lee 'Sprinkles' Bickley, Joe Jackson, J Henninger, JoJo, Jonathan Williamson, TuFF GoNG, Lening Gonzalez, Mackenzie King, Ares Wolfe, M.B.Schroeder, Matt Gorsuch, Nicholas Rocan, Noel Townsend, Patrick "biker dude" Anguish, Phoebe Wang, Robert J. Mosentoff, Ruth C. Jones (ruthiejones.com), Simon "Mort" Evans (who is definitely on the team!), Stephanie Letzring, Struan Findlay, Theresina Lloyd, Todd Ponto

If you are interested in joining the beta group and getting early access to the books, reach out to me at: bryce@bryceoconnorbooks.com

And, lastly to a very special group, my Patron on Patreon! Thank you all especially for the feedback and endless support you have provided over the last 6 months. Our dialogue, and your appreciation of the rough work you have received, has been priceless in keeping me moving forward.

To become a Patron, check out my Patreon page at:
https://www.patreon.com/bryceoconnor

- Robert Julian Mosentoff
- Neil Davis
- Cory C
- Daniel Shay
- daniel john gerhart
- Jackie Eqinox
- Devin Fucco
- Kelly Larson
- Ethan Alderman
- Eric Kramer
- Altoids
- Daniel Bacon

One last time, thank you all!

AS IRON FALLS

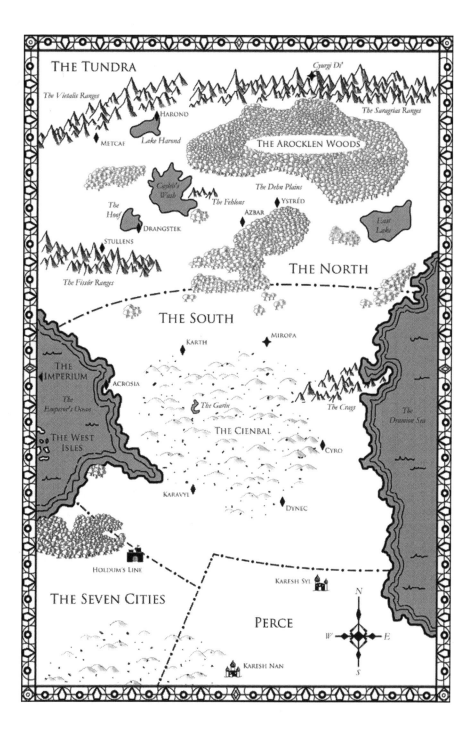

PART I

862 V.S.

PROLOGUE

"There is little to document the rise and fall of the last šef of the Miropan Mahsadën, due in large part to the brevity of his reign. Spanning hardly the breadth of two years, I have had a troublesome time producing credible records of his period presiding over the most vicious and secretive underworld society the South has ever suffered. Outside of what one might traditionally deem 'credible,' however, there is plenty to be learned. Compiling rumors and tales, drawing out of everything from the tattered journals of the Mahsadën's lesser officers to stories passed down as fables through generations, I have managed to come to several conclusions. Foremost among these: this last bastion of darkness ruled by more than the standard fare of respect and fear with which every šef before him had governed the society. Every recounting and myth I can dredge up from that time speaks of something greater within him, some dark power which he used to hold fast the chains of his lessers in a fist wreathed in white flames."

—*As Death Rose from the Ashes*, by Kohly Grofh

The man's hands trembled slightly as he clung to the fragile parchment of the letter, doing his best to clear his mind long enough to take in the words scrawled in hasty lines across the page. He wondered briefly if the paired couriers before him, kneeling to either side below at the base of the raised dais upon which his throne sat, could sense his trepidation. He doubted it. For one, their heads were bowed, half out of respect and half out of fear.

For another, enough deception had been sown into the ranks of the Mahsadën already to ensure the men were like to interpret his shaking as something altogether more wrathful.

"What is it, my love? What news has been brought to you?"

The voice, gentle as silk fluttering in a desert wind, dug into the man's ear like a nail. He did not jump—as he had done for the first few months the woman had sat in the smaller seat to his right—but he couldn't help himself from tensing or his fingers from twitching the slightest bit away when a slim hand reached out to settle on his wrist, the figure beside him leaning closer to read the letter as well.

"News from the North," the man said in a strong voice that had taken a long time to steady—it would never do for his subordinates to find more weakness in him than his crippled form already proved, after all. He handed the letter to the woman as she reached for it, then let his grey eyes settle on the two couriers once again. "You may go."

The men dipped their heads reverently, then scurried away like rats outrunning a flood. He couldn't blame them. He'd dismissed them deliberately, knowing the contents of the letter would not please the woman at his elbow.

And her anger was always a terrible thing to behold.

Indeed, even as he thought this, the man felt an unpleasant heat begin to radiate from his right, thickening the already dusk-choked air and chasing away what little coolness the throne room provided. It was early summer, and the cruel gaze of the Sun had begun its ravaging of the South, searing eyes and any flesh that dared expose itself to its hunger. The room, once the receiving hall of a former šef by the name of Imaneal Evony, had been designed to thwart—or at least minimize—this oppressive hotness of the summer days. Thin, spiraling columns held up a high, ribbed ceiling that trapped the rising air and funneled it through hatches in the top of each vaulting. Arched windows made up a majority of the walls on every side, their blue-green silk curtains pulled away now to coax in what little breeze made it through the streets of Miropa and the bustle of the main square outside. The floor was fashioned of white quartz, streaked with greys and blacks, and did not sting the bare soles of the feet as one made their way across it.

And yet, despite these measures taken, the heat continued to rise until the man could feel the sear of it on his cheek, radiating as the woman's wrath built up with every line read of the letter clutched now in her delicate hands.

"Months," she finally hissed. "*Months* I wait for the freeze to end and the paths to clear, and *this* is all the news I receive?"

"We know where he is," the man said evenly, not looking at her. "A temple in the mountains, north of the great forest. Secluded like that, he won't be able to—"

"I don't give a *damn* where he *is*, fool!" The woman cut him off with a snap, altogether abandoning the pretense of the calm lover she'd portrayed in front of the couriers. "I care about where he's *been*, what he's been *doing*. Your cousin's story grows with every passing moment, and with it the unrest in my city. Almost a year since he made a fool of you and your šef before fleeing, and more than half that since he made a fool of every man we sent to Azbar. And now *this*." There was the crunch of paper, and he could imagine her clutching at the edges of the parchment.

"In single combat, as well," the man said in a musing tone, careful to hide his underhanded delight. "It's my understanding this 'Kayle' must have been something of a formidable opponent, too…"

It was his little rebellion, his only outlet to shift even the slightest bit out from under the claws of the woman. Being the puppet of her uprising had its uses. In a way, he was untouchable, free of the threat her anger posed to so many of the lesser men within the Mahsadën.

At least for the moment.

"Look at me, Adrion."

A shiver ran down his spine at the words, and it was a moment before he could obey. Slowly, like a man attempting to delay his fate, Adrion Blaeth turned, his eyes finally meeting the lightning-blue irises of the woman beside him. She was a beautiful creature, as he'd always thought her. Her hair, which he suspected had once been a pure blonde some time ago, had been bleached to near-white after years in the Sun. Her smooth skin, still several shades lighter than the darker complexion of a true Southerner, seemed to glow like gold in the relative shade of the chamber. Even the curious scar, radiating out from her right eye in perpendicular lines to create a perfect X-shape across her face, did little to mar her comeliness, and there had been a time Adrion had felt equal parts pleasure and lust when he looked into those thunderous eyes.

Now, all he felt was nausea and a strange, quavering cold.

"Play your games while you can," the woman whispered in a deadly murmur, bringing a hand up to stroke his cheek as something like a smile teased her lips. "Enjoy what freedoms you are allowed. But consider, on the day you serve me no purpose, what things I might learn from *your* corpse when the time arises."

There was a crackle and a flash, and Adrion barely kept himself from crying out as pain seared up the left side of his face, making him jerk away. When he felt his cheek, of course, there was nothing, no visible mark, and the pain vanished in an instant, winking out without leaving so much as a hint of its passing. Still, his fingers rubbed at the place hers had lingered over, his mind convinced he could feel the tingle of magic still palpable on his skin.

"We know where he is," Adrion repeated angrily, not looking away from the blue eyes that continued to bore into his. "Whatever else, *that* carries value. The North is a great realm, with what cities it has left scattered across its forests and mountains. It took us this long to find him, though, which means you have to act quickly. If word gets out that we know... How long do you think it would take us to hunt him down again?"

That gave the woman pause, the heartless smile shifting slowly into a frown of annoyance as she heard the wisdom in his words this time.

"Too long," she admitted, straightening and tilting her head back against the throne behind her, fingers stroking at her neck pensively as she thought. "He can't be allowed to disappear again. We have trouble enough as it is without the common rabble hearing that he managed to slip through our fingers *again*."

Adrion sat in silence, knowing better than to say anything more even though he thought he could guess what the woman would do long before she made the choice herself. In that way he was much like their former master. Ergoin Sass had always been the even-headed one, the šef of sharpest wit and quickest thought, apart from perhaps Imaneal Evony himself. Adrion had learned much in his years of servitude to the man, and it was amusing to see that his fellow apprentice had not absorbed that keenness despite the pair's apparent closeness.

The skills she'd learned in its place, on the other hand, certainly had their uses...

3

Here we go, Adrion thought, seeing the woman settle on a decision, her eyes returning to the present before looking once more to the ground. Putting an elbow on the arm of her seat, she rested her cheek against her fist.

"Na'zeem."

She spoke the name quietly, like the one she wished to summon were standing over her shoulder, waiting for her call. Instead, there was a shift in what little shadows survived the beating of the Sun through the windows, and a figure stepped out from behind the back right-most pillar of the hall. Adrion tensed once more, as he always did when the man appeared, unsettled by the unnatural stillness of his form within the plain tunic that hung loose over his body. Pale grey eyes gleamed in the space between the maroon turban wrapped about his head and the black veil that cut across his face, hiding his nose and mouth from view. One hand hung at his side, the other wrapped expectantly around the well-worn leather grip of the saber sheathed across his lower back. He said nothing, nor did he so much as glance at Adrion. His eyes were fixed on the woman, dutifully awaiting her command.

"Approach," she said after a moment, and it seemed no more than an instant before the man stood at their feet, his clothes settling around him quietly as she held out the letter. "Read it."

Accepting the parchment carefully, Na'zeem did as he was told with dutiful efficiency. Adrion watched the man's eyes skim the contents once, then again, seeing what might have been the slightest presence of surprise in the subtle shift of his brow.

"'The High Citadel'," Na'zeem spoke at last. His voice was as soft as his master's as he handed the page back to her, if made heavy by the accents of the lower fringe cities across the Cienbal. "I do not know this place."

Beside him, Adrion felt the woman shift in what could only be excitement.

"But *I* do," she said smoothly. "Very well, in fact. Summon your shadows. You are about to depart on the greatest hunt of your lives."

Adrion—who had turned in disbelief at her words—did not see the shift in Na'zeem's eyes, the thrill bordering on bloodlust. A moment later, the man was gone, stepping away and vanishing behind his pillar once more.

"You know the place?" Adrion asked once he was gone.

For a long time the woman said nothing, the little finger of the hand she leaned into tracing the line of the scar that ran down across her cheek. After several seconds, she finally lifted her head, bringing the hand up before her and spreading it, as if presenting some gift to an invisible visitor.

There was a flash of light, and the now-familiar flames, white as the carved ivory sold as trinkets in the markets, bloomed to life within the cage of her digits. It flickered, exuding a cheerful glow that so harshly contradicted the violent nature of the magic the woman had ripped from the corpse of the woman she had once so efficiently pretended to care for. Adrion watched it apprehensively, nervous in its presence, hating the memories he held of the sorcery. He had nightmares, sometimes, of the screams of the men that fire had consumed before his very eyes. Failed soldiers, captured spies, often even just unfortunate messengers. It was a savage thing, hunger and rage made pure, and it devoured so cruelly and efficiently that no other soul except Na'zeem and his contingent—men the woman had taken under her wing directly and trained in the same arts Sass had so efficiently instilled in her— had ever witnessed it and lived to speak of the event.

As a result, it was Adrion, in the mind of his men and lessers, who so wickedly wielded the powers of a demon.

"The High Citadel," the woman answered finally, speaking so quietly he had to strain a little to hear. "Cyurgi 'Di. Yes… I know it."

"How?" Adrion pressed, still watching the flames in her hands. At his words he saw the woman's arm spasm, and the fire sparked and grew, encircling her fingers in a layer of flickering white tongues.

"It is the place I gained and lost everything," she snarled. "The place that gave, then took away."

Her hand was trembling now, and Adrion finally managed to tear his eyes from the magic to study her face once more. Her eyes were set, hard as stone and wide with fury, on the fire curling about her fingers. Adrion saw hate in that gaze, as clear and vivid as the hate he sometimes saw in the more willful of the men and women the Mahsadën had thrown into the Cages. It was visceral, born of a grudge the depth of which he didn't think he could ever fathom.

Then the woman's expression cooled, suddenly replaced by something like satisfaction. With a jerk she closed the fingers of her hand, extinguishing the sorcery with a sizzling *crack*.

"The High Citadel," Lazura cooed, smirking ever so subtly at the trailing sparks of arcane light that fell and faded about her lap. "Your cousin could not have picked a more appropriate place to die, Adrion."

I

"It is the naïve conscience that considers terror a product only of the material world. If you are of such a mind, take pause and consider this: if terror thrives in the plane of man, by what word would you thus describe the twisted product of said horrors after their corruption by the cruelest enemy of a fragile imagination: one's own mind?"

—*Dreamer's Dictation,* author unknown

Syrah awoke to the distant sound of children screaming.

The cries pulled her mercifully from the throes of a fitful night, lifting her upward out of the darkness and fear that had plagued her sleep. Images lingered above her, flickering against the faintest details she could make out of the stone ceiling above her bed. Cruel, bearded faces, made hungrier and uglier every time they visited her, their voices seeming to echo off the walls of her small room.

Instinctively, she reached out, her hand scrabbling at the side of the bed, seeking the comforting coolness of familiar skin.

Nothing.

Of course there was nothing. He had told her he would be gone before she woke, and it had been some time since Syrah had last suffered the night terrors. Almost three weeks, in fact. Three weeks of freedom from being dragged back to the confines of that small tent, the intricate details of the space reincarnated by memory with terrifying accuracy to paint her nightmares. It had been so long that Syrah had started to hope she might be free of the pestilence upon her sleep.

Now, though, that glimmer of optimism guttered and died. The nightmares had returned, and the strange face that always chased them away wasn't there, looming above her, outlined in the dark.

Abruptly Syrah realized her cheeks were wet, and she quickly reached up to wipe them clean with both hands. As she did, her fingertips moved over the divot of the scar that cut down through her right eye, bare to the chill air of the room, and she snatched them away with a gasp. Rolling onto her side, she felt about in the limited light cast by the outline of the door in the far wall, searching until she found the cloth folded in a neat pile on the crude table beside her bed.

Pushing herself up to sit on her heels atop the feather-stuffed mattress, Syrah quickly looped the black wrappings about her head with familiar ease, pulling them snug over her face. This done, she let her hands fall, sighing in relief.

Tomorrow, she promised herself, as she had every morning for the last six months. *Tomorrow, I won't be frightened of my own face.*

That hope, she still held firm upon.

Just then, more shouting rang faintly through the door to her room, and Syrah recalled what it was that had pulled her into wakefulness in the first place. The continued cries of the little ones rang distantly, their squeals and screams cutting dully through the dark. Echoing them, muffled but all-too-familiar, came the roars and bellows of what most anyone else would have assumed was some terrible beast let loose within the halls of the Citadel.

Syrah, though, only smiled, the sounds of that "beast" chasing away what shivers her nightmares had left her with.

Kicking away the furs tangled about her feet, Syrah swept her legs off the bed and stood before moving over to the massive wardrobe that took up almost the entirety of the room's north wall. Throwing it open, she took a moment to appreciate the solemn emptiness of the thing, the distinct vacuum left by the absent spaces along the shelves and pegs where steel and leather had hung almost untouched for months, until that morning. Now, all that was left to fill the vastness of the closet was a cloth shirt, some sewn leather britches, her boots, gloves, and a simple hooded traveling cloak.

After she'd pulled these out and setting them on the bed, Syrah couldn't bare the true hollowness of the wardrobe and everything it meant, closing it behind her.

She dressed rapidly, ensuring the cloak was snug about her shoulders before making for the door. As she opened it, she again paused to look back, taking in the chamber that had been her home for more years than she could properly remember. She looked about the space, marveling at how small it seemed in comparison to what lay ahead of her, and how she couldn't decide what she wanted more: to shut the door behind her, or to throw herself back into the fur blankets of the bed that had been hers since she'd been no more than six summers old.

In the end, she stepped across the threshold and pulled the latch shut, wondering if she would ever set foot in that room again.

Pale light, cast by the kicking flames of dozens of blue and white candles nestled about the base of the wall and in little recesses scooped right out of the stone, flickered around her as Syrah began to make her way north up the hall. The well-worn soles of her boots made little sound as she moved, and her shadows were faint as they danced and jumped about her. It was warm, despite the fact that summer had only barely reached Cyurgi 'Di, kept humid and comfortable by the great furnaces that channeled fresh air through copper pipes built into the great temple's very walls. Before long Syrah began to feel herself sweat as she grew hot beneath her layers, and it was with some relief that she turned down the main outer corridor of the Citadel and saw a familiar form slumped in a chair not far down the hall. As she neared, the figure stirred, drawn from his light sleep by the sound of her approach.

"Oh. Syrah." Dolt Avonair, the Citadel's head gatekeeper, spoke in a tired voice, blinking away the drowsiness and pushing himself to his feet with the grunt of an aging man as he peered at her. "Is it that time already?"

"It is." Syrah gave him a sad smile. "You'll be missed something awful, Dolt."

Before the man could answer, there was another beastly roar from outside, only barely muffled by the heavy timber door kept shut tight against the early-summer chill, and Dolt shivered visibly. The howl and squeal of children that followed seem to do nothing to appease him.

"Are… Are you sure about this?" he asked her in a sudden whisper, his eyes wide. "There's talk, you know. Many among the faith—"

"Aren't pleased that I'm leaving," Syrah finished for him in a huff, rolling her good eye and crossing her arms. "Believe me, I'm aware. I've spent most of the last month avoiding people trying to convince me to stay."

"It's not that you're leaving." Dolt was almost pleading now, something like real fear seeping into his watery eyes. "It's that you're leaving with *him*. Are you sure this is what—?"

His words were choked off as Syrah reached up, pulling the gatekeeper into a firm hug. After a moment of surprised hesitation, he returned the embrace.

"He's a good man," Syrah said quietly as they stood there, sharing a last goodbye. "Don't worry your head off over me. He's a good man."

Dolt didn't reply. Eventually, though, Syrah felt him nod, and she broke away from him. The Priest held her gaze a moment longer, as though looking for a final confirmation. When all she gave him was the same smile, he sighed, then moved to take the great iron handle of the gate with both hands. There was a groan of metal and wood, and the door crept open slowly. When it was just wide enough for her to slip through, Dolt stopped and looked back at her.

"Stay safe," he told her gently. "For Talo's sake, if no one else's."

Syrah squeezed his arm in promise, then stepped through the gate.

The outside world greeted her with one of the most glorious mornings she could recall. Shading her face against the gleam of the sun that had just started to peek over the walls of the Citadel before her, it was several seconds before her sensitive eye adjusted to the brightness of the cloudless day. A brief wind, cleverly sneaking its way over the ramparts that surrounded the inner courtyard before her, teased at her cheeks, pulling locks of her white hair loose to play in the breeze. She tucked them quickly behind her ears, making a mental note to braid her hair before starting the descent later.

Then she caught sight of the scene before her, and all other thoughts whirled away.

To her left, standing and sitting about the bottom of the short flight of stairs that led down to the cobbled floor of the courtyard, a group of men and women in the white robes of the faith were waiting, some in the shade, some with hoods pulled back and faces upturned to take in the sunlight. Syrah's stomach gave a nervous twitch as she looked down on the backs of the council members, particularly when she saw the black stripe running down the hood and spine of one of the robes. It had been months since the tragedy of Gûlraht Baoill's attack on the Citadel, but some among the faith had never forgotten the role she'd played in the battle, both in its victories and its losses.

Syrah herself least among them…

As several members of the council turned to look at her, noting the sound of the gate opening, Syrah shifted her attention to the second group taking up the courtyard. This, by far, was the odder of the two gatherings. Mountain men all, as varied in their markings, garmets, and sizes as they were by tribe. At a glance she saw examples of nearly every clan among their dozen or so. The scarred faces of the Kregoan, the painted cheeks of the Amreht, the animal skulls of the Gähs. The eastern tribes who called the Saragrias Ranges their home were also present, and there was even a single representative of the Sigûrth, an old man, only just starting to twist with age, his silver-white hair and beard braided and decorated with iron and steel baubles and carved wooden rings.

As though sensing her gaze, the tribesman turned to look at her, and Syrah frowned as the somber blue eyes of Rako the Calm met her pale pink one. There was a moment of tension, then the Sigûrth inclined his head respectfully. Stiffly, Syrah did the same, then turned her attention to the last of the wild men, sitting on a stone bench at their head. When this figure looked her way she smiled, seeing it returned at once.

Carro al'Dor was a much different man than the one she had known for most of her life. Not a year ago he'd been a respected member of the faith, a leader amongst the Laorin, even seated at the council he now stood separate from. With the fall of the Kayle, however, many things had changed. His face was content but weathered, the distinct scar of his Breaking transecting it in perfect diagonal lines from around his right eye. He'd always had the braided and beaded hair of his Sigûrth heritage, but instead of the white robes of a Priest, Carro now sat bedecked in leathers and furs. Similarly, where once his great hands had held firm to the patterned steel of a Priest's staff, they were now wrapped about a curious wooden stave, solid in its build and beautiful in its craftsmanship. Carvings crowned its upper quarter, depicting peaceful, pensive faces of a number of bearded, bright-eyed men.

It was an antithetical representation of the Stone Gods—the brutal deities of the mountain men—Syrah hoped to see much more often in the future.

As she watched him, Carro's eyes abruptly grew wide, and he opened his mouth as though to shout a warning. Before he could say anything, however, Syrah noted the clambering of a dozen little feet, and she turned just in time to witness no less than six or seven small, squealing forms rushing up the stairs at her. She'd been so distracted by the presence of the council and Carro's mountain men that she hadn't yet looked to the last group taking up space in the courtyard. She would pay for her lack of awareness for several days after as the children collided with her, screaming happily and laughing as they knocked her back, landing her on her rump on the hardened stone of the top step behind her.

Syrah hardly noticed. Instantly she was laughing and shouting along with the children, tickling the smallest and wrestling the bigger ones off one after the other. For several seconds they played, ignoring the cold ground beneath them in the warmth of the sunny day, enjoying the freedom summer had delivered.

Then their frolicking was interrupted by a deafening roar that seemed almost to make the air itself shiver.

"AHA! BREAKFAST IS *SERVED!*"

At once the children scattered, darting off in every direction as they shrieked with delight, running away from the great shadow that had risen to loom over them at the words. When they were all gone, dashing to be far clear of the man who'd come up behind them, Syrah finally managed to right herself, sitting on the edge of the step to look up into the strange face she had missed that morning.

No one in their right mind would have the gall to call Raz i'Syul Arro ugly, whether to his face or otherwise. For one thing, most of the world knew him by a reputation that lent itself to fear any variety of terrible retributions for such a slight. For another—at least in Syrah's opinion—there was a unique beauty to the atherian, a sort of awe-inspiring wonder one might witness in the lithe form of a mountain lion, or in the dangerous geometries of a viper's curves. At over seven feet tall, the Dragon of the North towered above nearly any other man, including the several lumbering Kregoan standing behind Carro along the far wall of the courtyard. His eyes shone above a serpentine snout, their vertical pupils bisecting an amber that was the color of a sunrise made liquid. His scaled skin was dark almost to the point of black, hinting at a sheen of green where the light hit it just right. His spined ears were webbed, their membranes a reddish gold and lined with the faint outline of threaded veins. This was even more noticeable in the great wings he had half-folded against his back, the delicate skin between the more prominent arching bones frayed along their edges, giving them the impression of worn sails in a slow wind. He stood on the balls of his feet, his clawed toes *clacking* against the stone as he took two steps up the stairs, his heavy tail snaking along behind him as he came to a stop in front of Syrah.

Smiling down at her—or giving her the twisted baring of his fangs that the Priestess had long since learned to be a smile—he reached out a clawed hand for her to take.

"Up and at 'em," the Dragon said with a chuckle and a wink. "We don't have all day for you to sit around staring."

Syrah laughed, taking his hand gratefully. As soon as they touched she felt herself relax, like the warmth of a fire had filled a cold room she'd been standing in. It was that touch she had sought out as she'd woken from her night terrors. That cool, sharp softness, like silk sliding over the edge of a blade. She allowed Raz to pull her onto her feet, where she stood two steps above him and yet still not quite eye to eye. He gave her another grin, and made to let go of her hand and turn away, but she wouldn't let him. When he glanced back at her, examining her face quizzically, she answered with a small grimace.

"Just… Just a second," she said, squeezing his fingers. Raz's expression grew concerned, and he turned back to look at her fully.

"Nightmares?" he asked so that only she could hear. Syrah gave a quick nod, and in response she felt his long, strong fingers tighten around her more delicate ones. He didn't say anything, but the motion spoke volumes.

I won't let you go, it said, and it was all she needed to know.

Still holding his hand, Syrah pushed herself up onto her tiptoes, leaned in, and gave him a quick kiss on the cheek before the atherian could stop her. Then she stepped around him, chuckling herself as she patted him affectionately on the chest.

"Time to get going. We don't have all day for you to stand around staring."

If Raz had been capable of blushing, he was quite certain that would have been the moment his face might have turned the same color as his ears. As it was, he wasn't so sure he was incapable of succumbing to death-by-embarrassment, so he allowed several seconds to compose himself before turning and following down Syrah to the base of the stairs. Waiting there already—and not a few among them watching him with mixed expressions ranging from amused to awkward to outright revolted—the Citadel council waited. As those who'd been sitting got to their feet, so too did Carro and his mountain men make their approach. The children—whom Raz had passed the last half-hour with after his morning exercises, chasing them around the courtyard to their great delight—lingered behind the adults, torn between wanting to continue playing and understanding that something beyond their youthful comprehension seemed to be taking place. Motioning one of the eldest over, Raz knelt down to get eye to eye with the little girl as she scampered closer, or as close to it as their discrepancy in height would allow.

"Ema, take the others and go play with the horses," he told her quietly, indicating the far side of the courtyard where a massive black stallion and a slighter, beige-colored mare stood loose by the tunnel that led through the outer wall. "Mind Gale's hooves. Don't want any of you losing a foot, do we?"

Ema giggled and shook her head, then turned and ran back to gather her friends. Standing up again, Raz watched the children—all dressed in the plain rough garbs of Laorin acolytes—hurry over to the mounts, reaching up with little hands to stroke the smooth sheen of their hair. The mare took a few moments to adjust to the sudden attention, having arrived at the Citadel not more than a few days prior at Carro's summoning. Gale, on the other hand, dipped his great black head down at once, offering the ridge of his nose for petting. Both horses were tacked and bagged, the thick cloth traveling sacks hanging off either side of their saddles already heavy with provisions, blankets, and spare clothes. In addition, the hilt of Raz's gladius jutted skyward from where its scabbard had been strapped to Gale's left shoulder, and the leather bag that covered Ahna's wicked twin tips could be seen protruding from where the dviassegai had been lashed to his right side. Similarly, Syrah's steel staff, the defining symbol of her Priesthood among the Laorin, hung off the side of the mare, within easy reach.

Neither of them was fool enough to expect an untroubled journey out of the faith's lands.

"…horses are stocked with three weeks' supplies. It should be enough to get you both through the Arocklen and beyond the Dehn, but we can have more brought up from the larders if you think it prudent."

Syrah had already started to say her farewells, and Raz turned his attention back to the men and women before him, gathered in a half-circle around the Priestess.

"No, no that's quite all right," Syrah was replying to a slight, bespectacled man when Raz moved to stand over her shoulder. "The temple's reserves are strained enough as it is, given the extra mouths we had to feed this freeze. I'm sure the Woods will provide, should Raz and I find ourselves short."

Jofrey al'Sen nodded sagely, causing the black strip of cloth sewn along the top and back of his hooded robes to shift. The High Priest of Cyurgi 'Di was a smaller man in comparison to many Northerners, but there was a quiet confidence about him Raz had always found intriguing. Skilled in diplomacy and the arcane arts granted to his faith by their god, Laor, Jofrey had come into power suddenly the year before upon the unexpected death of his predecessor. Despite this, he'd risen well to the demands of the position, and Raz had found his respect for the man steadily solidifying over the duration of the winter.

"If you're sure," the High Priest said to Syrah before glancing up at Raz with a twinkle in his eye. "Given I've known your companion to consume more on any given day than a small family, though, I'd say the possibility of that is high."

Raz snorted, and Syrah bounced back into him affectionately. "If that's the case, then he can go hunt his own dinner every night," she said with a sly smile, looking back at him.

"Sounds like fun," Raz said with a shrug.

Jofrey nodded, his eyes not leaving Raz's. "I know I've said it before, Master Arro, but I hope you understand *why* I must ask you to leave our mountains. We will always be grateful for what you did for this Citadel, but the sort of life you live—"

"And as *I've* said before," Raz interrupted him gruffly, raising a hand to stop the man, "I *do* understand. There's no need to rehash the facts, Jofrey. Cyurgi 'Di cannot be seen to harbor a killer. It's as simple as that."

From behind the High Priest, Raz heard the quiet mutter of someone whispering "You mean *murderer*, lizard," and he raised his eyes to meet the defiant glares of old Valaria Petrük and her favorite lackey, Behn Argo.

If Jofrey heard the murmured insults, he chose to ignore them. Instead, the old man nodded. "Your understanding is appreciated. On a related note, however," he turned his gaze on Syrah again, "we received a bird from Ystréd yesterday evening. Tana Atler wanted me to tell you that her temple's doors are open to you both, and she will be happy to accommodate you until such time as you find other lodgings."

Raz and Syrah glanced at each other. Ystréd had indeed been their first intended destination, at least for the time being, though they'd planned on camping outside the city walls while Syrah took trips into the town to gather news while they formed their plans. The temple in Ystréd was a smaller one, particularly in comparison to the Citadel, but the faith had a significant enough presence across the North as a whole to make anyone think twice about approaching them while under Laor's protection. Raz didn't see too much harm in accepting the offer of shelter, particularly if it meant a true bed for Syrah to sleep in, rather than the grass under whatever tree they could find…

Eventually Raz shrugged, then nodded, and the Priestess did the same as they silently agreed.

"We would be pleased to take the High Priestess up on her offer," Syrah told Jofrey, facing him again. "If you have a chance to respond, please extend our gratitude to her."

"I'll make sure to do that," Jofrey agreed. "In return, I hope you'll find the time to send us a bird when you reach the city. It will do us all good to know that you arrived safe." He looked at Raz again. "Both of you."

"We will," Raz promised him simply, and Jofrey seemed to take that to heart, because he smiled before glancing over at the man who'd come to stand by his side while they spoke.

It had taken Raz some time to warm up to Carro al'Dor when they'd first met, nearly a year past now. The former Priest had been rigid, in Raz's opinion, too set in his ways and unable to compromise. However, after weeks spent on the road together as they'd set off for Cyurgi 'Di in the company of the Citadel's former High Priest, Talo Brahnt, Raz had developed an altogether different opinion of the man. He was fair, strong of will and heart, and had made the greatest sacrifice a faithful of the cloth could offer in order to save his people. As a result, he'd lost much, his Priesthood being the least of those things, and the scar that marked that loss was one he would bear across his face forever.

But with a price paid often comes something in exchange, and in the absence of magic and the companionship of the Laorin, Carro had gained much in return. The mountain men called him "the Peacekeeper," because in the span of a few short weeks Carro al'Dor had managed to disband the great army of their former Kayle, returning to the clans the freedoms they'd lost under the boot of Gûlraht Baoill. In doing so he had garnered the respect—and even the love—of many among their ranks. The dozen that stood behind him were only the closest handful of nearly five thousand warriors of various tribes who had elected to stay with the man they saw as their new Kayle, a more just and compassionate ruler than any they had known in their time. Even the old Sigûrth, Rako, seemed more than simply subservient to Carro now. The most level-headed of all Baoill's former generals, Rako had sought to lend his knowledge to the Peacekeeper after the battle that had claimed the former Kayle's life, as well as those of dozens of Priests and Priestesses of the faith. He'd proven himself indispensable in the end, even loyal, and though they had never been able to bring themselves to *like* the Sigûrth, Raz and Syrah had eventually come to respect him.

He had, after all, been integral in placing a great man in a position of immense power.

"Syrah," Carro said affectionately, stepping forward and spreading his arms wide to grip the Priestess in a bear-like hug. "I will miss you dearly, child."

"And I you, old man," Syrah said in a hushed tone, and Raz heard true sadness in her voice. "Stay safe, will you?"

"I think those were meant to be *my* words," Carro said with a smirk, pulling away and holding the woman at arm's length so he could take her in. "Ystréd first, it sounds like?" He glanced up at Raz. "Do you have a plan after that?"

"No." Raz shook his head. "No plan, and it's for the best. The Mahsadën undoubtedly still want me dead, and we both know there are still factions among your tribes that yet favor Gûlraht Baoill's vision of the North.'" He uncrossed his arms to put a clawed hand on Syrah's slim shoulder. "No plan means no one can guess where we are, or at least where we're going."

Carro nodded in understanding, letting go of Syrah before looking over his shoulder and nodding to a Gähs warrior who was waiting there expectantly.

"No plan is the best plan," Carro summarized as the mountain man ducked back between his companions, then reappeared holding what looked to be several layers of heavy pelts. "I see. If that's the case—" he motioned the man forward, and the Gähs stepped up to Syrah at once "—let us assume you may well end up in less friendly climates."

Carro reached out with his free hand to peel back the topmost furs and reveal what lay beneath. There, folded neatly over itself, was a mantle out of what seemed almost another life to Raz. A clean, pure white, it had been cut and crafted from what looked to be thin, breathable silk. Even folded as it was it shimmered in the faint breeze of the summer morning, and for a moment Raz was taken back to the ripples of the Garin, the desert lake around which he and his family had spent his childhood summers in calm comfort. The desert shined in that silk, somehow, as though the Sun above saw fit to reflect the best and worst memories of Raz's life back at him from the fabric.

"Carro…" Raz began, stepping around Syrah and lifting a hand slowly, hesitantly, to run a hand over the mantle's layers. He had no other words, however, as he felt the familiar texture settle between his fingers, like wind made tangible.

"You recognize it?" Carro asked him, watching his face.

Raz nodded, looking back at Syrah. "It's the mantle I gave to you, the day we first met." As Syrah's eyes widened, he turned back to Carro. "Where in the Sun's name did you get it?"

"Talo kept it," Carro told him, looking at the silk almost fondly. "Jofrey and I found it while cleaning out the High Priest's quarters." He indicated the man standing just behind him with a nudging elbow.

Jofrey inclined his head in agreement. "We thought you should have it back. I'm sorry our laws prevent us from replacing your lost weaponry, but we hoped this would be some small recompense of our gratitude."

For the first time in several months, Raz felt the absence of a familiar weight on his hip. The war-axe that had once nestled there, looped into his belt, was the most inconsequential of the losses suffered that day, the day Gûlraht Baoill came knocking on the very doors of the Citadel. Still, it had taken its small toll on Raz after the battle was done. The weapon—like all his gear—had been crafted by Allihmad Jerr, the South's premier blacksmith, and one of less than a handful of friends he'd left behind upon fleeing the fringe cities. Its absence was something of a dark realization every time he thought about it, like a hole in the few good memories he had.

The silk in his hands, however, was a gift of an altogether different caliber. It had been commissioned specially for him by his family when he'd grown too large for any of the capes or cloaks the other men could pass down to him. It would be somewhat short on him now, he knew, but Raz didn't care. He'd just been handed back a piece of his old life. It was a small thing, an article he had taken for granted when he'd lived among the Arros as a thing of necessity against the cruel gaze of the Sun.

Now, though, vivid as the men standing before him, he recalled his father handing him the mantle, making a joke about its cost and how Raz had better stop growing before his food and clothing ran the clan's coffers dry.

"Thank you," he managed to get out, carefully lifting the cloth from the furs with both hands. "This… this means much to me. Thank you both."

Jofrey smiled and nodded, but Carro glanced over at Syrah. "There's something here for you as well."

Syrah, who'd been staring at the white silks as Raz held them almost reverently in his hands, blinked and looked around. Raz, too, lifted his head at the old man's words, and almost laughed at what he saw.

There, revealed now that he'd removed his own gift from atop them, were several more distinctive articles of clothing. Raz recognized them at once, noting first the paired gloves of thin, pliable leather bleached white, then the ivory robes they were folded atop, woven of silk. They were the very garments Syrah had been wearing when he'd first laid eyes on her, and he'd thought her mad for it. Whatever loon was fool enough to wear leather and full-length robes during the hottest time of year in the South had to be insane, after all.

Glancing at the woman now, though, he relived his folly all over again. Her pale, ghostly skin echoed the snows of the Northern lands he had come to love so much. Her hair, loose over the black wrappings that covered her missing right eye, was whiter than bone, and her good eye, pale and pink, had a sharpness to it that spoke volumes of the depth of the mind beneath.

Albinos never made it past infancy beneath the devouring light of the Southern Sun. He hadn't even considered it an option as he'd strolled past what he could only assume was a madwoman in the busy market streets of Karth.

"Talo kept these, too?" Syrah groaned, stepping forward and lifting one of the gloves up with distinct displeasure.

Clearly her gift wasn't having the same sort of impact on her as Raz's had.

"He did," Carro chuckled, "and he repaired them. Whatever else you might think, they could come in useful."

"Not likely," Syrah grumbled, pulling the glove onto her right hand and flexing her fingers. It still fit. "The robes just tore when I was taken. I lost the shawl and veil completely.

The grin that passed between Carro and Jofrey then was so mischievous, one might have thought the two of them were nothing more than a pair of misbehaving children. At once, Raz had a suspicion of what was about to happen. Slowly, like a magician pulling a cloth out of some hidden pocket of his coat, Jofrey drew what looked like a length of yet more ivory silk from the folds of his sleeve, holding it up for her to see.

"Is that so?" he asked through a half-suppressed laugh.

It was a new shawl, dangling alongside what looked to be a thin, breathable white veil.

Syrah's audible curse drew laughs from the entire crowd, this time.

Raz felt strange, stopping and turning one last time with Syrah to wave back at the mouth of the tunnel that was Cyurgi 'Di's outermost entrance. They stood, side-by-side between their horses, in the center of the wide plateau that acted as a sort of outer courtyard for the Citadel, a flattened space that hugged the mountain cliffs on one side and fell off into oblivion on the other. Looking back, Raz felt what could only be described as ironic disappointment overwhelm him, the sort of conflicted sadness that comes when one is leaving behind something they found themselves distinctly surprised to have enjoyed.

He recalled the first time he had laid eyes on the lumbering outline of the bastions that flanked the outer entrance, black-and-grey monoliths looming like living giants out of the endless snow of the winter storms. Raz had, in that moment, understood for the first time in his life the absolute truth of his insignificance in the greater existence that was the larger world. He'd felt small, powerless, even afraid. The stone had exuded a callous coldness to him, a lifeless quality he had feared, like the scaled skin of some dead titan fallen across the mountain's face.

And yet now, taking in the outlines of the walls against the crisp blue of the cloudless summer morning, Raz could feel only the sudden absence of the Citadel's warmth around him. It had taken him some weeks to forgo his distaste of enclosed spaces—particularly when said spaces were often half-a-mile below anywhere that saw the Sun—but in time he'd discovered himself coming to terms with, then even appreciating, the closeness of the stone around him, the kind heat of the tunnels and fresh breeze of the narrow windows.

Eventually, the place had started to feel almost like a home…

The others had followed them out, gathering around the mouth of the tunnel and raising their hands to return Raz and Syrah's final goodbye. Jofrey stood close to Carro, their respective entourages on either side of them, the ranks of which had swollen significantly in the last quarter-hour. Raz brought his hand down over his eyes to peer against the Sun's light, seeing some hundred other figures crowding the entranceway, many with their hands in the air, others watching them go with tight lips and narrowed eyes. There was the sound of laughter, and Raz looked up to the ramparts high above, seeing the children of the temple clambering onto the crenellations to wave. He smiled, chuckling as he returned the gesture.

He was just about to turn around again when Syrah inhaled sharply from beside him.

Raz looked at her, only to find the woman staring at something along the very edge of the large group standing outside the Citadel walls. He followed her eyes, and it only took him a moment to find what she had seen, the familiar visage jumping out at him from the throng.

Reyn Hartlet had not changed as much as Carro in the last months, but his was still a face far different than the youthful one Raz had known in the first days of his arrival at the mountain temple. Once clean-shaven and strong-chinned, the young Priest now bore a heavy beard which gave him the look of a man twice his age. His hair, half-a-year ago kept clean and kempt, hung long and lank, loose strands falling across his eyes. It was in those eyes that Raz had seen the greatest change. It had come on slowly at first, a measured build of mixed heartbreak and confusion, but as the weeks passed, so grew the anger. Blue irises, once bright with life, were now dark, filled with something heavy and boiling as they took in Raz and Syrah. Disappointment. Disgust.

Hatred.

Beside him, Syrah let out a rattling exhalation, and Raz reached out once more to take her by the shoulder. He felt her turn toward him, seeking the comfort of his gaze, but he couldn't grant it to her just yet.

As Raz's hand had fallen on the cloth of her tunic, Hartlet's darkened eyes had snapped to his, and the pair now waged their silent war.

For a long time they glared at each other, blue burning against amber-gold. There seemed no bottom to the depth of the revulsion that swam in the Priest's face, itself an energy by which he appeared to sustain his will.

In the end, though, something seemed to break, and Reyn Hartlet finally looked away, ducking back into the crowd and disappearing for the last time.

Only then, after the man had vanished among the other white robes of the Laorin, did Raz turn his eyes down to Syrah and smile.

"Ready?" he asked her simply.

Without hesitation, she nodded, and together they made for the first steps that would lead them down into the woodlands below, horses plodding dutifully behind.

II

"The roads between the realms of North and South are never so bustling as during the brief periods at the beginning and end of the summer season. It is in that time, taking advantage of the lack of the sundering heat of the Sun or the harsh cold of the freeze, that merchants and border traders ply the greatest labors of their professions, hauling in goods and crafts from one land to the other and sometimes back again. It is a generally pleasant thing to make the journey in this time. The roads, lonely and desolate for much of the year, become a hive of thriving, vibrant life, with all the sights and sounds of the Miropan markets, yet none of the oppressing heat or wrenching wails of those poor tormented souls left to the cruelties of the Cages."

—*A Study of Modern Economies,* by Marret Vern

Cahna couldn't help her little eyes from growing wide as her family made their way down the forest road, though she was careful to keep a tight hold of her mother's skirt even as she stared around. They had been traveling for nearly a week now, their little three-wagon caravan grinding along southward, handling the mud and stone churned up by the storms that saw fit to pass overhead every other day or so. Despite this, Cahna still couldn't help but marvel at how the world changed around her one evening after the other. As each day failed, the carts and merchants they traveled alongside or passed by going in the opposite direction would call a halt to their respective journeys, leading their draft horses to the side of the road before reining them to a halt. Once everyone was settled, somewhere along the path one family or another would haul flutes and drums out from where they were stowed, and before long the night sky would be alive with music and the flickering colors of camp and cooking fires. The smell of food and the sound of laughter grew heavy on the air, and after dinner the families would mingle, sharing news and bartering for goods they thought might sell well wherever it was they were traveling to.

Cahna, despite her shy nature—which she heard her mother often say was certainly to be expected at her age—often found that she enjoyed these nightly family excursions, meeting and visiting all manner of people on the road. There was always something new to discover, someone different to encounter. Most borderers were of some mixed blood or another, like Cahna and the rest of their family, but others made the trip at the beginning and end of summer just as well. There were true Southerners and Northerners, the former often boasting the tanned skin and grey eyes of their people, the latter seeming almost delicate in their paleness and fair-haired complexions. There were sometimes West Islers, narrowed eyes kind despite their rigid cultures, and Percian, black skin gleaming in the gentler sunlight of these cooler days. Others were dispersed between these, but Cahna had no sense of where they might have come from, knowing little of the rest of the world. Of course, as young as she was, questions like "Where are they from?" and "Where are they going?" very infrequently came to mind compared to queries such as "Can I have a funny hat like that?" and "Why are some of her teeth made of gold?"

Needless to say, it was fortunate for Cahna's parents that she was innately quiet around strangers.

"Eren! Eren! Here! Over here, man!"

Cahna's father—leading her mother by the hand while Cahna herself trailed behind the pair of them—stopped at the sound of his name, braided, dirty-blond hair shifting over his shoulders as he looked around. Catching sight of a tall figure attempting to wave them down from within a group of people sitting around a fire along the east edge of the road, he smiled broadly, starting for them at once.

"It's Naro!" Cahna heard her father say excitedly over his shoulder as they moved, dodging strangers and stepping over puddles that reflected the firelight around them. "I was wondering if we would pass him this year!"

As they got nearer, it took a few moments for Cahna to recognize the man still smiling at them, his hair—the same color of rusted straw as her father's—cropped short around his ears. Her uncle Naro lived in the South, she knew, having met and married a woman there some time before Cahna's grandfather had passed away last year. She didn't know Naro well, but as they got nearer she grew excited in the way only small children can upon seeing extended family, knowing it probably meant gifts of treats and toys before the night was through.

Sure enough, as a young couple shifted over from where they sat on a fallen trunk to let her and her family by, Cahna saw her uncle's eyes drop to her, and his smile broadened immediately.

"Little Cahna!" the man bellowed jovially, dropping down to one knee and opening his arms to her. "Look at you, taller than a tree now! Come give your Uncle Naro a hug!"

Cahna hesitated, looking up at her mother, who smiled and nodded encouragingly. Gathering her courage, Cahna took several shy steps forward, allowing her uncle to sweep her up and spin her around. Unable to help herself, she giggled, then laughed in truth as the sound spurred the man to bounce her into the air before easing her back to the ground and looking her up and down.

"You've got more of your mother in you than your poor father, don't you, girl?" Naro said with a chuckle, patting her hair and looking past her at her parents. "This one's going to be tall as you, Myna."

Cahna's mother, who stood some two inches above her husband, laughed. "Taller, according to her grandmother. Apparently she's half-again my height when I was her age."

Uncle Naro whistled before looking back down at Cahna. "Growing girl! Do you know what helps growing girls, little Cahna?"

Cahna said nothing, but smiled and shook her head vigorously. In response, her uncle inched forward to cup her ear with a hand and whisper something to her.

"Lots and lots of sweets."

Cahna's smile only brightened as she felt the man press what felt like a large chunk of toffee into her little hand.

They spent a generally pleasant evening after that, or at least Cahna did. She met and took a liking to her aunt, Sammar, examining her tanned skin and bleached hair with childish curiosity while the woman told her stories of the South and its Cienbal desert and its infamous *sarydâ*. After that, she sat eating her candy while the adults spoke over the fire, their words mingling with the lively atmosphere of the night around Naro's camp.

"How goes life below the border?" Cahna's mother asked her uncle, warming her hands over the flames. "We've heard some unpleasant rumors, even through the freeze."

"With good reason," Naro responded, his face twisting into something of a scowl. "Unrest is growing, particularly in the northern fringe cities. After the Monster cut apart the Miropan šef last year, the society has seemed a lot less untouchable. Whether that's for the better has yet to be seen, but the problem is the Mahsadën *know* they appear weak right now."

"Which means what?" Cahna's mother pressed.

"It means things are worse than ever," the husband of the young couple on the log spoke up for the first time since their arrival. "There's a new šef in Miropa, a man called Blaeth. Word is he was the right hand of Ergoin Sass himself before Raz i'Syul Arro butchered the man, and they say he's even more ruthless than his former master."

Naro nodded in agreement. "It's been a hard year. Even in the other fringe cities the Mahsadën have grown vicious. The South has seen they aren't invincible, and the šef are looking to make examples of anyone fool enough to think they can take advantage of that fact. In Karth they've taken to razing the slums every month or so, leaving the dwellers to the elements in an attempt to keep them from uniting. In Acrosia the rings have started publicly drowning smugglers and slave traders attempting to make use of the ports without paying the society's dues."

"And the Monster?" Cahna's father asked, leaning in with excited eyes. "Did they ever find him? We heard nothing after word came from Azbar, looking for fighters to pit against him."

"They call him 'the Dragon' now, I hear," Aunt Sammar said with a frown, joining in. "And no, no news, which undoubtedly means they haven't tracked him down."

"Agreed," the woman on the trunk now spoke up. "If they had, Blaeth would have had him flayed alive in the Miropan Cages for all to see."

"Without a doubt," Uncle Naro said with a dark chuckle. "That news would have traveled fast. And they can't *pretend* to have caught him either, as he's bound to show his face again the minute they do, just to prove them liars. It's a no-win situation for the Mahsadën right now. Small wonder they're doing everything they can to find him."

It was as her uncle said these very words that something strange seemed to come over the night. Gradually, like a steadily rising tide, the mood of the evening changed around them. Cahna paused in her chewing, the sweet taste of the toffee dulling as she realized that the music had stopped in the camps to the south of them, and that this strange silence appeared to be nearing. Sure enough, as the adults around her noted the same stillness and turned their heads, the families closest to them quieted as well, the wash of apprehension passing along like a chill. By the time it reached their little fire, Cahna had made out what it was that had brought this emptiness to the festivities of the roadside camp.

A line of some twenty or so horses were making their way steadily through the cooking fires, plodding along with bobbing heads, the dull *clop* of their iron shoes against the muddy stone the only sound of their passing. The horses themselves were unimpressive, a motley mix of all breeds and colors and sizes, like the mounts had been hurriedly assembled, gathered in whatever order they became available.

Much more frightening, however, were the men astride their backs.

Had Cahna been a little older, she might have been more frightened of the figures, all of them little more than silhouettes despite the flickering light that washed over them as they moved by. She was afraid as it was, but her young eyes did not register the glint of the smoke-blackened sword-grips that protruded over most of the men's saddles, nor the plethora of knives and smaller blades some had strapped about their chests, hips, and shoulders. Rather, what Cahna took in were the men themselves, and it would be many years before the memories she formed would fade away into oblivion.

Like shadows made solid, each of the riders was little more than a human-shaped blotch against the night. They were garbed in loose layers of dark cloth ranging from slate grey to pitch black. Every inch of them—down to the gloves that held the reins of their horses—was covered, hiding the men and anything that might have identified them. The only exposed part of their persons was a narrow slit above the bridge of their noses, barely extending ear to ear. Watching their faces as they passed, it wasn't until half of them had gone by that Cahna caught even the faintest glint of eyes in that gap, assuaging her greater fear that there might very well be nothing at all beneath the wrappings. Still, the fact that the men didn't so much as turn their heads to examine the people they passed was unnerving, particularly when coupled with the absolute stillness of their forms, the calm, deathly demeanor with which they swayed only with the rhythm of their mounts, all other movement limited to the point where—after the men had come and gone—many of the adults would wonder aloud if the riders had been living things, and not perhaps twenty corpses strapped to their saddles as some horrifying joke.

The shadows made no motion to interact with anyone as they rode through the camp, the stillness they had brought with them bearing the distinct aura of danger they carried about them like a smothering cloak. One after another they passed, their single careful line bisecting the families as absolutely as a river. No one spoke while the men were within earshot, and even afterward no one dared do more than whisper until the back of the last figure had long vanished into the confusion of smoke and tents and overhangs.

After that, though, the hum of conversation that started up had a distinctly darker measure to it than the festive banter which had filled the night before the riders' passings.

"By the Sun," Uncle Naro finally managed to choke out as the buzz of nervous voices began to rise like the thrum of a disturbed wasp nest. "Let's hope the Moon looks favorably on whatever poor bastard crosses *that* lot the wrong way."

All about Cahna, heads still turned north in the direction the men had been trudging along, the adults nodded together. While Cahna did not understand exactly what her uncle meant by these words, it didn't matter. She learned more by way of her confusion, as she looked to her parents to see if they might explain it to her.

There, in the faces of the two people from whom she had known only strength and kindness and courage, lay heavy something Cahna had not thought she would ever see. It terrified her, the emotion she saw lining the creases that had just started to frame her mother's eyes, as did the tension she saw in the firmness of her father's jaw.

For, as all children know, when one's own parents show fear, it is very nearly the end of the world.

III

"There is no day in which I would find the Arocklen Woods anything less than breathtaking. It is true that for much of the year the forest is dreary and cold, almost all light smothered by the snow and ice which packs its highest branches, but even in those depths of winter there is a wonder to the place, a mesmerizing quality which exists heavily in the muffled silence of the evergreens and the frozen stillness of undergrowth and rivers and hills.

That being said, I am not fool enough to claim that such icy fascinations are not outweighed by the true magnificence of the Woods when taken in under a summer sun..."

—private journal of Talo Brahnt

Raz stood a ways behind Syrah, the reins of both horses held firm in one hand while he allowed the woman her much-needed moment of solitude.

They stood at the base of the stairs, the wide space of cleared land that separated the Saragrias Ranges from the forest devoid of the wind-blown snows that had covered it every other time Raz had visited the place. He looked around, noting with an unamused grunt that the changing of the seasons left behind not even a hint of the violence and butchery which once plagued the ground around his feet.

It had taken them nearly a week to manage the mountain path in its entirety. Without Syrah to keep him company, Raz thought he might have found their crawling pace maddening. Instead, he'd discovered he couldn't help but enjoy the time they spent navigating the winding steeps, easing the horses down each step, one after the other with careful deliberation. Syrah kept his mind from straying too often to the dark cloud of worry that started to hang over him the moment they'd left the safety of the Citadel's walls, her presence and spirit guiding his thoughts constantly elsewhere. She'd pointed out the gracious flight of the cliff falcons, their calls echoing against the crags above their heads. She'd forced him to stop earlier than he would have liked every evening, grabbing hold of his arm and tugging him along the path until they found a spot in which the Sun could be seen setting over the distant horizon in a painting of colors. She'd spent the evenings telling him stories of her childhood in the Citadel, often repeating tales he'd heard half-a-dozen times before, but he never cared. It kept his mind from straying, kept him focused on her and the world she saw, so filled with beauty and wonder that he was often more than a little jealous of her understanding of life and all its value.

Jealous, that was, until this moment.

Raz watched the woman carefully, ignoring the tug of the reins in his hand as Gale and the mare—Nymara, Syrah had decided to call the animal— shuffled about looking for particularly appetizing tufts of grass. He took in the tension of her shoulders, noting the shake of the hand that grasped the steel of her Priestess' staff. It was newly forged, that steel, worked metal to replace the weapon lost to her in this very spot, as the past freeze had just begun to take hold. Raz wondered if Syrah realized this fact, though he doubted it.

It seemed a paltry connection to make when compared to the other things that must have been going through the woman's mind.

Syrah was facing south, away from him, her one eye taking in the thick line of trees that waited for them some hundred paces across the grass. Raz felt an odd sadness well up within himself as he followed her gaze, taking in the forest of his own accord. To him, the place spoke of welcome and anticipation. As a cool breeze blew down from the mountains, the branches of the old firs and towering pines tilted and swayed, back and forth like hands enticing him to approach. His sharp ears made out songbirds crafting their music in the greenery, and even here he could see patches of the Sun's flitting light dance brightly across flowery underbrush. He'd loved the place even in the harshest night of winter, taken something very much like comfort in its solitude. Now, though, he wanted nothing more than to experience its magnificence in all its Sun-lit glory.

And so his sadness grew as he looked again to Syrah, who—he knew all too well—was feeling a very different set of emotions as she took in the Arocklen Woods.

She'd lost much, in this place, her eye being the least of those things. Raz fought back anger as he remembered the state he'd found her in, a tortured soul torn down to little more than bruised skin and bone by the gruff hands of the Sigûrth as they'd declared their war against her kind. He'd been the death of many men that night, the cold touch of iron vengeance which had stolen the lives of a score and more of her captors.

It was one of the few rampages in his life Raz could look back on without so much as an ounce of regret.

After several minutes, Raz decided it was time to pull Syrah back from the dark waters of memory. Looping the reins together so that Nymara wouldn't stray too far from Gale, Raz moved quietly through the grass, the silk mantle Carro and Jofrey had returned to him whispering around his calves, the old weight of his gladius comforting across his back. When he was a pace behind her he allowed the woman another few moments, seeing now the true intensity with which she looked into the shadows of the Woods.

Then, gently, he took the last step forward and settled a lithe arm around her narrow shoulders.

Syrah jumped only slightly as the weight of his limb fell across her, but even then she did not look away from the Arocklen. It was a few seconds before she made any motion, in fact, finally reaching across herself to grasp the fingers of his hand.

"It's a stupid fear, isn't it?" she asked him in a hushed voice, still not looking away from the trees. "There's nothing there. I *know* there's nothing there, and... and yet..." She trailed off.

"It's not," Raz told her, following her eye through the twisted evergreens. "What you feel is as justified as anything else in this world." He looked down at her again. "I told you, we don't have to do this. We can go around."

Syrah snorted, and Raz was pleased to see a smile play on her pale lips as she raised an eyebrow. "It's adorable that you think that's an option," she said in an amused tone. "Even on horseback that would add weeks before making it to Ystréd, not to mention what time it would take to hunt once we ran out of provisions."

Raz shrugged. "We could make it work."

Syrah cocked her head up at him. "The sooner we reach the city, the more time we'll have to figure out our next move. Summers are short here, Raz. The freeze will arrive again before you even get a chance to feel the sun on your skin."

Raz frowned, though not at her words. The tilt of her head had shifted her hair, revealing the warped knot of scarring that was all that remained of most of her right ear. It hurt him to see that, hurt him to realize he had not been there to stop it.

And it hurt him now, dwelling on what she was about to put herself through.

"We don't have to do this," he repeated, looking her carefully in the eye. This time, she smiled in truth, seeing the depth of his concern. She let go of his hand and reached up to rest her palm against his cheek. Her skin was warm to the touch, her fingers gentle against his scales.

"Yes, we do," she said, and despite the softness of her voice he heard the finality in the statement.

Making this out, Raz gave in and nodded. As she drew her hand away he turned north, whistling once. Immediately Gale raised his broad head from the grass it was buried in, and a few seconds later he and Nymara were trotting over, the mare snorting in an annoyed sort of fashion as she was pulled unwillingly along by the stallion's stronger frame.

A minute or so later they were mounted and approaching the edge of the tree line again, the warmth of the Sun fading slightly when they trotted into the shadows of the branches. Syrah did not pause as they passed into the Woods, though Raz saw her start to tremble the slightest bit when the trunks began to close in around them. He let her be, wanting her to draw from her own strength to overcome her terror, and it wasn't long before he heard the woman take a deep breath, letting it out again as the shivering subsided. For nearly a quarter-hour they traveled in silence, Raz keeping Gale close to Nymara's flank, never straying far and only taking his eyes off the woman's back when it came to guiding the horse over streams or around fallen trees. Before long they were deep within the trees, the space between the pines, firs, and hemlocks growing wider while the trunks thickened until some of them were so broad Raz doubted he knew any five men in the world who could link hands around their bases. At this point Syrah began to relax in truth, the opening up of the forest floor seeming to relieve a little of the weight bearing down upon her shoulders, the brightness of the light streaming between the leaves warming away some of the lingering tension. After a time she finally turned around in her saddle and—though her face was strained—spoke in a calm, steady voice.

"It's beautiful, isn't it?"

Raz nodded at once, allowing himself to look around in truth now that Syrah seemed to have found some measure of control over her fears.

The scene around him felt like witnessing a finished masterpiece after seeing only the rough attempts of its early creation. The Arocklen, in winter so calm and still, was now practically vibrating with life. Everywhere he looked, the green of the forest was almost overwhelming, moss-lined bark melding with swaying saplings, dipping flowers, and colorful underbrush. All around them the sounds of the Woods played like a distant orchestra, with the calls of birds and the rush of a nearby river colluding with the wind through the leaves until the hill they were traversing felt like an amphitheater of earth and stone and grass.

It didn't take them long to find the path south. During the freeze it had been harder to distinguish, the dirt of the worn trails difficult to make out against the frosted brown of the forest floor. In summer, however, it was a clear road, twisting its way cheerfully through the Woods as space allowed, sometimes wrapping around lichen-covered boulders or else trailing along streams for a time until the waters became shallow enough to cross.

It was so drastic a change compared to the trek north Raz had experienced that it took him a while before he realized some of the surroundings were starting to become familiar.

A tree with a particularly noticeable bend. An odd shift in the earth where a thick root partially protruded out of the ground. A clearing in which— where once there had been only snow and fallen branches—now grazed a small herd of deer, their ears flicking up at the dull *thumps* of Gale and Nymara's hooves on the trail. A few hours into their journey Raz felt some of the joy of the woods fade, replaced by a tense echo of a fear he hadn't realized he'd forgotten.

When they started climbing upward, the echo became claws scraping at the back of his mind.

"What on earth...?" Raz heard Syrah demand under her breath as they reached the ridge of the hill, pulling her mare gently to a halt. She was a short way ahead of him, and had come across the markings first. Whereas winter's passing had obliterated any hint of a fight from the stone steps along the base of the mountain path, the grassy floor of the Arocklen had not fared so well. Where once the face of the incline might have been a uniform of green speckled with the reds and purples of flowers, there were in places now the unmistakable scars of what could only have been fire scorching earth. As Syrah urged Nymara forward, peering closer at the patterns in the damaged grass, Raz's eyes read the ground like a book, the black and brown spots and lines little more than the words of an old story. Here, the blast of magic.

There, the ring of flames. Raz could almost smell the seared flesh and the crack of bone as the wolves had died one after the other.

Abruptly, Raz felt his throat tighten. "Syrah," he managed in a hard voice as he started to pull Gale about, "come with me."

The Priestess tore her eyes from the scorch marks to look around, confused. "Where are we going?" she called out after him as Raz kicked Gale into a slow gallop back down the hill, in the direction they'd come.

Raz answered, but spoke too quietly for her to make out the words.

"To say goodbye."

It took them the remainder of the morning to find the lake. Raz possessed little more than a general idea of where the place might be, and they ended up circling back to the path frequently as a point of reference in their search. Rather than grow irritated, however, Syrah became only more determined with each loop they made through the western Woods, her face set from the moment he had explained to her what it was they were searching for.

Fortunately, their perseverance eventually bore fruit.

Raz stood by the woman this time, the pair of them sharing their moment of silence at the edge of the water. It was still, shimmering only when the occasional breeze blew down from the canopy above, and so clear they could see the bottom all the way from where it dipped into the deepest parts until it rose again to form the small island in the center of the lake. Upon this little plot of land grew a single tree, a gnarled pine, half-bent with age. It had the look of a wise old man, the weight of his life twisting him almost to his knees, and yet its thick, spiny foliage was hearty and green with life. With each gust of wind the tree's branches would shift, and every time Raz would peer carefully into the shadows beneath, seeking out a very particular shape.

Finally, there was the glint of metal in the shifting pattern of the Sun.

"There," Raz said, lifting a clawed hand and pointing.

Syrah followed his finger, but it was still a few seconds before she, too, caught sight of the thing. When she did, he heard her try to repress the shaking gasp that overtook her.

The shape of the staff, black beneath the branches, then gleaming in the light, stood out to them like a beacon, guiding their eyes. Raz followed it down as the tree shifted about once again, and it wasn't long before he found what he truly sought.

Outlined against the trunk of the old pine, there appeared to be the form of a man at rest, seated with his legs outstretched, his back against the roughened bark. His hood was pulled up over his face, the white outlines of his sleeves bent to give the impression that his hands were resting in his lap. The Sun danced over him, and from this distance anyone else might have thought the figure was only taking a midday nap in the calm brightness of the summer day.

Raz felt his throat constrict again, and he swallowed hard.

Talo Brahnt sat where he had died, his last breath spent at the end of the very blade now slung across Raz's back. By either twisted luck or merciful magic, his body seemed not to have been disturbed in the months of winter it had lain there, propped up and at peace in the shade of the tree that had become the man's only remaining companion in death. Despite all attempts, Raz couldn't help but frown as his mind wandered back to that night, seeming an eternity ago, the three of them illuminated in the golden light of the healing spells Carro al'Dor had been casting with desperate fervor.

But Talo had been too far gone, and steel had been the only mercy left to him.

The touch of Syrah's fingers about his wrist made Raz tense, then relax. He realized he'd been clenching his fists at his side, and he loosened them, feeling his palms throb where his metal claws had dug through the leather of the gauntlets to the skin beneath.

"Where did it happen?" Syrah was asking him, and it took a moment for Raz to clear his head. When he did, he pointed to the western surface of the lake.

"There," he told her hoarsely, finding he could say little else. Syrah nodded, her eye on the surface of the water he was indicating. She let go of his hand and started moving around the edge of the shore, leaving Raz to gain control of the anger and sadness that threatened now to overwhelm him.

When he managed it, he turned and moved to join her.

Syrah stood quietly, her eye still gazing into the water, apparently not noticing that the tips of her boots were under threat of a good soak as she sank into the loose earth. Raz could guess what she was looking at before he reached her side, and it didn't take him long to find the object of her interest.

Most of the ursalus' body, unlike Talo, had been ravaged by the beasts of the freeze. Whether it was wolves or other bears or some different manner of creature, it looked as though little was left of the terrible animal which had stolen away the High Priest's life with nothing more than a swipe of its great clawed paw. The bear, though, had been a horror of massive proportions, easily outweighing Raz five times over, and some parts of the corpse looked to have been simply too big to drag away into the relative shelter of the trees. From where he stood Raz could just make out the staggered line of what remained of the thing's spine, an odd pattern of what might almost have been pale stones from which bent and broken ribs extended upward, creating a maze through which little fish darted even as he watched. It looked as though one limb might have survived the scavengers as well, though the long bones of the paw were now half-buried in the rock and stone of the lake bottom.

More prevalent that either of these things, though, was the skull that sat, lopsided and leering, several feet from the rest of the body.

In death the ursalus had lost none of its ferocity, and Raz felt his blood curdle as he looked into the empty sockets where once dark, viciously intelligent eyes had stared him down. He remembered facing off against the beast, remembered the sheerness of the terror he'd had to wrench himself from, a fear unlike anything he had ever—and hopefully *would* ever—experience. He remembered the certainty with which he'd entered their fight, the same certainty with which he had crossed blades with Gûlraht Baoill.

It was an iron absoluteness, an inflexible understanding that only one combatant would have the chance to walk away with their life.

I hope the Sun burns hot in whatever hell you're in, Raz thought, glaring at the skull and wishing, for a moment, that he could cut the bear's head off all over again.

He could have guessed Syrah was thinking something similar, even before she leaned forward and, with deliberate malice, spat into the water of the lake. After this her eye lifted again, seeking out the form of her fallen mentor, and for a minute she stood quiet, whatever prayer she was reciting meant only for herself, Talo, and the Lifegiver they'd both sacrificed so much for.

When she turned away from the island, it was with an almost pleading look in her eye.

"Let's go," she said sadly. "I can't be here anymore."

Raz nodded, shifting to allow her to step past him, back into the shadow of the trees. As she did, he himself glanced back one last time, seeking and finding the gleam of the staff through the shifting branches.

"May you find yourself among the highest of Her Stars," he told the wind.

Then Raz turned away from that place of sorrow, following Syrah into the Woods.

IV

With no more distractions to sway their course, it took Raz and Syrah only a little more than a week to make their way through the boundaries of the Arocklen, the Priestess' uneasiness fading with every passing day. It was clear, though, that she never managed to appreciate the Woods as Raz did, her head so often set firmly forward on a stiff neck save when they were talking, or when some sound would make her jump and whirl in her saddle. Her nightmares, too, had returned in force, and each night as they stopped to rest Raz made sure to keep the blaze of the campfire high until Syrah fell asleep, usually curled up against his chest in an effort to keep the terrors at bay. Neither the flames nor his presence ever did much to help, though, and Syrah awoke so often crying out that some nights were spent altogether sleepless for Raz. By the time the trees started to thin around them again, he found himself praying to the Twins that her dreams would be kinder when they were beyond the borders of the Woods.

Fortunately, he was assured of this the moment they stepped back into true daylight once again.

"Oh!" Syrah exclaimed in delight, standing in her stirrups to peer out over the lands before them, demonstrating something other than a stoic face for the first time in days. Raz almost laughed with relief to see it, but found himself sharing in her excitement too much to tease her.

Before them, the land rolled like calm waves in a solid pasture of swaying grass. The last he'd seen the Dehn Plains, they had been a canvas of white under the winter snows, an unbroken blanket of purity reflecting the rolling grey of the storm clouds above. It had been beautiful in its own way, but— like the Arocklen whose tree line was some dozen yards behind them now— that beauty paled in comparison to the life that had overrun the land as summer fell. The Plains still held themselves in uniform color, but instead of white the crests of the hills now shimmered with shifting shades of green as the wind caught the rising fields and played with them in patterns and waves. Far in the distance, the unbroken horizon bent and twisted across the end of the earth, shearing the somber blue of the sky accented with wispy clouds moving along lazily overhead.

Raz had to lift a hand over his eyes as they adjusted to the direct gaze of the Sun once again, smiling into the warmth of a true summer day. He watched the grasses in the distance bend, bowing in their direction, and a few seconds later the gusting breeze reached them with a *whooshing* song of wind across the hills.

"I never get tired of this view."

Raz looked around at Syrah's words. The woman was beaming, still standing above her saddle, pulling her hood down off her head. He couldn't see her good eye from where he sat on her right, but her smile was earnest and hearty, and he warmed at the sight of it.

"I wouldn't imagine it would ever be possible to," he agreed. "It's a different world to the one I saw on my way up, mind you."

Syrah looked at him suddenly. "I hadn't thought of that! You passed through the Dehn in the middle of winter!" She looked suddenly excited, sitting down again and leaning toward him, the interest bright in her eye. "What was it like? Was it beautiful? It must have been magnificent."

Raz nodded, looking to the horizon again. In his mind's eye he recalled the wash of untouched snow, dipping and rising across the world.

"It was," he answered, putting his heels into Gale's sides, nudging the horse into a steady walk along the path that still extended before them, winding across the Plains. "It reminded me of home, in fact."

Pressing Nymara into a brief trot to catch up to him, Syrah pulled the horse up when they were side-by-side, looking out over the land before them with a perplexed expression. "Home?" she mumbled, obviously not making the connection.

Raz nodded. "Have you ever seen the Cienbal? Did you get a chance when you took your pilgrimage?"

"No," Syrah said with a shake of her head, and she sounded genuinely disappointed as she ducked her head under a rocky outcropping that jutted over the path from one of the hills to her left. "I never had the opportunity..."

"I imagine sightseeing was low on the list, after we met," Raz said with a dark chuckle.

"To put it mildly," Syrah grumbled. Then she brightened, looking around at him in full. "What is it like? Can you tell me about it?"

"Depends on how much you enjoy the heat and the Sun."

Syrah scowled. "Ugh," she huffed, grimacing. "What kind of realm exists without winter?"

Raz grinned. "Seems only fair, given that your own lands seem to be nothing *but* winter."

Syrah laughed at that, and they spent the rest of the day in pleasant conversation, Raz telling her about the sands he'd grown up in and the cities he and his family had traveled between during the South's predominantly cooler seasons. There was nothing new to share with the woman about the Arros themselves, of course. In the seven months they'd spent cooped up within the warmth of Cyurgi 'Di as the freeze battered away at the outer walls, Syrah had learned almost all there was to know about Raz's old life. He'd spared her no details as they'd gotten to know each other, and they'd grown closer for it. In the end they'd made an odd pair, their days spent almost entirely in each other's company.

It had earned them the disapproving glares of not a few among the Laorin.

By the time evening fell and they guided the horses off the road to make camp among the hills, Syrah had asked Raz a hundred different questions about the geography and history of the South, taking to the subject with surprising interest. As a Priestess of Laor she was as familiar as anyone with every valley town of the North, but of the Southern cities she'd seen only one, and Raz took great pleasure in assuring her that Karth in particular was a nest of rats, filthy and ragged as compared to the other municipalities that surrounded the Cienbal. They passed a calm evening under the stars, Raz describing in detail the towering marble spires of the wealthier districts of Miropa, and the small oasis the city had been built around. He told her of the ports of Acrosia, where a hundred ships from around the world were docked on any given day, their sails and flags a shifting rainbow of colors as they came and went. He told her of the Crags, the mountain ranges which dipped into the eastern edge of the desert, and of the lower fringe cities like Karavyl and Dynec, whose economies relied much on the trade they did with the lands of Perce and the Seven Cities, even further south.

"Have you been there?" Syrah asked him excitedly, propped up on one elbow on her bedroll, which she'd laid out parallel to his. "To the kingdoms beyond the South?"

For the first time all day, Raz frowned, his eyes on Her Stars far above as he lay on his back, their glimmer dimmed slightly by the white glow of the campfire at their feet.

"No," he said after a moment. "And I don't intend to."

"Why not?" Syrah asked curiously. "You came this far north. Why not further south?"

Here, Raz hesitated, pondering his words. Then he lifted both hands overhead, palms facing down.

He'd taken off his gauntlets when they'd stopped for the evening, and the pale rings of colorless flesh were distinct against the otherwise-black scales of his wrists and the night sky beyond.

"Do you know how I got these?" Raz asked Syrah quietly.

The woman nodded, looking up at his wrists. "You've told me," she responded gently. "And Talo before you. Apparently it wasn't hard to figure out your story, even as we fled Karth."

"Not too many atherian living free in civilized society," Raz said with a nod. He had meant it as a joke, but he heard the hard edge in his voice. "Only one, in fact."

Syrah said nothing, waiting for him to continue.

Eventually, he did.

"I don't remember the chains, exactly. I was too young, I think. But I remember the pain of them. And the weight. And I remember the men. Not the details of them or their faces, of course, but more what their presence made me feel. Terror. Hate. Hopelessness. Rage."

He rolled his hand over, looking at the back of the scars now. "I don't know what happened to make them leave me behind. When I was old enough my father told me he and my uncle found me with two other bodies, men who'd obviously been among the slavers. He thought it was I who had killed the pair, and when the others tried to stop me they knocked me out cold.

Whether they thought I was dead or just intended to leave me regardless, I don't know. Either way, abandoning me to the sands was the kindest thing they could have done."

Raz's frown deepened. "If they hadn't, Perce or the Seven Cities is where I would have ended up, just another body on the auction block, sold like chattel to the highest bidder."

Syrah gave a small inhalation of outrage, her eyes widening in realization. "They keep your kind as slaves?" she demanded, her tone disbelieving.

Raz nodded, letting his arms fall to his chest and looking to the sky again. "Your faith did well to ban the practice," he told her. "Even in the fringe cities, the slavers only work as an open secret, and most of their 'goods'—" he said the word like it left a bad taste in his mouth "—are shipped south, generally to Perce. It's a civilization of wealth and plenty, I'm told. They pay the most for the best among the stock." He grit his teeth. "Apparently, that includes the atherian."

Beside him, Syrah's mouth hung slightly agape. For a time it seemed she was lost for words. After a minute or so she eased herself down on her back, lying beside him as she, too, took in the heavens.

"Life isn't kind, is it?" she asked finally.

Raz rolled his head around to look at her. Her pink eye was clear, reflecting the Moon above them, and the loose ends of the black wraps that shielded the scarred right side of her face lay about her head. Her white hair shifted over her shoulders as a warm breeze tumbled down off the hill behind them. She looked sad, like she was navigating some unhappy contemplating.

"What do you mean?"

In response, Syrah reached out with her left hand to take Raz's right, curling her fingers between his before pulling them up, lifting both above their heads. Outlined against Her Stars, their matching scars seemed to loop through each other, his a pale circle between black scales, hers a pink ring around her slim wrist.

It hurt him, seeing that blemish, the disfigurement of her otherwise smooth skin. It hurt every time he caught sight of it or its counterpart on her other arm, like some deity or another was intent on making him suffer at least a fraction of the torment she'd been through to earn them.

"I mean that the Laorin go out of their way to teach the children of our faith one thing," Syrah finally answered. "We teach them that life is a gift—the greatest gift, in fact—to be cherished above all other things. We teach them that life is a beautiful, perfect thing, filled with wonder and adventure and excitement, and must therefore be protected at all cost."

She sighed, letting their arms drop between them again, though she didn't let go of his hand. "But it's not perfect, is it? It's not even beautiful. It's filled with hardship and misery, challenges and pain. I don't think I ever understood that before... before..."

She trailed off for a moment, and Raz felt her fingers tighten around his. He knew all too well where her mind had gone, and he returned the pressure comfortingly, intent on keeping the nightmares far at bay for this one night at least.

After a moment, Syrah found her voice again.

"It's not kind," she said again. "And just when you start to come to terms with the hardships of your own life, you discover that someone, somewhere in some far-off place, exists in a world that makes the difficulties of yours pale in comparison."

The sadness in her eye deepened, and she smiled in a rigid, sorrowful fashion. "Do those people even know what hope is, Raz?" she asked. "What it means? Do slaves still hold on to purpose? I had hope, when Kareth Grahst had me. I always had hope. Even if I died there, in the cold and misery, I knew I would be reborn in warmth and comfort, born into the arms of loving parents as Laor returned me to the cycle of life. But what do people who have nothing live for? How do they carry on?"

For a long time, Raz didn't answer her, pondering her words. He looked back to the sky, his eyes trailing across the infinite blackness, seeking the place of solace he knew he would always find there. It took several seconds, but eventually he found them, two bright points of light crowning a smaller, calmer one.

"There was a time I thought I had nothing."

Syrah tensed slightly at his words, as though she'd been unsure he would answer. As Raz continued, he felt her relax again.

"For a long time, in fact, I thought I had nothing. No family. No home. No hope. For years I merely existed, like some empty shell of a man, trying to find meaning in all the wrong places. I *was* the Monster, in truth then. I lived with no purpose but to devour, to take vengeance on a world that had left me alone and without reason to be."

He smiled, then, still watching the trio of Her Stars glimmer against the night.

"But I wasn't that person forever. I found my reason, eventually, in the work I did, or at least I found some semblance of it. As misguided as I was, allowing myself to take up arms for the Mahsadën, I found a glimmer of something in my labors, my efforts to eradicate the vermin from the city I came to call my home. It was twisted, I admit, and it took me a long time to fully understand that, but when I did, that glimmer bloomed into purpose."

Finally, he pulled his gaze away from the heavens, looking back to Syrah.

"Life is never perfect, no," he agreed. "And life *is* ugly. But consider the fact that maybe, just maybe, it's from all that ugliness that many of the best things come. If there was nothing to pull us down, to bring us to our knees, then there would never be any reason for us to stand up taller than before, to better ourselves and rise above. Life may not be innately beautiful, but it can be *made* beautiful. In one way or another, it can be made to have purpose. Slaves are not things, are not creatures. They feel, and they hurt, and they die. But that means they also love, and fight, and live."

He squeezed her hand again. "Don't belittle the trials you went through, Syrah. Don't attempt to minimize that crucible simply because you learn that someone else has it harder. You said it yourself: you kept your faith. You kept your hope. Through everything you suffered, your spirit found a way to persevere. So don't discount the will of the broken. Even if you think they have nothing—even if *they* think they have nothing—there is always something to live for. There is always something to fight for and hold on to."

It was Syrah's turn to be silent for a time, her eye on his. Raz knew, though, by the stillness of her face, that the woman was no longer present. She'd taken his words and traveled far away with them, allowing herself to be carried off.

After several minutes of silence, Syrah rolled over, allowing her body to settle against his. Her head came to rest against his chest, her hair spilling out over his shoulder and neck. She hadn't let go of his hand, and with her other she played absently with a button of his cloth shirt.

"Maybe," she said finally. "Maybe they have something... But don't you wish you could give them more? Don't you wish you could give them everything...?"

In response, Raz moved to run the claws of his free hand carefully through her white locks, his eyes again on the sky.

"All the time," he murmured to her as the Arros glimmered far above. "All the time."

It was as they lay there, under the gaze of the Moon and Her Stars, that Syrah fell asleep against him. For the first time since they'd left the mountains behind she didn't thrash or scream in her sleep, the nightmares mercifully left among the shadowed trunks of the Arocklen. Despite this, it was many hours before Raz, too, found the peace of dreams. For the better part of the night, in fact, his mind stayed too busy to settle, his thoughts preoccupied with horrid considerations of what his life might have been like had he never escaped the bloody irons that had left those scars upon his wrists.

Two days later, Syrah and Raz got their first glimpse of civilization. An old cart loaded high with greens, turnips, gourds, and all manner of other fruits and vegetables rumbled towards them on the path, pulled along by a single worn-looking draft horse. At first, the old man seated at its front barely gave them a glance as they passed, raising his hand politely before freezing and slowly turning to gape at Raz as his cart wheeled on by. Raz and Syrah, for their part, did little more than return the wave, both willing themselves not to look over their shoulders, feeling the farmer's eyes linger on their backs.

"Guess that's to be expected," Raz grumbled when the grind of the wooden axels began to fade.

Beside him, Syrah sighed. "You're still sure you want to stay on the road?"

Raz nodded. It had been a matter of debate between them even before they'd left Cyurgi 'Di, whether they would keep to the main path or not as they made for Ystréd. The Woods had been one thing. Syrah, Carro, and Jofrey all had promised him that the only travelers they were likely to cross paths within the Arocklen would be Priests and Priestesses headed for the Citadel, or perhaps converts or pilgrims intent on doing the same. They'd ended up seeing no one as they trekked south through the trees, but the assurance had still helped him sleep better at night.

Now, though, as they traveled further and further from the certain safety of the forest, Raz didn't feel quite as confident. Syrah had pressed him time and time again to consider pulling Gale and Nymara to ride off the beaten path, even if it meant simply paralleling the main road and guiding the animals through the hills. Raz had debated the wisdom of the suggestion often, knowing it would be safer for them both to stay away from prying eyes for as long as possible, but he always refuted her in the end. He'd given Syrah every excuse in the book by the time he finally managed to convince her to stop bringing it up. He'd told her it wasn't worth the risk to the horses, pushing them over unfamiliar terrain. He'd told her they couldn't afford the time, using her own reasoning against her, arguing that even the two or three days they could lose might make all the difference in the end, given that they had no plan. He told her that the North was already well aware of his presence, that he'd already made a scene when he'd last left Ystréd with Carro and Talo, and that the name he'd made for himself in Azbar would keep away the rabble that might crowd them on the common way. He'd told Syrah everything she needed to hear and more.

In the end, the only thing he *didn't* tell her was his true reason for wanting to stay put:

Raz was tired of running.

It had been very nearly a full year now since he'd been forced to flee Miropa, forced to leave the fringe cities—and the South as a whole—behind. Apart from the weeks he'd spent openly defying the Mahsadën in the Azbar Arena, it could be argued he had been hiding ever since, always running from the shadows that followed him wherever he went, lurking hungrily at his back. Even the months he'd spent with Syrah in the Citadel had often felt to Raz as though he were cowering behind the walls of the great keep, secluding himself from the world where it was safe and warm and dry. He'd enjoyed his time there, of course, enjoyed the company of what friends he'd made and the opportunity he and Syrah had had to learn about each other. It had distracted him enough to keep him away from the hint of madness that seemed to so often scrape at the borders of his mind, like a voice screaming in the far-off distance. The walls of the Citadel, so cramped and so small. The milling of the faithful crowding the great hall and corridors at the busiest times of the day. The ever-present feeling that something waited for him, beyond the confines of the stone. The Mahsadën, the council of Azbar, the enemies he'd made among the tribes of the mountain men who had not so calmly gathered beneath the banner of Carro al'Dor. It was a madness that had nagged at him, whispering in his ear even as he sat by Syrah's bed while she slept, forcing its way through his concentration during his exercises in the Citadel's practice chambers, slinking into his thoughts as he'd prepared for their departure.

And the longer it had ground at his mind, the more Raz realized it would hound him until the day the shadows no longer nipped at his heels.

He was tired of running.

They passed two more parties later that same day, and both times Raz was greeted with similar reactions to the one the farmer had given him. A messenger on horseback nearly lamed his animal as he pulled it up short to gape at the Monster of Karth, and a few hours later a mother on foot shooed her two children as far off the road as they could get, watching Raz and Syrah pass with wide, terrified eyes. Syrah did her best to put these strangers at ease each time, smiling brightly and blessing them in the name of the Lifegiver, but it did little more than earn a perplexed blink from the rider and a scowl from the woman.

The following morning, things only worsened. Ystréd was close now, Syrah told him, gauging they were likely to arrive in the early-afternoon of the following day. This was mostly a relief after nearly three weeks ahorse, but as they approached the valley town the road became steadily busier and more well-traveled. Before noon they'd passed a half-dozen different groups, some farmers or farm hands, some families coming to and from the city, and even a patrol of soldiers and lightly-armored scouts bearing Ystréd's colors. This last party had made Syrah nervous, Raz could tell, because she'd glowered at them as they'd gone by, returning the glares and stares not a few among their number gave the pair of them. He'd chuckled to himself, pleased to see the spark in the woman's eye, though he didn't tell her he'd heard some of the soldiers mumbling about the price on his head once they'd thought they were out of earshot.

In the end, though, the men had kept to their north-bound route, and Raz let them go in peace.

Their first bit of true trouble came later in the day, well after the Sun had passed its zenith in the bright sky. They'd been discussing their plans after Ystréd, thinking perhaps of making for what was left of Harond and Metcaf along the Vietalis Ranges far northwest of them. Syrah had many contacts there from her time spent working with the mountain tribes—though if any still lived after Gûlraht Baoill's sacking of the towns was up for debate—and they both had little doubt Raz could find work of one kind or another among the efforts to rebuild that were bound to be going on now summer had come. Raz was busy staring off over the Plains, wondering if he would be allowed to get by as nothing more than a simple laborer, when Syrah's lowered voice brought him back to the present.

"Raz. Ahead."

Slowly, without looking away from the Western horizon, Raz reached up and pulled the white hood of his mantle over his head. This done, he casually faced forward, careful to give no indication that Syrah had given him warning.

They were six in all, he saw, four men and a pair of women, their mismatched chargers plodding along at a slow, lazy pace in the same direction Raz and Syrah were headed. Even with their backs to them Raz could tell they were a rugged lot, their leather jerkins worn and sweat-stained, the bare skin of their arms and necks streaked with dirt and grime. Pieces of plate and chainmail hung from their saddles, too hot and heavy to wear while riding under the glare of the Sun, and light gleamed off the pommels of swords sheathed over shoulders, the steel shafts of a couple of maces, and the bare blades of a twin-headed battle-axe one man kept across his lap.

Syrah and Raz were approaching them too quickly, he realized, and he put a hand out, gently gesturing her to slow down. Soon they were trudging along at pace with the group, some fifty yards behind them, and Raz wrinkled his snout as he made out the distinctly unpleasant reek of too many bodies left unwashed for too many days.

"Do you think they'll let us by?" Syrah asked him under her breath.

Raz narrowed his eyes, trying to make out anything else he could about the rough-looking band. "I don't know," he answered truthfully, listening as the woman furthest to the left broke out in a roar of hard laughter, apparently amused by some lewd joke one of the men had made. "Maybe, but they're well-armed and not bearing any colors I can make out."

"Mercenaries," Syrah said, reading his mind. "If they're making south then they might have broken off from the forces Drangstek and Stullens sent to assist the northern valley towns before the freeze."

Raz nodded. This wasn't the first group they'd passed who'd looked as though they, too, were making for Ystréd, but all the others had been families and individuals of little note. This was different. This was a road-hardened lot, dirty and unkempt, but their weapons gleamed clean and their horses looked to be well cared for, the sorts of things soldiers on the march put first, priorities for men and women who were always ready for a fight. A few lice and muddy boots could be ignored, but a rusted blade could get stuck in its sheath, and a sick horse was no good in a charge or retreat.

Still, Raz thought with some impatience as he felt the sluggish clop of Gale's hooves beneath him, *at this rate we'd make better time crawling to the city.*

He glanced back to the Plains, considering once again the option of taking to the hills, if only for the few minutes they would need to get around the group. As they'd traveled further and further south, though, the rolling of the land had subsided substantially, and what had once been great waves of green grass were now more calm swells of a settling sea. Short of waiting till nightfall, Raz thought they would have a hard time masking their presence by going around the mercenaries, and he had little doubt the group would grow suspicious if they caught sight of a pair of riders obviously going out of their way to get around them.

In the end, he decided on a different gamble.

"We'll pass them," he said, pulling his tail under the folds of his mantle and tucking in his wings before making sure the hood was low over his face. "Stay on my right. We move quick, but not too quick. Try to look like we have somewhere to be, but not that we're *trying* to outrun them."

Syrah nodded, and Raz watched her hand stray, almost subconsciously, down to her staff, still strapped to Nymara's side. When she was sure the weapon was still there, Syrah pulled the mare back, then around Gale, urging her up until she was even with Raz's right side.

"Ready?" Raz asked her.

Syrah's gave a small jerk of her head. "When you are."

Raz couldn't help grinning slightly at the firmness of her voice. Then he put his heels into Gale's sides, clucking the stallion into a quick trot.

They passed the group as intended, Syrah keeping carefully to his side. The stench of the sellswords was powerful as they went by, and Raz couldn't help but think that he would be—at the very least—pleased to be upwind of the party. His silks blew about him a little more than he would have liked, but there was nothing to be done about it in the moment. He could only pray the men and women hadn't caught a glimpse of his wings or tail.

They rode like that for several minutes, pressing Gale and Nymara a little faster once they were sure they were well out of sight. After a quarter hour or so, Raz motioned that he thought they were clear, and he and Syrah pulled the animals back, slowing them down until they cantered once again along the road.

"Anything?" Syrah asked him when they'd found a steady pace, watching Raz pull his hood down again and spread his spined ears.

It wasn't long before he shook his head. "Nothing, at least for the time being. We should keep moving, though. I think we were convincing, but there's no telling if they noticed me or not."

Syrah glanced up at the Sun. "We still have a good few hours of light. It shouldn't be too hard to get far enough ahead if they keep at their slower pace."

"That's a big 'if,'" Raz grumbled, still listening. The wind was making it hard for him to hear anything other than Syrah and the huffing breath of the horses.

"Well, the other option is to sit here and wait for them to catch up," Syrah said with a sarcastic half-smile. "Maybe you can ask them politely if I made a decent decoy."

"Oh, I'm sure the men were distracted plenty," Raz retorted with a laugh. "The women, on the other hand..."

"It's poor manners to assume," Syrah responded with an offended sniff. "You might be surprised by people's inclinations." She gave him a flirting, wicked smile. "Even those closest to you."

That brought Raz up short, a strange sort of warmth twisting his stomach.

"Wait…" he started, finding himself tripping over his words. "Hold on…"

In answer, Syrah only gave him the same half-alluring, half-teasing smile, then laughed and pushed Nymara once more into a slow gallop, pulling away from Raz and Gale.

"Oh, this is a story I need to hear," Raz muttered to himself, and a moment later he and the stallion were in hot pursuit, the beat of Gale's run doing much to hide the faintest sound of hoof-beats along the road behind them.

V

"Damn."

Syrah looked to Raz, brow knit in concern.

"What's wrong?" she asked in a worried voice. "Are they coming?"

Raz raised a finger to his lips, and the woman fell quiet. He was listening again, trying to make out if the sound of horses, driven hard along the road at their back, could be anyone else. It had been several hours since they'd galloped by the mercenaries, and he'd relaxed as the Sun had started to dip over the horizon to their right, the clear blue of the day turning steadily to a somber orange. He hoped, for a moment, that perhaps the riders coming up behind them were more messengers, or even the scouts sent back to report for the patrol of Ystréd soldiers they'd crossed earlier in the day.

When he made out the distinct sound of several voices urging their mounts on, though, reverberating over the hoof-beats and the clink of armor plating, Raz suspected his hope was vain.

"It's them," he said quickly, pulling Gale up short. The stallion snorted, kicking up dirt as he stomped in protest of the abrupt stop.

"But—" Syrah started, obviously as confused by Raz's sudden halt as the horse was. "Wait. What are you doing? We need to run!"

No, a harsh voice snarled inside Raz's head. *No more running.*

"It'll be night within half-an-hour," Raz said hurriedly, reaching down to pull Ahna free from where she was strapped beneath his left leg. "We can't risk running the horses hard in the dark, and even if we did, their chargers would run Nymara down before long."

"I can light the path!" Syrah exclaimed in a huff. "I can give us as much light as we need!"

"And they're likely to have torches," Raz countered, pulling Gale around, the dviassegai held in one hand at his side. "Even if they don't, they might risk the night. Last I heard, there's enough gold on my head to buy them each a dozen war-horses and then some." He looked back at her. "Go. I'll catch up to you when I finish here."

In retrospect, Raz thought he should have known better than to say those words. A shadow passed over Syrah's face like a storm cloud, and all at once the tension and worry vanished from her features. In their place, something very much like anger lingered, lighting a fire in her eye.

"Like I would leave you," she sniffed sourly, and she, too, pulled Nymara around, drawing her staff free of its straps and guiding the horse over to stand beside and slightly behind Raz. "Just do me a favor: try not to kill them all."

If it had been any other person, Raz would have laughed. As it was, however, the words were more perplexing than anything, and he looked at her curiously. Syrah's face was set, her eye on a bend in the road some hundred yards north of them. He thought about voicing his concerns, but before he could put the question together the sound of the approaching riders rang clear, and one after the other the group came around the hill.

They were a far different-looking lot than the rag-tag bunch they'd seemed earlier in the afternoon, and at once Raz saw why it had taken them so long to catch up. Whereas a few hours ago their armor had hung uselessly from their saddles, the mercenaries were now collectively attired in full gear, some with heavy plate and round-helms, others with leather over chain and scale-mail shirts. At their head, one of the women led the band, her brown hair cropped short about her ears, revealing an ugly scar that split around her right eye and cleaved though her cheek. For a moment Raz was reminded of an old friend, the Doctore of the Azbar Arena, but whereas Alyssa Rhen's eyes were a bright, sharp green, this woman's were a dull, damp brown, hungry in the pursuit.

Hungry, that is, until they found Raz and Syrah waiting for them in the center of the road.

At once, something strange came over the group, something which Raz couldn't explain. As expected, blades and maces and axes were drawn immediately, the woman at the forefront of the party pulling a long bastard sword free from where it had been sheathed at her knee. After this, however, Raz had presumed the mercenaries would attempt to ride them down, using the momentum of their charge to great advantage.

Instead, however, the woman in front yelled "Whoah!" pulling back on the reins of her mount. At once the steed, a grey stallion splotched with white, slid to a halt, snorting as rocks and tufts of grass came loose under its shoes. At the woman's back, the other riders did the same, some of their horses whinnying in surprise as they were brought up short, then settling and stomping nervously.

They were less than fifty feet away now. Raz could see the details of their faces, read their stunned expressions and hear the words passed to one another in hissing whispers. It took him aback, catching those hints of their sudden conversation.

"Arro," one man was saying to his companion, his voice strained.

"Monster," another said, apparently to no one in particular.

"Dragon," breathed the second woman, seated in the center of the group.

It took several seconds for Raz to make sense of their apparent surprise. When he did, however, his body stiffened, his arms flexing in a spasm of concerned realization.

"Syrah," he hissed, and from the corner of his vision he saw the Priestess glance at him, "stay here. Don't move."

He could almost hear the woman's teeth grind in annoyance. "I told you," she said in a frustrated voice. "I'm not going to leave y—"

"They're not here for me," Raz told her sharply, not taking his eyes off the mercenaries, who still hadn't moved from their place up the path. "Please. Do as I say."

That caught Syrah's attention.

"What do you mean, 'they're not here for—'?"

"Dragon!"

Syrah's question was cut off by the shouted hail. As Raz looked on, the group's leader guided her horse forward one step at a time, like she was unsure of the approach. It was she who had spoken, and her dim brown eyes watched him expectantly.

"I see you know who I am," Raz called coolly back as Gale hooved at the ground in annoyance, not appreciating the uninvited approach of the sellsword's charger. "It's impolite not to introduce oneself in such circumstances."

The woman blinked, then smirked. It was a hard, almost cruel smile.

Raz didn't like it one bit.

"My apologies," she said in a scornful tone, halting her horse when she was some twenty feet away. "You can call me Thera, if it pleases you. My friends and I are known as—"

"I couldn't give a *shit* what you and your playmates call your little gang," Raz snarled, interrupting her and allowing the red-orange of his neck crest to flare dangerously above his head. "Instead, you can tell me why you've decided to follow us halfway to Ystréd, and taken the time to don your armor to boot."

Thera—if that was indeed the woman's name—looked none-too-pleased to be cut off, her lip curling. "Watch your tongue, scaly," she spat. "I'm attempting to be polite because we didn't know it was *you* we were chasing, and I'm not convinced you're worth the trouble even for twenty thousand Southern crowns."

Bounty's gone up, Raz thought, and he would have been almost pleased with himself if the woman's other words hadn't bothered him so much.

"Explain yourself, mercenary," he growled, narrowing his eyes. "If you have no business with me, then you have no business with us, and I'd much rather be on my way than sitting here wasting my day on foul-mouthed rubbish such as you."

Thera didn't respond at once, her glare flitting away from Raz to linger on Syrah.

"How much is the faith paying you to escort her?" the woman asked finally, obviously attempting to keep her voice even. "A hundred gold? Two hundred? Hand her over, and I'll see to it you get five times that."

Something icy slipped up Raz's spine and into his mind as he caught on, putting everything together.

"How much?" he asked, hearing the building rage in the barely-controlled shake of his voice.

Thera frowned. "As I said, if you tell me how much the Laorin are paying you, I'll make sure—"

"No," Raz snarled, baring his fangs, "I mean: how much is the price on the Witch's head?"

The words hit Syrah like an avalanche, slamming into her in a blow of cold and fear and confusion. At first, as she heard the title—that vile name the worst of the mountain tribes had given her over the years—she was hurt, stunned that Raz would so casually use the phrase.

Then she caught on.

"What?" she hissed, startled and looking from Raz to the woman—Thera—and back again as she struggled to make sense of the question. "A price? What price?"

Raz spoke to her over his shoulder, though his golden eyes, the same shade as the rapidly closing day around them, never left the sellsword. "I was an idiot. They didn't even see me, when we rode by. They didn't know I was there. But they saw you. You would have been hard to miss."

"White hair, white skin, white robes, and missing an eye." Thera smirked, speaking as though quoting some description she'd been given. "It would take a fool not to notice Syrah Brahnt passing you, even at a run."

Syrah felt the iron grip of shock clutch at her heart. It wasn't the fact that the woman knew her name—she was a well-known figure in certain circles among the North. No, rather, it was the way the mercenary was leering at her, the way *all of them* were leering at her, when she looked back at the others still mounted a dozen yards behind their leader. It was a look Syrah knew well, the insatiable, cruel gaze of one driven by greed, by a desire for all the pleasures and glories and riches the world had to offer.

It was the same look Kareth Grahst used to have whenever his gaze fell upon her.

At the thought of the man, Syrah felt her chest constrict, felt her breath tighten and grow short. For an instant she was back in the cramped tent in which the Sigûrth had chained her, to starve and freeze and violate at their pleasure. She saw the faces of the men, the dozens that generally only plagued her now in nightmares, and she drew a ragged, heavy breath.

Then a hand, cool and smooth and strong, closed around her wrist, ripping her back into the present.

Raz hadn't turned away from Thera and her dirty band. His eyes were forward, never giving the woman so much as an instant to believe he was distracted. Despite this, he seemed to have sensed the shift in Syrah's emotions, felt her drop down into a place she never wanted to be. With his free hand he had reached back, seeking her out, seeking to tell her silently what he knew she needed to hear.

Come back to me, his hand said, light but firm about her arm.

Abruptly, the icy grip of fear melted away, once again leaving behind only hot, raging fire.

"They put a *bounty* on my head?" Syrah almost howled in fury at Thera, Nymara sidestepping nervously beneath her as white flames sparked and guttered unbidden around her hands. "After everything they did? Bastards!"

The mercenary shrugged as though the whole topic bored her. Raz, for his part, let go of Syrah's wrist, apparently satisfied she was back in her right mind.

"You didn't answer my question," he told Thera coolly. "I asked you how much. What's the price?"

At this, the woman hesitated. Syrah thought she knew what the mercenary was thinking. She was probably wondering—after seeing Raz's apparently more-than-professional touch to calm her—if attempting to sway the atherian to her side was such a good idea after all.

Greed, though, makes all men fools.

And women, too, it would seem.

"Five thousand gold pieces," she admitted finally, not looking happy about it. Then she lifted the hand not clasped around the hilt of her bastard blade, as though offering a sign of peace. "We're not unreasonable, though. We can share. Twenty-five percent to you, seventy-five to us."

There was some grumbling from the men and woman behind their leader, but Thera turned in her saddle and glared at them, shutting them up.

Beside her, Syrah watched something strange come over Raz. Whereas a few seconds before he'd been tense and rigid, almost shaking with outrage and disgust, abruptly his body was growing still, his face transitioning from enraged to calm, then almost impassive. At first Syrah didn't know what to make of it, but then she saw the look in his eye, the flat, deathly sheen, like an animal had replaced the man she knew. She'd seen that expression before, and it chilled her to the bone.

It was the same look she'd witnessed on the night he rescued her from Grahst's clutches. The same night she had witnessed him cut down a half-dozen men as though they were paper beneath his blades. The same night he had carried her across a snowy field of corpses, butchered in the wake of his desperate search to find her.

"Raz, no," she said quietly, starting to reach out for him. "Wait. Come back. Come back to me…"

But the man would have none of it. He raised his free hand, cutting her off. He eyes, cold and flat and predatory, were still on Thera.

"Even split," he said, edging Gale forward a few feet. "Fifty for you and yours, fifty for me."

VI

For a long time, Syrah thought she hadn't heard him correctly, his words a muffled ring through her ears, like a tolling bell from beneath the surface of a lake. When it registered, however, when she truly understood what had been said, it rocked her.

"Raz?" she gasped in disbelief, staring at the back of his head. "Raz, what are you—?"

"Keep your mouth shut, woman!" he barked, looking away from the sellswords for the first time as he whirled in his saddle. "I've had enough of you as it is! Stay there, stop talking, and maybe I'll hand you over with all your limbs attached."

At once, common sense won out, and an idea formed, complete in Syrah's mind. She wanted to catch Raz's eye, wanted to see the confirmation there, but Thera was already speaking again, and the atherian had turned back to face her.

"Ruthless as the legends claim, Arro," the woman was saying with a laugh, sounding almost approving. "No wonder they used to call you 'the Monster.'"

"Small titles made by small men," Raz snapped, heeling Gale forward another few steps, as though eager to forge their deal. "Now: I've said my offer. Fifty to you, fifty to me."

Thera's eyes narrowed again. "Thirty and seventy," she countered.

"Fifty," Raz repeated again slowly, the menace in his voice punctuating each word, "fifty."

Thera was looking more nervous by the second as Raz came within ten feet of her. The mercenaries behind her, too, were sounding agitated, but their irritation seemed more a result of the deal that appeared to be slipping further and further out of their favor by the second.

"Forty-sixty," Thera finally said in an insistent rush. "Take it or leave it, Dragon. Anything else isn't even worth the three weeks we would need to drag her back to the Vietalis Ranges."

The confirmation of her suspicions—that some aspect of the western clans, likely still within the Sigûrth, were responsible for this mess—registered distantly with Syrah. She had just enough time to consider that Carro probably had more dissent within his growing ranks than he realized when Raz spoke, interrupting her thoughts.

"Fine," he said, though he sounded none-too-pleased about conceding. "Forty-sixty, but I stay with you and your lot the whole way. She's never out of my sight. Agreed?"

"Agreed," Thera said hastily, looking as though she wanted nothing more than the conversation to be over. "She'll be a lot less trouble with more eyes on her, anyway."

Raz nodded slowly, glancing back at Syrah as though considering this. There *was* something in the dim glint of his eye meant for her, but it wasn't the confirmation she'd anticipated. Instead, there was a hint of something like sadness, glimmering at her despite the cold deadness of the gaze.

I'm sorry, his face told her.

Before Syrah could come to terms with what it could possibly mean, however, Raz turned back and pressed Gale forward the last few paces, lifting his right hand to Thera.

The mercenary, still looking nervous but pleased that she had managed to strike a bargain with a legend, reached out to clasp it at once.

"Deal?" she asked in a tentative, eager voice.

In response, Raz leaned in with a cruel, reptilian smile Syrah had never seen, and spoke a single word.

"Not likely."

And with that, his gauntleted fingers tightened around the woman's. With a quick, powerful pull he jerked her forward, and Thera's face barely had time to shift from excited to terrified before Raz brought Ahna up, gripping the weapon just below the head of her twin blades.

There was the sound of steel cleaving through flesh, and Thera's body and sword fell to the road only a second after her head.

As the woman's corpse tumbled from the saddle of her charger, Raz was already moving. He didn't trust that the abrupt death of their captain would incline the rest of the group to flee. Between him and Syrah, their heads were worth enough to buy up half of Ystréd, and even clever fighters were often made idiots by that amount of gold. Sure enough, as he yelled "Hyah!" and drove Gale right at the group, the rest of the mercenaries made no move to run. A few sat still in their saddles, staring in stunned rapture at the headless body of the woman who had been their leader, but some were quicker, hefting weapons and shields.

The advantage of the charge, though, was now in the Dragon's favor.

Old skills flared to life in Raz's body as the stallion careened forward, limbs drawing from memories of years passed among the Arros. Holding tight to Gale's sides with his knees, Raz released the reins completely, drawing his gladius from over his shoulder just as he bulled into the center of the group, roaring all the while. Even with their weapons already drawn, the mercenaries found themselves immediately on the defensive. The foremost man went down as Raz rode into them, Ahna skewering his chest even as Raz parried a hasty sword slash from the right with his gladius. Leaving the dviassegai stuck in the sellsword's chest, Raz maintained his momentum, Gale—a good two hands taller than even the largest of the mercenaries' mounts—little more than an oversized cannonball with legs. They broke through the back of the party with relative ease, Raz ducking the swing of a mace as they did, allowing Gale to gallop several strides before pulling him around as though to make a second pass.

The four remaining were cursing, trying to bring their own horses about to meet him in anticipation of another charge. Raz made a show of pressing Gale forward again, his gladius whirling about his head as though to build momentum for a devastating slash.

Fortunately, Syrah was quick to take advantage of the opportunity he had given her.

There was a series of bright flashes, followed immediately by a *sizzling* like burning meat. The remaining woman and one of the men howled in pain as something like a whip wrapped about their necks, the lash looking like it was made of bright, ivory fire. They yelled again as the magic strained, both of them dropping their weapons to reach up and pull at the rope-like flames with gloved hands, but too late. A second later they were toppling off their horses, hitting the earthen ground with echoed *thuds* and the crash of armor.

The lashes remained, their shining lengths leading back to where Syrah still sat ahorse on the other side of the group, the ends of the arcane whips wrapped around her right hand. About her left, still clenching the patterned steel of her staff, a blaze of pure white fire lit her pale face in bright shadows as it flickered.

"Bad idea to turn your back on a 'Witch,' isn't it?" Raz asked the last two men still left ahorse, grinning nastily at them. "I'd have expected better of you."

The pair looked terrified, sweat gleaming on their faces in the fading light, heads twisting this way and that as they tried to keep both Raz and Syrah in their sights. One hefted a twin-bladed battle-axe, the other a sword and banded shield, but both looked unsure of themselves. Penned on one side by the Dragon and on the other by the magics of a Northern god, the two men appeared to be struggling with a decision.

Raz made the choice easy.

"HYAH!" he screamed, slapping Gale's flank with the flat of his sword. The stallion reared and lanced forward, head plunging and mane whipping with every great stride of his strong legs. The two mercenaries yelled and brought their mounts around, driving them desperately toward Syrah in an attempt to escape Raz. Before they got within twenty feet of her, weapons held ready at their sides, the flames in Syrah's right hand solidified into two twin points of brilliant white, which shot forward in parallel streaks to meet the pair. The spells made no sound as they flew through the air, whisking toward the men like birds of prey on silent wings. One took the axe wielder square in the chest, and immediately the man went limp, toppling from his running horse.

The other, though, *pinged* harmlessly off the iron ribbing of the second man's shield.

Syrah's eyes went wide in alarm. The sellsword howled in triumph, barreling forward the last ten feet. His horse screamed as he drove it even faster, urging it forward for the kill. His sword came up, ready to descend on the woman's exposed neck. The steel shone, lethal and terrifying in the orange glow of the setting sun and the arcane gleam of the fiery whips the Priestess still held stubbornly in her right hand.

He was just about to drive the sword down, about to claim her head for his own, when Raz's skillfully thrown gladius took him squarely between the shoulder blades.

Thunk.

"*Urk!*" was the only sound the man made, his own weapon falling harmlessly to the road, his horse charging past Syrah so closely Raz saw the wind of its passing blow about in the loose strands of her white hair. The man made it another twenty feet or so, looking as though he were clawing at the blade that must have been protruding from his chest, before he too keeled from his saddle, landing in a bloody heap on the ground.

After that, the evening settled again, the only sound coming from the crackle of white fire and the groans and yelps of the pair who still had the magic wrapped around their necks. Gale's hooves clomped dully over the grassy earth as Raz nudged him forward, reaching for Ahna's haft and jerking her free from the ribcage of the first man.

"Close one," he said as he drew Gale up alongside Nymara, watching Syrah. "I didn't expect him to deflect the stunning spell like that."

He had presumed the woman would be shaken, anticipated that she would stare at him blankly, or look down at the blood dripping from Ahna's blades with disgust, maybe even horror. He was taken aback, therefore, when she did little more than sigh. The only expression she had—casting over the remnants of the fight, over the men and women scattered dead and alive across the road—might have been slight disappointment.

"I didn't either," she said, sounding like she was chastising herself, her mouth twisting into a frown. "I should have. I'll know better next time."

Raz stared at her, stunned, at a loss for words.

When Syrah noticed this, she cocked her head at him. "What?" She glanced down at herself in sudden concern. "Am I bleeding?"

Raz blinked, thinking of what he could say, then looked away. "No." He nearly tripped over the word. "It's nothing. We'll speak of it later." He shook off the confusion, indicating the twitching and yelping man and woman Syrah still held leashed in her lashes, and the unconscious man she'd stunned. "Let's finish this."

At that, Raz finally witnessed what he'd expected to see. The Priestess blanched, looking at him sharply.

"'Finish?'" she quoted, as though unsure what he meant. "They're done, Raz. Beaten. You don't have to—"

"I'm not going to kill them," Raz said with a half-amused snort, throwing a leg off of Gale as he dismounted, tossing Ahna over his shoulder once he did. "What sort of man do you think I am?"

Syrah hesitated, then looked sad. "Sorry," she said after a moment, what little color she had returning to her cheeks. "I-I wasn't sure. There was a second there, when you were pretending you'd split my bounty with that woman…"

Raz laughed and gave her a lopsided grin. "Who says I was pretending? I asked for fifty-fifty. She didn't give it to me."

Syrah scowled. "Not funny." But she seemed to relax a little.

Raz chuckled again, then turned and started making for the pair of bound sellswords up the road. "It's a little funny. Now, can you release the spells?" He tapped one of the lashes of solidified fire with a steel-clad finger as he walked, making the magic vibrate. "I've been on the end of these things before. They're not comfortable."

Behind him, he heard Syrah grumble something like "It's *not* funny," but a second later the flames dissolved in a shower of white dust, glistening and vanishing as it tumbled toward the ground. Before him, the mercenaries began to hack and cough, breathing clear for the first time in well over a minute. The woman was the quickest to attempt to get on her feet, pushing herself shakily onto one knee and going for a long knife on her belt as she did.

"Oh no you don't," Raz told her, taking the last few steps in a flash. In three quick moves he caught her wrist with his free hand, twisted the knife out of it, and swept her legs from under her once again. The woman landed on her back in the dirt for a second time with a hard *thud*, gasping as the wind was knocked out of her. A moment later, Raz had stepped away from her, moving toward her companion just as the man managed to push himself unsteadily up onto his hands and knees.

"And you," Raz snarled, slamming the bottom of his gauntleted fist into the back of the man's head. "Stay down."

With a puff of dust and a grunt, the mercenary did exactly that.

By the time Raz turned around again, Syrah had dismounted and moved to stand over the armored woman, who was still struggling to catch her breath as she lay flat on her back in the road.

"What's your name?" Syrah was asking her in an—in Raz's opinion—unnecessarily kind voice as he stepped back to stand on the other side of the fallen figure.

The woman glared at her. "Fuck off," she grumbled between groans. "If you're gonna kill me, then kill me, and be done with it."

"Killing's finished for now," Raz growled at her. "Answer my friend's question, then you can take what comrades are still breathing and get out of our sight."

The sellsword continued to glower, but whereas Syrah's calm query had done little to persuade her, Raz's less-patient tone seemed to loosen her tongue.

"Alana," she grumbled through a clenched jaw.

"Alana," Syrah said with a smile, setting the tip of her staff into the ground and kneeling beside her. "Are you hurt? I can assist you, if you are."

Alana the mercenary looked at Syrah as though she had three heads. "Back off, Witch. I don't need none of your damn sorcery."

Raz growled. "Watch your tongue. I had half-a-mind to cut it from your head already, and that was *before* you opened your mouth."

Immediately the woman shut up, eyes widening in fear. Sure he had her attention, Raz set the heavy steel point of Ahna's bottom end suggestively close to the mercenary's ear and grinned wickedly at her.

"So, then," he said, his crest rising once more behind his head and his wings spreading several feet to either side of his body as he spoke. "You don't look hurt. You can thank the Moon for that. You'll stay that way, too, if you do as we say and answer our questions. Understood?"

Alana swallowed, but didn't hesitate as she nodded up at him. On her other side, Syrah looked on in silence.

"Good," Raz said, not moving the dviassegai's pointed tip away from the woman's ear even as she glanced at it nervously. "First question, then: who put out the bounty?"

The answer was prompt, and expected.

"Mountain men," Alana said quickly, her eyes flicking to his. "Western tribes, as the freeze ended."

"What tribes?" Syrah pressed her. "Sigûrth?"

Alana shook her head, complexion paling as she looked at the Priestess, like she didn't want to give the answer she had. "I don't know. I don't think Thera knew, either. We were assisting with the rebuilding efforts and security in Metcaf. When winter broke, we heard the Kayle's army was no more, and how it happened." She glanced at Raz again. "They released most of the mercenary groups from our contracts just so they wouldn't have to feed us through the summer. We heard about the bounty on the road."

Raz frowned at that. "Then anyone could have posted it. Who were you supposed to deliver her to, if you found her?"

Alana looked even more nervous. "Any of the tribes," she answered in a shaking voice. "Rumor was any of the Vietalis clans would be willing to pay for the Witch's head."

Raz looked up at Syrah, catching her eye and raising a brow.

This complicates things, his look said, and she nodded briefly in understanding and agreement.

"Who knows about the price?" Syrah asked the woman. "How many groups like yours were in Metcaf?"

"Just in Metcaf?" Alana asked with a harsh snort. "A hundred. In Harond, though, there was half that again."

"And they were all made aware of it?"

Alana shrugged, taking the opportunity to scoot her head an inch or two away from the steel point still buried in the ground beside her. "Enough," she said eventually, "but that was weeks ago…"

"And by now most of the North would know, if not all of it," Syrah finished for her, eyes distant. After a second or two of thinking, she looked up. "Shall we let them go?"

For a moment, the mercenary looked relieved. Then her face tensed in fear as Raz answered.

"No. Not yet."

With a jerk he pulled Ahna's tip out of the ground, twisting her so that her blades plunged down toward Alana's neck like a guillotine. The woman screamed and Syrah gasped, but Raz stopped the dviassegai just short of the sellsword's throat. The blood dripped off Ahna's blades, trickling down to spatter the mercenary's dirty skin, and the woman's whole body shook from fear as she continued to stare up at Raz.

"You're going to deliver a message for me, Alana," he said in a low, dangerous voice, leering down at her. "You're going to hear what I have to say, and share it with any of your kind you come across. Understood?"

The woman's nod was an almost-imperceptible twitch as she swallowed, like she was nervous any greater movement would leave her as headless as her former captain.

"Good," Raz snarled, "then listen carefully. The bounty on the Witch's head is void. Any who would attempt to claim it can count their lives as forfeit."

He lifted Ahna away from the mercenary's throat then, throwing her over his shoulder once again and allowing himself to be outlined against the rising moon at his back, like some winged demon of the night.

"Tell them the Dragon says *no one* touches Syrah Brahnt."

VII

"Thank you."

Raz looked at Syrah, taking her face in beneath the light of the new day. It was the morning after their little battle along the north road, and these were among the first words she'd spoken since retrieving Raz's gladius and leaving the mercenary Alana to gather her living companions and be on her way. Syrah had been strangely quiet for the short remainder of the evening they'd spent ahorse, and had even kept her silence when they'd stopped to make camp and settle in for the night. Raz had wanted to press her, wanted to ask her the questions boiling about his brain since the moments before the fight, but thought better of it in the end. Syrah had something on her mind, that was clear enough, and when she'd settled into her habitual spot beside him, curling up against his chest to sleep, Raz decided he'd give her the evening to gather herself.

Now, as they set about saddling their horses in preparation for their last few hours before reaching Ystréd, he suspected he was about to have his answers.

"For what?" he asked in response, strapping his rolled-up bedroll to the back of Gale's saddle.

She glared at him. "You know what," she said, and he was pleased to hear more of the old fire in her voice. "For the sword… the man… last night…"

In his mind, he saw again the flash of the rider's sword, ready and waiting to cleave her head from her neck.

"I killed that man, Syrah," Raz said evenly, not looking at her as he double-checked that he'd packed what little provisions they had left.

There was a pause.

"I know," Syrah finally said. "And I'm glad you did."

At this, Raz looked around at her. His concern must have been plain on his face, because Syrah looked suddenly strained, barely managing to give him a twisted, forced smile.

"I *know* I'm not allowed to say that," she said in a tense voice. "Believe me, I know. But…" She stopped, glancing down at the reins she'd been in the process of getting over Nymara's head.

"Are you doubting, Syrah?"

It was the heaviest of the questions Raz had been fumbling with, and—if he was honest with himself—it was one he'd been harboring for much longer than just the one night. He hadn't known the woman all that long, in truth, let alone before he'd pulled her from Kareth Grahst's cruel clutches. Still, Raz had developed the distinct sense over the course of the winter that something—*No*, he thought. *Many things*—had changed about the woman during those months of the freeze. He'd noticed it less in his own interactions with her than he had in her interactions with the other occupants of the Citadel. Syrah had conceded her post on the council as soon as she'd been given a free moment to do so, but she'd still been a well-known and popular figure within Cyurgi 'Di's walls. Men and women and children of all ages recognized her and sought to speak to her, wanting to ask her how she was, or what had happened, or what she expected for the future of the faith and the Citadel.

It had been hardest at first, in the weeks following the fall of Gûlraht Baoill. As far as Raz knew, he was still the only man she would allow to touch her, but in the month or so after the disbanding of the Kayle's army, Syrah could barely function if he wasn't by her side, if he wasn't there to pull her back when the darkness took over. After a time, that passed—largely because the men of the Citadel came to understand and respect her aversion to them—but even once Syrah returned to what Raz thought was very likely to be most of her old self, something was off. He saw it in the concerned looks her friends gave her as they ate in the great hall, heard it in the toneless manner she spoke her prayers and blessings. He felt it in the manner others sometimes pulled away from her in conversation, like her opinions had suddenly become taboo. He witnessed it when she'd requested to be relieved of all teaching responsibilities except for combat instruction in the keep's practice chambers.

Only there, beneath the cavernous arched ceilings of the rooms where the men and women of the faith learned to channel and control their bodies, staffs, and magics, did Raz ever get the feeling that Syrah really and truly became herself again.

But it hadn't mattered, then, Raz thought privately as he considered this.

At the time, Syrah was safe among friends and comrades who cared for her. As she'd recovered, learning to move past the violence and horrors Kareth Grahst and his men had visited upon her, she'd been in an environment of warmth and love, and Raz hadn't worried too much about it. She would find her balance, he had told himself. With his help, she would come to terms with the brutality she'd suffered. The nightmares had started to pass, becoming less and less frequent until she'd had almost none for a month before they were set to depart. Raz had dared hope her soul had found that steadiness he'd prayed to the Sun for every day.

But now, out in the brightness and warmth and savagery of the world beyond the safety of the Citadel's ramparts, he was getting the sense that that steadiness was not as solid as he'd hoped.

"'Doubt'…? No… 'Doubt' isn't the right word."

Syrah's answer pulled Raz out of his whirlwind of thoughts.

"Oh?" he pressed her gently.

Syrah nodded, looking out over the southern horizon, which was growing flatter by the hour. "I don't doubt, Raz. The Lifegiver is to me as your Sun and Moon are to you. He exists as a part of me, as alive as any limb or organ or soul." She frowned. "I'm not doubting his existence, or his plan for the world. I just…"

She trailed off, looking as though she were struggling to find the words.

"Wonder if your faith views him in a brighter light than it should?" he finished helpfully.

Syrah's eye went wide in surprise, and she looked at him.

"*Yes*," she breathed, like he had managed to put words to some feeling or thought she hadn't yet been able to pinpoint. "Exactly. How can I not? After Carro? After your duel with Baoill...?"

Raz nodded in understanding. He had suspected as much. It had taken the Breaking of Carro al'Dor, the wisest and kindest man he'd ever met—other than perhaps Talo Brahnt himself—for Raz to fully understand the rigidness to which the Laorin held themselves by the cardinal rule of their faith: no death knowingly committed or allowed at the hands of a worshiper of Laor. Carro had thrown away his trust in that rule, thrown away his robes and steel and power and pride when he'd understood that the world existed in a much more complex state than the strict doctrine of his faith allowed for. He had permitted Raz to give Talo—the man he'd loved—mercy by the sword as the former High Priest lay suffering a slow and horrible death. He'd condoned the killing of a dozen men of the tribes in order to break through their siege of the Citadel and bring a glimmer of hope to the thousands of Priests and Priestesses trapped there upon the mountain, then again when he'd tasked Raz with seeking out and rescuing Syrah. He had thrown everything he'd ever known away to give the men and women of his home even a slight chance at avoiding a cold and brutal death at the hands of the Kayle, and in thanks the Laorin had stripped him of his rank and title, torn the magics from his body in an agonizing ritual, and banished him from their halls forever once summer came.

And then, when faced with the same choices he had been given, the faith had chosen to allow Carro to challenge Gûlraht Baoill to a duel to the death, and to nominate Raz as his champion.

In the end, it seemed even the Laorin as a whole had not been able to deny the wisdom of sacrificing one life so that thousands could live...

"Are you wondering where the line is drawn?" Raz asked her, watching Syrah carefully and letting Gale and Nymara amble along the grassy road.

Syrah's face darkened. "Honestly... I'm more wondering if I've simply been a fool these last twenty years of my life."

Raz smiled wryly. "No, not a fool, Syrah. Perhaps you were *fooled*, mystified by some notion of your god that you'd come to believe as an ironclad reality, but you're far from anything I'd call a fool."

"Then where *is* the line, Raz?" she demanded abruptly, sounding suddenly angry. "If I'm no fool, explain to me why I can't see it, can't find it. I had a rule, a law by which I could live. *Then*, I saw the line. *Then*, I understand that there was a boundary that couldn't be crossed. Now..." She swallowed, her knuckles whitening as she gripped Nymara's reins so tightly they shook. "Now, I can't see it. Now, there is no line."

"Exactly."

Syrah blinked and looked around at him.

"What?" she asked in disbelief.

"Exactly," Raz repeatedly darkly, watching a covered wagon roll by, the young couple at its front ogling him with terrified surprise. "There is no line, Syrah. There is no *rule* by which the world works. Do you think I stop to think every time I have to spill blood? Did you think I stopped to consider, stopped to calculate your value against his, when I killed that man last night?"

He frowned, pulling Gale over as the stallion strayed too close to Nymara, briefly knocking he and Syrah's knees together. "You're still attempting to see the world in black and white, just with the boundary skewed differently. You're still trying to fit life into categories of 'acceptable' and 'unacceptable.' But that's not how it works, Syrah. That's not how life is. There is no uniform color. There aren't even shades of grey, as any clichéd poet will be tempted to tell you. Life is not a spectrum that can be measured and weighed. It's a damn ocean, sometimes calm and pleasant, sometimes black and churning, but in either case at no point do we have *any* idea what lies more than a few feet beneath the surface."

He lifted a hand, waving about at the settled hills of the Dehn. "It's all right to have rules, guidelines. Laws are a necessary thing in a world that would otherwise be chaos, but to live a life like ours it's important to come to terms with the fact that laws are not some celestial decree which holds men firm like a dog chained to a wall. They can be bent, broken, even ignored outright. And there are places which have no laws, have no rules. This road, for example—" he swept the hand before him now, indicating the path down which they traveled "—do you think Thera and her men were concerned with whether or not taking you fell in the black or white? Do you think they paused to value your freedom against what they were there to do? No."

He paused, then brought his hand to his face, studying the steel of his claws. "Your god—or rather the teachings by which your faith has had you adhere to—does not allow for reality. They do not allow for chance, or mistakes, or situations in which there is simply no good option. Talo thought of it as 'the lesser of evils,' which is apt enough. The Laorin would have you believe that there is always another way, that one needs only consider all the options. But it doesn't work like that. If I had 'considered all the options' last night—"

"I would be dead," Syrah finished for him, nodding. "I know. I understand. But is it right for you to value my life against his?"

"You talk like you can quantify what one is worth. Like there's an equation for it."

Syrah shrugged. "Isn't there?"

Raz sighed. "None that I know of." Then he blinked. "And even if there was, you make my point for me."

"How so?" Syrah asked, giving him a sharp look as Gale and Nymara started across a wide bridge of wood and timber, their iron shoes *clomping* hollowly over the timber slats beneath them.

"If you want me to try to reduce your existence to basic arithmetic, then I can't," Raz said with a shrug once they'd stepped off the bridge. "I can only give you the facts of what I know to be true. That man was a killer. They all were. You felt better, I'm sure, leaving half of them alive, but if you think for a moment Alana and the other two are off to pick up basket weaving or blacksmithing, you've got another thing coming. They'll spend a day or two nursing their wounds, then they'll be off to form or join another cohort and ply their trade somewhere else. By the logic of your faith, we let three murderers walk away unscathed, free to kill again. By sparing them, we have allowed for the death of others."

"You don't know that," Syrah said quietly, but she didn't sound as though she had much faith in her words.

"No," Raz admitted with half-a-shrug, scratching at Gale's mane as the horse shook his great head. "I don't. But neither do you know that they *won't* lift their swords against another, that they *won't* spill blood within so much as the fortnight, much less the rest of their lives."

Syrah said nothing, her head bowed as she listened.

"But you," Raz said slowly, eyes back on the road. "You are something else, Syrah." He gave her a sidelong look. "You're a fighter. I would never argue otherwise. But you're also a healer, a woman who cares *genuinely* about the betterment of the world. By killing that man, not only did I keep him from murder for the rest of his life, but I saved you. And in saving you, I saved the dozens of souls your smile and your magic might spare from death before their time."

He paused, contemplating his next words carefully. "Essentially, by killing one man, by taking one life, I may have prevented the death of a hundred more."

Beside him, Syrah was quiet. For several long minutes they rode in silence, the Priestess not taking her eye off the back of Nymara's neck, lost to her thoughts. Raz let her be, allowing himself his own contemplations, wondering if he'd said too much.

Finally, Syrah's head lifted. When Raz turned to look at her, the first thing he saw was that she was smiling.

The next was that she was crying.

"I think," she began slowly, her voice uneven, like the words were hard to say, "that I serve a god of death, as much as I serve a god of life."

In response, Raz gave her his own sad smile. Reaching out, he carefully wiped the tears from her cheek, then brought her head down to rest against his chest as they rode slowly along.

Pressing the end of his snout into her white hair, his voice was gentle when he spoke.

"You can't have one without the other, Syrah. You can never have one without the other."

It wasn't more than an hour or two later that the hills of the Dehn Plains finally broke in truth, and the low walls of Ystréd came into view at last. They had been on the road for almost three weeks, and the sight of civilization was enough to make even Raz—who'd never been a fan of the crowds and noise of the cities—sigh in relief.

For Syrah, the excitement was much more visceral. She had brightened significantly since they'd finished their talk, seeming to come to terms with at least some of the confusion that must have been racking her since the previous evening. Now, though, the rest of the darkness lifted from her, like overcast clouds breaking in heed of the Sun.

"Thank *Laor*," she practically groaned, leaning forward to rest her forehead on Nymara's neck dramatically so that the rest of her words came muffled through the horse's mane. "The minute we're within the walls, I'm sending Atler a messenger spell asking to have water heated. I need a *bath*."

"You and me both," Raz said, grimacing and fighting the impulse to sniff at the dirty cotton of his shirt. "I don't hate the idea of a proper meal, either."

Syrah turned her head so that her mangled ear rested against the horse. "Glutton," she teased.

"I'm shocked food wasn't your first thought, too," Raz said with a snort, clucking Gale forward. "I've had enough salted venison and dried potatoes to sate me for this life and anything after it."

Together they took the last dip from the Plains, pushing the animals into a quick trot until they could make out the details of the city wall. From there, they guided Gale and Nymara in behind the short line of families and carts waiting to be allowed through the small northern gate, Raz lifting his hood as high over his face as he could and tucking his wings and tail away once more. For several minutes they were left in peace, the man in line before them doing nothing more than giving them an uninterested glance as he led an old mule and the weapon-stocked cart it was pulling a few steps forward. As they waited, Raz and Syrah talked quietly about whether Jofrey had ever managed to get a bird to Tana Atler, the High Priestess of Ystréd's temple, to let her know they would be arriving, and whether or not Carro had left the Citadel yet. They were having a disagreement about how long they should stay in the city and where they should go from there when the man ahead of them was given leave to pass into Ystréd, and they were waved forward.

They had less trouble getting through the gate than Raz had expected. The last time he'd crossed paths with the Ystréd guard, he'd been forced to lay one of them flat on his ass to make a point, and he was worried the soldiers stationed around the north entrance would have heard the story and held a grudge. Instead, though, the three young men, dressed in simple uniforms bearing the city's colors, only looked at him with the same horrified fascination as anyone else, then directed their questions at Syrah once they'd shaken themselves free of their shock. Where were they coming from? Where were they headed? How long would they be in the city? Syrah navigated each question pleasantly, smiling at the men as she did. Before long, the soldiers were only ever glancing at Raz, their attentions fixed most assertively on the Priestess as she spoke. None of them saw the tension of her shoulders, or the way she shied away from one of the men when he stepped forward and asked to look through her saddlebags. Raz allowed it to happen, trusting Syrah to let him know if she needed him to speak up. A minute or so later, though, they were waved on, and Syrah bid the men a pleasant day before leading Nymara through the gate.

"That's a first," Raz laughed once they were well out of earshot, weaving their way through the simple timber-and-stone buildings of the city proper.

Syrah looked back at him curiously. "What is?"

"Riding away from a group of armed guards, and only half of them are staring at me. I think you had them smitten."

Syrah rolled her eyes. "I'm glad my charms amuse you," she said dryly. "A simple 'thank you for getting us through without half the town being alerted to our presence' would have been fine."

"Oh, I don't know," Raz continued to tease her. "I'm pretty sure most of them would have gone to one knee if you'd given them half-a-chance. Sure the city life doesn't suit you?"

Syrah grimaced, then gave him one of her special, tauntingly enticing smiles. "I'm sad you think I'd settle for a simple guardsman, gallant as they may be. You should know I have higher standards for myself, Raz i'Syul Arro."

At that, Raz snorted, but said nothing more. They spent the better part of a half-hour negotiating the cobbled roads of the city, traveling deeper in as the buildings became grander and more elaborate around them. Raz thought he could have gotten them to the temple eventually, vaguely recalling the way from when he, Talo, and Carro had last left Ystréd, but he didn't say as much. For one thing, he wasn't in any hurry, enjoying—as he always did—the feel of the town rising up around him, all wood and stone lined one against the other, broken up only by the occasional towering tree, or fountain now flowing with water in the warmth of the summer day.

For another, though, it was definitely best to let Syrah have the lead, making it very clear that he was *her* guest on this venture, and not the other way around.

Ystréd's roads had been crowded when last he'd visited the city, people milling about with families and horses and oxen as they'd sought to take advantage of the last week or so before the winter storms came in truth. Now, though, the streets were well and truly packed, writhing to the point of bursting with men and women and children out enjoying the rare months of warmth and sunlight. On one hand, it was pleasant to witness, to see the residents of the frigid lands of the North living life as any other people might have in more temperate climates, their voices raised in a rumble of sound, some shouting back and forth as they sought each other in the crowd.

On the other hand, it gave Raz an instant headache, and the irritated expression he must have been carrying across his face as they rode could have done nothing to help the sudden breadth of silence that followed him and Syrah like a ring of sickness while they pressed carefully through the city.

It had been a long time, Raz realized, since he remembered causing such unease among people. To the south, in the fringe cities, he was a known anomaly, a figure Southerners tended often to ignore or glower at, but rarely stare. In Azbar, his name had become synonymous with the thrill of the Arena, and after the first week or two of his arrival the residents of that city had been more likely to cheer him or ogle him excitedly than they'd been to gape at him in terrified silence. Even when he'd traveled through Ystréd last—along this very road, in fact—the people of the town had only been hesitant to approach, many of them overcoming their fear of the newly-dubbed "Scourge of the South" in order to receive benediction from a High Priest of Laor.

Now, though, despite a few of apparently greatest faith and courage reaching out to Syrah so that she might bless them with the sign of the new day, Raz found the otherwise still and silent crowd unnerving.

"Maybe this wasn't such a good idea," he muttered under his breath to Syrah, urging Gale up so that they rode abreast again.

Syrah finished her prayer over a baby girl who'd been raised up to her in her father's hands, then straightened in her saddle. "It's all right," she replied, smiling into the crowd of gawkers around them in a clear attempt to assuage their fear. "Maybe they've just heard what you did to the Kayle. Thera and her band knew. There's no reason these people wouldn't."

Raz nodded slowly, glancing about. "Hadn't thought of that," he admitted. "Still, if they were grateful—or even just relieved—you'd think we'd see a few happier expressions among them."

Syrah shrugged, still not looking around at him. "Don't take this the wrong way, Raz," she began, "but if anything, you may be more beast to them now than ever before. 'The Dragon.' If that's the name they've heard on the wind, then there isn't much reason for them to feel any more comfortable around you."

"'Comfortable?'" Raz repeated with a grunt. "Syrah, some of these people look like the only reason they haven't run away screaming is because *you're* with me."

At that, it seemed Syrah couldn't help but blush a little, glancing at him. "Well, I guess that means you'll have to keep me around, then. For morale, of course."

Raz, though, was not feeling in the mood to play her game. "Whose morale?" he asked. "Mine?" He indicated the throng around them with a tilt of his hooded head. "Or theirs?"

"Why not both?" Syrah replied with something almost like a giggle.

Raz just rolled his eyes.

They rode on for another ten minutes or so, guiding Gale and Nymara carefully through the streets, doing their best to avoid trampling on anyone's feet. Syrah stopped a few times to ask for directions from a varied assortment of women, thanking each and giving them a smile before moving on, and it wasn't long before Raz became sure he recognized their surroundings.

"That way," he said eventually, reaching out to tap Syrah on the thigh and point down a wide fairway leading west. Syrah blinked, then nodded, pulling Nymara about slowly as she and Raz went around a vendor shouting for all to come view the clay and porcelain wares he had displayed on a covered stall on the corner.

Another few minutes of struggling through the streets, and the temple came into view.

Compared to the likes of Cyurgi 'Di, the Laorin temple of Ystréd was a pitiful thing. Two stories tall, it was a squat sort of building accented with a modest garden that now bloomed a hundred different colors, its overhanging upper level designed to shelter the front door from the wind and snow during the freeze. When last he'd seen it, the temple had carried the same cold, mournful air about it as most of the North's buildings in winter, its withered plants hidden beneath white frost, its ledges and lips teethed with icicles. Now, though, the temple was animated, glass windows shining in the brightness of the day, the garden alive and vibrant as a half-dozen men and women in the plain brown tunics of acolytes and the white robes of the ordained moved about it, gathering its bounty and caring for the plants.

When they were near, Syrah raised a hand and hailed the Laorin, a few of whom stood straight and turned at her call. A look of surprise darted across each of their faces—though for once there was no hint of disgust or fear at the sight of Raz—and one older Priestess said something quickly to a younger acolyte at her elbow. A second later the boy hurried off, disappearing into the open doors of the temple, likely fetching the High Priestess.

"Welcome, Syrah Brant," the woman said with a kind smile once Raz and Syrah led Gale and Nymara off the street. "We've been expecting you." She turned her blue eyes on Raz, and he was relieved to see that her smile didn't fade. "And welcome, Master Arro. We were pleased to hear you had made it safely to the Citadel after you left last winter."

Raz ducked his head in thanks.

"You received word from Jofrey, then?" Syrah asked, starting to dismount as another acolyte, a young woman, hurried forward to take Gale and Nymara's reins.

"We did," the Priestess said, motioning for the acolyte to lead the horses around the back of the temple before indicating the doors of the building. "But please, come inside. I'm sure the High Priestess will want to fill you in herself."

Raz too, dismounted, giving Gale a reassuring pat before allowing him to be led away, and followed Syrah as they trailed the Priestess back toward the house. The other faithful in the garden around them watched him as they passed, but there was still no apprehension in their gaze. Instead, they looked more impressed, excited, just as the crowds of Azbar had when he'd wandered through their streets with Arrun and Lueski.

Seems 'the Dragon' made a name for himself here, too, Raz thought in exasperated amusement.

They entered the temple one after the other, Raz having to duck under the low overhang of the front door before straightening up again. They were in the building's small common hall, a large portion of the space occupied by an old wooden table where the faithful took their meals. Past that, a large hearth—which had been bright and roaring when last he'd seen it—was cool and dark, and a doorway at its left led back to what he seemed to recall were the kitchens. Ahead of them and to their right, a set of stairs led upward to the second level, open over their heads. He could see the tops of doors over the lip of the walkway above them, the private chambers of the temple's residents. There were other rooms on the bottom floor as well, some with their own fireplaces and windows, though Raz couldn't recall which one he'd been cooped up in for the short duration of his recovery.

"Priestess Brahnt," a gentle voice called out. "Master Arro. Welcome to Ystréd. I hope your trip wasn't too troublesome."

Looking around, Raz watched a woman in the robes of the faith coming quickly down the stairs, the white cloth of her hood crested with a single stripe of black. Tana Atler was a short, plump woman of some thirty years, with wavy blonde hair that hung from beneath the hood. Her eyes were a lively shade of hazel, and they took them in jovially as she reached the bottom of the flight.

Or at least took in Syrah jovially. When they glanced to Raz, he saw a coldness there he realized suddenly he might have expected.

Syrah, apparently, noticed nothing. "High Priestess," she said with a respectful bow. "You have our thanks for sheltering us. We hope we won't inconvenience you for more than a few days, perhaps a week or so at most."

At that, Atler tut-tutted like an old woman, waving Syrah's bow away like it was embarrassing her. "Please, call me Tana. After having the pleasure of your Priest-Mentor under my roof, I can only imagine you will be much the same." Her face softened. "Incidentally, you have our condolences for your loss. It's my understanding you and Talo were very close."

Syrah smiled sadly and nodded. "We were," she said quietly. "And thank you. Talo gave his life fighting to save another, as anyone would have expected him to. It also helps—" she gestured at Raz "—to have the man who avenged him as a companion."

"Yes…" Atler said slowly, her voice hardening ever so slightly, looking again to Raz. "We heard about the ursalus. It's a pity you weren't by his side sooner, Master Arro. Talo Brahnt was a great man. His loss will be felt for many years among our faith."

63

This time, Syrah heard the coolness in the High Priestess' words, and her brow knitted in confusion. She looked about to ask as to the meaning of it, but Raz stopped her with a hand on her shoulder.

"I couldn't agree more, High Priestess," he said with an inclination of his head, doing his best to make the woman feel the sincerity of his words. "Of the many things I regret in my life, I doubt Talo's death will ever be surpassed. I wish for nothing more than to have been able to be there, to have reached him sooner."

"Raz," Syrah started in a startled whisper, eye widening. "What are you talking about? It wasn't your fault. You couldn't have—"

But again Raz silenced her gently, squeezing her shoulder, his eyes on Atler. The woman, for her part, looked at him a little more kindly, as though his admittance had managed to redeem him ever so slightly in her eyes.

"Yes," she said finally, shaking the harshness from her voice, "well... By now Talo Brahnt has been reborn to the world, and we should all pray to be fortunate enough that his soul finds its way back into the arms of the faith. For the moment," she nodded to the older Priestess who had led them into the temple, now standing quietly to the side, "let's get you out of those clothes and see to it that you're fed. Kerren will show you to your rooms. Kerren, if you wouldn't mind?"

The Priestess—Kerren—bowed and, after Atler told them she would see them both come dinnertime and took her leave, stepped between them and started for the stairs.

"Your packs and personal items will be brought up as soon as the acolytes finish caring for your horses," the woman said over her shoulder once she was sure they were following her. "If they've left anything of importance, please feel free to retrieve them. The stables are around the back of the temple, and can also be reached through the kitchens."

She paused at the top of the stairs, glancing back at the hilt of Raz's gladius nervously. "We do ask, however, that any weapons other than staffs be kept either with the horses, or in your quarters, Master Arro. We hope that's not an unreasonable request."

Raz shook his head at once. "Not at all. I'll leave the sword in my room. The rest of my equipment can stay with Gale, for the time being."

Kerren looked relieved, then turned and led them along the walkway, stopping before a pair of doors in the wall directly above the great empty hearth of the dining hall below.

"Your arrangements," she said to Raz, opening the innermost door to reveal a small, comfortable room with a single bed, a simple dresser, and a shuttered window in the back wall, now open to the light of the day. "You are welcome to stay as long as you need, and please let us know if you require assistance in making provisions should you decide to take your leave from us."

She shut the door, then stepped over and made to open the other, closer to the wall. Before she did, though, she hesitated, and looked around at Syrah.

"I hope this isn't overstepping," she said quietly, "but I thought you would prefer to take this room, Priestess. It was the one High Priest Brahnt and Priest al'Dor stayed in when last they were here."

Then, as Syrah looked on in disbelief, she opened the door.

The chamber wasn't all that different from the first Kerren had shown them. It was a corner space, with an open window set into the wall above a small escritoire that looked out over an alleyway. The bed was a little larger, but not by much, and Raz had a moment of amusement as he tried to imagine how Talo and Carro—both men of some breadth and bulk—ever fit comfortably on it together.

I'll bet Carro made Talo sleep on the floor, he thought, chuckling to himself.

"It's…" Syrah started, sounding at a bit of a loss for words as she stepped inside. "It's wonderful. Thank you, Kerren. And please, call me Syrah."

Kerren nodded but said nothing more, moving aside and allowing Raz to duck into the room behind Syrah.

"Two rooms, huh?" he said under his breath, coming up behind her. "Will you be all right on your own?"

In response, the Priestess gave him a roguish wink over her shoulder. "Guess you'll have to sneak out and join me," she whispered, making sure Kerren couldn't hear. Her eyes gleamed mischievously. "Reminds me of when I used to sneak out of my room in Cyurgi 'Di and—"

"I *don't* need to know," Raz said with a snort, putting a hand on her head and shoving her away playfully as he turned back to the door. "I get the feeling you and I had *very* different upbringings in that respect."

Syrah snickered, then turned to take in the room once more. An odd look crossed her pale features, like she was simultaneously happy and heartbroken to be standing there, in the center of the place the man who had been everything but her father had once occupied. Raz glanced back at her, and when she didn't look his way, he stepped through the door and reached back to close it behind him.

"Let's give her a minute," he told Kerren quietly. "In the meantime, would you be so kind as to point me in the direction of the nearest plate of hot food?"

VIII

"There are many who will frequently make the claim that whores and courtesans practice the oldest trade in the history of man. Such scholars insist that no craft could possibly have started before—or is likely to last beyond—the trade of selling one's body to the masses. I, however, must disagree. There is one vocation which I believe will outlast any other. Should our civilization ever advance to a point where the act of selling pleasure is a folly of the past, there is a profession which will continue and endure so long as man suffers from the affliction of his own nature. After all—if we agree to accept that all things have a price—should it not be taken into consideration that the only thing of more value to a person than their own flesh is, perhaps, their life itself?"

—*Living Shadows: A Study of the Art of Death,* by Elot Acker

He's here.

The thought slipped across Na'zeem Ashur's mind in an infinite loop, seeing fit to keep his focus from settling. He sat, arms crossed over the dark layers of his shirt, back against the rotting plank wall of the rundown building he and his lessers had claimed for themselves upon their arrival in the city, rousting the slum runners and beggars who'd initially called it home.

They were four days into the week Na'zeem had allotted them to stay in Ystréd, a week in which he'd planned to find new horses for him and his twenty men, gather what information he could on these "Priests of Laor," and set about making preparations for their assault on the great mountain keep his mistress had simply called "the Citadel." The city was—he was told by the men he'd sent out in stolen clothes—the last true bastion of civilization before the wilds would swallow them up for nearly a month. It would be their last opportunity to purchase any provisions and equipment they might need and so—considering the good three months of summer still ahead of them— Na'zeem had elected to take the time to make sure everything was right before they returned to their arduous journey north, making for the Vietalis Ranges.

And then Ehmed had returned from the markets, where he'd been seeking out a seller of salted meats and traveling rations, with news that had rendered every one of the group's carefully plotted plans entirely inconsequential.

He's here, Na'zeem thought again, eyes on the back of Ehmed's head as the man knelt before his master. *The Monster came right to us.*

It had been a consideration he'd made a few times as he and the others journeyed north, across the border, past the great city of Azbar, and finally to Ystréd. He'd wondered briefly—and with a certain level of trepidation— what they would do if the lizard wasn't where their mistress believed him to be. The bird which had borne the news that Arro was holed up in the place the Northerners called "Cyurgi 'Di" must have been at least a week reaching

Miropa, and even leaving the fringe cities the following day it had taken well over a fortnight for Na'zeem and his comrades to make it to Ystréd. All in all, the information was already nearing a month old, not to mention the weeks more it would take them to reach this fabled keep in the mountains.

As there was nothing to do about these facts, however, Na'zeem had eventually pushed them aside. If the lizard wasn't in the Citadel, then they would hunt him across the North until they caught him. In Miropa the Monster had always been a figure of renown, a sellsword of legendary prowess and terrifying savagery, but here in the North it appeared Arro was developing a reputation of an entirely different caliber. In Azbar they had called the man "the Scourge," and even on the road Na'zeem and his men had heard whispers about "the Dragon." Arro had made a name for himself—or multiple, for that matter—and if his trail had been at all difficult to follow before, now the news of his passings alone would have been enough to stalk him to the ends of the earth.

And, in the end, it was that same reputation which had delivered unto Na'zeem the fact that Arro was there, in Ystréd, waiting like an unsuspecting doe in a clearing, unaware of the wolves that lurked in the shade of the trees.

"Where?"

Na'zeem spoke the word slowly, the first sound he'd made since Ehmed had knelt before him and delivered his news.

"We don't know yet," the man answered at once, head still down. "But we will. I sent Eram and Fah'zer out as soon as I returned, telling them to find out what they could. I didn't see him myself, only heard from the throng that the beast had arrived some time before through the northern gate. I wasn't sure I believed it, but the news is spreading across the city. I find it hard to believe it's only a rumor."

Na'zeem nodded. "Good. What else did you hear?"

Ehmed finally looked up, his face uncertain. "The cityfolk believe he travels with a woman, but her description seemed odd. Albino, they say. White hair and skin, and missing an eye. I wouldn't have believed it, but many seemed to know her name."

"Brahnt?" Na'zeem asked.

If Ehmed was surprised, he didn't show it. "Yes," he said. "Syrah Brahnt."

Na'zeem nodded, frowning. It was a name he, too, had heard a few times when he'd been out and about the city. Not as frequently as Arro's, but often in the same breath, and occasionally on its own. If the mutterings were true, then Syrah Brahnt was a woman to be reckoned with, a skilled user of the strange magics the Northern deity, Laor, was said to grant his most devout followers. Na'zeem had seen that magic at work, had seen the power with which it could be wielded. He wondered briefly, if his mistress was truly as imposing as she seemed, how she would match up against a spellcaster who'd trained for a lifetime to harness the powers of their god.

He shoved this thought quickly aside, fearing the blasphemy of such a consideration.

Even if she is no master of sorcery, she has other ways of making those who challenge her disappear among the sands...

Regardless, this "Brahnt" woman was likely someone to be wary of...

"When Eram and Fah'zer return, gather the men," Na'zeem said, the fingers of his right hand absently playing with the hilt of the curved saber strapped behind his lower back. "For now, tell everyone you can find that the lizard is not to be touched. He's formidable on his own. If his companion is even half as dangerous, then there are considerations we need to make."

Ehmed nodded once, then was gone, little more than a shift among the rays of dust cast as the Sun filtered through the broken and rotted planks of the walls. Na'zeem, after the man had taken his leave, tilted his head back to rest it against the flaking and splintered wood, watching the patterns whirl about in the light.

Silently, he thanked the Twins for his good fortune.

He's here.

IX

"There is much in life one should value. Much one should take care to gather and cherish. Your mother might say otherwise, but I do not think it unwise to appreciate the material things that give life much of its meaning. Wealth has its place in the pursuit of happiness, after all. That being said... Do not ever lose sight of that which truly matters. Never stray so far from the path that leads you back to family..."

—Agais Arro to his eldest child, Raz i'Syul

Raz and Syrah spent the better part of the next four days generally avoiding the topic of where it was they would be heading off to next, as well as when they would be leaving. They both agreed—despite the assurance of Tana Atler—that they could not tarry about Ystréd for too long, as delaying their departure would eventually result in their being largely trapped in the city by the winter snows. On the other hand, there was something to be said for enjoying the hospitality and presence of others, particularly after nearly a month of no other company but their own.

Atler hadn't quite shaken the cold shoulder she tended to give Raz, but he didn't mind. He'd failed her, in a way, when Talo had died, and he understood her unwillingness to welcome him back with open arms. Syrah had asked him repeatedly as to the reason the High Priestess seemed consistently distant with him, but he'd done his best to dodge the question every time.

He just hadn't found the courage to tell her that, before he and Talo and Carro had last departed the temple, Atler had pulled him aside and practically begged him to protect the High Priest with his life.

Even if he hadn't intended to, he had failed her.

Syrah eventually gave up on getting her answer, and life settled into a pleasant routine for a time. Raz would always wake before the rest of the temple, even those with early morning chores. He'd never needed much sleep—the Grandmother had theorized it was a character of his race, when he'd been younger—and he enjoyed the quiet of the dawn, enjoyed the opportunity to be up and about before the thrum of the city set his head to aching again. He would wake up, briefly ensure Syrah wasn't trapped in the throes of any nightmare, then make for the downstairs kitchens where he'd help himself to a plate of raw beef or chicken or whatever other meats the Laorin had stowed away in the cabinets they kept magically cooled. After this, he would go outside to tend to Gale and Nymara—it had only been in the last week that the mare finally stopped shying away at his approach—brushing the horses down and speaking to them calmly while feeding them handfuls of grain and sugar from a chest at the back of the small stable.

Once the animals were groomed, it was time to practice.

It was a habit Raz had fallen into in the weeks of travel with Carro and Talo, and it was one he'd worked to maintain ever since. In the past years Raz had had to do little in the way of training, his work as a sellsword providing all the opportunity he ever needed to keep his skills sharp and his body fit. Now, though, in a happier time when bloodshed wasn't quite as frequent an occurrence, he'd returned to a daily rigor he hadn't committed to so thoroughly since his earliest days learning to wield Ahna and his other weapons.

Raz danced for almost an hour each morning, taking advantage of a small, well-trodden paddock the horses would spend the day in if the weather allowed. He practiced unarmed, then with the gladius, and finally with Ahna, pushing his body until his legs burned and his arms ached. He found a place apart from himself in those fights with invisible opponents, found a spot in his mind from where he could safely peek into the abyss down which he knew the animal lay dormant, waiting to be called on. It was a calm space, one devoid of any of the noise and lights and vigor of the world around him. It was a space into which he could escape, pressing his physical and mental limits again and again and again.

Raz only ever stopped when he heard the temple start to wake behind him.

When the *thump* of feet and the splash of washing basins rang clear from the windows, he knew it was time to put his weapons away and move inside to take a seat among the faithful as they broke their fast. Syrah was generally up and about by then, and saved Raz a wide chair beside her every morning. Atler was not unreasonable in her disapproval of him, always making sure there was something for him to eat among the fruits and grains the others partook in. On the first day, Raz was treated to salted bacon and spiced sausages. On the second, a slab of ham so large Syrah had ended up helping him finish it, to her great amusement. On the third, roast duck marinated in a plum jam.

After the morning meal, the temple started its day in truth, the acolytes, Priests, and Priestesses setting about their chores or greeting congregants who came as groups or pairs or individuals to seek the blessings of the Lifegiver. During this time, Syrah would always drag Raz out into the city, forcing him to tail her about Ystréd as she delighted in the shops and markets. Ordinarily it would all have been a painful ordeal for him, his sensitive ears and snout rebelling against the tumultuous sounds and smells of the town. Unsurprisingly, though, Raz always found himself hard-pressed not to enjoy himself at least the smallest bit around Syrah's infectious excitement.

He eventually decided the woman's energy could only have come from a childhood spent mostly locked away within the walls of the Citadel. Whatever the reason, Syrah made it seem like she could have spent her life wandering the bustle of the city and never gotten bored. She pulled him along, day after day, each time to a new quarter of Ystréd, so taken by the buildings and bustle of the place that at times she seemed almost to forget the darker cloud that

70

loomed above her head. Only on occasion did Raz have to step between her and a man who strayed too close, or stiff-arm the crowd as it pressed in around them, making her blanch. Fortunately, the aversion of the people of Ystréd generally worked in their favor, most none-too-keen on being within reach his at any given time.

Even better, it was easy for Raz to ignore the annoyed flutter this ignorance evoked when Syrah smiled and dragged him by the hand to the next shop along the bazaars.

It was always well-past noon by the time they returned to the temple, and Syrah and Raz typically had a late lunch alone in Syrah's room. This was the time, every day, that they pretended they would spend planning their next move, working out where they were off to next, but it never worked out that way. They always found a reason to stray from the topic, to speak of everything and anything that wasn't what the future held for them. They tended, in fact, to speak of Talo, and Syrah's childhood with him, talking of the trouble she'd caused and what kind of father he had been. It felt right, remembering him together in that space where they could almost feel the old Priest's presence.

When their lunch was done, Raz and Syrah sought to earn their keep. Syrah would assist the other Priests and Priestesses in instructing the acolytes in the art of spellwork, teaching the children and converts of the temple how to fight and defend themselves, or else showing them how to weave the magics together into spells and runes of protection or warmth or light. While she did this, Raz set about putting his strength to use, joining in with the other men as they split timber to pile behind the stables in preparation for the coming freeze, or made repairs about the building. It was arduous work, to the point where even Raz—despite his body's general preference for warmth—usually had his shirt off by the time he and the others called an end to the day, allowing his scaled skin to cool in the shadows. Afterward, the men would all briefly retire to their chambers to bathe and clean up, and then it was time for one last meal together.

After supper, as people split off one after the other for bed, Raz and Syrah would take their leave. Raz would retrieve his gladius from his room, then quickly make his way to Syrah's, wondering every night what the Priests and Priestesses would think when it was discovered that his own bed had never been slept in.

Finally, Raz would settle into his habitual place, seated on the floor facing the room door, his back against Syrah's bed, the sword resting against his shoulder.

"I'm going to miss this," Syrah said slowly, surprising him.

It was their fourth evening spent in the hospitality of the faith. Syrah's window was open, letting in the cool breeze of the late evening, the Moon illuminating the stone wall of the alleyway opposite. The candles she had lit about the chamber flickered in the shifting air, making warm shadows dance about. She lay on her back on the bed, her head hanging off the edge to rest on Raz's shoulder, looking up at the angled slope of the ceiling as her hair fell over his neck and chest. They hadn't been talking for several minutes, and Raz was just beginning to think she'd fallen asleep there, propped up against him, when she spoke.

It took him a moment to catch on.

"It's hard, walking away from everything you know," he said with a slow nod, reaching across himself to run his claws carefully through her hair. "This is your world. I admit I'm hesitant to take you away from it…"

"If you're about to ask me if I'm sure I don't want to stay behind, don't waste your time." Syrah closed her eyes in appreciation as Raz's fingers ran gently over her head. "That's not what I'm trying to say. I'm more afraid you're going to take off in the middle of the night without me than I am of anything I might be leaving behind."

"I'm not going to leave you," Raz promised her, his eyes on the shapes passing under the jamb of the door as residents of the temple bid each other goodnight on the walkway outside.

Syrah gave a small shrug. "I wouldn't put it past you, casting me off here because of some misguided understanding that I'm not meant for the world beyond walls like this." She lifted a hand to wave about the room.

Raz snorted. "You were doing just fine before I came along," he told her. "The people of the North knew your name a long time before they learned of 'the Monster,' or 'the Scourge.'"

"Or 'the Dragon?'" she kept on, half-teasing.

It was Raz's turn to shrug. "The point is that I know you can handle yourself. If I didn't, then I would never have agreed to leave the Citadel with you in the first place."

That seemed to cheer the woman up a little, because he felt her smile. Still, when she spoke, she didn't sound altogether convinced. "If I can handle myself, then how did I end up with this?" She waved a hand at the bandage still wrapped about her right eye. She said it casually, as though she were merely keeping up the conversation, but Raz knew better.

Just as he knew well how she'd come to receive that scar.

"It was you and a few against hundreds," he told her, leaning his head back so that it rested on her own shoulder, staring up at the dance of candlelight against the ceiling. "If you think I could have done any better, with odds like that, then you're delusional, and I *should* leave you behind."

That got a laugh out of her. "Maybe." She reached up, running the fingers of her hand between his eyes and over the crown of his head. "In that case, though, maybe we *both* need to get stronger."

"If we stay together, we're plenty strong," Raz mumbled as he, too, closed his eyes in enjoyment. "Wherever we end up."

"And where is that going to be, exactly?"

Raz tensed, then smirked grimly. He'd been wondering which of them would bring it up first, would be willing to break the brief spell of peace they had found there in the temple.

Seems we know which of us is the braver one, now.

"West," he told her. "We can find passage across the Emperor's Ocean, and make for the Isles, or the Imperium. Apart from some sea trade, I don't imagine either empire has much love for the South or the Mahsadën, and I doubt they've ever even heard of Gûlraht Baoill. With any luck, not too many people would bother either of us if we can make it."

"'If we can make it...'" Syrah repeated slowly, and Raz caught the concern in her voice.

He didn't bother telling her that it was shared.

It was far from a perfect plan. For one thing, he was fairly sure easy passage across the Emperor's Ocean could only be found in Acrosia, the South's western port. He hadn't been there in almost ten years, having last visited when he and the Arros still traveled the Cienbal's routes as one of the nomadic trading caravans. He knew well, though, despite this, that Acrosia was as firmly under the thumb of the Mahsadën as any of the other fringe cities. Even if they waited out the summer in Ystréd, making South once the cooler season had returned, it would prove difficult to get into the city. Beyond that, Raz didn't even bother contemplating how they would find a captain who might agree to take he and Syrah on rather than turn them over for the prices on their heads, much less sneak himself onto a ship.

No, it wasn't a perfect plan, but with the South removed as an option and the North still a hunting ground for him—and now Syrah—it was the best he had been able to come up with.

There was a flicker of a shadow outside the window, and Raz glanced around. It must have been some slum runner, darting across the alley below, because it disappeared at once, and Raz found himself looking out at the light of the Moon illuminating the mortared granite of the building opposite the temple. He got the feeling, abruptly, that if they decided on this path, decided on making for the West Isles or the Imperium, that he would be praying to Her and Her Stars all too often in the coming months.

Beside him, Syrah sighed. "Maybe we should *both* stay here," she said glumly, rolling over and off him as she made for the head of the bed. "We could lock ourselves in this room where no one can get us."

Raz chuckled, turning to watch the Priestess slide under the covers. "I'm sure Atler wouldn't mind. We can commandeer an acolyte or two to bring us our meals and empty our chamber pots a few times a day."

Syrah grunted in distaste, fluffing her feather pillow before laying down, her good eye meeting his. "Pleasant," she said sarcastically.

Raz grinned. "It's that, or the Sun of the South and a boat west."

Syrah groaned. "Chamber pots don't sound so bad when you put it that way. You're sure there's no better options?"

"None that I can come up with," he told her with a shake of his head. "We've done a good job of making ourselves poor company in most of the known world, it seems."

Syrah didn't reply immediately, toying with a loose piece of straw sticking out of the stitching in her mattress.

"Why do so many bad souls exist?" she asked after a time, pulling the straw loose and rolling onto her back as she turned it absently between her fingers. "I believe in a god who is supposed to purge the world of the wicked, and yet as I get older I see only more darkness all around. Your Mahsadën. These factions within the clans who still want my head. Cutthroats like that woman Thera and her band. Why couldn't Laor have given us the power to simply wipe them from the world, and be done with it? If they'd never existed, we wouldn't have to run."

"It would certainly be easier," Raz mused, contemplating the question. "Then again, if they didn't exist, neither would we."

Syrah paused in her fidgeting, considering his words. "I suppose," she said eventually, resuming her toying with the straw. "It's a balance, in the end. Where there is light, there is shadow."

"I think it's more the opposite," Raz said, though he nodded. "Where there is shadow, there must be light."

Syrah smiled, but it was a cool, disheartened smile. "'You can't have one without the other,'" she quoted what he had told her on the road. Then she frowned and looked his way with sad eyes.

"I'm happy to be with you," she said. "But… I wish we didn't have to leave…"

No more running, a snarling voice chimed in from the back of Raz's mind, but he pressed it back.

"Not for long," he told her gently. "I promise."

In response, Syrah just nodded. Then, after a minute, she threw the strand of straw to the floor, rolled onto her side, and started to undo the eye-wraps with one hand as she raised the other above her head.

"Tomorrow we can tell Atler we're leaving," she said. "Goodnight."

"Goodnight," Raz told her, settling down himself. "Wake me if you need me."

And with that, Syrah extinguished the candles with a flick of her wrist, leaving Raz with nothing but the night wind and Moon's light for company.

X

"Plan. Plot. Prepare. These are the essentials of your trade, the essentials of your survival. I can teach you to mold your body into a weapon, can teach you to become as lethal as the blade you hold in your hand. It won't mean anything, though, if you are not ready, if you are not poised to strike when and where the moment arrives..."

—Ergoin Sass

As the light in the corner room the Monster had been sharing with Syrah Brahnt winked out, Na'zeem couldn't help but feel his heart jolt with anticipation. He calmed himself at once, taking a breath of cool evening air to steady his excitement, and continued his wait.

For four days now, he and his men had been patient, studying the comings and goings of the Laorin with keen eyes from the roofs and corners and awnings of the buildings all around the temple. Na'zeem hadn't risked setting disguised watchers on the place, concerned someone would notice the sudden presence of one or more distinctly tanned Southerners lingering about the temple's entrance. It had been harder to convince himself not to set a tail on the atherian and his woman as they'd taken their leave into the city every day, but in the end he'd opted not to for the same reasons. His mistress' crippled puppet had been all too clear that Raz i'Syul Arro was not a man they could expect to trap by conventional means. If the lizard so much as caught a whiff of Na'zeem or his men, the Monster would vanish, and it would be next to impossible to find him until he chose to make himself known again.

And so Na'zeem—ever a patient man—had set his shadows to the task of gathering all the information they could, and waited. Now, as more lights went out behind the slatted shutters of two more rooms, he could feel the time fast approaching.

Na'zeem crouched, still as stone, in the darkened recess of a mortared chimney on the roof of the building adjacent to the temple's east wall. The Moon was bright tonight, She and Her Stars shining down from a black heaven speckled with tendrils of thin clouds. All about him, in a dozen different directions, he knew his men lay in similar wait, each having taken their places as the day died. It had been two hours since, two hours of watching the temple steadily still from one minute into the next, like some squat, large animal slowly falling to sleep. More candlelight in windows faded and winked out, a few of the dozens of eyes closing in slumber. Ten more minutes passed, then thirty, then another hour, then two. Finally, as the Moon began to approach Her peak in the sky, the last room went dark, leaving only the flicker of a single torch along the bottom floor near the temple's main doors.

Allowing another twenty minutes to pass as a precaution, Na'zeem finally set his tongue against his teeth. In a careful pattern he gave several quick, sharp chirps, exactly like a cricket in the night.

Then, with no more sound than a breeze against the slate slats beneath his feet, Na'zeem darted down the rooftop, took hold of a gutter-pipe along the corner of the building, and slid earthward to the alley floor.

By the time he reached the ground, Ehmed stood ready at the front door of the temple, a small crossbow in his hands, the bolt attached to a length of rope two other men held loosely behind him. As he darted quickly forward, Na'zeem watched a fourth shadow move to knock quietly on the door.

By the time he was vaulting over the low stone wall that wrapped around the garden at the front of the building, the door had cracked open.

The Laorin kept a single watcher at the door after nightfall, presumably to greet any faithful who might come seeking their "Lifegiver's" grace after dusk. It had been the same boy each of the last three evenings, a tall youth with a splash of freckles across his nose and curly brown hair that fell over a pinched set of blue eyes.

Ehmed didn't even have to correct his aim, the crossbow raised to exactly the right height well before the night watcher had so much as heard the knock.

There was the dull *clunk* of the firing mechanism, and the bolt took the boy through the throat, snuffing his life out in near-total silence as he made to peek out into the night. Before the body could fall back under the force of the shot, though, the two men who'd been waiting took hold of the rope which had zipped through their hands, heaving on it quickly.

Barely a drop of blood had hit the stone floor on the inside of the temple before the watcher's corpse was hauled out and stowed quickly among the thick flowers and plants of the garden behind them.

Then, like black water seeping through a crack in a wall, Na'zeem led their foursome inside, knowing as he did that all around the temple other shadows were crawling up the walls and dropping from the rooftops around them.

Tana Atler awoke with a start she couldn't explain. She thought, at first, that it was perhaps early morning, and that the dim light filtering through the slats of her closed window was simply portent of the overcast dawn of a rainy day. As she sat up in bed, however, she realized quickly that that wasn't likely. There was no bustle outside the door of her High Priestess' chambers, no noise and rumble of the temple coming awake around her. When her eyes had cleared, too, she saw very distinctly that it was still moonlight streaming in through gaps in her shutters, and she frowned.

Inexplicably, she had a bad feeling. It was as though Laor himself had driven her up from her dreams, seeking to wake her.

Suddenly nervous, Tana lifted a hand and willed her magics into life with a thought. Instantly the room was aglow with white light, every bit of the lingering dark driven away by the wave of flames balled into an orb above her palm. It took a moment for her eyes to adjust to the sudden brightness, but when they did she blinked and cast about, seeking some explanation for her apprehension.

When she was sure she was alone in the room, Tana relaxed a little, letting the magics fade until the light was nothing more than a guttering flame, like a candle in her palm.

Still… Something didn't feel right.

Kicking off her covers, Tana threw her feet over the edge of the bed and found her boots quickly, slipping into them. Standing up, she retrieved her staff from where it waited, propped against the wall to her right, then made her way carefully to her door in little more than her nightgown. The feeling of disquiet intensified with every step, as though something dreadful waited for her out there on the walkway.

When she stood before it, she let the magics die completely, took a breath, and wrenched the door open.

Nothing.

Tana blinked, then stepped across the threshold of her small room. Everything seemed normal, quiet, the only light coming from the single torch left alight by the door of the temple below, encouraging any who might need Laor's guidance to feel welcome at any hour. She glanced around, up and down the walkway, but heard nothing but the gentle whistle of the wind against the walls and roof. Steadily, her unease died, and she relaxed.

Did I have a bad dream? she thought to herself, trying to recall if it had perhaps been some nightmare that had woken her.

Then Tana noticed the chair, empty and still, by the front door.

Where is Toman? she wondered, confused, peering over the railing at it. It wasn't like the young man to leave his post until he was relieved in a few hours. The acolyte was dependable and firm in his faith, and wouldn't have been dragged away unless it was necessary.

The feeling returned, sharper and colder with fear, and Tana turned back toward her room, intent on donning her robes and rousing some of the older Priests and Priestesses.

When she did, though, she froze.

Before her, the room waited, a dark maw into nothingness save for the light of the moon shining across her bed through the open window. For a moment, Tana couldn't understand what had petrified her so, her conscious thoughts racing to catch up with her own mind. She stood, tense and unmoving, until terror rocketed through her like a lightning bolt.

The window. The *open* window.

The two seconds Tana Atler spent stricken, staring at the dim brightness of the night outside as she scrambled for some rational explanation, cost her her life. She'd just decided to shout a warning, just started to lift her free hand to blast the room with ivory fire, when the darkness before her seemed to melt outward. In a flash a man took form from the blackness, tall and lithe, the curved shine of a knife glinting at his side. He was on her in a blink, and Tana only had time to glimpse the coldness of his grey eyes between the wrappings that covered his face before the blade took her just beneath the sternum, ripping up and into her, through lung and straight to her heart. The High Priestess only managed a single, shallow *"Gah!"* of surprise and disbelief before the pain roared outward from her chest, swallowing her whole. As her mind fell victim to shock and horror, Tana made out a second figure clawing out from the shadows, this one moving with the speed of a snake for the steel staff that had fallen from her limp fingers, catching it before it clattered to the wood and granite of the walkway. She felt rough hands grab her under her arms, dragging her back into her room. Her head flopped, and she was forced to look back in agonized denial at the thick stain of red she left across the floor.

Then the men dropped her unceremoniously onto the cold stone, and the last thing Tana Atler saw before blood began to pour from her mouth were the paired figures silhouetted against the light of the hall, closing the door and leaving her to die, alone and shivering, in the dark.

XI

"There comes a point in every great man's life where his reputation outstrips any of his intentions. A general who learns to desire peace will find it difficult to outrun his past deeds. An assassin pained by the lives he's taken will never earn the forgiveness of his victims. Eventually, even those with the best intentions may fall prey to their own legend, discovering—on the very day they wish to put down the sword—that their very name prevents them from ever truly sheathing that blade…"

—The *Art of Sword & Shield*, by Kelo ev'Ret

It wasn't anything in particular that roused Raz from his slumber. It wasn't a noise, or a movement, or the shout of voices. Rather, Raz thought it was the utter stillness about him that had pulled him into consciousness, dragged him up from sleep, still seated on the floor by Syrah's bed.

Everything was silent. Nothing stirred. There wasn't so much as the distant sound of snoring in other rooms, or the faintest rumble of the faithful mumbling in their sleep.

The world around them, it felt, had died.

For several long seconds Raz sat, unmoving and listening, his eyes on the floor. His crest twitched in unease behind his neck, like the rising hackles of a wolf, and he was about to push himself up to his feet, thinking he'd take a look out in the hall, when he smelled it.

Blood.

Raz was up, the gladius hissing out of its sheath even as he turned toward the bed. Syrah woke violently as he pressed a hand over her face, just as he expected her to, her body tensing and bucking as soon as he touched her. Now without her wrappings, both eyes rolled in fear and anger as they flew open before fixing on him, one healthy and shining, the other dead and dull and white in the crevice of the vertical scar that bisected it. She looked terrified, as though he were a nightmare made real, but Raz didn't have time to feel sorry for her.

"*Syrah,*" he said in a desperate, quiet hiss. "Don't speak, just listen. Something's wrong. Get up and get dressed. *Now.*"

Instantly the fury and fear vanished, replaced by wide-eyed alertness. For a heartbeat after he pulled his hand away from her face Raz was afraid she would protest, maybe refuse to move until he told her what was going on, but the woman only threw the covers off and got quickly out of bed, moving to where her robes hung on the back of the chair by the escritoire beneath the open window.

"What is it?" she finally whispered as he heard her struggling to pull the clothes over her head. "What's happening?"

Raz didn't answer immediately, his eyes narrowing at the faint light of the jamb beneath the door again. He was listening hard now, and it seemed almost that he could hear the patter of footsteps all about them, so quiet he couldn't be sure his mind wasn't playing tricks on him.

The smell of death, though, still lingered in the air.

"Get your things," he said, starting to turn toward Syrah, intent on developing a plan of escape. "Someone's in the temple. We need to—"

He never finished the statement, his blood running cold as time seemed to warp and slow about him. There, her white hair gleaming like a silvery waterfall in the glow of the Moon, Syrah stood. She was watching him with nervous anticipation, waiting for him to tell her what to do, her hands clenched by her side. Her eyes were wide, less fearful than firm, and her jaw was tense and set.

And behind her, crouched like some terrible bird of prey on the sill of the window, was a man garbed in dark layers, the curved dagger in his raised hand gleaming wickedly in the evening glow.

Raz moved like a whip, so fast he didn't even have time to raise his sword. Syrah gasped and started to shout in surprise as he shoved her aside unceremoniously just as the figure struck. The blade took Raz in the arm, lodging in the roped muscle of his biceps, and he roared in pain and anger even as he thundered into the writing desk, smashing it to pieces.

His right shoulder, though, caught the assassin squarely in the chest, blasting him back out of the window with such incredible force that the man smashed into the wall opposite the temple with a screech of pain before tumbling in a crumpled, unmoving heap to the alley floor.

Instantly, the sound of footsteps all around them became distinct, attracted by the sound of the fight.

"Syrah!" Raz roared, whirling toward the door and tearing the dagger from his arm. "Out the window! NOW!"

In an instant, Syrah was at his side. There was a flash of magic, and Raz had to dodge as the Priestess' staff flew over the bed from where it had been resting against the far wall, zipping by him and into its master's hands.

"But the temple!" Syrah was saying in anguish. "What about Tana and the rest of the—?"

Just then, though, the door slammed open, and they were both bathed in a broad line of dim firelight from the walkway.

With it, pouring in like black water against the glow, came a flood of writhing shadows.

"GO!" Raz howled again.

Without waiting to see if Syrah had listened, he leapt forward, blades flashing.

It was like fighting smoke, the shapes of the men—or what he *assumed* were men—slinking in and out of the dark, whispering beneath almost every slash and lunge he threw at them. They were silent even as they moved, like the dead themselves had risen to haunt him, seeking his end in the night. They shifted about in a whirl, flickering and keeping away from the illumination of the open door, making it hard for even Raz to make them out.

Sometimes he thought there were only two, sometimes five, sometimes ten. He couldn't tell, the shapes constantly flowing around each other or melting back into the darker corners of the room. Most men would have died a dozen times over in the two or three minutes Raz battled the shades, victim to the slashes of blades coming from every direction.

But Raz i'Syul Arro, the assassins soon discovered, was a much greater task than any of them had anticipated.

Raz roared and snarled as he danced, compensating for his opponent's own attempts to surround him by never staying still, never giving them the chance. He rolled and leapt and dashed, his blades gleaming as they whirled around him in a never-ending wail of razored steel cutting through air. For a time he couldn't do more than keep them at bay, even then suffering several shallow stabs and slashes he wasn't able to completely duck or parry. He fought only to survive, to avoid the silvery flashes of the men's curved knives and swords. Even from the depths of the battle fog Raz wished he had fought to keep Ahna close to him, fought the Laorin and their foolish fear of even allied steel. He was starting to worry that his gladius and the borrowed dagger wouldn't be enough, that there were just too many men and he was bound to tire before all of them did, when he began to see the pattern, began to see the form in their ghostly choreography. This was a unit, a phalanx of blackened shades. This was a brethren of killers, each as familiar with the other as he was with himself. Ordinarily, Raz was sure this would have meant a certain end to whichever life the group chose to set itself upon, the comfortable, familiar rhythm working with such terrifying efficiency there could be no escape.

Against the Dragon, though, this meant only that it was nothing more than a matter of time before the advantage changed.

Ducking and rolling under the high slash of one man's blade, Raz allowed for another few engagements to assure himself that he was right. His eyes flicked this way and that, sharper than man's in the limited light, keeping pace with a number of the shapes and the patterns in which they were moving.

This moment of assertion cost him a narrow gash along the ribs, but he made well sure it was worth it.

Over the course of four seconds, the tide of the battle shifted.

Raz feinted forward, making as though to leap into the middle of the room, but in midair he put a foot on the sturdy corner-post of the bed that had been Syrah's and shoved sideways, changing direction. For the first time he heard a noise from the men who surrounded him, a single hiss of shock from the one he was suddenly lancing toward.

Then Raz's borrowed knife slashed, parting the thick tissues along the side of the figure's neck, and the hiss turned into a wail of agony and horror.

After that, things changed quickly.

The others about the room didn't so much as blink at the dying howls of their comrade, but nor did they adjust quickly enough to Raz's deduction of their movements. In the space of three heartbeats the gladius flashed twice more as he careened into the group with a warcry that might have shaken dust from the rafters. Before they knew it, two more of their number died, one screaming as the sword caught him across the face in a vicious slash, the other silent as the bloody dagger drove itself into his left eye. After that, though, the men realized their mistake, and instantly the pattern of their approach shifted. Within seconds Raz was hard-pressed once again, fighting off the converging attacks of what he believed to be three left standing.

As they collapsed on him all at once, Raz decided it was time to make his exit. Kicking splintered wood from the escritoire up into the face of one of the men, he darted forward and bulled him over, knocking him out of the way.

With two bounding steps, he tucked and leapt bodily out the still-open window.

The fall was brief. Without time to get his wings out to slow himself down, Raz landed hard in the alley below, rolling to his feet and nearly slamming into the far wall as he stumbled over the still-groaning form of the man he'd shoulder-checked off the sill. When he managed to steady himself he stood, expecting to find the side-street empty or—horribly—a group of shadowy figures standing with dripping blades over Syrah's limp body.

Instead, Raz gaped as he discovered he was standing at the center of a world on fire.

It was a battlefield. One end of the alley—to Raz's left and toward the back of the temple—was smoking, charred lines of what could only be expended magic etched into the ground and walls on either side. Around him, the sorcery still burned—if faintly—webbing everything with streaking lines of white flames, like lightning branded across the stone. To his right, at the far end of the alley, a literal *wall* of fire rose up two stories, extending from building to building, completely blocking that end of the way.

It was against this barrier of magic, pushed so hard that her back was almost touching the flames, that Syrah was making her final stand.

For a single breath, Raz couldn't move as he took her in. Despite the half-dozen or so figures that pressed her, he stared in utter amazement at the Priestess, seeing the woman for the first time in what could only be her true element. He had witnessed what he thought to be incredible spellwork before, had seen Carro al'Dor holding a ring of flames about himself and Talo as they'd fought off wolves in the Arocklen Woods. Back then, Raz had been impressed. Now, though, he recalled he'd been told more than once that Carro had never been one for fighting.

Now, taking in Syrah Brahnt as her robes and hair whirled about her, caught in the rising heat of her own fire, he truly understood what a mastery of battle magic must look like.

Three men were pinned ten feet up against the walls, two to Syrah's right and one to the left, their hands and feet fettered to the timber and granite by the same ivory fire she'd used against the mercenaries on the road to Ystréd. Two more lay motionless at her feet, the flames eating at their darkened tunics, obviously fallen victim to the hard steel of the staff she held before her in a defensive position. Another pair were slumped and scattered between Raz and the far end of the alley, blasted into unconsciousness by what could only have been stunning spells. It was an impressive sight, and for a moment Raz debated whether the woman needed any help at all, or if he would do better waiting for the assassins undoubtedly already chasing him out the window.

Even as he thought this, though, the flames around him flickered, and one of the figures tumbled free of the wall, the magical ropes binding him there failing. Syrah herself staggered, clearly exhausted.

In an instant, Raz was nothing more than a flash of scale and cloth, blades shining in the arcane glow roaring all about him.

Syrah was nearing the very end of her limits.

Even as she realized this she felt her grip on the magics slip, and all about her the flames faltered and guttered briefly. The wall of fire at her back, conjured to keep the assassins from taking her from behind, shrank somewhat, reaching only halfway up the second story, and one of the men she'd managed to trap against the wall above their heads dropped to the alley floor as his bonds gave way.

Shit, she thought to herself, her staff heavy in her hands as she held it at the ready before her, gaze flicking from one set of veiled grey eyes to the other. *Not good.*

She'd leapt from the window as soon as the door of their room had opened, following Raz's command. She would likely have broken an ankle were it not for the small amount of magic she'd been able to push into her legs, strengthening them. She'd rolled clear, anticipating—or maybe just praying—that Raz would be right behind her.

Instead, she'd come up right in front of a tall, thin man, his entire body wrapped in dark grey-and-black clothes.

Syrah hadn't hesitated, her hand moving even before she saw the sword he held at his side. She'd blasted him with a stunning spell at point-blank range, the force of the magic throwing him back into the wall. After that, she'd bolted left for the back of the temple, hoping to reach Gale and Nymara.

She hadn't been quick enough.

More shadows had fallen in around her, dropping from the roof and windows of the temple to cut off her escape, and from there on it had been a battle for her life. They'd pressed her back in rapid succession, moving about her like ebony liquid, doing their best to get beside or behind her. Syrah had managed to keep them at bay only barely, her staff and free hand working faster than she'd ever thought herself capable of to weave the steel and spells into a defense the assassins had never quite managed to penetrate completely. Still, their assault kept her constantly retreating, one step after the other, and it wasn't long before the white of her robes was stained with red, blood seeping from slashes and jabs in the cloth that she hadn't quite managed to escape. Sweat dripped down her ruined face, and her breath came in ragged heaves as her legs and arms became heavier and heavier under the toll the magic took on her body.

Now she'd been pressed to the very opposite end of the alley, and there was nowhere left to run. She knew that if she was forced back any further, into the openness of the dark street, she would be done for. The men before her were professionals, cold-eyed killers, and the silent understanding with which they moved about one another made it clear they were good at their work. She had no doubt there were at least one or two already lying in wait beyond the mouth of the alley, patient in their anticipation that she would be forced into their expecting blades. Like a cornered animal Syrah now fought in desperation, putting every ounce of energy that remained to her into the magics, the one true advantage she had at her disposal, the one reason she wasn't already lying dead at their feet.

Suddenly, one of the assassins lanced forward, clearly trying to take advantage of her fatigue. Adrenaline surged through Syrah, and she managed to deflect the lunging blade away with one end of her staff, then slam the other end into the man's side, sending him flying. In the same moment, though, another had darted forward to flank her, ignoring the flames that had eaten away his shoes and the bottom of his pants with professional disinterest, his own knife striking up at her neck. Syrah twisted and punched out, the blasting force that erupted from her fist blowing the man back ten feet over the heads of his comrades.

After that, though, she knew she didn't have long. Syrah tripped back, barely managing to stay on her feet, struggling to focus and draw some magic into herself to refresh her exhausted body. It worked a little, a measure of strength pulsing back into her aching limbs and her head clearing, but the barrier behind her shrank yet again, and a second man fell free of the wall.

Shit, Syrah thought again, watching the figures before her take a collective step forward.

And then, from the back of the group, somebody screamed.

There was the shearing sound of steel through muscle and bone, and Syrah blinked as a spray of blood streaked across the wall to her right, smoking where it made contact with her flames. Immediately following this there was a *crack* of some limb or another breaking, and another man howled in pain, then went silent. As one, the assassins before her hesitated, several glancing back to see what was happening at their rear.

That was when Syrah saw him, a demon of fire and blades, his towering form and great wings outlined against the white glow of her magic, his sword and the stolen knife screeching as they moved like a wind storm about his body.

Raz had charged right into the assassins' rear line, crashing into them with such savagery and power he might have been the incarnation of war itself.

Making a split-second decision, Syrah allowed the wall at her back to dissipate, drawing the magic back into herself and focusing it throughout her body. Instantly she felt refreshed, and took advantage of the sudden distraction of the men before her to whirl and meet the attack she knew would come. Two shadows leapt at her from the street, just as she'd expected. Where they had anticipated to find a beaten and defeated woman, however, they instead came face-to-face with a fiery-eyed Priestess of Laor, brimming with power. They were practically in midair, in fact, when Syrah's lash took one about the waist and whipped him sideways, smashing him into his partner so that both men went careening violently into the temple garden.

By the time she turned around again, Raz had cut his way to her.

"With me!" he growled, already whirling to face their opponents again.

Without hesitating, Syrah followed him right back into the fight.

Together they pressed through the men still standing, watching their step as they navigated the carnage Raz had left in his wake. Syrah fought hard to ignore the smell of blood and smoke and burning cloth as they moved, Raz forging their way forward, she watching their backs. Eventually they were in the middle of the alley again, pinned on either side as they each fought four men, Raz snarling and parrying and lashing out with blades and claws and teeth and tail, Syrah focusing what magic she had left into whips and stunning spells and blasts of fiery heat that sent her opponents staggering. For several long minutes they battled on, his back pressed to hers, each trusting the other with their life. Despite their being penned in, the advantage had turned. There were no dark corners left for the assassins to hide in, no openings for them to attack from the sides or back. Steel cleaved through skin and flesh. Magic rocked the air. Screams filled the night. Light flashed across the sky. Raz and Syrah ignored the wounds they suffered, ignored the blood splattering against the stone around them when they swung sword and knife and staff, roaring in defiance. Nothing existed in that moment but the shapes of the men before them and the feel of their bodies moving together, reassuring each the other still lived.

More fell before them, dead at Raz's feet and unconscious at Syrah's. Before long, the four they each battled became three, then two, and finally one. When this happened, the pair of assassins left standing seemed at last to come to terms with the fact that they were well and truly outmatched. The one before Syrah, his curved saber held overhead like the hovering tail of a scorpion, made a chirping sound like a cricket in the night, and in a flash both men were retreating, vanishing back into the shadows at either end of the alley before Raz or Syrah had a chance to realize they were running. At once Raz began to follow, a hungry, animal-like snarl building in his throat, but as his body left hers Syrah reached back with her free hand and caught his arm, restraining him.

"No, Raz," she said over the snapping of the fires that still burned all around them, her eyes not leaving the mouth of the alley where her opponent had vanished. "Leave him."

She felt the muscle beneath her fingers spasm, then relax, and Raz didn't make to step any further away.

When she let go of him, her hand came away wet and dark with blood.

Syrah didn't know how long they stayed like that, standing together among the white flames of Laor. It felt like hours, though in truth it couldn't have been more than half-a-minute. Neither moved. Neither spoke. Each listened and watched, their eyes flicking to every twist in the light, their bodies flinching toward any sound they could make out above the fire. They did not trust the night, did not trust the darkness beyond the glow of the flames. For that brief period the blackness of the evening was alive around them, writhing with invisible shapes and the glint of curved blades.

Eventually, though, Syrah forced herself to believe that the fight was over, and the fires all about her shimmered and winked out as she collapsed to the alley floor.

"Laor's mercy," she croaked, sucking in ragged breaths of cool air, staring wide-eyed at the ground as her body began to shake violently. "Laor's *fucking* mercy."

Behind her she felt Raz stagger, and when he spoke it was in a shaking, rasping voice that told her all too well that he, too, had about reached his limit.

"Syrah," he said between gasps as he fought to catch his breath. "Syrah, we have to go. We have to *go*!"

At first, Syrah barely heard him. She understood, from some distant part of her own mind, that she was going into shock. She'd fought before, true, even fought for her life, but never had she faced something so cold, so empty and vicious as the hunger she'd seen in the grey eyes of the shadow men. She stared, unable to move, gaping at the splotches of her own blood dripping down from her body, arms, and hair.

"By the Lifegiver," she heard herself mumble over and over again. "By the Lifegiver. By the Lifegiver. By the—"

"*Syrah*! Get UP!"

Raz's voice, this time so desperate it was almost anguished, finally managed to cut through the fog. She blinked and looked around at him slowly. He was standing, one shoulder pressed against the wall to her left, still breathing hard. He still had his blades, the gladius and the borrowed knife he had saved her from, but barely. They hung loose at his sides, both sheened crimson in the moonlight, and looked to be trembling as he tried to hold on to them.

"Get *up*!" he was yelling again. "*Please*! Get *up*!"

The sight of him, bloody and battle-worn and screaming at her as though their lives depended on it, was all she needed to shake herself free. Slowly, feeling like her entire body was on fire, Syrah planted her staff and forced herself onto her feet, her bloodied, sweating palms slipping against the steel.

"Can you walk?" Raz asked her, slightly calmer now that she was standing.

Syrah took a moment, forcing her legs to take her weight, then nodded.

"Good," Raz said, grimacing and spasming in pain. "That's good. The horses. We have to get to the stables."

For the first time, the sounds of the world rushed back to Syrah. Where before the fight there had been nothing but the wind rustling through trees and across rooftops, she heard now the shouts of men and women in the homes and buildings all about them, heard the thunder of approaching hooves in the distance. Behind her, Syrah made out the noises of Gale and Nymara screaming and whinnying in fear, the smell of death and fire likely driving them half-mad in their pens.

From the temple, though, came not a sound.

"The Laorin!" she gasped, stumbling as she took a shaking step toward the street, intent on the front door of the building. "Tana! Kerren! We have to—!"

"We can't, Syrah!" Raz said with a groan. "There's nothing we can do! They're gone! We have to *go*!"

Syrah meant to keep walking, *wanted* to keep walking, but some part of her made her stop. The old her wanted to run, wanted to ignore the fatigue of her body and the fragility of her mind and rush for the temple, calling the names of the men and women she had come to know. That part wanted to scream for the approaching city guard, wanted to beg the help of the people shouting to each other from the windows.

But she became aware, in that moment, of a harder part of herself, a colder, calmer portion of her own conscience. It had been there for some time now, she realized. It had lingered in the corners of her mind, waiting for the moment it would be needed.

It was a fragment left to her, a shard of the world she had been abandoned to in the days after a blade had claimed her right eye.

No, this part spoke within her mind in a hard, dead voice. *They are gone. You cannot help them.*

And she knew it to be true. No light shimmered into life in the temple rooms. There came no slamming of doors as Priests and Priestesses came pouring out from the front and back of the temple, seeking to lend a hand or treat the injured. The assassins, it seemed, had been thorough in their work, purging any who might have been able to come to her and Raz's aid.

They are gone, the voice said again. *You cannot help them.*

Syrah allowed one racking, tearless sob to take her, trembling through her body like a blow as she gasped, understanding what had been lost on this night. She stood for half a moment more, gazing at nothing and everything, allowing the realization to grip her.

Then, still shaking, she turned and limped back to Raz, helping him to stand.

It took them more time than they would have liked to calm Gale and Nymara, the animals' fear redoubling at the ghastly sight the two of them must have made. Once they'd managed it, though, they moved as quickly as they could, abandoning everything but Ahna and Raz's gear and their gifts from the Laorin, all of which Raz stuffed quickly into one large traveling bag and slung from the end of the dviassegai. He had lost the scabbard of his gladius in the fight, and so he shoved the sword and the knife in with the rest of his armor. Not even bothering to saddle the horses, they each grunted and ignored the pain of their bodies as they clambered onto the backs of their mounts. Grabbing fistfuls of mane in lieu of reins, they held tight to their weapons with their free hands and pulled the horses about before kicking them into a full gallop out of the stables, around the temple, and into the street. From there, Raz turned west, leading them thundering down the road just as Syrah made out the clear sound of the city guard turning the corner behind them, headed for the temple.

They rode hard for some time, neither speaking. Syrah rapidly discovered that she was no good at handling a horse bareback, but was too tired to complain and in too much pain already to notice the discomfort of Nymara's spine beneath her. She didn't even have the energy, for a time, to realize that she had no idea where they were going, nor to consider if Raz did.

Only after nearly a quarter-hour, in fact, as they slowed abruptly to a trot, did Syrah realize that she didn't know where they were.

Through tired eyes she took in their surroundings, noticing the run-down state of the buildings about her, as well as the hovels and shanty-towns raised here and there wherever there was space. The road was less stone than flattened earth now, ignored and unattended, and the whole place had a distinctly dirty feel. No oil-fed streetlamps glinted above them to cast any sort of light on the area, and under nothing more than the gaze of the moon and stars the place looked dark and foreboding, like a graveyard in the night.

The slums, Syrah realized with a hint of fear.

"Raz?" Syrah said hoarsely, speaking for the first time since they left the temple as she continued to peer into the darkness of the crossroads and side-streets. "What are we doing here?"

Raz, though, didn't appear to have heard her. She looked around at him, and the cold that rushed through her then woke her up more thoroughly than any magic she might have been able to summon.

"Raz!" she yelled, heeling Nymara desperately forward.

The atherian was slumped where he sat, half-bent over Gale's neck as Syrah came up beside him. His golden eyes were partially closed, fluttering even as they flicked up to her, and she saw with a thrill of fear that the hand not grasping Ahna's shaft across his thighs was no longer holding on to the horse's mane.

Rather, Raz had brought it up, pressing it against the wound in his arm, trying to staunch the trickle of blood that seemed intent on escaping through his fingers.

"Oh no," Syrah hissed, sliding off Nymara's back and hurrying forward to urge Gale to a stop. "No, no, no. We need to get you off the street."

Raz nodded sluggishly, allowing the dviassegai and his sack of gear to tumble unceremoniously to the ground with a *crash*. Then, with what appeared to be great effort, he dragged a leg over Gale's back and dropped to the ground, only keeping his feet because Syrah caught him as he staggered.

"Over there," he breathed, lifting a single finger to point toward the nearest building, a single-story home with no front door and half its roof having long-since caved in.

Syrah glanced at it, and with a nervous shiver noticed several dark shapes watching them from the shadows of the place, eyes wide with what looked to be some combination of amazement and fear.

"Raz, I don't think—" Syrah began, but Raz gave a quick shake of his head, cutting her off.

"Over… there," he said again, each word coming in a weak, single breath.

Syrah wasn't happy about it, but she helped him toward the home one fumbling step at a time, leaving the horses to nicker nervously in the street.

As they approached the home's single entrance, Syrah made out the shapes still watching them from the dark. A dirty-faced woman, looking awestruck, with two small boys clutched to her thighs. She didn't flee as Syrah heaved Raz through the door of the building, though she did shrink away from them into the furthest corner of the room.

"What now?" Syrah asked in a rushed whisper as Raz let go of her and set his shoulder into the wall, sliding down to the hovel's dirty floor. "Raz, we need to get you help. I can't heal a wound like that alone."

For a moment, Raz said nothing, breathing in shallow huffs that made Syrah's heart skip in fear. Then he lifted his head.

When he spoke, though, it wasn't to her.

"The Carver," he said in a weak, ragged voice, eyes on the slum-woman and her children. "Get me… Get me the Carver of Ystréd."

XII

"Of the many aspects of the Mahsadën I have found fascinating in my studies, few compare to the sheer will of the society. This was not some loosely gathered band of miscreants out to make a name for themselves. Rather, this was the singular most cohesive collection of criminal minds the South—and perhaps the world—has ever known, intricately winding itself into the very fabric of government and establishment in the old fringe cities around the desert that was then known as "the Cienbal." They maintained this grip on the municipalities in their control—as well as the order within their own ranks—through one shear measure: an utter, unbending willingness to act as needed in order to survive and thrive."

— *As Death Rose from the Ashes*, by Kohly Grofh

With a grunt of exhausted effort, Na'zeem shouldered his way through the rickety door of their rundown hideout, promptly heaving the unconscious form of Eram off his back and onto the floor. Ehmed followed on his heels, laying Kailee down more carefully before straightening.

"That beast…" the man began in a horrified sort of groan, but he seemed unable to finish his thought.

For once, Na'zeem didn't berate him for the moment of weakness.

They had witnessed the Monster of Karth in his element, this night. He had thought themselves prepared, but looking back on the battle Na'zeem wanted to flay himself for his own foolishness. Despite every argument he could offer to the contrary, he'd approached the fight with the utmost confidence, especially after they had successfully silenced the Laorin who might have come to Arro's aid. To be fair, Na'zeem rather thought they *would* have taken the lizard's head that night, had he not made one crucial miscalculation.

It wasn't the atherian, after all, that they seemed to have underestimated…

Syrah Brahnt's face flashed across his mind, and Na'zeem allowed himself the space of a moment to memorize it, to etch the details of it into his memory. Her pale skin. Her white hair. Her one rose-colored eye reflected like through a broken mirror by the ruined ugliness of the other.

Gritting his teeth in fury at himself, Na'zeem shoved the thought of Brahnt away, convincing himself that was a satisfaction he would need to seek another day. For the time being, they had more pressing concerns.

Eleven dead. Eleven…

Even Na'zeem couldn't help but be staggered by that number. Whatever Adrion Blaeth might say to the contrary, he *had* listened to the damned cripple's warning, *had* listened to his and others' descriptions of the lizard's prowess. He'd planned accordingly, leading the assault himself into the Monster's room with five others. Enough, Na'zeem had thought, to force him and his woman into a retreat. The plan worked almost perfectly, eventually pressing the pair out into what was supposed to be a collapse attack in the alley by the others. He had expected casualties, had expected losses when their mistress had told him he and his men would be sent out on the "hunt of their lives."

But eleven? he seethed, gripping the hilt of his curved sword so tight it made his hand hurt.

Still… That fact alone cut their work out for them.

"Five men?" he asked aloud, not turning to look at Ehmed. "We're sure the city guard took only five?"

"Yes," the assassin answered at once. "Zafree, Aseri, Caluso—"

"I don't care *who* they took," Na'zeem snapped furiously over his shoulder. "Just how many. Five… By the Sun…"

He couldn't help but linger once more on the fact, on that shocking thought that—whereas an hour ago they had numbered a full score—they were now only nine, and more than half of that count by now already locked away in some cell in Ystréd's barracks.

"See what can be done about waking these two up," Na'zeem told Ehmed, finally turning and motioning down at the two unconscious men laid out at their feet. "It's my understanding the woman's magic won't kill them, so you should be able to rouse them eventually. When you do, I want all three of you back on the streets. Find out where the guard took the others. We'll need to retrieve them as soon as possible."

Ehmed dipped his head in agreement. "And you?" he asked, almost hesitantly. "What will you do?"

"Our mistress will want to be apprised of our new circumstances," Na'zeem said morbidly, turning away again and making through the darkness of the space toward the back wall of the room. "I'm going to draft her a missive. After that—" he forced himself to unclench the fist still bound about the handle of his sword, stretching his fingers and fighting the urge to strangle the next living person he saw "—we hunt once more."

"The Monster won't let himself be found again so easily!" Ehmed called after him in warning. "He'll be long gone by the time we manage to gather our numbers."

Na'zeem stopped at that, tilting his head back to look up at the patchwork of Her Stars he could see glimmering through the large open spaces that had long fallen from the roof.

"Then we'll look everywhere," he hissed into the night.

XIII

"It can often be heard said by the grandest mystical minds of our time that dreams are much more than a simple dive into one's subconscious, a ludicrous theory repeatedly proposed by the so-called "scientists" of this era. Through study, meditation, and contemplation, it is not all too difficult to grasp the fact that the worlds we visit in sleep are not mere manifestations of subliminal thought. Rather, they are glimpses into other realms, other realities and planes of existence.

Perhaps, with the right mindset, one should even consider that dreams are a hint at what awaits us on the other side of the darkness that eventually claims all…"

—*Dreamer's Dictation,* author unknown

Raz was dreaming of the Garin again. He stood, still in the quiet of the desert dusk, clawed feet toeing the edge of the crystalline waters as a warm breeze made the lake shiver before him. It was his favorite dream, and he smiled when he made out the sound of the clan at his back, men and women going about their chores of preparing for the evening meal while the children shouted and played around them. He didn't turn around. He *never* turned around when he found himself in the welcome stupors of this particular place, afraid that if he did there would be nothing to see except smoke and ash and flame. It was enough simply listening to the Arros move about, laughing and talking, though he could never make out their words. Somewhere at his back his mother and father, Agais and Grea, still lived, in their own way. His uncle Jarden would be fiddling with his pipes, or teaching the younger ones how to use the bleached-wood staff he'd always carried with him. Ahna would be sitting by the fire, giggling and pretending with her favorite straw doll. Raz even thought he could make out the happy voices of Lueski and Arrun Koyt joining in with the others, and the sound made him smile.

Not for the first time, he wondered what would happen if he simply didn't wake up. He wondered—as men who live by the sword often do— what he would find on the day his sleep became eternal. Would there be nothing, there in the light of the Moon? Would he be given the honor of ascending to shine among Her Stars? Would he be allowed to exist in this dream, perhaps, to join his family at the edges of the Garin?

There was very little he had ever wished for more fervently.

Abruptly, Raz felt something cool about his feet, and he glanced down. The lake, which had only been at his toes a minute before, appeared to be rising, rapidly climbing up to his ankles, then to his knees, then his hips. Raz felt no fear as the water continued to build around him, understanding that it meant his time in this place of happiness was at an end. He gazed down at his own reflection as the lake reached his chest, promising himself he would hold on to the hope of one day being allowed to stay for good.

Then the water was at his neck, and a moment later he was submerged completely beneath the cool, comfortable depths of the Garin.

"You're a damned *fool*, Raz i'Syul Arro."

Slowly, Raz opened his eyes, blinking several times as the world about him came into steady focus. He became aware that he was lying in some sort of bed, a stiff, short cot judging by the way his feet were sticking well off the end. The air smelled strange, a mixture of fire and herbs combined with the faint smell of blood and sickness, and he heard shuffling and the groans of men and women all around him. He was swathed in bandages, several about his abdomen and chest, though most were tied over his left arm, binding it like a white cocoon.

Then his vision cleared, and he made out two feminine faces tipped to stare down at him from either side.

Syrah had lost her eye wraps when they'd fled, but appeared to have replaced them with a length of black cloth that looked like it might have been sheared from some larger piece of fabric. She had clean cotton dressings wrapped about her neck—as well as what looked like several sutures under the right line of her jaw—and seemed to be holding a wet compress to Raz's forehead, the excess water trickling down between his ears. He smiled when he saw her, seeing relief brighten her good eye.

Then he rolled his head to the other woman, the one who had spoken.

"Eva," he said hoarsely, grinning. "It's good to see you too."

Evalyn Zall, the Carver of Ystréd, glowered down at Raz in a half-amused, half-annoyed sort of way. She was a pretty woman, her skin several shades darker than any true Northerner even in summer, particularly when compared to Syrah. Her grey eyes, so distinct of her desert heritage, were sweeping across his body, taking him in critically behind several strands of black hair that had fallen across her face. She looked more worn than when he'd last seen her some months past, her face a little thinner and a darkness building under her lids, but she also looked invigorated, as though whatever was keeping her from sleep was nothing she would ever trade the world for.

"I didn't say it wasn't good to see you," Eva said in a huff, crossing her arms in irritation, "but just once we should have a reunion that doesn't start with you *unconscious on my table.*"

Raz chuckled. "Where's the fun in that, though?" He started to sit up, wincing as he did, and Syrah quickly put the compress aside to help him. "Got to keep your skills sharp somehow."

"Trust me, I have ample opportunity already," Eva said with a roll of her eyes once Raz had managed to steady himself on the edge of his cot. "Even without *you* bleeding out all over my floor."

Looking around, Raz's brows rose in surprise. "Yes... I can see that."

He sat, his back to the wall of a massive room that he could only compare to the infirmary of Cyurgi 'Di. Two massive fireplaces burned on either side of the chamber, cut right into the stone, their light bathing the space in bright warmth. Above, a high vaulted ceiling arched over them, with several ladders set into the walls leading up to a second-story catwalk stocked with wooden boxes and barrels of supplies. All about them, on the ground floor, a score of beds just like Raz's were spaced across the room in several even rows. Almost all of them were full, and he noticed with a brief jump of gratitude that he had been placed in the furthest corner from the occupied cots, as far from prying eyes as could be managed. Several attendants moved about the room checking on patients, some changing bandages, some applying salves to wounds or assisting in eating or drinking. There were others, too, about a half-dozen heavier-set men and women in plain clothes lingering about the edges of the place, hands tending to rest on the pommels of the swords they had strapped to their waists.

When he noticed this, Raz tensed.

"It's all right," Syrah told him at once, coming around to sit beside him on the bed. "They won't bother us. Eva's assured me."

Sure enough, not a one among the armed men and women looked to be paying him any attention outside of a curious glance here and there. Rather, they appeared intent on the patients, watching them closely, as though keeping an eye out for trouble.

"Seems you've been busy," Raz grumbled, glancing at Eva. "Don't tell me you had all of this the last time we met?"

In response the woman snorted, then half-turned, arms still crossed, to look back at her operation. "Hardly," she said. "After that fiasco at the start of the freeze, Sven decided it was time to retire. He left not long after you, with a caravan for Azbar to stay with family there, and ceded me his list of... uh... clients." She smirked.

Raz could understand her amusement. He had first met Eva over a year ago now, when he'd still worked as a dog of the Miropan Mahsadën. Chained up among the slaves the society had attempted to trick him into collecting for them, the woman was part of the brutal understanding Raz had come to that night, the realization of what he'd become, and what he was doing. Rather than turn them over to the šef—the ringleaders of the Mahsadën—Raz had helped Eva and the others escape and flee northward, though not before the woman had put her skill as a surgeon's apprentice to use in healing several broken ribs he'd suffered in the process.

Ever since then—with no apprenticeship and no mentor to vouch for her legitimacy—Eva had been establishing a name for herself among the only people of Ystréd who didn't give a rat's ass that she wasn't a fully-trained physician: the slum dwellers and criminals of the city. Raz had stumbled across her again some eight or nine months ago when a local hack—Sven, Raz recalled as the surgeon said the name—had been hired to save his life by a band of mercenaries he'd managed to get himself captured by, half-frozen and half-dead as he was. Sven had gotten word to Eva, who'd in turn reached out to the Laorin faith for assistance and managed to rescue Raz from the group before they'd had a chance to drag him back to the South as a living gift for the Mahsadën.

And now, it seemed, Sven had given up the trade, leaving Eva with a city's-worth of vagrants and miscreants to tend to.

Abruptly, Raz understood why she needed the guards.

"You must pay them well, if you're not worried they'll try to collect the prices on our heads," he commented, still eyeing the men and women along the walls.

Eva nodded. "I do. It also helps that each and every one of them is only alive today because of me." Her face softened. "They feel they owe me."

"Not just them," Syrah said quietly, her arm slipping into Raz's, though she was looking at the woman. "Eva... Thank you. I don't know what I would have done. And again, I-I'm sorry about..."

She hesitated, sounding embarrassed. Raz glanced at her, confused, then at Eva.

"By the time word reached me and my men and I got to you, you were unconscious," Eva explained. "Unfortunately, Syrah—" she nodded to the Priestess with an amused expression "—didn't know to trust us. She almost blew half the building apart before I managed to explain who I was."

Beside him, Syrah blushed in embarrassment. "I'm *so* sorry," she mumbled awkwardly.

Eva waved her apology away, hiding a smile now. "Don't be." She glared at Raz with a meaningful, almost motherly expression. "It's good to know that this oaf isn't wandering alone anymore, especially if he keeps managing to get wounds like *that*."

She poked Raz's bandaged arm playfully, making him wince.

"You still need to work on your bedside manner, I see," he grumbled, moving the limb about in an attempt to lessen the throb. "This isn't how you build loyalty among your clientele."

Eva raised an eyebrow. "This is the third time I've patched you up in a year. I would say my bedside manner hasn't stopped *you* from becoming a repeat customer."

Beside him, Syrah snorted and lifted a hand to her mouth as she tried to stifle a laugh.

"I'm not sure I like having you two in the same room together..." Raz grumbled, eyeing the Priestess in feigned annoyance.

"Oh, hush," Syrah said, squeezing his arm in hers—which earned them a second raised eyebrow from Eva.

Seeming to think better of asking, though, the woman's eyes looked suddenly concerned. "Teasing aside... Raz, you need to tell me what happened. Syrah tried, but we figured you probably knew more. Were they really assassins? Your injuries... You looked like minced meat when we carried you down here. How many attacked you?"

Raz frowned, feeling their collective mood darken, Syrah going still and silent beside him. "I don't know," he said after a few moments of contemplation. "Twenty, maybe more. It was hard to tell. The way they moved…" He paused, glancing around. Catching sight of his gear, shoved in a corner to their right, he pointed at it. "Can someone bring me my things?"

At once, Eva looked around. With a word, two of the closest guards detached themselves from their places along the wall and moved as commanded, starting to drag Ahna and the bag still attached to her end over with some effort.

"Lifegiver's tits," Raz heard one curse under his breath as they moved. "Dragon he must be, if he can bloody well carry this lot around with him all day."

Raz smiled to himself, nodding in thanks to the men as they deposited his things at his feet.

It took him only a moment to find what he was looking for, rummaging through the bag carefully so as not to cut himself on the blade of the gladius, still bare and bloody within. Finally, his hand closed around the handle of the item, and he pulled it from the bag for the three of them to examine.

He hadn't had much of an opportunity to examine the knife during the fight, but looking at it now he realized it wasn't going to tell him anything he hadn't already deduced. It had a narrow, straight hilt with a black cloth handle and a large, semi-circular pommel. It's broad cross-guard was unadorned, and the blade curved wickedly along its length, then more sharply toward the tip. Overall it was a plain, simple dagger, though exceptionally well-crafted. He'd seen a thousand such weapons of its ilk.

He'd even sold not-a-few of them himself, in his years among the Arros.

"Southern," he grunted, turning the blade over to see if there was anything more meaningful on its flipside. "But I could have told you that already."

Beside him, Syrah nodded. "Their eyes. Grey. All of them," she said.

Eva's own grey eyes blinked in muted surprise. "The Mahsadën?" she asked Raz, who inclined his head at once.

"Undoubtedly." He brought the blade right up to his face, peering at it closely, but the steel stubbornly refused to reveal anything of interest. "And worse than that… They were *too* good. They used the shadows like nothing I'd ever seen before." He glanced at Eva. "It was like witnessing every story I'd ever heard about Ergoin Sass."

Eva bared her teeth in anger at the name, making Syrah blink.

"Sass…?" she said slowly, like she thought she were treading on thin ice. "Your contact in the Mahsadën?"

"My handler," Raz spat, tossing the knife back in with the rest of his gear. "I'll say it how it was. And one of the more evil bastards I've ever had the misfortune of working with, to be sure."

"But…" Syrah kept on, confused. "Isn't he dead?"

Raz nodded.

Ergoin Sass had been the šef in charge of handling all the society's assassination contracts and bounties. As a result, he'd been Raz's primary go-between, reaching out whenever the Mahsadën had a situation which required a particular touch, or if they needed to send a message of the kind only the Monster of Karth was capable of delivering. Sass had been a vile, corrupted soul, having gained his power by his own hand, killing off what competition came along, and had thrived in his position as master of the group's cutthroats and assassins.

It had made cleaving him half-in-two the previous summer almost enjoyable.

"He's dead," Raz confirmed. "But if he managed to pass his skills on to a group like the one we fought, that bodes well for no one. Men like that won't give up, even if I killed half of them off. They'll collect themselves and very likely try again." He grit his teeth, turning to Syrah. "Making for Acrosia isn't an option now. If we get caught on the road we'll be done for, and if we survive until we make it to the city then the assassins will have the support of the Mahsadën, not to mention how much harder it will become to sneak into the port."

Syrah paled, looking as though she were thinking quickly. "We can still make west?" she offered. "Stullens and Drangstek are much larger than Ystréd, and the Laorin have a much greater presence."

"No," Raz said at once with a shake of his head. "I won't put the faith between me and these men. Not again." His shoulders slumped. "And I don't think you want to either, after what's happened here…"

Syrah tensed at his words. He could feel her arm begin to shake against his, and he took her hand.

"No," she finally said. "No, you're right. We can't."

A tear glimmered in the corner of her good eye, and her gaze was distant. He couldn't blame her. She had borne witness to the death of a good score of her kind and, though she might bear a strong face now, Raz knew it would weigh on her.

And it's my fault, he couldn't help but think. *Once again… my fault.*

He shoved the guilt aside, allowing it to be replaced by a seething anger at the men who'd done this. He wanted to go out, wanted to take Ahna and hunt down every one of the bastards who might have escaped. He gave himself a moment to bask in that anger, to gain focus from the hate he had for the men who would so callously throw away the lives of dozens just to ensure the death of one.

He was just calming himself down when Eva spoke.

"You're looking for a way out of the North?"

Raz and Syrah both looked up at her in surprise.

"We are…" Raz said, watching the woman closely. "Why?"

"But not via the fringe cities?"

Raz nodded, but said nothing more.

Eva hesitated, apparently mulling a thought over in her head.

"Do you have an idea?" Syrah pressed her.

"I do…" Eva said, still sounding as though she were considering the options. "But I'd need to send a bird. Find out if it's even an option."

"What is it?" Raz insisted. They were getting desperate, he knew. Any opportunity was worth considering at this point.

"Well…" Eva began, sounding almost nervous and not meeting Raz's eyes. "There's a man I know. A captain, actually."

"Of a ship?" Raz felt his interest swell with a sudden intensity. "Could he get us to the Imperium? Or even just the Isles?"

Eva shook her head. "Not likely. He doesn't sail the Emperor's Ocean."

That made Raz frown. "Then he sales the Dramion?"

While the Emperor's Ocean lay far to the west, playing host to the island nations of the West Isles and the more distant Imperium, the Dramion Sea was much closer, likely no more than a week or two's ride east. The problem, though, was that it was an endless, landless expanse. Raz recalled old Kosen and the Grandmother telling him and his young cousins stories of the sea, speaking of hydras and serpents and other great monsters lurking in the depths of the vast emptiness. They had told him a hundred tales of adventurers who had sailed out, seeking distant shores at the edges of the world, never to return again.

They might have only been stories to frighten children around the evening fire, but Raz felt a chill as he realized he hadn't even considered the Dramion an option for he and Syrah.

Eva nodded. "He does. Every five or six months he makes the trip, back and forth. He's has a… a shipping business. Some of the medicines, the herbs and compounds I need can't be found in the North, and are too expensive to ship by traditional routes." She blushed. "Garht can generally get me what I need."

"He's a smuggler," Syrah said flatly, sounding suddenly very disenchanted.

Eva shrugged helplessly. "And a thief, I think," she sighed. "But he seems a good man, outside of all that."

Syrah grumbled something under her breath that even Raz didn't catch, which made it easy to ignore her. "But you think he would be able to grant us passage out of the North?" he asked.

"I do. And I don't think he'd want to draw attention to himself by turning you over to the šef. He's refused to do business with them in the past, and I don't believe they were happy about it."

"Why did he refuse?" Syrah asked, her eyes narrowed.

A muscle twitched in Eva's jaw. "He never told me outright, but let's just say I choose to work with the man because he appears to have more morals than others of his ilk. Specifically when it comes to livestock of the two-legged kind…"

Raz's felt his face darken. "He wouldn't traffic slaves for them," he said simply. "No wonder he'd be out of favor with the šef."

"Oh," Syrah said, sounding a little more enthusiastic at the prospect now. "Well, if that's the case..." She paused, her brow furrowing in sudden confusion. "But if your captain is sailing out of the North and doesn't end port in the South, then that means..."

Right then it clicked for Raz as well, and he groaned in frustration even as Eva spoke.

"Yes. Garht's ship should raise anchor before summer's end, making for Perce."

XIV

Syrah was the one who told Eva to send the bird, utterly ignoring Raz's protests. Initially he refused, point-blank, to plot them on any course that would land them in the realms beyond the South, telling her over and over again that he wouldn't set foot in an empire that had been built on the back of slaves, human and atherian alike. They argued several times over the next few days, Syrah pointing out repeatedly that they had no other good options and that suffering their pride in Perce was better than suffering a knife in the back anywhere else.

"Where would you have us go, then?" she'd demanded furiously the last time they'd had it out. "In the North we are hunted, and in the South you would be as good as dead." Her expression had grown sad at that. "I won't lose you, Raz. Not you, too."

And then she'd walked away, leaving him in his cot with nothing more than his frustration and sudden desire to call after her and apologize.

It was the better part of a week, in fact, before Raz was even remotely open to the idea, time that both women forced him to spend mostly bedridden, healing from his wounds and allowing his body to recover. For the first day or two he didn't mind, the fight with the Mahsadën assassins— for he really couldn't think of anyone else who might have sent the men— having taken more out of him than he would admit to either Syrah *or* Eva. By the end of the third day, though, Raz was tired of being cooped up. Between his body's own natural healing prowess and the spells Syrah worked into his flesh every morning, it wasn't long before he was on his feet again and itching to move.

Eva, however, wouldn't hear of it.

"I don't care how good you feel," she told him on more than one occasion, shoving him back down on the cot. "You lost a third of your blood volume, easily. It's going to be hard enough getting you and Syrah out of the city already. I won't have you fainting before we manage to even get you within view of the gates."

Raz—having long since been used to being shouted down by healers— would always grumble and sulk, but eventually give in. In the end, he had to rely on Eva's people for information on what was happening about the city, and the news was never good. The morning following the attack, word reached them that the massacre at the temple had indeed been discovered, and was being investigated by the Ystréd guard. Syrah spent much of that day in silent grief. Not a single Priest or Priestess had managed to escape their home with their life.

They were the only survivors.

Two days later, a slum boy arrived with several rolled-up parchments, handing them to Eva before stealing an awe-struck glance at Raz and darting back up the stairs, out of the infirmary. Eva had unrolled the sheaf and looked the papers over, glowering at whatever they contained before throwing them into one of the room's great fires without a word.

Only after a lot of pressing had she admitted to Raz that they'd been notices the boy had found in the market streets, each bearing Raz or Syrah's crude likenesses and a request for any information that would lead to their whereabouts.

That was the moment Raz's determination had started to waver, when the fear had started to sink in. He wasn't worried about what happened to him. If the Mahsadën men came again, then they came, and fate would decide once more who would survive that second fight. But he had others to consider. He'd dragged Syrah into the muck now, truly pulled her into the blood and violence that was his life. He doubted the city guard thought them perpetrators in the slaughter of the Laorin, given the bodies they must have found at the scene, but if they were taken in even for questioning, then they would be trapped. Regardless of whether the assassins took advantage of that vulnerability, there was still the price on his head—on *both* their heads. All it would take was a couple of greedy souls, out to make their fortune in the world, and he and Syrah would die with soldiers' swords in their backs.

Beyond that, there was Eva, now. She was stretching her small network to its full extent, he knew, making sure she had ears on the ground at all times. She was making excuses with her current patients to keep them from leaving, knowing all too well—as Raz did—that given the opportunity not a few among them would go straight to the guard in hopes of a reward, or gather their friends and return with the intention of making a play for his head themselves. Within four days her people were having to lay out spare bedrolls in corners to make space for the sick and injured who came stumbling in with handfuls of coin and stolen valuables as payment. By the fifth day the woman—who'd already been strained when Raz and Syrah had first arrived—looked in poorer health than some of her patients, struggling to balance seeing to all the men and women in her care and keeping Raz's presence secret. Every time he saw her, the shadows under her eyes clear now, Raz felt a little of his conviction flake away.

Unfortunately, it wasn't till another three days after that a bird came from the east, bearing a response from the captain.

Raz saw the girl arrive in a hurry, a narrow scroll in her hand as she took the steps to the room two at a time before looking around frantically for Eva. She wore ratty, baggy pants and a thin shirt, and her bare feet left dusty footprints across the ground once she caught sight of the woman and hurried over. They exchanged a few words, Eva's eyes gleaming excitedly as the girl told her who the message was from, and she handed the slum runner a copper from her pocket before thanking her and sending her off again. Before the girl was back up the stairs and gone, Eva had broken the seal on the letter and started reading.

It must have been a short reply, because a few seconds later she was hurrying over to Raz.

"Where is Syrah?" she asked him at once.

"Over there," Raz told her, nodding toward the far end of the room where the Priestess was assisting some of Eva's attendants in their tasks. "Did you hear back from your man?"

Eva nodded without looking at him, catching the eye of one of her guards and indicating the woman with a jerk of her head. At once the man lumbered over to speak into Syrah's ear.

"I did," Eva finally answered as Syrah began weaving her way through the beds toward them. "And it's better news than I expected."

Raz blinked, unsure what to make of this statement.

"What's going on?" Syrah asked quietly, reaching them and looking between he and Eva. She was still dressed in her white robes, but the sleeves had been rolled up, revealing the scars along her wrists as she wiped her hands clean with a moist towel. Similarly, her white hair had been pulled back and tied into a ponytail behind her head, though she'd left enough loose to hide the mangled remnants of her right ear. Unlike Raz, Syrah had found a way to keep busy over the last week, assisting in the treatment and healing of what patients she could.

Before responding, Eva handed the letter to Raz. "Garht says he's willing to grant you passage," she said as he began reading the response for himself. "I'd asked what it would cost you, but he says he won't accept any payment in exchange."

Though he didn't look up from the parchment in his fingers, Raz rather thought Syrah's silence was indicative of his own feelings: surprise and confusion.

And—above all else—suspicion.

He read the response carefully several times, trying to discern anything amiss in the captain's words, but there was nothing more there than Eva had said. The handwriting was ugly, the hasty, rugged script of a man struggling with his letters.

Willing. Payment not necessary. Details upon your arrival.

-Garht Argoan

"A man of few words," Raz said evenly, handing the letter to Syrah so she could review it herself. "Though the fact that he's refusing payment concerns me."

Eva frowned. "I've never received a letter like this from him. It's like he was in a hurry to agree."

That did little to assuage Raz's worry, but he said nothing of it. On one hand, he had never known a smuggler or thief of any kind to work for free. It bothered him. On the other... He and Syrah had no gold with which to pay their passage. What little they'd been granted by the council of Cyurgi 'Di had been abandoned when they'd fled the temple, leaving them without so much as two copper barons to rub together. He supposed, considering it now, that the pair of them might have attempted to work off the price while on the ship, but if this 'Garht Argoan' was truly offering them free passage…

It's too good to be true, a cold voice said in the back of his mind.

Raz was inclined to agree.

"We don't have any other options."

Syrah, too, had apparently read the letter's single line more than once, and was now handing it back to Eva. She didn't look happy, but her eye was resolute as she looked around at him. "Raz, we have no other choice."

"Even if it's a trap?" he asked her darkly.

Syrah bit her lip. "Yes. Even then. I don't like the fact that he's refusing payment any more than you do, but Eva trusts him." She looked at the surgeon uncertainly. "Don't you?"

Eva hesitated, then nodded slowly. "As far as I can trust a man of his vocation, I suppose."

Syrah nodded. "Then—as much as I wish he'd put them in ink—there's a chance he has his reasons. Even if it *is* a trap, I'll take the odds of us against whatever he and his crew might have in store over our just staying here, waiting for the Mahsadën to strike again. It's a risk we have to take."

Raz didn't respond to her, looking instead at Eva. "What did he mean, 'your arrival'? Would you be coming with us?"

"I would," she said, crossing her arms, as was her fashion. "Along with a few others. Garht won't risk his goods to a middleman, and I need to take stock of what he has for me, as well as haggle a price."

Raz felt a little better, knowing that. He was still concerned, but he trusted Eva about as much as he trusted anyone else in the world, and he thought it might be bad business for a smuggler to risk one of his patrons by involving her in something like a trap.

And yet, he still hesitated.

Perce, he thought to himself, the land's name sounding like a curse even silent within his own mind.

He could list a hundred reasons why they shouldn't go, *had* listed a hundred reasons why they shouldn't go. He hated the idea of it viscerally, feeling almost nauseous as he considered every other alternative once again. He turned everything over in his head a last time, fighting with every ounce of desperation he could muster to try and find a better solution.

In the end, he came up empty, like he knew he would.

Eventually, Raz looked up at Syrah. "If I promised to convert, do you think Jofrey would allow us back into the Citadel?"

Syrah laughed, a bright, sad sound of relief, anticipation, and fear.

Then she politely asked Eva to send a reply at once, telling Garht Argoan they would be taking him up on his offer.

They departed Ystréd the following evening. While the north, east, and west gates were all barred to traffic after sunset, the south gate was kept manned at all hours to greet any messengers and travelers from Azbar and the surrounding villages who chose to ride through the night. For this reason, it was in that direction that their little party headed first, leaving Eva's illicit infirmary in the slums behind.

Smuggling Syrah out of the city, it turned out, was a simple matter, if a little tedious. Eva had her attendants wrap the Priestess from head to toe in cloth bandages, obscuring everything from her fingers to her hair to her face. After that, Syrah allowed herself to be bundled in several layers of dirty blankets, then laid down in a thick bed of straw along the bed of the narrow wagon that had been hitched to the mount of one of Eva's men. By the time they were ready to depart, Syrah Brahnt, Priestess of Laor, looked like nothing more than some miserable leper headed out to die among family in the Plains.

It didn't hurt that her blankets and straw also hid the three small chests of gold and silver Eva would exchange for Garht's stolen medicines.

Raz smiled, watching the gate guard wave them through after hardly a minute's inspection, those who weren't staying well away from the cart outright unwilling to do more than glance at Syrah's bandaged form before shuffling back. He waited until they were well-clear of the walls, following the group as they took a turn in the road to make east, before lifting himself out of his crouch to look out over the city.

There was a beauty to the sprawl of the valley town. From where he stood on the sloped roof of the three-story cobbler's shop overlooking the gate, Raz could see most everything. Ystréd spread like its own small world before him, the glint and glimmer of fire and lamps and candlelit windows carpeting the earth like a million stars reflecting up at the night sky above. Beyond it, though, there was little more than darkness, the Moon shedding just enough light over the land to draw away from the suspense of the black. If he peered closely, Raz could just make out the jagged outline of woodlands to the south, then the waving shapes of the Dehn's horizon to the north. For a time he took it in, wondering—as he had when he'd left the Citadel—if he would ever have a chance to witness the warm glow of the Northern cities ever again.

Then, with several bounding steps, he launched himself over the gap of the road between him and the buildings opposite, landing on the wooden roof of a blacksmith's forge with a dull *thump*.

Raz moved quickly and quietly, keeping the wall of the city to his right as he ran. It felt good, being on the rooftops again. He hadn't had the opportunity in some time, since well-before he'd left the walls of Azbar behind, and the world opened up for him as it always did when he was above the horizon. Even in full gear—Ahna clenched in one hand and his gladius strapped in a borrowed sheath across his back as he watched the shadows for signs of life—he sped over the homes and shops and buildings, winding unseen up and down the inclines and declines of the town, between chimneys, over open-air balconies, and under the overhangs and eaves of higher rooftops. He moved beneath the gaze of Her Stars above, dropping into the darkness of unlit alleys as needed, then back up the half-timber walls and into open air once more. The stiffness of the last week left him bit by bit, fleeing his limbs and chest as he pushed himself to go faster. Muscle stretched and lungs expanded, and eventually Raz was starting to feel a little bit himself again, the night sky whisking away the frustration of having been cooped up indoors for too many days.

After about a quarter-hour, maybe halfway between the south and east gates, Raz decided his fun was at an end. He shifted his course to trace Ystréd's curved wall more closely, granting himself one more minute of tumbling and leaping across the skyline.

Then, sure he was in the clear, he vaulted onto the roof of a split-level home, turned sharply, and launched himself into the air toward the emptiness of the night beyond the brightness of the city.

For a second or two Raz allowed himself to fall, thrilling in the lurch of freedom and fear that comes when one is prisoner to the harsh judgment of gravity. When he was sure he was beyond the lip of the wall, Raz spread his wings to their extent, feeling the jolt of his momentum cut short and the shaking strain of the muscles in his back, unused to such stress.

He held them firm, however, and a moment or two later hit the grassy earth beyond Ystréd with a *thud*, rolling to his feet and twisting to come up with Ahna at the ready, facing the city.

Nothing.

For thirty long seconds he watched the outline of the rooftops he'd leapt from, his eyes flicking toward every shiver of light or whip of curtains through windows. Finally, when nothing rose or tried to follow him from the shadows, Raz turned and began hurrying east, his clawed feet pounding over the soft summer earth, the dviassegai over one shoulder.

He made them out not five minutes later, waiting at the crossroads Eva had described, all ahorse and peering expectantly through the night in his direction. Syrah saw him first, having freed herself of the disguising bandages, and he heard her give a distant exclamation, then raise a hand to wave. He slowed down as he approached, crossing the dirt road at a jog and accepting Gale's reins with a nod of thanks as one of Eva's guards handed them over.

"No sign of them?" Eva asked as he put a foot in the stirrups and heaved himself up into the stallion's new saddle.

"None," Raz confirmed, guiding the horse around so that he, too, could look back at the city. "Either they're better than I gave them credit for, or they never managed to figure out where we were."

"Truth be told, I don't know how many of them could have been left," Syrah added thoughtfully, nudging Nymara up to snort at the grass beside Gale. "I left six or seven unconscious, at least, and I don't know how many you dealt with."

She said the last two words as casually as she could, which almost amused Raz.

"Not enough," he said coolly. "There could be a half-dozen left in play. Likely more."

"That's assuming the Mahsadën hasn't already sent reinforcements," Eva said darkly. "I haven't known them to ever give up easily…"

Raz glanced back at her. She sat astride her own horse, frowning at the light of the city to the west. Beside and behind her, three of her retinue waited patiently, two men and a woman, the cart yoked behind the left-most's dappled gelding. None of them *looked* nervous, but it was clear by the way their eyes shifted between Raz and their employer that they found the conversation unsettling.

"All the more reason to put as much space as we can between us and this place," Raz told them all, turning and heeling Gale into a canter down the east road, Syrah right behind him.

XV

"The further I delve into what little I have found on the man known as Adrion Blaeth, the more terrifying the picture becomes. I hesitate indeed to put some of my findings to text, as I fear the speculations I've been able to make may indeed deter many of my readers. The man's apparent violent nature, the horrible powers he seems to have wielded in a time when magic is largely considered to have been reserved only for a chosen few… I wonder if I do not challenge our understanding of the period too much, with too little to show in defense of such claims…"

—from the journals of Kohly Grofh

The messenger arrived in the evening, just as supper was being set out. The man had been ushered into the hall by one of Adrion's attending servants, and at once he saw Lazura's lip curl in distaste across the table from him, though he couldn't venture a guess as to whether it was due to the interruption, or simply the state of the runner himself. He was filthy, the thick furs wrapped about his shoulders to fend off the biting chill of the desert night matted with dust, his face streaked with lines of sweat. He looked as though he had run full-tilt to deliver the message.

Add that to the fact that whatever news he bore was apparently enough to warrant disturbing their meal, and Adrion instantly felt apprehension dampen his appetite.

The messenger, to his credit, didn't waste time with apologies or explanations. As soon as he was let in, he made a line for Adrion, who took a moment of amusement from the further ire this seemed to cause Lazura. *She's growing tired of the game*, he thought as he wiped his fingers on the napkin in his lap and accepted the rolled message with a nod of thanks to the man. He was about to dismiss him when the seal caught his eye, and a sudden chill overcame Adrion despite the warmth of the room.

There was the black circle of wax, embossed with the letter "M" of the Mahsadën. It was the same stamp he saw up to a dozen times on any given day, with nothing particularly remarkable to be noted at first glance. There was a detail that stood out in the impression, however, one few others would have even given a second look. The shape of the band that wrapped around the symbol was broken in two places, like the ring that had been used to make the seal was dented in a diagonal manner.

Na'zeem's mark, Adrion realized at once.

The letter was not meant for him.

For a second he froze, earning himself a curious blink from the messenger and a piercing look from Lazura. Coming to his senses, Adrion handed the message back to the man. "This is a missive for my consort," he said with a nod toward the other end of the long table. "She has been expecting word from family in the North regarding a private matter."

The runner took the roll in fumbling fingers, managing to get out a stumbling "Yessir" before turning and hurrying to the woman. Apparently unable to restrain herself, Lazura snatched the letter up and stood, breaking the seal and unrolling the paper as she stepped away from her dinner.

"You may go, runner," Adrion said hurriedly, not taking his eyes off the woman as he watched her cold blue eyes tick across the message quickly. He had seen that look before.

As he'd guessed, the news wasn't good.

The messenger had just finished stammering a hurried "Thank you, sir" and started to turn toward the door of the hall again, when Lazura spoke.

"No. Stay."

The words hissed from her lips like ice made ethereal. Though she had no true power over the society as far as anyone outside of Adrion and her pet shadows were aware, the utter fury in the command grabbed the messenger firm, and he froze where he stood.

"Lazura… Adrion said warningly, but she took as much notice of him as she did the chair she had just vacated. She was breathing hard, the parchment crinkling in her fingers as she gripped it furiously. Before his eyes he saw the letter start to smoke, and his apprehension solidified into something very much like true fear.

"Na'zeem has failed."

She said it quietly, but the words were sharp as daggers against Adrion's skin. Had he not been worried about the more imminent dangers, he might have taken some small amount of satisfaction in this news. He'd suspected it might come, after all, though the delivery was much earlier than he'd expected.

As it was, all he could do was stare at her, silent and unmoving, hands gripping the arms of his chair so hard it hurt.

"He was 'forced to retreat'," Lazura quoted in a deadly tone that made the candles jump and flicker around them. "He and three others are all that remain. Another five were arrested by the local guard, though he assures me he will have found a way to retrieve them before this letter reached us."

Adrion's brows furrowed in confusion. "'The guard' arrested his men? I didn't imagine these Laorin would have such men under their employment…"

"They don't," Lazura answered, not looking up as she read the letter for what had to be the fourth time. "The Monster came to them. They seem to have crossed paths in Ystréd, one of the Northern cities."

That explains it. Adrion almost felt sorry for Na'zeem and his subordinates if they had approached the fight under the impression that Raz i'Syul Arro had been delivered to them by the Twins on a silver platter. More than *half* the assassin's men had been wiped out in their initial assault. They were whispers in the night, fabrications of darkness that weren't supposed to exist. As far as Adrion knew, neither Na'zeem nor any of his men had ever been caught in the act of carrying out Lazura's orders, much less been killed in the attempt.

Adrion wondered, with no small amount of satisfaction, if this disastrous failure would do something to wipe away the smug, cruel confidence Na'zeem's eyes had always boasted on the few occasions they'd met.

"Is something amusing?" Lazura asked him, the question like broken nails scraping across the back of his neck. With a jolt of fear, Adrion realized he had been smiling ever so slightly.

"Not at all," he answered at once, sitting up straighter in his chair and thinking fast. "I was just considering that the Monster is still within our grasp. Na'zeem has options yet. If he's managed to free those captured by the guard, he'll still have a force of almost ten men. Now that he's faced Raz once, perhaps he will know how best to approach his next attempt."

A chill swept through the room, like the fire in the back wall had suddenly stopped exuding warmth, exposing them to the cruelty of the desert night. Again the candles danced, and in that half-moment of dimmed light the outlines of Lazura on the floor and walls around her seemed to combine into some twisted, terrible form.

"The beast," Lazura said, her words almost echoing over the deathly silence that followed Adrion's suggestion, "has fled. The Monster is in the wind once again."

For several seconds, nothing happened. Lazura stood, so still she might have been made of ice and stone. The quiet of the chamber took hold once more, not even the wind outside seeming brave enough to disturb her. Adrion began to relax ever so slightly, thinking perhaps she'd managed to keep control of herself this time.

And then the air about the woman began to shimmer, like a mirage across the hot sands of the Cienbal, and Adrion's blood ran cold.

"Run," he managed to get out, struggling to stand.

The messenger, who still hadn't moved from his place by the door, looked around at him. "M-My lord?" he asked foolishly.

"RUN!" Adrion bellowed, making a desperate swipe for the crutch leaning on the table beside him.

Too late.

Lazura let loose a scream of such wrathful fury, Adrion felt it vibrate in his teeth. In the same instant, the parchment the woman had been holding in both hands blew apart as though by a terrifying blast of wind, and a wave of incomprehensible energy rippled out from her form. Adrion had a moment in which he saw the magic coming at him, saw it shatter glassware and send books and wine-filled goblets and lit candles hurtling, before it caught him. When it did, he was thrown backward with such force he might as well have been kicked in the chest by a horse, and he missed tumbling into the fire by mere feet. Instead, Adrion was slammed into the granite wall, breaking an old oil portrait of a caravan trundling across a dune-laden horizon, and fell heavily to the floor.

109

Flames erupted around him even as he heaved and gasped for the breath that had been pummeled out of him. The hearth roared, the candles now scattered across the floor blooming into ravenous life as they answered the call of the magic. Lazura was still screaming, howling in rage as the fires rippled higher. Consumed by desperation, Adrion forced himself to roll onto his stomach, still heaving for air as he began to scramble for the next room.

It didn't take him more than ten seconds to make the arched way, but in that short time the inferno was raging in truth, a torrent of ravenous brilliance churning out of control. Adrion could smell his own hair burning, and when he reached the sudden coolness of the fire-free space he immediately rolled himself about, putting out the small flames that had caught on the edges of his pants and shirt sleeves.

Behind him, within the cacophony of the white fire which now devoured what had been their dining hall, he could still hear Lazura's bitter screams. She howled, shrieking in hateful denial, untouched within the cage of colorless flames which licked at the ceiling. Beyond her, though, was another sound. Within the depth of the beast's gullet, another voice rose.

The wailing, pitiful cries of unfathomable agony as a man suffered the horrid fate he had delivered with his own two hands.

XVI

"It is not always in prayer that one may bear witness to the greatness of one's gods. Rather, where better to bask in the glory of one's creator than in the infinite wonder of creation itself?"

—*Studying the Lifegiver*, by Carro al'Dor

There'd been a period of several days, as Raz had set course with Talo and Carro the previous year for the Citadel, in which the winter storms had buffeted them about and ripped their words away. It had been hard, then. The cold had dug into them as they rode, kept at bay only barely by the Priest's spells of warmth and protection. The wind bit like a blade through their cloaks and furs, cutting through the magics all too frequently. They'd moved at a crawling pace, unwilling to risk their horses by pushing them into anything faster than a plodding walk through the snow. Patience wore thin quickly, and it wasn't until the blizzard cleared that Raz had been able to take in the wonder of the lands about him in winter.

Now, as they traveled further east with every passing day, he was reminded of that time, and suspected that he should have been miserable.

The rains had started not a few hours after their sixth morning on the road broke an early dawn. Raz had sensed a heaviness to the air when Syrah woke him, a denseness that must have had something to do with the grey and black clouds broiling overhead, blotting out the Sun. Soon after, he'd felt the first *ping* of a drop against the steel of his pauldron, and he had wiped up the trail of water running down the steel, staring at it in stunned amazement.

Before midday came and went, the six of them were guiding their horses through puddles and coursing streams that cut furrows across the mud of the road, the downpour blinding even Raz to anything beyond some fifteen feet ahead.

In the day since, he hadn't been able to stop smiling.

"Raz!" Syrah shouted with a laugh. "Stop that! You're going to catch cold!"

Raz grinned, tilting his head down from where it had been upturned toward the clouds. Water streaked his face, slipping in narrow lines down the sleek skin of his snout and between his ears. His hood was pulled back so that he could feel the rain, marveling at the sensation of it against his scales.

"This is incredible," he said for what must have been the hundredth time. He pulled his hood up again and shifted Gale closer to Nymara, slipping into the ward of warmth Syrah was casting about herself. "Incredible. It's endless!"

"You mean relentless," Eva grumbled from the Priestess' other side, pulling her thin leathers tighter around her shoulders. While the magic kept them all from catching a chill, it couldn't defend them from the storm completely. Everyone was soaked, and Eva and her entourage were huddled miserably over their saddles, the hoods of their traveling capes pulled high atop their heads.

Despite the strain of a week's ride, the wonder of this amazing event had yet to wear away for Raz. Even within the ward he looked up, appreciating the infinite thrum of the storm overhead with nothing short of reverence. When he'd experienced snow for the first time, it had been an incredible moment. Something so delicate, so magical. It had enthralled him, that wonder, but at the same time it had been strange to him, a concept he'd only been able to imagine until it finally fell, dulling the world like a spell of white and cold.

But rain... Rain was an altogether different matter.

Water was life in the South, a substance treated with such reverence that Miropa, the greatest of the fringe cities, had been built up around an oasis like a crown. In the depth of the Cienbal itself, the Garin had been a place of peace and plenty in a world of heat and strife and hardship. Water was that which gave all, that which granted life.

And so, on the three occasions in his life Raz had witnessed rain fall upon the sands, it had been cause for nothing short of worship and ceaseless praise to the Twins.

He was remembering those times now, looking up into the storm suspended above them like the head of a great hammer hovering above the world. He couldn't help it, couldn't stop himself from *feeling* the water in a way none of the others seemed able to. It would have saddened him, were he not so engrossed in the memories of another life, in a place where such bounty would have led to dancing and festivals and rejoicing that transcended pettier things like class and wealth and vocation.

Raz heard a familiar laugh, and he looked around again. Syrah was watching him, eyebrow raised, clearly amused by his continued fascination with the sky.

Raz sighed. "You don't understand," he told her. "And I clearly can't explain it well enough."

"Because you're bloody mental," one of Eva's men—Jeck—grumbled from where he and his mount towed the cart behind them. "It's *rain*, Arro. Nothing more."

There was a mumbling of assent from the other two—Fara and Samet— and Raz shook his head in disagreement. "Just imagine if you could have the Southern Sun in the middle of the freeze," he said. "Even if it was just a day or two."

"I'd still rather take the damn cold," he heard Eva sniff from across Syrah. Jeck, though, made a face that said he might have gotten Raz's point.

"The world is fascinating in that way," Syrah said, still studying the storm. "We live in lands that border each other, and yet the rains we consider only a necessary nuisance are something else entirely to you."

Raz nodded, holding out a hand so that it passed beyond the boundary of the ward to his right, watching the downpour course across the worn leather of his gauntlet. "That's the least of it. You should have seen me when I stumbled into your woodlands for the first time. I used to call deer 'ponies,' before Arrun Koyt taught me otherwise."

Syrah's gaze dropped back to him, eye so wide you'd have thought he'd just told her he secretly knew how to fly. Several of the others snorted in amusement as well.

"You did not!" she hissed in delighted disbelief.

Raz nodded, pulling his hand back and shaking it dry. "I did. I also thought I could find myself a cave or something and weather out your winter until the snows passed—not that I even knew what snow *was*. I've since learned that would not have been my best option…"

The others all got a good laugh out of that, even Eva, though Syrah looked suddenly pensive. She was quiet for so long that Raz eventually had to nudge her with an elbow and give her a "spit it out" look.

"I was just thinking," she said so that only he could hear her as the others started their own discussion about who would tow the cart on their way back to Ystréd. "Talking about new lands… I don't know much of Perce, other than what I've read in books."

Raz scowled slightly, though he looked away so the Priestess wouldn't notice. The further east they traveled, the land around them shifting from plains and woodlands to grass-strewn rock and slate as they approached the coastline, the more he wished he had never committed to this foolhardy plan. It was an act of desperation, a trade of dangers he wasn't convinced was balanced in their favor.

Still, Syrah was right: they couldn't stay in the North, and Raz supposed that a wild shot at freedom was better than an eternity fleeing bounty hunters and assassins.

"It's supposed to be a beautiful country," he admitted reluctantly. "Not in the same fashion as all of this—" he waved a hand out to the lushness of the grass and brush that waved in the wind over the rain-darkened stone "—but in its own way. My father and uncle used to tell my cousins and I stories of the world, when I was younger. Perce was actually the realm I wanted to see most, until I learned more about its practices…"

"Really?" Syrah asked, sounding surprised. "What made you wish that?"

Raz reached up and wiped rain off his snout. "The Percian might be cruel and ignorant, but the lands beyond the lowest border of the Cienbal's sands are rich and abundant. My father used to tell me that Perce and the Seven Cities share the plains and savannahs, and that the world there was brimming with life. He said the Sun was kinder, too, and that the days weren't as unbearable in their heat and the nights weren't as cruel in their cold. He said that animals unlike anything I could ever imagine roamed the land." He smiled slightly as he remembered the delight he'd taken in the stories, looking forward at the road again. "Striped horses. Birds as tall as a man that couldn't fly, but could outrun all but the best riders. Beasts with necks as long as my body." His thoughts were far away now, giving in to the memories. "I remember begging my father to take us."

"But he couldn't," Syrah said, almost sadly.

Raz shook his head, the recollections fading away into the rain. "In another life, maybe. His father had taken the caravan south a few times, when he was younger, but when the Arros took me in…"

"It wouldn't have been safe for you." Syrah looked dejected. "How sad that a place as wonderful as that would be so closed off from the world."

"Not the world," Raz said firmly, feeling his apprehension returning. "They're happy enough to do business with the likes of the Mahsadën. We won't have any friends in that place, Syrah. We will be on our own."

Syrah nodded, but reached out and squeezed his arm comfortingly.

"Then we'll just have to make some," she said with a half-hearted grin. "And—" she looked suddenly mischievous as she pulled away again "—we'll have to find me a striped horse."

At that moment, Nymara chose to make a disgruntled huff, as though annoyed, and both Raz and Syrah choked on their laughter, earning themselves not a few odd glances from the others.

Despite the storm, they made good time. The rains subsided after a day or so, and—all of them already too soaked to care about getting a little dirty— they started up a good pace at once, ignoring the mud that splashed up around them to coat their pants and boots. After a few more nights spent camped out along the main road, Eva finally led them off the beaten path, along a narrow trail barely wide enough to allow for the cart as it wound between the stony outcroppings. The next day, after they broke their fast, Eva informed them they'd be arriving within a matter of hours.

Neither Raz nor Syrah had bothered asking "arriving where?"

All around them, the stone and rock jutted up and over the path, massive edges of slate and shale layered with waving tufts of blueish grass and green-and-black moss. Above them, the sky was clear once more, the lingering trail of the storm having long-since faded to the west, revealing the welcome warmth of the Sun. Raz had been able to smell the ocean since the evening before, but now, as they started off again—single-file with Jeck and the cart bringing up the rear—he thought he could make out the cry of distant gulls on the air. He told Syrah as much, and they'd spent an amusing several minutes as she cupped a hand over her good ear and strained to hear before giving up. Not long after, though, the shrill call of the birds was distinct, and even as the Priestess looked around at him in excitement Raz made out another, softer sound.

The distant crash of swelling waves, lapping against the earth.

Even Eva and her men looked excited now, and without any explicit order they all picked up the pace, hooves clacking against the hard ground beneath them and the cart rolling loudly along behind. After another ten minutes the wind was picking up the salt spray, peppering them and dampening their clothes even more, but this time no one complained. The roar of the water was near, now, rising all around them in undulating rhythms. They took a last turn in the path, passing beneath an overhang of earth and rock that hung like a ceiling overhead.

Then they stood in the light of day once again, looking out over a breathtaking sight.

"By the Sun," Raz said under his breath.

It was not the first time he'd been along the coast. Acrosia, after all, was a port city. For this reason it had been a place of verdant life unlike any of the other Southern municipalities, the shoreline dotted with palm trees, the sands thinner and cooler from being churned up over and over again by the surf. It was a place Raz had enjoyed, an image he'd held on to once it had been decided they would be accepting Garht Argoan's offer of passage. Calm, white-tan beaches dotted with the thin outlines of swaying trees. Slum-children playing in the shallows, or fighting over coconuts they had climbed up to harvest. The water warm, waves lapping against the sand.

What greeted Raz instead was something far more spectacular.

They were standing at the edge of a cliff, the world bottoming out before them. The ledge wound infinitely to the north and south, a sheer drop some hundred feet at its lowest point and at least twice that at its highest, its jagged line disappearing off in either direction. Far, far below them, a beach unlike anything Raz had ever imagined stretched from the base of the bluffs. It looked to be made of black pebbles and sea-smoothed stone, and here and there, scattered like the pale bones of long-dead giants, the Sun-bleached trunks of massive trees had washed aground after who-knew-how-long at sea. The tide foamed as it lapped against the dark shore, marking the water's edge in a white line along the coast.

And before them, extending away into an endlessness which the mind of man would never quite manage to fathom, was the Dramion itself.

The water shifted in a hundred shades of grey, green, and blue, so clear Raz could follow the ocean floor until it faded into the depths. It was a calm day, the waves licking at the beach gently, back and forth over the pebbles, and yet despite this it reminded him of the storm they had weathered to reach this place. This sea was powerful, omnipotent to him in a way the Emperor's Ocean to the west had never seemed. Whether it was something about the water itself, or merely just the fact that he was taking in the Dramion from some two hundred feet up above the rest of the world, Raz suddenly understood why he'd heard of cultures that revered the sea. There was a presence here, as real and heavy on his mind as the beat of the Sun above.

He wondered, briefly, what god he would be praying to before their journey's end.

"Raz." Eva's voice interrupted his reverence. "This way."

Raz blinked and looked around. The surgeon was indicating a wide path that had been cut into the cliffs to their left, looping back and forth along the ledge below them. Jeck had dismounted and was already leading his gelding down slowly, easing the cart along the descent as Fara and Samet followed close behind, ready to assist. Eva herself was still ahorse, having pulled her animal up to stand by Gale, with Syrah and Nymara cantering up on the other side of her.

"We'll take the path down and walk from there," Eva was telling them both. "Carefully. The horses won't do well on the beach." Then she pointed southward, down at the coast to their right. "That's where Garht should be waiting for us."

Raz followed her finger and made out the place she was indicating with some surprise. There, bisecting the beach maybe a quarter-mile down-shore, an inlet ran, a wide line of deep water that shifted and swelled with the waves of the sea. From this angle, Raz couldn't make out where it led to, but he suspected it didn't simply crash up against the bluffs and end there.

Studying the place, Raz nodded. "Lead the way. We'll follow."

Eva pulled her horse back at once, moving around Syrah and heading down the path. Raz and the Priestess locked eyes briefly and—though neither said anything more—he could tell the woman's excitement and curiosity had bloomed to match his at the sight of the Dramion. For a little while, Raz had no qualms with setting aside his fears and concerns regarding the journey ahead.

For the moment, he desired only to bask in the wonder of the sea.

It took them more than twenty minutes to descend the winding path, Jeck and the cart slowing them down significantly at their head. It was apparent, as they moved, that the men who'd carved the track into the stone had likely not been skilled masons. There were portions where the incline was so steep Raz considered dismounting himself, and certain turns were too narrow, to the point where more than once he made out the *thud* of one of the wagon's wheels dropping down as Jeck was forced to pivot sharply or risk tumbling off the cliff. By the time they reached the beach, Eva was cursing Garht Argoan, her guards were swearing in the Lifegiver's name, and Syrah was praying under her breath. Even Raz, bringing up the rear, breathed easier once he felt the stones *crunch* under Gale's hooves.

As one they dismounted and, at Eva's word, started leading the horses across the shore, toward the channel of water in the distance. At the base of the cliffs the wind was almost nonexistent, blocked by the ledge they were following to their right, but the sea still churned and sprayed, rumbling a greeting as it surged back and forth toward and away from them. Raz had hoped he would be able to make out their destination once they reached the base of the path, but no luck. A twist in the peaks hid the mouth of the channel from view, but as they got closer Raz's excitement and suspicion grew. It wasn't until they were almost at the edge of the inlet, the horses grunting as they followed and the cart rumbling along behind them, that he finally made out where they were headed. For the second time, he swore by the Sun

It was Syrah, though, who put his amazement into words.

"By the Lifegiver," she managed to a gasp. "Incredible..."

All Raz could do was nod numbly.

The sight before him was like something out of the stories he'd heard around the evening fires as a child. The channel to their left led up to the sheer face of the cliffs, spilling in and out of a massive, oblong opening which had been carved like a crooked mouth out of the rock face by the sea. Beyond it, a cavern gleamed with Sun and firelight, the latter flickering out from a hundred different lamps and torches, the former streaming down from a number of narrow cracks in the roof of the cave. On one side, built high up against the wall of the massive space on spindly timber legs, something like a large tavern sat well clear of the water. A number of other buildings had been constructed along the face of the smooth rock as well, though these were smaller, like individual boarding quarters. A wide walkway of wooden planks, like the wharf of a port, encircled the wall just above where high-tide must have settled, with five jetties cutting out into the main body of the lagoon. Only three were occupied now, but this did nothing to offset the bizarre scene of a longship and two tri-masted frigates anchored beneath a ceiling of stone and earth, swaying ever so slightly as the ocean swells pushed in and out of the cavern.

"Welcome to Highmast Cove," Eva said, looking around at Raz and Syrah and chuckling at what could only have been utter astonishment on both their faces. "Now clam those mouths up. You don't want anyone here thinking you don't look like you belong in a smuggler's den."

The pair of them did as they were told, though it was still a moment before they managed to stop ogling the cave and follow Eva forward. A minute or so later they passed into the damp shelter of the cove proper, the sound of the Dramion behind them muffling somewhat as the earth encircled them in a massive, lopsided sphere. Without pause Eva led them forward, around the lip of the space, until they reached a short set of wooden steps that led up onto the pier.

"Leave the horses here," she said, pulling the hood of her traveling cloak back and looking around. "Samet will stay behind and watch them. Jeck and Fara, you're with me. Raz..." She paused, her features shifting into something between amusement and hesitation. "Try not to kill anyone. It would be bad business for me."

Raz wasn't sure if she was joking or not, so he didn't respond. Syrah, on the other hand, looked uncertain.

"You think we might be at risk?" she asked Eva nervously, hurrying forward to walk with the surgeon, the pair of them stepping up onto the wharf together. "I thought you said you trusted this captain."

"Garht, I trust," Raz heard Eva say with a nod after he, Jeck, and Fara fell in behind the two women. "But those ships aren't all his."

Two crews she knows nothing about, Raz thought when he realized what she was trying to say. He glanced out over the lagoon again, studying the boats. The longship was a single-mast, with enough space on the deck to look like it might have boarded some thirty or forty men. The other two, though—the frigates—were larger. He was suddenly aware of the fact that he and Syrah were very much exposed in this place, with nothing more than Eva's men to watch their backs and the word of a smuggler that they weren't walking into a trap. He considered hurrying back to Gale to retrieve Ahna from where she was strapped in her habitual spot off his saddle but, glancing up, thought better of it. The dviassegai likely wouldn't serve him well in a crowded room anyway, and it looked like Eva was leading them right up to the tavern.

They climbed for several minutes, taking a half-dozen different sets of steps that wound this way and that along narrow platforms and jutting rock ledges on which the smaller rooms and buildings seemed to be perched. Finally, they crested the highest stairs, and Raz made out a sign hanging above the front entrance of the place, swinging gently as Eva pulled the door open to a clamor of laughter and shouting. "The Highest Mast," it read, and Raz couldn't help feeling like he was in some bizarre dream. He glanced over his shoulder again. There sat the ships, some fifty feet below, docked in the middle of the cave.

Shaking his head in wonder, he followed Fara and Jeck into the warmth of the building.

The Highest Mast was nearly exactly like any other tavern Raz had ever seen. It reminded him acutely, in fact, of the White Sands Inn where he had lived for the last years of his life in Miropa. The same smells greeted him: stale ale, smoking tar, the rich aromas of hot food, and too many bodies in one place, though here these all mixed in with an underlying edge of sea air and fish. Men and women were howling all around them, some in raucous laughter, others in fury as they leapt at one another over rickety old tables that all looked like they had seen too many fights already. The common room itself was massive, much larger that it appeared from the outside, and looked to have been carved right out of the earth judging from the rough-hewn walls. Fire and lamplight flickered joyfully over wood and stone, the torches bracketed to the timber and stone in what looked like large spiraled shells the length of Raz's arm, the chandeliers hanging from the ceiling crafted out of old ships' wheels. In the center of the space, the bar had been built like a four-sided island. A group of girls in blush-worthy attire were running the counter, deftly pouring ale while managing to dodge or slap away the innumerable hands that reached out at them drunkenly. At the back of the room, a stairway led up to the second floor, and Raz wondered if that, too, had been carved right out of the rock.

He didn't have time to contemplate this for long, however, because almost at once the room started to quiet, all eyes slowly turning in their direction.

Raz was well-used to public establishments growing suddenly shy when he walked in, the uproar that generally held sway over any swillyard dying away like it was being strangled. He never *liked* the effect, per se, but he had come to understand it, even appreciate the privacy it brought him and the respect it indicated.

Now, though, surrounded on three sides by what looked like almost a hundred roughened sailors all staring openly at them, Raz was suddenly feeling very ill-at-ease. Before the hubbub of the common area could die completely, he began to make out the whispers. As the fights quelled and the conversation trailed off, he heard the names carried to him over the silence. *Monster. Scourge.*

Dragon.

Some said the words with fear and reverence, others with something that could only have been greed. No one moved for a time, and Raz watched as dozens of different sets of eyes shifted steadily over their little group, always flicking back to him. Slowly, Raz reached out and took Syrah by the elbow, pulling her back and stepping around her so that his body was between her and the sailors. The woman didn't argue, and he thought he could feel the air shift about her as she swept the room anxiously, already drawing power into herself in preparation for a fight.

To their right, a man finally stood, pushing himself to his feet from among a thick knot of ruffians who appeared to have been playing dice on the floor. Unlike most of the group he was stepping out of, *this* seaman looked sober, his hands steady as they rested on the basket grip of the cutlass he kept on one hip and the hilt of the long knife on the other. He was a thin, wiry fellow, but he looked to have lived a hard life at sea, his skin bronzed and wrinkling around his eyes, his long hair bleached by the Sun and kept at bay under a band of cloth looped over his forehead. His clothes were loose and stained, his leather boots worn and cracked, but he stood with such firm confidence before them that he might as well have been royalty among his kind. For a second, Raz allowed himself to hope that this was Garht Argoan.

When the man spoke, though, that optimism was dashed away.

"You, Southerner," the sailor said, dark eyes dropping to Eva, who still stood at their head. "You the one in charge a' this lot?"

"For the time being," Eva replied distractedly, not looking at the man. "We are expected by the captain of the *Sylgid*. Is he here?"

Behind him, Raz felt Syrah stiffen suddenly, and he snuck a look back at her. The Priestess was frowning at Eva, as though something the woman had said had taken her aback.

"The *Sylgid?*" he heard her murmur to herself.

"Argoan?" the man before them asked with distaste, spitting at Eva's feet. "Why ya' botherin' with tha' whoreson? If it's passage South yer seeking, my *Drake*'ll get you there twice as fast." His eyes lifted to Raz reflexively, then away again. "Better yet, why don't ya' consider leaving yer 'cargo' ta' me? I'd be happy to buy it off you at a good price, say… five thousand Southern crowns?"

Raz smirked at the offer, and in front of him Eva scoffed, finally looking around at the man. "My friend is not for sale, captain," she said in a warning tone. "I would recommend you take that to heart now, before you rub him the wrong way."

Backing her up, Raz allowed his neck crest to rise above his head, a wild, low growl building in his throat. The man—clearly the captain of one of the ships docked outside—paled slightly, but stood his ground.

"You'd do better ta' watch yer tone, miss," the man said, sounding as though his patience were wearing thin. As though to make a point, he brought two fingers to his mouth and gave a shrill whistle, like he was calling a dog to heel.

At once, forty or so men and women rose to their feet all about the tavern, glaring in their direction. Raz saw the rusted grips of swords and knives tucked into any belt or sash they could fit. Axes and cudgels hung from hips and over shoulders. They were a ratty bunch, a mismatch of fighters and good-for-nothings who looked to have armed themselves with whatever weapons and spare pieces of armor they'd managed to steal or pillage.

But they were all defiantly staring him down, not even blinking as their commander continued speaking.

"You walk in here with twenty thousand gold on yer arm—" he stared at Raz, now, though his words were still directed at Eva "—and ya' don't think we're going ta' ask ya' ta' share? I'll say again: five thousand, and you and the other three can walk away."

As he said this, though, a female sailor with short-cropped hair sidled over to him, leaning in to whisper something in the man's ear. He blinked at her in surprise, only looking around again after she nodded in confirmation.

This time, his eyes fell on Syrah.

"Seems I've been hasty in my offer," he said, leering excitedly at the Priestess. "I'll give ya' six thousand, if yer kind enough to leave the one-eyed one with me as well. Apparently, the scaly ain't the only one worth a copper or two."

Raz felt his patience slip, and he took a step forward between Fara and Jeck. "Try it, little sea man," he snarled, coming to stand beside Eva and allowing his wings and tail to ripple out behind him. "Your boat won't be more than a ghost ship by the time we're through."

This time, unfortunately, the captain only smiled, his courage bolstered by the presence of his crew all around him.

"I've heard yer good, Monster," he said with disdain. "But don't pick a fight you can't win."

"He's had worse odds," Eva said with a shrug, though Raz could hear the tension in her voice. "I wouldn't gamble on you winning this fight just yet."

"So you ain't willin' to take my generous offer?" the captain asked, leering at her with a twisted smile. "Last chance."

"Take your offer and eat it, Captain," Eva said loudly, but she sounded more worried than annoyed now. Looking around at the other sailors still lounging and standing about the common area, she spoke to the room again. "We are looking for Garht Argoan. Is he here?"

Before her, the nameless captain's face twisted in anger. "I'll make sure to let him know you was lookin' for him," he snapped, starting to draw the cutlass with one hand and raising the other to signal his crew. "If you want to do this the hard way, then—!"

WHAM!

Several candles on a nearby table flickered and danced under the rush of Raz's dart forward. His shoulder hit the man like a battering ram, squarely in the chest. At the same time, one clawed hand took him by the throat, the other grasping the basket grip of the sword. With a twist Raz rolled, slamming the captain into the wooden floor and drawing the blade in the same motion.

In half-a-second the captain was spread-eagled, coughing for a clear breath of air, staring down the edge of his own sword while his face looked as though he were struggling to figure out what had happened.

His crew hadn't even had time to draw their own weapons.

"Blades on the ground," Raz said calmly, looking around at the men and women who encircled him as though this were a perfectly normal situation. "Drop them all, or your captain loses an ear."

Whether it was solidarity, uncertainty, or simply the fact that the man wasn't well loved by his ship's company, not a one among the crew moved to do as Raz asked. None of them made to attack him either, though, so he thought it likely they merely needed to be galvanized into action.

With a whip and a *thud*, quicker than any of them could follow, the cutlass plunged down, piercing the man's left ear and pinning it to the wood beneath it. As the captain screeched in pain, twisting and grabbing at the blade in a desperate attempt to wrench it free, Raz straightened to stand over him.

"I'll say it one more time," he told the throng before him, reaching up to draw his own gladius slowly from the borrowed scabbard over his shoulder. "Blades on the ground. *Now.*"

This time the hesitation was only brief. There was a dull *clang* as an axe and iron shield hit the timber slats of the inn's sticky floor, then another as a pair of daggers fell. After that, it was only half-a-minute or so before the forty members of the ship's crew stood unarmed. To a one they stared at him in stupefied awe, eyes only moving away to glance nervously at the gladius in his right hand, or to grimace at their captain, still writhing and howling at Raz's feet.

Then the clapping started.

Raz looked around, baring his teeth in the direction of the sound, suspecting mockery. When he caught sight of the source, though, he nearly choked in surprise.

A group stood on the stairway at the back of the room, apparently having descended from the floor above to see what the commotion was about. In their midst, a broad man was bringing his hands together in slow applause, grinning as though he'd never seen anything so entertaining. The stranger was balding, the monk's ring of long, scraggly hair about his head a greying brown, just like the heavy beard that was braided and plaited halfway down his wide chest. He had deep, twinkling blue eyes surrounded by laugh-lines, squinted now in mirth as he clapped. He was dressed, in large part, much like any of the other sailors scattered about the room. A thin leather vest was pulled over his baggy cotton shirt, blotched yellow with old sweat and age, and his wool leggings had been tucked into the wide brim of his black boots. At his side, a war-hammer was looped into his belt, one head flat and the other a single, wicked-looking spike. Raz might have thought this an odd weapon of choice for a seafarer, except for one other detail that made the man stand out clear from the crowd.

Across his face, in three diagonal lines, red war-paint had been streaked with skilled, ritualistic practice.

Behind him, Raz heard Syrah hiss in alarm.

"Well fought, Dahgün," Garht Argoan said, his grasp of the Common Tongue marred only by the thick accent of the mountain clans. "As to be expected of the slayer of Gûlraht Baoill."

XVII

'The Sylgid,' it transpired, was the name of the benevolent spirit of water the mountain clans prayed to for safe passage when crossing the frozen rivers and lakes of their treacherous homelands. Syrah had explained this quietly to Raz as they'd allowed themselves to be escorted by Argoan's crew through the common area and up the stairs, leaving the still-unnamed captain of the other ship to be freed by his own once they were gone. She told Raz she'd thought it must have been some odd coincidence, at first.

Now, obviously, not so much.

"Please, sit," Argoan told them as he moved around the end of a wide, oval table, pulling out a bench for himself as he did.

The Highest Mast had at least three levels, it turned out. Another set of stairs, a bit shorter than the first, led to another floor, but Argoan had ignored these after he'd led them up from the common area. Instead, they were now in a back corner of the second story, which was even larger than the room below. All around them a haphazard assortment of tables, benches, and chairs took up every square foot of the space, many of them occupied by sailors and mercenaries sharing food and drink as more tavern wenches moved about the room, taking orders and carrying away empty tankards and dishes. As the mountain man sat, several of his men rousted a few of the closest tables, suggesting—with feigned politeness—that the current occupants would do best to vacate.

No one had to be asked twice.

Eva sat as soon as Argoan extended the invitation, giving Raz and Syrah little choice but to follow suit. As soon as they'd done so, the crew of the *Sylgid* took their own seats, filling the tables all around them until Raz, Syrah, Argoan, and Eva were well and truly surrounded by a wall of roughened seafarers, ensuring their privacy. Seeing this, a couple of the serving girls started to move in their direction, but scurried away again when several of the sailors gave them cold glares.

For several seconds, Argoan sat and waited, looking between Raz and Syrah, clearly expecting them to speak first.

Syrah obliged.

"Strange to find an Amreht courting the sea, Captain," she said evenly, meeting his eyes despite the fact that her hands were balled into fists under the table. "I admit: you've taken us by surprise."

Argoan nodded slowly. He was watching Syrah intently, as though trying to size her up, but when he spoke his voice was cordial, almost friendly. "My apologies for that. I suspected you would be… uh… *less inclined* to consider my offer if you were aware of my lineage."

To Raz's right, Eva looked around in confusion. "What are they talking about?" she whispered to him.

In response, Raz shook his head ever so slightly, trying to say he would explain later. Eva, fortunately, seemed to get the hint, and said nothing more.

"I'm not sure I'm inclined either way," Syrah was saying, frowning as she did. "You'll forgive me, but Raz and I were already suspicious that you would so generously offer us a place aboard your ship. In light of these new circumstances—" her good eye lingered on the paint streaked across his face "—you can appreciate that our concerns are not alleviated."

"*At all*," Raz added, narrowing his eyes at Garht Argoan. He wondered, perhaps, if the captain would sneer at them and say they shouldn't look a gift horse in the mouth. He thought the man might grow angry, maybe even command his men to throw them from the tavern.

Instead, Argoan just grimaced unhappily.

"I am not surprised," he said with a slow shake of his head, sitting up on his bench and sighing. "Not in the least bit, in fact. I imagine it would be hard to trust most anyone with my features at the moment. I had considered, in fact, having my first mate pretend to be me—" he indicated a tall, strong woman with dreaded hair and a chunk missing from her nose standing over his left shoulder "—but suspected Evalyn wouldn't know to play along." He looked to the surgeon. "Apologies, my friend. The politics of our lands are a bit more strife-ridden at the moment than I fear you might be aware of."

Eva said nothing, though her brow furrowed in an obvious sign that she still didn't have a grasp on what was going on.

"Why extend the offer at all, then?" Syrah pressed him, leaning forward. "If you knew Raz and I wouldn't trust you, why bother?"

"Oh, it's not complicated, really," Argoan said, crossing his arms over his broad chest and shrugging. "Simply put: I owe you a debt."

It was Raz's turn to frown. "A debt?" he asked, confused.

Argoan nodded. "The both of you. As individuals, and as a pair."

Raz still didn't follow. He was just about to suggest—none-too-gently— that the man speak plainly, when Syrah made a small sound of realization.

"The Amreht," she said, like she was putting together the pieces of a puzzle. "Baoill's conquest of your tribe…"

"Was brutal," Argoan finished with a nod as the woman trailed off. "Yes, in so many words. I'm all too aware of the horrors the Kayle perpetrated on your valley towns, believe me. I would not belittle that. But I don't know if *you* are aware of how he went about conscripting the other clans for his army."

"He held families hostage," Syrah said at once. "I heard as much straight from the mouth of Kareth Grahst."

"*After* he'd already brought them to knee, yes," the captain said, and he sounded now as though he were having a hard time keeping himself in check. "But to break them in the first place… Baoill allowed no law or tradition to stand in his way. He butchered any chieftain who didn't pledge their allegiance to him in advance, which was nearly all among the Amreht. Their loved ones were treated no better, often given over to the army as spoils of war. Wives and sisters and daughters were made into battlewives, sons and brothers into camp slaves. There was no mercy, no decency."

Argoan brought his gloved hands together, winding his fingers about one another to stare at them. His eyes were distant as he continued. "My own brother was a minor chieftain in the northern reaches of the Vietalis. Mercifully, he hadn't yet taken a woman to wife, but our sisters..."

He paused again, clearly struggling to find the words. Eventually he looked up, meeting Syrah's eye directly. "I left the Amreht of my own volition some thirty winters past. The way of the mountain clans was not in my blood, I fear. Still... I have returned, many times. Every few years if I can manage it. My family did not hate me, did not shun me. They welcomed me back each time. We are not *all* the monsters the Sigûrth have become."

At that, Syrah shuddered and looked away from the man, and Raz thought the captain seemed rather saddened as his gaze traveled across the woman's face. Raz wondered, briefly, if any of his sisters had survived the war, and what state they were in, now...

There was a moment of silence, then Argoan took a deep breath, sitting back again and forcing a smile. "I was thrilled, you see, when Evalyn told me you sought passage from the North. I'd heard of you before, Syrah Brahnt. Stories and rumors whispered throughout my village, telling of a woman who was brokering a peace with old Emreht Grahst. I wasn't surprised when I heard tales in the smaller ports north of here that you'd had a hand in tearing Baoill from his throne, though the company you were said to keep was more astonishing." He looked around at Raz. "I am less familiar with you, Master Arro. I heard your name come out of Azbar, I believe, but I confess not to have paid it much mind."

"I don't take offense," Raz said with a shrug. "I'm pleased to hear of *anyone* who didn't heed Quin Tern's call."

Garht Argoan glowered in distaste. "I never understood man's insatiable desire for violence. It's among the reasons I left the clans, truth be told. The Arena was never a point of interest for me."

At that, Raz couldn't help but crack a half-hearted smile.

"Have I said something amusing?" Argoan asked, eyeing him suspiciously.

"No," Raz said, attempting to regain his solemn composure. "It's just..." He glanced at Syrah briefly. "I suddenly realize that you remind me of someone. A friend of ours. A man named Carro al'Dor."

He could tell, by the quiet "oh" of surprise from Syrah, that she hadn't been expecting that. It was Argoan, though, who looked the most astounded.

"The Peacekeeper?" he said, sounding as though he didn't know whether to be confused or pleased. "I... I believe you've paid me a great compliment with that, Dahgün."

"I have," Raz said coolly. "So make sure you don't prove me wrong."

Out of the corner of his eye, he thought he saw Syrah hide a smile.

Argoan nodded at once, then continued. "As I was saying, yours is a name I'm much less familiar with. Only after I'd heard of the 'Dragon' that had felled the Kayle did I ask around. Needless to say, your reputation precedes you."

"Clearly not enough," Eva said dryly, speaking to the table for the first time. "Otherwise, your colleague downstairs might still have both his ears intact."

"Wylsh is a fool." Argoan spoke with distinct annoyance. "He won the *Drake* through mutiny and murder, and has held onto it with violence and fear." He glanced at Raz. "One can only hope the lesson you taught him will set, for once."

"Doubtful," Raz said bitterly. "I've known too many of his kind, in my life. He'll seek revenge before he seeks wisdom."

"All the more reason to take you away from these shores as soon as possible. The *Sylgid* is ready to depart. We were only waiting for you. We can set sail at first light."

"No one has agreed to come with you," Syrah said quickly, giving the man a sharp look. "You assume much, Captain."

"I *assume*," Argoan said firmly, "that you have little choice. If you had other options, I can't imagine you'd have come all this way in the first place." His brow knit in something like concern as he looked between Raz and Syrah. "You *have* considered this, haven't you? Perce is a wondrous land, in its own ways, but not necessarily a kind one." His eyes lingered on Raz. "Especially to you. I'm about as averse to the trafficking of flesh as I am to the violence of a place like the Arena, but I am in the minority. Your race are property in Perce. Do you know this?"

"All too well," Raz replied stiffly. "It has been a topic we've circled around for nearly a month now."

"And yet you still wish to go?"

"I'm confused as to whether your interest is in granting us passage, or convincing us it's a fool's errand?" Syrah said slowly.

"My interest is in paying a debt, Priestess," Argoan told her, and for the first time he sounded as though his patience was being stretched. "It would be a poor fashion of doing so if I dumped you on Percian shores without ensuring you have at least the slightest idea of the hellhole you could be walking into."

"And yet, as you say," Raz interrupted before the exchange got too heated, "we have little choice."

Argoan nodded, his entwined fingers tightening. "I have no desire to sway you one way or the other. I am merely providing a solution, but an imperfect one. You need to escape the North, and the Mahsadën of the fringe cities. It will take two months to reach Perce, and that's only if the Gods bless us with fair weather all the way. At the very least that gives time for your trail to cool, and for you both to come up with a plan on what to do next. Evalyn's letter said your original goal was the West Isles, or the Imperium?" He glanced at Eva, who nodded in confirmation. "There are ships which make that crossing from the Seven Cities. I'm not saying it will be without its own troubles, but I imagine you will have an easier time getting across Perce than you would the South. Your name might be known, Dahgün, but your face is less so."

Raz scowled at that. "My face?" he started in disbelief. "The details of my features are hardly important, don't you think?"

Argoan looked at him blankly. "How so?"

"I'm not too difficult to make out in a crowd," Raz grumbled, wondering if the captain was pulling his leg. "No matter what we do, how long do you think it would take for the Percian to discover me if I'm the only... if I'm..."

His argument lingered and died, the words fading when he realized what Argoan was getting at. It struck him like he'd been dunked into a vat of cold water, a fact he had been aware of, but hadn't yet truly come to terms with.

"I wouldn't be the only one anymore," he said in a low mumble. "By the Sun..."

For the first time, that simple reality resonated with him. He had been so focused, so enthralled with the idea of escaping their pursuers, that he hadn't really paused to consider the implications of the journey Garht Argoan was proposing to them. He'd been aware that man and atherian alike were enslaved in the lands of Perce and the Seven Cities, but it hadn't yet settled in his mind what that meant, what that *really* meant. Despite their situation, despite the state he feared he might find them in, there would be other lizard-kind in the realms beyond the South.

I wouldn't be the only one, he thought again, privately this time, momentarily struck speechless.

Syrah must have realized where his mind had gone, because she squeezed his fingers beneath the table. "We might be able to hide in plain sight," she told him gently, voicing the whirl of realizations he himself was making. "At least in the cities. You do a good job of concealing your wings already. We could pretend..."

She trailed off, apparently not liking where her own idea was going.

Raz was pretty sure he had followed her, though, and the thought churned his stomach. "A slave," he grunted distastefully. "If we pretend I'm property of yours, we would have a lot less trouble crossing through Perce and the Seven Cities. Maybe even gaining passage west."

Syrah's face was red, and she refused to nod in assent. Raz felt a swell of affection for the woman at that, knowing she was holding herself back from saying something like "it's the smart thing to do."

It is *the smart thing to do,* he thought.

But the darker, colder voice spoke up in the back of his head, reminding him that he was so, *so* tired of running.

"We can discuss the details at a later point," Raz said brusquely, wanting very much to move away from the topic. "As Syrah said: we haven't agreed to go."

Argoan's face darkened, but it wasn't anger. There might have been some impatience there, Raz saw, but in truth the man looked less irritated and more… worried.

"I understand your hesitancy," the captain said. "I do. But hear this: I extend you this opportunity as an offering of peace, an effort to do my small part in repayment for the violence my kind has wrought upon your people, and for the kindness and respect you have shown them despite this." His eyes moved to Syrah. "I cannot, however, endanger the livelihood of myself and my men by sitting on our thumbs, waiting for you to decide what you should or shouldn't do." He started to stand, the bench scraping loudly against the wooden floor as he pushed it back and out of the way. "The *Sylgid* lifts anchor at dawn. I expect to have your answer before then. Evalyn," he looked to Eva, "we still have business to attend to. Might I suggest we leave these two to their deliberations, and see to our own interests for a while?"

Eva nodded and got up at once, looking around at Fara and Jeck as she stepped over the bench. "Stay here. Keep an eye on things."

"Aye," Argoan agreed as the man and woman nodded, "a good idea. Lysa—" his first mate, the woman with the scarred nose, stood to attention by the wall "—pick twenty of the crew and stay put. I wouldn't be surprised if Captain Wylsh comes looking for a fight again. The rest of you, with me."

As one, a majority of the *Sylgid*'s company got to their feet from their chairs and benches, the only ones remaining in their seats doing so after Lysa gave each of their tables a nod. Argoan and Eva made to head toward the back stairs, but the captain paused as he passed Raz and Syrah.

"You may not trust me," he said flatly, frowning down at them as his men hovered around him, waiting. "That's fine. But the way I see it, you are on a road where nothing but darkness lies behind, and the only possibility of light may be found ahead. Give us a chance. Perhaps we will surprise you."

And with that, he moved off with Eva between the tables, vanishing down the steps to the common room below.

For a long time Raz and Syrah sat there at the table, neither saying anything, each battling their own reservations and hesitations. Raz's thumb rubbed absently over the scar that ringed Syrah's wrist, allowing his mind to catch up to the points Garht Argoan had made.

"Can we trust him?" Syrah asked under her breath after several minutes, clearly attempting to avoid being overheard by the first mate, who was still watching them calculatingly from her spot against the wall.

"No," Raz said with a small shake of his head. "I don't think we can. But it comes down to the same problem each time: do we have a choice?"

Syrah nodded slightly. "I don't think we do, Raz. I really don't."

He didn't reply, giving her hand a comforting squeeze before looking up at Lysa. He almost hoped to see the woman tense as his eyes fell upon her, hoped she would blink nervously or glance around, just to give him *some* solid indication that it was a trap, a hint by which he could act. The first mate, however, met his gaze without so much as a flinch of fear or skittishness. She didn't watch him with the greed and selfish desire he had come to expect from cutthroats and sellswords. Her eyes, sharp and intelligent, said nothing of danger, gave no clue as to what Raz and Syrah should do. Rather, they were calm, almost impassive, taking in Raz expectantly, as though the only thing she anticipated from him was an answer.

But then, just as Raz started to look away from her, the woman spoke.

"Ask us why we follow him."

Raz and Syrah both blinked, turning to the first mate again.

"Sorry?" Syrah, eyeing the woman warily.

In response, Lysa finally stepped away from the wall, slipping onto the bench to seat herself across from the pair of them. She had green-blue eyes and a hard, weathered face that might have been pretty once, but was now ravaged by the Sun and the scar that had ruined her nose. Her hair was bleached and dreaded down her back, though shaved to the scalp along one side. Her gaze was intent, moving from Raz to Syrah and back again, scrutinizing them carefully.

"Ask us why we crew the *Sylgid*," she said, waving a hand at the twenty men and women seated all around them, not a few of whom were now watching the conversation with interest. "Why we *choose* to follow Garht."

Raz stared her down. "You think your opinion would make a difference? One shouldn't ask a hound what it thinks of its master."

He had wanted to get a reaction out of the woman, wanted to shake her in the hopes of making her slip.

All he succeeded in getting was a crooked smile.

"You compare us to dogs," Lysa said in amusement. "It's true enough, in a way. We are loyal, and would be happy to tear your throat out should you give us cause to."

"How enticing," Raz said sarcastically. "Please, continue. You are doing a wondrous job of convincing us to trust you."

The woman's face grew hard. "At sea, there are many kinds of captains, Dragon. There are men like Wylsh, crafty bastards who control their ships through fear and cleverness. There are men worse than him, also, men who treat their crews as cattle, who throw the insubordinate overboard with an iron weight chained to their ankles. Most aren't so cruel. Most value their men in their own ways, understanding that they are nothing without the hands that help them wrestle the ship. They take great care in selecting those they allow within the ranks of their company, building that bond of trust any good employer fosters with their subordinates."

"And Argoan is such a captain?" Raz said with a raised eyebrow, indicating he wasn't impressed.

"No," Lyssa said shortly. "He is not."

Then she looked past him.

"Kelen," she said, and Raz and Syrah both turned to see a young Southerner, maybe sixteen or seventeen years of age, sit up straight. "Tell our guests how you came to be with us.

"Was a stow 'way," the boy said, blowing a loose strand of curly hair out of his eyes. "Cap found me elbow deep in a barrel a' salted mackerel he was supposed to sell to a merchant from Cyro. Thought he was gonna slit my throat an' use me for shark bait."

Behind them, Raz heard Lysa shift, looking in a different direction.

"Jan, what about you?"

"Parents was fixin' ta' sell me ta' a head trader from the Seven Cities," a borderer in her twenties said from the right. "Captain bought me up instead."

"Eko?" Lysa asked next.

A dark-skinned Percian who looked much too old to be a sailor spoke up in a raspy voice from the left. "The First Hand of Karesh Nan wanted my head. Argoan gave me refuge. Had this been discovered, it would have cost him much."

And it kept going. For several more minutes Lysa would indicate one of the crew, asking them to share their story. Most were prompt, answering at once, but others were hesitant, as though memories of their old lives were not something they wished to relive. By the time the first mate looked around at Raz and Syrah again, they had come to know the history of more than half of the men and women seated around them. Runaways. Criminals. Former slaves. It was not all that strange a mix to find among a ship's crew, Raz thought, but their recountings seemed heartfelt. Either they were telling the truth, or Garht Argoan had gone out of his way to employ some *very* good actors.

"There is a reason Garht trusts us enough to leave you in our care," Lysa said to the pair of them after the final story had ended, extending both arms to indicate her sailors. "He does not 'believe' we will not selfishly attempt to claim your bounties for ourselves. He *knows* it. Without a shred of doubt, he knows it. I do not pretend to grasp your history with the mountain clans—" her eyes flicked to Syrah here, studying the patch over her right eye "—but if nothing else you should understand that there is a reason Garht left the Amreht. It is the same reason, I believe, that your Carver trusts him." She indicated the place Eva had been sitting with an inclination of her head. "Garht is a good man."

"Can smugglers and thieves be 'good men'?" Syrah asked sardonically.

Lysa gave her a half-smile, then looked at Raz. "Can mercenaries and murderers?"

The question seemed to do the trick, because Syrah fell silent.

"Garht said we would have to be patient with you," Lysa continued, crossing her arms over her leather breastplate. "It is difficult for us, sitting here and watching you debate this. We—" she indicated the men and women around them again "—would wish for nothing more than the ability to make you understand the man we know. The man we follow."

She paused long enough to allow for several nods of assent from the crew before pressing on. "It is difficult for us to witness you deliberate over the hand he has extended toward you, much at his own risk. I don't need you to see what we see in him. I don't need you to feel as we feel." She was gazing at them hard now, like she was trying to *will* them into understanding. "All I need from you is to consider the possibility that maybe, just *maybe*, Garht Argoan is everything you need him to be. Then—" she wound her fingers together on the table in front of her, much as her captain had not five minutes before "—I need you to consider if that possibility is worth the risk, or if you'd rather stay and wait for whatever enemies are hounding you to finally catch up."

There was a long pause as Lysa finished, Raz and Syrah watching her silently. After a while, Raz looked around, taking in the faces of the men and women of the crew, meeting every eye he could. Again, he almost hoped to see deceit in their stares, hoped for some hint that they were being tricked. It would have been easier, would have made getting up from the table and leaving that much simpler.

All he saw, though, was the fierce devotion of a crew he rather suspected might have jumped from the tavern roof if Argoan had asked them to.

Eventually Raz looked around at Syrah, meeting her eye, sure the question was plain on his face. The Priestess took one shaking breath, as though preparing for a plunge into the frigid depths of the sea beyond the cove.

Then she nodded.

XVIII

They set sail as the first tendrils of dawn crept over the eastern horizon. Raz and Syrah bent over the port rail of the *Sylgid*, waving in final farewell to Eva and her cohort, who stood at the end of the jetty to see them off. They'd all broken an early fast an hour before, saying their goodbyes and hugging the woman as they thanked her for all she'd done for them. Now, watching Eva pull away while ship's hands pushed them far enough off the pier to start rowing for the cavern entrance, Raz could only hope it wouldn't be for the last time.

"Who am I going to get to patch me up?" he shouted after her.

In response, Eva cupped both hands over her mouth. "How about trying *not* to turn yourself into a bloody mess in the first place!" she called back. "Syrah, keep an eye on him, will you?"

"I'll do my best!" Syrah yelled, grinning. "I make no promises, though!"

The surgeon laughed, then waved one last time as the nose of the ship passed through the opening of Highmast Cove and out into the early light of the summer morning. Raz watched Eva turn away from them and motion to Jeck, Fara, and Samet behind her. Together, they moved back to the now-laden cart waiting for them at the end of the pier.

When they had faded into the concealing shadows of the cave, Raz finally allowed himself to look east, the sight that greeted him making his heart soar.

Beyond the raised bow of the frigate, the Dramion extended like a mirror across the world. In the farthest distances the Sun had just begun to rise in truth, a single point of yellow-white brightness stretching out in an orange band along the horizon. The sky, still mostly dark as the Moon and Her Stars gave way to the day, was as clear as newly blown glass, not so much as hinting at clouds for as far as the eye could see. Raz watched the blue of the morning slowly claim the heavens mile by mile, losing himself to the sound of the crew shouting to one another in the masts and the snap of the sails as they were dropped to accept the ocean breeze.

And before him, like a beautiful spirit of winter basking in the light of the new day, Syrah stood quiet, her gaze, like his, on the rising Sun.

Despite the awesomeness of the dawn before him, Raz couldn't help but watch the Priestess a moment more. He would never grow bored, he realized then, of taking in the loose strands of her braided white hair as they traced around her ears. He would never tire, he suspected, of gazing upon the icy smoothness of her skin, like forest snow woven into something soft and warm and real. Her hood was pulled back so that the warm wind could whisper about her face. Her neck lay bare, and Raz couldn't help but gaze at it, studying the graceful curve from the base of her jaw until it disappeared beneath the shoulder of her robes.

As though feeling his eyes on her, Syrah looked back, and for the space of a heartbeat Raz was lost in the depths of her rose-colored eye, happily drowning in its gentle warmth. The woman said nothing, but she smiled upon seeing him watching her, and that simple act filled Raz with such fire he felt it shiver up his spine and down his arms and legs.

He took a step forward, then, keeping one hand on the rail but wrapping the other about her, pulling the woman against him. At once she reached up to grasp the forearm hugging her, allowing her body to press back against his chest as he dipped his head down to rest along the crown of her head. How long they stayed like that, neither of them would ever know. For that time, there was nothing more in the world than each other, the cool spray of the sea around them, and the warmth of the slowly rising Sun over the ocean to the east.

Together, they sailed off into the brightness of the new day, leaving the dark shores of the North far, far behind.

XIX

"Never seen a man move like that... The lizard, sure, but he was a different beast altogether, if you'll pardon the wit. But a man... No. Never before, and hopefully never again."

—Dhristie Idris, captain of the *Hollow Arrow*

When the door of the Highest Mast opened and the two strangers stepped into the orange glow of the common room, Captain Callum Wylsh saw his chance to reassert himself. He'd lost face to the Monster of Karth—a lot of face—and had spent the last three days fighting to regain it. The side of his head, wrapped in a swath of dirty bandages, still throbbed, and he knew the crew had given him a name behind his back. "Half-Ear," they called him when they thought he wasn't listening. He'd already locked two in the *Drake*'s brig for doing so, and had given the cook a new scar when he'd overheard the fat lump snickering about how they'd all have been better off if "the lizard had left just enough of the captain to make soup out of." All of that had helped somewhat to bring his sailors back under his thumb, but when all was said and done, Wylsh didn't think he'd made much progress.

They still feared him plenty, but with every passing day it seemed that fear was measured off with more and more contempt.

And so, when the front door of the inn opened and two men stepped out of the dim light of the cave outside, the captain saw his chance.

"Ho, friends!" he hailed them, pulling himself away from the bar and lifting a tankard as though to greet the strangers. "You lost yer way?"

All around him, his crew began to still, turning in the direction of their captain's voice. It would have been exactly what Wylsh needed, drawing their attention to an opportunity for a little fun, except for one issue: the two men ignored him utterly, not even glancing in his direction as they moved toward the bar.

This did nothing to improve the man's temperament.

"Oy!" Wylsh called angrily as the pair reached the counter, each stepping through several layers of sailors like water through loose stone. "I'm talking to you, uglies!"

This time one of them glanced his way, and the captain felt a stone drop into his stomach, a sensation he didn't like in the least.

The man's eyes were grey as dry slate, set over a pointed nose above a beard that looked like it might have been black had it not been frosted and bleached by the sun. His skin was bronzed, though perhaps lightened by the Northern climate, and his clothes were nothing of note; a brown tunic atop cotton pants, with black boots that looked to have been very finely made. A sword, a wide-bladed saber, was slung diagonally at the back of his belt. All in all, the man looked as though he could have been the older brother of the tanned bitch who'd arrived with the Monster not half a week past, except that there was something missing in his gaze, like a light that should have been there had gone out.

When the man looked away again, it took Wylsh several seconds to regain his composure. Then, though, his anger at being ignored flared in truth, and the next thing he knew he was shoving his way through the crowd.

"OY!" he yelled again, louder now as he approached the two men. "I'm bloody well *not someone you'd best ignore*, hear?"

This time, the entire room went quiet. All around Wylsh men and women were ducking away quickly, taking their cups and tankards with them. He could almost feel the gaze of his crew on his back, and knew there was no backing down now. Once he'd won this fight, he'd give leave for them to pick the bodies clean. *That* would earn him back some of the respect he'd lost.

But as the two men turned to face him, the space around them suddenly clear of patrons, Wylsh felt some of his confidence slip away.

Their eyes… It was like looking into the faces of the dead, like their souls had been cast aside in favor of a stiller, hungrier emptiness that lay there in wait.

"We've no business with you," one of the men—the one who hadn't looked at Wylsh when he'd last yelled—said coolly. "Begone."

He spoke with the accent of a Southerner, which was hardly surprising given the pair's complexions. This man, though, was clean-shaven. He was a little shorter than his companion, as well as younger, but the way the other stood slightly over and behind his shoulder made it clear this was the one in charge.

Wylsh sneered. "If you've come ta' the Cove, then you've business with me. The *Sylgid's* been gone three days now, and the *Hollow Arrow* leaves port tonight. Ain't gonna be nothin' left but my *Drake*."

"Is that so?" the man asked with distinct disinterest, turning toward the counter once again. "Unfortunately for you, we do not come seeking a smuggler."

"Then what did ya' come for?" the captain asked, gritting his teeth at this continued indifference.

"The Monster of Karth," the stranger said, loud enough for everyone in the vicinity to hear him, though he never turned away from the counter. "We are seeking Raz i'Syul Arro."

At once the quiet that had fallen over the room thickened, weighing down like dark clouds threatening rain. Behind him, Wylsh heard someone among his own men snicker, and he fought back the urge to whirl on them and roust the offender.

Instead, his just gave the travelers a nasty smile.

"That so?" he asked with feigned sweetness, his hands moving to the hilts of his cutlass and long knife. "Ya' friends of his, or somethin'?"

The one in charge stilled, then turned slowly to take Wylsh in much more carefully.

"Or something, yes," he replied simply. "Why?"

"'Cause Wylsh's left ear ain't a fan o' the scaly!" someone shouted from the back corner of the room to a roll of laughter from his fellows. Again, the captain had to work hard to ignore the taunt.

"I see," the stranger said slowly, his eyes moving to take in the browning bandages that encased the side of Wylsh's head. "That means he was here, I take it. When?"

Wylsh frowned at that. "Ain't yer business when," he spat. Then he grinned, getting an idea. "You want information, you pay. Tha's the way of the world, ya' know?"

The stranger's mouth tightened, and he shared a look with the older man.

"We are willing to pay for good information," he said after a moment, turning back to Wylsh. "Tell us what you know."

Wylsh chuckled, shrugging and slowly drawing the sword from his hip. "Ya' got coin on you, you mean? Tha's good. Maybe if it's enough then we can tell yer corpses before we throw them into the sea."

"Eram."

The shorter of the men said the word coolly, like he was sighing in exasperation. In response, however, there was a blur of silver and grey, and Wylsh howled in pain and was forced to release the cutlass as his wrist was enclosed in an iron grip and pinned with crushing force against the bar to his right. The sound was cut short, though, as the gleaming silver edge of a saber appeared under his chin, pressing him until he was bent backward over the counter. Instinctively his free hand groped for his long knife, but even as he found the hilt a voice growled in his ear.

"Try it, and I bleed you dry."

The older man stood over Wylsh, pinning his wrist with one hand and pressing his head back and down against the bar with his sword. The captain, for his part, couldn't do more than blink up at him in confused surprise. The stranger had moved so fast it was almost like facing the Dragon again.

This time, though, he didn't hear any of the crew draw their weapons in protest.

"Smuggler."

Wylsh turned wide eyes to his right. The shorter of the men had come to stand behind the captain's captor, looking down at him impassively even as the razor edge of the saber tickled his neck.

"Eram will not hesitate to separate your head from your shoulders," the stranger said calmly, his dead eyes boring into Wylsh's. "Of course, if you tell us what you know, that won't be necessary. Now—" his grey eyes narrowed warningly "—when was the Monster here?"

Wylsh would have liked, in that moment, to spit in the man's face and tell him to go fuck his mother. To his credit, he almost managed it, his face twisting in preparation. Then the man standing over him—Eram—pressed the sword in ever so slightly, and the captain felt the skin of his throat burn as it parted like paper beneath the blade.

"Th-three days!" Wylsh said hurriedly, his words choking as he swallowed with difficulty. "He was here three days past!"

The shorter man, nodded slowly. "Good. Where did he go?"

"Boarded the *Sylgid!*" Wylsh answered at once, feeling his back start to ache at the cruel angle he was bent. "Sh-ship belongs to Garht Argoan! Headed for Perce!"

The stranger looked surprised at this. "Do you know where and when it's scheduled to arrive?"

Wylsh tried to shake his head, then thought better of it. Beneath him, he felt spilled ale soaking through the back of his shirt. "H-he makes stops en route. All along the coast. Slows him down. Sh-should be about eight weeks, if weather's good."

For another minute or so they questioned him, and Wylsh told them everything, ignoring the warm wetness he felt seeping down the lines of his collar. He told them of the one-eyed Priestess the Dragon had been traveling with, and the Southern woman who had accompanied them both. He told them of how Argoan set sail with them at first light of the following day. He even, in his panic, told them of how he himself had challenged the atherian, and essentially lost his ear as a result.

For some reason, *that* tale seemed to strike a nerve with the two men, as though hearing of the Dragon's prowess rubbed them the wrong way.

Apparently Wylsh wasn't the only one to have lost a fight to the lizard.

"Anything else?" the shorter man asked finally.

"No," Wylsh said at once. "No, nothing. I swear on Laor himself."

Eram sneered at the name of the Northern deity, but glanced over his shoulder. The unnamed Southerner nodded once, and in a flash the sword was lifted from Wylsh's throat and his right wrist released. He sagged to the floor at once, rubbing his neck and coughing as his hand came away bloody.

When he lifted his head, the crew of the *Drake* stood about him in a loose circle, not one among them looking like they held even an ounce of sympathy in their glares. Abruptly, Wylsh realized he had just lost his ship, and the blood rushed from his head, leaving him cold and shivering. Through his daze his eyes moved, seeking those at fault.

The two men were walking away, back toward the entrance, without giving him so much as a second glance.

Wylsh saw red.

His saber still lay where it had dropped to the floor beside him. Snatching it up with one hand, the captain scrambled to his feet, drawing his knife from his hip as he did. Shoving a few onlookers out of the way, he stumbled after the strangers, cursing as he did. He caught up to them just as they reached the door of the tavern, and with a howl he lunged, looking to plunge pointed steel into the men's turned backs.

The blades never got within a foot of either of them.

It was not Eram, the taller one, who moved this time. Instead, it was the clean-shaven man, the younger of the two. One moment he was facing the door, away from Wylsh, and the next he was facing *toward* him. The Southerner didn't even bother drawing a blade. Instead, he twisted and struck out, dodging the saber and dashing the knife from Wylsh's other hand. Unable to stop his own impetus, Wylsh tripped forward, his cry strangling desperately in his throat. The man moved around him like smoke, spinning and ducking before slamming an elbow into Wylsh's lower back. With nothing left between them, the captain slammed headfirst into the door.

Then, before he could even begin to recover and turn around, he felt the saber ripped from his grasp.

Shlunk. Crack.

Pain unlike anything Wylsh could have ever imagined erupted from his abdomen. His breath came in a hot inhalation, and he screamed as the agony spread through his body, rocking up his back and through his limbs. He pounded and scrabbled at the wood he was pressed up against, unable to comprehend why he couldn't step away from it, why he couldn't move. When he managed look down, he saw the bloody width of a blade he recognized all too well protruding from his gut and disappearing into the timber planks of the door.

He had been impaled, pinned to the wood with his own sword.

It was as he made this realization that the shock began to overcome him. The pain began to subside, and Wylsh felt numbness tickling up from his fingers. He would have stopped moving, perhaps, except that someone reached for the latch next to his hip, and in the next moment his feet were being dragged over the floor as the two men opened the door they'd nailed him to.

He didn't see their faces again, but even over his renewed screams as the cutlass shifted through his torso, Wylsh heard them speak.

"Ehmed," the one called Eram said quietly, stepping through the opening and back out into Highmast Cove as though nothing had happened, "shall I send a bird?"

The other man—Ehmed—responded at once. "Yes. Immediately. Tell Na'zeem the Monster sails for Perce."

PART II

XX

"There is power in this world, Hana, magic none among our people or any other truly comprehend. You may not possess it, but there are those who do, those who have been touched by the Daystar or the Night Eye. Believe in that power, my child. I hope it will bless your reign as often as it has blessed my own..."

—Shas-ronah Rhan, Last-Queen, to her daughter Shas-hana

Uhsula of the Undercaves awoke to darkness.

There was nothing strange about that. She had lived too many decades already in her blind solitude, depending on others to tend to her needs. It had become comforting, even, not to have to see the pity and weariness in the faces of those around her, many of whom she was sure believed—with perhaps good reason—that she had long outlived her usefulness.

But now, on this day, Uhsula smiled into the blackness, the images of her dreams lingering in the shadows of her empty vision.

A winged ship, sailing beneath the arcing gaze of the Daystar, cutting through blood-red waters and leaving behind a frozen sheet of frosted waves.

"Mistress?"

Uhsula slowly rolled her head left, in the direction the voice had come from, ignoring the painful creak of her neck against the furs that layered the flat stone bed she rested upon. It took her a moment to sense the handmaiden's presence, but eventually she found the female, lingering near the wall on the other side of the room.

"Water," Uhsula croaked through a parched throat. At once she heard the handmaid hurry to the far corner, then approach accompanied by the slosh of a full pail. After a few seconds a clawed hand slid carefully behind Uhsula's head, gently lifting it as a ladle was pressed to her lips. She drank greedily, commanding the female to assist her twice more before she felt satisfied.

"Will that be all, mistress?" the handmaid asked quietly after she had eased Uhsula's head back down on the bed.

The old seer shook her head. *"No,"* she said hoarsely. *"Fetch the Queen."*

She felt the female shift uncomfortably beside her. *"Th-the Queen, mistress?"*

Uhsula nodded slowly. She couldn't blame her young assistant for her uncertainty. It had been nearly a year since she'd called up Shas-hana Rhan, though the Queen made a point to visit herself when she could. Since the start of the last cool season, Uhsula had had no visions, had been able to provide no news of the state of their larger plan. Her sight had not extended beyond the realm of the Daystar, the First Born. It could not penetrate the natural magics that separated the sands from the cold lands of the northern woods.

But now the visions had returned. Now the sight took life before her blind eyes once more.

Uhsula couldn't help cracking a quivering, toothless smile.

"*Fetch the Queen,*" she said again. "*Tell her our great hope has started to make his way home. Tell her he returns with a woman of ice and snow on his arm.*"

XXI

"Heave-ho, heave-ho, a seaman goes,
sailing as the captain says!
Heave-ho, heave-ho, a seaman goes,
as they toss him to the depths!"

—excerpt of a sailing song, c. 860v.S., author unknown

Clang! Woosh. Clang!

Steel struck wood in a dull echo over the emptiness of the ocean. Syrah ducked under a blow, then leapt clear over the haft that would have taken her at the ankles before moving forward to strike again.

Clang!

"Better!" Raz shouted from off to the side. "Now take her down!"

Syrah didn't know who it was he was encouraging, but decided to follow his advice. She was close to her opponent now—too close, truth be told, given that she herself was wielding her Priestess' staff—but Raz was slowly drilling into her that focusing solely on one's own advantages often left you blind to opportunity in a fight. In that moment she saw her chance, and she took it. Sidestepping quickly before her adversary could retreat and reclaim some range, Syrah feigned a high swing, turning it at the last second into a spinning jab that placed the rod of steel squarely between the woman's legs. Syrah twisted the staff, complementing the move with a spinning kick that caught her opponent in the chest.

Lysa, the ship's first mate, gave a rough "*Oof!*" as she tumbled to the deck, her feet suddenly no longer beneath her.

There were shouts and applause from all around them as Syrah stood straight, wiping the sweat from her brow and smiling broadly before turning to face the spectators. Thirty or so men and women, most of the third of the crew who weren't on duty at the time, were lounging about in a crescent around their little cleared space on the deck. Some had their legs over the *Sylgid*'s rails, alternately watching the fight and the blue-green water flowing by below them. Some were perched in the riggings and lowest booms overhead, cheering or groaning as they passed coins back and forth from won and lost wagers. Most, including Raz himself, were seated or standing among the covered crates and cargo tied down mid-ship. The atherian was clapping and grinning with the rest of them, and Syrah beamed at him before stepping over to extend a hand to Lysa.

"Lifegiver's arse, girl," the woman grumbled, accepting the help getting to her feet and rubbing her rear. "Did you have to take me down so hard?"

"Sorry," Syrah said sheepishly. "Are you all right?"

At that, Lysa laughed, then threw an arm around her shoulders, steering her back toward Raz and the others. "Aye, fine! We'll count it as payback for my knocking you into the wash-bucket yesterday."

"My robes *still* aren't dry," Syrah grumbled in agreement, looking down at her cloth pants and sleeveless tunic.

Lysa grinned deviously, then lifted her arm from around Syrah's neck to look around. "Who's next?" she shouted to the onlookers. "You lot only got these two for another month! Don't be shy now!"

There was a general cheer from the onlookers, and Syrah glanced around happily at the shouting and laughing faces of the crew of the *Sylgid*.

They had been at sea for just over four weeks now, and it had been a far different journey than either she or Raz would have predicted. The first several days had been the hardest, as might be expected, primarily because both of them struggled early on to gain their so-called "sea legs." They had discovered, also, that Raz's physiology apparently made him unable to vomit, a fact which Syrah wasn't sure if she envied or felt pity for. The first two nights, she'd only been able to sleep after hurling a majority of their lunch and dinner over the side of the boat.

Raz had kept his meals, but she didn't want to see the scales of his face that unfortunate shade of green ever again.

Worse than the seasickness, though, had been the struggle of getting to know the crew. At first, no one but Lysa and Garht Argoan himself had been really willing to speak to them, the distraught tension built from base mistrust and a larger fear of Raz's appearance and reputation. It was amusing in its own way, considering it all now. For those first half-dozen days or so, Syrah and Raz had been on constant edge, always watching each other's backs. They'd been on the lookout for any sign of betrayal, always being careful on the rare occasion they approached or were approached by one of the sailors, fearing trickery.

Looking back on it, Syrah was fairly sure the men and women of the *Sylgid* had been just as suspicious of her and Raz as they'd been of *them*.

It had been a slow process, building a mutual respect. They'd made three stops so far on their route—once at a small coastal village along the border and twice in other smugglers' hideaways along the shore of the South—and with each sojourn Raz and Syrah began to worry less and less. They stayed stowed together in the stores every time, hiding away in the straw-strewn quarters where Gale and Nymara were being kept, but not once had they seen so much as a hint of deceit, much less actual Mahsadën agents storming the ship.

Then, one day, a few of the younger sailors had gathered up the courage to ask Raz if they could see him fight, and things had rapidly improved from there.

What Raz had initially called an opportunity for him to keep limber had quickly turned into a daily event for the crew as a whole to enjoy. There were a few fine fighters among them, but most came from the scattered backgrounds of outcasts and runaways, with little to no experience with a blade to their name. Learning this, Raz had started working with the least competent of the group, and within a fortnight he and Syrah had gone from unwelcome curiosities on the ship to cheered guests in the crew's quarters for evening meals, dice games, and stories. It was pleasant—far more so than their lonely dinners in their guest quarters—and Syrah was slowly getting better at tolerating the proximity of men around her, though she still didn't stray from Raz's side around the crew.

And now, as the first month of the trip came to an end, Syrah was starting to realize she was going to have a hard time leaving some of these people behind once they made the shores of Perce.

"Dragon! Dragon! Dragon! Dragon!"

Syrah rose from her thoughts to the chant, sniggering as Raz rolled his eyes and shook his head, waving a hand as he attempted to refuse the call. It always happened, when they opened the floor to sparring like this. For a while everyone had a good enough time watching and learning as Raz shouted encouragement and feedback to the fighters, all of whom were armed with staffs or wooden weapons they'd spent several days whittling from broken oars stolen from the lower deck and rowing galley. Eventually, though, they always wanted a taste of the main attraction.

"Get up," Syrah said, moving to plop down beside the atherian and giving him a shove for good measure. "Give the people what they want."

Raz scowled at her, though it was a look accented with more resignation than annoyance. She didn't think he'd exactly *warmed* to the idea of allowing himself to be used as entertainment—Syrah suspected the shadow of the Arena still hung over him, in that way—but he'd come to accept that it bolstered spirits and served as a good opportunity for him to keep his own skills sharp.

"Dragon! Dragon! Dragon! Dragon!" the chant continued from all around.

"Fine!" Raz huffed in mock frustration, throwing his bare arms up as though in surrender before pushing himself to his feet. "It's your funerals."

There was a resounding cheer from the ship's company, and Syrah felt her own sense of anticipation, watching him move to the center of the cleared deck. Raz wore nothing more than a loose pair of cloth shorts, the emerald gleam that hid among the black scales of his body shining clear beneath the midday sun. He stretched his wings, allowing their red-and-orange membranes to bask in the warmth before pulling them flush to his back again. Muscle writhed and flexed along his legs, arms, and chest as he moved, and Syrah heard a giggle from overhead when he bent to pick up a large staff from the pile of wooden weapons, spinning it experimentally.

She gave the two women sitting in the rigging above a sharp look, head cocked and the brow of her good eye raised in warning, and the pair of them blushed and fell silent.

It had been too long, Raz had told her, since he'd been able to feel the freedom of the wind against his skin. In the North he'd worn a shirt or thin furs, even in summer. He was always saying that he enjoyed the feel of the Southern sun, and Syrah couldn't really blame him. While she had a more tenuous relationship with his god, she'd come to enjoy the heat herself, shedding her robes whenever she could. The daylight was less harsh this far out at sea than she'd expected, and only on a few particularly harsh days had she been forced to dig out the miserable veiled hood the Laorin had gifted her as a parting farewell.

"So?" Raz was asking, looking around expectantly. "Who's it going to be?"

One would think very few people might be fool enough to voluntarily pit themselves against a man known most commonly as "the Dragon," but Raz always had his pick of those wishing to learn. He selected three of the dozen or so who stuck their arms in the air, and a minute later the fight was in full swing. Raz twisted and darted around the deck, dodging and ducking and parrying as he shouted suggestions to his opponents and pointed out things for the rest of the spectators to observe. "Look at Davos' positioning here," he'd say, or "Olona, grip that sword higher." He would maintain the dance for a while, giving them the opportunity to practice their movements and positions while he himself took the chance to loosen up and stay nimble.

Then, in a blur, all would be reminded of how Raz had earned his name. *Whack! Clunk. Whack! Thud!*

Within five seconds, each of Raz's adversaries were brought to ground, two having lost their weapons, the other looking down the end of the atherian's wooded staff from flat on his back.

"Excellent!" Raz said encouragingly, pulling the staff away and glancing around with a smile as the three sailors gained their feet to the rising applause of their comrades. "Much better, all of you. Now… Who wants to go again?"

The sun was dipping well past its zenith before Lysa called a halt to the games, citing that all had tasks they'd been avoiding long enough. With grumbles of disappointment, the crew disbanded, some up the mast and ratlines to see to the sails, others about the deck or down into the frigate's belly below. Lysa herself took her leave of them shortly after, telling them both they were expected to sup with the crew that evening, which Raz and Syrah accepted heartily. Then, at last, they were left to their own devices.

"Maybe we shouldn't be bothered with disembarking," Syrah joked as they gathered up the wooden weapons and made for the door that led down into the rowing galley, toward the stern of the ship. "Maybe we could be sailors. Seafarers and scallywags!"

Raz gave her an amused look, heaving the door open with one hand, his bundle of whittled swords and axes snug under the other arm.

"Scallywags?" he asked her with a snort. "On the contrary, if you're starting to speak like that, we should tell Argoan we'll be taking our leave at the next port."

Syrah grinned. "Lysa told me Cyro is within a week's ride of our next docking. Perhaps the Mahsadën there would be more accepting of you?"

"If you mean they might consider just taking my head, rather than the drawing and quartering I'm sure the new šef of Miropa have in mind, then yes, *much* more accepting."

Syrah scoffed darkly, reaching the bottom landing of the twisted stairway. "Somehow, every time we discuss the South, Perce just seems so much more alluring…"

"That's the idea," Raz told her, ducking as he, too, stepped down into the below-deck. "To make it seem like the viper's nest is a better idea than the sandcat's lair."

The rowing galley was the largest single chamber in the ship, with twenty rows of flat one-person seats on either side of a narrow walkway. It could hold forty oar-men, though Argoan had only rarely put more than twenty or thirty at a time to the task of rowing when the winds weren't in their favor. Now, as the *Sylgid* rode a healthy southeaster gust that hadn't quit for several days, the place was abandoned, the majority of the crew set to checking the state of the sails, cleaning, and maintaining the ship. Gale and Nymara were kept among the storage rooms at the fore of the frigate, past the crew quarters, and so Raz and Syrah paid them a brief visit before heading back up to the top deck.

The *Sylgid* was a glorious ship, a true pride for any seaman. She was a triple-mast with a high stern that housed the captain's and guest quarters— where Raz and Syrah had been offered a bed and kept their things—and a curved bow crowned with the effigy of her namesake: a young woman whose hair flowed about her bare chest and shoulders like water. Argoan had confided in them that she wasn't the fastest of what he affectionately called the "smugglers' fleet," but she was well-built, dependable, and had yet to fail him. She'd out-sailed pirates, could navigate the reef-strewn Northern coastline, and could haul half-again what most ships her class were able to. Syrah considered that she and Raz might indeed be in the process of getting spoiled by the journey. Forgiving the frigate their first few nights of discomfort, the *Sylgid* cut across the ocean smoothly, bouncing and bobbing only with the swells of the shore when they approached land.

They spent the rest of the afternoon in their quarters, talking while Syrah practiced her spellwork and Raz sharpened Ahna and his gladius for the hundredth time since they'd left Highmast Cove. The captain had lent them a few books from his private collection, and they spent an interesting hour working on Raz's understanding of Northern letters, which were slightly different from the script used in the fringe cities. They joked and thanked their respective gods that both Perce and the Seven Cities still kept the Common Tongue as their primary languages. After that, they took to the ship's top-deck once more, marveling in the sunset over the western horizon.

It was nearly dark, in fact, before the cook's bell rang. Syrah and Raz allowed themselves a last few minutes to watch the dusk close off the day and the moon and stars to shine overhead, then headed below to sup with the crew not on the night watch. It was a pleasant evening, the plain meal of hardtack, bread, and salted meat over sauerkraut offset by raucous laughter, lecherous jokes, and enough ale passed around that by the end of the night Syrah had the hiccups. Raz eventually bid all goodnight for them before helping her to her feet, chased up to the deck by the boisterous catcalls of the men and titters of the women. They chuckled together and talked until he got her back to their lodgings and into bed, helping her kick off her boots before tucking her beneath the layers of wool blankets.

"It's nice, isn't it?"

Syrah watched Raz stir and look around at her question. He had just been in the process of settling down in his habitual place at the edge of the bed, his golden eyes glinting in the glow of the room's single candle.

"What is?" he asked her, finishing easing himself to the cabin floor. Ahna and Syrah's staff lay along the far wall—they hadn't wanted them falling with the rocking of the ship—but he had his gladius in its mismatched sheath in one hand.

"All this?" Syrah said, her face half-buried in the pillow even as she waved her hand about them. Dimly, she became aware that she was much, *much* drunker than she'd thought. "Life. Friends. Without worrying if we are going to get stabbed in the back as we sleep."

Raz said nothing, turning to look at the door of the guest quarters. Slowly, he set the gladius aside, though he didn't get up from his place on the floor.

"It is," he said after a while.

"But it can't stay like this, can it?" Syrah mumbled, feeling the sway of the ship claim her as the candle flickered by her bed.

"No, I don't think so," came the quiet reply.

Syrah nodded into the pillow, closing her eyes. She hiccupped once. "Guess we'd best enjoy it while we can, then."

If Raz answered her, she never heard it. She felt his hand, the one usually kept grasped around the hilt of his sword while she slept, reach out and take hers. She smiled, mumbled something unintelligible, and allowed herself to drift away into a peaceful sleep, comfortable and calm as the waves lapped against the side of the ship.

It would be another two weeks before the quiet of this new world of wind and water would finally betray them to the cruelties of the sea.

XXII

"There is a truth to the ocean that has always captivated me. On land, I have found that nothing is ever certain, that the bends in the road are not honest in their portrayal of risk and danger. Even among the clans, among family and blood, I thought man to be untrustworthy, to be deceitful. At sea, there is no such duplicity. The water never lies, never attempts to shield you from the fact that there is danger there, as much as there is beauty."

— from the private journals of Garht Argoan

"Lysa. With me."

As one, Raz, Syrah, and the first mate all turned toward the open door of their guest quarters, where Garht Argoan stood outlined against the Sun's light. It wasn't all that strange for the Amreht to visit their cabin, but he usually came in high spirits, bearing books or food or telling them to come look at something in the water, like the dolphins that sometimes danced through the wake of the ship or whales leaping from the ocean in the distance.

On this occasion, however, Raz felt at once that something wasn't right.

There was a tension in the captain's bulky form, a tightness to his painted face that stood out like an ill omen. In one hand he clenched a spyglass—a collapsing instrument sailors used to see things at long distances. The other rested on the head of his war-hammer, fingers drumming anxiously against the steel. Lysa, who'd been sitting on the bed with Syrah going over a map of the Percian shore while Raz looked on from his place on the floor, leapt up at once.

"Aye, sir," she said in a rush, hurrying to follow the man out onto the top-deck without so much as a glance backward. When they were gone, Raz and Syrah exchanged a look of confused concern.

Then, together, they clambered to their feet and made after the captain and his first mate.

It appeared, at first glance, to be yet another wonderful summer morning at sea. Raz's skin tingled as he stepped into the Sun's warmth, sending a shiver up his spine after the relative coolness of their cabin. The gulls, which had followed them since leaving the southern coast yesterday morning, were gone, flying back to the safety of land. Before them—southward—the sky was a dark azure that might have been a perfect reflection of the Dramion, were it not for the choppiness of the water. Raz frowned as he noticed this, eyeing the swells. This far out to sea, waves breaking gently about the *Sylgid* was a strange sight. Instinctively his forked tongue flicked out to taste the air, and his disquiet grew. There was a humidity to the morning, a denseness to the breeze that fluttered in the sails above. The tang of salt was lessened, somehow, and for a moment Raz couldn't comprehend why.

Then he noticed the ship hands leaning over the frigate's sides, looking north with uneasy expressions.

"Come on," he told Syrah, turning and making for the aft steps that led first up to the quarter-deck and the captain's quarters, then the top of the stern. As they hurried up the stairs, Argoan and Lysa appeared once again, standing along the banister at the very rear of the ship. The first mate had the spyglass now, and was peering into the distance as the boat swayed beneath them. Beside her, the captain was leaning against the railing with both hands, shoulders tense. As Raz and Syrah came up to stand behind them, Lysa brought the glass down from her face.

"Looks to be a nasty one," she was saying gravely, handing the instrument back to the captain. "And definitely chasing us south."

"Explains this fortune we've had with the wind," Argoan responded, bringing the glass up to his own eye and squinting through it. "Should have guessed our luck wouldn't hold."

"What's wrong?" Syrah asked uneasily, looking between the man and woman.

The Amreht grimaced in response, then handed the instrument to her. "See for yourself."

It took a moment for Syrah to figure out how the spyglass worked, lifting it to her good eye and shifting the collapsing tubes into focus. When she managed it, her mouth dropped open in tentative awe. For several seconds she swept the instrument slowly across the northern horizon, then pulled it away and made to hand it to Raz, but he refused it with a shake of his head.

He didn't need help to see what it was they were all observing.

Far, far in the distance, little more than a growing dark line over the edge of the sea, smoky clouds billowed in a solid sheet across the sky. Even as he took them in through narrowed eyes the wind picked up around them, bringing with it the cool scent of rain from miles away. There was a flash—imperceptible to the others, likely—momentarily lightening up a patch of the writhing grey as a shivering line of light struck down at the water.

A storm, he knew. *And coming right for us.*

"Should we make for port again, sir?" Lysa asked, turning to Argoan. "We're barely a day from Weary's Rest."

The captain shook his head. "Weary would have us sailing into the storm." He pointed northwest, back toward the port they had left the morning before. "We'd never make it. And I don't want to be caught near the shore if we can't find harbor. Anchor won't hold in Southern sand. Too thin. We'll be beached for sure."

Lysa took a shaking breath, but didn't argue. "We'll weather it, then?"

Argoan looked none-too-pleased, but grunted in confirmation. "Aye, we'll weather it. There's no outrunning a beast like that." He looked around at his first mate. "Tell the crew to raise and bind the sails. Don't want any masts splintering. Double-check all cargo is secure, above and below deck, and have the men on standby in the rowing galley. Full seats."

"Aye, Captain." Lysa snapped to attention once, then hurried down to the main ship again, shouting orders even as she took the steps two at a time.

Behind them, Raz heard the boat come alive, sailors rushing about to secure the *Sylgid*, some thundering down into the hull, others shouting to one another as they clambered up the main lines to lift and secure the sails.

"What can we do?" Syrah asked hurriedly, stepping forward. "How can we help?"

Argoan turned to look at them. His expression was tired, the face of a captain who knew well the gauntlet they were about to brave.

"We've three sets of gods aboard this ship right now," he said darkly. "Maybe that's fortunate. Maybe if we pray to them all, someone will get us through this in one piece."

It was evening before the storm caught up to them in truth.

For the remainder of the day it had gathered around the *Sylgid* like a growing fury, first darkening the Sun as the leading clouds began to creep across the sky, then pattering the frigate with steadily building rain. Raz and Syrah did what they could to assist the crew, she rushing back and forth to help clear the main deck of anything that might be tossed around or overboard as the ship began to rock on growing waves, he clambering up among the masts and booms with spare line and canvas that would have taken any other man twice as long to lug. By the time the light failed them, night creeping across the clouds above like a black tide through grey glass, the Dramion churned and boiled around them, lifting and dropping the ship five, then ten, then twenty feet at a time. Argoan kept to the helm, roaring curses up at the storm in his guttural native tongue and laughing as the water began to cap and break to *thud* against the hull. Lysa was constantly on the move, still shouting her orders as she clung to ropes and railings and anything that was tied down. The planks of the deck were slick, the rain pounding down about their heads, and more than once someone slipped and slid several feet before finding something to catch hold of as the *Sylgid* listed and groaned beneath them.

Midnight must have come and gone before there was nothing else they could do, and at the shouted order of the captain every spare hand— including Raz and Syrah—took shelter below on either end of the rowing galley. Syrah moved about the space, using her magic to warm and refresh as many as she could, careful not to fall into the rows of seated men heaving at their oars and trying to keep the ship moving forward through the gale. For an hour or two they stayed like that, huddled in the limited light of a couple of oil lanterns shifting back and forth from their hooks in the rafters. Few bothered trying to sleep, preferring instead to do their best to converse in an attempt to drown out the roar of the wind and the *boom* of thunder as lightning lit up the oar-holes. Salt sprayed into the chamber with every *thump* of waves against them. The world rocked, sending individuals who had the misfortune of choosing that moment to stand tumbling sideways.

And then, in the earliest hours of the morning, Raz heard something truly terrifying over the wailing of the storm. A *snap*, followed by another, then another.

Then, like a hundred whips, the cracking sound of wet, flailing cloth.

He straightened up from where he and Syrah had been sitting together against the stern-side wall of the rowing galley, surprising her and making her lift her head from his shoulder.

"What is it?" she asked, watching him apprehensively as Raz stared up at the deck above.

He was about to answer that he wasn't sure, that he only thought he had an idea, when there was the *slam* of a door being thrown open and a clamber of footsteps down the stairs to their right. Two seconds later a sailor appeared—a Southerner Raz was pretty sure was called Perro—so thoroughly soaked he looked like he'd been dunked in the sea. He stood at the base of the stairs, shaking in what might have been cold, except that his voice was filled with fear as he shouted.

"THE SAIL!" he howled, pale as a ghost. "THE MAIN SAIL IS LOOSE! WE'RE GOING TO LOSE THE MAST!"

All around them the sailors came alive with panicked energy. Some shouted and yelled, screaming after Perro as the man turned and hurried back up toward the top-deck, but *all* moved. In a rush, every spare body was hurrying for the stairs, not a few among them tripping and falling into the cursing oar-men as the ship swept some thirty degrees portside. Without more than a quick look at each other, Raz and Syrah pulled themselves up and joined the crew, scrambling up to the deck.

The world that greeted them was a more awesome scene, more terrifying and enthralling, than Raz had ever witnessed.

He was grateful, in that moment, that he could make out the sea swelling around them in mountainous waves better than the others. If they'd witnessed the true power of the elements they were battling against, he wondered if their sailors' bravery would hold out. In every direction the water rose and fell fifty feet at a time, giving the impression that some colossal creature was writhing and roaring just beneath the surface, its great limbs pushing and dragging the black sea up and down as it flailed. Rain still hammered them in an endless torrent. The wind screamed, shrieking against them, chilly despite the heat of the summer morning they'd had less than twelve hours before.

Then lightning flashed, thunder ripping over their ears, and Raz made out the sight above with a thrill of horror.

The center sail had come loose of its ties, falling down to hang from its primary boom. It was still attached—though tattered along the bottom where it had ripped loose of its tethers—but the storm was pressing it against the main mast, folding over the pole until it hung like two wings spread wide against the storm. Even as he watched there was a creaking shriek, and Raz knew the wood wouldn't hold out to the abuse of the wind against the canvas. They might be able to do with two of their three sails, but if the main went it would likely crash down onto the foremast.

Even if they survived the storm, they would be largely stranded.

"Syrah!" Raz howled even as he bolted forward. "Lights! *Lights!*"

He didn't know if the woman had heard or understood him, but there was no time to wait and find out. With four steps and a massive lunge he lanced past the aft-mast, vaulted atop a covered cargo crate in the waist of the ship, then launched himself into the air with a massive leap, extending his wings. The wind did exactly what he'd hoped for, catching him and propelling him forward. He almost missed the jump, almost lost to the storm and would have been thrown out to sea, but he managed to tangle himself in the rigging, earning an ample opportunity to grab hold of several of the lines lashing about behind him. Steadying himself as the rain and wind continued to batter his body, Raz started to climb with quick, efficient heaves.

He'd just reached the top of the primary boom, pulling himself up to hug the mast with one arm, when the ship below him was suddenly lit in a blaze of brilliant light.

Raz blinked and looked down, allowing his eyes to adjust. Far beneath him, a number of glowing orbs about the size of a man's head were scattered about, floating some ten feet above the deck. They bathed everything in a gold-white glow, blinding him to the ocean beyond them, for which he was grateful.

Thank the Sun for that woman.

Under him, Raz noticed the outline of a dozen men and women clambering toward him. Wiping rain from his eyes, he realized he'd reached the top of the mast before anyone else had gotten even a third of the way up.

"WHAT DO I DO?" he bellowed against the roar of the ocean, cupping his free hand over his mouth.

At his shout, the leading figure looked up, blinking at him in surprise. He recognized the woman's scarred face.

Lysa.

"CUT THE SAIL FREE!" she hollered back, making a chopping motion with one hand as others overtook her.

Raz looked around. There was so much line, looped and tied and knotted in a thousand intricate ways about his feet in either direction. He had no idea where to start.

"HOW?" he screamed back even as a bolt of lightning ripped across the sky to the west, striking the heaving sea with a flash and crash of thunder.

Lysa was just about to yell out an answer, looping one leg into the netting to cup both hands around her mouth, when there was another *crack*.

Off to her left, one of the lower booms, caught in the soaked embrace of the flapping canvas, broke loose and spun away into the black water.

"CUT IT ALL!" Lysa's answer came, shrill with desperation. "CUT EVERYTHING!"

Raz didn't hesitate.

With no knife on him and his gladius likely skittering around the floor of their cabin with the rest of their gear, he resorted to the only tools he had left. Alternating hands to clutch at any hold he could find and using the talons of his feet to great effect, Raz moved along the boom foot by foot, slashing at the ropes. He would have preferred a blade, but his claws made short work of the ties regardless, and within a minute the port side of the sails fell away. Instantly the mast beneath him bent, torqued by the sudden shift in pressure, and Raz nearly lost his footing, barely keeping himself from swinging down on a loose length of rope into open air. By the time he found his balance, several others had reached the main boom, and were working feverishly to hack at the starboard side.

Moving as quickly as he could, Raz made his way over, swinging himself around the mast to join the effort. His claws slashed again, left and right, and the canvas came free not a moment too soon. There was a *snap*, and yet another section of the rigging came loose, crashing to the deck this time and sending sailors screaming and throwing themselves out of the way. The soaked sail tumbled down to hang from what was left of the lower boom, where others rushed to lug it free and drag it to the base of the mast where it lay, a wet mass of useless cloth.

"Good work!"

Raz looked around, blinking into the onslaught of rain. Lysa was grinning at him, though her face was pale and her eyes showed a lot more fear than she would have ever let her men see. He nodded, then pointed downward.

"Shall we?" he hollered, and the first mate nodded. Together they dropped with the others, sliding hand over hand down loose rope until they reached the main starboard ratline. Lysa continued to descend from there, but Raz allowed himself to fall, landing on the deck on all fours among a rush of men and women moving about the ship, hauling people to their feet and helping them toward the stairs to the galley as the ship bucked. There were wounded, he saw, several individuals with shards of wood sticking from limbs and torsos from when the booms had failed, as well as one still form who looked like he might have fallen from the mast.

"ARRO!"

Raz turned, lifting both hands to shield his eyes from the rain and blinking in the light of the magic orbs. The first thing he saw was Syrah, standing with her hands outstretched before her in the center of the ship, water steaming off her body as the spellwork she was maintaining cast shimmering heat about her form. When he lifted his eyes, he made out the figure of Garht Argoan still manning the helm, outlined by his own sphere of light hovering behind his shoulder.

The captain was looking right at him.

"GET EVERYONE BELOW DECK!" Argoan yelled, struggling with the ship's wheel as the *Sylgid* listed portside again. "TELL LYSA I WANT THE OAR-MEN ROWING AT DOUBLE-PACE!"

Raz raised a hand to indicate that he had heard. He turned and bolted, making the starboard railing just as the first mate reached the deck, dropping to the ship floor.

"Argoan wants everyone back in the rowing galley!" he yelled over the storm. "Told me to tell you the oars need to go at 'double-pace'!"

Lysa wiped her sheet of plastered wet hair out of her eyes. "Aye!" she yelled back. "I'll tell them all fore-side! Can you take the aft?"

Raz was about to answer, about to tell her that he understood, when another bolt of lightning lit up the blackness beyond the ship's rail. It was only a moment, only a brief glimpse of the Dramion behind Lysa, but Raz felt his entire body stiffen. What he saw was not the raging swell of the ocean, nor the dips and hills that had been throwing them up and down for the last several hours.

Instead, what Raz saw was nothing less than a solid wall of water, curved into a true wave, so high he didn't even have time to find the top in the flash of the storm.

Without thinking, Raz grabbed Lysa by the arm and hauled her back, ignoring her yell of pain and surprise. He had just enough time to turn, just enough time to make a mad dash for the middle of the ship, when he felt the deck lurch and start to lift beneath his feet. This time it didn't stop, though, didn't bob back down and even out. It continued to list, twisting until Raz felt like he was running downhill. He reached Syrah just in time, still pulling the first mate along behind him.

The Priestess yelped in shock as he collided with her, slamming all three of them to the deck, sliding in a tumble of limbs and bodies over the wet wood until they collided, hard, with the portside railing. Raz had just enough time to loop an arm through the banister, encasing the two women in an iron embrace with his other as they both shouted in confusion, when the wave fell over the ship with a *crunch* of unfathomable weight.

Never in his life had Raz ever felt such brute, terrifying power. The water struck and rushed over them with the force of a falling mountain, crushing their forms into the railing. Nothing existed in those ten seconds other than the rush of the ocean over and between their bodies, simultaneously ripping at them and pushing them down against the ship. All the air was forced out of Raz, and it took every ounce of his willpower not to gasp in a lungful of seawater. It didn't last long but, as the blast of the wave spilled over them to flow back into the ocean, Raz knew he had never been closer to death than in that moment.

As he felt the ship right itself beneath them, swaying dangerously starboard, Raz finally opened his eyes. The *Sylgid* seemed to sparkle. Water dripped from everywhere, everything more thoroughly soaked than any amount of rain could ever achieve, glinting in the fading light of the orbs that seemed to be dying as Syrah's concentration no longer provided for them. In his arms, the Priestess herself coughed and vomited up seawater, joined shortly after by Lysa. They hacked and heaved, Syrah looking up at Raz in mixed relief and terror. The first mate, though, looked upward.

Her eyes went wide in panic.

Raz knew, somehow, what he would find as he turned to follow her gaze. Cold ripped at him in that moment, settling into his soul to churn with the horror the dark sea was breeding within him. He twisted around, bending back to look where he knew the first mate was staring. There, in the dimming glow of a magic orb, the helm spun free, a lonely silhouette atop the stern.

Garht Argoan was gone.

XXIII

"NO!"

It was Lysa who howled the word, her scream ringing with terror and desperation. She scrambled to her feet as Raz, too, fought to stand, his mind whirling.

"Syrah!" he shouted, gaining his footing and digging claws into the slick timber. "The water! Put the lights in the water!"

"Raz, what are you going to—?" the Priestess started to yell, trying to get up herself, but Raz cut her off.

"DO IT!"

Then he was off, running after Lysa.

Rope was never lacking on any seaworthy ship. It was everywhere, curled around itself in corners and looped over handles nailed into the railings for the exact purpose of *not* getting swept overboard. Raz had spent the day toting line up and down the masts, so he knew exactly where to go. Even as he dashed after the first mate he snatched up a massive coil of the stuff from where it had sat in the semi-sheltered nook beneath the aft stairs, throwing it over one shoulder. He took the steps four at a time, and it was just as he reached the top, rushing to join Lysa to lean over the portside rail, that the world went dark around him. The orb that had been lingering by the helm, fading slowly, suddenly blinked out, as did every other source of Syrah's magic on the ship. For the two seconds it took for Raz to bolt from the top of the stairs to Lysa's side, he was blind.

Then, just as he reached her, the ocean began to glow.

If it had been any other moment in his life, Raz might have said that what he witnessed over the side of the ship then would have been the most beautiful thing he had ever seen. The sea danced before him, rising and falling in growing and shrinking swells, but it was no longer black. It roared, pounding against the hull of the *Sylgid*, but the mystery of it was revealed, opening up before them under the warm glow of golden white light that seemed to rise without source from below. The water flowed, still opaque in its depth and its surface textured harshly by the rain, but alight for a hundred feet before them. Even as he searched he heard the awed gasps of dozens of sailors on the deck below, their combined amazement beating out even the wind.

There were shapes, shifting like inverse shadows in the water, illuminated from beneath. Debris floated over the surface of the ocean. Shattered oars, splinters of wood and torn cloth from the broken booms, loose and broken cargo. There were bodies, too, the floundering forms of a half-dozen men and women who had been swept from the ship by the wave, and a few more who were already unmoving. Raz forced himself to ignore them, forced himself to look away from the slighter bodies silhouetted by the light, hoping the others would be able to reach them.

"THERE!" Lysa shouted, pointing to a spot near the center of the magic. Raz's eyes followed her finger, desperately searching the sea. Sure enough, the shadow of a large, balding man was submerged feet below the surface. The flow drew him back and forth, whisking him up and down with the swells.

Raz didn't hesitate. Praying the rope was long enough, he bit down on one end, took three steps back, and hammered forward again.

Then, planting a foot on the railing, he launched himself head-first into the sea.

He hit the surface of the water with a mind-numbing *crack*, stars erupting across his vision as he plunged downward into the dull silence. The current was surprisingly warm as it churned around him, pushing him this way and that. He forced himself to open his eyes, ignoring the burn of them as he kicked himself forward, fighting to reach Argoan's dark outline. Unfortunately, Raz had only ever been a poor swimmer. The Arros had taught him well enough as a boy, but the depths of the Garin were home to caimans and crocodiles, and his wings and smooth skin had never served him well in water. He struggled forward, praying to the Moon for help. Within fifteen seconds his chest started to ache. Before long he forced himself to kick upward, breaking the surface again and taking the rope from his mouth to gasp in a lungful of air as the howl of the storm and rain returned. Without pause, he plunged downward again, Syrah's spell still shining to cast Argoan's outline upward from the depths.

The ocean toyed with him as he swam, pushing him back, then forward, sometimes drawing the captain's form closer, then whisking it away. Still, Raz fought, resolved to battle the forces of nature itself as he drew himself through the water, struggling against the waves. With every passing second, with every inch he got closer, he feared it would be too late. He was twenty feet away. Raz could hear the dull howl of the storm. He was ten feet away. His stomach pitched as both he and the captain were dragged upward. He was five feet away. The shapes of debris flashed between them. He was a foot away. He reached out, feeling his lungs screaming for air. The claws of his hands just managed to catch the loose layers of the cotton shirt swaying about the man's chest.

Raz had him.

At once he made for the surface, struggling with everything he had left to pull them both upward. He was seeing stars again, the edges of his vision going black, the endless murk of the sea pressing in all around him. It was suddenly ten times harder to move, Argoan's bulk fighting him as much as the current. Raz could feel himself slipping, feel himself fail. Abruptly, he realized the cruel joke the Dramion had played on him. He understood that, even though he'd been allowed to reach the captain, the sea would never let him haul the man back to the ship.

Raz knew, suddenly, that he would have to let the man go if he wanted a chance at surviving himself.

I'm sorry, friend, he thought as the black continued to pool across his vision. *May the Moon see you up into Her Stars.*

He started to loosen his grip, started to untangle his claws from the wet folds of Argoan's loose shirt.

Then, just as he was about to let go completely, Raz felt a sharp tug against his teeth.

The rope was being pulled back in.

With a surge of hope Raz snatched the captain up again. Taking hold of the line with his free hand, he spat it out and stopped fighting. At once the water began moving faster around him, whipping by as what must have been a dozen sets of hands towed them back toward the *Sylgid.* A moment later they broke the surface, and Raz nearly passed out from the influx of oxygen as he sucked in the most wonderful breath of air he'd ever had in his life. The sounds of the raging storm returned, the rain pounding at him almost painfully. He blinked and tried to make out where he was, but could tell only that Syrah's magic had faded, the water around them dark and foreboding once more. His eyes stung. His head hurt, and his chest felt as though he had been stepped on by an elephant. He continued to heave in breath after breath in an attempt to fight away the heaviness of his arms and legs, the shakiness of his grip. He hacked and gasped as the wake kicked back at him, spilling seawater into his mouth.

They reached the frigate just as Raz thought his strength would fail him. Hands grabbed at him as soon as he felt his shoulder knock against the hull, and from the clatter of wood on wood and the bleary outlines he could make out through his blurred vision, Raz realized a pair of rope ladders had been thrown over the side of the ship. He felt the captain taken from his grasp and hauled upward as voices shouted all around over the scream of the wind. He thudded and scraped against the boat, feeling the world go dark, and in some distant place he realized the tow line was sliding from his grasp. He fought not to sink, fought with all he had left to hold tighter to the rope, but to no avail. The warmth of the ocean called to him, an almost soothing song. The abuse of the rain faded as he slid beneath the surface again, salt filling his mouth once more. Inch by inch the line slipped, more as the ocean pushed him this way and that in the current. He felt the end slide against his wrist, then his palm, then the very edge of his fingers. He was too tired to be frightened, too beaten to give much thought to his own death. He regretted only what he would leave behind, seeing a glint of white shimmer high above the surface of the water. He watched that ivory glow even as the rope slipped away completely, wondering if she would be safe without him.

Then, with a *crack* and shriek of boiling water, the white exploded through the surface. Something hot and brilliant and flickering with painless ivory flames snaked downward, wrapping around his wrist. A moment later he was hauled upward again, breaking once more into the roaring wind of the storm.

Raz's head lolled back. He had only the time to grin stupidly up at the indistinct outline of the woman leaning over the railing above, her white hair whipping about her pale face, the fiery lash gripped tight in one hand. More forms hurried down the ladders on either side of him, and as strong hands took him under both arms, Raz had time for one last thought before he dropped into oblivion.

Thank the Sun for that woman.

Warmth was the first thing Raz felt as he came to. The feeling of the Sun against his face and chest, and the brush of a breeze rustling against his bare skin. At first he thought he was dreaming of the Garin again, but when he tried to open his eyes he groaned and blinked repeatedly, not anticipating the dry, stinging achiness of the attempt, nor the brightness of the day.

"Lysa!" a familiar voice called from beside him. "Come! He's awake."

Raz forced himself to squint and turn his head. Slowly, the light of the day pounding at him like a cruel headache, he made out Syrah's form side-sitting by his right hip. Eventually her face came into focus, and the smile he tried to give her came out as a pained smirk even as he made out the sound of boots on steps. A second later, the blurred outline of the first mate approached over the Priestess' shoulder.

"I take it we made it through?" Raz asked, half-teasing, letting his head fall back to the wood of the ship's deck and bringing an arm up to cover his face. "Ooooww. My eyes."

"Salt water will do that," Lysa's voice answered, sounding all-too relieved that he was back among the living. "A good rinse and a few days, and you'll be fine."

Raz nodded, not moving his arm, enjoying the cool darkness of the inside of his elbow. "How long have I been out?"

"Just a few hours," Syrah said. "We kept you and Argoan in the captain's quarters until the storm passed. He's still there, but I told them the sunlight would do you good."

Raz tried to peek with one eye at the sky again. He caught only a glimpse of thick clouds patterning a pale blue before his eye ached, and he covered it back up. "He made it, then," he said with a groan. "That's good. How is he?"

"Fine," Lysa answered first. "Took a good hit to the head and gagged up enough of the Dramion to raise the tides after we hauled him back on board, but no lasting damage overall. He's asleep now."

"Can't blame him," Raz muttered, suddenly realizing how heavy his body was. "I feel like I haven't seen a bed in years." He frowned suddenly, thinking of something else. "And the rest? I saw others, in the water. Were we able to get to them?"

There was a moment of sad silence.

"We managed to rescue two," Syrah said sadly. "We tried to get ropes to the others, but the current pulled them away. We've been searching all night and morning but…" He felt her shudder beside him. "It's my fault. I couldn't hold the spell any longer. As soon as we saw you reach the captain, I had to let go. I barely had enough strength left to keep you from drowning once you made it back to the ship."

Raz was about to reach out to her, to comfort her and tell her that none of it was her doing, but Lysa beat him to it.

"It is anything *but* your fault," she snapped, sounding genuinely irritated. "We would have made this trip regardless of your presence. If anything, you two are the only reason we managed to save even those two, not to mention the captain or the bloody *mast*. A storm like that is a rare curse. We were lucky to have you on board."

Raz nodded in agreement, then decided it was time to get up. With a groan he lifted his arm from his face and started to push himself into a sitting position, keeping his eyes shut. At once he heard Syrah curse under her breath, then felt her slim hands on his shoulders as she helped. "She's right," Raz told the Priestess after he managed to steady himself, ignoring the throb of his head as he blinked at the ground. It was easier opening his eyes, this time, without the Sun glaring directly into them. "You saved a lot of lives last night, Syrah. Mine included."

"*All* our lives," Lysa corrected. "The both of you. If the main mast had gone down, it would have taken out the foresail in that wind. We would have had to row against the wind and current back to land, and we've only provisions for a week or so, until our next docking. It would have meant disaster."

Their words seemed to help. Syrah didn't say anything more, but Raz felt her relax beside him. Slowly he looked up, still unable to do more than squint as the glare of the new morning stabbed at his eyes again.

They were seated on the raised bow, the *Sylgid*'s figurehead rising up behind Raz's back. Before him, the top-deck was a mess. Apparently no one had bothered yet with worrying about cleaning up, likely too preoccupied with the search for their missing shipmates and caring for the wounded from the previous night. The sail they'd cut down remained where it had fallen, loose and limp in a wet pile wrapped about the base of the main mast, and what was left of the lower boom splintered out in either direction ten feet above them. From his place above the deck, Raz could easily see the loose rigging flapping about overhead, as well as the dent and scrape from where the broken beam had fallen and crashed to the ship floor. A chunk was missing from the portside railing, and it looked as though a significant amount of the covered cargo hadn't withstood the wave that had nearly capsized them.

"We're lucky we made it through…" Raz muttered to himself.

Neither of the women contradicted him.

It took a while before Raz was ready to try standing in truth. He'd been worse off, he decided as he got to his feet—thinking in particular about a time he had taken a crossbow bolt in the side—but he still felt like he'd been thrown off a building head-first. Between the desperation with which he'd fought to cut the sail free, the brutal crush of the wave, and the unplanned dive into the sea, his whole body was largely *not* happy with him. He limped along, using Syrah's shoulder like a crutch, following Lysa as the first mate descended the bow steps to the waist, then down the ship toward their cabin. All around them, sailors whose names he knew and didn't hailed him, but all Raz could do was wave and grimace in attempted cheer. The morning Sun did indeed feel good on his back—they were sailing southwest now, meaning they must have been blown off-course by the storm—but the ache in his head didn't fade in the glare. When Lysa opened the door to their quarters and helped Syrah get him inside, he couldn't help but feel relieved in the relative darkness of the lodgings.

"How many did we lose last night?" he asked after they'd eased him to sit at the edge of the feather-stuffed mattress. Syrah sat down beside him, taking hold of his hand with surprising firmness.

"Seven in all," Lysa answered, sounding as though she had to fight to keep her voice even. "Six to the sea, but Perro fell when we were trying to free the sail." She sighed, reaching up with one hand to rub her temples. "He died a few hours ago."

Raz thought of the sailor sadly, remembering the desperation in the Southerner's voice as he'd rushed down into the rowing galley, yelling for help. He thought, too, of the others, damned to the waves. He didn't envy them their deaths, couldn't fathom the fear that must have drowned them as thoroughly as the sea itself. He shivered, shaking his head slightly, and Syrah's hand tightened even more in his.

"Poor bastards," he said quietly. "Let's hope the Moon was quick in claiming them."

"Aye," Lysa agreed. "They were good sailors." She hesitated, looking at Syrah. "Would you pray for them for me? Let the Lifegiver know... Let him know they deserve to be reborn into the world?"

If the Priestess was surprised by this request, she didn't show it.

"Of course," she said with a sad smile. "Do you have their names?"

The first mate gave them to her, and Raz felt his heart sink as he recognized nearly every one. Men and women he had sparred with, eaten and joked with in the crew's quarters.

Poor bastards, he repeated to himself.

After that, Lysa left them to check on the captain. For a little while Syrah fussed over Raz, asking him how he felt and checking his wounds. His head was the worst—Raz suspected he'd managed to give himself a mild concussion when he'd dived into the water—but he'd also managed to scrape up his back, right arm, and the limb of his right wing against the barnacled hull of the ship. In the muddled ache that was his entire body he hadn't really noticed, but after the woman worked some magic over his shoulder he felt much of the hidden pain subside.

"Better," he groaned, easing back before pushing himself gingerly up to the head of the bed and lying down against the pillows. The throbbing headache lessened somewhat as he relaxed and closed his eyes again. "Thanks. If the crew wasn't pleased to have us on board the ship before, I'll bet they are now. That magic last night… I didn't know you could do something like that."

Syrah didn't say anything. After nearly a minute of silence Raz cracked an eye open to look at her curiously. She still sat at the edge of the bed to his right, turned away from him, and he realized with a start that she was shaking. Her shoulders were quivering as she slouched, and she seemed to be refusing to meet his gaze.

"Syrah?" he asked, ignoring the pain in his head as he rolled to push himself up onto one elbow, reaching out to place his other hand on the small of her waist. "What's wrong?"

For a while longer, the woman didn't respond. She'd stopped shivering at his touch, but her breaths were short and broken, like she was fighting to control them. He couldn't see her face, but Raz was almost sure she was crying.

"What were you thinking?"

The question came in a ragged, quiet voice that took Raz by surprise. The words brimmed with any number of emotions—anger, sadness, grief, disbelief—and it stabbed at his heart more sharply than any knife. It took him a moment, but eventually he thought he knew what she was asking.

He just wasn't sure he had a good answer for her.

"Would you rather I'd have let him drown?" he asked gently.

Syrah gave a mirthless laugh, and he saw her left arm shift as she wiped at her face.

"And what about you?" she demanded, still not looking around. "What if *you* had drowned? I saw you in that water, Raz. You don't swim well. You had to have known that, and yet you jumped in anyway. What if we hadn't been able to pull you back? What if the rope had slipped, or hadn't been long enough? What if…?"

The questions trailed away, and Raz gave the woman a moment to get ahold of herself again.

"I had to try," he said after she'd stilled. "I owed him that, don't you think? Argoan's taken us in at no benefit to himself. It's all a risk to him, to his crew. I owed him the attempt. I owed him—"

"*You.*"

Syrah whirled on him, cutting him off. The anger and hurt in her voice was sharp, and as he met her good eye Raz saw that she had indeed been crying. Her cheek was wet, and her lips quivered downward in the way they do when one is fighting off more tears.

"*You* had to try," she hissed shakily. "*You* owed him. *You* risked your life. *You* almost drowned."

Raz blinked at her, unsure of what he was expected to say next.

Then she asked her next question.

"What about *me?*"

He saw it then, all that he hadn't yet noticed. Whether he'd missed it due to the pain or the fatigue or his own bottomless stupidity, he couldn't quite say. Every feeling he had made out in her voice was there, plain across her face, but there was something more as well, more than the base anger and sadness. Clearer than any of it, shining like a fire in her eye, was fear. *True* fear. Syrah, above all else, was terrified. Terrified by what he had done. Terrified by the utter lack of doubt with which he had done it. He had frightened her in a way he'd never considered, risking it all as he'd done to save the captain.

"You're not alone anymore, Raz," Syrah continued as though reading his thoughts. "Everything you are, everything you mean and are a part of... It's not just *yours* anymore. When you jumped, when you threw yourself into the sea... It was like watching you pull Gûlraht Baoill over the cliff all over again. You could have died. You could have..." Her eye became bright with tears again, and her repeated words came through a barely controlled sob. "You could have *died.*"

Raz watched her, open-mouthed, taking it all in. For the first time, it really fell into place for him. He had been on his own for so long, had forgotten to fear something as trivial as death so many years ago... It seemed strange, now, realizing it wasn't just *him* he was responsible to anymore. It wasn't a bad feeling, by any means. Despite the state of Syrah, despite the crying, shivering woman before him, the idea filled Raz with a confusing warmth of emotions, building up in his chest like his heart were suddenly too big for the small space it had been allotted. He stared at her, reflecting for the first time on how he would feel if *she* had thrown herself overboard, if *she* had risked leaving him behind to save a man they hardly knew.

"I'm sorry," was all he managed to get out. "Syrah, I... I'm so sorry. I didn't think..."

"No," Syrah agreed with an angry jerk of her head that shook a tear from the smooth skin of her cheek. "No, you didn't. Don't ever do that to me again. *Please* don't ever do that to me again."

He nodded numbly, pushing himself up to kneel on the bed, feeling the sway of the ship beneath them. Silently he pulled the woman toward him, and Syrah responded at once, turning and crawling into his arms, burying her head in his chest and letting the sobs come in truth now. For several minutes they stayed like that, Raz holding the woman tight and stroking her white hair carefully while she cried and hugged his waist tighter than he would have thought possible.

"I'm a fool," he told her softly once she'd finally calmed down, though her face still stayed buried against him. "I'm sorry."

Syrah shook her head against him, but didn't look up. "I don't know what I would have expected you to do instead," she said with a sigh. "I don't think you know how to be anything else. I just…"

She couldn't seem to find the words, so Raz tried finishing for her.

"Wish I'd hesitated?" he asked. "Wish I'd thought of you?"

Syrah didn't say anything for a moment. Then, finally, she lifted her face from his scaled skin to look up at him. Even with her eye ringed with red and the loose strands of her hair clinging to the wetness of her face, she was a beautiful sight to behold.

"Maybe," she said, wiping her cheek dry with a corner of her tunic. "I don't know. I don't want you to be anything less than you are, but I think that scares me as much as the thought of you becoming anything else."

"Sounds infuriating," Raz said with a grin down at her.

Syrah couldn't help but laugh, punching him lightly. "Very. Why couldn't you have been a farm-hand, or a soldier? Life would be *so* much simpler."

"Of all the differences between us, you think the fact that I'm not a *farm-hand* is the most concerning?" Raz asked her dubiously, raising an eyebrow. "Maybe the captain wasn't the only one to get hit over the head last night…"

As Syrah dropped her head back to his chest, he felt her smile against him. For a time they were silent again, but when the woman eventually spoke, her voice was calmer.

"I don't want you to be anything less than you are," she said again, mumbling against him. "I just want you to remember that *what* you are doesn't just belong to you anymore. Please."

Raz dipped his snout down to rest in her hair. Despite the weeks at sea, her smell reminded him of a life long-past, of spending the broiling summer days at the edge of the Garin, of dawns and dusks rising and falling over the palm groves as the desert wind shook the trees. It brought him back to another time when he had belonged to more than himself.

"I will," he said into her hair softly. "I promise."

This time, when he lay down again, Syrah came with him, and before long they were asleep in each other's arms, giving in to the gentle rock of the ocean.

XXIV

"...But the Twins, in Their infinite wisdom, knew well that they could never stand before their creation, lest the vision of Their true forms render mankind mad. For the first half of eternity They debated this, seeking a solution, searching for a way to have Their voices heard. In the end, it was the Sun who found the way. Seeking out a chosen child, He bestowed upon him all the powers of a god, while the Moon granted the boy all the wisdoms of the world. It was in this way that They were able to speak for the first time to their child, reaching out through the line of men that passed the crown from head unto the other."

—*Creason i'Raz* or *"Creation of Child,"* ancient Percian holy text

"All kneel before His Greatness, Gift of the Sun, Blessed of the Moon, Tash of the mighty city of Karesh Syl!"

It took everything he had for Ekene Okonso not to roll his eyes as he was announced to the court. There had been a time—as a younger man—when he'd taken great pride in hearing his name echo through the silence of the gilded hall. He had been quicker, then, easy on his feet and handsomer by far, and the gazes of his courtiers had always been adoring, respectful, even awestruck. He had been a well-loved ruler, as impressive in his physique as he'd been in shrewdness and will.

Now, though, as his grandchildren began to think of bearing sons and daughters of their own, the strength had long left Ekene's limbs. The Moon had mercifully allowed him to retain his mind, but he fought mightily not to show the strain it took to climb even the dozen short steps that led up to the three staggered thrones raised over the west end of the hall. When he reached them, he turned on the room, the white-and-red robes his wives had selected for him that morning twisting about his bent form as he settled into the center-most of the three seats. At his right, the chair lay empty. Yseri Suro, his First Hand, was negotiating tariffs with the Tash of Karesh Nan, and wasn't expected to return for another week at least. At his left, Naizer Ima, his Second Hand, lounged lazily, studying the gathered crowd below them with distinct disdain.

"Look at them," he grumbled to Ekene, his voice thick with annoyance. "Ask them for their support in trade deals or men to guard our caravans north, and they shy away like cockroaches in the light. Let slip the rumor of an interesting visitor, however, and they flock to your court like ants to sugar."

Ekene didn't respond, his mood dark enough without Naizer's mutterings. His Second was indispensable in his grasp on the city's commerce and markets and the average values of a slave on any given day, but he'd never made for pleasant company. If it had been possible, the Tash would have had the younger man permanently locked in his offices on the top floor of the palace.

Still, Ekene thought, reaching up to stroke the silver of his beard as he looked out over the court, *he's not wrong.*

It had been a long time since he had seen so much of the nobility flock to his halls. There were always a few at every audience, known faces that came seeking either to gain his favor with their consistent presence, or to see what scandals they could gather to whisper about in their social circles. Today, however, it seemed that the better part of the inner city had deigned to grace him with their presence, though it was small wonder as to why. His attendants had informed him that a strange party of men had arrived overnight via the north gate, claiming to be messengers of the fringe cities. Ekene had been none-too-pleased to hear this, of course—the Mahsadën were another entity he would have preferred to hide from sight—but he had to admit it was a curious event. Usually the society preferred to send their envoys in pairs at most, seeking to keep their presence in the politics of the lands an open secret rather than an outright obviousness.

So, when Ekene had heard that a group of nine men—all armed and all claiming to be envoys of the šef—had arrived, he'd been quick to accept their audience.

And with that, he thought privately, his gaze drifting over the crowd below, *the gathering of the insects.*

The nobility of Karesh Syl looked like nothing short of a hundred colorful birds flocking around a watering hole. They milled about now that Ekene had taken his seat, moving in groups, each more lavish than the last. The ladies of the city looked as though they'd spent most of the morning preparing for whatever excitement they might be privy to once his guests arrived, their ringed black hair rowed or woven into feathers and jewels and metal plates of a thousand different colors, their dresses and gowns looking as though each was trying to out-scandalize the others. The men appeared more reserved, a few among them even looking to be murmuring seriously to one another, but all the same the trims of their coats were lined with furs and gems, and several looked to have what appeared to be live snakes wound about their necks. Ekene had heard that such a fashion was coming into prevalence. One of his wives had even asked him for a python a few nights before.

The Tash had had her lashed for daring to bleat such brazen idiocy in his presence.

Ekene forced himself to look around at Naizer. "What do you know of these 'envoys'?"

The Second Hand frowned, his cropped black beard twisting and his bald head shining as he leaned over. "Likely not much more than you've been told," he said quietly. "Nine men, in simple clothes. General Saresh almost turned them away at the gate until one presented him with a scroll sealed with the Mahsadën's mark. Your 'Third'—" he said the title with blatant repugnance "—believes to know from which city the men have come."

"Oh?" Ekene asked, curious.

Naizer nodded. "He suspects they hail from Miropa."

That caught the Tash's attention. Miropa, the Gem of the South. Each of the fringe cities had their own ring within the Mahsadën, but Miropa was largely considered the most powerful of the municipalities, even by Perce. Beyond that, it was said that the place was now controlled by a *single* šef, a cripple who'd survived the massacre of his betters the summer before and had somehow pulled the tattered remnants of the society together under his boot.

If these envoys were from *this* man, this audience might be worth having after all…

At that exact moment, there was a *clunk* as the massive iron-bound doors at the other end of the hall were unlocked from the outside and began to grind open. The court itself was largely beneath the earth, with only the top quarter of the chamber extending over the ground above them. A line of thick glass plates crowned the apex of the ceiling, however, casting a long pillar of light to bisect the room from one end to the other, and after a second the old Tash made out a number of shadows moving toward them, flickering in the dust settling through the Sun's rays. There were nine in all, he counted quickly, moving in three rows of three, flanked on either side by armed guards in spiked helms bearing kite shields in one hand while the other rested on the hilts of their matching swords. They wore loose, plain tunics of various materials of both Southern and Percian make, and had it been any other group Ekene would have had them thrown to the lions for daring to present themselves to his court in such a state of disarray.

Instead, though, the Tash couldn't help but feel a chill as the men approached, moving together with such quiet confidence they might have been a pack of wolves. Their grey eyes flicked steadily about the room, taking in every detail of the place. The high ceiling, the polished marble floors, the white banners woven with the crossed golden spears of the city that fluttered from the pillars. They seemed to miss nothing, only one of them not casting about as though memorizing the space around them. This man led them, walking slightly ahead of the other eight, his own eyes fixed on the thrones. Ekene didn't know why—there was nothing particularly different about this one figure compared to the others trailing behind him—but he had the distinct impression that this man in particular was not one to be trifled with. Each of the envoys had had their weapons confiscated at the palace gates, of course, but there was something strikingly lethal about the leader of the group, clearly just as confident without a sword as he might have been with one.

Ekene knew of only one other man who moved with such lithesome deadliness, like a cobra shifting silently through high grass.

"Koro," he said under his breath, speaking to the empty air, "be ready."

Nothing answered his command, not the faintest clink of metal or shift of leather, but Ekene felt better all the same.

"The šef bid you well, Your Greatness, Tash of the great city of Karesh Syl."

The envoys had reached the bottom of the dais and taken a knee, most of them bowing their heads respectfully. Only their leader, half-a-step before the men on either side of him, was looking up at Ekene, hailing him.

"I am Na'zeem," he continued in a calm, firm voice. "I bring news from the fringe cities, as well as a plea for your assistance from my master."

"Right into it, then?" Naizer muttered in irritation from Ekene's left.

The Tash ignored him.

"Should you be who you claim, my home welcomes you, strangers," Ekene answered formally, lifting a wizened hand and sweeping it across his court. "I understand you bear a letter from your betters that may confirm this?"

The man—Na'zeem—nodded, motioning to a soldier at his right. "It was claimed by your guard, Your Greatness. They will need provide it to you."

The soldier procured the roll of parchment from behind his shield at once, moving toward the throne. He stopped several feet from the bottom of the dais, not daring to get within even a foot of the lowest step. Ekene gave his Second a nod, and Naizer heaved himself up with a grumble, hurrying down to the court floor.

Snatching the letter from the solider without so much as a glance at the man himself, he moved back up the steps, studying it as he climbed.

"The seal looks real," Naizer told Ekene so that only he could hear. "I would assume it is safe to open."

The Tash held out his hand, and his Second deposited the scroll in his palm before returning to his own throne.

It took a moment or two for Ekene's shaking fingers to break the wax insignia, a black circle embossed with a curving letter "M". When he managed, he unrolled the parchment carefully in his lap, squinting down at it. After his tired eyes finally found their focus, he read the contents slowly, carefully taking in the words, his mood growing more troubled with every line. When he finished, he handed the message back to Naizer, then addressed the kneeling group on the court floor.

"'Adrion Blaeth.'" He quoted the signature which had been scrawled along the bottom of the page. "At last I put a name to this infamous master of Miropa."

For the first time, Na'zeem twitched, his face—only for the briefest instant—curling involuntarily into something like irritation. When he spoke, though, his voice was even. Ekene made no comment to the behavior, but noted it well.

A man who did not respect his master was a man who needed to be watched.

"A great man," Na'zeem agreed. "And the danger he wishes to warn you of is just as great."

"'Raz i'Syul Arro,'" Naizer iterated from the Tash's left, his eyes still on the letter. "We've heard that name before, I believe. Some months ago..."

"Yes..." Ekene said slowly, pretending he needed a moment to place the name. "The atherian responsible for the death of the former šef of Miropa. I recall. We hosted many riders, carrying the news and spreading word of the bounty." He paused, considering the figures still kneeling below him. "You believe he is coming here? To Perce?"

In response, Na'zeem looked over his shoulder at the man on one knee at his right. "Speak," he commanded simply.

At once, this second face lifted to the Tash.

"I have it on good authority that the Monster sails south even as we speak," the man said. He was younger than his superior, but carried himself with nearly all the same calm power. "A captain, in a smuggler's hideaway along the eastern coast of the Northern realm. He assured me the atherian boarded a vessel headed for your shores, great Tash, a ship dubbed 'the *Sylgid*.'"

Ekene glanced at Naizer, but when his Second shook his head he turned back to the speaker. "We do not know of this vessel. When did you hear of this news?"

"Ehmed gathered this information nearly seven weeks past, great Tash." It was Na'zeem who spoke again now, and his man—Ehmed—ducked his head respectfully again. "It has taken us that many weeks to assemble and ride hard for your lands to deliver it."

"If you intended to do nothing more than 'deliver news,' a bird would have sufficed," Ekene said stiffly, shifting to sit more comfortably in his throne. "What is this 'assistance' you seek?"

Na'zeem bobbed his head in agreement. "Indeed, great Tash. We come personally because we have been tasked by our master with delivering the head of the Monster ourselves. In the lands of the South and North, he wouldn't have been hard to track. Within your borders, however..."

"He'll have an easier time moving in plain sight," Naizer finished, rubbing his cheek thoughtfully. "Yes. I can see how that would be a problem..."

"What is it you would ask of us?" Ekene demanded, resting his elbows on the arms of his seat and leaning forward. "A trap, I'm assuming?"

Na'zeem, though, shook his head. "No, great Tash," he said. "At least not as of yet. We do not at present know where or when the beast will land. He could already be on your shores. Your esteemed Second—" he nodded respectfully to Naizer "—is correct, however. Even winged, it would be easy enough for Arro to conceal himself among the enslaved of his kind. It will be difficult to rout him alone."

"'Alone?'" the Tash repeated with a frown. "You imply he travels with others?"

"One other," Na'zeem corrected, and a cruel smile spread across his face. "A woman. A Laorin Priestess of some renown, named Syrah Brahnt."

"Brahnt?" Ekene rolled the strange syllables over his tongue curiously. He had heard of the Laorin, a faith of pacifists and mages, but he knew little about the specifics of their ranks and practices. "So he travels with a Northerner. How does that help us? Our borders are open. She will not be the only fair-skinned woman in the land, even in the company of lizard-kind."

"You might be surprised," Na'zeem said, his smile growing wider. "Syrah Brahnt is an albino, and has only one eye."

Ekene raised an eyebrow. "An albino, you say? And one eye…" He leaned back in his chair, contemplating this.

The lands of Perce were not as harsh as the Cienbal and the fringe cities north of them. It was a verdant, lusher land, a place where the Sun's gaze was kinder in the day and the nights—under the watchful eye of the Moon and Her Stars—were always cool and pleasant even in summer. Albinos were not unheard of, to be sure. They were curiosities, in fact, often sold by parents to the slavers for a good price at a young age, but they could survive nonetheless. Still… an albino woman, and with only one eye…

Surely she wouldn't be *that* hard to find.

"And in exchange for my assistance?" Ekene boomed. "What is your master willing to offer? I assume you don't expect me to grant the services of my spies and soldiers freely."

"Certainly not," Na'zeem answered with a nod. "The bounty for Arro's head stands at twenty thousand, and it appears the Priestess has earned a price on hers as well. Some five thousand Northern gold."

"Just over twenty-six thousand, five hundred Southern crowns total," Naizer whispered to Ekene, doing some quick conversions. "A sizable sum."

Despite this, the Tash narrowed his black eyes at the group below. He knew well how to play the negotiator. "A mere pittance," he said flatly. "Barely what I allow my attendants to spend on clothes and perfumes for my wives. Come, surely your šef knows to do better than that."

Na'zeem no longer looked amused. His eyes were cold, dead things, and his mouth was a flat line.

"I have been given permission, also," he said flatly, "to offer Your Greatness a deduction on all heads provided by the Mahsadën through the fullness of the next cool season."

To Ekene's left, Naizer sat forward abruptly. "What sort of deduction?" he asked almost greedily.

"Three percent."

Naizer's eyes went wide, and he drew an abacus from the sleeves of his robes—a sort of wooden frame with hollowed beads slotted across a number of perpendicular iron rods, used for calculating sums. With a dozen quick motions he did the maths, and when he looked around at the Tash he seemed impressed.

"Nearly two hundred thousand crowns," he said in a hissed whisper. "Assuming averages of the last five seasons."

Ekene couldn't keep the surprise from passing over his face. "Your master must desire this 'Monster's' head quite desperately, to offer that," he said, turning back to Na'zeem. Then he narrowed his eyes again. "I assume I am expected to provide you and your men with food and lodgings in the meantime? If I had to venture a guess—" his eyes moved over the nine kneeling forms "—I would say you plan to see this through to the end."

Na'zeem nodded slowly. "You will find us very useful, I think, once we root out the lizard and his whore. He owes us a debt, you see. In the meantime, I am to place myself and my men at your disposal."

Ekene grunted at that, then sat back in his throne and waved them away. "Have word sent to Blaeth that I accept his proposal. My Second—" he glanced at Naizer "—will see to it that you are housed and fed, as well as provided with clean clothes and servants."

"With pleasure," Naizer said quickly, standing up and brushing out the creases from his robes before starting down the dais. "Anything to get out of that damn chair."

"Thank you, Your Greatness," Na'zeem said, standing up. The other eight copied him as quickly as reflections in a mirror. "My master will be most pleased."

Ekene mumbled something, pretending he held little interest in them now that the matter was done. He watched, though, as Na'zeem and his men followed Naizer out of the hall again, still flanked on either side by the palace guard. When they were gone, the courtiers—who had been mercifully stricken into silence throughout the entire audience—all began talking at once. For a minute or two Ekene allowed the drone of their voices to wash against him, he himself sitting quietly as he turned over this new information in his head.

When he'd had enough, the Tash sat up straight in his chair, pointing to the doors.

"All of you!" he thundered. "Out!"

Silence fell over the room at once, and a hundred faces turned toward him.

"Your Greatness," simpering Lord Ubede Nyko began, braving an approach of the dais, "should we not stay? Perhaps you will be in need of our council. The Monster of Karth is a subject of great interest to all our—"

"I couldn't care less what fuels your circles of gossips, Nyko" Ekene snarled. "As for your council: when I need advice on how to powder my nose, I will ask for it. Now—and you are all fools to make me repeat myself—I. Said. OUT!"

This time his words struck true. The lords and ladies of the city sensed the danger, because with many bows and terrified glances back at him, they scurried for the open doors. Ekene watched them hasten up the great steps to the entrance, many of the women tripping over dresses that were too long or losing shoes so ludicrous they never should have been thought of in the first place. When the last of the nobles had gone, vanishing up to the palace's ground floor, the Tash leaned back.

"Koro. Attend me."

This time, in the absolute silence of the hall, Ekene heard the whisper of movement behind him. Like a wraith, a man appeared at his side, stepping out from behind his throne to stand at his left, between his seat and Naizer's recently vacated one. He was dressed all in black, his leather armor and the dyed hilt of his sword all as dark as his skin, making him seem like night made real. Only the whites of his eyes contrasted with the rest of his figure, and when his spoke his teeth were bright behind his lips.

"You were right to fear that man," the Third Hand said. "Na'zeem. He seems to possess all the potential of a powerful adversary."

"Or ally," Ekene said, looking down at the spot the man in question had been kneeling. "Truthfully, he reminded me of you."

The Third Hand smirked at the thought, and it was a look that sent a shiver up the Tash's spine. The man had appeared in his bedchambers some six months past without so much as a whisper, much less a cry of alarm from the soldiers of the palace. Once he'd made it clear he intended to do Ekene no harm, the Tash had immediately taken him into his service, informing only Yseri and Naizer of the choice. Koro was not well-loved by either of the other Hands, but—in Ekene's opinion—had of late proven more useful than both of the others put together.

"So Arro comes here?" the Third said pensively. "Good."

"Could you defeat him, if it came down to it?" the Tash asked, watching the man carefully. "Your spies speak of him like they would a ghost, or a god. They call him 'Dragon' now, correct?"

The man nodded, his dark eyes on the light of the Sun streaming through the glass above them. "They do. I'm told he earned that title besting the greatest warrior of the Northern mountain clans. He is formidable, without a doubt. Perhaps even more so now than when I knew him."

"But can you beat him?" Ekene repeated, annoyed.

Beside him, the man's eyes narrowed as he considered the variables. "Alone? Doubtful. With some help from our new friends, though…" His gaze dropped down to where Na'zeem and his men had knelt. "Clearly I am not the only one holding a grudge. Assuming these 'envoys' could have killed everyone in this room without so much as batting an eye, nine seems an odd number for such a detachment, doesn't it?"

"You think there are more?" the Tash asked with a frown, suddenly fearing *more* visitors in the night.

"No," the Third said with a shake of his head. "I think there *were* more."

The chill within Ekene deepened.

Dragon, he thought privately. *What kind of beast has the Sun seen fit to deliver onto my lands?*

"See to it," he said sharply. "I put Na'zeem and his company in your hands. I want the lizard dead before he gets the idea that he can do to us what he did to the Mahsadën."

When the Third answered, his voice brimmed with nothing short of predatory anticipation.

"With pleasure," Azzeki Koro said.

XXV

"Is it not fascinating to consider the varied cultures of the world? Even within the borders of any known realm, society splits and diverges. The city-dwellers of the South, for example, have little in common with the nomadic trade caravans or the desert mercenaries they call the 'sarydâ.' To the North, it is only the will of the Laorin that maintains a tentative balance between the valley towns and the men of the mountain clans. Most interesting—and terrible—of all, though, are the savannahs of Perce, where the citizens of Karesh Syl and Karesh Nan wish nothing more than to bring the wild kuja under their thumb, all while ignoring the largely more savage culture which has bred itself along their coasts…"

—*An Expanded Study of the Modern World,* by Adolûs Fenn

Almost two weeks after the storm had nearly dragged them to the bottom of the sea, the call came. Raz was in the captain's quarters, playing an odd game of cards and dice with Argoan on the small table bolted into the corner of the cabin, when they heard the shout. At first it was faint, dulled by the closed door, but as Raz's ears perked up he made out the word clearly when it came again.

"Land," he repeated for the captain. "They've spotted the coast."

Argoan blinked in surprise, then his painted face split into a grin. "See?" he asked gruffly, hurrying to scoot himself from under the table and climb to his feet. "Told you I'd get you there without much trouble."

Raz snorted. While Garht Argoan had never outright thanked him or Syrah for saving his life, the man had made his appreciation clear in other ways. They'd spoken in the weeks before the storm, of course, even been friendly at times, but as their journey came to a close the captain seemed intent on making it clear their assistance had not gone unnoticed. He'd taken to inviting the pair of them to share meals with him, which meant much better rations than the hardtack and salted meat in the crew's quarters. What leisure time his position allowed he sought to spend teaching them the ways of the sea, and the little the pair of them had picked up in the first month-and-a-half of the passage was soon eclipsed by everything they took in under the captain's guidance. They'd spent several days learning how to harness the wind from any direction by shifting the angle of the sails, then how to measure depth and speed using knotted ropes dipped into the water. He'd shown them how to communicate between other vessels they passed in the trade lanes via a pair of small mirrors he and Lysa kept in their pockets, then even how to handle the ship's wheel itself. Most useful of all, on clear evenings he convinced them to leave the warmth of their lodgings to learn how to read Her Stars, showing them how to navigate by night. Before long, both Raz and Syrah felt as though they could have helmed the *Sylgid* on their own.

By the time they entered Percian waters, Argoan—despite apparently being unable to voice his gratitude aloud—had made it clear they'd earned their places aboard his ship several times over.

As the captain passed him, Raz threw his cards on the table and stood to follow the man. He blinked against the brightness of the day when Argoan pushed open the cabin door, shading his eyes before stepping out into the Sun. It was another mercifully clear day. The gulls, which had returned to the ship earlier that morning, seemed to have multiplied in the hours they'd wasted away at their games, circling the masts and settling to flap their wings and call to one another along the railings of the ship. The sails—the main having long since been repaired and brought to bear again over a spare oar they'd whittled down to replace the broken boom—fluttered gently in a calm wind. The sky was mottled blue, peppered by a scattering of wispy clouds that did nothing to block the Sun's glare at its peak high above them. As Raz glanced skyward, closing one eye and squinting up with the other, he made out the hazy outline of the crow's nest at the very top of the rigging. A sailor—he couldn't make out who against the light—was still calling out, pointing westward.

"LAND!"

Together, Raz and Argoan joined two score of the others on the deck below in turning in the direction the lookout was indicating. There, like a rippling mirage, the horizon had gone from a shivering line of white and blue to a darker band of tan, brown, and green. Even Raz couldn't see much through the undulating heat, but as he peered at the approaching shore he could just barely make out the broad leaves of palm trees and the pale sands of a broad, barren beach.

"Perce?" he asked the captain.

In response, there was a familiar *click-click*, and Raz glanced over his shoulder to see Argoan bringing his spyglass up to his eye. After a moment the captain took it down again, then offered it to him.

"Aye," Argoan said with a frown and a nod as Raz accepted and lifted the instrument to peer through its eyepiece. "Though we've still at least half-a-week of sailing before making port. We're a fair ways more north than I thought, judging by the thinness of the trees."

Raz didn't miss the worry in the man's voice as he made out the shore in truth. Indeed, the palms stretched as far as he could see in either direction, by they were small and sparse, nothing more impressive than anything he'd seen along the Garin or the shores of the Emperor's Ocean around Acrosia.

"Why do I get the feeling that's not good news…?" Raz asked, bringing the glass down to squint at the horizon again.

Argoan chewed at the corner of his lip nervously. For a man who'd literally laughed in the face of a storm that had nearly pulled him to the bottom of the ocean, it was a concerning expression.

"Nothing we should have to worry about," he answered after a moment's contemplation. "The shore villages and I have a long-standing bargain. We shouldn't have any trouble from them."

Raz stared at him blankly, making it clear he wasn't about to let the man off so easily.

Argoan sighed. "The locals survive mostly off fishing and pirating. There aren't enough ships that pass seasonally for them to ransack without scaring the rest away, so they strike deals with most of the captains who sail through their waters. They make some easy gold, and we get to pass by undisturbed. Nothing complicated."

Raz whistled darkly. "First storms, then pirates. I'm glad we didn't run into any sea monsters, or I'd start to think I was living in some far-fetched fantasy."

Argoan paled as he said this, then mumbled something quick and unintelligible Raz was fairly sure was a prayer in the man's native tongue.

"Don't speak of such creatures, Dahgün," he said when he was done, licking his lips and glancing down at the water shimmering below them. "It is bad luck to summon their names aboard a ship."

Raz hid a smirk by looking down at the main deck of the boat. Along the portside banister, facing west, more men and women had gathered to gaze out at the shore in the distance. Among them he quickly made out an oddity, a pair of women, one in what looked like a white hood, and he had to stop himself from laughing again.

"Let's pray your bargain holds firm, Captain," Raz said with a chuckle, moving around the man and handing him back the spyglass as he made for the steps behind him. "I can't imagine what beasts would turn up if I have to toss a bunch of dead pirates into the sea."

Then, laughing to himself as Argoan cursed under his breath, Raz descended to the deck.

The men and women of the ship's company had embraced the heat of the day with a lazy fervor, stripping down to nothing more than pants or shorts and thin shirts as they went about their tasks. Some, with nothing to do in the kinder climates of these strange waters, were lounging about in the ratlines, or seated over the edge of the *Sylgid*'s rails, enjoying what sea spray they could get to cool themselves off. As Raz passed by and beneath them, several called out asking if the crew would get to spar that afternoon, but he gave them vague answers and generally dodged the questions, distracted by the figures still leaning over the portside banister.

"You look hot enough to enjoy a dip," he said roguishly, coming up behind the closest of the women. "Shall I toss you over?"

Syrah turned on him at once, glaring. At least, he suspected she was glaring. Her face was largely hidden, masked behind a pale veil of thin silk that hung from a wide hood of the same fabric she'd pulled up over her head. He could only make out the vaguest details of her features through the cloth, as well as the distinct black outline of her eye-wraps against the paleness of her skin, but even that was enough to tell him she wasn't happy with her situation.

"Damn your sun, Southerner," she said in a huff, glancing up at the sky in annoyance. "I would have preferred to say I'd seen the last of these clothes. If we ever return to the North, I swear by the Lifegiver I'm burning them and dancing for joy around the fire."

There was a chuckle, and at Syrah's side Lysa turned to lean back against the rail, looking the Priestess up and down. The pair had grown closer over the last fortnight, and could almost always be found together when Syrah wasn't with Raz. It was easier for her, he suspected. She could speak and touch Lysa as she pleased, whereas she still had trouble spending any time alone around the men of the crew, Argoan included.

"Oh, I don't know," the first mate said with a wink. "I think it suits you. You could be some noble's daughter, come in a veil of innocence to be given away to a Percian noble." She gave Raz a sidelong glance. "She'd make a fine bride, wouldn't she, Dragon?"

"Quit your teasing, Lysa," Raz grumbled, looking Syrah over himself, "or it will be *you* I throw overboard instead."

The Priestess had seen fit to bedeck herself only partially in the gifts the Laorin had provided her as they'd left the Citadel. Her hood was attached to a light robe that hung to her ankles, with sleeves that tapered to her wrists. She wasn't sporting the thin gloves and boots of bleached leather Raz knew she had stowed away somewhere in their cabin, and he couldn't blame her. She was likely to develop a sunburn on her hands and bare feet before the day was done, but he flashed back in that moment to the first time he had ever seen the woman, strolling along the market streets of Karth nearly a decade ago. He'd thought her mad to suffer the oppressive warmth of the clothes and, even now, in the more temperate light of the Percian shore as the cooler season began to take hold, he didn't envy her outfit.

"Stop staring," Syrah grumbled, snapping him out of his memories. "It's rude to stare."

Raz started. "Sorry," he said quickly, but he couldn't help but grin slightly. "I was just recalling the first time I saw you."

"Ooh, *here's* a story I need to hear," Lysa said scandalously, shoving herself up to sit on the banister as the ship swayed under their feet. "Do tell."

He wasn't sure, but Raz thought he saw Syrah smile beneath the veil. At the very least, she looked away from him, toward the first mate.

"You're terrible," she said with a snort. "It's nothing like that. Raz just..." She hesitated. "He pulled me from a dangerous situation. That's all."

Raz thought he knew why she seemed tentative. His rescue of her had been the trigger that had burned his old life to the ground. There had been a time, in fact, when he had tried to blame her, tried to hate her for that fact.

He'd never managed it.

"A *very* dangerous situation," he prompted her, pretending to egg her on, hoping she would understand that it was all right. "Syrah had managed to get herself trapped by some local slavers."

"*Slavers?*" Lysa said, sounding amazed. "How?"

"They tricked me," Syrah said, sounding relieved that Raz appeared to be comfortable talking about the subject. "One of them—Bastard. I still remember his rat face—fooled me into thinking he needed my help. From there…"

After that, they spent much of the afternoon in Lysa's company, trading tales with the woman. Argoan joined them several times, at one point uncorking a rare bottle of wine for the four of them to share as they ate an early supper on the *Sylgid*'s raised bow. It was a pleasant evening, all in all, and as night fell and the Moon and Her Stars appeared once more across the heavens, Raz couldn't help but begin to feel a building excitement stoking itself to life in his gut. As the four of them talked, exchanging stories of their lives and the people they had met over the course of their adventures, Raz could feel the shores of Perce gliding by at his back, a presence that pulled at him like someone calling his name from far away. They'd drifted closer over the course of the day, the horizon growing more distinct, and the trees had thickened and grown as they'd moved further south, hinting at the verdant splendor he and Syrah had been promised. He was starting to feel—despite whatever evils and cruelties lurked in these new lands—that thrill of eagerness which inevitably comes with the discovery and exploration of new worlds. He recalled his elation upon stepping over the Southern border into the North, then his awe when he'd first set eyes upon the great city of Azbar, thousands of stone-and-timber homes enwalled against a bottomless canyon. He remembered the breathtaking minutes it had taken the silence of winter to settle over him as he'd ridden into the Arocklen Woods, then the sense of infinite irrelevance when the ramparts of Cyurgi 'Di had risen above him for the first time, looming out of the winter storms.

Maybe, just maybe, the Twins would be kind, and he and Syrah would be allowed a moment or two like those before the hardships of Perce came to weigh down upon them.

Whoosh! Whack-whack-whack!

"Good!" Raz said, backing away from Syrah and shouting to the crew gathered in their familiar spaces about the deck and above them. "Now, watch carefully. Syrah is going to disarm me in three moves, then sweep my knee and take me to the ground. Are you ready to—?"

Wham!

Raz staggered back, the unexpected blow catching him in the stomach. Fortunately the woman pulled the strike, or he would probably have had trouble breathing. He'd just started to recover, bringing his gladius up defensively, when the steel of Syrah's staff looped under the sword's cross-guard and twisted it out of his hand. An instant later the other end of the staff took him in the back of his left leg, and he twisted as he dropped to one knee.

There was a roar of approval and amusement from the crew, several whistling and shouting good-natured insults as Raz fell.

"What was that you said?" Syrah asked sweetly, moving to bend over him, one hand around her staff and the other planted at her hip. "Did you say 'three' moves to disarm you?"

"Apparently, I was mistaken," he grumbled with a snort, picking up his blade from the deck before shoving himself back up to cower before the woman in mock fear. "I've definitely taught you too well."

Syrah feigned an indignant scowl. "'*You've*' taught me too well?" she scoffed. "Talo is rolling in his grave at the thought that you would claim credit for all his hard work."

Raz chuckled, sheathing the blade over his shoulder. Syrah had been able to forgo the hooded robe and veil the previous day had forced her into. It was another bright day, but the sky was studded with clouds that fell thickly over the Sun every few minutes, and the heat was much more tolerable. Her white hair had grown over the course of their journey, well past her shoulders, and she'd allowed Lysa to wind it into a plait that fell along one side of her neck. The scarred remnant of her right ear was bared to the wind, and Raz was almost pleased to see it. She was becoming more comfortable with herself, comfortable with the hard sacrifices she'd had to make to survive. It was good to see her laughing again, especially in the company of other men.

"All right, settle down!" Raz shouted to the crowd, raising both hands as he looked around at the gathered crew. "Believe it or not, it isn't the first time I've lost a fight, and I doubt it'll be the last. Now, did everyone see how Syrah did that?"

There were scattered mutters and general nodding from everywhere.

"Excellent!" Raz clapped his hands together as Syrah moved to sit down again. "The let's have volunteers. Three pairs, alternating offense and defense. Who would like to—?"

He was about to start picking from arms, already being thrown in the air, when a shout cut Raz short.

"PERCIAN SAILS! PORT AND BOW! PERCIAN SAILS!"

There wasn't more than half-a-moment of stillness as the words reverberated over the emptiness of the ocean.

Then everyone leapt up at once.

From an outsider's view, it would have seemed then that the deck of the *Sylgid* had been thrown into instant chaos. Men and women rushed about this way and that, calling to one another as they did. Some climbed up into the masts, while others scattered along the portside railing. For almost a minute they milled like bees, the nervous buzz of excitement and concern palpable in the thrum of their voices. Over everything, the captain and his first mate could be heard shouting orders, the former calling out names and assigning posts and positions, the latter ordering for weapons and supplies to be brought up from below deck.

When the ship finally settled, however, it could not have been more apparent that there had been a distinct order to all that commotion. A solid line of sailors stood at the portside railing, blades sheathed but every hand on the hilt of their swords and daggers. Above their heads, a dozen others had perched themselves in the rigging and were busy stringing shortbows—retrieved from the stores at Lyra's command—and checking their quivers of arrows were well stocked. Tension was palpable in the air, not helped by the fact that someone must have disturbed the horses below deck, because the animals were now screaming shrilly and stomping against the wooden floor of their lodgings.

They had come across other vessels over the last month. It was nothing unusual. They were—aside from the few days they'd lost making repairs after being pushed several miles out to sea by the storm—largely using the common trade lanes that spanned the eastern seaboard of the world. It was bound to happen. On each of those occasions, no alarm had ever been raised, no cause for concern ever made.

Now, though, the lookout in the nest above had made a distinction.

Percian sails.

Raz had pulled Syrah out of the way as soon as the crew started running about around them, tucking them both against the covered crates and cargo in the center of the ship that had survived the journey. As everything stilled, he glanced toward the stern.

"Let's see what's going on," he said, jabbing a thumb to indicate the aft-deck. Syrah glanced in the direction he was pointing, then nodded. Together they hurried along the clear starboard rail, making for the steps that led up to the helm.

Lysa appeared to be among those lined up along the portside, but the captain was still at the wheel, the diagonal red lines across his face wrinkled as he frowned toward the southwest. Raz and Syrah had just started up the stairs when he caught sight of them, and he blanched.

"No!" he hissed, his voice a shrill whisper, like he was afraid of being overheard. "Down! Stay *down!*"

Raz and Syrah both froze, then crouched. From their place at the bottom of the steps they could barely make out Argoan's head over the lip of the stern.

"What's going on?" Syrah asked him impatiently. Her question was apparently louder than the captain was comfortable with, because he stiffened.

"Probably nothing," he told her in a voice steadier than his posture conveyed, but he glanced down at Raz. "A ship from one of the local villages I was telling you about yesterday. They're likely just looking to collect their fee for passage."

Raz nodded. Once again, though, the captain's nervousness did not make him feel any better.

"What should we do?" he asked, glancing south and west. Over the heads of the *Sylgid*'s crew, he could just make out the indistinct shape of grey and maroon sails in the distance. "Do you want us to be ready?"

"No," Argoan said quickly. "I don't want to put the crew more on edge than they have to be. These exchanges are always tense enough already. Have you seen Lysa?"

Raz and Syrah shook their heads.

"Find her," the captain ordered, turning the helm slightly east as the nose of the *Sylgid* started to drift toward the shore. "Tell her to get you into the hatch, and quick. Go!"

With a nod, Raz took Syrah's hand and—still staying low as he moved—led her back up the ship.

They found the first mate near the bow, holding onto a tethering line as she leaned out over the water, her free hand shielding her eyes to peer at the approaching ship. They caught her attention, getting her to swing back down onto the deck, and she frowned as they relayed the captain's orders.

"The hatch?" she said, looking disconcerted as she continued, apparently mumbling to herself. "If he thinks they might search the ship, then he's more worried than he's letting on…"

Then she looked up, her green-blue eyes fiery.

"Follow me."

Still holding on to each other, Raz and Syrah trailed the first mate back toward the stern once again, careful to stay below the heads of the sailors standing shoulder-to-shoulder to their left. Without pausing, Lysa led them down the looped stairs to the hull, stepping out into the rowing galley and hurrying across the walking platform that bisected it. From there they moved through the crew's quarters, then into the stores, Gale and Nymara's screams getting louder with every step.

"You'll have to calm the horses," Lysa said hurriedly, pulling open the door to the last compartment, where the animals were kept. "The hatch is beneath them."

"Beneath them?" Raz repeated in surprise, but Lysa didn't reply. Instead, she stepped into the space, motioning that they follow her at once.

The place stank of horse, as it had for the better part of the journey. The floor was cleared daily of manure and loose feed, and the straw had been changed every week or so, but there is only so much one can do when confining a pair of animals the size of Gale and Nymara into a space they could barely pace around. They'd settled into the journey well enough at first—better than either Raz or Syrah, in fact—but ever since the storm they'd grown increasingly restless. Now the hull was dented in a dozen places with hoofprint-shaped depressions, and the wood around the door was starting to splinter from being gnawed at. The horses themselves settled when Raz and

Syrah stepped into the compartment, but they still hoofed and snuffled nervously, sidestepping and bobbing with the motion of the ocean.

"Shh, boy," Raz said gently, moving over to Gale quickly as Syrah did the same with Nymara. "Hush now. We're almost there. Another few days. I need you to be quiet now, though. Quiet."

The stallion calmed further at Raz touch, bowing his black head to allow his muzzle to be stroked.

"Move them out of the way," Lysa said after she'd allowed a few seconds for the animals to understand that they were safe. "As far to the sides as possible."

It took some time and maneuvering, but they managed it. When Gale and Nymara stood on either side of the hull, Lysa got to one knee and started shuffling around in the thick straw, ignoring the droppings that hadn't been cleaned out yet. After a minute or so of searching, she appeared to find what she was looking for, and with a grunt of victory she pulled upward with both hands.

With a creak of hidden hinges, two doors, each about a third the width of the room, opened toward the ceiling. Gale and Nymara snorted and stomped again as the secret hatch was revealed, but Raz and Syrah kept them quiet. Then, together, they stepped away from the horses to peer down through the opening.

It was a smuggler's compartment, that much was obvious. It seemed silly, thinking about it now, that Raz hadn't considered the fact that the *Sylgid* likely had any number of similar hiding places, given the nature of the ship's purpose. He wondered, abruptly, how many concealed nooks and hideaways he had walked past or over, never glancing at them twice. He doubted any of them were half as large as the one before them now, though, or as cluttered. At a glance he made out dozens of different items, all carefully tucked against each other. Several large timber chests, wooden crates of all sizes, and a pair of massive clay jars sealed with paper and marked with the word "pork" in Northern script had been shoved under the floor beneath their feet, making it clear the hatch extended further than just the expanse directly below the opening. A number of heavy carpets of fine-looking craftsmanship were rolled up lengthwise in the center of the space, penned in by a multitude of smaller items. A couple of statues, a bundle of plain steel weapons, canvas bags that looked like they might have been filled with books. It felt, to Raz, like seeing a treasure cave opened up before him, enticing him to enter. The hatch had an old, musty scent to it that added to this illusion, like some ancient tomb, though the faintest trace of vinegar and brine wafted from the sealed pots.

"Get in," Lysa told them, looking over her shoulder nervously, as though she expected someone to be lurking through the ship behind them. "Hurry."

Raz and Syrah glanced at each other, and the Priestess shrugged. With a final comforting pat to Nymara's neck, she stepped around the door and into the pit, putting a foot atop what looked like a small, gold-gilded table before easing herself onto the rolled carpets. Resting her staff lengthwise beside her, she laid down over the woven cloth like a bed.

With a grimace, Raz followed her lead.

When they were both side-by-side, Lysa eased the doors closed over them again. Raz felt a wrench in his gut as the hatch shut with a *thud* over them, shaking loose pieces of straw and splinters across their faces. Through some slim gaps in the boards, he made out the first mate bending down again.

"Stay quiet, and stay still," she said. "I'll come get you when our business is done."

"What if you need us?" Raz asked her, his own voice loud against his ears in the tight confines. By the Sun, he *hated* cramped spaces.

Lysa laughed dryly. "If you hear screaming, then I guess you'd both better come running."

Then, with several sweeps of her hands, she covered the boards in straw again, walked out of the storeroom, and shut the door behind her, leaving the pair of them in near-total darkness.

XXVI

Neither Raz nor Syrah knew how long they stayed like that, tucked beneath the boards of the storeroom as Gale and Nymara clomped about above them, sniffing curiously at the floor. Of course, neither of them managed to stay quiet long, and soon they were whispering about what the worst-case scenarios of their situation might be. Syrah was worried the approaching Percian knew they were on board. Raz feared the same thing, but didn't say so, filling her in instead on what the captain had told him about local pirates demanding fees in exchange for safe passage.

"*Pirates?*" Syrah had hissed in shock at this.

In the end, though, they agreed there was nothing to be done about it, and so they waited in the dark. At one point, the crueler part of Raz's mind got the better of him, and—as soon as the horses had cleared the doors— he'd reached with both hands to press up on the floor ever so slightly. It gave under his push, causing the animals to snort in annoyance near the back of the room. Syrah had snatched his hands away, giving him a glare through the gloom, but the fact that she didn't berate him made Raz think that, if only for a moment, she'd had the same fear. The doors, though, weren't locked.

The crew of the *Sylgid* did not seem intent on betraying them.

It must have been twenty minutes or so before Raz made out a new sound over the constant churning of the sea against the hull around them. It became rapidly more distinct, the swishing, churning gurgle of a ship—a different ship—cutting through water. As he thought this, he heard the distant voice of Garht Argoan shouting for the sails to be raised, and almost at once the *Sylgid* began to slow.

"They're near," he said into the darkness, feeling Syrah tense at his words. Instinctively he reached up, making sure the gladius was still slung across his back as he continued to listen.

Before long he could make out the groan of the approaching boat, feeling the presence growing closer. Eventually, the sound of it was right beside them, and the *Sylgid* stopped in truth, the wash of the sea stilling somewhat around them. There was a heavy *clunk* that sent a shudder through the entire ship, and Raz made out the faint strikes of booted feet on wood.

"Gangplank," he said, recalling the word Argoan had taught him as he reiterated what he heard for Syrah. "Men boarding the *Sylgid*."

Beside him, the Priestess lay in silence, listening intently.

"Voices," Raz said. "Can't make them out exactly. They're talking about… about fees? Yes. A fee. Argoan is asking them what the cost is this time." He frowned, not catching the sum. "He says he'll pay it. Lysa's not happy about it. Apparently it's too much."

He thought he saw Syrah's mouth twitch in the dark.

"She's arguing about passage fees when we're stuck in the hold?" she asked in amused exasperation.

"Probably trying to make things seem normal," Raz told her quickly. "I doubt there's a smuggler in the world who wouldn't try to bargain for a better deal. Now hush, they're talking again."

He listened hard, his brow furrowing.

"What is it?" Syrah asked, apparently unable to help herself.

"They want to search the ship," Raz answered with a frown. "I think… No, they won't say why. Lysa isn't happy again. She's telling them where they can search instead."

Syrah had to stifle a laugh, and Raz would have cracked a smile too, except that right then there was a faint storm of boots on wood.

"Some of the other crew have crossed over. A lot. I don't know how many. Lysa is *livid*, but it sounds like Argoan is telling her to let them look."

The boots moved across the deck, some hovering overhead, others moving down the ship. Nothing else seemed to happen for several minutes. Raz shut his eyes, trying to make out anything he could. There were shouts as men with Percian accents called out that they'd found nothing of interest. For a while, Raz hoped they'd gotten away without issue.

Then he heard footsteps coming down the stairs near the stern.

"They're coming," he hissed, his eyes snapping open and his hand moving to the grip of his gladius again. "Be ready."

Almost at once the air warmed around him. Syrah hadn't summoned her flames for obvious reasons, but Raz could feel her drawing strength into her body. The heat mixed with the dust and ever-lingering smell of vinegar in an unpleasant way.

The booted feet approached steadily, first taking their time along what he thought was the rowing galley, likely checking under every seat, then into the crew quarters, where they took even longer. It was at this point that Raz realized it wasn't a single set of steps he was hearing, but rather several. Three at least, maybe more. He started making out the voices more clearly, too, hearing them speak to one another in quiet tones they clearly thought no one could overhear.

"They're arguing about whether or not they should pilfer the crew quarters," Raz whispered to Syrah. "Apparently it's bad luck to steal from another sailor."

Syrah didn't answer, all her concentration apparently on her magic. Raz kept listening, picturing the men moving down the long cabin, then into the storage compartments. When they were right outside the door of Gale and Nymara's storeroom, he clicked the gladius loose ever so slightly, letting Syrah know. He felt her stiffen beside him, and the air rose another degree.

The door opened with a creak. Though he couldn't make out the details of their features through the layered straw, here and there he caught a glimpse of dark-skinned faces, and the glint of steel and iron.

"Horses?" one man asked aloud in the strange accent of his people, obviously surprised. "Why would they bother shipping horses?"

185

"Someone who thinks Percian breeds aren't good enough?" another offered, taking a step into the room. "Look at this beast." He moved toward where Raz was fairly sure Gale was standing. "A *fine* animal. Northern, without a doubt. What I wouldn't do for a—AYE!"

There was a snap and a huff, and the man leapt back, landing with a heavy *thud* directly over Syrah's head. It seemed the pirate had gotten too close to Gale, or offered his hand, and the stallion had attempted to take a bite out of him.

Good man, Raz thought, his eyes following the shadows through the straw above them.

"Bastard!" the man in question was cursing. "Nearly took my finger off!"

There was a guffaw of laughter from the other two.

"There's nothing here," one of them said through his chuckles. "Come, Ykero. Before the beast decides you look anything more like his midday meal."

There were further curses from the man who'd approached Gale—Ykero—as well as even more laughter from his companions, but a moment or two later they left. Raz heard them go, walking through the crew quarters and rowing galley much faster now, but it wasn't until he made out their footsteps on the stairs that he realized he'd been holding his breath.

He exhaled in a deep sigh of relief.

"Laor's mercy," Syrah muttered beside him, and Raz felt the temperature of the hatch start to cool as she let the spells go. "That was closer than I would have liked."

Raz nodded, but said nothing else. Above, voices were starting up again, but they were too garbled for him to make out. He heard what he thought had to be the clinking of gold being handed over, and a minute later there was a grind as the gangplank was lifted. Soon after he heard Argoan shout for the sails to be brought to full again, and then the *Sylgid* lurched and began moving once more. At the same time, Raz felt the presence of the other ship fade away, splitting west and south again, in the direction it had come.

"They're gone," he said finally, speaking in a normal voice. "The Percian ship is leaving."

Syrah was about to say something, but a hurry of footsteps cut her off. A few seconds later the door of the compartment opened above them, and Lysa's familiar voice called out.

"They've gone," she confirmed, shooing Nymara out of the way before bending down and brushing aside the straw once more. "Damn dogs wanted *twice* what they asked for last winter."

There was grind and a creak, and the doors lifted open over them.

Raz blinked as his eyes adjusted, sitting up. "No trouble, though?"

"Not that I could tell." The first mate shook her head, reaching out to offer Syrah a hand getting to her feet. "They wanted to search the ship, though. That seemed odd."

"A few of them came down here," Syrah said as she allowed herself to be hauled up onto the floor proper, her staff in one hand. "Gale chased them away." She reached out and gave the stallion an affectionate pet.

"They didn't say why they wanted to look, though?" Raz asked, heaving himself out of the hatch before turning and helping Lysa to close it behind them. "They didn't give you a reason?"

"None." With a *thud*, the hidden doors disappeared once again. Lysa spent a couple seconds kicking straw around to hide the handle thoroughly. "That had me worried, but if they found anything worth mentioning, they didn't say so in front of us. Still… It's bad for business, if they're insisting on searching every vessel they're demanding a fee from. Gonna make captains worry about carrying precious cargo."

"You think that's what they were after?" Syrah asked as she and Raz gave their horses one last pat before following the first mate out the door. "Precious cargo? Not us?"

Lyra didn't seem too sure. "I don't know…" She frowned as they passed through the crew quarters and into the rowing galley. "What are the chances we are the only ship being searched? They'd have to know you were aboard, and it certainly doesn't seem like they looked very hard."

"Maybe they found what they needed," Raz snorted. "Check to make sure all the diamonds and chests of gold you keep in plain sight are accounted for."

Lysa gave a dry laugh, but didn't say anything more as they started up the steps.

When they stepped back out onto the deck, the first thing Raz noted was that none of the tension had left the ship. Many of the crew were no longer lined along the portside, but no one had taken their eyes off the sea to the west. The ratlines and mast ropes were crawling with sailors, most of them shading their eyes to peer across the water. Weapons—swords and daggers and bows—hadn't been stowed away either. Frowning, Raz joined them in gazing out over the Dramion, making out the stern of a narrow two-masted vessel pulling away from them quickly.

All-in-all, it felt like no one was convinced the danger was over.

Argoan didn't turn to look at them as Lysa led the way over to stand beside him. His spyglass was collapsed in one hand, the other resting on the head of the hammer in his belt, and he was watching the pirate ship go with a distinctly unsettled expression.

"Problem?" Raz asked, and the captain finally glanced around at him.

"Don't know," he said truthfully, looking back over the sea at the withdrawing boat. "I don't like it, though. That search felt… targeted. They can't be asking that of every ship. Captains would stop sailing through their waters within the year."

"So you think they knew about us?" Syrah asked in a worried tone.

Argoan chewed on his lip, the bald pate of his monk's ring of long hair shining with perspiration. "I don't know what else would have given them cause. We're not hauling anything else of particular value. But how would they know?"

"Someone could have informed the Mahsadën," Raz said darkly. "A bird to the right place would be all it took."

On his other, Lysa bristled. "No one aboard this ship would do such a thing," she snapped defensively. "No one would go against the captain's wishes, much less his orders."

"I don't think Raz means anyone of the *Sylgid*," Syrah told her placatingly, reaching out to put a calming hand on the first mate's forearm. "There were a hundred other men in the Highest Mast. Two full crews who saw us arrive and leave with you."

Raz nodded. "And before that, Eva and her cohorts."

That made Syrah frown, turning to him. "You don't think…?"

"That Eva would have sold us out?" Raz completed her thought in a hard voice. "No. But her word that her employees wouldn't doesn't hold as firm for me. Not to mention the šef have more ways to extract information from an unwilling witness than I care to consider."

All of them were silent at that, if only for a second.

"But it doesn't matter," Lysa said with a relieved sort of sigh, plopping down to sit on a coil of rope by the mast behind her. "They didn't find anything, and they took the payment for safe passage. We should be in the clear, at least until we make port." She looked up at Argoan, who was still watching the grey and maroon sails of the ship in the distance. "How long before we arrive?"

"A day," Argoan said without turning. "Two at the most. Still, this business has me nervous. If word has reached Perce that you're arriving by ship, I wouldn't be surprised if trouble waits for us at the docks." He looked over his shoulder at Raz and Syrah. "Gather your things, and have everything ready to saddle your horses. We might do best to drop you off in the shallows north of the harbors tomorrow. Your mounts will have to swim for the shore, but at the very least you'll avoid—"

"Our things."

Everyone turned to look at Syrah, who'd cut the captain off. The woman had gone rigid, her eyes on the distant sails, her face losing what little color her pale skin allowed her. Her eye was wide, panicked almost, and Raz was about to ask her what was wrong when she spoke again.

"Our… our things," she repeated slowly, sounding as though some terrible realization had just dawned on her.

There was a brief pause as the other three stared at her. Lysa had just started to stand again, clearly intent on approaching her friend and asking what was the matter, when Syrah spun on her heel and bolted back to the stern.

"Syrah!" Raz called after her, starting to follow hesitantly. "Where are you going?"

The Priestess, though, didn't respond. Reaching the door of their guest quarters, she pulled it open and hurried inside. Before Raz could even look around at the others in confusion, though, Syrah stepped out into the light again, looking shaken.

Once more, her eye found the retreating stern of the pirate ship, and her expression was utterly horrified.

"Syrah?" Raz asked, more gently now, stepping toward her cautiously. "What is it? What are you thinking?"

When she spoke, though, it wasn't to him.

"Did they search our quarters?" she asked. Though her gaze never left the far-off sails, her question was obviously meant for Argoan and Lysa.

The first mate frowned, giving her captain a confused look before nodding. "Yes," she said curtly. "It was one of the first places they looked."

Abruptly, Raz understood. He gaped at Syrah, his eyes falling to the staff she still had in one hand, the weapon she had happened to be carrying when the call had come of Percian sails on the horizon. He himself had had his gladius, but...

"Ahna." Syrah told the others, her voice a tone of forced evenness. "Ahna is still on the floor of our cabin. They know we're aboard."

XXVII

The pirates returned within hours, and this time they brought friends.

There was no need for a lookout to shout a warning, now. The entire crew had been put on alert, and those not going about the minimum tasks of keeping the *Sylgid* moving south stood along the rails and in the masts, scanning the horizon in every direction for the first sign of the enemy. It was Raz, naturally, who spotted them first, making out the indistinct shapes against the tan-and-green line of the distant shore.

"There," he said calmly, pointing southwest with a steel claw. "Two ships."

He was in full gear, now, and for the first time in many years the steel plating felt heavy, his body unaccustomed to the weight after nearly two months without it. Ahna was slung over his right shoulder, retrieved from his and Syrah's lodgings, her curved blades gleaming dangerously in the Sun. He'd thrown his mantle back around his shoulders as well, allowing the white silk cape to flutter behind him in the ocean breeze.

If he didn't have the element of surprise, then at the very least he was going to do his dammed best to cut an intimidating figure.

At his left, manning the helm, Argoan squinted in the direction he was indicating, Lysa and Syrah doing the same on his right.

"You sure?" the captain asked grimly. "I don't see anything."

"Give Lysa the wheel. Look closer."

Argoan didn't have to be told twice. He relinquished control of the ship to his first mate, stepping away and pulling out the spyglass from his shirt. They all looked on in bated silence as the man brought the instrument up to his eye, and there was a tense moment as he scanned the horizon.

Then Argoan hissed under his breath.

"Aye," he said somberly. "Aye. I see them."

He pulled the spyglass away and looked down at the deck, giving a sharp whistle. At once, every one of the crew—from the figures leaning out over the hull to the duo peering north and south atop the crow's nest—turned to the stern. Raz watched expectantly as Argoan allowed himself a moment, just a brief second, to take a deep, calming breath.

Then he bellowed over the ship.

"BATTLE STATIONS!"

The *Sylgid* came alive in a flurry. Sailors rushed about the deck once more, moving to their assigned positions. Figures climbed up and down the rigging. Some took to the bow, others to the port and starboard rails. Everywhere, this time, there was the flash of metal, blades being drawn with shrieks and scratching hisses from their sheaths. Arrows were nocked, and boiling sealing tar—usually used to patch leaks as needed—was hurriedly lugged up from the belly of the ship in large, bubbling buckets. Within five minutes, as the paired enemy ships became distinct and split away from each other to approach in a pincer maneuver from east and west, the *Sylgid* smelled of iron, sweat, and smoke. To their credit, the men and women of the crew didn't balk, all of them tense and ready, shouting encouragements to one another or hurling taunts at the distant vessels.

Raz felt a thrill of excitement he couldn't quite repress. He looked around at the others, his eyes settling on Syrah.

"I'll handle the portside. Can you support the starboard?"

The Priestess looked pale, but nodded.

"Be careful," she said insistently. "Remember your promise. Please."

Raz couldn't help it. He flashed her a grin he thought might have seemed just a touch maniacal.

"Me?" he asked in feigned offense. "I don't know what you mean. I'm always careful."

And then, before Syrah could offer a retort, he leapt from the raised stern down to the deck below.

The ship's company cheered him as he slipped through their ranks, shouting his name like he was one of their own while he moved up the ship, headed for the bow. He ignored them all, this time, giving himself over to the battlefog, his golden eyes on the closest of the ships, approaching quickly from the east. When Raz reached the front of the ship, he vaulted up onto the raised part of the deck behind the water-spirit figurehead, then pushed his way through several other sailors to take hold of one of the foremast tethers and pull himself up to stand on the rail of the bow itself. He hoped Syrah would forgive him his foolishness. He knew all too well what would happen if he fell into the sea, weighed down as he was by Ahna and a hundred pounds of steel armor, but there was a purpose to his recklessness. He stood there in full splendor at the head of the ship, the dviassegai held confident and loose by his side as he towered behind the wooden woman's right shoulder, bouncing masterfully with the bump of the waves beneath him.

Been a long time since it was you and me, huh, sis? he asked the weapon silently. *Think we've still got what it takes?*

If the weapon had an opinion, she didn't see fit to share it.

For a long time he waited, watching the approaching ship, only occasionally glancing westward to see where the other was. One minute went by, then two. Raz waited, forcing himself to be patient. It was nearly five minutes, in fact, the distance between them warped by the vastness of the sea, before he could make out the details of the enemy vessel. It was the same one from earlier in the day, a narrow, two-masted beast with mottled grey and dark red sails. A brigantine, he thought it was called, shuffling through the various facts Argoan had hammered into his head in the last weeks. As a whole it was a plain thing, with nothing but a simple black flag to act as a figurehead and a weathered look to the hull, but it cut through the water cleanly even against the winds, a half-dozen oars pulling it along on either side. Lining its own rail, Raz made out a thick group of about two-score dark-skinned men, each bedecked in a motley assortment of what must have been stolen or salvaged armor from the ships they preyed on. Chain and platemail gleamed, as well as iron-studded leather and even hide or fur greaves and chest pieces that reminded Raz of the Gähs of the Northern mountains. The only common thing many shared, in fact, was a silver round-helm capped with a single long spike, sometimes complemented by a chain neck-guard. He had seen such helms before, in the Azbar Arena, always worn by the Percian.

Raz made a mental note not to land on any heads if he could help it today.

Their weapons, too, were an odd mélange. He saw falchion blades and cutlasses, as one might expect aboard a pirate ship, but also a multitude of other swords, axes, knives, and even spears and pikes. Some had timber-and-iron shields hefted on their arms, and they were banging them against the rail of the ship so that soon the sea began to ring with the bashing sound of metal on wood. Shouts went up, howling hollers of excitement and bloodlust, and behind him Raz started to hear muttered prayers to various gods and murmurs of fear. The Percians' intent was to intimidate, to let their enemy know that the only thing they felt regarding the upcoming battle was excitement and anticipation. Indeed, the pirates seemed to be building themselves into a frenzy, their battlelust so charged that, when they caught sight of him standing on the bow, they screamed and jeered in victory and glee. Where most men would have blanched and thought twice about what they were about to do, the approaching pirates only became more elated, their calls and war-cries building as they neared. Within two minutes they were close enough for Raz to make out the scarred details of their faces, see the white of their gnashing teeth and smell the sweat off their bodies. Despite this, Raz waited a minute more, waited until he saw the coiled ropes in many of their hands, ends capped with barbed iron hooks.

When he began to feel true fear start to bubble up in the crew at his back, Raz decided it was about time to even the battlefield.

With a *whoosh* of wind his sunset-red wings extended out to either side of him, their twenty-foot wingspan blocking the entire front bow of the *Sylgid*. His neck crest flared over his head, and with a deep breath he leaned out over the hull of the frigate, Ahna pointed right at the approaching ship.

Then Raz roared, pouring every ounce of hunger and defiance he could muster into the scream.

The sound pitched over the empty churn of the Dramion, vibrating in the wood beneath his feet. It seemed to shake the air, shivering over the Percian sails as it washed over the boat and the pirates lined up eagerly along its sides. It reverberated, rippling across the water, making it seem like the shallow waves lapping at their hulls were a product of Raz's own power.

All at once, Raz watched the anticipation drain from the dark faces of the pirates, their smiles wavering as the Dragon made it all too clear he, too, was eagerly awaiting their arrival. A moment later, like an echo, Raz felt a surge of courage and strength from the men and women along the deck behind him, and their combined voices ripped across the sea, thundering over the quiet.

Then, with a *thrum* of ripping air from above, the first arrow was let loose, and the battle began.

The Dragon's roar crushed over Ykero Kalae and his comrades with the force of a tidal wave. In one moment he and the entire crew of the *Moalas* were building themselves up, pressing each other into a hungry madness as the *Sylgid* came within reach. They had seen the atherian already, of course, made out his form against the head of the ship. The sight of him only drove their anticipation higher. They had howled and jeered, each and every one of them ready to strike down this beast that dared to stand tall among his betters.

And then the atherian had spread his wings, bellowing a challenge that sent shivers up each of their spines, and for the first time in his life Ykero felt fear in the face of the lizard-kind.

Winged? he thought in alarm, recalling tales and stories which did nothing to quell the bloom of terror that had welled up within him at the sight. *He's winged?*

Just then, though, there was a *zip* and a *thud*, and directly to Ykero's left his friend Aideh fell screaming to the ground, clutching at the fletched shaft of an arrow that had taken him in the thigh.

Then the gap between the ships closed, and all was madness.

Regaining some of their courage, his comrades whooped and howled, the men closest to the bow whirling their grapples even as half-a-dozen more arrows rained down over them. With heaves and shouts they launched the ropes across the water. A few fell short, tumbling into the sea or thumping harmlessly against the hull of the frigate, but most caught hold, and with triumphant yells several hands grabbed and heaved at each of the lines. Aboard the *Sylgid*, several sailors were howling, running up and down the portside to hack at the grapples.

"Archers!" Captain Omara thundered from somewhere behind Ykero. "Loose!"

There were twangs of bowstrings being released, and two of the men who had been attempting to free the enemy ship fell with shrieks of pain away from the rail. In response, a number of flaming arrows came arcing over the gap, digging into the deck of the *Moalas* with whooshes of spreading fire as the tar they had been dunked in splattered everywhere. At once, several men rushed forward with thick blankets, and Ykero couldn't help but grin. He and his fellows were well versed in the art of boarding, despite their frenzy. As smoke billowed up around them and more flaming shafts struck masts and cargo and scraped across the deck, he and the rest of the crew kept their heads. He could taste victory again, feel his own fear subside as the panic grew aboard the *Sylgid* once more, fearful shouts going up from across the gap as more grappling lines found anchors. Through the chaos, Ykero made out the looming form of the *Red Turor* flanking their prey's starboard side, penning them in. At once many of the *Sylgid*'s crew, including the archers in the rigging, turned to meet this new threat, giving Ykero and his comrades the time they needed to close in on the ship.

With a grinding *crunch* of wood on wood, the two hulls met.

More cheers went up, but over everything Omara could be heard yelling for the gangplanks to be brought forward. The smoke was heavy now, the men fighting the fires rushing about as the flames sought to spread across the deck. The air was thickening fast, the outline of the *Sylgid*'s masts growing harder to see by the second. The planks were brought forward, three heavy lengths of thick wood hauled by four men each, and with echoed *booms* they were lifted up, then dropped to span the space that remained between the decks of the two ships. With elated roars the men of the *Moalas* started to cross. One after the other they slipped into the gloom, their figures bare outlines through the smoke. There was a minute of fierce combat, Ykero making out nothing of the others other than flashing steel as they clashed with the enemy, more hurrying over to join the battle aboard the frigate.

Then, like some terrible animal hiding in the night, there came a snarling growl from within the smoke, and the sounds of battle redoubled. There was the shearing and wrenching of steel cutting through metal and flesh, and a few seconds later several men howled and tumbled into the sea, the gangplank they had just been crossing, closest to the stern, jolting and sliding with a grind to follow them into the waters below. Ykero felt the thrill of fear return even before there was another splintering crunch, and the far end of a second plank thudded free of the *Sylgid* to clatter off the hulls and splash into the Dramion.

There were several tense moments, the sound of fighting aboard the *Sylgid* subsiding. Then the last gangplank, only slightly off to Ykero's right, shuddered as well. The two men who had just started crossing it, though, didn't fall. Instead, they screamed in pain and fear as they appeared to be thrown clear of the plank, one disappearing into the sea, the other unfortunate soul getting caught just as the hulls slammed together again on the waves, killing him with a wrenching *crunch* that left both ships' sides stained with blood when they drifted apart again.

Ykero, though, barely registered this horrible event. His gaze was instead trained on the same thing every other eye on the *Moalas* was focused on.

A figure, terrible in its size and form, loomed out of the smoke. Seven feet tall at least, it appeared to be walking casually across the plank, materializing bit by bit as it approached. All about him Ykero felt his comrades freeze, just as he did, gaping at the shadow as it revealed itself. First came the glint of steel, shining in the light of the Sun above the flickering remnants of the fires that hadn't yet been put out. Then came the lithe, muscled limbs, black scales encased here and there in finely-crafted armor or thick leather wraps. Clawed gauntlets shone wet with blood, both wrapped about the haft of a massive, twin-bladed spear that itself made Ykero want to cower and run.

Then, at last, the beast's face came into clear view, and what courage Ykero might have been able to hold onto fled him completely.

He had heard the tales of Raz i'Syul Arro, of course. Everyone had. In Perce, though, they laughed at the stories, jeered at the fear and awe the rest of the world seemed to hold for the famed "Monster of Karth." The atherian could be dangerous, sure, but only when not dealt with appropriately. The legends of the so-called "Dragon of the North" had been circulating for weeks now, spread wide at the command of the Tash of Karesh Syl to the west, but men like Ykero had scoffed at the warnings as readily as they'd salivated over the size of the bounty. A creature like this "Arro" had likely simply never come across a group who knew well how to deal with insolent lizard-kind. When the captain had told them that the weapon described in the contract, the wicked spear now held before them, had been found aboard the *Sylgid*, they'd all rejoiced, cheering over the riches they were sure would be spilling into their hands soon enough.

Now, though, looking into the face of the Dragon himself, Ykero was quite sure gold was the last thing that was about to be spilled.

Arro dropped down from the gangplank almost casually, his amber eyes—like molten sunlight—scanning them one after the other. His gaze was so calm, so impassive, Ykero felt like the atherian was about as threatened by any of them as they might have been by the laundry they hung up to dry in the sea breeze. He couldn't blame the beast, either. Seeing him now, Ykero understood every rumor, every warning the notices and riders had spread of the man. Ykero had spent his life among subservient lizard-kind, as any but the *kuja* did, and he saw now how that had skewed his understanding of the titan before him, how it had made him underestimate the stories. It was as though all his life Ykero had only ever known the feel of summer rains, but now stood before a lightning storm, cowering beneath broiling black clouds of such terrifying power they seemed capable of sweeping away all that was the world.

Arro's wings flickered on either side of him, blood-red and sunset-orange. His reptilian head turned as he looked at each of them. The webbed blade along the back of his neck and head rose. When he spoke, it was a dark growl, like the storm had a voice of quiet thunder.

"Who is the captain here?"

Beyond the Dragon, the battle continued to rage. Ykero could make out continued screams, the clang of blades and the *whoosh* of more fire. There were flashes of strange white light, the grind of wood of the hulls of all three ships moving against each other.

And yet, to every man who had heard the atherian's question, no other sound existed.

Captain Omara did not volunteer himself, though whether this was out of surprise or fear, Ykero couldn't guess. Even with more than twenty men left aboard the ship, not a soul was moving toward the atherian, each and every one of them held firm by their fear. It was that same crew, though, that gave the poor man away, several heads swiveling in his direction at once. He stood, suddenly separated from his company as those closest to him stepped quickly away, like they wanted to distance themselves from whatever punishment the Sun had seen fit to deliver upon their captain on this day.

The atherian's eyes settled on him instantly.

"Captain," the beast said, taking a step further onto the deck and lifting his two-headed spear up onto one shoulder like it weighed as much as a toy sword. "I'm surprised at you. I would have thought a man of such distinguished rank wouldn't fear a lowly creature such as me."

In response, the captain stiffened. Omara was a tall man, well over six feet in height, and he had earned his title the hard way, by fighting for it. His dreaded hair fell halfway down his chest from beneath the spiked half-helm, and he held a curved scimitar in one hand matched by a pirate's sagaris—a long-handled axe with a narrow steel head balanced by a slim spike—in his other. His skill with those weapons was well-known, almost legendary along the coastal villages of Perce, and yet now, standing before the Dragon, the sword and axe seemed almost limp in his grasp.

As the atherian called him out, however, some of the captain's courage returned.

"Your kind do not address their betters directly, in this land," he said fiercely, managing to keep the tremor out of his voice that Ykero could clearly see in the shake of his arms. "You will learn this swiftly, I think."

The atherian's brows rose in what was very obviously mock surprise, though he appeared to eye Omara's sagaris with interest even as he replied sarcastically. "Oh, will I? Do tell me how. Are you planning on instilling this lesson now, or will I have to wait until you chain me up with the slaves of your village? Personally, I see no need to wait."

"You assume we intend to take you alive," Omara spat, moving a brave step forward and motioning for the rest of his men to follow his lead. Only a few did, including Ykero. "The Tash has not stated that as a requirement to collect the bounty on your life." He smiled cruelly. "We could just as easily take your head now. Maybe pin your body up by your wings in the galley, so the others can see what happens when you do not bow to those you are inferior to."

Right then and there, Ykero knew the captain had crossed a line. Where a second before the atherian had been relaxed, almost amused in the way he spoke and held himself, now his body told a different story. His wings stiffened and stilled, his face hardening into something almost feral. His arms and legs flexed, the great black tail at his back going rigid. Around the haft of his spear, his hands tightened abruptly, and his eyes almost glowed with anger as they bored into Omara.

196

"You have slaves here?" he asked, his voice a deadly hiss. "Here? Aboard the ship?"

The captain must have sensed the danger, but it seemed as though Arro's spell of fear was failing as Omara glanced around, realizing just how many men he had left compared to the Dragon alone. With another nod, he took a second step forward, and this time the entirety of the crew began to press in around the beast.

"Aye," he said with another cruel smile, bringing his scimitar and axe up in preparation. "You should have heard them, as we set sail. Whispering amongst themselves and praying to every god of the world. Apparently you're something of a hero to their kind. Let's see what happens when we—!"

Shlunk.

Arro moved so fast, Ykero thought he had blinked and missed it. There was a moment in which the atherian had been standing before the gangplank, still as stone, listening to the captain speak. Then in a blur, he was suddenly in front of Omara, materializing like some great dark shadow in the smoke before the man. No one saw the spear move. No one saw it arc back, then rip around with all the force of a sharpened battering ram.

All they saw was their captain falling to the deck, his body severed in half, cleaved in two from hip to armpit.

There was a space of two heartbeats in which all was silent. The world itself seemed to still, the sounds of the battle echoing over them as though from far, far away. Every eye was on the body of Omara, his chest, arms, and head convulsing as his legs kicked weakly some three feet away. Terror, unlike anything he had ever felt or *thought* he could ever feel, washed over Ykero.

"I'm sorry," Arro said, lowering the spear slowly and bending down over the corpse to tug the sagaris free of Omara's twitching fingers. "I had intended to challenge the man. I'd hoped to end this without more bloodshed."

He hefted the axe experimentally as he stood up again, slashing it through the air as he tested its weight. Apparently satisfied, he brought it to his face, studying the narrow steel head with interest.

"You've made that impossible."

And then the Dragon was moving again, a black blur streaked with silver and gold, and all the world was blood.

XXVIII

"There is a place for all in life. There is a place for happiness and sadness, for joy and grief. There is a place for gain and loss, for friendship and betrayal. To an extent, one could argue that there is even some small place for the ravages of madness…"

—*the Grandmother*

Raz saw red.

It had been some time, he realized distantly, since the animal had managed to gain any amount of control over him. He'd found peace, these last eight months, first among the Laorin as a whole, then with Syrah alone. The woman had been the keystone of his willpower, his strength in keeping this monstrous part of his soul at bay.

Now, though, he had relinquished that control, and his body moved without thought, taken over by a will all its own.

The pirates fell before him like wheat beneath the scythe. These were not the fighters of skill and reputation he had felled in the Arena. These were not the great warriors of the Sigûrth, molded by Gûlraht Baoill himself. These were not the living shadows, the trained assassins of the Mahsadën. These were mere men, mere vessels of human greed, who thought so little of the freedoms they so dispassionately stole away.

Raz was more than happy to steal something greater in return.

Like an armored hurricane he barreled around the deck of the brigantine, Ahna and the strange new axe he had stolen from the captain's corpse leaving a wake of death and destruction in his stead. He did not stay tethered to the ground, instead leaping and sliding, somersaulting off the rough wood of the masts as he slashed downward, jumping up onto the railings as the dviassegai arced out before him, ducking beneath swinging blades to cut at knees and guts and groins. Screams filled his ears, trembling through his skull, but Raz— even the conscious part of his soul which had so willingly allowed the animal to rise—felt no pity. He struck and slashed, kicked and punched. Men died clutching at their wounds, howling in agony and writhing on the ground as limbs were severed and tumbled away, or struggling to keep themselves together as organs tried to escape from great gashes in their chests and guts. Some tumbled overboard, or were thrown, screaming as they plummeted, too late as they scrambled to free themselves of the heavy armor that would drag them to the bottom of the sea. Blood painted every surface in great arcs and smeared splatters, sometimes even slashing across the sails above their heads. The wood became slick and slippery, and Raz had to dig in with his talons to keep his footing. His weapons moved about him without effort, and for a time he forgot the weight of his own armor as he extinguished all life around him.

A few men put up better fights than others, managing to block a blow or two before falling. Raz would have almost liked to take his time with these individuals, to drive in the terror that weaker men feel when the will of someone stronger is pressed upon them. He would have liked to make them suffer, to punish them for daring to wield their talents as an advantage over those who had no defense. He wanted to tear them apart with his bare hands, to toss them in several pieces over the rails into the waters that were steadily reddening around the ship.

Instead, he satisfied himself with breaking their spirits, allowing them to understand just how weak they actually were as he knocked aside their weapons to cleave them half-in-two or crush their skulls with hammered steel.

After a time, though, the weeks at sea began to betray him. Raz's movements became heavy, his blows slowing. A dozen or more lay dead or dying about the deck, but another ten still stood scattered, slipping and tripping in the blood that glossed the planks beneath their feet. Soon Raz was fighting harder, shifting about as quickly as he could to keep them scattered, keep them from managing to gang together. He feinted toward one, then twisted Ahna around as another tried to take advantage of the opening, severing the attacker's right leg from his body. Before the screaming pirate had even fallen to the ground, another died, the man behind him unprepared for Raz's sudden bull over his dying comrade, or the axe head that took him through the stomach and ripped out his side. After that, a pair managed to get their wits together and push him at once, trying to pincer him in from either side, and Raz just managed to get out of the way of their falling blades, deflecting one with Ahna's blades and feeling the other whistle past his ear as he sidestepped. He shifted around them, succeeding in spearing one with the dviassegai's weighted tip, but before he could try for the other the remaining five were rushing him, and he found himself backing away quickly. He was just starting to wonder if Syrah would be screaming her frustrations at his corpse before the battle was over when there was a roar from off to his left.

Lysa appeared, leading a dozen sailors through the smoke over the gangplank.

They took the pirates in the flank, crashing into them one after the other. The Percian whirled to meet them, but within seconds they were outnumbered. Raz allowed himself a respite, dodging back as far as he could and breathing hard. He gave himself five seconds, ticking them off against the hard drumming of his heart. He realized the animal had faded, and he cursed the weight of his armor, realizing he had been a fool to allow his body to learn how to move without it again.

Then, with a snarl, he rejoined the fray.

The pirates didn't have a prayer. The crew of the *Sylgid* had numbers on their side, now, and that was before Raz—tired as he was—returned to the fight. It was a short, brutal battle, and Raz was glad he was in control again. In the chaos it was already hard enough to distinguish friend from foe. He wondered, distantly, if this was what war felt like, if there was that constant hesitation in every strike, wondering who you were about to fell. He was almost careful as he fought, using Ahna for parrying and defense for fear her sweeping reach might do more harm than good. His new axe, with its long handle, worked better in the confines, the long spike on the back of its head punching cleanly through leather and iron in quick, efficient blows.

A minute later, the last of the Percian pirates tumbled to the ground, attempting to stem the blood coursing through the hole Lysa had carved across his chest. As the man died, Raz half-expected there to be a roar of victory from those of the *Sylgid*'s crew left standing. Instead, though, the men and women looked around, gaping in horrified fascination at the scene around them. Glancing about as he fought to catch his breath again, Raz could understand why. It was very possible the first mate's charge had saved his life, but even then the crew had only had to cut down a half-dozen pirates.

Scattered about the deck, a battlefield outlined in smoke, blood, and dying fire, some fifteen others were already still, and more corpses that hadn't sunk could be seen floating off on the waves around the ship.

"By the Sun..." someone hissed quietly, and another voice muttered a prayer to the Lifegiver. One sailor, a young woman, stumbled to the closest rail and vomited over the side of the ship.

Lysa managed to shake herself first, though she looked pale as she stepped over bodies to get to him.

"Raz..." the scarred woman said, blinking around at the carnage. "Raz, this is... this is..."

"Why they call me 'Monster,'" Raz finished for her with a grunt, grimacing at the scene. "Vile, isn't it?"

Lysa didn't seem to have an answer for him, her eyes fixed in disgusted awe upon the bisected corpse of the man who had been the pirates' captain.

"*Lysa*," Raz snapped, shaking the woman out of her trance. "There will be plenty to gawk at when this fight is done. Get your people back to the *Sylgid!* There's still fighting to be done."

The first mate looked shaken as she met his gaze. "What about you?"

"I haven't finished here." Raz couldn't help but growl, his eyes finding what he thought might be the hatch to the lower galley. "I'll join you soon. Go!"

Lysa cast about one last time, as though not believing her eyes, then nodded. With a quick order she led her group back to the gangplank and over the gap, disappearing into the smog and sounds of battle.

When they were gone, Raz moved quickly.

Flicking the axe clean, he slipped its handle into the loop of his belt where another weapon had once hung, feeling it settle about his hip with a nostalgic sort of weight. As he did so, Raz hurried over to the great double doors in the center of the deck. They'd been latched shut with a heavy padlock, either to keep boarders out or whatever was below in. Slipping Ahna's end through the iron lock and into the wood, he used her like a lever, straining up on the top of her haft with a grunt. There was a *crack*, then a *crunch*, and the padlock tore free of the door completely. Raz pulled it clear of the dviassegai's tip and tossed it into the sea before reaching for the closest handle.

The moment he hauled the hatch open there was a defiant howl, and Raz was forced to dodge out of the way as a blade streaked up from below, slashing at his legs. The pirate rushed out from the lower deck to meet him, closely followed by a second. Raz might have had to retreat to gain back the advantage, but the bloody scene about them seemed to shake the pair, because their war-cries faltered and strangled off as they stared in disbelief at the slaughter.

Distracted as they were, Ahna made quick work of the two, adding their bodies to the dead.

A set of steep steps led down into the belly of the ship, and another Percian met Raz at the base, charging him with a lowered spear. Raz sidestepped and took hold of the weapon's end with his free hand, smashing Ahna's haft up into the pirate's nose. There was a *crunch* as shattered bone was driven into the man's brain, and Raz pulled the spear free as the body fell convulsing over the steps. Twirling the weapon about, he hefted it over his shoulder as he heard the thumping of yet another set of boots. A fourth figure appeared in the doorway some ten feet in front of the stairs, rushing through just in time to take the borrowed spear squarely in the chest. When Raz was sure he could make out no one else running to meet him, he moved forward to step over the body.

A second later he found himself in the rowing galley, and he almost choked as he took in the scene before him.

The space was much the same as the *Sylgid*'s, but a good deal smaller. Bloody water could be made out through a dozen oar-holes, and a raised walkway bisected the compartment, leading to yet another doorway at the back of the space. On either side of it, bolted into the floor, two cylindrical iron cages stood empty, about six feet tall by four feet wide. Overhead, a trio of oil lanterns, dark now in the light of day, swung from hooks in the ceiling, and at Raz's feet a single large, animal-skin drum lay abandoned, as though one of the men he'd just butchered might have been standing over it a moment before. The sticks were nowhere in sight.

Likely they had rolled away, dropping into the sunken rows that lined each side of the hull, disappearing among the shackled feet of two-dozen of the most miserable souls Raz had ever seen.

The slaves sat in pairs, two to a seat, twelve to a row. It wasn't their bodies that nearly brought Raz to his knees, looking over them. If anything, they looked almost healthy, lean and muscled, as though their masters had wanted them strong enough to handle the oars all day and night if need be. They were men, all, of varying ages, but each sporting thick arms and weathered, callused hands. Their garb was plain and minimal, often nothing more than a simple set of cloth shorts and rough, sleeveless shirts, but the clothes looked as though they'd never once been washed, and every figure he could see was barefooted.

But it was their eyes—in every gaze that stared up at him in unfathomable silence—that made Raz rasp out a harrowed sob of misery and relief.

They were not the eyes of dead men, per se. Rather, they were the eyes of men who *wished* to die, but had never been given leave by the gods to do so. They watched him, empty and hollow except for a gleam that looked to reflect every emotion Raz himself was feeling in that moment, like more than a score of mirrors shining with pain, desperation, and even hope. His breath grew shallow as he looked them over, his body shivering. There weren't any atherian among them—a fact he wasn't sure if he was grateful for or not—but aside from that there couldn't have been a greater variety of men in any given place in the world. To his surprise, nearly a third of them were Percian themselves, their dark skin marked and blemished with dozens of pale scars, most bearing geometric and spiraling tattoos across their chests and shoulders in symbols Raz didn't recognize. There were Southerners, desert and city-born both, all with marred, tanned skin. There were blond-headed Northerners, including one hulking figure at the back who had to have mountain clan blood in him. There were West Islers, with their straight black hair and narrow eyes, and Imperialist, their dark curls dirty and lank over their faces and their olive skin weathered by the sea. Raz even thought a few of the figures, scattered here and there, might have been of the Seven Cities, with lighter hair and somber eyes over heavy beards.

Each of them, though—every single one—shared the same empty blankness in their gaze, like none truly dared believe there might be hope standing before them.

Raz did his best to shake himself free of the wash of emotions that were threatening to drown him, but his voice still quavered as he spoke.

"Do you know who I am?" he asked them simply.

For a long time, no one moved. Nothing could be heard over the creak of the boat and the coursing of the water outside, mixing with the ring of swords and shouting of the battle still raging aboard the *Sylgid* above.

Then several of them nodded slowly.

"Are there more?" Raz continued, waving behind him at the bloody bodies on the floor.

Again, no one answered. The silence extended so long he began to dread that the men before him might not be *able* to speak.

Finally, though, from the aisle in the middle of the portside rows, a single voice rose, ragged and harsh, as though it hadn't been used in many years.

"Three. In the crew quarters. They heard you coming."

Raz studied the man. He was one of the Percian, and looked older than most of the others. His roughly-cropped black hair was strained with grey, and his face was crinkled like hardened leather. He seemed—given the odd combination of his apparent years and the broadness of his muscled shoulders—rather like an aged general who still preferred to lead his troops into battle, and there was a strength to his eyes that was lacking in those of the others.

Will, Raz thought he recognized, meeting the man's gaze.

"Three," he repeated. "You're sure?"

The slave nodded.

"And the keys?"

At that, there was a shiver among the group. Not a single voice spoke, not even the Percian's, but every single eye dropped to look past Raz's feet. He turned, finding the prone form of the pirate he had speared through the chest, his body spread-eagled with the haft of the weapon sticking out of his sternum like a flagpole.

Raz glanced back around, his eyes on the distant door behind which the last three lay in wait.

"Is there one among you whom you all trust?" he asked the slaves.

Again, no one answered. Despite this, after a few seconds heads started to turn. Their mute fear held, but soon nearly every face had shifted, some looking over shoulders, others staring at the back of the man's head, singling him out.

Could have guessed that, Raz said, his eyes settling on the old Percian again.

Then he eased himself to one knee, patting the dead pirate down until he heard the jingle of metal, and he drew a simple iron ring from his pocket from which dangled a trio of rusty keys.

Raz moved quickly between the slaves, toward the end of the boat. He could feel their eyes on him, feel the hunger with which they watched those keys pass. When he stopped beside the Percian, he looked down at him.

"What's your name, old man?"

At the question, the slave started and stared up at him, like this was a question he never expected to be asked. Eventually he opened his mouth to answer, his silvered beard scraggly about his chin and cheeks, but no words came. For a while he seemed pained, as though he couldn't remember the answer.

Then, with a twitch of his lips that spoke of a pleasant memory pulled from somewhere far, far away, it came back to him.

"Akelo," he croaked in answer, like the syllables were hard to get out. "Akelo Aseni."

Raz nodded in greeting.

"Well then, Akelo," he said, holding out the keys to the dark-skinned man and looking back to the door at the far end of the galley. "Shall I kill them, or would you rather I leave them to you and your men?"

XXIX

"There is a trope so commonly used in literature and poetry, always some variation of 'there is nothing more dangerous than a cornered animal.' I cannot help but glean some grim amusement from this, for I often wonder if the authors of these clichés have ever in their life witnessed the far more frightening sight of a cornered man…"

—the Lifetaker

Syrah was feeling hard-pressed by the time Raz showed up with help.

For nearly twenty minutes she and Argoan had been battling along the starboard side of the *Sylgid*, sometimes fighting to press the pirates back off the ship, sometimes simply battling for their lives. They'd done well so far, in her opinion. The captain himself stood like a wall, his hammer flashing left and right, striking down anyone fool enough to step within reach. His crew had managed to cut loose many of the grappling hooks lashing the frigate to the enemy, as well as topple one of the four heavy gangplanks into the sea, and Syrah had managed to blast another to ash. For a time, the battle had been even.

Eventually, however, they'd started to lose ground.

The Percian who managed to cross over began pressing them back, pushing them into the openness of the *Sylgid*'s deck as others poured in behind their comrades. In a matter of minutes the fight turned, shifting away from an attempt to keep the pirates from boarding into an all-out battle for the *Sylgid* herself. Syrah moved like a demoness about the ship, summoning spells and striking out with her staff wherever she found the opportunity. She silently thanked Raz a dozen different times for the practice he had put in with her and the rest of the crew over the last months. She'd been good before, she knew, a capable fighter, but now she could feel the difference in her encounters, could witness the lessons he had worked into her body revealing themselves subtly, but to great effect. She never stopped moving, never stood in one place longer than she needed to. She became more than a single warrior in the battle, her constant shifting allowing her to cast her magic in a hundred different ways as she tried to keep the tide of battle even. For a while, she did well for herself. Runes blasted under the pirates' feet. Stunning spells streaked through the confusion to knock men unconscious. Lashes flicked out to tie victims to the railings and masts and tangle them in the ratlines.

But, eventually, it dawned on Syrah that they were losing.

They caught a brief reprieve when Lysa—who'd gone after Raz when no one had seen him for several minutes—returned with her party. For several minutes the fight was at a standstill again, but they'd already lost so much ground that the first mate's arrival only delayed the inevitable. Now Syrah, Argoan, and Lysa were being borne down on, forced beyond the mid-point of the ship, past the masts. A few more yards and they would be fighting with their backs against the portside banister, the pirates having claimed most of the *Sylgid*.

And then, with a thunder of clawed feet and a war-cry that rang clear over the sounds of fighting, Raz careened out of the smoke at their backs, launching himself over their heads and into the melee, plunging right through the ranks of the pressing Percian. Syrah would have laughed for joy, relieved that he was alive and fighting, but several *thuds* told her others were crossing over from the ship at their backs. She whirled, concerned that enemy reinforcements were coming from behind, but what she saw instead confused and mystified her.

A large group of heavyset men, all ragged and wild-eyed and dressed in a filthy assortment of worn garments, were following Raz off the gangplank onto the *Sylgid*. They had a haunted look, each casting about as though they hadn't seen the light of day in a long time, and in their hands they clutched such a mismatch of bloodstained weapons they might have come from the very pirates Syrah was fending off now. Their clothes, too, were bloody, splattered and stained, and many of their hands were dyed red. Seeing this, Syrah noticed another common mark among them, something that made her catch her breath in sad surprise.

Scarred rings, thick and old, banded each of the men's wrists and ankles.

She made the connection just as the small army of slaves roared and charged after Raz into the fight, fearless despite their utter lack of armor, desperate in their savage, furious slashes and strikes.

After that, the battle was won. Syrah and the crew fought on, but they could just as well have stood back and watched the slaughter unfold without them. The Dragon revealed himself in all his horrifying glory, Ahna screaming through the air as he darted about the deck like black lightning, an axe Syrah had never seen flashing in his other hand. The slaves, too, fought like wild animals, several falling with howls and wails, but most simply refusing to die as they battled with such vicious savagery that the Percian seemed utterly outmatched by the sheer *will* of the men assaulting them. Within a few minutes the pirates had been pressed back, and soon after there were yells to retreat. The men who hadn't fallen to Raz or his unexpected army scrambled and fought to be clear of the *Sylgid*, several falling with shrill screams of terror into the Dramion as the two remaining gangplanks suddenly became overrun in the flight. The grappling lines went slack, released or cut from the enemy's side, and with a groan the planks themselves tumbled into the water, abandoned as the ship began to pull away.

For one terrifying second, Syrah knew Raz was going to leap the growing gap onto the deck of the retreating ship. He almost managed it, his head snapping around from the last lingering skirmishes as he heard the boat pull away. He began to run, his clawed feet pounding over the body-strewn deck, and he was barely three yards from the starboard rail when Syrah screamed his name.

"RAZ! NO!"

The atherian stumbled, like he'd tripped over something that wasn't there. He managed to stop himself slamming into the banister only by catching hold of the main ratlines over his head, coming to such a sharp halt Syrah thought she saw splinters fly from beneath his talons. He didn't look back at her, though. Instead, Raz roared as he watched the ship flee, the sound ringing out over the ocean half-furiously, half-despairingly.

Then the vessel pulled away, and the atherian crumpled, half-sitting, to the deck.

"VICTORY!"

It was Garht Argoan who raised the cheer, bellowing in a booming voice as he thrust his gory hammer into the air, his bearded face and leather-clad body wet with blood and dust from the smoke. In response, the survivors of the *Sylgid* echoed the hurrah, their combined voices booming out in triumph. Sunlight glinted across the ship, reflected a thousand times against blades raised and waved about in the sheer ecstasy of the moment.

Syrah heard none of it.

"Raz!" she said desperately, running to him and stumbling to her knees at his side, her staff rolling away uncaringly to settle against the rail. "Raz! Look at me!"

He was a bloody sight. Only once before had she ever witnessed him in such a terrifying state, on the night he'd rescued her from the clutches of Kareth Grahst. On that occasion, though, there had at least been a light behind his eyes. Now, as his gaze turned to meet hers, she saw the dimness there, the dead coolness of the Monster.

"Raz!" she yelled, shaking him. "Come back!"

The man gave a shudder, blinked once, and seemed to return to himself.

"Syrah," he groaned by way of greeting, giving her a lopsided smile. "Careful. You're going to get your robes bloody."

Unable to help herself, Syrah choked back a small sob, then threw her arms around his neck, almost toppling them both.

When he'd found his balance again, Raz chuckled. "Guess you don't care." Gently, he forced himself free of the embrace, pushing her back to hold at arm's length. His gold eyes looked her up and down. "Wish you hadn't done that, though. Now I can't tell. Is any of this yours?"

Syrah looked down at herself. Indeed, the white robes of her faith were now covered in red, patterned crudely in the same manner of Raz's armor.

She gave a short, gasping laugh, shaking her head. "No, none of it." Now it was her turn to take him in, feeling worry rear up inside her. "What about you?" she asked, reaching out to wipe some of the blood from his chest and face. "You look ghastly. Are you hurt?"

Raz shook his head, bemused. "Believe it or not, I don't think so. I might have made it out without a scratch, this time."

"I *don't* believe it," she said firmly, getting to her feet. "Stand up, let me see."

Raz grumbled, but did as he was told, pushing himself up with a groan before turning unsteadily for her, Ahna still held in one hand, the odd axe in the other. Sure enough, apart from one or two shallow lacerations across his back and the exposed part of his right arm, there was nothing, and Syrah sighed in relief.

"Better than usual," she admitted grudgingly, pulling him around to face her again. "You're still a mess, though. Let's clean you up and—"

"Arro."

A stranger's voice cut across their conversation, and Syrah turned to find herself facing one of the slaves who'd followed Raz off the brigantine that had attempted to board their portside. He was a tall, muscular Percian, his dark skin scarred and leathery, and he looked to be of a surprising age. He might have seen fifty summers for all Syrah knew, but it was difficult to tell. She'd seen many slaves in her time working with the tribes of the Vietalis. After years of hard labor, it could be hard to judge their age merely by their appearance.

This man, though, held himself with surprising strength, given where Raz must have found him. His black eyes, set in a worn face framed by a heavily-silvered beard, gazed over the ocean beyond Syrah and Raz's shoulders, watching the shrinking sails of the fleeing ship. He was nearly as much of a mess as the atherian, his threadbare shirt and shorts blotched with red splotches of crimson over old dirt and grime, his right eye rapidly swelling shut above a bloody lip. In one hand he gripped a shortbow likely salvaged from some dead pirate, the wood cracked and dented like he'd used the weapon as a club when he'd run out of whatever arrows he'd managed to scavenge. Behind him, five or six of the other slaves stood silently in similar states of reddened filthiness, shifting uncomfortably and looking nervously about, as though unsure if they were allowed to stand at all.

The rest of their number were scattered across the deck, kneeling and shaking over the mangled bodies of those who hadn't survived the fight.

"There were many more of our kind aboard that vessel," the Percian was saying in a low, rough voice, still watching the retreating sails. "It is a terrible thing, to see it sail free…"

Raz nodded wearily. "I know. I'm sorry. I—" He staggered, and Syrah barely managed to catch and steady him before he fell to one knee. "I'm all right," he told her gently, finding his balance. "Just a little tired." His golden eyes fell back on the slave. "I'm sorry, Akelo. I would have liked the opportunity to free them of their chains as well. Believe that of me."

Realizing what they were talking about, Syrah glared at the Percian. "Look at him," she said angrily, holding tight to Raz's arm to make sure he didn't keel over. "He can barely stand. You think he would have survived taking on *another* crew on his own?"

The man—Akelo, Raz had called him—started and looked around at her in surprise, his swollen eye twisting half of his face into an involuntary grimace. He seemed to take her in, as though noticing her presence for the first time, black irises flitting over the pair of them as Syrah continued to support Raz. Akelo's expression was almost confused, like the sight of them—the atherian leaning into her, half-dead from exhaustion—had a meaning he hadn't even begun to consider.

Then the bow fell from his grasp, clattering against the wood of the deck, and Akelo's whole body began to shake violently as he brought his bloody hands up to look at them.

"I... My... My apologies. No. Of course not." His voice quavered, and he appeared unable to see anything more than the scars about his wrists. "It has been... has been many years since I have not felt the weight of iron on these arms. It's not... It's not real."

"It's not real for any of us," one of the men behind him, a short West Isler, echoed quietly, his eyes on his own banded marks.

Syrah felt her anger dissolve. Helping Raz find the boat rail to lean on, she quietly asked him if he could stand on his own. When the atherian nodded, Syrah gave his arm one last squeeze, then stepped carefully toward the Percian. He flinched at her approach, like a dog accustomed only to beatings, but did not move away. His shaking became more pronounced, however, more violent, as she slowly reached up, hesitating before she could touch him. She wanted to, wanted to take his hands in her own and comfort him, but she couldn't bring herself to do it. All the same, the motion caused her sleeve to slip up her arm, revealing the grey-red ring of knotted flesh around her wrist.

The man gaped at it, inhaling like he couldn't believe what he was seeing.

"It *will* be real," she promised him, lifting her other arm to reveal the same ring. "In time, it will be real. For months you will wake up each morning terrified, convinced that your deliverance was nothing more than a cruel fabrication of dream. That will fade. You will find your place, your purpose. You will learn to live life again."

"Live," Akelo repeated shallowly, speaking like it was a foreign concept to him. "I... I-I don't know if any of us know the meaning of that word anymore..."

Syrah smiled up at him, ducking her head so that he was forced to meet her eye again.

"You will," she said encouragingly. "Trust me on that."

The Percian nodded.

"Where are you from, Akelo?" Raz asked from his place leaning against the boat behind Syrah, and the Percian blinked before lifting his eyes to him. Around them, the shouting and cheering of the crew was dying down, replaced moment by moment with the moans and screams of the dead and dying.

"The heartlands, to the south," Akelo answered slowly. "But that was a long time ago..."

"Do you want to see it again?"

"Raz…" Syrah said warningly, dropping the Percian's hands and stepping aside as the atherian pushed himself off the rail with a grunt of effort and moved to stand beside her, leaning heavily on Ahna. "Maybe this isn't the time…"

"Do you want to see it again?" Raz repeated, ignoring her as he stared at the slave intently.

Whereas most would have quailed under that gaze, it seemed only to invigorate Akelo.

"More than anything," he said firmly, and Syrah felt a thrill as she saw something shine in the onyx depths of the man's eyes. Light returned to him, a brief glow of life, like the first sparks of a fire catching hold.

"Then you know how to live," Raz told him. "You have a reason. Hold onto that. Fiercely. With desire comes purpose. The rest… that will come with time, as Syrah said."

The Percian's face tightened, but it wasn't in pain, or misery. Rather, he looked instead to be a man fighting to contain the overwhelming rush of a hundred different emotions as he realized, for the first time in what might well have been the better part of his existence, that he wasn't living for the purposes of another anymore.

Indeed, as they watched, a single wet line traced down the old man's wrinkled cheek, trailing from his blackened eye to cling to the coarse, silvering hair of his beard. Slowly, in twitching attempts that made it clear he hadn't managed such a thing in a very long time., Akelo smiled.

Then he fell to his knees and began to laugh, staring at his hands once again as more tears fell to pattern the bloody scars that marked both the end and beginning of his life as a free man.

XXX

In the aftermath of the battle at sea, there was much to do. Fires required putting out, and the damage to the *Sylgid*'s hull and structure had to be accounted for and addressed. Blood needed to be scrubbed from the deck, and the wounded were carried down to the crew quarters where they were laid out in any cot, atop every table, and along any spare space of the compartment floor that could be cleared. Syrah spent the afternoon hurrying from patient to patient, treating what injuries she could with spellwork, but more often assisting in suturing lacerations or bandaging glistening burns that smelled of cooked meat. On several occasions she was called on to help in even more gruesome businesses, such as removing two arms and a leg that had been maimed beyond saving, or removing an arrow from the skull of a Southerner who miraculously still breathed. By the time most of the injured had been attended to, Syrah was in a grislier state than she'd ever been during the fight. She had traded her robes for a simpler tunic, but the state of her shirt and wool pants was so morbid she doubted the clothes could be saved. The edges of her rolled-up sleeves, once the worn paleness of undyed cloth, were so red they were almost black, and the front of her shirt and pants looked more like she had spent the last hours slaughtering livestock than rushing about the makeshift sickbay. Even as she weaved her magics to help the last of the wounded fall into a dreamless sleep, it took every ounce of her constitution not to crawl into the nearest corner of the cabin and hug herself while she fought to keep at bay the keening screams and sobs of pain and misery that lingered in her ears.

As evening fell, the dead were given to the sea. The *Moalas*—Akelo Aseni had given them the name of the captured vessel while staring up at its grey and maroon sales in loathing—remained tethered along the portside, and spare sheets from the pirate ship were used to wrap the bodies of the *Sylgid*'s fallen, as well as the seven slain slaves. In all, the still forms lining the starboard side of the deck numbered eighteen, the mismatched colors of their cloth coffins glowing a dim orange and red in the sunset. Argoan, scrubbed clean and in fresh clothes—though he sported a new scar across his left cheek—stood over the dead and said a few words. His wet eyes threated to ruin the newly applied war-paint across his face, but his voice was strong as he spoke, praising the bravery and sacrifice of the men and women before him. When he stepped away, Lysa shouted for a salute, and as one the survivors snapped to attention over the swaddled forms. Finally, the bodies were given to the waves.

The corpses of the *Moalas'* crew, along with the rest of the slain pirates, Argoan had ordered be thrown into the Dramion without ceremony or fanfare.

After that, the entirety of the *Sylgid*'s company ate together atop the main deck. It was a celebration the likes of which Syrah didn't know if she would ever be able to replicate, a simultaneous marking of their victory and a commemoration of the lives lost to win it. Argoan pulled out all the stops, opening up his small store of private rations for all, and the cooks had managed to prepare a decent stew of salted pork, softened hardtack, cheese, potatoes, and dried fruit flavored with various herbs and spices. Three full caskets of ale and mead were brought up from the hatch—Syrah hoped they wouldn't be missed by whoever they'd been intended for—and within an hour or two a vast majority of the ship's company was roaring drunk beneath the glow of a dozen torches and lanterns, alternating between singing bawdy tales and exchanging stories about the sailors who had passed on this day.

This time, Syrah stayed away from the alcohol.

Feeling much refreshed in a loose leather vest and clean cotton shorts she'd manage to borrow from Lysa, she sat with the first mate in the loudest corner of the frigate, at the base of the stern stairs. Several steps above them, Argoan was roaring like a madman, swinging his tankard aloft and bellowing along with the songs as his free arm hung playfully about the neck of one of the female sailors. He appeared about as inebriated as the rest of the crew, but Syrah had a feeling it was much an act for the sake of his men. Not once had she seen the captain get up to refill his cups, or relieve himself over the edge of the ship, and she frequently caught him gazing sadly at the moonlit water over the starboard bow, where the shrouded bodies had faded into the depths not so many hours ago. When he noticed her watching him, the captain just winked roguishly and returned to his singing, clearly intent on keeping up appearances.

All around them, some fifteen sailors sat on stools and coils of ropes they'd dragged up from below deck, or else leaned against the cabin walls and railings as they laughed and talked and occasionally burst out into random bouts of cheering or fighting. A few of the freed slaves, including Akelo and the West Isler Syrah had heard speak briefly earlier in the afternoon, lingered among them, scrubbed clean now. They were dressed in borrowed clothes and armor they'd pilfered from the dead pirates before the corpses had been heaved overboard, and now sat with wide eyes and stiff bodies as they attempted to weather the onslaught of sensations that was the celebration. The others, Syrah was pleased to see, were dispersed among the smaller parties of men and women about the ship, sticking together in quiet groups of threes and fours, but all looking as though they were at least attempting to have a good time. It warmed her heart in a curious way to see them like that. As strained as many of the men seemed, as much as they flinched from the touch of the sailors and clung to their bowls of stew like they were afraid the food would be ripped away from their hands at any moment, Syrah found her spirits lift as she watched them try.

The only person distinctly *not* having a good time, in fact, was the figure sitting on the deck at her feet, leaning back against her knees.

As the evening stretched on she had tried several times to drag Raz into conversation, but with little success. Sometimes Lysa—who was getting progressively redder in the face as the moon rose above them—would attempt to help her, punching the atherian in the shoulder and insisting he recount some particularly gruesome aspect of the battle, or demanding to know how many drinks he was in. He answered each time with feigned enthusiasm, but—similar to the captain seated above them—always returned to his somber silence, never attempting to engage any of the others around him as they talked and laughed. Syrah didn't press him too hard. It had taken the help of several of the crew to lug enough water up from the sea to wash Raz's scaled skin of blood, even after they'd removed his armor. She thought, perhaps, that the man was simply lost in his own consciousness, or maybe dwelling on the fact that he'd allowed the second vessel—the *Red Turor*, Akelo had called it—to escape unscathed with its hull full of slaves.

Her worry grew, though, when several hours into the festivities Raz abruptly stood and left their ring of celebrators, stepping through the group into the less-crowded space of the ship's deck.

No one else seemed to notice him leave. Lysa was deep in her own conversation, slurring her words as she flirted with a handsome seaman she'd pulled down to sit beside her some time before, and Argoan was once again staring out at sea with sad eyes, his female companion dozing against his shoulder and hiccupping pleasantly. Raz managed to slip through without anyone calling him to come back, or hailing him once more as the hero of the battle, and Syrah let him go, wanting to give him his moment of peace. For a time he stood at the ship's edge, staring at the reflection of the moon and stars in the water, and she wondered if he, too, was thinking about the souls that had passed on this day. She couldn't blame him. She was struggling with the deaths herself, still fighting to come to terms with this new understanding of the Lifegiver that her eyes were slowly being opened to. Still, she watched him, wondering what it was that he was tormenting himself with now.

And then, like a shifting of the light, Raz slipped across the *Sylgid*, sliding through the shadows like he was made of them.

Syrah's eyes narrowed as she watched him deftly avoid the scattered pockets of other men and women drinking and enjoying themselves in the torchlight. She thought, for a moment, that he might simply be heading for their guest quarters, desiring to retire undisturbed. He made no move for the door of the cabin, though, and in the end she followed his dark outline toward the port rail.

Then, quiet as death, Raz stole across the gangplank that still spanned the gap between the *Sylgid* and *Moalas*, disappearing into the darkness of the night onto the captured ship.

"Excuse me," she said at once, getting up so quickly she nearly spilled Lysa's drink as she bumped into the woman's elbow. She moved gingerly through the group, doing her best not to draw too much attention, but as she managed to push herself clear of the ring of sailors she thought she saw Akelo watching her, the former slave's good eye following her across the ship.

She didn't glance back to see if she was right.

Syrah discovered quickly that she wasn't nearly as adept as Raz when it came to maneuvering undisturbed through the celebrations. On three different occasions men and woman caught sight of her and attempted to drag her into their merrymaking, requiring her to bow out politely and wave away offered mugs of frothing mead. By the time she made it to the end of the gangplank, Syrah knew at least a few people were watching her curiously, but she ignored them. Hauling herself up onto the makeshift wooden bridge, she was positive that no one would want to follow her onto the deck of the *Moalas*. The bodies Raz and Lysa's group had cut down had been cleared, tossed into the sea to feed the bottom feeders along the ocean floor.

No one, though, had wanted to waste more time on cleaning the rest of the deck.

Syrah found herself pressing a hand over her nose and mouth as she dropped off the gangplank onto the pirate vessel, the hard heels of her leather boots *clomping* onto the old wood. The air was sour about her, almost rancid, and she could taste iron in her mouth as she looked about for a sign of Raz. The blood had dried in the hours since the fight, patterning what she could make out of the deck in shapes and splatters and slashes of black beneath the moonlight. Flies buzzed even in the night, and though the *Sylgid* wasn't more than ten feet behind her Syrah felt as though the sounds of the crew's festivities were distant here, like the cheer of the other ship was dulled by the distinct aura of death that hung over the *Moalas*. She felt a chill as she took in the outline of the boat against the shimmering water beyond it, the utter stillness of the place bringing to mind stories the others had told her of ghost ships that sailed the seas, steered only by the dead.

Making matters worse, the atherian was nowhere to be found.

"Raz?" Syrah called out softly, hands clenched in fists by her side as she tried to swallow her fear. "Raz, where are you?"

No answer.

Taking a shaking breath, she stepped further onto the deck, feeling the boards creak ominously beneath her feet, still casting about for signs of the man. The twin masts towered above her, sails lifted and strapped so that the booms and riggings looked like giant skeletons leering down at her. Rats skittered along the rails, making her jump, and there was a groan as the boat swayed, the helm to her left spinning slowly back and forth with the current.

It didn't take long for Syrah to figure out that Raz wasn't on the top deck, and the realization made her insides squirm as she caught sight of the open hatch in the floor near the aft, like a dark mouth leading down into the belly of the ship. She approached it cautiously, unable to shake the fact that she distinctly did *not* want to descend into the dark. When she stood over the opening, peering into the blackness below, the feeling redoubled.

"Raz?" she called down quietly. "Are you down there?"

Again, silence was all that answered her.

Given that she was fairly sure Raz hadn't jumped overboard, Syrah began to feel annoyed, which did much to bury her anxiety. Lifting a hand up, she willed her magic into being, and ivory flames flickered to life in her palm. They cast the ship in a bright, cheerful glow that chased away the rest of her apprehension, and carefully Syrah stepped into the gloom, avoiding the slick sheen of blood that covered the right half of the stairs leading down.

Raz was waiting for her in the rowing galley.

As she stepped through a doorway at the base of the steps, her flames bathed the compartment beyond it in white light, casting shifting shadows over the space. They danced between the dozen benches set on either side of a raised walkway, tilting with the swing of a trio of dark lanterns in the rafters above her. The fore wall of the space was a collage of light, shining through the narrow bars of a pair of cages set in the floor at the back of the galley.

And there, in the center of the starboard row of seats, Raz sat with his back to her.

Syrah didn't say anything as she approached him, her steps pulling away flakes of the dried blood that painted the raised walkway from the back door of the chamber in a faded streak. She stayed silent, too, when she stepped down to join him, taking a seat at his side and following his eyes to the fore wall, where the twin cages stood like still, dead things. She didn't touch him, didn't reach for him, but she kept the flames alight in her hand, trusting in the warmth of the magic to find him in whatever dark place the man had sunk to.

After nearly a minute of nothing more than the quiet rush of the sea through the oar-hole to their right, Raz finally spoke.

"Did Akelo tell you why there weren't any of my kind aboard?" he asked her, his voice sad and grave.

Syrah frowned, then shook her head slowly. "No. I didn't ask."

Raz nodded, like he would have been surprised to hear her answer any other way. "Food," he said simply, still staring at the cages. "He told me atherian made poor ship slaves because the amount of meat needed to sustain them on long journeys was never worth the cost." He laughed, but it was a dull, hollow sound. "Apparently atherian are almost exclusively property of the city-states, for that reason. They have such little value, there are some tasks not even pirates will put them to, just because they aren't worth the trouble. I think I'm more vexed by that than I would have been if we *had* found a ship full of lizard-kind. Is that strange?"

Syrah said nothing, knowing Raz wasn't actually looking for an answer.

"There were another thirty on that second ship, Syrah," he told her, his shoulders quivering. "The *Red Turor*. I wish you hadn't stopped me."

"You would have been killed," Syrah told him softly, reaching out now to slide her free hand into his. "You could barely stand as it was."

Raz made no attempt to contradict her, and his shaking subsided at her touch. "I know," he told her as the wind picked up outside, whistling through the holes around them. "And I know I made you a promise not to do anything rash. But..."

"You still wish I hadn't stopped you," Syrah finished for him with a nod. "I know. And truthfully—" she sighed unhappily "—if I'd had a moment to consider what letting the ship escape meant, I would have been tempted to let you go."

That managed to get a smile out of him. It was a weak, paltry thing, but it was a smile nonetheless. With a flick of her wrist, Syrah transformed the flames into an orb of light, letting it float free in the air above their heads as she leaned against him, resting her head on his shoulder.

"Akelo and the others are free because of you, Raz," she continued softly, looking at the cages as the shadows of the bars continued to swim against the wall behind them. "Don't lose sight of that. You won't always be able to save everyone."

Raz grunted in frustrated agreement. "I'm *never* able to save everyone. Not the Arros, not the Koyts, not the Laorin…"

It was Syrah's turn to smile sadly. "That doesn't mean you should give up trying."

"Giving up is the last thing I'm thinking about."

Syrah's brows knit at that, and she sat up again to look at him directly.

"What *are* you thinking about, then?" she asked apprehensively, not sure she wanted to know the answer.

For a while, Raz didn't answer her, his jaw moving like he was chewing on his words.

Then he turned and looked right at her, golden eyes glinting like dusk over the ocean waves.

"I'm *tired* of running, Syrah," he told her in an exhausted sort of voice. "I'm so, *so* tired of running. I told myself when we were still in the North that I was done turning tail every time trouble reared its head, and look how well that's worked out. It's been over a year since I fled Miropa, and in all that time all I've been doing is running and hiding and running some more."

Syrah frowned. "Yes…" she said, choosing her words carefully. "But isn't that the point of this journey? First Perce, then the Cities, and from there the West Isles, or the Imperium. If we reach the Emperor's Ocean, you won't have to run anymore, Raz. You'll be free."

"I *might* be free," he corrected her somberly, and his eyes were dark with sadness and anger. "And it's not just me now, Syrah. It's us. So long as you're with me, you are running. Hell, even if we parted ways, there's a bounty on your head now. You might never be safe again."

Syrah felt all the heat leave her body at those words.

"Is… is that what you came here to think about?" she asked shakily, pulling her hand from his. "To figure out how to tell me you're leaving? Is that what this is all about?"

In response, Raz gaped at her, the look on his face so dumbfounded she might have just punched him in the snout.

Then he laughed, the sound echoing hollowly against the empty hull around them.

"Gods, no," he managed to get out finally, smiling in truth now, like he couldn't help it, before reaching out to take her hand back. "*No*. I'm not sure I would have had it in me to make it to the Isles with you, and certainly not *without* you. No. That's absolutely *not* what I came down here to think about."

The warmth returned to Syrah's body, relief washing over her, but something kept her happiness in check.

"'Would have had'," she quoted uncertainly. "What do you mean, 'would have had'?"

Raz stilled, the amusement in his eyes dying as he realized he had let something slip. The smiled faded, and his face grew slowly hard, firm with what Syrah could only describe as conviction.

"I'm tired of running, Syrah," he said again, like he was goading her toward some understanding. "I'm so, so tired of running."

Syrah watched him, disconcerted, her good eye flicking back and forth between his, looking for additional clues as she struggled to find the answer in his gaze. At first she thought he was telling her that he wanted to stay as a part of Argoan's crew, but that didn't fit. She doubted he would have the heart to sell Gale off at port—much less make the horse suffer a life of confinement at sea—and while this passage across the Dramion had been unforgettable in its own way, the role of "sailor" had never fit either of them quite right. Syrah herself hadn't felt more alive in the last two months than she had during the battle, defending her life and that of her friends. She was a fighter, had *always* been a fighter, from the moment Talo had first taught her how to hold a staff. She required more from the world than the typically monotonous repetition of a smuggler's day.

Even more so, that vibrancy, that glow of energy, had been reflected tenfold in Raz as she'd watched him combat the Percian. The atherian might claim not to take pleasure in the deaths dealt by his hand, but there was reason for him there. There was meaning in the protection of those he cared about, *and* in the punishment of those who wronged them. Raz was born to wield a blade. It was his essence, these wars he waged, this bloodshed he brought to the feet of those he deemed deserving. It was his purpose.

Purpose, Syrah thought, and the word made her think of the fervor with which Raz had encouraged Akelo to take hold of this second chance at life.

Then, abruptly, it clicked.

"You want to stay!" she hissed in astonishment. "You want to stay in *Perce!*"

Raz hesitated, then nodded.

"For a while, at least," he told her. "Not forever."

"But *why?*" she asked in disbelief. "What for? Almost twenty people died today because of the simple fact that Perce is *not* our friend, Raz. And that's not counting the pirates slain to win that battle. If anything, this land is going to be even more daunting than we thought! Why would you want to stay?"

This time, Raz was much longer in answering her. For a while he didn't meet her eye, staring down at his own feet. When he was silent so long she began to get annoyed again, Syrah glanced down too, intending to demand what *in the Lifegiver's name* was so enthralling he couldn't be bothered giving her a reason for this sudden change of heart.

She choked on her anger, though, when she saw the floor of the boat beneath her.

The oar that would have slotted through the hole in the hull at their right when needed had been slid out of the way, half-hidden under the raised walkway to their right. Of the section she could see, though, Syrah made out worn divots in the haft, smooth as stone, but discolored with dark red splotches where blisters had burst and blood had run free over the wood to stain it like spilled wine. Beneath this, tangled about each other like discarded bear traps, two sets of manacles were bolted into the floor, one for each foot of the paired rowers who would have taken up the bench she and Raz now occupied. Thinking of this, Syrah reached down and pressed shaking fingers to the surface of the seat. She felt where the coarseness of the plain timber block faded into a glassy smoothness, polished down by so many men shifting and bending for hours on end to pull at the oars.

Lastly, her eyes lifted to the cages, where she imagined the pirates had imprisoned the captives they took on their raids, allowing them a glimpse of the life they were likely to live as they gazed out over the broken slaves laboring miserably to get them back to shore.

Even before Raz finally gave her his answer, Syrah understood.

"Because I want a chance to save *everyone*, for once," he told her in a calm, cool voice as they sat there in the dim glow of her arcane light.

XXXI

"After the fall of Karesh Nan, the Mahsadën sought to prepare themselves. They gathered every ally they could to their banner, and—when that wasn't enough—nearly emptied their coffers enlisting whatever sarydâ and other mercenary groups could be mustered to their cause. The last šef of Miropa, a man by the name of Adrion Blaeth, ended up amassing an army the likes of which the South had never seen before.
What good that did the society in the end, though, can be witnessed in what remains of the Mahsadën today…"

—*A History of War & Peace*, by Marret Vern

After he'd explained the details of his plan to Syrah, Raz led the way out of the galley, up the hatch stairs, and back over the gangplank onto the *Sylgid*. There were whistles and catcalls from the drunker of the figures still celebrating about them as he dropped onto the ship and turned to help the Priestess down, as well as quite a few odd looks from the more sober sailors, undoubtedly wondering what they could have been up to aboard the gruesome scene that was the *Moalas*. Ignoring all, Raz took Syrah by the hand and made a line straight back toward the largest knot of festivities, where Argoan and Lysa were still seated along the steps.

"Captain!" Raz shouted over the noise of conversation and laughter and clinking tankards. When Argoan turned to look at him, Raz pointed a clawed finger at the door of the guest quarters, off to his left. "A word, if you please!"

The Amreht looked puzzled, but nodded, inclining his head at his first mate quizzically. Raz nodded, indicating that he should bring the woman as well before turning and stepping toward the cabin. As he did, he felt eyes on his back, and he glanced over his shoulder.

While he could have sworn Akelo Aseni had been watching him a moment before, it seemed the old Percian was now deep in conversation with one of the other freed slaves.

Shaking off the feeling, Raz moved with Syrah into their quarters.

Argoan and Lysa joined them not a minute later. The captain, Raz was surprised to find, was quite steady on his feet for a man who'd been clutching a flagon of ale all night. The first mate, on the other hand, half-stumbled into the room, leaving the door open behind her while muttering about being dragged away from the "fine work of a man" she'd been nuzzling with.

She sobered up quickly, though, when Raz and Syrah told them what they intended to do.

"You want to *what?*" the woman practically shouted, the flush of her cheeks doing nothing to reduce the shock painted across her face.

"We're going to stay, Lysa," Syrah repeated calmly. Raz had let her take the lead on the explanation, thinking the pair would trust her as the more level-headed of the two. "In Perce. For a time, at least."

Lysa gaped at her, then at Raz, then back at Syrah, her mouth moving all the while like a fish out of water.

"Th-that's... madness," she finally managed to get out, falling back against the bow wall of the room and sliding to the floor, one eye drooping as she struggled to overcome her cups. "Why? Why would you... want to stay?"

"There's work to be done here," Raz told her evenly. "Syrah and I are clearly already infamous in these lands, thanks to the Mahsadën. There's a chance we can use that to our advantage, or at least to the advantage of others. Regardless, it's clear we're going to find about as much peace in this place as we would have if we'd made straight for the fringe cities."

"Exactlyyyy," Lysa insisted, drawing out the word drunkenly. "You shouldn't... shouldn't be here *at all*, let alone be talking about... this! Stay with us." She gave the pair of them an affectionate—if distinctly inebriated—smile. "S-Stay on the ship. No more pirates." She raised her arms and closed her eyes, still smiling. "No more... Perce."

"We can't stay on the *Sylgid*," Syrah said, regarding the woman with sad fondness. "It would be too dangerous for all of you. You need to sail. Let anyone who asks search the ship. When they realize we aren't aboard, they'll leave you be."

"We're done running," Raz finished, speaking with every ounce of conviction he could muster.

"B-but it's madness," Lysa insisted again, turning to look at Argoan and blinking like she was seeing double. "Tell them, Garht!"

The captain was leaning against the starboard wall of the quarters, staring into the hollow of his tankard as he swirled the swills of his drink absently. When the woman addressed him, he looked up, frowning at Raz and Syrah.

He didn't, though, agree with Lysa outright.

"You *are* welcome to stay," the man said steadily, looking between them. "The crew would have you in a moment, and you've saved my ship—my *life*—twice now. There is a home for you both here, if you desire it."

Raz's fingers prickled, so surprisingly touched was he by the offer. He knew he and Syrah were appreciated—the captain had already made that clear ten times over—but he hadn't realized just how much their presence on the boat meant to the man until that moment.

Despite this, though, he had to shake his head.

"No, Captain," he said, hoping he at least sounded a little disappointed. "For one thing, the *Sylgid* would never have come under attack if we weren't here. For another... Syrah and I aren't meant for the sea."

At that, Argoan shrugged. "Neither are men of the mountains."

Raz chuckled. "Point made." Then he shook his head again. "But no. The offer is appreciated—greatly, even—but we can't accept. I chose my path a long time ago, and it's time to see it through." On his lap, he turned his hand over, palm up, and looked down at the pale ring of skin that wrapped around his wrist like a bracelet. "It's been over a year since I butchered the

Miropan Mahsadën. Before that, I was lost. Wandering through life one bloody step at a time." He lifted his hand, making sure the other three could clearly make out the scars left by the manacles he didn't even remember. "When I met Eva, I was working for the wrong side, refusing to acknowledge that I was a building block of the society itself. I found her chained with a dozen others, half-frozen and half-starved, each one having given up all hope of regaining the life they'd been torn from. Only then, when what I'd become was put right in front of my face, did I realize how far gone I was."

He grit his teeth, and his hand tensed unwillingly, clawed fingers curling inward so that the tendons of his forearm stood out along the scale-less band he still stared at. "I wore myself to the bone fighting to destroy everything I'd inadvertently helped to build. I bled and I killed and I almost died a half-dozen times in a matter of weeks. I thought I'd made a difference. I thought I'd rid the world of a piece of the corruption eating at it, at least for a time."

Abruptly, he shifted his hand to point at the open door of the cabin. "Do you see how hollow those men are, out there?" he asked Argoan. "They are free, now, and yet despite this there is so little left to most of them that they fear their own shadows. Can you tell me how, in the end, I made a difference? How I changed the world for the better?"

The man said nothing, frowning at him, though he did glance out onto the torch-lit deck as though contemplating Raz's point.

"Y-you killed half-a-hundred pirates all by yourself," Lysa cut in, her words slurred as she waved her empty right hand about, like she were swinging a sword. "Bast-bastards won't be slaving anyone again any-anytime soon!"

"And I let a ship get away with thirty souls who will likely never know what it's like to take a piss without being told to," Raz growled angrily. "*Thirty* men who will be worked until their hands are bone and their backs are broken. How does that *make anything*—?"

Syrah's hand looped under his arm, and in an instant he calmed. He didn't look around at her, but he felt his fury with himself, his anger at his own failings, recede at her touch.

Taking a breath, he continued in a more even tone. "The point," he said to Lysa, "is that I started my war against the Mahsadën to make a change, and I didn't manage it. I realized today that there's a fight I never finished. One I need to see through."

"This fight is like to see you killed, Dahgün," Argoan said darkly, but his eyes were on Syrah. "Have you come to terms with that?"

In response, Raz felt Syrah shift beside him. Without removing her arm from his, she lifted both hands up. In the faint white light of the candles, the reddish scars about her own wrists showed pink against her pale skin.

"There are some things worth risking it all for, aren't there?" she asked the Amreht.

Argoan sighed in response, bobbing his head as though in defeat. "Very well." He sounded like a man resigning himself to a terrible fate. "If you're going to do this, will you at least let us help?"

Raz felt measured relief lift a weight off his shoulders, and he nodded and spoke before Lysa—who looked ready to pass out from either disbelief or the ale—could interrupt again. "We were hoping you might. We could use provisions, and we need to be taken to shore, obviously." He hesitated, glancing at Syrah, worried about his next request.

"Also—" the Priestess took the lead calmly "—we were wondering if you could spare a man. Anyone familiar with Percian lands and customs."

The captain looked suddenly pained, and he chewed on his beard a moment before speaking. "Shore and provisions are easy enough," he said with a nod. "But a guide is trickier. I lost eleven good sailors today, and that's not counting the injured. I'm not sure I have enough hands to man the ship safely as it is. Even if I did, I couldn't just order one of my own to follow you. They would have to volunteer."

Raz grimaced, seeing the man's point. He suspected he and Syrah could survive well enough on their own for a while—given how verdant the land seemed to be—but there was little point in wandering the wild plains of Perce without direction. They had little enough of a plan to go on *without* struggling to find civilization in what he was coming to understand was a realm full of its own dangers.

He decided to press his luck.

"A guide would be the greatest boon you could grant us," he said. "Even a volunteer. Syrah and I know less than we would like of this place. I couldn't even tell you who this 'Tash' is, or why he's intent on my head. If *anyone* would be willing to at least help us—"

He stopped abruptly, though, because all three of the others had reacted differently to his plea. Before him, Argoan scowled suddenly. On the floor, Lysa started hiccupping, eyes wide again, suddenly looking far soberer than she had all night. Even at his side, Syrah tensed.

"Raz!" she hissed in surprise. "You didn't tell me that!"

"What?" Raz asked, not understanding as he glanced around at each of them. "What did I say?"

"Where did you hear that?" It was Argoan who asked the question, his voice thunderous. "Who told you of the Tash?"

Raz looked at him, brow creased in confusion. "The captain of the *Moalas*," he said uncertainly, disliking the sudden edge of fear he could taste in the room. "He told me someone called 'the Tash' was the one spreading the word that Syrah and I were aboard the *Sylgid*."

Argoan cursed in rapid mountain tongue, and Lysa started hiccupping again. Disliking being out of the loop, he turned to Syrah.

"What is it?" he demanded in frustration.

Syrah grimaced.

"I'm not the best person to explain," she said uncertainly. "I know the Tash are rulers. Powerful ones." She swore under her breath, muttering to herself. "Lifegiver's arse, I was never good at cultural studies." She blinked and look back up at him. "I think the Tash are masters of the city-states of Perce. They are... kings, in their own way."

"The Tash," a new voice said from the entrance of the cabin, "are the blessed chosen of the Sun and Moon. They are considered the Twins' emissaries in the mortal world. Their Hands are thought of as the secondary voices of the gods."

Everyone turned to the open door. There, as the echoes of cheering and laughter mixed with the sounds of fighting and breaking clay flagons from behind him, Akelo Aseni stood framed against the light of the deck. Whereas the sailors of the *Sylgid* had doffed their gear and weapons after the battle had ended, Akelo—like most of the other former slaves—had refused to part with the items he'd managed to scavenge from the bodies of their former masters for fear he wouldn't get them back. The man had attired himself in looted clothes and armor, a rough set of hardened leather plating fastened over a torn red shirt that almost hid the dark weep of blood staining its left side. The bow he'd found was still slung over his back, and an empty quiver hung from his right hip. On his left, a battered scimitar was sheathed in a wooden loop off a worn belt. In the crook of one elbow rested one of the Percian spiked half-helms, complete with a neck guard made of woven leather straps, and his free hand was at his side, fist clenched nervously. He had the look of a man unsure of whether or not he was about to be welcomed with open arms, or hurled from the room.

"Akelo," Raz greeted him in surprise, waving him in. "Come in. And close the door behind you."

The Percian hesitated for almost five whole seconds, clearly uncertain if doing as Raz said was in his best interest. At last, though, he stepped into the cabin and shut the door after him, muting the cacophony of the festivities.

"I apologize for eavesdropping," he said in that rough voice, like he was only now realizing he could speak after a lifetime of silence. "I..." He paused, uncertain of himself. "I wondered what it was you were planning to do, now that you're free to sail again."

The way he said it made it sound like he was asking the group as a whole, but he never looked away from Raz.

Raz, in turn, took him in. Though the aging man looked a good deal better off now he was clean and his dirty rags had been thrown to the sea with the dead, he was still half-a-mess. His right eye was completely swollen shut now, the hard crust of a scab forming over a large section of the bruise where some pommel or club must have caught him. He clung to his new helm and kept his other fist clenched tight, but still didn't manage to hide the shake of his hands completely. He might have stood tall and strong, but his face was gaunt and the hollows of his bearded cheeks and good eye were dark, like a man who'd only ever been fed just enough to keep his body strong for the task at hand.

Despite all this, though, there was still that will in his gaze that Raz had noted the first time the man had spoken up, seizing on the chance to see him and his comrades freed from a life in chains.

"We were wondering the same," Raz answered him, appraising the former slave. "We were just addressing some concerns regarding what our next move might be."

Akelo nodded in a jerking fashion, but said nothing more.

"Concerns you seem to have some of the answers to, Akelo," Syrah pressed the man gently. "You sound like you might know more of the Tash than any of us…" She looked to Argoan and Lysa, who nodded and shrugged respectively.

Again, Akelo hesitated, clearly out of his element. Raz felt Syrah lift a finger from where her hand rested against his forearm, and in almost imperceptible increments the white flames of the candles grew, steadily chasing away the shadows of the cabin.

There are no cruelties lurking in the dark, here, she seemed to be trying to say. *There are no evils lying in wait.*

As the light brightened, so too did the freed man's confidence. He took a quick breath, chewing on his lip for a moment more, but his hands stopped shaking.

"The Tash are the blessed chosen of the Twins," he repeated again, his voice much calmer now, and it was Syrah he addressed this time. "The Sun and Moon. They are men held in the same level of reverence as Her Stars, considered something like adopted children of the gods. Their Hands—the First and Second—are their proxies, individually chosen to aid them in ruling the lands around the city-states of Karesh Syl and Karesh Nan." His eye flicked to Raz. "If one of the Tash has put out the word of your arrival in Perce, then the entire realm is like to be on the lookout for you."

Raz ground his teeth at the words, and he felt Syrah stiffen beside him.

"Is there something we could do?" the Priestess asked him. "Some way we could appease them?"

At her question, the Percian's face twisted in what might have been disgust. "You would not want to make the attempt," he said flatly. "And you would have little sympathy from me if you tried. The Tash are not worth the reverence they are given. They bask in their privilege, seeking only to hold onto their power and appease the masses of their cities." He swallowed, like the words came hard, and looked at Raz again. "I may have been mistaken, but you seemed surprised to find so many of my kind aboard the *Moalas*…?"

"I was," Raz answered at once. "I hadn't realized the Percian preyed on their own, let alone in such numbers."

Akelo nodded. "Nearly half of all the enslaved in Perce come from within the borders of its lands. No other race comes close, not even—" he inclined his head in Raz's direction meaningfully "—the atherian."

Raz felt himself bristle.

"It's just like the South, then," he muttered furiously, feeling his neck-crest twitch in outrage. "Cities devouring their own. Sun burn them all!"

"No," Akelo said firmly. "The walls of Karesh Syl and Karesh Nan protect residents. Any born to a free father within their borders are guaranteed their liberty. Outsiders, on the other hand…"

Beside Raz, Syrah was watching the man in concern. "Is that what happened to you?" she asked. "Were you born outside the cities?"

In response, Akelo smiled. It was a light, happy expression, and Raz knew well the face of a man lost to old memories. For a second the Percian looked at peace, drawn back into his own mind by the Priestess' query.

When he spoke, his voice was as distant as his gaze.

"I had never even been within a hundred miles of Karesh Nan when its soldiers fell upon my tribe." Akelo reached up, tugging at the neck of his shirt to reveal a swirling pattern of white curled under the dark skin below his collarbone. A tattoo, much like the ones Raz had noticed on most of the other Percian slaves as well. "I was—No, I *am*—*kuja*."

Argoan made a sound then, like a slow exhale of understanding. Raz and Syrah glanced at him.

"'Man of the plains,'" the captain translated for them, studying the tattoo with distinct interest. "Families who live in the savannah, separate from the laws of the cities. We trade with them often." His eyes met Raz's. "They're how I manage to get my hands on the herbs and medications for Evalyn."

Akelo nodded, releasing his shirt so the white ink was hidden once more. "I was the shaman of my tribe—the chieftain, you would say. Another family wished to control a number of watering holes in our territory. After we rebuffed them for several seasons, they sought help from Karesh Nan in routing us." The man's lip twitched at the memory, combining with his bruised eye for a moment to make him look demented. "They sold my tribe to the slavers. Whereas we could very well have continued repelling them each year on their own, they fell on us with a hundred extra men, all bearing leather armor and steel. We were no match. Ours homes were burned to the ground, our livestock slaughtered. Even after we yielded, they murdered those too old to be of value and drowned the infants and babes." Abruptly, his left eye became wet, his bad right already weeping tears. "My own family… I-it's been… It's been…" He inhaled sharply, rasping in a breath and shaking free of the spell of his own story.

When he had regained control of himself, Akelo's eye fell on Raz and Syrah again. "I tried to count the years, but eventually you stop caring. You have no *purpose*." He injected the word with meaning. "I would have you give me a purpose, Arro. If you would be willing. Many of the others, too, I think, should you grant them the opportunity…"

The proposition took a moment for Raz to comprehend. He blinked at the Percian, then around at Syrah, who looked about as surprised as he felt.

"You want to join us?" she asked, sounding taken aback.

This time, Akelo nodded at once. "I do," he said. "You told the captain you require a guide. Many years may have passed, but the lands of the savannah do not change so easily. You will find none better than I. In addition—" he inclined his head respectfully to Argoan "—we are most grateful for his hospitality, and his food. This way, none of his company need leave him."

"A-and the others?" Syrah followed up, tripping over her words like she had trouble believing them. "They would want to join us as well?"

At that, Argoan interrupted with a splutter. "I had intended to offer them a place aboard the ship," he admitted, looking sheepishly around at Raz and Syrah. "As I said, we are short-handed…"

There was a hiccup, and off to the side Lysa mimed lifting a drink to the heavens.

"To the dead," she muttered, then lapsed back into silence.

After a pause, Akelo turned back to the captain. "You should make the offer," he agreed. "I believe a few, at least, are hoping you might. Most of us have spent many years at sea, and not just pulling the oars. You will find any who agree to sail with you valuable additions to your crew." He eyed the man then, as though unsure. "So long as you treat them well, that is…"

"He will," Raz cut in before Argoan could struggle to form a response. "I will vouch for the captain, Akelo. You can tell your men that."

That seemed to satisfy the former slave, because he relaxed, then faced Raz and Syrah once more.

"We know your story, Arro," he began slowly, speaking cautiously. "You are laughed at by the freemen of Perce, I will not deny it, but among those bound in iron your tale is very much alive, and often repeated. We have heard of what you did to the rulers of your fringe city, and what happened to the governor of that valley town in the North. You are a myth to the enslaved, a dream many of them cling to. You are often the hero our children pretend to be, imagining themselves descending on their homes to free their mothers and fathers from their chains." His eyes were fiery, bright in the candlelight. "If you seek to make a difference, know that you would not be alone in doing so. There are thousands—*tens* of thousands, even—in this land who would rise and join you if you would give them the chance. There is an army waiting for you, bound and shackled, that you need only free."

Raz felt a shiver go down his spine, and he wasn't sure if it was a jolt of excitement or fear.

"You're talking about starting a war," he said cautiously.

To his surprise, Akelo shook his head.

"No," the man said, his voice growing stronger. Then he raised his own hand, as Raz and Syrah had before. There, ringing his wrist in an even darker shade of black than his skin, was the scar that marked where the irons had bound him for more years than the man had been able to count.

"I am talking about finishing the one you started."

XXXII

In the end, eleven of the surviving freed slaves—including Akelo—cast their vote in favor of joining Raz and Syrah. When all was said and done, such a number was likely a small thing—they were apparently considering bringing their fight to the doorstep of some god-king of Perce, after all—but in the moment Raz wasn't sure he had ever felt more honored, or more terrified. One by one they stood, pushing themselves up from where they'd all been sitting in a group on the deck under the next day's early-morning Sun to hear out his and Argoan's respective proposals. As each of the men got to his feet to volunteer themselves, Raz had felt a thrill of apprehension and excitement. The captain, too, hadn't come out too poorly. Four men, a Northerner, two Southerners, and a Percian, elected to stay aboard and join the crew. While this might not have been the numbers Argoan would have liked, he seemed pleased enough with the result, extending his hand to each man as he came forward and officially welcoming them aboard the *Sylgid* while cheers rose up from the ship's company all around.

Two men—both former *kuja* themselves, judging by the tattoos of different colors spiraling over their bodies—chose not to join either group, stating that they planned instead to strike out on their own into the wild plains in search of the families they had been taken from.

When the decisions came to an end, Raz found himself between Syrah and Akelo, standing before a clump of ten men who were all looking at him with nervous expectancy. There were a few faces among them that he recognized, Raz realized, looking each over carefully. There was the short West Isler, his black hair looking like it had been recently shaved tight to his scalp, his grey-green eyes bright but cautious. At the back of the group, the big form of the man Raz suspected to have mountain blood in him stood silently, the top of his blond head looming half-a-foot over the others, apparently not noticing the anxious glances Syrah kept shooting his way. There were others, too, scattered throughout. Men he had witnessed battle with savagery and desperation as they fought for their freedom, whom he had seen weep over the still forms of fallen comrades.

He decided the best place to start was with honesty.

"Akelo has told me that many of you believe you know who I am," he said firmly even as he heard Argoan start his own speech for the newcomers at the far end of the ship. "Through stories and tales, you've been made to believe that I am some great hero, come to deliver you and the world from your bindings. What I will ask of you first—" he met each of their eyes individually "—is to cast that understanding aside."

There was a disquieted shuffling from the group, as well as some uncertain mutterings, but Raz kept on before anyone could voice their confusion.

"My intention when Syrah and I entered Percian waters—" he gestured toward the Priestess at his right "—was not to fight. I did not board your ship with the intent of freeing you. I boarded the ship because your former masters attacked us, seeking to drag me down in the same irons that they held you. I boarded the ship because those men would have kept me from my larger goal: to flee Perce through the Seven Cities, and on to a better life in the western realms of the Emperor's Ocean."

There were hisses of disbelief, but he raised a hand to quell them.

"I tell you this not to break your spirits, or to change your mind, but to offer you the basic truth: I am—for lack of a better metaphor—as human as any of you. I am capable of foolishness, of cowardliness. I am able to fall, able to bleed, able to die." He raised both arms, showing off the bandages Syrah had bound about his chest to cover the wounds he'd received the day before. "I am not invulnerable. I am not invincible. I tell you this because if you intend to follow me, you need to understand that you follow a man, not a myth."

He paused, allowing the words to sink in. This time, there were no sounds of disgruntlement.

"All that being said, I will not deny that the stories are true. I challenged the Mahsadën of Miropa, and I emerged victorious. I tore the ruler of Azbar from his throne, and left him to die in the winter snows. Some of you—" his eyes raised to the large man at the back of the ten "—may even have heard that I slew the greatest warrior of the mountain tribes of the North, shattering his armies."

The large man blinked in surprise, but made no other sound.

"You have heard them call me 'Dragon'," Raz pressed on, motioning to the crew of the *Sylgid*, clumped about their captain and new recruits some fifty feet away, "and though you'll hear me say I find such titles distasteful, *believe* that I earned it. I fought with everything I had to earn it, in fact, fought with everything I had to keep the darkness of this world away from a people I learned to care for, even love."

Syrah made a quiet sound at those words, but he didn't look around at her.

"You *must* understand that I am not infallible, that I am not untouchable. But give me reason to, and I will fight just as hard for you and your kind. Give me reason to, and I will prove to you that man can be just as great as myth, when driven to his limits." He waved a hand at the weapons the men had strapped over shoulders and at hips. "I can offer you training. I can offer you discipline. I can offer you a reason to live and a reason to fight. I can even offer you some small taste of revenge." He frowned at the group, making it clear he was measuring his words. "But for that, you will have to let me lead you into a war you should never have been a part of. For that, you will have to lay your life on the line, and place others before yourself. I can give you much, but it is likely that I will ask for even more in return."

Again, he looked over the group, searching for hesitancy.

Surprisingly, he found none.

"You are already delivered from your bonds," he said, waving a hand at the two *kuja* who sat along the bow, talking to each other about their plans to search for their families. "You have the right to walk your own path. If that is what you desire, I urge you to take it. Follow me, and the road inevitably leads to pain, to blood and hardship."

"Arro…" Akelo whispered warningly, like he was concerned Raz was pushing them too far.

But Raz gave him a sharp look, and the Percian fell silent.

"But *if* you follow me," he insisted, "then that road might—just might—also lead to something greater than yourself. I do not promise this. I do not promise to be able to grant freedom to every person, to every soul who screams out in the night, fearing the day and the pain it will bring. I do not promise to liberate your families, your friends, your loved ones. I do not promise to rid this world of cruelty, of greed and pettiness."

He stopped for a full second, willing the words to sink into the men.

"But give me reason to," he finished slowly, "and I *do* promise to fight for all of that with every ounce of my will and being… or die trying."

There was a long, heavy pause as he ended. For a while nothing could be heard over the drone of the sea and the call of the gulls overhead as the wind drifted lazily through the empty rigging of the ship. For a while, no one spoke, every eye on Raz.

Then, abruptly, the West Isler stepped forward, loosening something on his belt as he did so. For a moment Raz was confused, unsure of what the man was doing, but then the former slave pulled the curved saber he had been wearing on his hip free, scabbard and all.

When he reached Raz, he dropped to one knee and placed the sword on the deck in front of him.

"In my land," the man said in his sharp accent, loud enough for all to hear, "it is believed that there is no greater honor than to serve a cause one believes in with all their heart. I am Cyper Edalos," he looked up at Raz once, then bowed his head, "and I am yours, Dragon."

After that, though none of the others took a knee, one at a time they nodded, eyes steely and resolved, looking at Raz in a new light.

It was nearly noon before they got to say their farewells. It didn't take long for Raz and Syrah to gather their things—not to mention that their new entourage quite literally owned nothing more than what they carried on their bodies—but it was almost an hour alone before Gale and Nymara allowed themselves to be guided up from their compartment, then carefully onto and over the width of the swaying gangplank and back down to the deck of the *Moalas*. The Sun was practically overhead before Syrah and Lysa broke apart tearfully, both women promising the other that they would meet again. As several of the crew moved back and forth between the *Sylgid* and the *Moalas*, toting sacks of provisions and two small barrels of fresh water, Raz clasped arms with Garht Argoan.

"You'll be missed, boy," the captain said with a melancholy grin. "You're sure we can't at least escort you to land? It'll be tricky, manning the ship with only the lot of you."

"I'm sure," Raz said grimly as their hands fell apart. "We've wasted enough time as is. The *Red Turor* could return with reinforcements, and I want you and the *Sylgid* as far away as possible before that happens. We'll manage just fine." He indicated the Sun with an upward nod of his head, then the shore of Perce along the western horizon. "Clear sky, friendly wind, and land in sight. We'll get there in one piece."

"Aye, if you say so," the captain said with a shrug. Then he turned to watch Syrah and his first mate, who hadn't yet quit consoling one another. "Never seen Lysa in such a fuss. She'll be heartbroken for weeks, I tell you."

"Good friends are hard to find," Raz said, watching Syrah's newly-laundered robes catch the ocean breeze and blow westward about her feet.

"Aye," the captain agreed simply, and for a while the two stood without speaking, content in each other's company, watching the two women exchange a last few words.

A quarter-hour later, Raz stood at the helm of the *Moalas*, watching the gangplank being pulled back onto the still-bloody deck as the last of the grappling lines were hacked free. With a groan of wood the two ships began to drift apart, the *Sylgid* tacking for a southern route, and Raz brought the brigantine slowly around, taking full advantage of a fortunate westward tailwind while those among his miniscule crew who knew what they were doing climbed up the ratlines and masts to drop the sails. As they turned, Syrah moved along the stern rail, waving for as long as she could to Argoan and Lysa. When he was sure they were on a direct course for land, Raz lashed the wheel in place with rope, then made to join the Priestess at the edge of the ship. Together they bid farewell to the *Sylgid*, even long after the details of the captain and his first mate were lost to the distance. Raz, though, could just make out the glint of the spyglass turned in their direction, and he guessed Argoan wanted to see them safely toward shore for as long as he could.

He smiled gratefully into the wind.

When the sails of the vessel were nothing more than vague shapes in the distance, he finally brought his hand down, resting it gently on Syrah's shoulder.

"Do you think we'll see them again?" the woman asked him, not looking away from the southern horizon.

Had Raz been a better man, he might have told her the truth: that he didn't know, that he wasn't even sure he and Syrah would be alive in a month's time, much less thinking of old friends.

Instead, he lied.

"Without a doubt."

He suspected the Priestess could sense the dishonesty in his words, but she seemed to appreciate them all the same. Reaching up, she took hold of his fingers, as was her fashion, and together the pair stood quietly at the rail until the *Sylgid* was gone completely from sight.

They only broke apart when Akelo and the West Isler, Cyper—who seemed to have assumed a sort of second-in-command position to the Percian—joined them on the aft.

"Neret says we'll make land within a half-hour," Akelo told the pair of them as they turned to meet the two men. He was in full armor again today, and his right eye was a little less swollen between the viewing slots of his spiked half-helm. He was pointing, as he spoke, to a blond Northerner at the crown of the foremast, squatting on the flat platform that topped it to act as a poor excuse for a crow's nest. "He says we'll need to reef the sails soon, or risk running the ship aground."

At his words, Raz looked around at the deck of the *Moalas*, taking in the blood-splattered wood and the flies that still seemed to buzz about despite the healthy wind.

"How hard is it for you both?" he asked the men without glancing back around at them, his right hand thumbing the strange axe—the 'sagaris,' Argoan had called it—he had scavenged from the corpse of the vessel's former captain. "How difficult is it to be back on this ship?"

He realized he hadn't considered this when they'd made the decision to take the brigantine. Argoan had been willing to chart the *Sylgid* inland at the nearest estuary and anchor along the river-mouths, but Raz and Syrah had squashed the idea. The captain had no use for the *Moalas*, with his crew already depleted, and the boat could serve at least one last purpose.

Akelo and Cyper exchanged a dark look.

"We will manage, Dragon," the West Isler said with forced certainty. "A small price to pay, to say the least."

Raz looked around at Syrah, seeking her opinion silently. He was pretty sure the woman understood what he was trying to ask, because she smiled in a satisfied, cold sort of way, and nodded. .

Raz turned back to the paired men.

"I told you I'd give you some small revenge, at least," he said with a hard grin. "Tell the crew to brace for impact."

XXXIII

They started the fire in the rowing galley.

After beaching the *Moalas* at full speed with a crashing *crunch* of the keel over the white sands, Raz had Akelo coordinate the men into lowering the gangway and carrying their provisions up the shore into the safety of the palm trees. As they did this, Raz and Syrah led Gale and Nymara down onto the beach, both horses going half-mad with joy the moment they realized they were on firm land again. Raz couldn't help but laugh as he let the stallion go, allowing the animal to tear down the shore at full gallop for nearly a quarter-mile before calling him back with a long whistle.

Once the horses were settled in the shade with a drink of fresh water, the ship was stripped of anything of use or value. Raz then gathered the men in the galley, where he personally broke each of the twenty-four oars in half by placing them at an angle between the hull floor and the raised walkway, then stomping on them. By the time he was done, Raz's foot was numb and there were splinters everywhere, but each of the freed men held a length of wood a little taller than they were. When he nodded to her, Syrah had moved about the group, taking the shattered timber of each piece in hand—though ever careful not to touch the men themselves—and willing them to take flame.

Then the two of them had left the eleven to their task, walking together down the gangway and clambering up the shifting beach once more just as smoke began to furl from the port and starboard oar-holes.

For a long time Raz and Syrah sat in the shadows of the trees, listening to the wind rush about them, bearing with it the thickening smell of smoke and burning wood. Together they talked and watched the dipping Sun glimmer in and out of sight through the thick, fan-like leaves high above them. They'd lain out one of several pieces of spare sailcloth salvaged from the *Moalas*, unfolding it like a blanket over the sandy earth of the grove. All around them their scavenged goods had been deposited like an eclectic collection of merchant wares. Several caches of iron and steel weapons, some sharp and well-cared for, others rusted through. Additional provisions, including a bag of candied toffee and fresh fruit discovered under the bed in the captain's bunk. A small chest they'd found in the same place, brimming with silver and gold crowns, gems, and jewelry, which Raz suspected would come in useful. All in all, it made for a pleasant early-afternoon, sitting in the semi-seclusion of the palms, both chuckling as they watched the men by the shore laughing and dancing in maddening satisfaction before the rapidly burning skeleton of the pirate ship, the tide rolling steadily in around them.

After an hour or two the ocean waves had risen enough to begin lapping at the still-burning husk of the *Moalas*, and the men seemed finally to have enough of spitting on the wreckage and hurling curses into the heat. They moved as one up toward the trees, Akelo and Cyper at their head, wet booted feet slipping and sliding as they walked.

"Thank you, Arro," the old Percian said in a hoarse voice when he came to stand before Raz and Syrah, pulling his helmet free of his bruised face and sweaty hair. "I don't know if you could have given us a greater gift."

Raz nodded in turn, watching the men settle around them. The group indeed seemed much more at ease as they found clear space along the edges of the cloth. A few were even smiling.

"It wasn't a gift," Raz said after Akelo had sat down on his left, his eyes on the rising smoke as he made out the *hiss* of the ocean starting to spill over the crumpling sides of the burning ship. "No sane man would have dared take that right away from you."

The Percian shrugged, accepting a pear with a word of thanks as Syrah handed it to him. "All the same," he said, polishing the fruit with his sleeve, "you have our gratitude."

"How did it feel?"

It was Syrah who asked the question, using a knife from their salvaged weapons to cut herself a chunk of salted pork before passing the meat and blade carefully to Marsus Byrn, a Southerner who'd taken a seat at her right.

Akelo seemed not to understand the question, taking her in with a look of confusion.

Syrah grimaced, half-amused, half-disappointed. "If I could have had the chance to burn Grahst's camp to the ground…" she started, but trailed off, looking suddenly uncomfortable.

"Don't." Raz cut Akelo off as gently as he could as the man opened his mouth to ask Syrah what she was talking about. "Just don't."

The Percian gave him an odd look, but then his good eye fell on the ring of scars around the Priestess' wrists. His expression softened, and he didn't pursue the matter more.

Gratefully, Raz also noted that he hadn't answered the question.

They ate their late lunch in relative silence, which didn't surprise him. He and Syrah spoke, as well as Akelo and occasionally Cyper off to their left, but the others seemed generally content in their lack of conversation, intent on their plain meals. As they ate, Raz cast about the group, testing himself on every name and what he knew of the men. They'd made introductions that morning, before shipping off on the *Moalas*, and he wanted to be sure he remembered each face.

Marsus, beside Syrah, was the only Southerner of the group, a balding man with a scar across the left line of his jaw. His grey eyes unnerved Raz somewhat, reminding him all-too distinctly of another life, but during the battle with the pirates of the *Red Turor* the man had looked to know his way around the steel round-mace he kept slung at his hip.

At Marsus' right, a threesome of Percian sat in silence—Kalin, Odene, and Zehir. They seemed most comfortable keeping to each other's company, which Raz supposed he could understand. All three had *kuja* tattoos running across their torsos and shoulders like Akelo, though the inks were red, greyish blue, and a purplish-green, respectively. The group had fought well together, from what Raz could recall, though their knowledge of the swords leaning against the trunk of the palm behind them had appeared rudimentary at best.

Beside these three and across the circle from Raz and Syrah, a pair of Northerners were sharing a large chunk of pork and washing it down with swigs of water from a flask they passed between themselves. Neret and Aemen had claimed spiked Percian half-helms, like most everyone, but had opted not to take them off as they ate. Perhaps the armor made them feel secure in their freedom, or perhaps they were afraid someone might take the helms away if they removed them. More likely, though, Raz thought their refusal to doff the armor had something to do with the nervous glances they kept shooting at the lumbering outline of the man seated at their right, further away from the group than anyone else, half-hidden in the shadows of the grove.

It was Akelo who had had to give Raz the mountain man's name: Hur. As it transpired, Hur was mute, his tongue having been cut out at some point in the years he had spent in chains. The Percian had added, as an aside, that it was commonly believed the man was a eunuch as well, but Raz didn't believe that. He'd seen castrated men in the fringe cities before, beggars who'd lost their manhood as punishment for crimes, or attendants who were well-compensated to give them up willingly by masters who didn't want functioning men in the presence of their wives and courtesans. The poor bastards had always had a unanimous softness, a delicacy to them as the rough edge of masculinity abandoned their bodies.

Hur—despite the fact that his name apparently came from the dull sound he made when he breathed—was none of those things. The man was a chiseled wall of power, his arms and legs thicker even than Raz's, though he stood six inches shorter when not sitting. His long brown hair hung straight and lank over startling blue eyes, and his beard was thick about a square, solid chin. Despite the fact that he was doing nothing more than licking his fingers free of the juice of the peach he'd just scarfed down, muscle rippled over his shoulders and neck, like snakes writhing beneath his skin. His hands were massive, and though Raz had seen him fighting with a club and shield the day before, it looked like Hur had abandoned the selection in favor of a large, single-headed battle-axe they'd found among the caches on the *Moalas*. It sat across his crossed legs, glinting in the fire. Raz felt a twinge of worry as he looked at it, remembering another axe-wielding mountain man. He couldn't blame Neret and Aemen, who looked to have been raised in the valley towns of the North, for being skittish.

Nor could he blame Syrah for the semi-frightened looks she kept shooting in Hur's direction, despite the fact that both Raz and Akelo sat between them.

Closer to the flames, on Hur's right, Cyper sat in the middle of the last two men. The West Isler had also replaced his blade with one they'd salvaged, trading the saber he had presented at Raz's feet that morning for a longer, narrower straight-sword which made Raz grimace as he noticed. The blade must have been a traditional weapon of the Isles, because he'd come across its make once before, when Sury Atheus had nearly run him through the back with it in the pit of the Azbar Arena.

Of the other two, Raz knew little, and neither had presented much in the way of clearing that up. The first was an older man—of an age with Akelo, even—who'd given only his first name. Arnus had greying hair that looked to have once been thick and ringed, but now hung limp, flaccid and mostly lifeless. His despondent features, however, stood in direct contrast to the skill with which Raz had seen the former slave wield the six-foot spear that protruded from the sand by his knee. In addition, it appeared the older man had commandeered the round-shield Hur had set aside in favor of his axe, as it now hung from a notch in a tree at his back.

Spear and shield. Raz thought he'd been told somewhere that this was the preferred style of combat among the Imperium's legionnaires, which offered some inkling as to where the old man might have come from...

The last man, Erom, was fortunately less of a mystery. Though he, too, had given nothing more than his name, he had faintly tanned skin—not quite as dark as Marsus' Southern complexion but nowhere near the pale tone of Neret and Aemen, the Northerners—and blue-grey eyes under wavy, dirty-blond hair which gave him away as a borderer. A mismatched set of grips stuck out from either side of his lower back where he'd strapped a pair of long daggers, and the pommel of a smaller knife could be made out over the cuff of his right boot. Though Raz hadn't had the opportunity to see the man fight, he had the distinct impression that Erom was—or had at least once been—well-versed in the use of such blades.

All these men, Raz took in one after the other. It felt strange, in so many ways, to look around at the group and realize how suddenly he'd become responsible for the lives now sitting around the circle, quietly eating a late lunch. A part of him—a small, cowardly part—grew cold and wondered if he could get away with convincing them all to hide forever in the cool shade of the palms, trusting in the trees and the sea to provide for them. He didn't want to put these men at risk, didn't want them to fight his battles for him. Despite whatever he'd said to the contrary, he had the impression the former slaves still saw him as something more than a man.

He was contemplating this, watching Hur chomp at another peach with a look of pure delight flickering over his sunken eyes, when Syrah's gentle touch brought him back, her hand coming to rest at the base of his neck.

He looked around at her, and thought perhaps the woman was able to tell where his mind had wandered to. She smiled, almost in amusement, her gaze very clearly saying "*It will be fine.*" He took heart in that, drew faith from her confidence in him.

Returning the smile briefly, he turned his attention to Akelo.

"Do you know where we are?" he asked as the Percian wiped his mouth with the back of his sleeve, wetness from the leather skin he'd just swigged from glistening in his beard. "We can't stay here too long. The smoke from the fire is going to attract attention sooner or later."

It was part of the reason he had allowed the men to burn the ship. If the *Red Turor* returned, he was hoping the smoking ruins would give the *Sylgid* at least a bit of a lead.

At his side, Akelo nodded, passing the waterskin to Erom on his left. "Generally, yes," he said. "The village we come from is perhaps an hour to the south, down the beach." He pointed through the palms. "If we made inland, the groves would give way to the marshes, and the savannah a day's hard ride after that. If we reach the plains, I'll have a better idea."

"With only two horses, it's going to be slow-going," Raz muttered thoughtfully, watching Gale and Nymara pacing back and forth, munching contentedly on the salt grass they found along the base of the palms. "A day's ride is a long way on foot. How far to the nearest city?"

Akelo frowned in distaste, like he didn't want to think about the place. "Karesh Syl is north and west of here. If we had the mounts, we could make it within a week. As is... Three? At least?"

Raz groaned. Three weeks was a long time to be moving at a slow pace through unfriendly lands.

"And that's if we cut through the marshes and over the savannah?"

The Percian shook his head. "We wouldn't be able to manage the swamplands. They're treacherous, even for *kuja*. Footing is too unstable, and shell beds will slice through armor and cloth better than a knife if you're not careful. Crocodiles aren't uncommon, either, and I challenge even *you* to win a battle with one of those bastards if they drag you into the bog."

Raz made a face at the idea. Thinking of the struggle it had been to swim for Garht Argoan after the man had been swept overboard at sea, he was not keen on fighting for his life in the water ever again.

"What's our best option, then?" Syrah asked from Raz's right, jumping into the conversation. "How are we to make for the city?"

Akelo immediately pointed left, up the shoreline. "We follow the coast. There should be another village a ways north of here. I couldn't say exactly where—the *Moalas* only docked away from home when the storms caught us too far out—but it can't be more than two or three days' walk. From there, it shouldn't be too difficult to find safe roads inland."

Raz snorted at the image. "I'm not sure the locals will react pleasantly to our little group strutting straight into the village square."

Akelo half-smiled. "We won't have to. Once we find it, we can manage our way through groves. They'll be none the wiser."

"Until we're caught on the open road to Karesh Syl," Raz grumbled in annoyance, turning the problem over in his head. "Three weeks is too long. We need to find a way to move faster." He blinked as a thought struck him, and he turned to Akelo. "Would they have horses in the village? Could we send a few into town to buy more?"

Akelo nodded slowly. "Perhaps…" He glanced at the small chest of gold and silver in the center of their canvas sheet. "However… I won't pretend I know the cost of a horse anymore, but I don't imagine we have *near* enough to buy more than two or three, much less eleven."

Raz took in the treasure as well, feeling like it was shrinking before his eyes. He was just about to suggest *stealing* what they needed—he had a funny feeling the borderer, Erom, could help them with that—when Syrah voiced a thought.

"We don't necessarily have to move *faster*," she said, her eye—oddly enough—on the charred husk of the *Moalas* at the water's edge. "What we need is a way to move without being *found out*."

Raz wasn't sure he followed.

"How do you mean?" he asked, hoping he didn't sound *too* confused in front of his new men.

Syrah waved around at their group, most of whom were now watching their conversation intently. "You and I are the odd ones out," she told Raz, sounding like she was growing more confident in her idea with every word. "Without us, they could be anyone."

To their left, Cyper frowned.

"Are you saying you would leave us?" he asked suspiciously in his Isler's accent.

"No," Syrah said with a laugh and a shake of her head. "I mean that so long as Raz and I don't *appear* to be with you, there would be little suspicion cast upon the group by anyone we pass on the road. We could take all the time we needed."

While the concept made sense enough, Raz was relieved to see the utter confusion with which every other man was staring at the Priestess.

"Syrah," he said, almost imploringly. "You're leaving us in your dust. What are you talking about?"

In response, Syrah pointed down the shore. As one, every eye followed her finger, trailing over the initially unremarkable outline of the corpse of the ship, smoke and steam still furling into the clear blue sky as the water continued to rise over it. For several seconds Raz was still unclear as to what she was trying to show them. He was about to demand—with no small amount of frustration—that she explain herself, when his gaze settled on a pair of silhouettes.

Rising out of the crumbled hull, like fire-blackened omens, the iron cages stood lopsided and half-sunk into the sand.

With a thrill of anxious realization, Raz thought he understood Syrah's plan.

XXXIV

"In the end, I was as blind as all the others."

—Azzeki Koro, Third Hand of Karesh Syl

Ekene Okonso was in the middle of an audience when Osana interrupted them. Fortunately for the Tash, he had always prided himself on being more level-headed than the majority of his predecessors, and so when the woman slipped into the room—unnoticed by the court's guests—he did not immediately roar for her to be flogged for her insolence. Ekene had an understanding with his slaves, a balance that he always kept carefully tilted in his favor. They were treated well—even with respect—so long as they performed their duties to his satisfaction. Failing this, however, they were made an example of, used to give every other of their kind within the palace cause to redouble their commitment to serve to the best of their abilities.

With this in mind, Ekene held his tongue when Osana made herself known. If the woman—one of the few servants trusted enough to be allowed to stand unchained in his presence—had deemed the news she bore important enough to interrupt his meeting, then she likely had good reason.

The Tash sat in his usual place in the center throne upon the twelve-stepped dais that led down to the court floor before him. On his left, Naizer Ima slouched as he typically did in the seat of the Second Hand, one cheek resting against his fist in a distinct bid to leave little doubt he was as bored as a man could possibly be. On Ekene's right, Yseri Suro had returned from his diplomatic mission to Karesh Nan, and now filled the First Hand's throne with a quiet dignity that never ceased to impress the Tash. He'd discovered the young man some ten years prior, a second son of one of Karesh Syl's less-loved noble families. Yseri was paunchy, and anything but handsome. His bald pate and round, hairless cheeks always made it seem like the man was a child stuck in a body too big for him, and his dark eyes were unduly large for his face and not quite even. Despite this, though, despite how harshly the nobility must have initially judged him according to their petty ideals of beauty and presentation, Yseri had proven himself a master of social tact. Before the man was twenty he'd been in the process of rapidly building up to be one of the most popular members of the court circles, raising himself in the esteem of the lesser minds with nothing more than natural charm, wit, and a keen, calm intellect.

Seeing the potential there, Ekene had plucked him from the crowd, and within six years Yseri claimed his seat at the Tash's right hand.

Below them, several steps from the base of the dais and flanked by two guards each, five men stood in a half-circle, the rich cleanliness of their collared robes and tailored shirts contrasting sharply with the ragged, worn features of their faces. Three were Percian, while the other two—including the one at the head of the group—were Southern-born. It was this middle man, standing half-a-step closer than the others, with whom the Tash had been speaking when Osana made her entrance.

"Great Tash," Vashül Tyre was saying in a voice of forced calm, "surely you can understand our position. These new tariffs your First Hand has agreed to with Karesh Nan do not favor us." He glared briefly at Yseri with cold grey eyes before continuing. "If you consider this, and take into account as well the new ruling by the Mahsadën that we grant you a reduction on every head we bring you, you *must* see why you risk running us out of business."

"What the Tash 'must' do is not up to you to decide, Tyre," Yseri answered in Ekene's place as the Tash himself made a small motion that Osana should come forward. "Do not presume that you are owed anything, in this place."

The Southerner bowed his head in quick acknowledgement, though his jaw was set in irritation. "Of course," he said, continuing while several of his comrades turned at the sound of the slave's bare feet moving over the polished marble floor of the chamber behind them. "I beg your forgiveness for such disrespect. I merely wished to clarify for His Greatness the position we have been put in by these decisions. These tariffs and price adjustments cut sharply into our business—" he frowned, glancing around as well when Osana came to a stop at the bottom of the dais "—and will make it difficult for us to pay our men appropriately. We have families to feed, all of us."

As Yseri responded with a barbed comment about the irony of the man's familial concerns, Ekene motioned to Naizer. Even if his Second had been on the verge of dozing off, he was not brazen enough to ignore the instruction. With a muttered grumble he pushed himself from his seat and started down the steps, cutting across Yseri and Tyre's squabble. Ekene followed the man carefully, curiosity rising as Osana stood on her tiptoes to whisper into the Hand's ear.

"*Honored* First." Vashül Tyre enunciated the word like he wished for nothing more than the ability to replace it with a much more poignant descriptor. "Such erosion of our profits is something we cannot stand for. For these prices, we would be better off driving our merchandise the extra leagues to the Seven Cities."

"Then do so," Yseri said with a careless wave, sitting back in his chair. "Do not dupe yourself into thinking you will be missed. Where you stand today, tomorrow another will take your place. You are utterly—"

"*What?*"

Naizer's barked demand cut across the argument, jolting everyone into silence. If the Second noticed he had interrupted anything, though, he didn't care, still bent to listen to what Osana had to say. When the slave was done, he dismissed her with a snap of his fingers even as he turned and stormed up the stairs. She scurried off at once, almost running, clearly not keen to stay and see what consequences her news would bring about.

"Guards! Escort our visitors out!" the Second shouted, not looking back as he climbed. "*Now!*"

"What?" Tyre demanded furiously, taking a step forward. "You can't just—?"

"Guards," Ekene said coolly, choking off the man's words. "As Naizer says. We will finish the audience at a later time."

As he spoke, his eyes never left the Hand's.

There were angry mutterings of discontent while the five guests were led toward the great double-doors at the back of the chamber, but not even Tyre had it in him to argue with the Tash himself. The guards pressed them like a military line, shields held before them, right hands on their swords as if to say "Move, or else."

After the doors slammed closed behind them with a groaning *boom*, Naizer spoke.

"Raz i'Syul Arro was discovered aboard the smuggler's ship, as our Southern friends informed us. There was a battle. Two vessels from the eastern coastal villages coordinated their assault on the *Sylgid*."

"'Eastern coastal villages,'" the Tash repeated with a snort. "Such a polite way to say 'pirates.' And? Do they have him?"

"No." The Second shook his head. "They were both overcome. One ship escaped, losing more than a quarter of its men, and the other was captured entirely. Apparently, rumor has it Arro butchered the entire crew single-handed."

A chill settled over the three of them.

"Are you honestly surprised?"

Like a splotch of darkness detaching itself from the shadows behind the Tash's throne, Azzeki Koro stepped into view. His black eyes were on Naizer, and they twinkled with reserved amusement.

"I could have told you not to put your faith in the coastal villages," he said, and as disciplined as the man might have been, Ekene detected the slightest hint of smugness in his tone. "I have said before that you must not underestimate him. There is a reason they call him 'Monster.'"

"Foolish stories for foolish men," Naizer hissed in what he likely thought was a dignified tone, but came out only as squeamish denial. "If the lizard escaped, then he must have had assistance. The woman, Brahnt, perhaps."

Koro's eyes lost their glimmer, and he looked suddenly annoyed as his gaze moved between the three men. "How much proof will you need before you come to terms with the fact that Arro is *nothing* like the atherian you keep chained in the camps below us? I have seen what he can do, witnessed it for myself. You *need* to face this head-on, or risk greater troubles coming to pass."

"Indeed." Ekene raised a hand as he spoke, ending his Second's spluttered attempt at a retort. "This news is troubling, to say the least. Regardless of the circumstances, Arro's victory does not bode well." He dropped his arm to look at Koro directly. "A full crew all his own, she said…?

I'm partial to believing it. If it turns out the atherian *does* have help beyond his 'Priestess'…"

"It spells trouble," Yseri offered with a nod of agreement, contemplating the facts himself. "Alone, he and Brahnt pose less of a threat."

Azzeki Koro's lip curled. "You cannot think like that," he said to the First. "My last master carried that frame of mind, and he was as sharp as you, Suro. Do you know what Arro did with him?"

"Left him to die by the Northern freeze," Yseri said with a tilt of his head. "I am familiar with the story, Koro, but you misunderstand. I agree that Arro is a problem. I was merely commenting that it would be easier to deal with him and the woman alone than if they have garnered supporters."

"Precisely." Ekene's gnarled fingers ran through his beard as he spoke. "In fact, I would say this gives me cause to rethink your other concerns as well, Koro…"

Still standing before the three of them, Naizer scowled. "What? That the lizard will come *here*? Why would he? What would he gain from such a suicidal act?"

"Much and more," Ekene said slowly, considering. Every day since they'd learned of Arro's imminent arrival, the Third had been whispering in his ear that they needed to prepare, needed to be ready. The Tash had brushed the warnings aside, allowing Koro to take his Southerners and check the city's defense purely in an attempt to appease the man.

Now, though…

An entire crew? Ekene thought. *Single-handed?*

"There is much to be gained," the Tash said again, deciding to voice his thoughts. "Even if the likelihood of success is small, he may seek to repeat his feat in Miropa. It would certainly have a greater effect here…"

Naizer paled at that. "Repeat his feat?" he asked hesitantly. "You don't mean—?"

"That Arro would attempt to come for us," Yseri finished for the man, catching on to the concept, staring at the banners on the columns above as he thought. "Yes… that would certainly have an impact." He looked around at Naizer. "'Cut the head off, and the body dies,' as they say in the South. He succeeded in Miropa."

"To an extent," the Tash corrected, still tugging at his beard. "The Mahsadën have recovered. This 'Adrion Blaeth' seems like a formidable leader, to say the least."

"Karesh Syl has no such protections." Azzeki pressed his advantage. "Arro may see taking your heads as a chance to correct past failures."

"*Our* heads," Ekene corrected him absently, still mulling over everything. "But something like that, yes…"

For several seconds, they were silent, the three Hands watching the Tash expectantly.

When he came to a decision, Ekene looked to Yseri.

"Tell the Lord General I want staggered patrols along every eastern road," he ordered the First Hand sharply. "On foot, five men each. Tell him I want every troop provided with a slave, and one good rider with a fast horse."

"Five?" Naizer asked incredulously even as Yseri nodded and hoisted himself to his feet. "You think five men is enough? *If* these rumors are true—and I'm not saying they are—" he glared pointedly at Koro "—then I don't see how five will be a match for Arro."

"They don't need to be," the First Hand said, patting the wrinkles out of his robes around his paunch. "But if he's distracted, four should be enough to slow him down, at the very least."

"F-four?" Naizer nodded, clearly bewildered. "I... I don't understand."

"Which is why you are trusted with the bulk of the coffers, and *not* the might of the army, honored Second," Yseri said with a smirk toward the man. Then he gave Koro a grudging nod before bowing low to Ekene. "It will be seen to, Great Tash."

Ekene watched the man descend the dais. The First was nearly halfway across the court floor when he stopped abruptly and turned around.

"The ship," he called back, as though struck by a thought. "I don't recall the name..."

"The *Sylgid*," Azzeki Koro offered. "Given the time it would have taken for this news to reach us, chances are it's made berth in one of the smugglers' hideaways along the southern coasts already. Likely the Horn, or Dead Man's Haunt."

"The *Sylgid*," Ekene muttered, rolling the strange name over his tongue and frowning. "Yes... I'd forgotten about that little matter..."

"Would you pass judgment on it?" Yseri called from his place in the middle of the chamber. "For crimes against your throne?"

Ekene thought on that a moment.

When he answered, he barely managed to hide the satisfied smile that threatened to creep across his face.

PART III

XXXV

"The documented methods for punishing escaped and runaway slaves in the mid-era v.S. are among some of the most barbaric treatments of man by man I have ever encountered. It pains me now, outlining the chapters of the texts I will use to spread these findings to the masses, for in my desire to educate the modern world on the horrors of old, I know in my heart of hearts that out there, somewhere, I will be feeding not a few sickened minds..."

—notes by unknown author of *Commonalities of Ancient & Modern Society*

The fact that Aleem Osero had no idea what he was doing in the middle of the savannah utterly terrified him.

There was a rhythm, typically, to a slave's life, a repetition to the days and months and years. Aleem himself had been a serving hand in the Tash's kitchens for nearly a decade now, tasked with delivering the extravagant meals prepared by the cooks for Ekene Okonso and his guests. Overall, it was not the worst assignment to have within the palace. Aleem knew of a pair of women whose sole responsibility was hauling the palace's refuse and waste out of the city, and slaves died all the time in the menagerie, mauled by half-starved tigers or trampled under the feet of the terrified rhinoceros His Greatness kept for his personal entertainment. In comparison, the kitchens were tame, the slaves who worked there only punished when something went wrong with the food, or the dishes were spilled. When he'd first started, Aleem had been beaten almost daily, but he learned fast how best to serve and who to be wary of. Nine years later, he was hardly ever struck, much less thrashed outright. He'd started to consider himself of some value, an experienced hand. In fact, for the last few weeks he'd been building up the courage to ask the overseer for the right to be made cook.

Then his world was turned upside down. Soldiers had descended into the kitchens, grabbing him and a handful of others seemingly at random. In a few short hours Aleem and another thirty or so slaves from all about the palace had been outfitted with heavy packs stuffed with provisions and supplies for a long journey. They were offered no explanation as their ankles were cuffed and chained, like they were newly-bought and might still have dreams of escape.

A little over a week later, Aleem was shuffling along the east-bound roads of the wild planes of Perce, trailing behind the five-man patrol he had been assigned to, sweat dampening the rumpled cloth of the stained kitchen tunic he hadn't even been allowed to change out of.

Under other circumstances, the slave thought he might have been thrilled for the chance to travel beyond the walls of Karesh Syl. The savannah was a wonder to behold in its own right, a sprawling sweep of endless prairies flatter than the surface of a still lake. Elbow- and shoulder-high grasses of green and gold swayed on either side of the relatively cleared path that was the winding road, shimmering in the slightest breeze so that the scene all around them undulated, inhaling and exhaling like a living thing. Here and there acacias rose above the plains, a dozen bare branches reaching some fifteen feet in the air to hold up a thick canopy of leaves that were far out of reach of any but the tallest grazers. More impressive still, every now and then they would pass through the shade cast by towering baobabs, massive trunks so wide it was said the trees were the legs of long-lost giants who'd roamed the world before the Sun and Moon had been born to the heavens. Animals of all kinds thrived in the lushness of the savannah, any of them far more majestic than the poor specimens the Tash kept in his enclosures. Elephants migrated across the grasslands in herds of ten and more, giving the patrol a wide berth. Giraffes were often seen in pairs or small groups, sometimes with calves among them, and they paid about as much attention to Aleem and the soldiers as they might the tickbirds that leapt along their backs and heads.

More exciting still—and far more terrifying—predators stalked the grasses, sometimes made distinct only by the faint shadow of their passing against the waving surface of the plains. Hyenas and packs of wild dogs could be heard in the night, yipping and snarling as they shared in their kills. Leopards lounged lazily in the lowest branches of the trees, sometimes sleeping the day away, other times glowering at the men as they passed, clawed paws resting protectively on whatever game they'd downed and dragged up into their perches. Once, the soldiers had even been forced to draw swords and put tinder to flint, lighting several torches they kept for night-traveling and surrounding the troop's one horse defensively.

The lioness that had come too near, baring teeth at them from the edge of the road as she decided whether or not they were worth the trouble, eventually slunk back into the swaying stalks of the prairie.

Yes, perhaps under different circumstances, Aleem would have enjoyed this trek.

As it was, though, he felt only fear.

They were selling him off to the eastern villages as punishment. It was the only explanation he could come up with. Somewhere, somehow, he had offended the Tash or one of his visitors beyond forgiveness. The overseers never—or rather very rarely—killed the slaves they were responsible for. "The dead have no value" was a common phrase among such men, after all. Instead, slaves whom the Tash no longer wanted in his sight were sold off, forced out of the relative comforts of the palace. Usually they were traded at auction in the city markets, where wealthy farmers would buy them as laborers to be put to work, or merchants would purchase them with the intention of using them as pack animals. Sometimes slaves would even be snatched up by the local brothels, which was a fate no one envied. In the worst cases, however, the Tash had been known to send the slaves who had displeased him most greatly to the gambling pits, or to exist as fodder for the pirates.

Given the choice, Aleem would rather have been thrown to the wild animals of the pit and been done with it.

The very thought of the coast made Aleem shudder, the cooking pots hanging from the side of his pack clinking as he did. In his mind's eye he pictured himself chained to an oar, forced to row day-in and day-out until his mind and body broke. Helplessly, he looked down at his hands. Where many slaves had calluses and scars from hard labor and a difficult life, Aleem's fingers were smooth. His nails had even been manicured weekly, so as not to offend the Tash while serving, though now they were scraped and filthy.

He would not fare well to this change, he knew.

He'd tried, for the last nine days, to keep his spirits up as much as he could. The men he'd been assigned to were a calm lot, as far as soldiers went, and left him largely alone apart from the occasional snap from the sergeant—Rafik—to keep up. They appeared almost grateful, in fact, when it was discovered Aleem's only real value as a field slave came in the form of cooking, the five members of the patrol gobbling up the porridges and stews he made out of their provisions like they'd never had anything so good on the road. It made him hopeful, wondering if perhaps one of them might recommend him to his buyer as a ship's chef, rather than an oarsman.

Things changed, though, when the others came into view.

"Halt," Rafik commanded over his shoulder, bringing everyone to a short stop. It was early morning, the Sun glaring into their eyes from its low position in the eastern sky, making it hard to see. Raising a hand to shade his face, Aleem managed to make out a surprisingly large group approaching them along the road, travelling in the opposite direction. The caravan looked to be led by four soldiers in the spiked helms and the white-and-gold colors of Karesh Syl, two on horseback on either side of what appeared to be a young woman whose face was covered by a veil of purity, the other two on foot as they carried tower shields depicting the crossed spears of the city. Behind them, a wide, dual-axle cart rumbled along, towed by a short-haired ox. It was flanked by another eight men in mismatched leather-and-iron armor, a couple of whom were driving the animal forward with narrow switches. What Aleem thought must have been some sort of cylindrical cage with a domed top looked to have been bolted into the bed of the cart, but it was hard to tell. The enclosure—distinct only by the pattern of narrow bars—had been hidden from view by a large sheet of cloth hung over its entirety.

At once, Aleem could understand why the sergeant had called a pause in their march. This wasn't the first group they'd come across in the last week and a half. The roads of Perce, even these smaller trading routes, were well-travelled as the cooler seasons fell over the South and commerce was bolstered with the fringe cities. There was something distinctly odd, however, about this particular convoy, something not quite right. Glancing at Rafik, the man's narrowed eyes told Aleem he had noted the oddities as well, and the slave grew suddenly anxious.

For one thing, the soldiers of the approaching caravan appeared to have no order to their ranks. Even this small patrol, with only five men, a horse, and Aleem trailing behind, marched in form: the sergeant in front, two rows of two behind him, and the animal between them and their slave. The group coming toward them, on the other hand, looked scattered, dirty, and disjointed, almost like a cohort returning from battle. Aside from the two men ahorse on either side of the woman they appeared to be escorting, there was no method to their procession, the men on foot slogging along here and there, sometimes alone, sometime in small groups. What was more, even from this distance Aleem could say with certainty that the men's armaments included anything *but* the standard sword and shield of the army. Before long he could make out spears, axes, knives, even the gleaming head of what looked to have been a round-mace. Given that soldiers in service to the Tash *were* allowed to choose their own weapons from anything they claimed in battle, it might not have been all that strange to see one or two such oddities. In this case, though, only a single figure—one of the mounted soldiers—appeared to be carrying an army-issued blade, which did nothing to balance out the fact that he had a bow slung across his back.

Combined with the undisciplined order of the group's ranks, Aleem could understand why Rafik looked so tense.

They waited for the caravan to approach, nearly ten minutes spent baking in the heat of the morning, but for once Aleem was not so grateful for the reprieve from their eastward drive. As the rumbling of the cart became audible, the tension in the men before him redoubled, and with a word from the sergeant, Kano—a soldier who sported light cavalry armor as opposed to the heavier chain and leather of the others—hurried back to the horse and slung himself up into the saddle. Aleem watched this happen with a frown. It had been the same on every occasion they'd passed another group on the road. Rafik would call a halt, and Kano would mount expectantly, like he was waiting for a word from his superior to bolt. Inevitably, when the travelers passed and nothing out of the ordinary occurred, the sergeant would order the rider back off the animal, and the march would start anew. Aleem wasn't sure what was going on, but he had set his curiosity largely aside, reminding himself that it was not a slave's place to question the actions of his betters.

Now, though, as he made out the details of the men coming closer, he couldn't help that curiosity from lighting anew.

When the two groups were no more than twenty feet apart, the sergeant raised a hand, indicating that the caravan should stop. It did at once, a barked command from the man with the sword and bow bringing the entire procession to a halt. This soldier, indeed, looked to be the senior officer. He had the brass marks that denoted him as a captain fastened into the leather of the white-dyed cuirass about his chest, but they were pinned to the wrong side. Rafik seemed to take note of this, because his frown deepened as he spoke.

"Declare yourself, by order of the Tash!" he shouted across the space between their two parties. It was the same order he'd given every group they came across. Having never been outside of the city walls in most of the last decade, Aleem had no idea if this was procedure on trips to the coastal towns.

Before them, the man who'd spoken raised a hand in greeting.

"Hail, brothers!" He had a low, rough voice, like stones crunching underfoot, and as he heeled his mount forward—a massive black stallion that would have caught even Ekene Okonso's eye—he kept his hand lifted, like a sign of peace. "I am Akelo Aseni. My men and I are returning from assignment along the coast. We have been tasked by the First Hand with escorting the Lady Ilyane back to Karesh Syl unharmed." He motioned to the veiled woman with a jerk of his head over his shoulder. "She is to be his third wife."

That seemed to take the sergeant by surprise. The man looked uncertainly around at the mounted figure—the "Lady Ilyane," if this Captain Aseni was to be believed—giving Aleem time to take in the others with greater detail.

Aseni was surprisingly old for a lesser officer of the Tash's army. He was Percian, obviously, but the bush of his beard was streaked with silver, and his face was so leathery he would have fit better as a seaman than a soldier. His dark eyes were bright beneath his helm, his right encircled by what might have been the remnants of an old bruise, and despite his apparent age he was broad-shouldered and strong, his armor a little snug over his muscled frame. The army-issue blade at his hip was a splash of normalcy, but did not offset the bow slung about his shoulders, nor the quiver of arrows hanging from the small of his back. If the man was an archer, it seemed strange that he would have been sent out into the savannah as a mere escort. Marksmen were generally kept within the walls of the city in case of attack, or trained as game hunters so that the Tash was always a powerful contributor to the lucrative pelt and ivory trade between Karesh Syl and Karesh Nan.

The others surrounding the captain did nothing to help the oddity of the scene. The three soldiers were similarly built, broad men who looked to ill-fit their uniform, white-and-gold armor. They wore curved swords on their belts—none of which matched the other—and the two on foot were holding their shields improperly, as though they'd only been taught how to handle them recently. The last man, who'd stayed ahorse beside the Lady Ilyane as his superior cantered forward on his black stallion, look distinctly rigid in his saddle, like he was unaccustomed to riding.

The Lady herself was even stranger. A purity veil was common enough—though a tradition Aleem had heard was dying out with the younger generations of the Percian nobility—but traditionally wives-to-be chose only to hide their faces from view. *This* woman, on the other hand, seemed to have taken the concept to heart, because every inch of her body was covered, from the thin, white-dyed leather of her boots and gloves to the hooded silk robes that hung loosely about her frame. For all any of them could tell, she might not have been Percian at all. Odder still, Aleem guessed that the other men, beyond her and the soldiers, were sellswords under employ of the lady's family, because not one among them looked to be a son of Perce. Five in total, Aleem made out Southerners, Northerners, West Islers, and even a borderer. The strange part was, though, that—apart from one thin man at the back of the group whose mismatched armor looked almost to be falling off, it was so loose—the men were each as broad as any of the others, like whoever had put together the caravan had wanted only the largest and strongest guarding the veiled woman.

Something was definitely not right, Aleem knew. Everything was off about this escort.

Whether fortunately or unfortunately, Rafik was clearly of the same mindset.

"Your men are in disarray, *Captain*," the sergeant said stiffly, enunciating the last word like Aseni should take more pride in his title. "Should you present yourself to the city like this, I would not expect to be greeted well by the gate commanders."

In response, the captain smiled in a tired sort of way. Aleem might have imagined it, but for a moment before the man spoke he could have sworn Aseni's eyes flicked right to him.

"You are correct," the officer said in an apologetic tone. "We have had a difficult road. Are you familiar with the lady's family, the Ilyanes?"

The sergeant shook his head, still looking annoyed.

Aseni groaned resignedly. "I'm not surprised. The lady's father is only just growing in power. He is responsible for much of the head trade Karesh Syl has been building with the eastern pirates." He waved a hand back at the veiled woman. "A few days ago, we came under assault. We suspect he intended to kill the lady in retaliation."

"'He?'" Rafik asked incredulously. "Who is 'he'?"

Aseni looked unsure, glancing back at the lady as though asking permission. When she nodded, he sighed, as though hesitant to share the information.

"The lizard," he said simply.

Aleem, it seemed, was the only one not to understand the context of the man's answer. "Lizard" was a common enough slur. He had heard it a thousand times, muttered and hurled at the atherian slaves in the city and palace. For this reason, it seemed strange indeed that the sergeant and his men all stiffened as one, Kano hissing in a sharp inhalation of excitement from atop his horse.

"Arro?" Rafik demanded gleefully, taking several steps forward. "You have Arro?"

Abruptly, Aleem felt his hands go numb. Where "lizard" had meant nothing to him, that name, spilled with such excited anticipation from a soldier of the Tash's army, squeezed at his heart, making it suddenly difficult to breathe.

Arro. Raz i'Syul Arro.

"We do," the captain was saying with a nod, looking curiously down at the man. "You seem less surprised by this fact than I would have assumed."

"We were tasked with cutting the lizard off if he came by way of the eastern roads," the sergeant said hurriedly, all suspicion apparently forgotten as he took another step forward, scanning the group like he expected to see the atherian bound and chained among them. "Us, and some two-dozen other patrols like ours. The Tash wishes to know if and when Arro would have arrived at the gates of Karesh Syl."

This, oddly, made Aseni frown, and his helm turned to take in Kano.

"I see," he said, as though considering this new information. "A rider to return word to the city." Again, shockingly, his eyes fell on Aleem. "A slave to distract the man, and soldiers to slow him down. Very clever."

At his words, Rafik looked annoyed again, pulling his gaze from where it had settled on the covered cage.

"Arro is no *man*," he spat, like he'd been offended by some filthy vulgarity the captain had uttered in his presence. "He is an animal. No more than any other scaly."

"Of course," the captain said almost too quickly, clearly intent on correcting himself. "As you say: an animal."

The slip-up, though, seemed to rouse the sergeant from his momentary elation. The man was looking at the group with suspicious eyes again, like he was still deciding what to make of them.

"I'd like to see the creature," he said eventually, speaking in a surprisingly harsh tone for a man who was technically addressing a superior. "Where is he?"

As he said it, though, Rafik's gaze seemed to fall again on the shape of the cage.

Aseni made a face that looked a little *too* much like he was trying to seem unsure, though the sergeant didn't appear to notice.

"Are you sure?" the captain asked. "It's been four days since we killed him. His remains aren't anything you'd want to look at…"

"He's *dead*?" the sergeant demanded, and he almost deflated under the weight of this news. "I was ordered to return him to Karesh Syl alive, if possible."

Aseni shrugged apologetically from atop his horse. "I had no such orders, and he took us by surprise. We had to defend ourselves."

Rafik, in turn, grunted, clearly not happy with the circumstances.

"Very well," he snapped irritably. "In that case, I wish to see the body."

Again, the request came out as a command, and the captain took it without so much as blinking.

"As you say." Aseni looked around at one of the men standing on foot in front of the Lady Ilyane. "Zehir, show them to the corpse."

"No," the sergeant said quickly. "*I* will suffice. A moment, though."

Rafik turned his back to the mounted man, facing his patrol, and spoke in half-a-whisper so that only they could hear.

"Kano," he said first to the rider atop his horse, "if anything goes wrong, make for the city *at once*. Don't wait. Tell them what you've seen here. The rest of you," he looked around at the others, "be ready to defend Kano's retreat, with your lives if necessary. For the Tash."

"For the Tash," the soldiers all said as one in reply, the three on the ground moving hands to the hilt of their blades. When he was satisfied they were prepared, Rafik turned back to the caravan.

"Show me."

Swiftly the soldier who had been designated—Zehir, Aleem thought the captain had called him—led the sergeant toward the back of the procession. The rest of the patrol watched expectantly, tense and ready, Kano and his horse shifting side to side nervously. Quietly as he could, Aleem slid to the edge of the road, ignoring the rustle of the winds through the grasses around him as he did his best to steer clear of the rider's potential path.

Rafik passed Akelo Aseni and the Lady Ilyane without incident. He didn't even glance at the other soldiers as he marched by with a stiff posture, like he was modeling what a *true* member of the army of Karesh Syl should act like. He approached the cart, his helmet tilting up to take in the oddity that was the covered cage.

Then one of the lady's men—the borderer—stepped rudely across the sergeant's path, and no one even managed to blink before it was over.

Aleem had just enough time to reflect on how badly *he* would have been beaten if he'd ever been foolish enough to cut off an officer when Rafik staggered, stumbling into the side of the cart. He didn't make a sound, but there was a glint of steel, and Aleem thought he saw the borderer tuck a pair of blades away as the sergeant convulsed, turning to put his back against the wood and slide heavily down to the ground. He coughed once, spraying blood across the road.

Then the sergeant keeled over, one hand dropping from where it had been trying to hold together a massive gash that had appeared in his stomach, the other falling from the dissected remnants of what had been a whole, healthy neck not three seconds before.

There was a horrified shout from the patrol, and three swords were drawn in unison. Someone yelled "Kano! Go!" and the soldier's horse reared as Kano brought the animal around, kicking it into a gallop back up the road. Dirt and dead grass churned, tossing dust into the air. Aleem staggered back, nearly stumbling right off the road as the rider drove his mount by so quickly the slave felt the wind of their passing.

Then there was a *zip*, followed by an ugly *thud*, and an arrow sprouted like magic from the back of Kano's head.

The horse screamed in confusion as the soldier tumbled from the saddle, one foot caught in the stirrups. Aleem couldn't look away, staring after the pair of them, the mount dragging the corpse of its former master with it as it ran, Karo's limbs bouncing gruesomely over the stony ground. The slave had just begun to consider that he, too, might be in danger, when the wind shifted in the grass around him once more.

Only this time, Aleem was made to understand that it wasn't, in fact, the wind.

As lithely as a snake sliding out of its hole, a dark figure rose from where he had crept to lie in silent wait behind them, stepping out of the field onto the road. He was a behemoth of calm, supple power, his dark, scaled skin rippling and glimmering in the Sun, his golden eyes shining like fire against his reptilian face. The steel of his armor and clawed gauntlets glinted, as did the blades of his strange straight sword and the twin-headed spear Aleem would have been able to name in his sleep.

The winged form of Raz i'Syul Arro, the Monster of Karth, the Dragon of the North, stood before him, the legendary Ahna held in one hand like she weighed no more than a walking stick.

Aleem thought, in that moment, that he should have been terrified. As he gaped up at the atherian—who stood several inches taller than even the largest lizard-kind the slave had ever met—he thought he should have cowered in fear. Instead, though, he felt a warmth well within his chest, a spark of something he hadn't experienced in a long, long time.

Hope.

Arro's eyes fell on him, but there was nothing but a sad sort of kindness in that gaze. Without saying a word, he nodded toward the ground, like he wanted Aleem to sit. The slave did so at once, crumpling at the edge of the road and continuing to stare as the Dragon stepped past him, the earth *crunching* lightly beneath his clawed feet.

The atherian moved with all the grace of his kind, the nimble poise that was the first thing stolen away from lizard-kind slaves by the chains they were bound in. Still without speaking, he approached the threesome of soldiers who hadn't looked away from the caravan, blades out and shoulder-to-shoulder in a wall formation as the man who had called himself Akelo Aseni put arrow after arrow into their raised shields. His own "soldiers," along with the "Lady Ilyane's" men, were closing in on the patrol as well, weapons drawn, though they made no move to step within striking distance. Aleem would have wondered why, except then the Dragon stopped some ten feet behind the three's turned backs.

With a sharp whistle, he took their attention.

At first the soldiers responded with all the trained discipline of Karesh Syl's army. When they registered that someone was behind them, the rightmost flank rolled off the shield wall to turn and protect their backs. When the man found himself staring up at Arro, though, he made a choking sound. It must have been enough to shake his comrades from their focus, because they glanced around.

For just a second, no one moved, like the Dragon was giving the men a chance to at least turn and face him.

The moment they did, though, he struck.

The great spear's point lanced forward, piercing the middle soldier's wooden shield with so much force it pushed the man back, ripping it from his arm as he fell. In the same move, Arro himself targeted the left-most man, striking *his* shield with such a massive kick Aleem heard a *crunch* of cracking timber, and the soldier reeled so far he, too, tripped and landed with a puff of dry dust next to his comrade. Most unfortunately for the third man, this left him completely alone against the Dragon, who didn't waste any time. Ahna's tips were still embroiled in the wood of the first soldier's shield, so Arro fought one-handed, his sword blurring into nothing more than a streak of steel as his opponent tried to keep his guard up.

As it turned out, all the training the city could offer wasn't a match for Raz i'Syul Arro.

In the space of a single engagement, the soldier's blade was knocked from his grasp, the Dragon's sword reversing direction after the disarming to knock the man's shield out of the way. Then, with a quick step forward, the weapon was retracted and thrust forward, taking the man straight through the chest, Arro's sword driven up to the hilt by the force of the strike.

Without so much as a sound, the man tumbled to the ground, leaving the atherian's sword a uniform wet red as the body slid from the steel.

Almost casually, Arro turned to face the remaining two, who were just managing to gather themselves and get to their feet. Twisting his spear's head into the ground, he put a foot on the ruined shield and wrenched her free of the wood, tossing splinters into the air. This done, he advanced on the pair as they collapsed into a two-layered defensive posture, the soldier with the cracked shield half-crouched in front, the one without standing behind him, sword raised above his head like a scorpion's tail.

The Dragon looked about as threatened as he might have been by a pair of wet rags.

Again, he led the attack, and again he moved so fast it was hard to follow his movements. He was more careful, now, fighting two trained opponents at once, but from the moment steel struck steel it was apparent the soldiers were *several* classes out of their league. Arro's arms worked as though guided by two separate minds, his right wielding Ahna to engage the back-most man, the left bringing the sword out and around to parry a slash the front-most tried to make at the atherian's legs from behind his shield. The exchange lasted a little longer, this time, the pair managing to defend themselves for nearly twenty whole seconds.

Then Ahna connected with the base of the back soldier's sword so hard the blade shattered.

The man screamed, dropping the now-useless hilt and staggering back as he shrieked and clutched at his face. In a flash, Arro retracted Ahna and threw a shoulder into the top of the front man's shield. The thing gave with a grunt of surprise from its owner, and the atherian used it like a platform, rolling right over the man to land behind him, between the two soldiers. The sword slashed before either could react, cutting the shield-bearer mostly in two from behind.

Ahna whistled, her twin blades cleaving through the air, and the screaming ended as the last member of the patrol lost his head and the two hands that had been clawing at the steel shards embedded in his cheeks, nose, and eyes.

Aleem had expected a roar of triumphant cheering as the fight came to an end, but the savannah was as quiet as it might have been had no man ever set foot in the wilds of the plains. With wide eyes, the slave watched the atherian rise and turn. The beast didn't have a scratch on him, and was breathing as lightly as he might have if he'd just finished a casual morning jaunt. He flicked his blades clean, sheathing the sword over his shoulder with a snap, and turned to face the men standing not twenty feet down the road. With a jolt, Aleem realized that the entire group had abandoned their advance on the soldiers as soon as Arro had made himself known.

Then the Dragon spoke.

"Take anything of use," he told the men firmly, indicating the ravaged forms of the fallen soldiers. "Then bury the bodies, if you can. Deep enough that the dogs can't get them. We'll rest here for the time being."

Aleem had never seen any lizard-kind give orders, so it was odd—even if said orders came from Raz i'Syul Arro—to witness men hop to and do as he commanded. The slave stared, mouth agape, as the soldiers of his patrol were stripped of their armor and weapons, a few of the group even breaking off toward the still form of the sergeant near the back of the train.

There was the *clop* of hooves, and a shadow passed over Aleem, shaking him from his shock. He looked around, stifling a yelp when he found himself nose to nose with the long face of a great black stallion. He began to scramble away, but a low voice called out soothingly.

"Easy, friend. Easy."

Aleem looked around the horse's snout to see the man who had called himself "Akelo Aseni" dismounting, more dust fluffing up about his booted feet as he dropped to the road. Aseni—*if* that was his name—gave the horse a friendly pat before speaking to it.

"Gale, go to your master."

The stallion huffed in Aleem's face, like it didn't like to be told what to do, then shook its great head and tromped off. The slave watched it go with his mouth hanging open, following the animal until it stopped, amazingly, to nudge at Raz i'Syul Arro's arm by the cart.

Seeing this, Aleem found his voice for the first time.

"Who... Who are you?" he asked with difficulty. It had been a long time since he'd posed a question to anyone who wasn't a slave like him.

Aseni chuckled in response. His bow was back over his shoulder, but he reached up with gloved hands to pull the spiked helm from his head. He was old, as Aleem had suspected, his hair the same mix of black and silver as his beard. The old bruise darkened his right eye in a fading shadow, but his expression was clear, like a man with a purpose.

"My name *is* Akelo Aseni," he insisted. "As to who *we* are—" he turned his head to nod down the road toward the rest of the group, now paired off to haul the limp forms of the dead soldiers into the grasses of the plains "—that's more complicated."

At first, Aleem had no words for that. He simply watched the bodies being carried off, one after the other, until nothing was left of the patrol he'd been tasked with caring for but a pile of armor and weapons and a few rust-colored stains soaking into the dirt of the road.

"Are you going to kill me?" he asked finally, not looking away from the spots where the men had died.

He wasn't sure why he asked the question. In truth, he had come to the conclusion a long time ago that perhaps dying was the best thing he might be able to manage. His placement in the kitchens had been easy enough, sure, but there were no guarantees in a slave's life, no promises that things would always—or ever, for that matter—be safe or fair. Not fifteen minutes ago, in fact, hadn't he been worried about being sold off as just another body for the pirates of the coast to grind to nothing in the belly of some ship?

Now, though, faced with death, Aleem found himself wondering if life was truly something to be given up so easily.

So when the Percian standing over him answered, he felt that spark of hope, kindled into existence at the sight of Raz i'Syul Arro, shiver and grow.

"No, friend," Aseni said. "We aren't going to kill you. On the contrary. We are here to make sure you learn again exactly what it means to *live*."

XXXVI

"Of all the titles Raz i'Syul Arro gathered in his time on this earth, none ever resounded as far or wide as the one given to him by the wild tribes of the Northern reaches. As 'the Dragon', Arro became more than a simple name to be feared and respected. After the fall of Karesh Nan, 'the Dragon' rose as a symbol of the revolution, a figure to which all those who thought themselves helpless could flock to and learn that, together, they were anything but..."

—*The Atherian*, by Jûn fi'Surr

Raz gave his men till noon to rest. They hadn't been marching all that long—maybe three or four hours since the Sun had first begun to rise over the savannah—but the encounter with the patrol seemed like a good opportunity to grant them all a reprieve from the tedium of the journey they'd been on for a little over a week now, ever since leaving the groves of the eastern coast. Most of the men who hadn't gone off to bury the dead in the prairie lounged about the caravan, sitting against the cart wheels or lazing to nap with arms over their eyes along the cooler edges of the road. Raz didn't bother them. He himself had been walking along at the head of the train, unwilling to ride if the others couldn't, and he didn't hate the idea of halting for a while. They were in no rush. So far their cover had held, and no witnesses had been allowed to escape from the now *two* patrols they'd run into.

More importantly, it gave them a chance to take stock of the loot they'd been left with from the encounter.

"Five full suits of armor." Cyper looked pleased, counting off the folded piles of leather and chain on the back of the cart. "A little bloody here and there, but nothing we can't wash out at the next watering hole." He gave Erom, standing next to him, an exasperated look. "Must you *always* cut their throats?"

The borderer, in turn, glowered and crossed his thick arms defensively.

"Arro says ta' end it quick, I end it quick," he drawled, jerking a thumb at Raz, who stood between them. "Ain't a faster way ta' kill a man."

"Because you *insist* on using those damn things," Cyper pressed with exasperation, waving at the hilts sticking out behind each of Erom's hips. "If you'd let us teach you how to handle a sword, then—"

"Cyper, leave him be," Raz cut in, lifting a pair of gold-and-white leather greaves from the piles, its right leg stained coppery red. "If Erom wants to stick to knives, it's his decision. Sun knows he's got a knack for them."

"I can do something about the stains," Syrah offered helpfully from beside him, speaking from behind her veil to nip off any argument the West Isler might have made as Erom grinned triumphantly at him. "It's more a pity that we lost the horse. It would have done us good to have another mount."

"Aye," Kalin, one of the group's three *kuja*, said with a pained expression from where he sat on the edge of the cart above them, lifting a boot for emphasis. "If Karesh Syl doesn't end us, all this walking might still."

Syrah looked at his feet with what Raz assumed was concern, given that her face was hidden.

"Well small wonder, with footwear like that," she said worriedly. "They're too big. Here." She reached to pluck a pair of boots from the new piles Cyper had collected

"These will do better. Then give yours to Harnen. He's been complaining about his as well. And we can—"

Raz smiled, leaving Syrah to her work swapping and switching out the men's attire as best she could. She still didn't *like* being left alone without him, but over the last two weeks the Priestess had grown to trust these men, these former slaves they'd freed. She'd found it easier to be around them particularly after donning her white robes, gloves, and veil as the Sun became crueler inland, like the hiding of her face and covering of her hands shielded her from their touch. More importantly, though, she knew the men respected her. Respected her, in fact—Raz suspected—practically as much as they respected him.

It had been Syrah's plan, after all, that had borne fruit as they'd been struggling to figure out how to begin their journey west.

It was a simple thing, the morning after they'd beached the boat, to pry one of the cages from the wreckage of the *Moalas* after the tide had cooled the iron and receded. What wood had been left for the metal to cling to was burned and brittle, so Raz tasked Hur with breaking it free. The mute man had taken to his task with fervor, he and his axe making short work of the residual hull. After that, they'd hauled the thing out of the wet sand, rolled it up the beach, and let it dry in the Sun. Finally, they'd wrapped all their provisions and equipment together in the sail canvas, plopped the whole bundle into the cage, and tied the bars to Gale and Nymara's saddles.

By the evening, the group had been nothing more than a streak in the sand, surrounded by footprints for the tide to wipe away, leaving behind the ghostly remnants of the burned ship.

The village Akelo had spoken of, it turned out, was several days' march to the north. They traveled mostly at night, surviving on coconuts, roots, and the provisions that Garht Argoan had spared them, taking to the shade of the groves when the Sun was highest during the day. When they finally reached the village, Akelo and Odene, one of the other Percian, took Gale and Nymara into town, the pockets of their stolen pants heavy with most of the gold and silver from the *Moalas'* treasure. They'd returned several hours later with exactly what Syrah had asked for: a cart and a draft animal, the oafish ox the men had taken to calling "Omara," though they never explained the joke. Another day or so hidden in the groves a mile down the coast from the village, and they'd managed to get the cage up onto the cart and bolted securely into the wood with iron nails they'd salvaged from the ruined *Moalas* several days before. This done, they'd packed the rest of the bed-space with their gear and food, then covered the entire thing with the sailcloth.

When they'd left the beach for good, it was in a wide arc around the village through the palms, as Akelo had suggested, and within a few hours they'd found the road that had led them west, away from the coast, and deeper into the vibrant lands of Perce.

They made the marshes just after nightfall, so Raz hadn't gotten to take in the wonder of the wetlands till the following morning. This worked out for the better, though, because it offered yet another opportunity for Syrah to prove herself to the men when the unforeseen difficulties of *mosquitoes* descended on them in swarms as they left the palm trees behind. The men had to endure about ten minutes of cursing and slapping their necks and arms before the Priestess got a simple ward of protection up around them, disintegrating the insects within with a dozen zapping flashes like firecrackers. After that, they'd spent the evening in relative peace, all of them eventually tuning out the frequent *pop* as another mosquito drifted foolishly within the border of the magical barrier.

For the next few days, Raz had been allowed to enjoy the scenery of the marshes with little distraction, taking in the saltwater bogs and cattails and sharp-billed birds that strutted through the reeds on legs so tall they reminded him of stilt-dancers in the streets of Miropa. Every now and then he would make out the sound of approaching groups from ahead or behind them, and before long a rapid system was developed wherein Raz would whistle quietly to get Akelo's attention, handing Gale off to him before hiding in the sweltering darkness of the iron confines beneath the canvas until the danger passed. Not once had he emerged to find out the men had been given anything other than a curious glance or a raised hand in greeting, and Akelo kept assuring him they were unlikely to come across soldiers along the trade roads. Some of the smaller *kuja* tribes, unable to make ends meet for their families, had been known to set up ambushes for travelers, but the Tash had never before cared to do anything about it. Sure enough, for the two days it took them to cross the marshes, nothing more exciting happened than Marsus Byrn losing a shirt—and almost a hand—to a crocodile while washing his clothes in the waters one morning.

Then they'd reached the savannah, and it wasn't more than a day before things got more complicated.

Initially, the wild plains of Perce sang with a hearty vigor that reminded Raz, in a way, of the depths of the Arocklen Woods in summer. Life was tangible here, thriving in a way it never could among the blistering sands of the Cienbal and Southern fringe cities. Though at first glance the place seemed half-barren—particularly in comparison to the Woods—it didn't take long for Raz to understand the hidden depths of the grasslands, to see the intricate sentience of the place. Every few hours Raz would have to ask Akelo or one of the other Percian what some animal or another was, or be brought back to earth by Syrah calling his name after his mind drifted off in the soothing sway of the fields. Trees were sparse, with only a few distinct species, but they stood like landmarks in the flatness of the world, a gathering place of shade for land-bound animals and birds alike. The consistency of the marshes was replaced by scattered watering holes as they pressed inland, and at one point Raz and Syrah had allowed the convoy to go on without them for a minute or two, sharing a private joke as they gaped in fascination at a herd of black-and-white striped horse-like creatures Odene had told him were called "zebras."

Then, on the eve of their second day crossing the savannah, they'd encountered the first patrol.

Raz, Syrah, and Akelo, leading the train, had made out the figures easily enough in the flatness of the plains. Then a favorable wind brought the smell of the men to him, and it was that scent—that taste of iron and oil and sweat in the air—that had concerned Raz. He'd told Akelo and Syrah what he suspected, then proceeded to hide as he usually did, praying to the Sun and Moon that everything would go smoothly.

Unfortunately, the Twins appeared to have been preoccupied with other matters that day.

When the groups met, the encounter turned sour almost at once. Raz made out a brief exchange, but it wasn't more than a minute before he heard a stranger's shouted order, and the sounds of blades being drawn. Leaving Ahna where he'd leaned her against the cage in the dark, Raz had bolted from beneath the cover to join the fray, drawing his gladius and sagaris as he did.

He made it just in time to keep his men from getting slaughtered by the five trained soldiers they'd pitted themselves against.

After the fight, Akelo had explained quickly what went wrong. Apart from the five men in white-and-gold leather armor—the colors of Karesh Syl, according to the Percian—there had been a horse and sixth figure, a boy in tattered clothes, weighted down with a heavy pack and fettered by iron chains about his ankles. No one was able to say if it was typical for patrols to travel with slaves, but the concern had been irrelevant in the moment. Apparently Akelo and Syrah had had a difficult enough time restraining the men of the caravan from the moment they'd made out the boy.

Then the patrol commander had asked for Syrah to lift her veil and show her face, and the dam broke. The former oarsmen of the *Moalas* had charged, and Raz had been forced to finish the fight.

In the end, fortunately, no one but the soldiers of the patrol had been hurt, but Raz was forced to implement several changes to their routine. First, he'd called them all to gather, and together they'd formed the ploy of Syrah as the "Lady Ilyane," which Akelo and the other *kuja* thought would be a passable cover. Then, he'd started drilling his men daily on the basic skills of combat, enlisting Cyper as an assistant when the West Isler demonstrated himself to have been a skilled swordsman in another life.

The slave-boy, a Northerner who'd called himself simply "Esser," had joined them with all the enthusiasm one could expect from an adolescent who had spent his life dreaming only of freedom.

And like that, they army had gained its first new recruit.

Thinking of the lad shook Raz from his thoughts, and he looked up the road. There Esser sat, garbed in the loose bits of armor the others had pulled together for him, cross-legged in the dirt beside Akelo. The Percian had called him over after the fight, likely hoping he would be a voice of comfort for the slave who'd been attending this most recent patrol. Raz himself hadn't approached the man yet. The look the slave had given him when he'd stepped out onto the road to challenge the soldiers, so full of a confusing wash of terror and hope, still pulled at him, weighing him down. It reminded him of the war he was rekindling, of the hardship he was dragging himself ever closer to with each soldier of Karesh Syl he felled.

Himself, and every soul who braved joining his cause.

Raz spent the next quarter-hour with their now-three horses, seated in a patch of shade on the side of the path, using a claw to free Ahna and his gladius of the dried blood that had managed to cling to their blades. In that time, the men who'd gone off to bury the dead returned to the cart, making for Syrah as the woman continued to hand out the looted gear. Soon after, Akelo, Esser, and the newcomer pulled themselves to their feet. Together they approached, the Percian's hand resting on the slave's shoulder encouragingly, and Raz sheathed his sword and set the dviassegai aside carefully as they neared. Slowly he got to his feet, doing his best not to look too intimidating, but the look on the newcomer's face told him he wasn't succeeding.

"Raz," Akelo said when the three of them stopped before him, "this is Aleem. Like Esser, he was indentured in the Tash's palace in Karesh Syl."

"Welcome, Aleem," Raz told the man with a nod, trying a smile. "I apologize if I made a poor first impression. I judged the fight to be more pressing than the niceties of a proper introduction."

In response, all he got was a gaping mouth and wide eyes, like the slave couldn't believe what he was seeing.

Akelo coughed pointedly. "Aleem had some insights we agreed he should share with you. His observations generally confirm some of the suspicions we developed after what Esser could tell us."

"Oh?" Raz asked, watching Aleem expectantly.

Still, though, the man appeared unable to do anything but stare.

It was Esser, finally, who got a sound out of the man. With an impatient roll of his eyes, the blond-haired man jabbed an elbow into the slave's side, making the man yelp and jump.

"I-I am Aleem!" he shouted foolishly, his mind clearly struggling to catch up to the conversation that had happened around him as he'd stood dumbstruck. "I can be of service to you, great Dragon! I cook! I cook very well. I could cook for you and your men, provided you are in need of a cook.

I am not good at much else. I only cook. I was a hand in the kitchen. I was a—"

"Aleem," Raz cut across the poor man's rambling gently. "Calm yourself. You are safe here. You are free."

Again, Aleem seemed unable to speak. This time, though, the silence came from somewhere other than his shock. Raz watched the man's face quiver, his cheeks and lips twitching, his eyes beginning to grow wet.

"Free." He said the word like it were new to him, but full of enough wonder to make his voice shake. "F-free…"

Then, with a breaking gasp and a smile of endless relief, Aleem fell to his knees and began to sob into the palms of his hands.

Raz gave him the time he needed, easing himself down until he crouched before the man, reaching out to grasp one of his shivering shoulders comfortingly as Aleem howled in joyful disbelief. At his touch the man flinched, but did not pull way, one hand even moving from his face to clutch at Raz's wrist like it were the lifeline to this new understanding of his own value. Above them, still standing, Akelo and Esser looked on, the old Percian's face a heartbroken picture of pride, the young Northerner's full of embarrassed fascination.

By the time Aleem got control of himself again, the doubts Raz had been having about his path had long faded.

This is why we fight, he reminded himself, watching the man's shaking start to subside. *This is why we hold nothing back.*

"M-Master Akelo says I can be of h-help?" the former slave finally managed to choke out, wiping his eyes and looking up at Raz. "What can I do, great Dragon?"

"First," Raz said with a pained grin, releasing Aleem's shoulder, "you can start by never addressing anyone as 'Master' ever again. You have no master now, Aleem. On the same note, stop calling me 'great Dragon.' 'Arro' or 'Raz' is fine."

"Or just 'Dragon'!" Esser offered up excitedly, earning himself a raised eyebrow from both Raz and Akelo.

The boy lapsed back into silence at once.

"Next, though," Raz continued, returning his attention to Aleem. "Akelo says you might have information. I would very much like to hear anything you think might be of value to us."

The man's nod was jerky, his body still shaking. "I-I do. The patrol. The orders the sergeant was giving…"

It took some time, but slowly Aleem opened up, repeating for Raz everything he must have already told Akelo and Esser. As he spoke, Raz put the pieces together, sometimes glancing up at the old Percian to get a silent agreement on something, sometimes frowning as the breadth of what they truly faced was revealed to him a little more. In the end, the man couldn't offer much Esser hadn't already been able to tell them, but the confirmation of the Northerner's observations and Raz's own suspicions had great value all its own. The frequent stops the patrol made. The horse and rider. The instructions the unit's commander—Rafik, Aleem called him—had given just before Erom had put him in the ground.

By the time he finished, Raz thought he had a good picture of the situation they were walking into.

"Thank you, Aleem," he said gratefully when the man finally trailed off. "This *is* of great use to us. Now—" he looked up at Akelo uncertainly "— has it been explained to you where we are going? What we mean to do?"

Aleem's nod was stronger now, and his voice no longer shook. In fact, he sounded almost resolved. "It has. You are making for Karesh Syl."

"Yes," Raz said gravely. "Back to the city you just escaped. You offered your help, and we will gladly take it. Sun knows we could use a decent cook. But it is *your* choice. It is—"

It was Aleem's turn, this time, to cut Raz off.

"I wish to serve," he said firmly, lifting his face to meet Raz's eyes defiantly.

"You're sure?" Raz pressed him cautiously. "Think on this."

"I am." Aleem's gaze was hard as steel. "And I have. You have offered me the chance to give my life meaning again, Arro. I think *this* is the place I'd like to start doing that."

Raz studied the man a moment more, seeking doubt in him. There was nothing there, however. Aleem might not have the strength of Akelo and his men, or the enthusiasm of Esser, but even on his knees his determination was palpable, his conviction almost tangible.

Finally, Raz nodded.

"Esser will introduce you to Syrah," he said, standing up again and offering a hand for the former slave to take. "She will see to it you are clothed and armed, if you desire it. She can also show you where we keep our provisions. Noon approaches, and I for one am eager to see your skills at work."

Aleem accepted his help, pulling himself unsteadily to his feet. He seemed to have no more words to say, but his fingers lingered around Raz's palm, like he thought that if he let go, that lifeline to his freedom would be severed.

Then Esser put an arm around his shoulders, speaking with surprising gentleness for a lad his age as he turned and led the former slave away. "Come on, old man. Let me take you to the only one of the group who's prettier than the Dragon."

Together, Raz and Akelo watched them go, and it wasn't until they saw Aleem bowing to Syrah that the Percian spoke up.

"At least two-dozen patrols like this." The man whistled. "As far as I know, there are four or five ways that could be taken east from Karesh Syl."

"Which means we have another four or five encounters to prepare for," Raz agreed thoughtfully. "Assuming the Tash is spreading his men evenly across all possible roads."

"If memory serves, this is one of the smaller trade routes," Akelo said with a shrug. "There's a chance fewer soldiers were sent down this path."

"Or more," Raz responded. "If the Tash and his Hands guess that Syrah and I would have wanted to avoid the traffic and eyes of the main road, it's possible they planned to guard these smaller routes more carefully."

"Anything is possible," the Percian said with a shrug. "We'll prepare for the worst, regardless. Which means we should devise a battle-plan for these patrols. Five soldiers might not be enough to make you break a sweat, Arro, but it seems their orders are only to get word back to Karesh Syl if something is amiss. It's nothing more than luck the first troop didn't send their rider back at the first sign of trouble, like this sergeant Rafik was ready to. We're already planning to enter a city of sharks. Pouring blood in the water before we get there would not bode well for us…"

"No, it wouldn't," Raz grumbled in agreement. "Not to mention that Syrah pointed out it would be nice to have more horses. Now we know what we're up against, we can strike preemptively." He glanced at the bow slung over Akelo's shoulder. "Speaking of which, I have to commend you on that shot. If the rider had gotten past me, I don't think Gale would have had the stamina to run him down."

The Percian smirked, patting the top of the quiver slung behind his back. Their stores of arrows were minimal, but hopefully sufficient, given that Akelo had the only bow among them.

"I've been practicing," the man said. "While you work with the others every morning."

"So *that's* where you disappear to." Raz laughed. "I've had to hold Cyper back from going to look for you. He'll be pleased to hear."

Akelo gave a reminiscent sort of smile. "The *kuja* live off the land and its bounties. Mastering the bow and arrow is an essential of survival. I admit, I thought I'd lost touch with that part of my life…"

The Percian's attention drifted away, his dark eyes on the distant edge of the morning horizon to the south. Raz realized, with an uncomfortable pang, that he had failed to consider how Akelo and the other Percian must feel, entering the savannah again. He'd been so preoccupied with his own thoughts, burying himself in his own wonder at the place and worry after their skirmish with the patrols, that he hadn't had time to consider that his own feelings were very likely eclipsed by the emotions the former wild men must be experiencing.

"Are they out there?" he asked after a moment. "Your family?"

Akelo drew in a long inhalation, letting it out with some difficulty.

"No," he answered with a shake of his head. "No, they are gone. My sons were young when the slavers came. Too young. My wife, Xula… She didn't live long, after we lost them. She and several of the other mothers stopped eating, then drinking. They died before we even reached the city." He frowned, and despite his bulk the man looked suddenly very much his age. "It was a kindness, I think, in the end."

Raz sighed unhappily. "I've had the same thought, many times over the years. When I miss my mother and father, or my sister. I dream of them, sometimes. I like to think it's the Sun giving me a glimpse of the happiness they have now. Afterward, I always wonder who suffers more: those who pass on, even in terrible ways, or those they leave behind to struggle through life without them."

"One can only hope it's the latter," Akelo grumbled, crossing his arms and watching a line of gazelle bound across the prairie in the distance. "There's enough misery in life, don't you think? I admit I hold out hope that whatever awaits us in the Moon's embrace is better than this."

He held up a hand, and Raz thought with some disappointment that the man was indicating the vastness of the plains before them, glistening as the Sun rose overhead.

Then he realized Akelo was presenting his scar about his wrist again.

"You've given us a purpose, Arro," the Percian said with an appreciative nod, dropping his hand, "but I struggle to convince myself that whatever we achieve now will be worth the struggles we faced to reach this point. If you tell me that death is no better than this… Well…"

"Syrah's faith believes that we all return to this life, after we pass," Raz offered thoughtfully. "She believes her god, Laor, spends eternity plucking the wicked from the cycle, pushing the world to perfection with every death and every rebirth."

Akelo scowled, but his face softened quickly.

"If that is the cycle of life, then perhaps the process is simply slower than I can see. It is hard to comprehend such a view, once you have seen the auctions in the markets of Karesh Syl, or the slave-trains that run a mile long from the savannah into the city." He gave Raz a grim smile. "Perhaps you and I will earn ourselves an easier path, in the next life, then? Perhaps with what we do now, we will be granted all the comforts and wonders we would have in the Moon's embrace."

"Doubtful," Raz said with a dry laugh. "The Laorin believe that life is the most precious gift their god has provided for man. They see killers as little short of blasphemers, as men and women willing to spit right in His face." He looked around at Akelo. "If anything, I wouldn't be surprised if you and I fall under the 'wicked' side of things, in the eyes of the Laorin. Perhaps we are only meant to be plucked from the world by Laor and cast into oblivion in order to make the world a better place."

At that, Akelo cracked a smile, a real one this time, if a little dry.

"If that's the case," he said, reaching out to clap Raz on the shoulder as he started to move back toward the cluster of men at end back of the cart, "I think I'll stick to hoping it's the Moon that judges me, when all is said and done."

XXXVII

It was just under two weeks later that Karesh Syl announced itself on the horizon.

"What do you see?" Syrah asked.

Raz didn't turn as the woman led Nymara up beside him. His eyes were shaded and set westward, in the direction they'd been plodding along for well over half a month now.

"Towers," he grunted, dropping his hand to pat Gale's neck as the stallion huffed under him. "Still a ways off, yet."

Indeed, though they were faint, he could just make out the angular shapes against the wash of the early morning, like shadow puppets atop a blue-grey backdrop. The outlines were clearer now, though. For nearly a half-hour he'd *thought* he'd been seeing some detail in the distance, but the heat of the midsummer day rippled over the flatness of the grasslands in undulating rivulets, distorting everything at any distance. Now, though, he'd called a halt, allowing Akelo to echo the command to the men as Raz had heeled Gale forward another dozen yards up the road.

At the very edge of his vision, indistinct silhouettes of what looked like a mountain made of turrets and struts and thin, jutting buildings clawed at the sky itself.

On his right, Syrah sighed, the veil that covered her face fluttering lightly with the exhalation. "I don't know whether to be relieved or terrified," she admitted, glancing behind them. "I can't even imagine what *they'll* think."

At that, Raz too turned around, taking in his meager forces.

In the last twelve days, they'd crossed paths with no less than seven more of Karesh Syl's patrols. The men had kept their promises, leaving the majority of the fighting to him, and as a result their numbers had swollen as five more slaves chose to join their cause, falling in with Esser and Aleem so that Raz's army was now twenty strong if he counted Syrah and himself. In addition, they'd collected an additional six horses—having lost another when the animal bolted before anyone could snatch its bridle—as well as a plethora of armor, weapons, and gold and silver looted from the bodies of the Tash's slain soldiers. As the number of mounts grew, their party had started moving faster, taking turns riding and walking. Indeed, if the former slaves were to be believed, Raz hadn't expected to see the city for another two days, maybe three.

They seemed to have made better time than any could have estimated, because now Karesh Syl loomed like a disease on the open flatness of the savannah.

"Find Akelo," Raz told Syrah, still not looking around at her. With every moment the heat shifted, revealing more and less of the hundred knives that were the bastions and towers of the city. "The other *kuja* as well."

He saw Syrah nod in the corner of his vision, then pull her mare around and canter back to the main group. A minute or so later, she returned with the Percian, Akelo and Odene on horseback, Zehir and Kalin on foot accompanied by a newcomer, a youth named Rufari. Like all the other slaves they'd managed to free from the patrols, Rufari was slimmer than the former oarsmen of the *Moalas*. Whereas most of the now-seven recruits they'd gained had been couriers, footmen, and servants, however, the boy claimed to have been a laborer along the palace walls. His strong frame fit well in the soldier's uniform he sported—better indeed than the broad shoulders of Akelo and the rest—and he had a stern, calm face that lent itself well to the overall persona of a man-at-arms of the Tash's army.

Well... *usually* Rufari was stern and calm. As seemed common among the newcomers, whenever he was summoned before Raz for any reason the man appeared to have trouble maintaining his composure, staring openly with nothing short of awe.

It was flattering, in a way, but also exasperating.

"What's going on?" Akelo asked as the five dark-skinned men came to group around Gale, all of them—except the young Rufari—peering off in the eastward distance, following Raz's eyes.

Raz gave Syrah a quick, grateful look. She hadn't said anything in front of the rest of the men.

"The city is closer than we thought," Raz answered, keeping his voice low to indicate that the others should do the same. "Three, maybe four hours' hard riding, if I had to guess."

There was a collective hiss of surprised disbelief from the *kuja*. Even Rufari now turned to look out over the horizon.

"You're sure?" Akelo asked, and the question was a testament to the weight of this news. Raz didn't think the man had even once before questioned his word.

"I am," he said with a nod. "It's time. Syrah and I will bring the caravan as close to the walls as we think prudent. You five will ride on ahead, as we discussed."

Akelo nodded, his dark face a little paler than usual. In truth, there wasn't too much to worry about, in the short term. Their plan was simple enough, and one of the other freed men—a Southerner named Nudar, whose family had been dragged from their home in Karavyl some years prior—had been in charge of cleaning the chamber pots in several of the city barracks. He'd been able to pass on a few key bits of knowledge from his time among the Tash's soldiers, explaining the basic etiquette of the army, as well as how to identify most of the ranks according to the bronze markers pinned to the left side of a soldier's bleached leather cuirass. Akelo and the other four had even replaced all their preferred weapons with several of the standard-issue blades they'd pilfered. The bow the old Percian preferred was now kept with the rest of their weapons stocks, retrieved only when the *kuja* prowled the savannah every morning for the game that had kept them all fed over the last three weeks.

Now—and after several days of instruction from Raz and Cyper on the appropriate way to heft a shield—the five men were more than passable as a basic scouting unit.

"You lot," Akelo was saying, turning in his saddle to speak to Zehir, Kalin, and Rufari, still on foot around them. "Find horses, and grab what supplies we'll need."

The three men nodded at once, jogging back to the cart and the rest of the caravan. After they'd gone, Raz turned to Akelo.

"We'll make camp off the main road, in whatever cover we can find," he said. "*Don't* draw more attention to yourself than you need to. Be back before dark, if you can."

"Aye," Akelo said through a tight jaw, his eyes once again on the lightening horizon. "In, out, and report. None of us want to be in the shadow of that place longer than we must, believe me."

Behind him, as though to accentuate this point, Odene muttered a prayer to the Sun above.

They left not long after, riding west at a hard gallop in the order Nudar had advised them on: Akelo at the head, the other four in two pairs on his heels. Raz and Syrah saw them off, watching the dust of their departure linger and settle, and after a minute or two the five men were nothing more than an indistinct group of steel helms and white leather even to him.

At that point, he turned back to the caravan.

"I suppose we should tell them?" he asked the Priestess under his breath, studying the set faces of his remaining men, all either watching him expectantly or gazing after Akelo and his group.

At his side, shifting in her saddle as Nymara dipped her head to snort at a tuft of dry grass in the road, he thought he made out Syrah smiling sadly.

"On the road," she said. "Give them a little while longer believing their troubles are still a few days away."

The men, in the end, took the news with such stoic understanding, Raz couldn't help but be proud of his little army. He made his announcement as Syrah suggested, while marching at a leisurely pace ever eastward, and even the recruits—though one or two of them blanched and stumbled when he said they could make the city as early as that evening—swallowed whatever fear they must have all been suffering, taking the new reality in stride.

Raz left them alone after that, ceding immediate command to Cyper, and rode ahead of the group with Syrah in order to give them all the chance to speak among themselves, reassuring each other and bolstering one another's courage out of earshot. For a time he and the Priestess trotted along in relative quiet, taking in the wondrous golden-flatness of the savannah, watching birds take off in waves from the grasses and listening to the occasional breeze play its music over the plains. Raz couldn't help but be saddened by the deceptive peacefulness of this place. Again he was reminded of the Arocklen Woods, of the solemn wonder of the Northern forests. He remembered feeling similarly conflicted when traversing the Woods with Talo and Carro, torn between the magnificence of the scenery and nature around him and the ever-present fact that something dark and hateful lingered within its depths. Then, it had been Gûlraht Baoill and his army, the constant knowledge that at some point Raz would have to confront the wild tribes of the Northern mountain men. Here, it was the weight of Karesh Syl, like the city itself were pressing him down as he approached.

After a while, Raz had to allow himself, too, a reprieve from the tension. Eventually he managed to press aside his concerns, if only for a time, even managing half a smile as he gazed off over the savannah, watching gazelles bound in dipping patterns in the distance, as well as a pod of lions lazing about in the shadows of a massive baobab. He was able to clear his mind, to separate himself from the trouble he could feel so rapidly approaching. For a time, he knew peace, enjoying the ride and world.

Then Syrah gasped.

Raz—who had been staring off to the south for several minutes, trusting Gale to keep to the road—whipped around in his saddle, his hand jerking up to the head of the sagaris on his hip as adrenaline spidered through him like light through shattered glass. His first instinct was to expect an attack, maybe yet another patrol, but as his eyes snapped over the savannah to the north he saw nothing more than shivering grasses and what looked like tilled growing fields approaching as they trotted forward. He took in this farmland in a flash, initially noting nothing of importance other than the fact that he should have known a city-state would need some means of supplying itself with food.

He was about to ask Syrah what she'd seen, about to demand that she explain the rigidness with which she sat in her saddle, when he made out the workers.

• •

The fields themselves were impressive in their size. There were dozens, each cleared of grass to reveal rich, earthy soil from which all manner of colorful vegetation grew, most of which he didn't recognize. They were separated by hedges of uncut land, marking boundaries between the plots, and around each section two or three men were standing in the shade of rickety tool sheds and covered carts, or pacing about the edges of the fields. Percian all, they wore uniform light, sleeveless shirts, most heads shaved clean so the sweat that lingered across their scalps shone beneath the Sun. Each man carried a whip and cudgel with him, either on their belts or held firmly in hand, and many were shouting harsh orders at the top of their lungs over the hundreds of forms toiling amid the harvests. Dozens of figures were bent or kneeling in each field, tending to the plants in the cruel light of the full day, heads bowed against the heat.

"Raz!" Syrah's voice was distant to him as he stared at the workers. "Raz, come on. Come *on!*"

He knew, in some secluded part of his mind, that she was right. The slave drivers hadn't noticed them yet, it seemed. They had to go back, had to rejoin the main group they'd left nearly a quarter-mile up the road. They could lose themselves among the men, he knew, or stow away in the cage again.

And yet, despite this knowledge, Raz couldn't move.

He had been expecting it, of course. He had been working diligently to brace himself, to prepare his mind and soul for the moment he knew would come eventually. With each day they grew nearer to Karesh Syl, though, and with each step the reality of the event had loomed ever closer, like death creeping up on an aging man.

And now, staring off across the fields, Raz felt as though the reaper had finally caught up to him.

The atherian worked in complete silence, the only sounds from their efforts coming from the human overseers all around them. They were bound—each and every one—around the ankles, looped manacles linked by a short iron chain that made it visibly hard for any of them to do more than shuffle about the rows. They wore thin, threadbare clothes that hardly even covered them decently, and the cloth of those rags was so dirty and disheveled they could as well have periodically been lying down and rolling around in the dirt.

As Raz continued to watch, he noted once again the distinct aura that hovered about the figures, that almost palpable sense of a unanimously broken spirit. He remembered the hollow eyes of men and women he'd seen cruelly penned up in the Cages of Miropa. He recalled the utter lack of hope lingering in the faces of Akelo and the others when he'd first descended into the hull of the *Moalas*. Again he witnessed it now, could practically taste the despaired wretchedness of the beings before him. They seemed less person, somehow, even to him. They had been worn away, stripped of the life and spirit that Syrah would have said made one "human." The atherian before him had been fractured, hammered and beaten down into something almost less than living.

They seemed little more than *things*, machines that just happened to be breathing, utterly without hope and desire, because hope and desire had only ever led to pain and disappointment.

It wasn't the first time Raz had been close to lizard-kind, of course. He remembered little and less of the details of his life before the Arros had taken him in, but he *did* remember the occasions when his family had stowed him away inside their wagons during the summer seasons by the Garin, hiding him when the atherian came down from the Crags to the east to trade with the nomadic families. He'd never been allowed—not even as he'd grown older—to interact with them, which had taken him some time to understand and appreciate. He'd been an Arro, a man of the clan, son of Agais and Grea. He did not belong to the atherian, not anymore, and he'd eventually understood that he didn't *want* to belong to them, that to show himself might well have resulted in attempts to take him away from his kin.

Still, Raz hadn't been able to control his curiosity completely, and more than once he'd snuck out of the wagon ring to study the strange people that were of his blood, observing them from a safe distance and always, *always,* downwind.

Now, witnessing the hundreds of lizard-kind spread out across the fields in the distance, Raz was reminded of that time.

Unlike him, the scales of many of the figures were not a congruent shade of greenish-black. They were mostly of that same color, true, but many of them had markings or patterned patches of different hues, like wolves or dogs of the same breed might have. There were ripples of white, red, and even luminescent blue down the back of necks and the front of throats. There were mirrored slashes of purple and green across chests and shoulders, or shapes of yellow and orange that layered down arms and legs like sheets of armor had been painted onto their skin. Not a single form bore wings, obviously, but the males had crests that twitched and fluttered behind their heads, and all had tails adorned with yet more patterns, like thick snakes marked with geometrics and swaths of different colors. They were a beautiful people, Raz thought, remembering abruptly that he had made the same realization on the occasions he'd had the opportunity to observe them around the Garin.

A beautiful people, now chained and fettered and driven at the end of a whip like common livestock.

Raz felt himself reaching for Ahna, still lashed at Gale's side. He felt, for the first time since the *Moalas,* the animal stir within him, felt it raise its head in tentative anticipation. As the steel claws of his gauntlet closed about the haft of the dviassegai, he sensed himself being pulled away, submerged into calm, cool depths as something more terrible rose up in his place.

Had it not been for Syrah, he would have ruined everything then and there.

Her touch, as always, brought him ripping back. Her hand, though tense and shaking in what might have been any combination of sadness or anger or fear, was a comforting warmth against his scales. She had reached out—probably as soon as she'd seen him going for Ahna—lightly gripping the muscled breadth of his upper arm.

"No, Raz," she said in a shallow whisper, and her fingers dug lightly into him. "Not here. It isn't the time or the place."

Raz clenched his jaw, feeling his fangs grind in loathing frustration. She was right, of course—Syrah was usually right, after all—but that didn't mean he had to like it.

"I left you, once," he said bitterly, his hand still around the bleached white wood of Ahna's shaft. "I had the chance to save you, and I didn't. Look how that turned out."

"Yes," Syrah hissed with a nod, indicating herself with her other hand. "*Look. Look* how it turned out. I'm free. I'm whole."

"Mostly whole," Raz growled, feeling his anger flux as his gaze flicked to her face. Through the veil he could barely make out the outline of the frayed black wraps bound over her right eye. "Mostly whole."

To his surprise, Syrah managed a hard laugh. "Maybe, yes. But all this—" she motioned to her hidden, ruined features "—was done long before you or anyone else could have helped me. Look at them, Raz." She pointed west and north, toward the fields, though her own face didn't turn from his. "They are slaves of Karesh Syl. You aren't leaving them. You aren't abandoning them. The remaining days they spend toiling for the Tash will be hard, yes, but they will be worth it. Allow them to make the sacrifice. Allow them to give you a chance to save them all, not just those right in front of you."

Save them all, Raz thought, realizing she was echoing his own words back at him.

He watched the atherian continue their work. A few of the slavers had noticed the pair of them now, he could tell, turning to look up at the road curiously. No one raised any alarm, though, so he thought the distance and the Sun at their back must have been enough to distort their forms, alone and ahorse on the road. Still, despite the situation becoming more pressing by the moment, Raz couldn't look away, couldn't quite bring himself to break the spell of seeing his own kind for the first time in the better part of a decade. He couldn't pull himself out from under the weight of the moment, nor the desperate fury that still lingered within him.

Once again, Syrah came to his rescue.

Leaning over in her saddle, the Priestess reached up and took his face gently in one hand. With deliberate care she forced him to look away from the fields, forced him to turn and meet her masked gaze. He couldn't see her eye through the veil, but her voice was warm and tender, drawing him back from the edge he was toeing.

"Talo would have reminded you of the greater need, Raz," she told him. "Carro, too, if he were here. You're *not* abandoning them. You're just asking them to make a small sacrifice."

For several seconds more, Raz stared into the white silk veil, feeling as though the depth of it were drawing him up, pulling him back from the red-tinged world of his own rage.

Eventually, he let go of Ahna's haft, allowing the dviassegai to settle against Gale's side once more.

They returned to the main group at a casual trot, not wanting to raise any more concerns from the overseers who were still watching them curiously from the distant fields. When they rejoined the men, Raz handed Gale over to Hur, telling the mute mountain man to saddle up as Erom did the same with Nymara. After that, Raz gave quiet orders to Cyper, who spent the next several minutes moving about the ranks, organizing the men and warning them of the scene ahead.

Together, they passed the fields several minutes later, an inconsequential group of traveling mercenaries to any outside eyes, any trace of Raz and Syrah lost in the middle of the group and their remaining horses.

Karan Brightneck felt the presence pass unsubstantiated, ethereal as the shadow of a cloud drifting over the Sun above.

No… that wasn't true. Rather, it was more the opposite, like a moment of warmth and light breaking through the heavens on a cold, stormy day. The feeling was anything but dark, anything but cold. For no apparent reason, the sensation passed over Karan and left her scales tingling inexplicably.

She should have known better than to pause in her work, should have known better than to straighten and look around, searching for the source of the mysterious notion that something was calling to her, as subtle as the passing of a breeze. Slowly she scanned the field around her, ignoring the bent and working forms of the other atherian, as well as the masters loitering about by the tool shed, playing a game of dice in the shade.

She found nothing out of the ordinary.

To the east, several carrion birds were circling, marking the spot where some poor beast had met—or was actively meeting—its end. On the road to the south, an unimpressive party of mercenaries and soldiers was towing a cart along west, making for Karesh Syl. Further beyond them, Karan made out the ambling outline of a small herd of elephants, headed for one watering hole or another.

No, nothing stood out as an explanation for her strange feeling.

"OI!"

Karan jumped, the icy realization that she had been standing still for almost half-a-minute shooting up her spine like a cold blade. Quickly she bent double again, rushing to pull up the carrots around her clawed feet in an attempt to look like nothing was amiss.

The master wasn't fooled.

CRACK!

Karan barely muffled her scream as the whip lashed across her back, the pain of the blow causing her to stumble forward several feet. There was a second sound of shearing air, and this time she couldn't stop the shriek as she was thrashed for a second time, the braided leather catching her half-across her neck and face, missing her left eye by inches. She tripped and fell to the earthy field, basket tumbling from her arm, curling up around herself and covering her head with her hands as the *thump* of boots approached.

"What in the Sun's name do you think you're doing, scaly?" a man's hard voice breathed down on her. "I should flog you within an inch of your miserable, pathetic life. Now *get up!*"

Karan didn't hesitate, ignoring the pain across her cheek, neck, and back as she scrambled onto her feet to stand before the slave driver. She didn't recognize the man—a fortunate thing, given the overseers that *were* well known weren't often renowned for their kindness—and made sure not to meet his gaze even though she stood at least two inches taller than him.

"Pick them up," the Percian growled, pointing with the handle of his whip at the basket of spilled carrots lying in the row between them. "Get back to work. Half rations tonight, for all!"

He shouted this last announcement to the field, looking around at the rest of the atherian, as though daring someone to raise a word of protest. Not a single slave uttered so much as a sound. They all knew better, all knew that to voice their disappointment and anger would only land them their own lashes, as well as a full *week* of half-rations. Still, many of the lizard-kind at least had the backbone to glare.

Not all of them, though, were staring at the master.

Karan swallowed in nervous fear as she briefly met Brahen's cold golden eyes, narrowed in displeasure. She knew, without a doubt, that at the very least she herself wouldn't be eating dinner at all that night, her already-cut ration of meat most likely forfeit.

It wasn't just the masters who could be cruel, after all.

And yet, despite all this pressing down on her, as the Percian moved away Karan couldn't help but give one quick glance around, searching a final time for any sign of the presence she'd felt, even a hint as to what the sensation had meant. Still finding nothing—and with many of her fellow slaves still watching her angrily—Karan gave up, returning to her labors and thinking wistfully of the supper she'd sacrificed for no apparent reason.

In the sky above, framed a layer of thin clouds, the Sun gazed down on her, as steady and strong and full of hope as He could be cruel and unforgiving.

XXXVIII

"To live and to die at His whim. To serve and to submit to His will. To defend and to protect by His word."

—excerpt of conscription pledge, Karesh Syl, c. 720 v.S.

Caysus Eboha was having a very, *very* long day. His morning had been bad enough: arriving late to roll-call, then realizing he'd left his helmet in the barracks, *then* vomiting into the horse trough during the post-call drills. But then, as *punishment* for all that, he'd been assigned afternoon sentry duty on the eastern gate. Now, as the shadow of the city wall stretched inch by inch over the road and savannah before him, Caysus was busy sweating in his uniform and trying not to be sick again, swearing up and down and praying to every god he had ever worshiped—or heard of, for that matter—to give him the strength never to visit the Lion's Paw Tavern ever again.

To be fair, Caysus knew he had gotten off relatively easy. If his captain had truly wanted to teach him a lesson, he would have assigned him duty at the north or west gates, which were a damned *nightmare* this time of day. There were always hundreds of comers and goers to and from the city, arriving or leaving from and for the South or the Seven Cities respectively, not to mention the frequent messengers, ambassadors, and bureaucrats that required special attention and vetting. At the east gate, traffic was generally much slower, the visitors they received largely limited to farmers, hunters, delegates from the grassland tribes and villages, or emissaries and traders from the pirates along the coast. It was tedious work, checking trade permits, searching carts for contraband, and keeping the crowd in check when tensions grew strained, but it was easy.

Or would have been, were it not for Dulan Yazir.

Yazir was, like every other commander of the four city gates, technically a general in the Tash's army. Too old to be of any real use but possessing too many friends in the higher ranks to really be put to pasture, the aged officer should have been taking advantage of his leisurely post, enjoying the advantages it offered. Caysus knew for a fact that Saresh, the general in charge of the north gate, padded his pockets with bribes and gifts from the Mahsadën envoys in exchange for overlooking the fifteen-head limit slavers were generally held to per entry. To the west, Erras Panya had enough sense to almost *never* actually show up to his post, entrusting such menial work as monitoring the comings and goings from the gate to lesser officers and foot soldiers. Caysus sighed, allowing himself a brief moment of fancying the idea of Dulan Yazir taking such a lax approach to his duties.

Unfortunately, the general of the east gate was the sort of good soldier his subordinates jested most likely slept under a crossed-spears banner of the city with his sword laid out lovingly in the bed beside him. He was rigid and utterly unrelenting, holding the soldiers under his daily command to the minutia of military expectations, from posture to procession. The man had a single vice—the city brothels—but the whorehouses were frequented as often by diplomats, advisors, and even the Hands of the Tash himself as they were by the common rabble.

In essence, his penchant for prostitutes wasn't much of a stain on Dulan Yazir's sterling reputation.

"Single file!" the general roared, pacing up and down the growing number of arrivals, lining up one after the other along the road that led out from the gate. He walked with a stoically erect bearing—or as erect as a man his age was capable of—his braided grey hair neatly bunched in a single plait along the base of his helmet. The only time he unclasped his hands from behind his back was when he needed to shove some unruly individual into place, or point to the back of the line where he sent anyone who gave him lip. When he was sure the man wasn't looking, Caysus rolled his eyes.

"How long, do you think," he muttered under his breath, squinting as the fading daylight made his head throb, "before the Moon sees fit to pull our good general up into her embrace?"

At his right, his watch-partner chuckled dryly. Caysus didn't consider Habib a friend, per se. They were part of different cohorts, and therefore were the type of acquaintances who only crossed paths when their assignments happened to line up, but the man was pleasant enough, and always happy to joke at a superior's expense. Caysus had counted himself fortunate when he'd realized they'd be partnered for the afternoon.

It made the time go by a little faster, at least.

"Pray it's sooner rather than later," Habib responded under his breath, briefly releasing the hilt of his sword to scratch at the straps that bound his hefted shield to his left arm. "Rumor has it General Ima has started 'compensating' some of his men for their services."

Caysus groaned jealously. It was an open secret that Zale Ima, commander of the south gate, had long used the benefits of his post to run a fairly lucrative smuggling operation. All turned a blind eye—a general who happened to be the older brother of the Tash's Second Hand was largely untouchable, after all—and if the man had started slipping some of his profits down the ranks…

Caysus licked his lips unconsciously, thinking momentarily of how many pints a single bribe from Ima would afford him.

Then the image made his stomach lurch, and he pushed the thought away.

"You'd think, after sixty-something years under the Tash's boot, he would have learned to bend a little," he muttered, watching Yazir continue his ceaseless pacing up and down the line. "Maybe someone should clue him in that being an officer of the watch isn't the 'great honor' he was probably told it was when they kicked him out of the main army."

"Oh, don't do that," Habib said with mock sadness. "The poor man wouldn't be able to handle it. He'd probably drop dead then and there of a broken heart."

Both of them snorted at that, not altogether upset with the image.

Most unfortunately, Caysus hadn't yet had time to compose his face completely when Yazir's eyes happened to fall on him.

Oh, shit.

In textbook fashion, the general detached himself from his amusement of bullying the men and women of the line and made right for Caysus and Habib. Caysus felt his heart hammer in his chest as they instinctively straightened, trying to appear as much a pair of perfect soldiers as they were capable of.

Yazir, of course, didn't buy it for a moment.

"Something funny, you two?" the old general asked sarcastically as he came to stand before them, hands still clasped behind his back, posture still rigid. He gave off an air of pride and patriotism that might have been impressive, except that age had withered away his height so drastically that the man was looking up at Caysus and Habib from a fairly significant discrepancy. His hard brown eyes, though, were edged with disapproval, and neither of the men were fool enough to be smart in response.

"No, General," they said together, eyes over Yazir's helmet. Caysus ignored the throb in his head, forcing himself to stare dutifully off into the distance. A five-man patrol galloped by on horseback—a rare occurrence they had been seeing more and more of over the last couple weeks—and Caysus barely controlled a grimace of annoyance as he saw them slow and glance in his direction, likely enjoying the free entertainment of seeing him berated.

"Oh, is that so?" Yazir was asking, looking from Caysus to Habib and back again. "Strange… I could have sworn I heard you two laughing behind my back. Care to share the joke?"

Neither men said anything, Caysus keeping his eyes resolutely forward even as the lingering patrol finally galloped off.

"Let me rephrase," the general said in a flat voice. "You *will* share the joke, or I'll have it made known to your captains that you were inattentive at your posts. Is flogging still the punishment for failed duty in your toothless generation?"

Caysus clenched his teeth. *This* was the exact reason Dulan Yazir was so thoroughly disliked among the ranks. Not only was there little doubt he would indeed inform their cohort officers of the transgressions, but he would *make sure* the punishments—otherwise rarely actually enforced—were carried out to their extent. Caysus was just about to tell the general where he could stick his smugness, content enough to go all in if he was going to be whipped anyway, when Habib saved the day.

Or tried to, at least.

"Caysus was merely informing me of a rumor, sir," the man said quickly. "Apparently the Silver Grasses purchased a number of new girls at auction this morning. We were discussing making our way there after watch's end this evening."

Brilliant, Caysus thought with relief, seeing the look on Yazir's face shift ever so slightly. The man was as much a lecherous lout as he was a good soldier. If he thought the Silver Grasses—one of the most well-respected brothels in the pleasure districts of the inner city—had fresh whores, it might just save them some of his displeasure...

Sadly, Habib's plan worked *too* well.

"Is that so?" The general's question was slow and contemplative, and something like a smirk played at his thin, mottled lips. "Well, I would certainly hate to deprive you both of your chance to take advantage of such good news. Still—" he leered in truth now "—it's really for the best if you let better men break in the merchandise beforehand. For your benefit, of course." He pulled a hand out from behind his back, holding up two fingers. "Evening watch," he said with a loathsome chuckle. "Tonight, and tomorrow. The both of you."

Habib began to splutter and protest, and Caysus felt his face flush in anger. Evening and night watches, after the gates had been shut and barred for the day, were traditionally left to new recruits and useless soldiers who couldn't be trusted with more sensitive or complicated assignments. Karesh Syl had treaties and trading routes with both the Mahsadën of the South and the rulers of the Seven Cities, the two closest concerning powers. *No one* gained from attacking them, not even Karesh Nan to the south, given the fortifications that made the metropolis more fortress-kingdom than city-state. As a result, evening watch was left to a bare unit of eight men. Compared to the two-dozen soldiers standing about the gate now, partnered off in twelve pairs at the ready for anything during one of the busiest times of daily traffic, standing sentry after dark was lonely, cold, and unfathomably boring.

And Yazir had just tasked them with two days of it.

"Next time," Caysus told Habib in an angry whisper after the general finally walked away. "Remind me to find out if he stands so upright after I fit my shield down his throat."

XXXIX

"They say the Twins' greatest source of entertainment is man's foolish preoccupation with 'plans'..."

—Jarden Arro, Champion of the Arro clan

The expectation had been for Akelo and the others to return before nightfall. Therefore, when the sun began to set without any sign of them, embellishing the now-distinct outline of the tapering towers of Karesh Syl against a fiery dusk, Raz began to worry. They'd kept to the road all day, in the end, moving at a slow, ambling pace that served to slip by the overseers of the slave-worked fields they kept passing without arousing suspicion.

As night fell in truth, though, Raz decided it was time to call a halt to their march. For one thing, the path was dimming before them, the black silhouette of the city drawing and disappearing into the darkness of the evening. For another, as the Sun descended, the drivers had started calling their charges to attention, tasking them with loading up the day's harvest into their wagons before driving the chained atherian onto the road. More than once Raz and Syrah had *both* been forced to shelter in the covered cage, sometimes braving a peek through the sailcloth as the Percian pressed the lizard-kind in a split around their group, hurrying them back toward the city as fast as their bound feet would allow. Again it had been hard, letting them pass without action. Even when he didn't look out to witness the dejected forms of his kind being driven eastward at the end of the whips, Raz could smell their presence all around him, a musky, distinct scent that no man could replicate.

On the fortunate side, the emptying of the farmlands left them with ample shelter to safely settle in for the night.

Raz led them off the road at the first chance they got, making for a plotting of fields he was sure were already empty. He thought—if nothing more drastic had already happened—that at the very least the *kuja* might notice the flattening of the grasses left by the cart trundling across the plain and onto the cleared earth, ignoring the squashes and unripe tomatoes they bumped over in passing. Without speaking, the men set about making camp as best they could, hiding the ox and cart from the road behind a wide shed in which all manner of hoes and axes and tilling tools were stacked or hung. After that, Aleem set about making the evening meal over a small cooking fire Syrah conjured up for him. Despite a hearty supper—seared steaks of salted antelope meat Akelo had downed and dressed the day before, along with roasted tubers and some sort of juicy, edible root Odene and Rufari had scrounged up that very morning—no one appeared much in the mood to talk. The emptiness could be felt by all, even the newcomers. Everyone ate in silence, glancing frequently at the bare spot at Raz's left where Akelo always took his meals, or over to the cart where the other Percian typically sat. Their absence was tangible, and the occasional attempts to start up conversation usually trailed off and died within a few minutes.

Eventually, thanking Aleem for their dinner, individuals and pairs began to break away, seeking choice spots about the field or in the surrounding grassland to sleep. After a while, Hur—the last to linger, nervously whetting the edge of his battle-axe by the still-flickering fire—gave in as well, nodding mutely to Raz and Syrah as he stood and moved off into the dark.

Neither of them spoke, even after they were left on their own around the flickering warmth of the cooking fire. Syrah leaned against him, her head—finally free of the oppressive hood and veil now that the Sun had set—resting against the bare scales of his shoulder, his arm around her as he stared into the flames. They might have spoken, perhaps, might have discussed in worried, low voices so as not to alarm the others, the concern they both felt that Akelo had not returned. Whatever they each thought, though—probably that it was premature to fret, or there was nothing to be done regardless, or they would address the problem in the morning—neither said a word, choosing to hold their tongue and appreciate the comfortable coolness of the Percian night. Here the air did not shudder and freeze as the Sun failed, countering the harsh heat of a desert day with frigid, icy air. Instead, the evenings were brisk, but pleasant, much like the more temperate border lands between the North and South. The temperature dropped enough for the warmth of the sorcery to feel good against their skin, but not so far as to bite into the body. Together, Raz and Syrah allowed themselves to appreciate the night, at least until the Priestess began to doze against him. When he noticed this, Raz laid her gently down on the ground beside the flames, folding his silk mantle under her head like a pillow, and told her he would take first watch. When she mumbled something unintelligible in return, he managed a smile, then turned away to walk out into the field.

The others had preferred, naturally, to find nooks and corners in and about the tool sheds, accepting what little cover the structures provided. As a result, Raz had the emptiness of the razed land to himself, and he took full advantage, stepping along and over the rows of vegetables until he stood in the very center of the field. Once there, Raz looked skyward, searching the night for a familiar sight.

The Arros sat a ways further north in the heavens than he'd been accustomed to initially, but Raz had adapted rapidly enough. It only took him a moment to find the stars among the dozens of constellations Garht Argoan had taught him, the trio twinkling and shining between the traces of clouds that strayed over the face of the sky. Briefly, he did nothing more than watch them, dipping back into pleasant memories.

Then, with the thought of Karesh Syl weighing on his mind, Raz began to pray.

Akelo and his *kuja* returned just as the first light of dawn broke over the east.

Raz had been relieved of his watch by Marsus Byrn an hour or so before midnight, but still he'd risen nearly an hour earlier than the others, as was his habit. He'd already put himself through his morning routine, and was busy strapping Ahna back onto Gale's saddle when he made out the sound of approaching hooves. Snatching up his gladius from where he'd dropped it in the grass at his feet, he drew the blade and moved quickly around the stallion, looking westward. Almost immediately he made out the indistinct blotches of shapes approaching along the road.

Before he had time to consider warning the others, Raz relaxed, making out the familiar faces of the five Percian, and raised his sword high to get their attention in the semi-darkness.

"You had us worried," he growled, half in annoyance, half in relief once the men, still bedecked in their soldier's uniforms, had guided their horses off the path and onto the clear earth of the field. "I was afraid something might have happened."

Akelo, although he had the worn look of a man who hadn't slept the night, smiled broadly as he and the others dismounted.

"We have news," he said quickly, pulling off his spiked half-helm and leading his gelding closer. "Good news. We may have found a way in."

Raz gaped at him.

Their reconnaissance plan had been simple. If things had gone accordingly, the *kuja* had approached Karesh Syl on horseback, wearing their stolen armor, and looped the wall in the formation of a patrol, gathering what information they could. Nudar, the Northerner who'd worked in the army barracks, said it wasn't common for a five-man patrol to be mounted, but not unheard of. Given the extent to which the Tash had already gone in his attempt to deduce where and when Raz would be arriving, as a group he, Syrah, and Akelo had decided no one was like to question the presence of five more soldiers, even ahorse.

Still, it hadn't been completely without risk, so for them to have been out all night like this…

"Odene." Raz called on one of the passing Percian. "Wake Syrah for me, if you would. Then you and the others grab some sleep while you can. We'll have to vacate this field soon, before the workers come back."

The man nodded at once, rejoining the other three as they led their horses back to the group to the relieved cheers of those who had stirred at their arrival.

Raz turned back to Akelo, anticipation getting the better of him. "We'll catch her up. Tell me everything."

The old man, it seemed, shared all-too-much in his excitement, because the words came in a rush.

"We did as you said, at first. We reached Karesh Syl before noon, I think, and spent most of the afternoon circling the wall a few times. The west and north gates are a little grander, and more secure. Probably has to do with receiving their allies in the South and Seven Cities, if I had to guess. Either way, when we arrived there wasn't much of a line to enter or leave anywhere, but we didn't think much of it at the time. We were busy counting how many men were at each entrance, and along the wall—Kalin memorized everything, I think. Just as we were about to leave, though, young Rufari noticed something. I have a feeling we'll be thanking the Sun he chose to join us before this journey is at an end."

"What did he see?" Raz pressed him eagerly, sheathing his gladius before tying it off over his shoulder.

In response, Akelo grinned. "There was a discrepancy during the changing of the guard, later in the day. Like I said, we didn't realize how few were coming and going at the time of our arrival, but as the afternoon went on there was a line a hundred men long to get into the city at any entrance, and as many trying to get out, it looked like. They close the gates, you see, when night falls. To compensate for the rush, the afternoon guard is *twice* what it was when we first arrived, at least two-dozen at the east and south gates, and more along the north and west."

Raz frowned, his spirit guttering a little. "This doesn't sound like good news..." he said tentatively.

Akelo's eyes were bright over the darkness of fatigue. "It is. When we noticed this, we wondered if the guard would change again after evening fell, when no one is coming and going *at all.*"

Raz saw where the conversation was headed, and his enthusiasm returned.

"And?" he demanded excitedly.

The answer almost made his scales stand on end, and he hadn't quite managed to smother his anticipation by the time Syrah joined them, rubbing the sleep from her good eye to hear the story all over again.

XL

Karesh Syl was a monument of human triumph over the relative emptiness of the Percian savannah. The wall itself rivaled the grand fortifications of Cyurgi 'Di, a perfect, gargantuan circle of smooth granite nearly a mile in diameter that towered fifty feet into the air, topped with pointed crenellations and patterned with staggered slits for archers and crossbowmen to sight through. Suspended bastions jutted from the ramparts every twenty yards, bulbous protuberances from which great, fluttering banners bearing the crossed pair of white-and-gold spears hung. At any given time Raz could just make out a half-dozen men patrolling every hundred yards of battlement, each bearing the emblazoned shield with the same adornment. He spent a while counting and calculating their patterns, trusting his eyes could see them more clearly than the indistinct forms against the grasses he and Akelo likely were to the soldiers at this distance.

And there, beyond the wall, stood the city itself.

Karesh Syl rose in concentric circles from the limits of its expanse, each ring higher and grander than the last. At its edges Raz could make out the plainest and least obtrusive buildings, revealing themselves in a staggered pattern over the wall, some high enough to peek above the crenellations, others apparently not. After several layers of these humbler structures, however, the city grew rapidly more resplendent, lumbering constructions of brick and wood and stone transitioning into more and more delicate towers of white marble accented—shining in lines and sheets in the light of the Sun—in bronze, silver, and gold trimmings. In the center of the metropolis, at the very peak of the city, Raz couldn't help but gape at the single wondrous structure that rose above all others, topping Karesh Syl like a crown.

It wasn't hard to guess what the building was.

The Tash's palace was an edifice of unparalleled grandeur. Like the city that surrounded it, it had been built in concentric rings, though these appeared symmetrical to a fault. The outermost layer was comprised of several angular buildings, while the first inner layer was made of crescent, bending shapes that folded inward over themselves like petals of a flower about to bloom. At the very center, soaring above the rest of the building, the city, and indeed the world itself, a pointed structure jutted toward the heavens, supported by spindly arches that seemed impossibly narrow to Raz.

For the first time, he allowed himself some grudging respect for the people of the city, as well as the miracles they had accomplished even on the backs of others.

"They say it's a tribute to the Twins."

Raz blinked and looked over his shoulder. Akelo was crouched just behind him, staring—like Raz—up at the crowning glory of Karesh Syl.

"The Tash's palace," the man said unnecessarily. "They say that, if seen from the sky, one would recognize the gods in its form. The two center rings—" he pointed to the top of the building, at the jutting point and the layer of petal-like extensions "—form the circle of the Moon. The outermost towers—" he pointed to the pattern of angular shapes along its edge "—are Her Stars. When taken all together, though, they form the body and waves of the Sun."

Raz couldn't help it. He turned and gawked once more at the splendor of the palace.

They were as close as they dared get to the city, crouched in the high grasses of the plains that surrounded the circular walls in all directions. The farmlands had given way to nature once more as they continued their approach of the metropolis, which Nudar explained was so that the Tash had the option of burning the grasslands if anyone was fool enough to lay siege to the gates. They'd led the caravan to the edge of what Raz felt was the observable distance from the walls, pulling the cart off the side of the road before putting their plan in motion. Syrah had taken to Nymara's saddle while Zehir, Kalin, and Rufari all claimed their own horses. Raz had lent Gale to Odene, telling the animal to behave for the man. He would be sad when it came time to turn their other mounts loose, but he'd be damned if he was going to leave the stallion behind after all they'd been through.

After the five of them departed, Raz had had Hur take his axe to the spokes of one of the cart wheels, rendering it useless but giving them all a good excuse to linger along the edge of the road.

Then, leaving Cyper in charge once more, he and Akelo had taken to the plains.

For an hour now, they'd waited impatiently, Raz taking advantage of his sharp eyes to alternately study the magnificence of the city and check on Syrah's progress in the line of the east gate. As Akelo had said, the morning rush was staggering, well over a hundred coming and going at any given time. It had been a gamble, with travelers passing the broken cart as they headed for the city, but the crowd would hopefully play in their favor. As he watched, Syrah—a veiled bride in white in the center of an escort of four mounted soldiers—neared the entrance.

For obvious reasons, Raz had initially rejected the plan Syrah and Akelo had presented him, even going so far as to open the problem up to the rest of the men for suggestions. When no one was able to come up with anything better, though, Raz had been forced to concede, making himself feel better by spending the morning brooding over the Priestess and the *kuja*-turned-soldiers who would be accompanying her.

Syrah had laughed and smiled through all of it, calling his concerns "endearing," which hadn't done much to improve his nerves.

And now, Raz was waiting, about as on edge as he had ever been in his life, knowing that if something went wrong there was absolutely nothing he, Akelo, or even the Sun above could do about it.

"She's getting nearer," he said over his shoulder. "Not long now."

Akelo, still crouched, moved up until he was right beside him. He stood ever so slightly, just enough to peer toward the gate, but frowned in annoyance.

"I'll take your word for it," he said with a shrug, dropping down again. "I can't even see Gale from here."

Raz nodded, but said nothing more. Syrah and the others had just pressed their horses forward again. They were no more than third or fourth in line for entry to the city.

Come on, Raz thought privately, absently clenching and unclenching his hands around Ahna's haft across his knees. *Come on...*

Eventually, they made it to the gate. From this distance even Raz couldn't make out more than general gestures, but his anxiety betrayed him rapidly. Did that guard seem too suspicious? Was there a reason the watchers on the wall seemed to have paused? Why were they still stopped? Wasn't it too long to be questioned?

Raz could quite literally feel the fabric of his restraint degrading, and he didn't like it. He wasn't used to this, wasn't used to the sensation of losing self-control so easily, so rapidly. He didn't have to ask himself *why* it was happening, of course. He knew *why* it was happening. It was the first time he and Syrah had been truly apart for some four months, now. Even before that, they hadn't spent much time away from one another over the course of the freeze, keeping each other frequent company in the Citadel library, practice chambers, and dining hall as the wind and storms raged outside. Abruptly, Raz become aware of a throbbing absence in his chest, like a little piece of his spirit was missing.

No. He didn't like this one bit.

And then, in a blink, Raz saw the sentries wave Syrah and the disguised *kuja* by. Before he could think to catch one last careful glimpse of her, the Priestess was gone, allowed through the eastern gate of Karesh Syl.

All at once, as she vanished from his sight, Raz wanted her back by his side more fervently than he had ever thought possible.

"She's in," he said in a rush, turning and hurrying around Akelo, bent double as he moved. "Time to get ready. It'll be our turn, soon."

Caysus' mood was already sour enough without drunks straining his threaded patience. As it turned out, the Silver Grasses *had* purchased a number of new slaves in the last week, so in addition to the ignominy of a second night of having to stand sentry with a bunch of sniveling new recruits and idiots who weren't smart enough to know which end to hold a sword by, he and Habib had been forced to suffer Dulan Yazir smugly taking his leave at the start of their watch. The gate general hadn't outright goaded them—he was far too straight-laced for that—but he'd given them a knowing smile as he'd passed, even winking at Caysus.

The subtle jab had irked the soldier to no end, so when the young couple came stumbling out of the alley into the lamp-lit streets, clearly having partaken too heavily in the spirits of some local inn or another, Caysus was anything but amused.

"Ugh…" Habib said in exasperation from beside him. "Just what we need to improve the mood of the evening, aye?"

Caysus grunted in annoyed agreement. At first he watched the pair approach with relative indifference, thinking they were likely to slip back into the shadows of the city once they realized they were tripping their way toward four soldiers of the Tash's army. When the man and woman kept on, though, he saw with displeasure that the former of the pair *was* a soldier, his broad shoulders straining an unkempt uniform, his sword at his side but his shield nowhere to be seen. Caysus may not have been a perfect example of an army man—his own drinking had been part of the reason he'd landed this shitty assignment in the first place, after all—but even *he* felt indignant as this man-at-arms kept on, weaving a slow path in the direction of the gate and laughing loudly with his white-cloaked companion. On the other side of the road, the two recruits he and Habib had been paired with were glancing between them and the approaching couple, clearly unsure of what to do.

Great, Caysus thought with an internal sigh, giving in to the pressure.

When the soldier and his woman stepped into the light of the braziers on either side of the gate, not ten yards up the cobbled road, he took a quick step forward, resting his free hand on the hilt of his sword and hefting his shield threateningly.

"Halt!" Caysus called. "By order of the Tash, all residents and slaves of the city are forbidden from leaving or entering Karesh Syl after dark. Turn around now, or you will be detained!"

His words seemed to shake the strangers out of their stupor a little. The man looked up somewhat blearily, dark Percian eyes taking in the four soldiers like he was surprised they were there. At his side, on the other hand, the woman kept her head bowed and turned into the soldier's chest, hiding her face from view.

"Jus—jus' looking to get out for a bit," the man hiccupped, taking another step forward. "C-c'mon, brothers. For a man a' the army!"

He slurred most of his words, waving toward the personnel door behind Habib. Caysus glanced back at it. It was a small, rectangular frame set into the much larger mass of the gate itself, used to allow through couriers and emissaries who arrived in the night, as well as to relieve the foursome of guards who stood watch, like Caysus, Habib, and the idiots opposite them, just outside.

Caysus snorted. "Not a chance, *brother*," he snapped, spilling as much sarcasm into the last word as he could and noting with a quick glance at the man's insignias that both he and Habib outranked him. "Turn around, now, or you'll find you and your friend in lockup while I send a runner for your cohort captain."

The threat should absolutely have shaken the man. Any man-at-arms knew well what that sort of trouble would mean for him, outside of even the immediate threat of corporal punishment. Drunk in uniform. If the broad-shouldered soldier was at all afraid of being court-martialed, though, he certainly didn't show it.

The blank stare the man gave Caysus, in fact, set him on edge.

Habib, too, seemed to sense that something was wrong, because he spoke up from his spot by the gate.

"You there!" he boomed, addressing the woman who still clung to the inebriated soldier, obviously well-into her cups herself. "Show yourself!"

The woman stirred, but did nothing more. She held onto the man, and appeared almost to be shaking, as though the coolness of the night were getting to her, which seemed odd given her attire.

"I said show yourself!" Habib ordered again, stepping up to stand beside Caysus.

Again, though, the woman appeared either not to hear him, or ignored him.

Habib growled at the disrespect, and looked about ready to march on the pair and drag them both to the nearest jail. Before he could move, however, there was a *whooshing* sound of something falling through the air, and half-an-instant later a large, formless shape plummeted from the night above their heads, landing with a muffled *thud* and *crunch* on the cobblestone exactly where Habib might have been if he'd charged forward. Before Caysus had a chance to register what the thing was, though, a second shape plunged from the sky, striking the cobblestone with another ugly sound.

Only then did Caysus realize what he was looking at.

Two men in the white-and-gold leathers of the army—the two sentries who had been posted atop the wall to keep watch over the gate from above—lay in broken, bloody piles at he and Habib's feet.

Had he not been so utterly shocked by the sight, Caysus might have had time to raise the alarm, might have had time to shout a warning that would at least have been heard by the guards further down the battlements. Instead, he could only stare at the bodies in stupefied disbelief for a full two seconds, just as Habib and the two recruits across the road did.

As a result, he only barely noticed the woman moving.

If he'd been quicker, if he'd been faster in his recovery, Caysus could still have saved the day. He would have seen the soldier's companion detach herself from the man, seen her raise one arm and give a quick tug at the air, like she were pulling something loose from a shelf. He would have seen her bring her other hand up before her, seen the strange glow of white that began to build around her pale, bare fingers.

Instead, though, all Caysus saw was darkness when the braziers on either side of the gate were snuffed out as if by magic, dying in a blink along with every other lamp and source of light in the vicinity. He managed one pitiful yelp as there was a single flash of brilliance in the sudden blackness, and a splitting streak of white-gold light.

Then something hot and jarring struck Caysus squarely in the chest, and the world was lost to him.

Syrah was afraid she was going to be sick.

She stood, several paces away from where Odene waited nervously in the center of the road in the dark behind her, inhaling heavily and looking up at the sky. She'd pulled her hood back, hoping in vain that the cool evening air would help fight off a little of the nausea and baseless fear that was racking her body. She did not hug herself, *refused* to lower to that senseless weakness. Instead, she held her hands by her sides, fingers clenched into tight fists, until eventually the feeling faded enough for her to breathe easy again.

"Syrah, are you sure you're all right?" Odene asked for the third time, sounding genuinely concerned.

For the third time, she nodded, though she didn't turn and look around at him yet. "Yes," she said shortly. "Just... Just give me a moment."

She was getting better. It was the silver lining in this momentary misery. She hadn't even thought about how easy it had been to be alone among her five Percian "soldiers" until they'd infiltrated the city, once again using the guise of the "Lady Ilyane." Even then, the discomfort had been more of a dull anxiety than any real panic, and when she and the *kuja* had found a moment to form a plan on how they were going to disarm the guards at the east gate, she hadn't had to work too hard to convince herself she could certainly cling to Odene like a good little drunkard. It had been the first time in nine months she'd willingly touched a man who wasn't Raz.

As it turned out, it hadn't been as easy as she'd hoped.

Still, she'd managed it, reining in the instinctive panic and keeping her cool. Kalin, Zehir, and Rufari had managed their part aptly—though they apparently hadn't thought much of her request to try to keep the soldiers on the wall alive if at all possible—and Odene's acting coupled with her rapidly conjured stunning spells had done the rest. Syrah managed to glance over, taking in the bare outlines of the six bodies scattered about the road and gate in the dark. She was glad she couldn't see the blood of the two corpses that had toppled down from the ramparts, but she didn't berate herself.

Four of the soldiers were breathing, and Raz had promised he would do his best to keep the men on the outside of the gate alive as well.

There was a quiet sound of approaching footsteps, and Syrah finally turned around. A set of timber stairs, outlined in the bare light of the city behind them, led up to the ramparts along the wall to the left of the east gate. Through the dark, a trio of familiar figures in white-and-gold leathers was descending toward them, watching the steps carefully. As they reached the road, Syrah raised a hand and conjured up a dim, pale glow, only hardly enough to see by.

The *kuja* stepped into the light as one, coming to stand beside Odene, their already-dirty uniforms now speckled with blood.

"By the Sun," Kalin said with a low whistle, eyeing the motionless forms of the Tash's soldiers as Zehir and Rufari did the same. "I guess they didn't know what hit them."

"No, they didn't," Syrah agreed, glancing toward the gate. "But neither will we if we tarry too long. Get them out of sight, somewhere they won't be found for a while. And—" she gave them all a warning, only semi-humorous glare "—if anyone so much as thinks of drawing their swords on these men, I'll light your boots on fire."

Each of the Percian managed a crooked smile at that, even Rufari, but did as she commanded. As they moved in pairs to heave the dead and unconscious soldiers up from the cobbled road, Syrah herself made for the stairs, dimming her light until it was just enough to make out the wooden slats beneath her feet.

Reaching the top of the wall, she gave herself a moment to appreciate the scene around her.

In the darkness of the night, the savannah of Perce stretched out like an empty abyss. It might have been part of the heavens themselves, a continuation of the infinite darkness overhead, except for the conspicuous absence of stars in its midst. Opposite this void, on the other hand, the city was aglow, evening bringing with it its own brilliance. Rather than the rising expanse of spectacular marble and granite structures shining gold and silver in the day, Karesh Syl now bloomed with orange light, so many dotted points of fires and torches and lamp-lit streets washing together that a corona of brightness rose from the darker shape of the city, a crown of light over the man-made wonder. The sight doused Syrah in conflicting emotions, at once drawing from her admiration and amazement just as it brought forth anger, disbelief, and disgust.

Maybe, just maybe, by the time they were done with their work here, this place would truly be as magnificent as the façade it presented to the world.

Turning, Syrah approached the pointed crenellations and looked down. Below her, the glow of a pair of torches flickered over the bare dirt of the trodden space that extended out before the outside of the east gate. Listening hard, she heard voices, though she couldn't make out the four men she knew stood guard on either side of the entrance. She'd been worried, as she and Odene had guiled their way into approaching the inner gate, that somehow the outer guard would be tipped off and raise their own alarm.

Whether because the heavy wood of the doors was too thick, though, or the men below simply didn't care much what minor scuffle their comrades may or may not have had to deal with within the city, it seemed her concerns had been baseless.

Giving a small sigh of relief, Syrah lifted the hand within which she contained her light-giving magic. With a thought, the spell pulsed a single time, just barely bright enough that Syrah had to squint out at the dark grasslands of Perce. Silently, she began to count, ticking off the seconds as best she could.

When she reached thirty, Syrah closed her fist with a snap, extinguishing the magic, as well as the two torches flanking the entrance below.

There was a confused yelp from several of the men, but no shout of alarm. Most likely, if anything, they thought the wind had gotten to the flames. Indeed, at first Syrah heard nothing but a few loud curses, and what might have been one of the soldiers snapping for someone to find some flint. There was a brief shuffling and more swearing by the Twins and Her Stars.

Then there was a *thwap*, and an *urk!* of breath being cut short, followed by a rapid series of *thunks* that Syrah recognized all too well.

The sounds of a staff, or the haft of some heavy weapon, going about its hefty work.

Syrah hurried back down the steps, keeping one hand on the wall to her left until she reached the road again. She didn't bother summoning her light a second time, allowing her already-sensitive eye to adjust to the distant illumination of the city. Most of the bodies had already been moved, the *kuja* currently hefting up the last two to carry them off into the alleys north of the gate. Ignoring them, Syrah made a line straight for the smaller personnel door, fumbling with the latch for a moment before figuring out the mechanism and throwing her shoulder into the iron-bound wood.

It opened onto true darkness, the world beyond the city consumed by the night. Indeed, Syrah shivered when she saw several forms looming out of the blackness at her, and she moved aside to let them pass.

Akelo grinned as he stepped through the door first, his own bleached leathers contrasting sharply against the night, his bow thrown back over his shoulder.

"Nice work," he said quietly while the others filed in behind him. "As smooth as we could have hoped."

"Almost," Syrah corrected, watching Hur's lumbering form duck under the overhang. "Two soldiers dead."

Akelo gave her a pained look. "Two of ten, Syrah. That's really not—"

"I know," she cut him off, not wanting to discuss the matter further as the last of the former slaves passed through the gate. "I'm sure it couldn't be helped."

Akelo nodded, then turned to join her in watching the dark outline of the door. There was a grunt, then the sound of something heavy dragging across the ground.

Then, like a demon of shadow, Raz loomed out of the gloom.

In one hand, Ahna and Syrah's staff were tossed over his shoulder almost knocking into the overhang when he bent over to fit through. In the other, he was hauling along the unconscious forms of two of the four guards he must have laid low, his clawed fingers twined into the collars of their armor. As he caught sight of her, Raz gave her a half-relieved, half-impressed smile, his white fangs gleaming in the dark.

Syrah returned it, feeling the thrill of success chase away the residual nausea that had been lingering in her gut. They had done it. Against all odds, they had breached the gate.

Raz i'Syul Arro, Monster of Karth, Dragon of the North, stood tall within the very walls of Karesh Syl.

XLI

"Of blood will be born the next of score-and-four,
yet twice will be the cost.
The only of his kind, he will fall for a face of snow,
and follow and be followed to dark depths and icy summits.
Son of the Sun he is.
Son of the Sun he will be named."

—the Grandmother

"HHAAAAAAAHHHGH!"

Karan woke with a start, pulled from a fretful sleep by the sound of Abir's frightening gasp. All around her there were groans and curses as most of the others awoke in the same moment, the humans muttering in varied languages while the atherian growled angrily in their native tongue.

Even as she rushed to push herself onto her hands and knees, Karan could sense all eyes already turning toward her.

Quickly she scrambled across the wooden floor, doing her best not to crawl over too many bodies in the faint light of the room's only small window. Everywhere there were voices snapping at her to shut the man up, and when she reached the old Percian she didn't hesitate to grab him by the shoulders and shake him, hissing pleadingly as she did.

"Abir! Wake up! Wake *up*!"

For once, the man came to at once.

Usually, when the dreams took him, Abir was difficult to free from their clutches. Sometimes he lay in a half-doze limp in her clawed hands, while other times he fought back, occasionally even catching her an inadvertent blow across the chest or face as he struggled.

This time, though, the man's eyes flew open, irises black and wide in the night, and he sat bolt upright. His voice rose in a low moan, but it wasn't the usual garbled nonsense Karan was accustomed to. Abir claimed to have been a seer, in another life, but his "predictions" had always struck her as nothing more than the ravings of an aging, fading mind. For as long as she'd known him his mutterings had been broken and incomprehensible, his shouts in the night irritating and senseless. He was well enough when awake, but when caught in the throes of dreams and nightmares the man was anything but coherent.

And yet now, though he stared at nothing in the relative darkness of the cramped room, his every word rang clear:

"Sand and snow, they come as one,
fire and ice made whole.
The Dragon's blade, the Witch's might,

each will play its role.

On wings of war, freedom soars,
though death will claim its fill.
Stand and fight, all you chained,
as iron falls to will."

To a one, every soul in the room was silent. Even Brahen—who'd been growing more and more irritated in recent weeks at being woken up in the middle of the night—didn't speak up. For her part, Karan could do little more than stare at the old Percian, her hands still clasped around his shoulders. She gaped even as Abir shuddered, blinking rapidly and seeming to come to.

Shaking his head, he looked around in clear confusion for a moment before meeting Karan's eyes.

"What...?" he started uncertainly. "Where...? What happened?

"Abir...?" Karan whispered, though her voice carried over the quiet of the quarters. "Those words...? What... What was that?"

The old man didn't say anything for a moment, obviously fighting to remember.

Then he shook his head.

"I... I don't know," he told her, looking down at his hands like they'd once held something important that was now slipping through them. "I can't recall. I remember... I remember the words, but—"

"What do they mean?" someone hissed from the darkness behind Karan.

"I don't know," Abir said miserably, clenching and unclenching his thin, wizened fingers. "I'm sorry, I don't know."

Karan had never bought into the man's masquerade of prescience. He'd always been kind to her, had taken her in when she'd been sold into the city's labor forces and protected her until she was old enough to mostly look after herself, but she'd always thought of his tales as little more than stories he used to keep himself and the slave children entertained.

Now, though... Now she wasn't so sure.

Karan felt as though some realization was just at the edge of her mind, some understanding for which she already had all the pieces.

The Dragon...

She didn't allow herself to dwell on *that* hope. The legends and whispers they'd been hearing more and more of about the city were nothing grander than that to veteran slaves like her: legends and whispers. Karan had long since learned to toss away empty dreams, long since learned that the pain of shattered hopes was far worse than any lashing. She'd come to terms, years ago, with her life and fate. The manacles around her feet were as much a part of her now as her own limbs, an absolute from which there was no escape.

The Dragon, she thought again, wistfully this time.

After a moment, Karan managed to quell her moment of weakness. Her temporary consideration that maybe, just maybe, there was more to Abir's words than the ravings of a worn soul passed into limbo.

"Go back to sleep, old man," she said kindly, easing him back down onto his small section of the floor. "Get some rest. Maybe it will make more sense in the morning."

She didn't believe a word of the suggestion, but Abir seemed to take comfort in the idea, nodding numbly as he accepted her assistance, huddling back up against the wall. When she was sure he was settled again, his dark eyes closing slowly, Karan shifted herself around and crawled back to her own little corner of the room.

Lying back down, her tail curling about herself as she balled her body as tightly as she could in an attempt to stave off the coolness of the summer night, Karan's mind couldn't help but wander back to the words Abir had recited, turning them over one after the other in an endless loop.

The Dragon, the name came again, and she could do nothing to stop her thoughts from drifting through the stories that had been spreading from slave to slave, fables of bloody victories and deposed tyrants.

Finally, as dreams pulled her off into a world where iron was as soft as butter and food was a plentiful thing, Karan faded away from the cruel teasings of her own mind. Had she not drifted off again so soon, though, she might have noticed that Abir slept more soundly than he'd ever managed for as long as she'd known him. Had she stayed awake, Karan might have wondered at the faint glow cutting through the little window as the clouds shifted outside.

Had she not closed her eyes, Karan might have seen the Moon, bright and promising in the night sky, bathing the gently breathing form of the old man in a shaft of pale, dancing light.

XLII

"Despite the perverse practices and acts of the cities, one cannot deny the fiscal and political titans the ancient seats of the Percian Tash once were. In their prime, Karesh Syl and Karesh Nan were nothing less than walled nations, colossal gears in the machine that was ancient trade and economy.

It is sad, in some ways, to look back and witness the abrupt dismantling of such tremendous power..."

—*The Fall of Ancient Perce*, author unknown

"Raz, you can't be serious."

"I don't like it either, but we're running out of options."

"But here? *Here?* We're going to get caught. I'm telling you, we're going to get *caught.*"

"Not if we don't stay long. A few nights, maybe. We just need to lie low until we can find a better alternative."

Even in the shadowed darkness of the alley, Raz could tell Syrah's face was twisted into a doubtful scowl. He couldn't really blame her, given their predicament, but they had little choice.

A gamble was all they had left.

Finding shelter before morning was far more difficult than Raz could have possibly anticipated. Once inside the city, he'd honestly expected it would be a relatively simple matter to find some semblance of the slums he was accustomed to, some derelict quarter with ample hovels and abandoned huts they would be able to lose themselves—and any potential pursuers—in. Such places had been an absolute reality of every other municipality Raz had ever had the misfortune of exploring. The fringe cities of the South were half-dead, the greatest portion of their residents surviving on the streets or in the abysmal squalor of the shantytowns that barely offered them refuge enough to stay out of the Sun's blaze. In the North, Azbar and Ystréd's conditions had been less deplorable, but he'd experienced the depths of the freeze for himself and understood all too well why hundreds died every winter in the valley towns, victims of hunger and the cruelties of the storms. Indeed, Raz had been so sure they would find refuge in the poor districts of Karesh Syl that he hadn't even bothered considering other options.

And so, when he realized with no small amount of disbelief that no such slums *existed*, Raz, Syrah, and their little army had found themselves at a horrible loss.

The streets of the outer ring—which were very obviously what passed for the "poor districts" of the city—were not as clean-cut and well cared for as the shining towers and obelisks that rose up toward the night sky as one approached the Tash's palace. The stone slabs beneath their feet were worn and cracking, and many of the oil lanterns hanging overhead from plain iron or timber posts were dim or unlit, so that the darkness was heavy over the cobbled road and the cumbersome buildings rising up in staggered measures on either side of the street. Still, no emaciated forms blinked at them from the shadows, no beggars sat bent and lonely on the corners, pleading for food and coin all while keeping an eye out for the guard that would beat them senseless if they were caught. They had roamed the city for nearly two hours, Raz and Syrah ducking into the nooks and side-streets on the rare occasions they crossed strangers in the night, and for the first half of that time Raz couldn't wrap his head around it, couldn't come to terms with the utter strangeness of his surroundings.

Eventually, though, he realized that a city like Karesh Syl had better uses for the likes of vagrants and vagabonds.

In the end, with every passing minute a moment closer to the stowed soldiers of the east gate being discovered, Raz had realized they would have to turn to the most absurd solution possible. They needed shelter, a place to lie low, even for just a day or two, until the commotion that would inevitably arrive with the rising Sun settled down a little.

And so it was—Raz, Syrah, Akelo, and Marsus Byrn tucked into one alley with Gale and Nymara while the rest of the men lingered in the streets or hid themselves in other nooks nearby—that they had ended up in front of the Red Shield Lodge.

The outer ring might not have been the traditional bastion of famine and misery Raz would have expected in a city the size of Karesh Syl, but in their time circling it—dodging the occasional patrols and giving the gates as wide a berth as they could—they passed any number of unsavory inns and taverns. The beggars might have been dragged off in chains, but thieves and louts and ruffians were an undeniable reality of every municipality of any respectable breadth, as were the largely distasteful institutions that served them their drinks and meals. The sort of unsavory establishments that wouldn't blink twice at a near-score of rough-looking men with hollow eyes and mismatched armor lumbering into their common room, much less the coin they brought with them.

Once he'd realized they had no other option, Raz made his choice quickly, backtracking them a quarter-hour until he found the building again. He'd picked the Red Shield out of the dozen others for several reasons, the least of which was that it seemed the cleanest and most respectable, and might therefore be lower on the list of places to inspect if the army chose to take things that far. More importantly, the premises were surprisingly large, encompassing three floors of what looked to have been two buildings joined by several rickety walkways into a single structure. Better still, even this late at night the open door to the common area was filled with light and laughter, the sounds of shouted entertainment, thudding chairs, and clinking tankards and plates loud and boisterous.

If they were ever going to lose themselves in the crowd, the Red Shield would be the place. Raz doubted anyone would so much as look twice at his motley crew of former slaves, much less the *kuja* still bedecked in soldiers' uniforms.

Fortunately, Syrah had managed to magically cleanse most of the bloodstains from the dyed leather armor.

Still ignoring the Priestess' sour expression, Raz turned to Akelo in the dark. "Five rooms," he told the old Percian. "Four men to a room. You and Cyper make sure to claim one with a street-facing window. When you've settled in, send someone out for the horses."

If Akelo had reservations about the plan, he didn't voice them. Nodding once, he told Marsus to gather the others, and together the pair stepped around Raz and Syrah back out into the street, the Southerner splitting off to assemble the men. Raz watched Akelo enter the tavern first, his broad form vanishing into the light and smoke and crowd. After him, the other Percian followed, then the rest in pairs and groups. Hur, Erom, and Marsus were the last to file into the Red Shield, the Southerner turning briefly to give the alley Raz and Syrah were still lingering in a confident nod.

For the next several minutes, the two of them waited tensely, she slinking back into the dark to stand with Nymara, her staff tucked into her crossed arms, he crouched as close to the mouth of the street as he dared, Ahna resting across both shoulders. He couldn't help his steel claws from drumming nervously at the dviassegai's white wood haft, nor keep his eyes from flicking up to the front-facing windows he could see. Syrah obviously sensed his doubts, and took the opportunity to try to make her point again.

"It's a bad idea..." she warned from behind him. "If any of them get caught..."

"They won't," Raz told her firmly, more to assure himself than out of any real conviction. "Akelo knows what's at stake."

"We're too exposed, Raz," Syrah insisted. "If the army searches the inns—"

"Then we'll think of something," Raz growled in irritation, turning to look over his shoulder at her and the horses. "What would you have me do, Syrah? What other options do we have? The Sun will be up in a few hours, and there's *no way* there won't be a changing of the watch before then."

Syrah was leaning against the wall of the alley, the staff still looped into her elbow. She glowered at him, but the look in her eye was one less of annoyance and more of frustration.

"I don't know," she admitted finally. "I don't. But this..." She glanced up at the façade of the Red Shield doubtfully. "I just don't know, Raz..."

Raz sighed, turning back to the tavern too. "It's a risk," he conceded. "And it's my fault. We should have prepared better. We should have sent someone into the city first, to see what they could find."

"It would have been too dangerous," Syrah said, her voice gentler now that he was giving her some credit. "It was already a gamble for Akelo and the *kuja* to scout the outer wall, much less pass through the gates."

Raz shrugged, eyes still shifting over the windows. "I shouldn't have assumed," he said gruffly. "I didn't even *think* to consider we would have trouble finding somewhere to hide. This city…" He grit his teeth. "It hides its cruelties so well. It feeds on itself, like Azbar did, but it's so much better at it. It's the epitome of the argument my cousin used to make, when I found out he was working for the Mahsadën…"

"Mychal?" Syrah asked tentatively.

Raz hesitated, then shook his head. "No. I think Mychal vanished into the flames with the rest of the Arros. 'Adrion' took his place a lot longer ago than I've been willing to admit."

He looked over his shoulder again, but this time his eyes lifted to the glowing outline of the Tash's palace, visible over the buildings at the opposite end of the side-street. "The filth he started to believe in… He would always tell me of the 'value' of the enslaved, how those who didn't work were nothing but a burden on modern society. He used to argue that a life of servitude was better than a life of nothingness. Ergoin Sass taught him that, I think. Even if it took a few years, Adrion subscribed wholly to this notion the Percian follow, of excising the ugliness of the world and replacing it with 'productivity.'"

"Crushing free will in the process," Syrah said with a grim nod. "Still, I understand the theory."

Raz's gaze dropped to her, anger boiling up so quickly inside him he started to stand and turn to face her. Before he could get so much as a word out, though, the Priestess cut him off.

"I said I *understand* it, Raz, not that I appreciate or condone it. It's despicable, a deplorable act. Even the concept is little more than an excuse fabricated by those in power to advance their own agendas at little to no cost to themselves. 'Productivity.'" She snorted in disgust. "Life is the greatest gift the Lifegiver has granted us. I may be straying from the traditional beliefs and respect we give that law, but I stand by the essential truth of it. I see now, the greater good. I understand that death might be a sacrifice so that others may live. But to deny a person the freedom to live as they choose, to take away their life and bind them until they are nothing but a building block in a place like this…" It was her turn to glance back at the grand outline of the palace. "You would never be able to convince me it serves any greater purpose than those laid out by cruel men for their own gain."

"But you understand it…?" Raz asked tentatively, his anger not completely quelled.

Syrah huffed irritably, though clearly more at the idea than at Raz himself. "I do. Talo taught to put one's self in other's shoes, Raz. The Lifetaker would never have become High Priest of Cyurgi 'Di had he not allowed himself to witness the world through the eyes of the Laorin. *I* would never have convinced Emreht Grahst to sign the treaties with the valley towns if I did not allow myself to learn and appreciate the needs of the mountain clans."

At that, Raz felt his fury spike again, his neck crest twitching up as his fingers spasmed to clench at Ahna's haft.

Again, though, Syrah continued before he could speak.

"Maybe those are bad examples," she said in a hurry, frowning. "Yes. I'm sorry. They are bad examples. I don't mean to say that I sympathize with this place, Raz. I don't. If I did, I think I would rot from the inside out until I was nothing but a worm-eaten corpse."

"Then what *do* you mean, Syrah?" Raz asked, unable to keep his voice from sounding dangerous.

"I mean that it's important to have a grasp of what it is we are facing. That it's essential to understand this fight we are throwing ourselves into. If we have that, if we know our enemy as well as they know themselves, then what advantage could they possibly hold over us?"

Raz was quiet at that, watching Syrah in the dark. Slowly he felt his wrath cool, felt the crest along his neck settle and still.

"'Know your enemy,'" he quoted, turning once more back to the Red Shield. His eyes, though, rose to the heavens, where the Moon and Her Stars glowed from between a shifting pattern of clouds. The Arros weren't in sight, the threesome of glimmering points hidden by the building and wall to the north of him, but all the same Raz managed to crack a smile, finding himself carried momentarily back to fond memories.

"My Uncle Jarden used to tell me that," he said aloud, though he didn't look down from the sky. "And other things, too. You remind me of him, in a way."

Syrah made a choking, laughing sound.

"I hope not in *too many* ways," she said teasingly, and Raz made out the sound of her boots as she approached. "My complexion doesn't favor a tan."

"Or dreaded hair," Raz chuckled, finally looking down at her as she came to stand by his side. "Or a clan-chain."

Syrah winced, one hand reaching up to rub her ear like it suddenly hurt.

"No," she agreed quickly. "No, I don't think so…"

Raz laughed again. "I mean," he continued, glancing one last time at the heavens, "that Jarden would have liked you. They *all* would have liked you, I think."

There was a silence, the two of them standing side by side in the dark. After a little while, Syrah stepped closer and wrapped one arm around his waist, holding him tight. She didn't say a word, but her touch drove away the dull ache of grief that had just started to well up in Raz's chest. Letting go of Ahna with one hand, he wrapped his own arm about her shoulders, and together they waited like that in silence, faces turned toward the sky, watching the Moon and Her Stars drift their way across the night.

That was how Odene found them a few minutes later, stepping out from the noisy bustle of the Red Shield's common room and looking both ways down the road before hurrying across to the alley. They broke apart as he reached them, but the *kuja* didn't so much as blink.

"We have the rooms," he said quietly. "Akelo paid for three nights. The owner has a few thugs hired, and says the locals know better than to steal from her. I should be able to hitch Gale and Nymara up outside the tavern without any trouble."

"Good," Syrah said, sounding a little relieved. "I don't know how much use we'll have for them in the city, but you can't be too careful."

Raz nodded in agreement. "Did Akelo find a street-facing room?" he asked the Percian.

In response, Odene turned and pointed upward. Following his finger, it didn't take more than a moment for Raz to make out Cyper leaning out of one of the third-story windows, looking up and down the street to make sure all was clear. Apparently seeing nothing concerning, the West Isler waved them up hurriedly.

"Syrah, leave your staff here," Raz told the Priestess quickly, leaning Ahna against the wall to his left as he eyed the façade of the tavern, studying the walls and windows and ledges. "I'll come back for them after."

"After what?" Syrah asked in confusion, frowning up at Cyper. "What is he doing, waving at us like—?"

And then it dawned on her, and she groaned.

"Can't exactly go through the front door, can we?" Raz asked her with a wink, bending down to loop an arm around her waist.

XLIII

"There are always those who would see you fail. No matter how many friends you think you have, no matter how many allies you believe you can count on. When you sit upon this throne, you do not have the luxury of showing anger, of showing fear. You may not indulge in the display of fondness or appreciation. Such things can be taken as weaknesses, as opportunity for exploitation, or as opportunity to strike..."

—Koran Esente, Tash of Karesh Syl, to his First Hand, Ekene

CRASH!

"HOW?" Naizer Ima bellowed in half-panic, ignoring the shattered remnants of the porcelain vase he had just smashed into the ground at his feet. *"HOW?* WHAT HAPPENED?"

"Naizer, calm down," Yseri Suro told the man sternly. "You are a Hand of the Tash, not a child. Control yourself!"

"CONTROL MYSELF?" the Second Hand demanded, like he couldn't believe what he was hearing. "CONTROL MYSELF? HOW CAN I BE EXPECTED TO CONTROL MYSELF WHEN WE'VE LOST TEN MEN, AND THE CITY HAS BEEN BREACHED?"

"We lost two," Azzeki Koro corrected evenly, though he looked to be having a hard time not smirking at the Second's tantrum. "The eight others were merely incapacitated."

"'*Merely incapacitated*,'" Naizer repeated in a mocking tone, glaring at the Third Hand. "How does that change the fact that—for the first time in over *three hundred years*—enemies of Karesh Syl have managed to get *inside our walls?*"

"It does not," Koro said with a smug nod. "Which is why it pains me to point out that all this might have been avoided had my advice been heeded sooner."

At that, Ekene felt his temper flare, and he narrowed his dark eyes at his Third.

"Mind your tone," he said dangerously. "Our response was not lacking. Thirty of my own slaves, thirty of our fastest horses, and a hundred and fifty soldiers set upon the east roads. I find it hard to believe any man, legend or not, could have escaped the attention of the patrols."

"I have my doubts he dodged them at all, great Tash," the Third Hand said with a gracious incline of his head. "I have reason to believe he cut right through them."

That sent a shiver across the room. Even Ekene, who prided himself on his calm demeanor, felt the thrum of a troubling knot form in his stomach.

They were in his personal quarters this morning, a series of some dozen chambers consisting of his own rooms, those of his numerous wives and courtesans, a privy, and his private library. White-and-gold silks hung over the wide arched windows in the south wall of the space, drifting lazily in the breeze of the new day. Blue and red tiles—matching the numerous vases, one of which Naizer had elected to smash in his fit—decorated the ceiling, floors, and the spiraled pillars that adjoined the two. The sprawling expanse of Ekene's covered bed took up much of the wall behind him, but the Tash had elected to sit in the center of the room on a cushion in a plain oak chair one of his slaves had procured for him.

He didn't for a moment miss the hard, cold stone of his throne in the courtroom far below.

Ekene and his three Hands were alone in the chambers. His wives and lovers had all scurried off at his command, followed quickly by the servants and soldiers, leaving the four of them to their business. The news of the assault on the east gate hadn't reached him more than twenty minutes after its discovery with the changing of the guard a few hours after midnight, and by the time the Hands had been summoned—Koro appearing in his rooms as he always did, as though by magic—the ten soldiers had been found dead and unconscious. Ekene hadn't spoken to any of them personally, of course, but Yseri had departed at once to do just that, returning with disturbing news just before the Sun's rise.

"We're sure it's him?" Naizer demanded for the fifth time, the squeak in his voice betraying him all too well. "We're absolutely sure?"

This time, even Azzeki Koro rolled his eyes, though it was the First who answered.

"We're sure, Naizer," Yseri said testily, reaching up to rub a temple with the thumb of one hand, like the questions were giving him a headache. "If you insist, I'm sure Koro won't have a problem summoning up our Southern friends again, just to confirm?"

The Second scowled at that, but didn't respond. Indeed, he'd kept much the same silence when the Mahsadën assassin, Na'zeem, had appeared at Koro's command, much like the Third himself did. The Southerner had been quick to confirm what Koro had already told them: based on the descriptions of the men Yseri had interrogated, at least four of the eight who'd survived had been felled by Northern magic. The woman, Syrah Brahnt, was in the city.

Which meant the Dragon couldn't be far behind...

"What are our options?" Ekene asked, cutting across the tension of the moment. "If it is safe to assume that Arro has breached our walls, where do we go from here?"

Though he asked the question to the room, it was Koro his eyes fell on.

The Third obliged at once. "All the usual protocols for such a situation should be followed," he said thoughtfully. "Additional patrols in the streets, and searches of anywhere the beast might have holed himself up in. Karesh Syl is unlike any city I believe he has ever known. He won't find the shelter here he is accustomed to, and what friends he has he will likely have brought with him. He does not know the terrain of the fight he is picking. Let us use that to our advantage."

"Agreed," Yseri said at once, nodding approvingly at the man. "Even if we do not find him outright, we will very likely disrupt his plans, if he has any."

"Exactly," Koro concurred. "Keep him on edge. Keep him on his toes. Arro is not a man to be underestimated, great Tash. He's proven that twice to you, now, and many times over to me, which is all the more reason to keep him from becoming established."

"Involve the slaves, as well," Yseri pressed. "We know Arro has a weakness for their kind. We can use them as a distraction, or as bait."

"Yes…" Koro said, sounding almost impressed as he raised a brow at the man. "Distress their community. Less food. Harsher punishments. Random beatings. It's easy enough to pass off as a response to the events at the east gates. We don't want them getting it in their heads that we are weak right now."

Ekene listened to all of this, nodding in slow agreement. When they were done, though, his eyes didn't leave the Third Hand.

"And you?" he asked evenly. "Where will you be in all of this? I was under the impression it was the fervent desire of our Southern guests to bring the Monster's head back to their new šef?"

"It is," Koro answered, "but until such time as we have a sense of where Arro might be, their strength poses little value in such a routing. With your permission, we will stay by your side, night and day. Should the beast be found, we will reassess. Until then, though, I would feel better having you under the eye of the only men the Monster might not see coming from a mile off."

"AAGH!"

There was a second *crash* of breaking porcelain, and another vase smashed into a hundred pieces across the tiled floor.

"Naizer!" Ekene thundered, tiring of the man's childish behavior. "ENOUGH! If you see fit to lay your hands on anything else in these chambers, I'll have you thrown in chains and let it be known to the entire city who you are! I'm sure the other slaves will appreciate your presence in their midst!"

The threat did its job. The Second blanched, hurriedly bowing in apology. "Your pardon, great Tash," he said weakly. "I am merely… uh… *distressed* that it has so rapidly come to this."

"As are we all," Yseri said impatiently. "And yet *you* are the only one I see smashing the Tash's possessions like a spoiled infant!"

Naizer nodded shakily. "With your permission, Your Greatness, I will excuse myself. Clearly I am not in an even state of mind, and I have much work to do if we are to pay our soldiers for the time they will be spending scouring the city streets soon."

"Go," Ekene snapped at once. Then he looked around at the other two. "All of you. Leave me. Handle this business. I want updates every hour. Moreover, I want that beast's head *on a stick*, and the bitch sorceress' along with it."

At once, all three of his Hands bowed, bidding him the formal farewells before taking their leave, Yseri and Naizer through the door of the chambers, Koro through the nearest window. For a long time after they were gone, Ekene sat alone, staring at the shards of the shattered jars, the morning's events pressing down on him. Steadily, despite every effort to control it, the Tash's heart began to thud in his chest, faster and faster until his hands began to shake. The knot in his stomach tightened, twisting about itself as his breathing grew uneven and shaky.

Then, all at once, Ekene shoved himself up from his chair, snatched a third vase from where it sat on a pedestal beside him, and hurled it across the room with a shrieking, furious scream as it smashed against the far wall.

XLIV

"It... It was like nothing I've ever seen. Nothing I've ever imagined... By the time I got to my window, most of them were already dead. I... I didn't even have time to understand what was going on before he killed the others, too... Sun have mercy on us all..."

—witness statement, taken by soldiers of Karesh Syl

Raz knew no later than the following morning that he had done well picking the Red Shield Lodge. The small rooms were cramped—four men in a space meant for one or two would naturally cause some discomfort—and the fact that he and Syrah were utterly confined to their quarters while Akelo and Cyper were able to at least descend to the common room didn't help much. On the other hand, though, the Sun had risen with the expected chaos of soldiers thundering up and down the road outside, shouting orders and demanding that any with information regarding the events at the east gate come forward, and no one had bothered their little group.

Yet.

It was only a matter of time. Raz knew that. Syrah had been right in her own way, too, though he still wasn't ready to admit it just yet. The Red Shield appeared far from the first place the army was looking for the perpetrators of the crimes, but with each hour they got closer and closer to being discovered. They would have to move, likely sooner than later, but Raz was still at a loss as to where they could go next. They had the gold—Akelo had barely used half of what had been left to them of the *Moalas'* treasure and the coin and valuables they'd looted from the patrols along the road east—but was it so easy as to simply change establishments? Maybe they could find out what inns and taverns had already been searched, and make for one of them?

Somehow, Raz doubted it would do the trick. Erom and Aleem had returned from fetching bread and meat from the horses' saddle pouches with the news that gossip was circulating among the common folk. Though the soldiers Raz had heard outside the window had never said a word of it, apparently rumors were abound that 'the Dragon' had come to Karesh Syl.

If the Tash knew he was within the city walls, Raz thought it likely he needed a better plan than lying low in the dingy parts of town, and he needed it fast.

As it turned out, though, his and Syrah's stay at the Red Shield ended up being—for better or for worse—far shorter than any of them expected.

They made it the length of the day without disruption, which both of them would look back on in amazement later. The Sun rose and fell, Raz, Syrah, Akelo, and Cyper discussing in increasingly desperate terms what they should do next, the others cycling in to voice their opinions. Even Hur made an appearance sometime in the afternoon, thick arms crossed over a massive chest as he scowled at a ludicrous idea suggested by Harnen, one of the

Northerners, that they charge the Tash's palace outright while they still had some element of surprise. By the time night began to fall they had chased their tails in circles more times than they could count, sending out the group in pairs to scout the city in every direction as far as they dared, though no one brought back good news. Not a single half-decent option for their next hideout had been found, and everyone reported there were more soldiers prowling the streets than they liked. Several men returned with stories of the patrols unnecessarily roughing up anyone who looked suspicious, and Zehir and Odene had actually been stopped by one such group of guards.

Fortunately, the *kuja* had abandoned their filthy soldiers' uniforms that morning, and their old mismatched gear had been enough to hide the scars that marked their wrists and ankles.

Far more trouble arrived, though, just after the Sun had set in truth.

As the darkness of the evening settled over the city, Raz braved opening the room window to peer outside. He told himself it was just to get some fresh air circulating through the space—a score of men who'd had little opportunity to bath in several weeks had passed through the quarters that day, after all—but the truth was that he just needed to see the sky, even for a minute or two. He *hated* being cooped up. After nearly three months spent between the open air of the sea and the flat vastness of the savannah, the room felt as much a cage to Raz as actual iron bars would have.

Syrah, Akelo, and Cyper hadn't given up their conversation, but Raz only half-listened to the West Isler insisting they should consider trying to find an entrance to the sewer system, a network of tunnels beneath the streets that carried water and waste out of the city to Sun-knew-where. It would have been a good plan, except that it was perhaps the fifth time they had rehashed it, with Akelo shooting the hope down with all the same arguments once again. They had no idea where the entrances were, if there existed any. They didn't know how big the tunnels might be, or where they led to. Syrah even put forth that the city likely had some sort of flooding mechanism, in order to clear out the sewage that had to build up on occasion. If they were caught down there, they were as likely to be drowned in human filth as they were to be felled by spear or sword.

Raz sighed, closing his eyes and thumping his head gently against the frame of the window several times, trying to think.

The only thing it served to do was make the ache behind his temples throb, and no new stroke of brilliance erupted into being in his thoughts.

Clink. Clink. Clink.

Raz froze, eyes snapping open to stare at nothing as he listened. Behind him, the sound of Syrah, Akelo, and Cyper's worried conversation faded, trailing away while he focused, listening to the approaching sound.

Clink. Clink. Clink.

Raz knew immediately what it was, the noise as distinct as the screech of a drawn blade. He could picture the group in his mind's eye for more than a whole minute before he saw them, could visualize their beaten, heavy forms and their shuffling, tired gait. He said nothing, gazing emptily at the sky, blind to the heavy clouds that cloaked the Moon and Her Stars from view. Before long he could make out more than the shifting of the chains. He could hear the heavy, exhausted breathing, and the scratching sound of dragging feet over the slabbed road. The rumble of heavy carts came next, and the clopping hooves of the oxen that pulled them along over the stone. Raz smelled the group before they came in view, wrinkling his snout in repugnance before he could stop himself.

When they made the corner in the road, shambling along like a dark mass through the night, Raz ducked away from the open window and flattened himself against the wall beside it, peering carefully out at an angle into the street.

He hadn't seen the atherian being driven out into the fields that morning. He supposed it was possible he'd missed their passing, his attention diverted by more pressing matters, but he doubted it. More likely, he thought, the harvest-laden carts had to be unloaded somewhere out of the way, and so the slaves were forced to take a different path home in the evening. Whatever the case, he didn't know how he felt now, in the moment, seeing the lizard-kind once again, and in such close proximity. They neared in a slow, lumbering mass, their bindings keeping them from taking even a full walking step. Occasionally one would trip, but they were always hauled up by their comrades around them with hisses of fear and quick glances toward the overseers at the back and sides of the group. The slave drivers paid them no attention, apparently content so long as everyone kept moving.

Then, however, a female at the very back of the group stumbled and lost her balance, tripping over her own chains. With no one behind her to help and the atherian on either side too slow to catch her, she fell flat across the stone. Raz felt his hands go cold as he heard her breath catch, then come in rapid, fearful gasps as she scrambled to stand once more, desperate not to draw attention to herself.

Too late.

Raz saw the two men shout and fall back, saw the whips rise and fall. His vision shifted and blurred as he heard the female scream, collapsing to the ground again as the overseers yelled in anger, lashing her mercilessly. Three, four, five, six... The leather tails of the cruel instruments buzzed through the air, cracking with each landing. The atherian shrieked in pain and terror, her tail curling around her body, her arms over her face.

Something warm fell on Raz's shoulder.

He started and blinked, realizing as he did that he was clenching the sill with one hand, gripping it so tight his steel claws were crushing the already-splintering wood. He looked around, breathing heavily, his heart slamming against his chest.

Syrah wasn't looking at him. She—like he'd been—was staring out the window, a look of tired, hard disgust printed across her face.

"Bastards," she spat quietly, her hand tense on his arm. "Lifegiver take them."

Akelo and Cyper had come to stand behind him as well. Raz hadn't heard the three of them end their conversation, but that was hardly surprising. As he turned his attention back to the scene outside, he felt his blood boil in his veins.

The drivers had ended their torment of the female, and were in the process of hauling her to her feet. When she stood, Raz saw that even bent and shaking she was nearly as tall as the two men, though her thin, emaciated frame did little to make her otherwise threatening. She was dark of skin, like him, but had a single patch of yellowish scales that painted something like a large arrowhead beneath her chin, down her throat, and past her collarbones. She looked dazed, even from afar, her breaths short and shaking, the trauma of the beating taking its toll on her even after it was done.

In that moment, Raz wanted nothing more in the world than to drop down to the street and deliver on the two men—now marching her along after the main group—every ounce of the combined pain and suffering they'd inflicted onto others in all their miserable lives.

A voice in his head, though, reminded him that the woman would have to endure, for the benefit of all.

"I'm getting tired of our 'greater good,' Syrah," Raz grumbled miserably, turning away from the window and pushing himself between Akelo and Cyper, heading for the bed where Ahna and Syrah's staff lay, intent on flopping down beside the weapons to sulk.

"You're not the only one," the Priestess sighed, still looking down into the street below. "Talo would tell us to keep to the path, though."

Raz snorted derisively. "Don't kid yourself. Talo would have been down there in the street, relieving those men of their teeth. He would have—"

"*Stop!*"

It wasn't the command that cut Raz short, ringing up from the street below. He'd heard soldiers shouting orders all day, snapping directions at the citizens of the city and pulling anyone they saw fit out of the crowd to question. Raz wouldn't have thought twice about it, in fact, were it not for the sound of Syrah's choked surprise and Akelo's hissed exclamation.

"Raz!"

He was back up in a flash, Cyper dodging smoothly out of the way as he surged back to the window, utterly forgetting to stay behind the cover of the wall. Following Syrah's eye, Raz made out the slave drivers and their trembling charge some dozen yards down the road, in the direction the rest of the slaves had been going.

Now, though, they had stopped, the two men still holding up the female atherian by each arm as they looked back up the road.

Almost directly below the room Raz, Syrah, Akelo, and Cyper were spectating from, a five-man patrol of soldiers had appeared out of one of the side-streets across the way. They moved in their typical formation toward the three figures, the leader at the head of the unit holding up a hand in indication of the halt. There was nothing unduly unusual about the group, the standard swords and shields of the army strapped to their hips and arms respectively, their spiked half-helms shining in the uneven light of the underfed oil-lamps that had been lit a half-hour before.

Despite this, however, Raz got a bad feeling watching the soldiers pass below.

"Problem, officer?" one of the overseers asked in confusion when the patrol came to a halt before him, his fellow, and the still-shaking atherian.

"I could ask you the same thing," the soldier at the head of the patrol responded. Even from the first floor of the Red Shield, Raz could tell he was eyeing the female. "The lizard giving you trouble, was she?"

The slave drivers glanced at each other. Whatever was going on, Raz could tell it made them uneasy.

"…Nothing we couldn't handle," the other man said, lifting his whip as though to make a point. "It's been taken care of."

"Has it?" the officer asked mockingly, his voice falsely-impressed. "My, you will have to teach us that trick. A lashing always keeps the difficult ones in check, does it?"

Again, the overseers shared a look.

"Not… always," the first answered hesitantly. "Not at first, anyway. They learn eventually."

The soldier nodded sanctimoniously. "Of course, of course." Then he turned his attention back to the atherian. "Leave her here."

There was a splutter of outrage.

"Leave her?" one of the drivers demanded, like he couldn't believe his ears. "What do you… We can't just *leave* her!"

"Oh?" the head of the patrol asked, still in his mocking tone. "I do believe you can, as that's the order I've just given you."

"They'll dock our pay," the other man grumbled indignantly. "If we lose one on our watch, the cost comes out of our pockets."

"Then you can tell your supervisors that the army commandeered your slave," the soldier said evenly. "A city laborer, isn't she?" He waited for one of the drivers to nod reluctantly. "Excellent. Then she is the property of the Tash, to be dealt with at his pleasure."

Raz heard the two overseers grumble at that, but he could tell they realized they were going to lose the argument.

"And if they want to know what you needed her for?" one asked, his voice resigned and heavy with annoyance. "What then?"

The soldier shrugged, motioning to the four others behind him. "Tell them there is more than one use for a slave that causes trouble for her masters."

After several more seconds' hesitation, it seemed the men understood they weren't being given a choice. Raz watched them disengage themselves from the female slowly, then step away to leave her shivering before the patrol. With some last rebellious grumbles, the overseers turned and walked away, one of them even glancing back when they were a dozen yards down the road.

Was that pity Raz saw in the Percian's eyes?

Then the men were gone, leaving the atherian to stand, head bowed and clearly terrified, alone with the soldiers.

"Look at me, scaly."

The leader's voice was a strange combination of stern and excited, and he took a step forward as he said the words, coming to stand directly in front of the female. At once she did as commanded, lifting her eyes to meet his, revealing the bright markings along her throat again. It was hard to tell, but Raz didn't think she could have been more than sixteen or seventeen summers old, judging by the bluish-orange webbing of her ears.

"Tell me what happened," the officer continued, sounding almost kindly, except for something cruel behind his words. "Why were you causing trouble for your masters?"

"I-I tripped, sir."

The female's voice jolted into Raz, rippling in a chill down his back and arms. She spoke the Common Tongue as easily as the soldiers did, like she'd been born to it. It was bizarre and amazing and terrifying to hear it, to come to terms with the fact that for the first time he was perceiving his language from an atherian that wasn't him. It was strange, too, hearing her speak, like experiencing an echo of his own voice, though softer and higher.

"You tripped?" the soldier said, sounding saddened by the news. At his side, his hand rose into a two-fingered gesture. "You chose to be difficult because you tripped?"

In a flash, the slave was surrounded. At their commander's signal, the other four had moved at once to encircle her, cutting her off from every direction.

Raz felt the anger start to build again.

"I-I didn't mean to be difficult, sir!" the female squeaked in fear, her head flicking this way and that to take in the men who flanked her from every side. "I wasn't trying to—!"

Wham.

The blow fell so fast, even Raz didn't see it coming. The officer's hand came up in a fist, catching the poor slave across her serpentine jaw. She staggered with a cry and would have fallen, except that the two soldiers at her back grabbed her under the arms and shoved her forward again. The man punched a second time, this time catching her squarely in the gut as she stumbled toward him.

Raz heard the breath erupt from her lungs.

"No…" Syrah whispered in terrified realization beside him, watching the slave fall to all fours at the officer's feet.

It was the man, though, that Raz heard more clearly.

"The Tash," the soldier said, half-squatting, like he wanted to ensure the atherian could hear him from her hands and knees on the road, "has no use for troublemakers among his servants."

Then he stood straight, and sunk his boot into the atherian's side.

"No!" Syrah said again, louder now and turning on the room. "Raz, they're going to kill her! Please! They're going to—!"

Raz, though, was already gone. By the time the others knew what had happened, Ahna was in his hands, and the Dragon was out the window, dropping thirty feet to the road below on spread wings, little more than a black-and-red shadow in the night wind.

XLV

"You can't truly understand it until you witness it for yourself... It's as though Laor, in some fit of madness, took all that is terrifying in the world and molded it together to form a single man. There is no stopping him, once he begins his dance. I have a hard time imagining that death itself would be brave enough to meet his challenge, should he ever decide to give it..."

—Alyssa Rhen, on seeing The Monster fight

Karan knew she was going to die.

It was a strange sensation to experience, curled up there on the cold stone of the empty street as the Tash's soldiers pressed in around her, their leather boots and fists pummeling her body from every angle. Despite all the hardships of her life, despite all the misery and fear the existence of a slave entailed, Karan had never truly feared she might be killed. Her kind were an expensive commodity. Her masters even sent for physicians and surgeons when one of their charges fell ill or injured, because paying the fees for exams and medicines was far cheaper than replacing a lost head. For this reason, Karan had never been afraid of death, even though there had been plenty of times when she'd wished for it.

Now, suddenly, she was acquainted with that terror.

It was the presence that had led her to this torment, she realized. It was that damned sensation that something more lingered nearby, that something she needed to know was within reach of her. It had passed over her mind as she and her field-mates had been returning home after a long day of labor. Once more the warmth had broken through the dim misery that was her life for a brief moment, bearing with it the feeling.

It had distracted her so much, Karan's feet got caught in her own chains, and the tumble that followed had very likely cost her her life.

The soldiers ringed her on all sides, beating her thin form bloody. She didn't know *why*, exactly, they seemed so intent on seeing her dead, especially so brutally, but even as the blows rained down on her Karan couldn't help but think that it was never a slave's place to question. She didn't even fight it, honestly, didn't do more than yelp and moan when fists caught her in the neck and head or boots took her in the back or sides. All she did was pray, reaching up to the Moon and Stars above and asking that one of the men might draw their blade and end it, that someone would make quick work of her misery. She fought to listen, waiting desperately for the sound of metal on leather that meant a sword was being pulled from its sheath.

What she heard instead almost made her jump out of her bruised skin.

"RRAAAAAAAAAAAWR!"

The roar seemed to shake even the heavy stone slabs of the road beneath her. It shattered the night, drowning out the huffs and grunts and laughs of the five men as they pummeled her. It ripped across her ears, so deafeningly loud it left her skull ringing—or maybe that was just from her head being slammed into the ground a few too many times?—and even through dimming consciousness Karan realized blearily that the blows had stopped. Her mind struggled to catch up to her senses, fought to link what she had heard with what seemed to be a sudden hesitancy in the soldiers.

Then, though, there was the sound of shearing flesh, a howl of agony from one of the men, and something wet and hot splattered Karan's arms and cheek. Even before she pulled her hands away from where she'd been trying to shield her face, she tasted the iron on the air. She blinked uncertainly, staring at the crimson sheen of the blood dripping from between her fingers. She didn't understand, *couldn't* understand. Her heart hammering in the cage of her bony chest, she looked shakily about, wondering what had happened to the men.

That was when she saw him.

At first, between the scrambling legs of the shouting soldiers, Karan couldn't make out much. A darkness, solid and shifting, shining like silver and steel. It moved with incredible speed, a massive flicker in the waning light of the lamps overhead. Like an avalanche of power it surged into the four men left standing, fearless and roaring in fury, clawed feet scraping against the stone as it whirled and danced among the soldiers.

Clawed feet? Karan thought in confusion.

Then, though, the legs before her shifted, and she saw the wings.

They extended like omens of a bloody battle, whipping out to slam men aside or buffeting them about their heads and helmets as they screamed in fear. A deep, sunset red, they were beacons in the night, shifting and undulating to glow in the light cast from above.

The atherian from whose back they extended, though, was even more awe-inspiring.

He was the biggest male she had ever seen. Though he never stood straight as he fought, Karan was sure even Brahen would have had to look up to this frightening figure of claws, muscle, and steel. Finely crafted armor encased his right arm, left leg, and both shins, and plate gauntlets covered both his forearms, tipping each finger in a wicked metal claw. In one hand he wielded a strange, narrow-headed axe, while in the other he hefted the most terrifying weapon Karan had ever laid eyes on. It was some sort of spear, the broad, double-bladed head of the thing looking like it weighed a hundred pounds on its own, but in the atherian's hands the weapon looked to be lighter than the air it shrieked through. Even as she watched, the thing moved in an arcing blur that transitioned flawlessly into a series of stabbing slices, engaging two men at once while the male used his axe to meet a third.

The other two, including the officer who had put her on the ground, were already lying in ragged heaps on either side of her, twitching and coughing up blood as they died.

Even if Karan had been able to believe outright what she was seeing, the next thirty seconds did nothing to manage her stunned astonishment. As she watched, the winged atherian cut down the other soldiers in quick succession, felling them with such graceful, brutal ease he might have been little more than a skilled butcher handling a few fine cuts of meat. The first dropped as he stepped out of the way too slowly. He crumbled to his knees, howling in pain and clutching at his abdomen and the massive diagonal gash that had been carved into it by the cruel, curved edges of the spear. The second—fortunately for him—died much faster, the axe looping and crushing his sword hand, than zipping back to crash through the steel of his helmet before the soldier even had time to scream. Finally, with no other distractions to bother with, the atherian turned his full attention on the last man standing, bringing both spear and sword to bear.

The soldier didn't last more than a few seconds, shrieking in fear and pain as the male's steel sliced his flesh to ribbons, then becoming suddenly silent as a clawed foot caught him in the side of the head in a spinning kick, breaking his neck with an audible *crack*.

When this fifth body fell to the ground, there were a few seconds of stillness, the quiet of the night returning to the world except for muffled shouts of confusion and alarm coming from the buildings around them.

Then the male's eyes turned on Karan.

Had she noticed them during the fight, she knew it was those eyes she would have found most fascinating. More than the male's size, more than his strange weapons and armor, more even than his damn *wings*, it was his eyes. She had seen danger in the gazes of her kind before. She had seen wild savagery in slaves who had had enough, as well as protective ferocity in the mothers of those poor babes born into a life of chains. She had seen insanity and madness, brought on by hunger and fear and grief and every combination in between.

But she had never, not once, witnessed even a measure of the cold, confident lethality that shone bright in the amber depths of this male's stare.

And it was that, more than anything, that convinced Karan of the truth.

"Dragon," she managed to say, pushing herself up to a side-sitting position, wincing and almost passing out as she did. "You're... You're Arro. You're the Dragon."

The atherian blinked at her, almost in surprise. He looked about to say something, his mouth cracking open, when a shout from over his shoulder drew his attention.

"Raz!"

The male—Raz i'Syul Arro—turned quickly, and Karan looked past him. A human woman had come rushing out of a building along the east side of the road, one of the city inns that housed the hundreds of sellswords and travelers that passed through Karesh Syl on any given day. This particular woman, though, looked nothing like any mercenary Karan had ever seen. She was tall and fit, her entire body covered in white robes of thin, breathable silk that extended in long sleeves down her arms, a heavy steel staff clutched in one hand as she ran. Her hands were covered in bleached leather gloves, and her dirty boots were made of the same material, giving her the look of a shifting apparition as she passed beneath the staggered brightness of the lamps. In the night, she was about as strange a sight as the winged Dragon.

"Syrah!" Arro snarled in what seemed almost to be protective anger. "What are you doing? If they catch us out here—!"

"If they catch *you* out here, it would be problematic enough!" the woman—Syrah, the atherian had called her—snapped back as she rushed right past him. To Karan's utter surprise, she took a hurried knee directly in front of her. As she did, Karan noticed even odder things than the stranger's attire and weapon. The skin of the woman's face was ghostly pale, and a single, rose-red eye shone with concern as it took in Karan's shivering form, the other hidden behind a wrap of frayed black cloth. Her hair was bone-white and scraggly, like it hadn't been washed in too many weeks, loose lengths of it falling across her cheeks.

An albino? Karan thought, so stunned she didn't even think to flinch away when the woman reached out with a gloved hand.

"Poor girl," the woman murmured, sounding heartbroken as her fingers settled against Karan's cheek. "Hold still. This won't take a moment."

Karan didn't think she could have moved far even if she hadn't been rooted to the spot, staring between this strange, white-haired figure and the towering form of the Dragon looming behind her, head flicking this way and that at every muffled shout from the buildings above. Before Karan could think to ask what was about to happen, there was a flash of white light that left her blinking, and she started in surprise.

Then, like water draining from a bowl, the pain and the thrumming of her head faded, her thoughts clearing at once.

"W-what was that?" Karan demanded, scrambling back and realizing as she did that much of the ache of the beating had fled her body. "What did you do?"

"Only a small thing," the woman answered, trying for a smile and holding up her hand as though she meant no harm. "The magics will do what they can, which will hopefully keep you from waking up tomorrow feeling like you were trampled by a horse."

"Magics?" Karan repeated, unsure she had heard correctly. "What do you...? *Magics?*"

The woman only held her smile. "My name is Syrah Brahnt, a Priestess of Laor, the Lifegiver. This is Raz." Still kneeling, she gestured back to the atherian behind her.

"I know who he is," Karan said quickly, taking in the massive male again. "I've heard the stories."

Behind Brahnt, Arro grunted in annoyance. "I'll bet you have," he grumbled, still keeping an eye out for trouble. "I've about had enough of these damn 'stories.'" Then he looked down at the woman between them. "Syrah, what about the others? Are they going to—?"

"I told Akelo to stay put," Brahnt said quickly, using her staff to push herself to her feet. "He had Cyper spread the word to the others."

"Good," the Dragon grunted, looking like he was thinking fast. "We have to get off this damn street, now."

As though to punctuate his words, there was a *slam* above, and all three of them glanced up to see shutters being shoved open and a pudgy, ugly face peek out of the open window. The fat Percian blinked for a second or two as he peered up and down the road, beady eyes adjusting to the dark.

Then he saw them.

"There!" he howled, leaning out to point with a thick finger as he hollered at the top of his lungs. "It's him! It's *him*! Guards! GUARDS!"

The Dragon moved in a blink, too quick for Karan to realize what he was doing before she felt the steel claws of his strong fingers grip her under the arm, hauling her quickly to her feet.

"Can you run?" he demanded, already dragging her toward the mouth of the nearest alley.

"N-no," Karan stammered, staggering and almost tripping again, much of the ache returning to her legs as they accepted her weight.

Apparently, the Priestess' magic could indeed only do so much.

"Raz!" Brahnt hissed, following them in a rush. "The chains! The *chains*!"

The Dragon looked down as he pulled them into the shadows of the side-street, taking in Karan's manacles with a curse. Obviously, he had forgotten about them.

"Can you weaken them?" he demanded of the woman, though he didn't stop, half-carrying Karan deeper between the buildings.

"Maybe," Brahnt answered, catching up to them. "But I need a moment!"

"We might not *have* a moment!"

"Raz, let her go! We'll move faster if we get rid of them!"

Get rid of them? Karan repeated to herself, still reeling at the surreal situation, unable to follow what they were saying. Even when the Dragon swore again, this time halting and resting her roughly against the nearest wall before bending down at her side, Karan struggled to comprehend.

It wasn't until Arro dropped his great spear—'Ahna', she remembered from the legends—onto the floor of the alley, then took the manacle and chains about her left ankle, that she understood.

From a distant place of disbelief, Karan heard the male tell Brahnt to hurry. Indeed, her keen ears were picking up the hammering of feet and shouted orders and questions in the distance, undoubtedly soldiers come running at the shouted alarms now echoing tenfold all around them. Despite this, the albino woman took a second as she, too, bent down beside the Dragon, muttering what sounded like a prayer under her breath.

Then she touched the metal between his massive hands.

Karan felt a brief sear of heat as the chains began to glow, but then Arro grunted with effort, and with a screech of bending steel the links separated from the cuff. They repeated the same thing on the other side, and suddenly Karan was free, the winged male retrieving Ahna from the ground before standing up and handing her the still-cooling chains that had bound her for as long as she could remember.

"Freedom is easy to give, girl," the Dragon said as she accepted the broken length of metal links in stunned comprehension. "It's harder to keep. Stay, or come with us. It's your choice now."

And with that, he was gone, hissing to the Priestess to follow him. Brahnt gave Karan a meaningful look and a nod of encouragement, then hurried to follow the Dragon deeper into the maze of alleys.

Karan stood staring down at the chains in her clawed hands. She gaped at the metal, limp and loose across her palms, like a dead thing that had only ever been given life by her misery. It weighed as much as the world, and yet nothing at the same time, and Karan saw the path she had never wanted but always known, etched in the nicks and rubbings of the steel.

Then, with a single skip of her heart, she threw the chains aside and followed the Dragon and Priestess into the depths of the night.

For perhaps the first time in her life, Karan ran unburdened.

XLVI

"Shield us from the darkness of the world, as we seek to chase it away with Your light. Protect us from the wickedness of man, as we strive to bring out the best that You have woven in him."

—basic Laorin prayer, taught to first-year acolytes

As they ran, Syrah sent a messenger spell back to the Red Shield, letting Akelo and the others know that she and Raz were alive and in one piece. She'd wanted to say more, wanted to tell the men that they would find a way to reconnect when time allowed, but even that simple magic was hard enough to gather as they half-sprinted through the dark, trusting in Raz alone to guide them.

She would have to believe the old *kuja* was smart enough to know to keep the band's heads down until they found a way to regroup.

More than once, Syrah found herself cursing her missing eye in the dark. It had taken months of exercise and hard work in the practice chambers of Cyurgi 'Di to get back even some sense of the depth perception she'd lost, and here in the faintest light of the overcast night sky her damaged vision was punishing her at every turn. She tripped over stacks of wood and baskets left out by workers and weavers during the day, and nearly slammed into walls as they took sharp corners. Ragged clothes left out to dry came ripping off their lines as she tangled herself between them, and once she almost dunked herself into a horse trough that seemed to have magically appeared across her path. Had it not been for the female atherian behind her, yelping a warning just in time, Syrah would likely have ended up face-first in the water, or knocked her teeth out on the edge of the stone basin.

It was after this near-miss—and almost five minutes of half-panicked, haphazard running through the back-ways and side-streets—that Syrah decided they'd well and truly lost themselves.

"Raz, that's far enough!" she whispered as loudly as she dared. "It won't do us any good losing the soldiers if we can't find our own way out!"

Raz, apparently, had been having the same thought, because as he slowed and jogged to a halt he frowned and looked around at the shadowy faces of the buildings rising up around them. Syrah did the same, squinting up into the night, but could make out little more than the ragged edge of the roofs above.

"Idiot." Raz was berating himself under his breath, turning in a circle as he tried to get his bearings. Apparently, even despite his better vision, he had no more of a clue where they had ended up than Syrah did. "Where are we?"

"Laor knows," Syrah snorted, looking over her shoulder. "We have a moment to find out, though. I don't think they followed us."

"These are… the miller's quarters," a small voice said between ragged breaths. "Just… Just north of the outer markets."

Together, Syrah and Raz turned to face the female atherian, who was resting with her back against the wall, trying hard to control her gasps for air. Now, as they paused in their flight from the gruesome scene of the butchered soldiers, Syrah finally had a chance to study the lizard-kind in detail.

She was a tall, thin youth, like a child who had grown up too fast on too little food. Her skin was mostly the same dark shade as Raz's, except for a single upside-down triangle of yellow scales that led from the line of her jaw down her throat, the point settling at her chest. Her eyes were a similar shade, like the midday sun, a little brighter and lighter than Raz's amber irises. They were the color of warmth and joy, except that at the moment the female's gaze was averted from either of them, looking down at the ground as she kept fighting to control her uneven breathing.

It was Syrah's turn to curse herself, and she hurried toward the girl at once.

"I'm sorry," she said quietly, reaching out with her free hand to rest her fingers against the atherian's shoulder. "You wouldn't be used to running, would you?"

The girl didn't respond, but as Syrah's spell poured into her, rejuvenating her tired limbs, her golden eyes widened in astonishment.

"Magic," she said again, standing straight and breathing easier, watching Syrah's hand as she pulled it away. "Is it…? By the Sun…"

Syrah would have laughed, but Raz cut her off.

"What's your name, girl?"

At his deep, double-tenor voice, the atherian started, her eyes jumping to him before dropping back down to the ground again.

"Karan," she said hesitantly. "Karan Brightneck."

That got a chuckle out of Raz, which seemed to help the female relax slightly.

"Head up, Karan," he told her with surprising gentility. "Never refuse to meet another's gaze again. You are not a slave anymore."

The words shivered over the female, and Syrah watched with something like amazement as Karan's chin lifted slowly.

"Not a… Not a slave…" she echoed the words. "I'm… free?"

"You are," Syrah answered the question, feeling a well of pride and sadness as the female looked to her. "You are no one's property, Karan. You are yours, and yours alone now."

"Mine…" Karan said, bringing her hands up to stare at them. "Mine… alone…"

"And we want to make sure you stay that way," Raz told her, firmly now. "But to do that, we need your help. How do you know where we are? Is there somewhere nearby we could hide, at least for the time being?"

"Raz…" Syrah warned him quietly. "Give her a moment…"

"We don't have a moment," Raz responded impatiently, not looking away from the female. "Karan, I swear I will do everything in my power to ensure you have all the time in the world to dwell, but right now I need your focus here, with us. Can you do that?"

There was a moment's pause.

Then the female nodded, though she didn't look up from her hands.

"Good," Raz said, peering about at the dark backs of the buildings on either side of the alley once more. "Then I ask again: how do you know where we are?"

To Syrah's impressed surprise, Karan answered at once.

"Flour," the girl said, blinking and finally tearing her eyes away from her scaled palms. "Wheat. I can smell them."

Raz sniffed at their surroundings, and Syrah saw his forked tongue flick out to taste the air.

"Aye," he grunted in agreement. "And sugar and bread."

"There are bakers a few roads over," Karan nodded, pointing south, through the wall to their left. "The markets are just beyond them."

"Is there somewhere we could find shelter?" Syrah asked, looking up and down the road. "Where do they store the grain?"

Karan looked suddenly uncomfortable. "N-Not near here," she said fearfully. "Soldiers every night, all night."

"Karesh Syl is a big city," Raz said with a thoughtful nod. "They'd have to protect their food from thieves carefully."

"Not thieves," Karan corrected with a glance at either end of the alley. "Slaves. It's the slaves they worry about. We have it best, the city laborers, almost as good as the palace workers. They feed us enough to keep our strength."

Syrah felt a chill, and a queasiness in her stomach. "And the others?" she asked, though she wasn't sure she wanted to know the answer.

Karan's ears flattened miserably. "Hungry…" she said softly. "Always hungry…"

Raz and Syrah kept their silence then, she out of sadness and he—she could tell—out of fury.

"Where else, then?" he growled finally, and Syrah hoped Karan would understand that the subliminal anger in his voice wasn't remotely directed at the female. "We can't be caught out here, come morning."

"That's assuming they don't find us earlier," Syrah said with a grimace.

Both of them looked at Karan expectantly.

"There… There is a place," she said, but the words quivered uncertainly. "Somewhere they won't look. Not yet."

"There is?" Raz demanded, suddenly interested. "Where? Is it close?"

Karan nodded. Then, looking like it was the last thing she wanted to do in the world, she lifted a hand and pointed west, up the way, deeper into the city.

"Very close," she answered. "But we will have to wait a little while more."

"Wait?" Syrah asked, confused. "Wait for what?"

Karan was positively shaking as she answered.

"For the masters to drive the others home."

XLVII

It seemed strange at first, when Syrah considered it, to keep a slave camp in the middle of the city. The compound was utterly out of place, a large enclosure of some dozen simple two-story buildings separated from the streets and structures around them by an eight-foot wall of granite and timber. Karan explained to her, though, as the two of them had waited on their own in the shadows of the alleys to the east, that she and the others of Karesh Syl's laborers were responsible for much more than tending to the farming lands when the need arose. Only the atherian worked the fields, that was true enough, but this was simply because they could toil for longer under the sun with much less water than their human counterparts. In the city itself, the slaves worked frequently as hands on the outer and inner walls, repairing and constructing fortifications under the guidance of masons and smiths who were only slightly less cruel than the overseers. They maintained the roads of the city—and there were many, *many* roads—tearing up and replacing old cobblestone when it became loose or worn. They cleaned the sewers and water channels, worked as mules for the Tash's merchants and hunters, and were even responsible for ridding the city of refuse once a month, carting out whatever the residents of Karesh Syl deemed worthless to bury in pits in some barren part of the savannah to the south. Having the slaves in the city— particularly here, right on the cusp of the inner ring—saved time and energy, allowing the Tash to get the most out of his slaves. Karan told her there had to be at least three or four score such compounds throughout Karesh Syl, ready to serve at the pleasure of the sovereign.

Syrah, though disgusted, couldn't help but be impressed once again by the infuriating efficiency of the whole thing.

The Tash had mastered all the cruelties of practicality.

"How many are there?" she had asked at one point, trying to do the math in her head as she gave a guess as to how many bodies could fit in any one of the buildings. "How many slaves?"

Karan had only shrugged, her reptilian face growing harder and more certain than Syrah had yet seen it.

"Too many to count," she'd answered simply, "but one less, tonight."

The conviction in her voice lit a warmth in Syrah's heart, and she'd had to hide a smile.

It wasn't more than five minutes later, the pair of them waiting silently in the dark and ducking away as five-man patrols marched past their hiding place, that a massive form dropped lithely down from the roofs to land in a crouch before them.

"It's as you said." Raz looked at Karan. "There's a small army at the enclosure entrance, maybe fifty men, but only a dozen or so within the walls themselves. If we can get inside, it shouldn't be too hard to sneak by."

The female nodded, but some of the confidence faded from her face. Syrah wanted to reach out, wanted to comfort her, but knew there was nothing she could do. The girl was being braver than anyone she had ever met as it was, running right back into the arms of the beast that had kept her chained her entire life. She gave Syrah a new appreciation of the men, of Akelo and Cyper and Aleem and all the rest, who had followed her and Raz once more into the mouth of cruelty just for the barest *chance* at purging Karesh Syl of its rotten affliction.

"Is there somewhere we can get over the wall?" she asked Raz. "A good point of access?"

Raz frowned. "I don't know about 'good', but the west corner is something of a blind-spot, I think. One of the buildings blocks it from sight of the entrance, and the Moon is in the east." He pointed up at the sky behind them, the faded glow shifting behind a blanket of clouds. "The light would be in our favor."

Syrah glanced at Karan, thinking to give the girl some encouragement, but the atherian was staring apprehensively at the compound across the way. She looked to be steeling herself, gathering her resolve again, and Syrah decided not to distract her.

Turning back to Raz, she took a breath.

"When you're ready."

A minute or so later, Raz gave them the all-clear, and together the three of them darted across the broad expanse of the street, a much wider and well-worn thoroughfare leading toward the center of the city than the looping road they had navigated the night before, around the inside of the inner wall. It took them several seconds to cross the open space, Raz trailing to make sure no one spotted them or tried to follow, and in that time Syrah felt her chest constrict with the fear that they might be caught. She recalled, for a brief moment as she and the two atherian slipped back into the cover of the buildings on the other side of the street, a time not so long ago when she'd constantly felt such helplessness, such utter defenselessness in the face of a greater enemy. It saddened her to consider—not for the first time—what it must have been like to live a life in which there had never been any other understanding.

Stealing a look over at Karan again, Syrah's admiration of the young atherian grew once more, taking in the determination in her gleaming yellow eyes.

They reached the east corner of the compound without incident, and Syrah stopped to glance around the bend while Raz continued to watch their backs. Seeing a clear, narrow road, she whispered the order to move, and as one they took the turn, hurrying into an even deeper darkness. They made it to the end of the way, and without hesitating Raz took a running leap, vaulting atop the wall in the shadows of the building that loomed over the corner. Dropping Ahna down behind him, he turned back and extended a hand to Karan, who jumped and took it, grunting as he heaved her up and over the granite capstones.

Before he could do the same for Syrah, she drew her spellwork into her hands and arms, leapt three feet into the air to snag the top of the wall, and powered herself over to land beside Karan on the thin grass inside the enclosure.

Turning to look up, she grinned at Raz's astounded expression.

"Don't treat me like some helpless damsel," she whispered with a teasing wink.

Apparently, he decided no reply was the best reply, because Raz did nothing more than scowl back as he dropped down, snatched Ahna from the ground, and slipped behind the cover of the nearest building.

Abir Fahaji had hoped, for the length of a pair of blissful days, that the dreams had finally abandoned him. He recalled still the words he'd spoken in the thralls of his gifts as Karan had shaken him from sleep two evenings prior, but they meant no more to him now than they had then. More importantly, though, they'd been the last vestiges of the nightmares he'd suffered since. Abir had prayed to the Twins, pleading with them to continue to keep the cursed voices silent. He'd fallen asleep hoping to doze in continued empty bliss, something he'd only ever rarely experienced since the visions had bloomed late in his youth.

Cruelly, though, the gods appeared to have other plans for him.

Perhaps it was the smarting lashes Abir had earned himself that day, when he'd dropped a pot of wet clay intended for the top of the inner wall where he'd been assigned for the morning. Or perhaps it was the groaning ache of his belly, disgruntled and sad and hungering after the dinner Brahen had stolen from him, snarling something about "hoping he'd starve so the rest could sleep in peace."

Most likely, though, Abir thought the dreams bloomed from the fear he'd felt as the soldiers had come about to lock them into the room for the night, the very moment he had realized Karan hadn't returned with the others from the fields that day...

The thralls of his slumber took him deep now, plunging him down and down and down into the accursed caverns of his own mind. The voices whispered in his ears as he fell, and even in his disappointment at finding himself once more within the chambers of his gifts Abir didn't bother trying to block them out. When he'd been younger he had tried, attempted everything. He'd burned incense and herbs—his old life had allowed him such luxuries, then—in an attempt to rest peacefully. He'd plugged his ears with wax and cotton, and once even hired a minstrel for an entire night to play soothing music as he slept. Nothing had ever worked, and eventually the aging man understood that it was a nightly battle best surrendered.

Images flashed before his mind, drowning him in other senses. A bloody sword accompanied by the smell of burning ash and the salty air of the sea. The porcelain mask of a pale, feminine face, smooth and beautiful until it cracked in twin diagonal patterns from around its right eye, falling away to reveal the leering, worm-riddled skull beneath. Two images mirrored at the edge of a lake, a wounded snake staring at the handsome grey-eyed hawk looking back at it, the water so still and clear Abir couldn't be sure which was the reflection. A mountain turned upside down on its horizon, the white snows capping its crown melting into blood to drip down and splatter in constellations across the heavens below. Finally, an old woman, her skin bronzed by the Sun and her hair as grey as her eyes, bending down to whisper something in his ear.

And there, lingering behind every premonition, a blaze of golden light, drawing ever nearer, splitting into twin points like eyes as the images flickering about Abir suddenly fell into violent shades of red and black.

As his consciousness began to shake, like the caverns of his thoughts were crumbling around him, the old man made out two words among the whisperings, growing louder and louder as the darkness descended in a wrathful cascade around him.

"HE COMES!"

Abir came to all at once, howling the premonition and hurling upright, ignoring the pain of the raw lashings along the frail skin of his back. All around him the other slaves awoke abruptly, most muttering in annoyance and resignation, though a few groaned angrily.

"*Hrar a'sy.*"

The words came as a low, threatening growl, and at once the room fell silent. Abir was not all that well-versed in the throaty language of the atherian, but Karan had taught him enough in their years together to understand at least what the simple phrase meant.

"*Enough of this,*" Brahen had said, and it was as Abir translated the sentence in his head that he made out the dim form of the male climbing slowly to his feet from his space on the floor, towering up like a titan in the dark.

Though he couldn't make out the details of the lizard-kind's face, the old man could envision them plainly even as the lumbering figure began to approach, chains dragging and clinking across the wooden floor, humans and atherian alike scrambling to get out of his way. He could see Brahen's cruel golden eyes staring at him with that cold, almost-hungry expression. He could imagine the white markings across the scales of the male's hands and forearms, like he'd dipped them into one of the buckets of blanching paint the slaves used to bleach new walls and old stone. Abir could even pretend to discern the dark red blade of the atherian's crest rising over his head, announcing to the world that blood was about to be spilled.

For once, Abir's fear and common sense won over the lingering compulsion of the visions.

"I'm sorry!" he moaned in panic, scrambling away from the approaching figure as quickly as his weathered limbs would take him. "I'm sorry! I didn't mean to wake you!"

"You never *mean* to wake us, old man," Brahen growled in the Common Tongue, following Abir. As he passed by the faint light of the window, Abir briefly made out the atherian's broad, muscled chest. "And yet you do. You always do."

There were curses and angry yelps as Abir turned over and outright crawled on his hands and knees over any and all who got in his way, desperate to escape. Before he could get far, though, there was a quick shuffling of steps and shifting iron, and clawed fingers grabbed him by the grizzled hair along the back of his balding head, hauling him up. Abir started to howl in pain and surprise, but Brahen's other hand clamped about his mouth, cutting off the cry.

"You bring the masters down on us, old man, and I'll pluck your eyes from your skull and leave you to die blind and alone," Brahen growled in his face. The lizard-kind's breath smelled like rotten meat. "Stop fighting, and I'll end this fast."

Abir, of course, did nothing of the sort. In panic, his aged body fought harder for life than he'd have thought possible, his thin hands pummeling at the thick muscle that knotted the atherian's arms, his bare, callused feet kicking at legs and stomach. He managed to catch the male a decent blow to the gut, making him grunt and wince, but the act only resulted in Brahen's hands tightening in his hair and across his face. Abir felt his scalp stretch and tear, and the claws piercing the skin of his cheeks.

"You want to do this the hard way?" the male snarled furiously, lifting him right off the ground so that his neck popped and strained. "Fine! Then I'll—!"

The sounds of footsteps, light and hurried on the stairs outside, were audible even to Abir in his state.

Instantly Brahen let go of him, and the man would probably have broken something if he hadn't landed on some poor unfortunate's tail. The female, whoever she was, squealed in pain, then again as Brahen himself dropped to lie on the floor, half-crushing her beneath him. The atherian hissed at her to shut up in their native tongue, and Abir couldn't actually blame him. If any of them were caught by the Tash's soldiers up and about after the door was locked, they would *all* be whipped bloody.

If that happened, the whole room would probably turn on him.

Collectively, the slaves waited in frightened silence, every eye on the door, every ear strained for shouts of warning or displeasure from outside. Instead, though, they heard the footsteps reach the landing, then a brief rattle as someone tried the latch, like they didn't know it was locked. There was a muttering of voices Abir didn't think even the atherian would have been able to make out, then an altogether different sound, a sort of sizzling, like lingering lightning, or the doused flames of a fire.

Then, with a strange flash of white light that made everyone jump in surprise, there was a *clunk* of the lock sliding free, and the door creaked open.

Three figures, hunched and black against the barest glow of the night outside, slid into the room, one after the other. The first of them, a thin, tall outline Abir could have sworn he recognized, turned as the last entered, closing the door behind them.

"Should I lock it again?" a stranger's voice, a human woman's, asked in the renewed dark.

"Do it," the deeper, throatier growl of a male atherian responded. "If they catch us, you might as well blast it down. No sense in subtlety, at that point."

There was a pause, then a second flash as the latch *thunked* back into place. A few yelped at the sudden blinding brightness, but Abir couldn't have closed his eyes if he wanted to. He'd seen the three figures, if only for a moment, and did indeed know one of them all too well.

"Karan?" he demanded in a low hiss through the quiet. "Karan? Is that you?"

"Abir." Karan's voice sounded relieved. "Yes, it is. Everybody stay quiet."

"And shut your eyes," the strange male grunted. "Syrah, a little light, if you please."

And then, before anyone could get over their surprise or voice their confusion, the room was suddenly illuminated, the entire chamber revealed in a warm, ethereal glow.

XLVIII

"There are those, later in our lives, who would find reason to criticize our actions of those few days. They would call us brash, irresponsible, even arrogant. They would demand to know why we did not take pause, why we did not seek out another solution.
I tell all of such a mind to come back with me, into my memories, and tell me if their logic still holds true once they understand with their own eyes the horrors we witnessed that night…"

—Syrah Brahnt, Executor of Laor

Had she not already been crouched low to the floor, the scene before her would have brought Syrah to her knees.

Revealed by the pale glow of the three faint orbs of light she'd summoned over their heads, somewhere around half-a-hundred huddled forms were blinking in her, Karan, and Raz's direction from their places laid out or sitting up one against the other, packed like rats into a space that might have fit a quarter that many comfortably. The sight dropped a stone from her throat to her stomach, and her breath caught as she cast about the room, looking into every face. There was no consistency in age or gender or race. Slaves who looked to be no more than ten or eleven years old lay beside those who had clearly seen too many summers already. Girls and boys mixed with men and women, each having carved out their little spot on the floor. Humans and atherian alike were gaping at them with pained confusion, the former with hollow, lifeless eyes, the latter's sadness hidden behind the reflective gleam that shone back at them in dozens of twin points in the light of the magic. Together they formed a blanket of living beings, huddled together partially for warmth, partially because there was no space to spare. Along the opposite wall, a single bucket took up a valuable corner of the room, and the smell wafting from it spelled out its purpose all-too-well.

Discretion and privacy were strange concepts in this place, luxuries best never pined for.

"It's all right," Karan was saying, holding up her hands as several expressions shifted into terrified panic, no one understanding who they were, or what they were doing there. "They're friends. We just needed a place to lie low."

"'We'?" a throaty voice repeated from the back of the room. "What do you mean 'we', Brightneck?"

Along the rear wall, near a single small window that would ordinarily have been the only source of the space's light and fresh air, a figure shoved himself up from where he'd been huddled among several other forms. Syrah blinked as he stood, having to shake the striking impression that, for a moment, a reflection of Raz himself was getting to his feet across from them. The longer she looked, though, the more distinct the differences became.

Aside from the obvious lack of wings, the male was a little broader than Raz, his shoulders looking like they might have been three full feet across, but he was several inches shorter. In addition, his eyes were a harder shade of gold than either Raz or Karan's, like roughly-cut gems gleaming in his serpentine face. The scales of his clawed hands and thick forearms were white-washed, like he was wearing skintight gloves the color of bone, and the membranes of his ears and the crest that flickered over his head were burgundy, giving Syrah the impression that he was older, perhaps five or six years Raz's senior.

Aside from that, there was a distinct, harsh aura about the atherian that set Syrah immediately on edge.

"I-I'm not a slave anymore, Brahen," Karan was responding, though her voice faltered with doubt. "My chains... My chains are gone."

As one, all eyes in the room dropped to Karan's feet, and there was a rumbling moan of disbelief from the huddled bodies as the empty manacles were noticed for the first time.

At the back of the room, the face of the broad atherian—Brahen—twisted in rage.

"What have you done?" he demanded wrathfully, starting toward them, shoving and kicking a path through the cowering forms that didn't get out of his way in time. "What is this? If the masters find out you've slipped your irons—!"

"They're not my irons anymore!" Karan squealed, but she apparently couldn't help but take a step back, almost bumping into the wall behind her as the lumbering male approached. "They're not my masters anymore!"

"Fool!" Brahen snarled, the white claws of his hands flexing with every step he took closer. "First Abir keeps us from what little sleep we get, now *you* risk all our hides with your selfishness. I've had enough. I'll kill you both myself and be done with all of—!"

"Try it, friend," a deadly growl interrupted him, "and there might be just enough of you left to toss in the shit-bucket."

A massive form slipped between Brahen and Karan, then, blocking the older atherian's way when he was ten feet from the female. The collective inhalation from the slaves that followed, each of them taking in the terror that was Raz i'Syul Arro, cast a thrilling chill up Syrah's back.

She had always known Raz was big. At over seven feet tall, the man towered above most anyone he faced off against, the only notable exception she had ever known being Gûlraht Baoill, who'd been a giant in his own right. In her mind's eye, though, Syrah had never considered how Raz might measure up compared to others of his kind. If she contemplated it, she thought she might have always just assumed that the atherian were a generally large species regardless, having never come across another before their arrival within sight of Karesh Syl. Karan had reinforced this presumption, standing several inches higher than Syrah, who was already considered a tall woman among her kind.

Looking around now, though, Syrah saw that she'd only been half-right.

The atherian, apparently, were indeed a larger breed than their human counterparts. Karan, it turned out, looked to be of about average height, maybe even a little shorter given her age, and Syrah thought the other males—judging by those who'd sat up to follow what was going on—might have stood around six and a half feet tall had they been on their feet. Brahen, it seemed, was already a specimen of notable size, and the way the others scrambled out of the way or watched him apprehensively as he'd crossed the room said that he was all-too aware of this.

Which partially explained, Syrah thought, the look of utter shock printed across his serpentine features now.

Raz, indeed, was not as broad as Brahen, but he stood at *least* three or four inches taller. In addition, the Dragon cut a much more impressive figure than the other male, his armor shining in the glow of Syrah's magic, Ahna's blades gleaming wickedly from where he had her slung in her typical resting spot over his shoulder. He appeared utterly relaxed, but Syrah made out the cold warning in his eye, the subtle stillness of his amber gaze that spoke of a man who didn't make threats lightly.

Brahen, though, along with every other slave in the room, wasn't looking at Raz's face.

Instead, to a one, they were staring at his wings, extended loosely six feet on either side of him, casting the walls and ceiling about them in wavering shadows in the light of the orbs.

"Dragon."

The word started as a whisper, slipping across the room as it was passed from person to person. Even Brahen mouthed it, Syrah saw, taking a step back from Raz and nearly tripping over a human boy who couldn't have been older than twelve. A few of the older atherian, in addition, were murmuring another word, one she couldn't quite make out. Several of these figures started getting to their feet, reaching out toward Raz hesitantly with confused expressions on their faces.

And then, in a slow, uncertain wave, every head turned *away* from them, looking to the back of the room.

At first, Syrah couldn't figure out what had drawn their attention away, or what they were all waiting for. Then, just as she thought to ask Karan what was going on, a second figure pulled himself shakily to his feet, rising out of the same corner Brahen had stood from. An old man, his dark, wrinkled skin marking him as one of the many Percian crowding the room. A broken ring of greying hair crowned his mottled head, and his eyes, as dark and deep as any of his kind, were staring at Raz like they'd never seen anything so amazing in the world.

"Abir," Karan said as loudly as she dared from beside Syrah. "Abir... I think I found the meaning in the words."

Syrah blinked, looking between the young female and the old Percian. The man—Abir—took a stumbling step forward, still fixated on Raz, mouth hanging open.

"I... I don't believe it," he muttered to himself. "He's come... You've come..."

"Karan," Syrah said sharply, grabbing the female's attention. "What is this? What words?"

Before the atherian could answer, though, Abir began to speak:

"Sand and snow, they come as one,
fire and ice made whole.
The Dragon's blade, the Witch's might,
each will play its role.

On wings of war, freedom soars,
though death will claim its fill.
Stand and fight, all you chained,
as iron falls to will."

Once more, silence held sway over the room. Everyone, even Brahen, turned to face the old man, who'd continued his approach, humans and atherian scooting sideways to give him a free path.

Amazingly, it was Raz who broke the stillness.

"A seer," he hissed, almost reverently. "You're a seer."

In response, Abir's brown eyes filled with tears, and he smiled as he took his last few steps forward, reaching out. Syrah thought for sure Raz would pull away from the man, or swat his hand aside, but to her disbelief he did no such thing. Instead, he allowed the old slave to approach and reach up, touching the scales of his face gently.

"From sand then snow then sea, the dragon comes..." Abir said with a choking laugh, like he was quoting some old poem. Then his face stilled, and he looked suddenly stricken, as if abruptly remembering something harrowing. "The eldest of your family is gone, boy. I have seen it in my dreams. She wishes you to know you were the very last of her thoughts."

Raz stiffened at the words, exhaling in a sharp, broken sound of grief.

"Raz?" Syrah demanded anxiously. "Raz, what's wrong?"

It took a moment for the atherian to answer her, and even then he seemed unable to look away from the old man.

"My... My Grandmother," he said quietly, his voice shaking. "My Grandmother has joined the Arros among Her Stars."

Sadness welled up inside Syrah. There was a moment in which she processed the news, recalling all he'd ever told her of the old woman he'd left to the care of his cousin in Miropa, one of the few links remaining to his old life. Before she could stop herself, she took two steps forward, wrapping the arm not holding her staff around his waist.

329

"Raz... I'm so sorry," she said into the silk cloth of his white mantle, pressing her face against him. "I'm so sorry."

The atherian gave another rasping gasp, but didn't shake her off. His body shook, and then his legs gave out, dragging him and Syrah both to the ground as Ahna rested limply against him. Abir came with them, too, his face stricken, his hand withdrawn to clutch at himself like he was suddenly overcome by some terrible cold.

"Arro?" Karan's small voice rose uneasily from behind them. "What do you mean? What do you mean, Abir is a... a 'seer'?"

It took a long time for Raz to answer her, and Syrah could feel him trying to control the sorrowful quivering. After nearly a minute, he started to stand again, and she let him go, remaining on the ground with Abir as she fought to master her own heartbreak.

"Abir has been gifted with sight," Raz said, his voice flat as he half-turned to meet Karan's eyes. "He's been touched by the Twins. The Grandmother of my clan was the same. She read her signs in the old way, in the scattering of bones and stones, but she was the same." His attention fell slowly back on Abir, and his next words seemed almost meant for no one but himself. "I sometimes wonder, in fact, how she didn't see the end coming...?"

Syrah watched the old Percian across from her on the floor, now pulling at the worn rags that hung from his narrow shoulders, shaking like a man who'd come to understand his purpose for the first time in his life.

"But what does it *mean*?" Karan insisted, and others around her murmured the same demand, wanting to know more. "The words, what do they *mean*?"

"It means he can't win this fight by himself."

Syrah couldn't fathom why she said it, what possessed her to answer for him. All she knew was that—looking up to take in Raz's winged outline standing above her—the truth of the weight he carried had settled upon her all at once. At least fifty slaves lay in this room, chained and bound and forced to sleep one pressed against the other. There were like to be another fifty in the chamber below, she knew, which meant over a thousand in the compound they now stood in. If some four score such places existed around the city...

"Your Moon isn't prophesizing some grand victory," Syrah told the room coldly. "It's not telling you to be patient and wait for freedom to fall into your lap. The telling isn't even *meant* for Raz." She looked around at the startled faces of the slaves around her. "It's meant for *you*. It's meant as a warning, and as a call."

Blinking, she looked back up at Raz, who was watching her with sad fondness as she spoke.

"'*Stand and fight, all you chained, as iron falls to will,*'" she finished quietly. "The words mean that some wars cannot be fought alone."

There was a heavy pause as the men and women and children looked on with wide eyes. A few appeared more terrified than ever, hands twitching and some even clutching at their chains as though they were the only solid thing left to hold on to. More, though, seemed to be gazing at her differently, a change coming over them as her message struck true.

Then there was a derisive snort.

The spell broke, and Syrah turned to glare at Brahen, who was still standing no more than a few feet away, thick arms crossed over his broad chest and looking disgusted.

"A 'seer'," he quoted distastefully, eyeing Abir, who was still on his knees on the floor. "What a load of shit. 'Stand and fight,' *ha*! You would have us all die at the Tash's hand, on nothing more than the word of an old man I should have killed a long time ago." He turned to glare at Syrah, uncrossing his arms to point a pale finger at her. "And *you*. I don't know what you are, but it's clear you pray to different gods than ours. Magic." His lip curled at the floating balls of orbs. "There is a reason such a thing doesn't exist in the lands of the Sun. It's blasphemy. It's witchcr—!"

WHAM!

In all the battles they had fought, in all the times she had seen Raz in his violent element, Syrah didn't think she had *ever* seen him move so fast. Perhaps it was a trick of the light, or maybe just the small confines of the room around them that gave the illusion of speed, but whereas in one instant Brahen was standing, glowering around at them as he spewed his poison, in the next he hit the ground with a massive *crunch* that shook the floor, Raz half-kneeling beside him, his free hand around the male's throat. The older atherian, to his credit, roared in anger and defiance, slashing at Raz's restraining arm with his white claws but gaining no traction on the steel plating of Allihmad Jerr's masterfully crafted armor. Before anyone could stop him, Raz spun Ahna in his other hand and raised her above his head, twin points down.

Syrah's voice was only one of many to yell as the dviassegai plunged earthward.

CRACK!

Ahna slammed into the wood of the floor, splitting the planks on either side of Brahen's thick neck with a marksman's precision. Her scarred blades shoved through until the male was pinned to the ground, still howling and cursing, his hands scrabbling at the weapon's haft as he tried to pull her free. In the room below, Syrah heard muffled shouts of fear and alarm as the slaves beneath them likely saw the dviassegai's steel tips punch through the roof of their quarters.

Keeping one hand tight about the lowest of Ahna's leather grips to keep Brahen from tearing her free, Raz reached up and slowly drew his gladius from over his shoulder. The momentary relief Syrah had felt upon realizing the male *hadn't* been impaled or decapitated began to fade, then vanished altogether when Raz shoved the edge of the sword blade under the struggling atherian's chin.

Only then, at last, did Brahen stop fighting, his breath coming in a hiss as the razored steel pressed against the scales of the highest part of his throat.

"Right now, Brahen, you are filth."

Raz's words whispered out, as sharp as the gladius in his hand. Behind him, the frightened squeals and groans of disbelief were snuffed out like a candle in a soft, dangerous breeze.

"You think I don't see what you've done here?" Raz snarled quietly down at the man, meeting his wide golden eyes. "You think I don't know how you've gotten to be so strong, when those around you wither away? You use that strength as a weapon against your own kind, wield it as fiercely as the whips in the hands of the Tash's men to take from them everything you want, knowing not one of them can do anything about it."

Raz leaned in until their fangs were only inches from each other. "What would happen, though, if everyone in this room rose up at once? What would happen if I told them all to stand, to fight, to end the suffering, the theft of their food and water, the fear they feel in the night? On their own, sure, there's nothing they could do." A growl built in Raz's throat. "But all together?"

For the first time, Syrah thought she saw something like fear flicker across Brahen's face.

"Yes," she heard Raz snarl, discerning the same thing. "Yes. You see it now, don't you? Or did you always see it, and just worked that much harder to control them for fear they'd see it too?" He pressed the blade up a little, causing Brahen to grunt as his head was forced to tilt back. "You're strong, Brahen. Obviously. Chances are you're fast, too, and I don't get the impression you're a fool. Even with a life ruled by iron and nothingness, the Sun has seen to give you so much. You could have fought to protect these people. You could have stood by them, for them. Instead of fear and hate, you could have built trust and respect."

Raz snarled. "But you didn't. Instead, you beat them, you brought terror into the *one place* they might have been free from it. You wore them down, used them like stones to whet the blade you then threatened them with. So… Shall we ask *them* what should be done with you?"

Brahen's eyes widened even further, but he couldn't open his mouth to respond without risking cutting himself on the blade. Raz, for his part, looked up and around, taking in the room.

"Well?" he demanded, perhaps louder than was advisable given the ruckus they'd already caused and the rumbling of confusion still rising from the quarters below. "What of it?"

Syrah looked around, scared of what she might behold. She expected to see anger and hate on the faces of the slaves, to see hunger and vengeance painted across the tired hollows of their eyes. She thought even that voices would start ringing up before long, calling for Brahen's end.

What she found instead, though, surprised her as much as anything else she'd witnessed that evening.

To a one, every head was turned toward Raz and the pinned male, but there was no anger lingering in their gazes, no hate or grumblings of "off with his head!". On the contrary, most of the slaves' expressions were fearful, even concerned, and to a one they sat and knelt stock-still, like they were afraid a wrong move might take Raz by surprise, and the blade would slip.

"Arro... Please. Let him go."

Karan's voice didn't shake when she spoke this time. Instead, it was even, if worried, and when she turned to look at the female Syrah saw that her clawed hands were up and her yellow eyes were on Brahen, like he were a hostage Raz had taken without cause.

"Please," she said again, a hint of pleading in her voice this time. "Please. Let him go. You don't understand. You don't—you *can't* understand. There is nothing in this life but the next day, nothing but surviving to see the Sun come up again. Brahen is a brute, but wouldn't you be too, if that's what it took to survive?"

Raz said nothing, watching her silently, like he expected her to go on.

"Please," Karan insisted again, taking a step forward this time. "There is no value in killing him. If he didn't exist, chances are another just like him would. This life is nothing more than a fight for the next moment, a battle for the next meal, or the next night of sleep. Brahen is merely one example of the few ways those with little else to live for can get by."

Behind Syrah, she heard others echo her words. Even Abir, she saw as she turned to face to room, was nodding slowly, though he still hadn't looked up from the floor. Indeed, some of the slaves were getting to their feet, standing—whether uncertainly or with chins held high—to stare Raz down.

Abruptly, Syrah saw the game he had just won, heard it in his voice as the Dragon chuckled darkly.

Then, to everyone's surprise except hers, he got to his feet and wrenched Ahna free of the planks with a grinding *crunch*.

"Get up," Raz snapped down at Brahen. At once, the atherian scrambled to his feet, rubbing his throat and eyeing the dviassegai slung once more over Raz's shoulder and the gladius hanging loosely in his other hand.

"You beat them, and you starved them," Raz growled, not looking away from Brahen. "You made them fear for their lives in the only place they might not have had to. And yet—" he half-turned and swung the sword, making the male flinch until he realized the blade was indicating the cluster of humans and atherian alike who had stood in his defense "—still they understand. Still they wouldn't want you hurt."

He gave those words a moment to sink in, seeing Brahen's golden eyes sweep over the group, a little of the cruelty lingering there sinking away to be replaced by something altogether different.

"They would stand by you, despite knowing that you would never have done the same for them," Raz pressed, turning back to the man. "They would see you live, despite knowing what it would mean for them, perhaps for the rest of their lives."

With a flick, Raz tossed the gladius up. It spun twice in the air, then stopped as he caught it in a reverse grip.

When he presented it to Brahen, hilt first, there was a hiss of shock from the rest of the room.

"Right now, Brahen, you are filth," Raz repeated to the male, who stared at the blade with something between amazement and terror. "Personally, I think you'll try to run me through with this the minute I hand it over. They, though—" he jerked his head over his shoulder to indicate the slaves "—apparently think better of you than that."

He shook the gladius, indicating that Brahen should take it.

"So, what's it going to be?" the Dragon asked evenly. "Are you going to strike? Are you going to prove me right? Or are you going to use that strength of yours to show me you're worth a little of their appreciation?" His fangs gleamed in the light of the shimmering magic. "You feared them, when they might have risen together against you. Consider that, and the position you all stand in now."

For a long time, Brahen continued to stare at the blade. Nothing moved but the shadows as he took it in, gazing at the intricate grip like he couldn't decide if accepting it would mean his salvation, or his doom.

And then, as Karan and many others gasped around her, Syrah watched the male reach out, grasping the sword's leather hilt in a clawed, white hand.

In the sheltering shadows of the alley, Syrah stood with Karan once more, watching the camp burn. Abir shivered in a huddled ball behind them, which did nothing to relieve the ache that threatened to swallow much of her heart. For several minutes Syrah couldn't bring herself to look down at the entrance of the enclosure, couldn't bring herself to acknowledge the horror of the scene that extended across and beyond most of the road, up to and past the small gate in the south side of the wall. She gave herself the time she needed, allowed herself to seek the Lifegiver in the twisted shapes of the flames and the rising body of the smoke that blotted out what little light the moon had been able to provide.

When she was finished with her prayers, Syrah took a breath, steeled herself, and turned her eye earthward once more.

Hundreds of forms moved across the cobbled road, bent and lingering to crowd the aftermath of the battle as they pillaged what they could from the dead, or wailed out in grief while mourning over the bodies of the lost. Beyond them, the gate's single broad door, built into the south wall of the compound, was dented and bloody, swung wide to reveal the inferno-like hell that was all the blazing remains of the slave camp. Around it, in the grass of the compound and spilling into the street, the bodies shimmered, partially hidden by the living, but still and black in the shadows of the firelight. Syrah didn't try to count them, didn't even give it a thought. The battle had been quick and brutal, she and Raz leading the charge to challenge the soldiers manning the gate with the two-score slaves that took up with them, the other ten spilling out at their rear to break down the doors to the other buildings. At first the guards had put up a good fight, Raz's strength and Syrah's magic the only true weapon their little army had against their swords and shields. A dozen slaves or more died screaming within the first minutes of the fight, the Tash's men shouting alarms and howling for reinforcements. Some ten patrols who'd been nearby answered the call, bolstering the troops with fifty additional men and sending runners to the palace for more.

By then, though, the hundreds of others had been freed, and no armor or blade in the world could save the soldiers from the sheer mass of howling bodies that thundered over them as swiftly as an avalanche, the humans fighting with pilfered swords and anything else they could get their hands on, the atherian with chipped and broken claws.

After maybe five minutes, the slaves had won their freedom, paying for it in blood and pain and life, and before long the camp began to burn, fires lit with flint and tinder stolen from the pockets of the dead. Keys had been recovered as well, and even as she watched Syrah witnessed them being passed among the group.

The pain in her chest sharpened as she saw one shaking, sobbing boy even use them to unclasp the manacles from the still, prone form of a woman who looked just old enough to be his mother.

"This was the easiest part."

Over the crackling roar of the flames, the voice boomed out, making each and every figure in the crowd start and look around. Even Syrah and Karan had to gasp as Raz made himself known, appearing suddenly from the curling smoke atop the wall over the gate, his winged silhouette painted ten feet above the crowd against the shimmering firelight, Ahna hanging from his right hand while her blades dripped black.

Before long, even the cries of the grieving faded away as all turned to listen.

"Casting off your chains is only the first step in the journey ahead of each of you," Raz kept on, his head turning to sweep over the masses that swelled about the street before him. "You have not gained your freedom yet. Even now, the Tash's soldiers will be gathering." He raised his free hand to point toward the towering form of the palace in the center of the city. "Even now, the men who think to own you are learning that you are no longer bound in their irons. This—" he cast the hand back at the fires behind him "—is only the first of the battles that must be won. This is only the beginning."

He jerked his arm back then, hammering a clawed fist against his broad chest.

"You know who I am," he thundered. "Call me what you wish—call me Dragon, or Scourge, or Monster. It does not matter. You know what I have come to do, as you know I will not stop until I see that goal fulfilled. The

Tash will fall, and Karesh Syl will either crumble with him, or learn to stand on something *other* than the broken backs of the enslaved." He glared around at them, hefting Ahna onto his shoulder before crouching on the wall, like he wanted to whisper a secret to the group. "You are only the smallest part of the uprising you must become. You are only the seed, and so you are the hope. Consider that, as I say this: what is your choice? Will you stay and cower? Will you allow the army to come and throw you back in chains?" He raised a hand and clenched his steel claws into a hard fist. "Or will you seize this chance, this hope, and fight for the freedom of will and life *all* men deserve?"

The response was instantaneous. Like the building howl of a winter storm, the voices of the thousand or so that clustered up and down the street at Raz's feet rose in rapid unison. In seconds the sound was so deafening, Syrah saw Karan cover her ears, though the atherian screamed along just as loudly as any other.

Pride and courage slipped back in, then, replacing some of the grief that had been weighing at Syrah's heart as she'd witnessed death claim its fill that night.

As the cheer died, individual voices could be heard over the fire.

"To the camps!" one tall man was shouting, thrusting a stolen sword eastward, deeper into the quarter. "To the camps!"

"Free the others!" a female atherian with a slashing wound across her face howled, and there was a swell of thunderous approval.

"The Dragon fights for us!" several people screamed. "The Dragon fights for us!"

And then, with that booming chant catching to echo against the night sky, the crowd surged eastward as one, looking to gather its strength and grant others the same deliverance they had been given on this night.

When the last of them had thundered past, Syrah, Karan, and Abir were left alone except for Raz's dark form, still lingering on the wall. With the sudden absence of the living, the gruesomeness of the scene revealed itself in truth, and Syrah couldn't help but sob in helpless gasps as she gazed out over the street, the corpses of the dead already stiffening in the coolness of the evening air. There were the soldiers, of course, their white leathers slashed and torn and bloody, scattered in clumps here and there where they had been overrun. Far outnumbering them, though, were the other forms, haggard corpses of half-starved men and women and atherian, as well as smaller bodies Syrah just couldn't bring herself to look at. Instead, as she took in a racking breath she watched Raz drop off the wall, landing among the carnage to pick his way toward a place in the center of the battlefield. When he reached it, he bent down, hesitating over a large, still form.

When he stood up again, he brought his gladius with him, ever so gently prying its handle free from the heavy, pale-scaled fingers still grasped around its handle.

When he stepped around the body to approach their little alley through the butchery, Syrah saw that Raz's strong, righteous demeanor had been replaced with that of a man who bore all the weight of the world on his shoulders. It broke her the slightest bit, and as he reached the shadows they were hiding in, she stepped forward to meet him, wrapping an arm around his muscled frame for the second time in less than an hour, holding him tight.

Raz accepted the embrace with a relieved sigh, sheathing his gladius over his shoulder so that he could hold her in return.

When they finally broke apart, he gave her a silent look, conveying his gratitude before speaking.

"Take the old man, and fetch Akelo and the others," he told her quietly, nodding to Abir over her shoulder. "Karan likely knows the way. I don't know where you'll find me, but we need to regroup. It won't be long before the Tash gathers the army to retaliate, and we can't let that happen. Even if we managed to free every slave in the city…"

"Thousands would die in that battle," Syrah said sadly, studying his face with concern. "Yes, I know."

Raz nodded, taking a breath. "If we're to end this before it comes to that, we need to strike, and we need to strike fast. Tell Akelo I'll hear any plan. Tell him to push Aleem and the other recruits for *anything* they can tell us about the palace, no matter how trivial they think it might be."

Syrah gave him a half-hearted smile. "It would be stupid of me to tell you to keep your head down, wouldn't it?"

Raz found it in himself to return the grim grin. "It would, yes. They need to *see* the Dragon. All of them."

Syrah watched him a moment more, taking him in. Then she reached up, cupping his cheek, ignoring the stickiness of the blood that clung to his scales.

Lifting a hand to grasp her fingers briefly in his, Raz closed his eyes, breathing her in.

Then he was gone.

Sighing again, Syrah turned to the alley, moving to take Abir by the arm. The old man jumped at her touch, looking around at her.

"Is it… Is it real?" he asked her in a pleading tone. "Are we free?"

Syrah gave him a sad, warm look. "Soon, I hope," she told the shivering Percian. "Soon."

Then her eye moved to Karan.

"Do you know the way back?" she asked.

The female nodded at once, and before long they were hurrying yet again through the winding bends of the back roads, slower this time, allowing Syrah to watch where she was going, which she appreciated.

It kept her from dwelling on the fact that the war they had come to wage had arrived all too soon, and all too swiftly.

IL

"The great poet Arcel Larent of Acrosia is most celebrated for an oeuvre he composed at the deathbed of his greatest love. Even as she passed, he wrote of it, claiming later that in that moment, in that cohesion of fathomless grief and heartbroken inspiration, he was one with the Moon's divinity, following his beloved into Her Stars for the briefest of moments. In the last line of the poem, he speaks of his fall back to the earthly realm, and of how that final separation from her was "a thing beyond the pain of death, beyond the horrors of any torture and terror." I thought I had understood that passage, had come to terms with its meaning.

After this morning... I am no longer so sure Larent had it right..."

—final entry from the private journals of Yseri Suro

The smell of fire woke Ekene Okonso up long before the pounding on the chamber doors shook his wives and courtesans from sleep. He'd been standing along the rail of his balcony for nearly five whole minutes, in fact, looking out over his city as his black nightgown flapped around him against the summer wind, before the soldiers finally barreled in, escorting his First and Second Hands.

They faltered among the shifting curtains of the archways when they found him already studying the billowing plumes of scattered smoke that cut a score of thick lines against the night sky above the south-east district of Karesh Syl.

After several long seconds in which neither man braved an approach, Ekene chose to break the silence with a growled word.

"Explain."

"Your Greatness," Yseri started, his voice unusually tight. "Five of the outer city camps have rebelled in the last three hours, overrunning their assigned troops."

"*Five?*" Ekene demanded, whirling on the two men in outrage. "How did this happen? Why was I not woken?"

"The revolts were not coordinated, Great Tash," Naizer said in a stringy, strained voice. "We ourselves only heard of it in the last hour. It appears the earliest engagements all originated from a single location, the ninth district camp, which is not unheard of. The generals thought they could gain control of the situation, but..."

"It spread," the Tash finished for him, grinding his worn teeth. "Yes, *obviously*. If that's the case—" he leered at his Hands "—what are you doing to *fix it?*"

"I am having all available troops deployed to the outer rings as a counter-force," Yseri said at once. "Lord General Sulva estimates we can muster almost ten thousand men, but it will take the night and much of the day to organize them, not to mention recall the short-distance patrols from the savannah. Wall sentries have been halved and put on double-duty, and *all* entrances to the city have been sealed to anyone but our soldiers until this revolt is contained. If word were to reach Karesh Nan that we are fighting an insurrection—"

"Then his *'esteemed'* Tash Haji might feel inclined to send his 'assistance,'" Ekene finished for him with a glower. "Who would be all too happy to attempt to depose me while they have the chance. Yes. Fine. Keep the gates sealed until this is resolved."

"There's more," Naizer followed up with, biting his lip nervously. "Your Greatness… It's been reported by multiple sources that Raz i'Syul Arro has been identified at several areas of conflict throughout the night…"

Ekene wasn't the *least* bit surprised by this, of course. They'd flooded the streets with patrols as soon as the east gate had been breached, but there were literally *thousands* of places to look in a city the size of Karesh Syl. There'd been a skirmish the evening before, leaving *another* five men dead, but the Monster and his bitch woman—according to several city residents who had witnessed the attack—had vanished into the night as quickly as they'd appeared.

"Damn him," the Tash cursed, spitting bitterly over the ivory tiles of the balcony before storming between the Hands, sending soldiers backpedaling away from him as he passed through the silk-hung arches and back into his rooms. "We should have sent the whole damn *army* out along the east roads. Wiped the bastard off the map while we knew where he was coming from."

"It would have been inadvisable at the time," Yseri insisted, he and Naizer following Ekene into the chambers. "He's one man. No one could have known how much trouble he would be."

At that, there was a polite, sarcastic cough of derision from the room's entrance.

Instantly, the sentries all around them spun to face the sound, drawing their swords and hefting their shields with shouts of surprise. Every eye moved to the figure in black leather armor who'd appeared out of nowhere, arms crossed over his chest and smirking at the First Hand as he leaned casually against one column of the open archway. Behind him, another man stood, swathed in loose-fitting garments of varied shades of black and grey, one tanned hand casually resting on the curved saber slung diagonally across his lower back.

"I *hate* to contradict you, honored First," Azzeki Koro drawled smugly with a shrug at Yseri, "but I do believe you were given *exactly* such warnings, only to have them fall on deaf ears."

"Stand down," the Tash snapped as the soldiers around them began to creep toward the two newcomers, blades at the ready. "Leave us."

Several of the men looked confused at this, glancing at him and at each other, as though unsure of what to do.

"S-sir?" one of the unit's officers stuttered, not meeting Ekene's gaze. "You're… You're sure?"

Behind the Tash, Yseri growled. "His Greatness gave you an order. *Obey*, or face the repercussions!"

That got the soldiers moving. At once they sheathed their swords and hurried past Koro and Na'zeem, eyeing the two men warily as they did.

When they were gone, Ekene leered at his Third Hand. "You'd best have a good reason for showing your face, Koro," he seethed. Then he looked around the man to the Southerner behind him. "You *and* your pet."

If Na'zeem was remotely offended by the insult, he certainly didn't show it. The assassin merely watched the Tash and his Hands, grey eyes shifting between them constantly, like he was assessing and reassessing the factors of the room every few seconds.

"Your safety isn't enough of a reason?" Koro asked, detaching himself from the archway. "We cornered an animal, gave him little opportunity for action and even less avenues of escape. Now he's biting back, and tearing your city apart as he does so. He'll want to take advantage of the chance while he has it."

"What do you mean?" Naizer asked from the Tash's right, frowning at the Third. "What advantage?"

It was Na'zeem who answered, taking a step forward at once to speak.

"The 'chaos' you were just speaking of," the man offered simply. "In the confusion, Arro is very likely to try and use it to his benefit. You're all clearly aware of the coup the lizard managed to pull off in Miropa over a year ago. Are you familiar with the circumstances that gave him the opportunity?"

As one, the Tash and his Hands held their tongue, waiting.

Na'zeem nodded, apparently unsurprised. "I thought not. Sparing you the details, the former šef of the city set a trap for the Monster. A very intricate one, which required a mass coordination and planning by all involved. It nearly worked, but the beast just managed to escape, killing dozens in the process. The failure caused a panic in the ranks of the Mahsadën—as well as unrest in the city itself—resulting in several mistakes made on their part. Arro promptly exploited these, and within a few hours of the failed attempt, every one of the šef were dead."

The ringing silence that followed this account was so absolute, it seemed even to dim the Moon outside.

"You think he'll strike?" the Tash hissed, struggling to wrap his mind around the concept. "Now? So soon? He's been in the city less than a handful of days."

"Days in which we did everything we could to disrupt him and keep him from gaining any hold with which to anchor himself to," Koro continued for him. "We forced him to hide, might even have split him from his forces, if he brought any with him into the city. Even now he is still on the move, following the rebellion as it spreads. If he cannot establish a place of advantage on this 'battlefield', what value is there in waiting and allowing your forces to entrench themselves into familiar territory? Even if he manages to free the rest of the slaves in the south-east quarter *and* call them all to his banner, that leaves him with perhaps a force of twenty thousand untrained and largely unarmed bodies. Yes—" he nodded in Naizer's direction as the Second choked at the thought "—that is a sum, but it's doubtful he would be able to manage that in a day."

"By which time *our* ten thousand will have congregated." Yseri was scratching his smooth cheek thoughtfully, staring at the Third. "Even with half that, we could blockade them within the quarter…"

"I have seen your men fight, Your Greatness," Na'zeem offered with an inclination of his head. "Even if he manages to gather twice the number you bring to bear, neither your Third nor I foresee such a battle going in favor of the lizard."

"But that's good news!" Naizer erupted excitedly, looking around. "Isn't it? Arro has already lost!"

"And he knows it."

The words left Ekene's mouth unbidden, even as he registered Koro's point. He'd turned his head to watch the growing pillar of smoke he could see against the night through the arches to his right, pondering the facts Koro and Na'zeem had presented.

"He knows it, so he will attempt to manipulate the variables in another way," the Tash continued. "It would take a fool not to notice we've halved the sentries along the walls…"

"And Arro is no fool," Koro pressed. "He will expect our response, will know we are going to do everything we can to contain the situation, even if it means surrendering the south-east quarter until his revolt burns itself out or your soldiers stamp it into the ground."

"He'll see it coming, and react accordingly," Na'zeem continued for the Third. "As he did in Miropa. I can assure you Arro knows there is only one sure way to cripple your army absolutely, to give himself and the slaves a real chance for victory in this battle."

"My head," the Tash grumbled, understanding. "He'll come for my head."

"He will," Koro said, he and the Southerner nodding together. "And sooner than you might believe. If the First already has your soldiers gathering, Arro will realize the sand has started slipping through the hourglass."

The Tash grimaced, glaring at the ground.

"When?" he snapped finally.

Koro and Na'zeem glanced at each other.

"No later than tonight," the Southerner answered after a moment. "More likely much sooner."

"Today?" Yseri cut in, frowning. "Would he be so brazen? Would he truly make an attempt in the light of day?"

"The sooner the better, in his mind," Koro said as Na'zeem inclined his head in agreement beside him. "He *knows* the army gathers. I've no doubt he sees you are already starting to limit the fight to a single district of the outer city. I wouldn't be surprised if he was already on the move, in fact."

"There is no rule that insists an assassin must move in the night, honored First," the Southerner added. "If Arro believes striking under the gaze of the Sun lends him the greatest advantage of surprise, he will not hesitate to plan accordingly. It is what I would do."

For several seconds after this deduction, no one said anything. Only Koro, in fact, appeared brave enough to smile.

And it was that smile that connected all the dots for the Tash.

"You *expected* this," he snarled abruptly, taking an angry step toward his Third Hand. "*That's* why you supported Yseri's protocol, why you told us it would be a good plan to run extra patrols and keep the lizard on edge after he had made it into the city. You knew it would come to this. The both of you!" He jabbed a crooked finger at Koro and Na'zeem in fury.

The First, behind him, sputtered in outrage, but Koro cut him off before he could say anything.

"We thought it *might* come to this," the Third said with a conceding inclination of his head. "Truthfully, we hoped the patrols would rout him out, but we suspected it was unlikely."

"And so you led us into a *trap*?" the Tash howled indignantly, taking another step forward. "You allowed Arro to seed chaos and rebellion? For WHAT?"

"To turn the trap around on him," Na'zeem said simply.

As one, everyone in the room except the Third looked to the assassin.

"Turn it... Turn it on him?" Naizer asked in a weak voice. He had been unusually quiet throughout the exchange, and Ekene rather thought it was because the man sounded like he was about to faint.

Silently, he swore he would replace him the moment they ended this madness.

"Yes," Na'zeem said, his grey eyes on the Tash. "Your Greatness, just as the lizard sees your death as the blow that would bring your city to its knees, so can you look at him in the same light. If you bring an end to 'the Dragon', you bring an end to his rebellion. More than that, you *crush* the legend of the man, and with it any such desire for similar uprisings for the next hundred years. You have the ability. You have the numbers. The lizard is not invulnerable. He bleeds. I have seen it. I have *made* him bleed. If you could pit your forces against him on an even field, you would crush him with sheer force." His eyebrows rose, as though trying to make his point. "And to do that, all you need is to know *where* he is, and *when* he'll be there..."

Ekene considered these words for a long time, chewing on them as he turned them over and over again in his head. He was of half-a-mind to shout for the guards to come back, to order them to heave both his cursed Third and his pet shadow over the balcony and be done with it. His own hands itched to throttle the both of them, and in years long past he might have attempted just that.

With age, though, came wisdom, and—for better or for worse—the Tash saw the sense in Na'zeem's words.

With that conclusion, all the anger flooded out of him, and Ekene's frail body became suddenly overcome with fatigue. With a sigh he turned and slunk back to his bed, using the nearest banister to ease himself down to sit at its edge.

When he was ready, he looked up.

"So I am to be the bait," he muttered disgruntledly. "I suppose it's a pleasant change, knowing beforehand of the attempt on my life." He looked up at Koro with weary eyes. "Can I at least pray to the Sun that you have a plan?"

In response, the Third glanced at Na'zeem. The assassin bowed to the Tash before turning and hurrying back through the archway and across the greeting room to pull open the distant door that led out into the palace halls. He exchanged a few brief words with someone outside, then some harsher ones with what might have been the sentries. After a moment, he stepped away from the opening, allowing one of the soldiers to peer nervously through.

"Your Greatness?" the man called skittishly, his eyes on the floor. "I have a number of slaves here who are requesting entry? They claim that you would be expecting them, but they have—?"

"Yes, yes!" the Tash snapped impatiently. "Let the damned fools in already!"

The soldier started and nodded, disappearing again to shout an order at whoever waited in the hall. A moment later, several awkward forms appeared, carefully managing their way through the door, carrying with them a pair of very peculiar items. It took a moment for Ekene to recognize the figures as several of Na'zeem's men, half of the eight other Southerners the assassin had brought with him from the fringe cities. At first he thought his tired eyes were playing tricks on him, but with a blink the Tash realized that the foursome of figures were indeed dressed in the simple white tunics shared by the palace slaves, having apparently traded out their greys for less conspicuous attire, complete with manacles and chains around their ankles. It made him momentarily uncomfortable, wondering suddenly if he'd ever been in the presence of one of the Southerners without noticing it, thinking on how many times he might have allowed them to serve him his meals or bring him hot water for his baths.

The concern, however, was quickly pushed aside in favor of confused interest when he took in the two objects each pair of men lugged between them, hauling them across the greeting chamber, through the archway, and into the room.

"What in the Sun's name...?" he heard Naizer mutter to his right, and for once the Tash thought this an appropriate commentary.

They were a pair of massive, roughly identical plain clay pots. Each of them was about half as high as Ekene might have stood in the prime of his youth, and two or three times as broad. They'd once been sealed, apparently, though the fragile papers that had been pasted to their sides were now broken, and carved into their tops were the rough scrawlings of Northern letters the Tash barely made out as "pork".

Even from here, he could detect the sour scent of the vinegar likely swilling about within, and at his left Yseri raised a hand to cover his nose and mouth, grimacing in distaste.

"Are we to dine Arro to death, Koro?" the First asked sarcastically, eyeing the objects. "Is that your plan? Your time in the North lent itself to learning the beast has an insatiable appetite for pickled meats, did it?"

The Third only smiled in response.

"Oh, no," he said, turning and gesturing to the disguised assassins with one hand to open the pots. "Nothing quite so dramatic, I'm afraid. I did learn much of the man, though, during our shared time together." As the Southerners each took a side of a lid and lifted them free with matching grinds of clay on clay, his grin broadened. "For example, how and when to hit the lizard the hardest."

Together on either side of Ekene, his First and Second Hands leaned forward slightly to peer into the jar. Even the Tash himself, overcome by curiosity, pulled himself back onto his feet from the bed to look inside.

What they saw was enough to make even Yseri's dark face turn green, and Naizer heaved and stumbled back through the curtains, reaching the edge of the balcony just in time to vomit.

Ekene, though, only saw the largest piece of the Third's plan fall into place.

"And so," Koro said with a cool shrug, "I thought we could attempt a trick my old master once tried. With some changes, of course."

L

"The Gods always see fit to fell the tallest of the trees..."

—Sigûrth proverb

Akelo sighted carefully down his arrow, silently cursing—for the hundredth time—the bleached-leather bracers that encased his arms. The stolen soldier's armor he and the other *kuja* had donned once more was cumbersome, and not at all conducive to archery. The white dye was distracting, and the bowstring often snapped across the lacing.

They would very likely need the disguises, though, if they were going to even have a chance at carrying out Raz's deranged plan.

Mad, Akelo thought to himself, loosening the arrow and watching it fly upward, toward the top of the inner wall of the city. *They'll be calling him 'The Mad Dragon' by the time this is all said and done.*

The arrow struck true, taking the sentry he'd been aiming for squarely beneath the jaw, dropping him like a silent stone as it ripped up through his head, piercing the top of his mouth to settle somewhere in the cavity of his skull.

Shifting in the early morning shadows under the cloth awnings of several silent shops that paralleled the wall, Akelo drew a second arrow. Nocking and drawing, he stayed crouched as he sighted the center-most of the eight soldiers paired off on either side of the gate Raz had selected to make their entry by into the noble's quarters. As with the other dozen or so such gates scattered throughout the districts—at least according to Karan, the atherian Syrah had returned with in the earliest hours of the morning—it was a smaller entrance than the main gates of Karesh Syl's outer wall, barely wide enough to allow three or four men through standing shoulder to shoulder. Ordinarily there might have been one, maybe two sentries tasked with the tedious work of guarding the place, just enough bodies to ensure the commoners of the outer city stayed away from the wealthier quarters and out from under the feet of the nobility, but—after the pandemonium that had been raging all night—none of them had been shocked to find security increased. In fact, Akelo had honestly expected grander measures in place, especially given how patient they had had to be to escape the south-east where the army of freed slaves still waged their war. Then again, the lookouts on the inner *and* outer walls had very obviously been cut back, so perhaps the Tash was merely a little *too* keen on crushing the revolt as soon as possible, with as many soldiers as he could spare.

Whatever the case, Akelo tried not to dwell on the nature of their good fortune.

And so, with a prayer to the Sun that must have been just rising over the eastern horizon, Akelo made a piping sound like a common mousebird, and let loose the arrow.

By the time it struck its mark, taking the poor soldier through the throat to slam him against the wall behind his shoulder, a trio of flickering points of light zipped out from beneath a set of arched stone steps across the road from the gate, and three more men tumbled to the ground. The four left standing had just begun to shout in alarm, their cries falling on the dead ears of the wall sentry above, when Raz dropped from the roofs above, landing right in their midst, Ahna and his gladius already swinging.

The soldiers died before any of them could think to raise their shields in defense.

"On me," Raz whispered into the slowly brightening shadows of the streets around them. At once, Akelo rose from his hiding place and hurried to join him. As he did, nineteen other forms appeared from around various nooks and corners to do the same. When he and Syrah had both taken their places by Raz's side, the atherian peered into the group.

"Karan, Aleem," he said as he found the pair he was looking for, "do you know the way from here?"

The cook and the young atherian nodded together, stepping forward.

"It's not far," Karan said, pointing up through the gate at the towering form of the palace in the very center of the city. "The inner quarters aren't nearly as broad as the outer. I don't know if they'll have patrols or additional lookouts, though…"

"Let the rest of us worry about that," Raz told her, rapping his steel claws against the head of his sagaris pointedly before turning his attention on Aleem. "You're sure you'll be able to find the entrance?"

The former slave nodded timidly, pulling uncomfortably at the cotton of the kitchen-hand's tunic he was dressed in once again. Syrah had spent every spare moment they'd had using her magic to scour the white cloth, and—though it was still stained and dirty—it was a far-cry cleaner even than when they'd freed him from the patrol along the eastern roads. All the same, the man looked miserable in it, like it weighed him down as much as the chains that had once bound his scarred ankles.

When Raz had asked him if he would don the uniform again, though, the cook's hesitation had been only brief.

"The door is along the south side of the palace wall," Aleem told them, his voice high as his wide eyes stared fearfully at the distant structure. "Away from the main gates to the west and south. His Great-the Tash—" he caught himself, frowning as anger replaced some of his fear "—never would have wanted his guests to risk stumbling across it."

"Can't blame 'em," someone—Akelo thought likely Erom—muttered queasily from behind them.

He ignored the comment, however, watching Raz step aside to wave Karan and Aleem through the gate.

"Lead on," the Dragon said.

And with that, they were on the move again, slipping into the breathtaking sprawl of the sloping inner city.

The buildings that rose up around them felt like the stuff of legend to Akelo. From a distance, in the expanse of the grass plains as they'd approached Karesh Syl, they'd been impressive enough, a myriad of jutting and twisting towers woven upward toward the sky on narrow struts of white marble and other polished stone. The inner rings of the outer city had been beautiful on their own, he'd thought, the clean edges of the stone-and-iron structures unlike anything he'd ever seen, least of all the rickety homes and hamlets of the coast cities. Now, however, they moved through a maze of true wonders, the empty streets still in the brightening light of the morning, the silver and gold gilding along the ledges and lips and gables gently glowing in the first light of dawn.

Akelo felt as though they had broken into some massive treasure vault, its wealth of riches left out for all to take.

"Easier than I thought," he admitted to Syrah as they hurried up the street, dark eyes scanning the arched and narrow rooftops on either side of them for trouble, bow at his side and his free hand steadying the hilt of the soldier's sword on his hip. "Doesn't mean your man isn't still mad, though."

Beside him, the Priestess gave a pained snort.

"Just don't let *him* here you say that," she answered, and Akelo saw her glance at the atherian on her other side, whose gaze was fixed on the outline of the Tash's palace rising before them, growing more and more distinct as the darkness of the cloudy night chased itself westward.

Syrah had returned just before midnight, shouting for Akelo and the others from the common room of the Red Shield Inn. He'd been incensed, at first, not understanding why the woman would be so rash, until he and Cyper descended to find her waiting for them in blood-splattered robes, standing with a young atherian female and an old man they didn't know. The scars around the strangers' ankles, of course, spelled out everything that needed to be said, and it hadn't taken much convincing on Syrah's part before the men gathered their things and set out at once into the chaos the southeast district had become, leaving the old man—Abir, Syrah had called him— to keep an eye on the horses. All around them, Percian families had been fleeing their homes, shouting to one another and clogging the streets while pointing up at the mass of smoke and glow of fire that was blotting out the light of the Moon and Her Stars. As a result, it had taken them longer than they would have liked to catch up to the mass of slaves, at which point only Syrah's presence and Karan's assurances had saved them—in their stolen pirate's leathers and irons—from being lynched by the furious mob. Eventually, though, several individuals had been able to point them northwest, saying that's where the Dragon had last been seen.

When they'd found him, a few hours after midnight, Raz looked a terror. He'd been on his own, reprieving himself of the skirmishes that were happening in practically every direction, sitting with his back and wings against the enclosure wall of one of the burning slave camps. They'd almost missed him, the entire group running right past the corner he had tucked himself around until Karan caught his scent. Exhausted as Raz was, a little of Syrah's magics and a hurried conversation among the men had been all it took to get him on his feet.

When he'd started talking about "striking before things spiraled out of control," Akelo had wondered if the man had gone half-mad.

He'd seen the gathering soldiers with his own eyes, though, seen the battles breaking out all around the district as they'd searched. He could tell, as inexperienced as he might have been in the rules of war, that the Tash's men were assembling, and that no one seemed keen on pressing into the havoc of the district just yet. They were waiting, preparing for what could only have been a single, massive push to crush the rebellion before it claimed Karesh Syl as a whole.

It had been just enough to convince Akelo not to voice his reservations when Raz had announced it was time to act, especially after Aleem came forward, offering a risky—but plausible—opportunity they might just be able to work to their advantage.

An hour later—Akelo and the other *kuja* donning their soldier's uniforms once more while Aleem put on his slave's tunic—their little group had slipped by the perimeter of soldiers surrounding the outer ring, taking advantage of the army's preoccupation with gaining a foothold in the chaos of the battle.

And now, as the day announced itself anew, they'd already beaten the first of the major barriers Akelo had been worried about.

He was grateful, for the first time in his life, for the innate laziness he'd come to know among the nobility, including the minor gentry that presided over the coastal villages and ships he'd been enslaved in. In this earliest hour of light, before the Sun could even begin to show itself over the distant outer wall of Karesh Syl, only rarely was there so much as a hint of the residents and owners of the intricate buildings rising up around them. Not even a half-dozen people crossed their path, and most of these individuals were so taken by surprise at the group's appearance that Syrah had no trouble stunning them with a silent spell. Better yet, whether the inner city was generally presided over by few soldiers, or the chaos in the outer ring had drawn them all away, they came across only three patrols as they climbed the rising streets toward the palace. The first two they managed to avoid, scattering and ducking into any crooks and shadows they could find at the hissed signal of whoever saw them first.

The last had not been so fortunate, as Raz heard them coming around a corner in the road ahead, only one man even managing to begin a scream before the Dragon turned the bend to meet them head-on, Ahna and his gladius moving in patterned blurs.

They paused for a single minute, then, taking the time to hide the bodies down the narrow stairwell of an alley nearby, Syrah burning away the bloodstains from the cobbled street with white fire.

Not long after that, Karan led them around a large curve in the street, and the group found themselves looking both ways along the length of the palace wall. Twenty feet high, it was a beautiful, ornate masterwork of masonry. The only traces of metal were plated bands of hammered gold around staggered capstones along the top of the fortification, making the entire thing look like a massive crown encircling the form of the palace behind it. Its burnished surface had been carved and chiseled so that every ten feet a meticulous, deftly sculpted mural stood embellished in the stone, each work a separate depiction of some scene or event Akelo assumed must have been part of the history of Karesh Syl. It was so spectacular, the group as a whole couldn't help but stand and gape at it, Syrah even letting out a little "Oh…" of awe as she tilted her hooded head back to take in the nearest work.

Fortunately for all, however, it appeared to have been many years since Aleem and several of the other recruits had been remotely impressed by the wall.

"This way," the cook said, pointing west and taking the lead. "We need to hurry. The nobility might sleep in, but their slaves and servants do not."

It was enough to shake the others from their stupor, and as one they followed, hammering after the man.

Not two minutes later, the door appeared. It was a bizarre sight, Akelo thought as they approached, a heavy bronze thing that looked like it had tried to be crafted with respect to the beauty of the stone it was set in, but nonetheless felt like a stain against the pristine white. In addition, the nobles' residences across from the wall had been built a dozen yards further away here than anywhere else along the perimeter of the palace, like a little square around the small door. It might have made for a quaint spot among the busyness of the rest of the inner city, were it not for the distinct, pungent reek of the place. It was a putrid scent, at sharp odds with the beauty of the decor that ringed them, and by the time they slowed to a quiet halt by the door several of the men looked queasy.

On the other side of Syrah, Akelo saw Raz turn to him.

"You're up," the atherian said under his breath, inclining his head toward the door as he motioned for the men who wouldn't be needed to press themselves against the wall behind him.

Akelo nodded, gesturing for the other Percian to join him. Odene, Zehir, Neret, and Rufari fell into place behind him at once, hefting their shields. Akelo traded his bow and quiver with Marsus Byrn, who had been holding onto his own shield, slipping the heavy thing onto his arm and strapping it tight before leading the way over to where Aleem was already waiting for them by the door. When he and his "soldiers" were in place behind the cook, Akelo glanced over at Raz once, giving him one last "You're *mad*!" look.

The atherian just shrugged in reply.

Then, barely holding back a sigh, Akelo grabbed Aleem by the back of his kitchen tunic as gently as he dared, and reached up to pound on the brass body of the door.

LI

"If given the choice, follow the general who smells like piss and shit, because he's been digging the sewage trenches with the rest of his men. The others know nothing more of their troops than what the sycophants and assenters they surround themselves with are willing to tell them…"

—Jarden Arro, Champion of the Arro Clan

They didn't have to wait long before Raz heard movement on the other side of the wall. He stiffened, shooting Akelo and the other disguised *kuja* a look, telling them to be ready. Not a few seconds later there was the shuffling of approaching footsteps, and with a bang and the shifting sound of oiled metal, a slot in the upper third of the door slid sideways.

"The Sun's name is all this?" a rough voice demanded through the space. Raz couldn't see the man, but he could imagine the soldier glaring out at Akelo and his group, taking them in suspiciously. "What are you doing here, Captain? *All* spare units have been ordered to the outer city."

"We've just returned from patrol assignment along the east roads," Akelo answered, sounding artfully weary. The stained conditions of his armor didn't hurt in selling the lie. "Got routed through the south gate. Haven't even returned to barracks yet."

The voice on the other side grunted, apparently buying the story. "You're lucky the gate sentries didn't report your presentation to your superiors." He paused, then continued in what Raz couldn't help but think was a slightly suspicious tone. "The east road patrols? I was told we wouldn't be expecting any of you lot back for another moon, at least."

Akelo, fortunately, was a quick thinker.

"Got put on one of the minor trade routes, into the south-east villages," he said with an annoyed snort, like he didn't care for the assignment. "Looped into one of the major roads, where we ran into another patrol. Commandant leading the unit ordered me home. Said there wasn't much point on so many of us on one route."

Another grunt, then another question. "And your horse?" the man asked, though he sounded less skeptical.

Akelo grimaced. "Hyenas. Not a week out. Left this poor bastard—" he shook Aleem in his grip, as though to remind the sentry why they were there "—to carry everything."

The soldier on the other side of the door chuckled at that. "Not much point in them otherwise, is there? You work in the kitchens, slave?"

"Y-yes, sir," Aleem answered at once, choking on his words. His eyes fell and his face flushed, and Raz's grip tightened around Ahna and his gladius. He *hated* to put one of his men through this, after the life they'd already had to lead.

The sentry grunted for a third time. The was a shift of feet, followed by the sound of metal on metal as he slid the slot back into place. Then, with a quiet *clunk* of some lock or lever being lifted, the door swung inward.

"Give him here," the soldier said, extending an arm toward Aleem. "Then I recommend you take your men back to your barracks, Captain. I wasn't jesting when I said they've made a call for all hands. You're lucky I was even here to—*URK!*"

Raz slipped along the wall and into the arch of the doorway, sinking the gladius up to its hilt in the man's stomach, shoving upward. He barely glanced at the soldier even as the blade cut through diaphragm, heart, and lung, ending his life with nothing more than a pained gasp. Raz was already moving through the door, bringing the spasming body with him before it could bleed out over the road. The others poured in behind him, weapons out and ready for a fight. The courtyard they found themselves in was a small thing, an uneven triangle of grass and stone wedged between two walls of one of the palace's outer structures. Along the left-most of these, a trio of short steps led up to a plain wooden door set into the stone, far less ornate that the bronze one they'd just come through.

The only people waiting for them, though, were a pair of thin women in ragged, grimy smocks, startled eyes taking the band in from above matching clothes wrapped over the lower halves of their faces.

It was a sad, pathetic scene. The two slaves stood, frozen, on either side of a narrow, half-filled cart that must *just* have fit through the door at Raz's back. Each woman was ankle-deep in a massive pile of half-eaten and rotting food and refuse built up against the wall of the palace proper, each wielding a worn wooden shovel they looked to have been using to haul the rubbish into the cart. Raz took them in as his men cursed and muttered behind him, some at the state of the two filthy women, some at the renewed stench of the waste heap.

If even a day before someone had suggested that Aleem—*Aleem*, their kitchen-hand-turned-cook—would be the key to infiltrating the Tash's palace, Raz would have questioned that person's sanity. When the man had told them about the rubbish door, though, Raz had been one of many to outright gape at the former slave, as stunned by the simplicity of the idea as he was by the ridiculousness of the notion. It made sense, of course. The Tash's palace was obviously home to hundreds—maybe even thousands—of people. Diplomats. Soldiers. Servants. Slaves. The functioning sewer system of Karesh Syl was a wonder all to itself, but one couldn't simply toss the remnants of one's meal down the privy. Of *course* the kitchens would have to have a way to rid themselves of leftovers and spoiled food. Of *course* there would be a place for the slaves to toss whatever rubbish might otherwise accumulate in such a bustling place. From where he stood, Raz could make out the broken leg of a finely carved chair sticking out from a small pile of moldy apples, the leather sole of some worn shoe, and the torn remnants of what might have been old bedsheets or curtains under a heap of plucked poultry feathers. Best of all, of *course* the Tash would want such a system out of the way and out of sight—not to mention out of scent. His city was blessed, after all. He himself was ordained by the Twins. How could the majesty of its inner quarters ever be tainted by such mundane difficulties as wasted scraps and junk? Raz almost felt sorry for the unfortunate nobles who'd settled in the homes closest to the bronze door Akelo was now closing behind them.

Doing his best not to breathe through his nose, Raz lowered his weapons and stood straight, trying to look as unthreatening as possible as he faced the two women whose labors they had clearly interrupted.

"Do you know who I am?" he asked them slowly.

It took a moment to get a response, and even then only one of the pair managed to nod, the motion jerky and small as both of them continued to stare, clearly having difficulty believing their eyes.

"Then you understand what I've come to do?" he continued, taking a step forward, relieved when neither woman made to flinch away or scream in alarm.

Again, a simple, spasmed nod.

"Can you help us?"

Raz worried the request was too much, worried that he was going to push the slaves too far. Indeed, as he thought this, he saw their eyes shift from him to over his shoulder, much of their surprise souring into uncertain agitation.

Glancing around, it didn't take him long to realize what they were looking at.

"Akelo," he asked, getting the old man's attention from among his other *kuja*, "show them your wrist, will you?"

Fortunately, the Percian seemed to understand where his head was at. Without pause he fumbled for a moment with the lacings of the white leathers around his forearm of his sword hand, then tugged the soldier's armor off to reveal his bare skin. There was a sharp inhalation of understanding from the two women when they saw the scar there, the broad swath of knotted flesh where shackles had so often chained the man to his oars. As Raz looked back at the slaves, he was certain there was a new hope dawning there in their wide eyes.

Sure enough, while the woman on the right still seemed hesitant, the one who'd nodded spoke up almost at once.

"There's only Overseer Jareen today." Her words were slurred as she looked at Raz, voice heavy with the accents of the Southern slums. "The other two were called away, but they ain't tellin' us why."

"The Tash is desperate," Syrah said, coming to stand beside Raz and giving the women one of her encouraging smiles as she spoke. "The outer ring is in rebellion, and the fighting threatens to spread if it's not contained."

The slaves looked at each other, their partially-hidden expressions seeming half-amazed, half-dubious.

"They're... They're rebelling?" the woman on the right finally spoke, gripping the haft of her shovel so tightly it shook. "They're fighting?"

"For their freedom, yes," Syrah answered with a nod. "They must. All we could do was give them the chance, which is all we ask of you."

The slaves exchanged one last glance.

When they looked around, their faces were set, and the woman on the left reached up to pull away the mask from her face as she stepped off the rubbish pile. Her tanned face was so dirty the cloth cut a clean patch around her nose and mouth.

"Yleke has the keys to the door," she said to Raz, frowning down at the dead soldier on the ground beside him like she wasn't much bothered by his demise. "Jareen will be sittin' at the overseers' desk to the left side of the door, unless he's up hasslin' one a' the cooks or kitchen hands." She looked to Aleem, still standing in his slave's uniform over by the palace wall, but continued to speak to Raz. "Do you know your way from there?"

"There are those among us who do," Raz answered with a grateful nod. "Is there anything else you can tell us?"

"The... The Tash will be preparing to take audiences, at this time," the second woman piped up in a squeak, though she didn't brave leaving the heap as she kept ahold of her shovel. "In the court halls. He's likely to have his Hands with him, a-as well as their royal details."

Raz frowned at that, turning to Akelo, who was lacing his bracer back around his arm again. "The Hands," he muttered, trying to remember what the man had told him. "The voices of the Twins, or something?"

"The most powerful men in the city, behind the Tash himself," the Percian said with a nod, tugging the final knots in the armor tight. "There are two, his First and Second."

"And their retinues," Syrah added with a thoughtful frown, looking up at Raz. "I get the feeling this isn't going to be easy..."

"A lot of the palace guard weren't at their posts this mornin'," the Southerner offered up hopefully. "Maybe called away ta' the outer city?"

"*There's* some good news..." someone whispered excitedly from behind them, and Raz heard Hur grunt in agreement.

"It helps," Raz answered with a grim smile at the woman, feeling that the Sun might just be shining favorably on them this day. He caught Erom's eye and indicated the dead soldier beside him with a nod. As the borderer hurried forward to bend down and search the man's uniform, Raz turned back to the two slaves. "You have our thanks. Now... If you're amenable, I have a last favor to ask of you..."

Despite the early hours of the post, Jareen Ysente had never disliked his position of overseer in the Tash's kitchens. It was a comfortable, easy detail—

at least in comparison to some of the other assignments his commanders could have given him—and any problems with the food or service were almost always placed on the heads of the cooks and hands themselves. On a typical day, he, Arren, and Zeuni spent most of their time playing dice on the small desk they shared along the south wall of the kitchens, positioned by the back door to monitor the comings and goings as slaves came and went with scraps for the rubbish pile. Occasionally one of the three got up to do a round, or brought out their cudgel when a dish was spilled or some meal or another was ruined in one of the dozen cooking hearths cut into the walls around them. Ordinarily it was lazy work, stressful only when Captain Nalym decided to make one of his irritating "surprise inspections."

Today, though, Arren and Zeuni had been called away to assist with one of the slave rebellions that occasionally troubled the outer city, and Jareen had found himself suddenly burdened with a bit more than he was accustomed to.

Since before dawn, the slaves of the kitchen had been tense, distracted even. Half of the bread the palace broke its fast with had come out of the kilns burned, someone had added salt instead of sugar to one of the porridge vats, and the cooks had outright *forgotten* to send the First Hand his morning tea. Jareen had very unusually been on his feet from the moment the kitchens had begun their prep, spending the last two hours yelling and banging his cudgel on the pots and pans that hung from long hooks in the wood and stone ceiling overhead, sweating in the heat of the cooking fires as he hurried about, ensuring no other mistakes were made. By the time he felt comfortable finally returning to his desk, he'd cuffed a dozen different serving boys and girls, threatened violence on several of the hands, and outright sunk his fist into the gut of one cook who'd muttered something under his breath as he'd passed.

Jareen hadn't actually made out the insult, be he'd gotten the gist of the slave's irritated tone.

Now, though, things finally seemed under control. With a huff of relief, Jareen weaved his way through the cutting tables and chopping blocks, splitting a swath through the workers who stepped smartly around him out of habit. The sounds of the kitchen rang clear around him as he walked, echoing over the shouts as orders for meals arrived from the palace above and requests for ingredients or dishes were yelled out from every corner of the wide room. More pleasant were the smells: the rich aroma of the yeast in the baking bread, the sweet scent of cinnamon and lavender, the delicious perfume of bacon being seared in the hearth off to his left. Jareen had just started enjoying the hint of pepper and garlic-stuffed beef whispering through the swath as someone began carving slabs for the midday meals, when an altogether less-enticing stench ruined the experience.

Jareen grimaced in disgust, seeing the two women waiting for him by his desk, standing in the arch of the little hall that led back to the courtyard where they usually toiled. Their ratty clothes were stained and discolored from their unappetizing work, and their feet and chains were so filthy it made him nauseous seeing them in his kitchen. Noting that the two slaves were unattended—Yleke, as usual, apparently nowhere to be seen—a spark of disapproval flared up in Jareen, and he made a line straight for the filthy pair. As he approached, he noted they'd left the back door of the kitchens—set into a side wall of the hall at their backs—open wide behind them, and his annoyance sparked into true anger.

"Sun burn you, women!" he snarled, marching right up to the pair and shoving his cudgel under their noses. "What in the blazes are you thinking, leaving that damn door open? Close it! Before your stench fouls the Tash's meal!"

"Sir, Master Yleke told us to come get you," one of the slaves, a Southerner, said hurriedly, bobbing her head apologetically. "He says there's a woman at the back gate who's refusin' to go away. Wants to be let in."

Jareen frowned at that. "A woman? What kind of woman?"

"He didn't say too much," the slave answered, and he almost thought she glanced nervously at her companion. "Just told us she had a white hood on and white hair. He just wanted us to—"

"What?" Jareen demanded, cutting her off as the woman's words sent a shiver up his back. "White hair? He said 'white hair'?"

"Aye, sir!" the other of the two squeaked nervously. "A-and white robes!"

For half a moment, Jareen stared at the two women, dumbfounded.

Then he rushed through them, shoving his way through the pair and hastening down the hall toward the door.

It can't be, he thought to himself as he rushed for the faint light of the morning outside. Even that basic description was enough to set his heart to hammering. It had been drilled into him and his brothers-in-arms in the palace barracks every day for the last several weeks, almost as thoroughly as the details of Raz i'Syul Arro himself.

Syrah Brahnt.

Jareen's mind flitted over the wonders it would do to his life if he and Yleke managed to capture the Northerner, Arro's woman, the one he'd heard called "the White Witch." It might not be as great a prize as the Dragon, but the overseer couldn't help but imagine the Tash would still consider the delivery of Brahnt, bound and chained, a great victory, especially if palace interrogators managed to drag the lizard's location from her. Grinning like a schoolboy who'd been offered a sweet, Jareen half-ran for the door.

He didn't even make it out into the courtyard.

As he was about to cross through the open entrance and down the steps to the food-strewn grass, Jareen was forced to stumble to a halt, cursing. There, in a half-circle about the base of the stairs, the strangest collaboration of individuals he had ever seen was looking up at him, a fair number of them smirking in something like amusement. Jareen had half-a-second to blink and take them in, noting the group of four or five soldiers—or men dressed like soldiers, at least—the eclectic collection of worn leathers and iron armor of the other men, and the single atherian female standing near their center, slightly behind a tall woman in white robes, a long steel staff held in one hand. The overseer gaped at the Witch, tripping over his shout of alarm as his free hand fumbled for the whip on his belt.

Just as his fingers wrapped around the handle of the thing, a presence materialized behind him, stepping out from where it had been hiding behind the door at his side, leaning down to hiss in his ear.

"No more of that, soldier. Never again."

In the next moment, the whip was torn from Jareen's belt, and a massive kick thrust him forward, sending him tumbling down the stairs with a yell. He landed hard, losing his cudgel as he did, tripping over his own feet to fall awkwardly at the feet of Syrah Brahnt. His head struck the earth, and he saw stars, groaning as he settled onto his back, looking skyward. Standing over him, the Witch looked impassively down, and he saw with a muddled thrill of fear that she held what looked like a twinkling spark of white fire in her free hand. He had just enough time to cast desperately around for help, just enough time to catch a glimpse of the massive figure still standing in the doorway to the kitchens, when there was a brilliant flash of light.

The last thought Jareen had, before he was dropped into the black depth of unconsciousness, was to wonder how far he could get from the city before someone realized *he* had been the one to let the Dragon of the North and his men into the palace without so much as a fight.

LII

"There are fewer accounts than I would have liked of the fall of the palace of Karesh Syl. Even those I have managed to scrounge up are brief and without detail. It is as if those who survived had little wish to dwell on—or even recall at all—whatever it was they witnessed that day…"

—*The Fall of Ancient Perce*, author unknown

The Tash's palace was as much a wonder within as it was without. The kitchens themselves had been low and cramped, packed with slaves who gaped silently at Raz and the others as they followed Aleem through the chamber and up a wide set of steps, but once they'd made the palace proper Raz was hard-pressed not to stop and gawk every few seconds at some incredible sight they passed as they hurried through the cavernous halls of the place. The palace seemed to have no understanding of enclosed space, even as Aleem led them north, into the heart of the Tash's home. Almost every hall generally had one side that comprised of columned archways, looking out onto open-air cloisters decorated with fountains and greenery crossed by the bent shadows of the palm trees sprouting from every corner. Even the walls that *did* exist were light and airy, as often made of perforated brass and copper as they were of polished stone, repeating shapes decoratively cut into them so that the rooms within were hardly hidden from view. Sculptures rose from pedestals on every corner they took, towering upward so that their carved heads almost touched the vaulted, painted ceilings above, each as beautiful and meticulously crafted as the magnificent murals they'd seen on the palace walls outside. The Sun was still low in the sky, but the shadows of the place did little to mar the spacious wonder of it all. Raz couldn't help but draw comparisons to Cyurgi 'Di, trying to imagine what a group like the Laorin could have done with such a magnificent residence, if they'd been given the chance.

As it was, though, none of the beauty of his surroundings could take the foul taste from Raz's mouth, the heavy understanding that all of it—from the airy courtyards to the smooth tiles of the floors to the silk draperies that fluttered in the archways as they caught the morning breeze—had been built on the sweat and blood of others.

Fortunately, Raz didn't have to wait long for the opportunity to vent some of his disgust.

They encountered the first trio of soldiers within a minute of leaving the kitchens. Raz would have expected to run into trouble earlier, truth be told, but between the early hour and the apparent fact that at least a portion of the palace guard had indeed been drawn away to the outer city, he counted themselves fortunate.

Then the Tash's men appeared out of a side-hall a fair distance ahead of the group, catching sight of them well before anyone could do anything about it.

"HERE!" one of the soldiers bellowed as all three drew their swords. "HE'S HERE!"

That, though, was all the time it took for Raz to surge ahead, barreling into the three figures with a roar he hoped would shake the very foundations of the place, Ahna whipping around in a horizontal arc.

The first soldier did his best to fend off the dviassegai's heavy blow, but there is little and less thin steel and flimsy wood can do against the masterworks of Allihmad Jerr. Ahna shattered his shield like it were made of cheap glass, punching through the man's hasty defense and catching him a glancing blow to the throat. As he dropped his sword to clutch at the great gash that partially-severed the front of his neck, his two comrades bravely stepped forward, still shouting their alarm.

"HERE! THE DRAGON IS HERE! TO ARMS!"

Ignoring this, Raz ducked a blow and swept the feet out from under one of the soldiers with a leg, half-flipping him as he slammed into the floor with a wheezing grunt. Using the impetus of the turn, Raz leapt and dealt a second kick to the other's shield, blasting him backward so hard he tripped and slid five feet on the smooth stone floor.

He fell on the downed men with about as much mercy as a wolf pouncing on injured prey, the gladius flashing twice more in his hand before they were still.

"Raz!" he heard Syrah shout as the others caught up to him. "On your left!"

Raz whirled. Sure enough, two sets of guards were charging him from down the side-hall the first patrol had appeared from, shouting their own warnings even as they ran at him. In all directions, Raz could hear other voices picking up the cry, as well as booted feet coming nearer.

Better make this quick, sis, he told the dviassegai silently, already taking two bounding steps at a diagonal up the hall.

Leaping as high as he could, he planted a foot in the perforated grating that made up the left wall, shoving himself into the air. He heard the men of the right group gasp in shocked surprise as he fell down on them, blades already slashing. One fell before he even hit the ground, skull split through his helmet by Ahna's falling blow. The other two had better luck, swinging their swords at him as he landed. One caught him a shallow blow in the shoulder, slicing his scaled skin, while the other *pinged* off the ocrea that encased his leg. Barely feeling the wound, Raz spun and met them. By the time they lay bleeding on the ground, Syrah had two of the other group lassoed in her fiery lash, her steel staff *thudding* into their temples in quick succession.

The last—unfortunate soul that he was—was screaming as Raz's men fell on him as a howling mob, weapons rising and falling until the man was silent.

"Aleem!" Raz shouted. "Esser! The Tash's court! Which way?"

The young Northerner was the first to respond, looking up from the gore to point left, up the bloodied hallway. "There!"

"On me!" Raz roared, taking off at once. Syrah was right on his heels, and the others disengaged themselves from the poor soldier's mangled form to follow close behind.

The Tash, it turned out, had made a fool's choice when he'd allowed his guard to be split between his home and the outer rings. They encountered several more groups, some coming six, nine, even twelve strong at a time, but Raz's blades, Syrah's magic, and the overwhelming numbers of Akelo, Karan, and the men behind them always felled whatever the palace could throw at them before they ever got too bogged down. Within ten minutes Raz lost count of how many dead and unconscious men they'd left behind, just as he'd lost track of the turns and corners and flights of stairs they had taken. Esser continued to lead the way, one eye bloodied up by a blow he'd weathered from a shield across his forehead. At his back, Raz sensed that the rest of their little army had not come out unscathed either, but he didn't have time to look back and take stock of the price their incursion was claiming on the brave former slaves charging behind him. He could hear Syrah's familiar breathing over his shoulder, the clack of Karan's clawed feet, and Akelo's near-continuous shouts of encouragement to the others. He took courage from that, turning to follow Esser down a short set of broad steps and left up a massive hall whose staggered walls reached at least fifty feet into the air. Here, they ran into another half-dozen soldiers, but a quick rune from Syrah sent half of them flying into the air to be lashed to the nearest wall. Of the other three, Raz took one, Akelo and his *kuja* downed another, and the last lurched back with a howl as one of Erom's daggers *thudded* through the left eye-slot of his helmet.

"Not far!" Esser shouted as soon as the encounter was over, running up the hall again without looking back, reaching up to wipe some of the blood from his face with the back of his sword hand. "It's just up the way!"

Raz believed him. He couldn't stop to study their surroundings, but he realized that the massive space curved as they ran, like it formed some sort of colossal ring. He imagined they had to be the circling the base of the center of the palace. He could *feel* the presence of power here, looming up and over him. It wasn't the sort of power he had known in Cyurgi 'Di, of course. It wasn't the warm, arcane hum of energy that vibrated, like a living thing, from within the depths of the mountain the Citadel had been built from. The essence here was cooler, harder. There was nothing magical about it, its force coming rather from the sharp majesty of the cavernous vaultings above, the still, white-and-gold draperies that hung across the space overhead depicting the crossed spears of Karesh Syl, and the light of the morning that filtered pale and lifeless through the opaque glass in a series of round clerestory windows crowning the outer wall.

Yes, he knew, they were certainly getting close.

"There!" Esser shouted not half-a-minute later, pointing ahead of them.

Raz saw the hall open up, then, a sudden outward press of the walls to form a sort of pseudo-room that the way spilled into before continuing out the other side. It was a wide, spacious area, the colored pattern of tiles in the floor lit by the dome of iron and glass high, high above. Seeing it, Raz hammered ahead, using Ahna's haft to pull Esser back behind him, knowing what to expect. When he reached the space, he charged in some fifteen feet before any of the others, fangs bared and weapons at the ready. He spun in a quick circle, searching for his first opponents.

That was when Raz felt the first flutter of worry tap against his heart.

There was nothing. Nobody. Only a pair of massive, gold-plated double doors set in the outer wall, silver inlaid in the shape of the Sun over the brighter metal. As Syrah, Karan, Akelo and the rest of the group caught up to him, Raz's crest flared nervously over his head. He could see, easily, where there should have been sentries, and there should *certainly* have been sentries. There were four pockets, little annexes in the walls, diagonal from each other across the hall. He could even smell the past presence of the men, make out the distinct hint of dyed leathers. There were usually guards here, he knew that, and hard as he might, Raz couldn't bring himself to believe that—*if* these were indeed the Tash's courts—the man would go so far as to willingly dismiss the soldiers of his personal retinue so flippantly.

Not right, the harsh voice of the animal hissed in the back of his mind, stirring at his sudden fear. *Not right. Something's not right.*

Before he could say anything, though, he made out the shouts and footsteps of the chasing palace guard, convening on them from either end of the hall.

"Shit," Raz hissed, head snapping in either direction, trying to decide.

"Raz?" Syrah demanded, gripping him by the arm and shaking him, like she thought something was wrong. "What are you doing? This is it! Come on!"

Raz looked down at her, wondering if he should voice his suspicions. He wasn't sure and, glancing over her head at the rest of his men, he saw the fear in their eyes, and the worry.

He saw also, now that he had a moment to take them in, that they numbered far less than the eighteen they'd been when they'd first left behind the eastern shores of the Dramion Sea.

"Raz!" It was Akelo's turn to shout, nocking an arrow to his bow and sighting down the east hall as the sounds of the approaching guards grew louder. "The court! Into the court!"

Even so, Raz hesitated.

"Raz, what's wrong?" Syrah asked, this time only for him to hear, seeing the concern in his eye.

Raz blinked and looked down at her. There wasn't so much as a hint of panic in the smooth features of the Priestess's face, only stoic determination. She had come this far with him. She was ready to see it through.

"Be ready," he told her simply, hoping she understood the warning.

And then Raz barreled forward, slamming an armored shoulder into the metal of the doors so hard they crashed open with a deafening *bang* that echoed in the cavern of the room beyond.

"Bar the entrance!" Raz bellowed at once as Syrah, Akelo, and the rest poured in around him, already turning to help heave the doors closed again. "Hurry!"

The others leapt to it with gusto, shouting and grunting as they threw their weight against the massive things. Foot by foot they swung shut again, and Raz caught the briefest glimpse of the palace soldiers pouring out of either side of the hall, shouting in panic as they saw the doors closing. Then, with a second *boom*, the metal and timber met, blocking the way.

"Seal it!" Akelo commanded as the soldiers outside started banging on the entrance, shoving their bodies against it in a desperate attempt to get inside. At his side, Odene was already taking his shield and kicking it into the wedge of the bottom jamb. The other Percian followed his lead, the rest of the men ripping spare blades from sheaths or iron plates from their armor to do the same. Soon, with several screeches of metal on stone, the doors were well and truly blocked.

The most pressing matter attended to, Raz and Syrah turned to face the chamber behind them.

The Tash's courtroom was a cool, somber place. Less austere than the grandiose halls of the palace proper, it nonetheless radiated the same assertive presence, the same heavy sense of power. Several dozen marble columns about five feet wide flanked a heavy carpet that led down the center of the chamber, their beveled caps reaching up to support the ribbed vaulting of the ceiling maybe a hundred feet above their heads. More banners hung from these marble pillars, still as death in the quiet of the space, their white-and-gold fabrics settling handsomely over the curving of the stone. The shadowed walls on either side of the massive room were plain, but somewhat rough-hewn, and appeared to be comprised of interlocking blocks as high and wide as Raz was tall. Accenting everything, along the apex of the ceiling, a wide strip of what looked to be heavy clear glass crested the entire chamber, bathing the right-side columns and floor in a solid ray of dusted, early-morning light. There was an age to the place that removed it from the rest of the palace, a still tranquility that made Raz feel, standing with Syrah at the top of a long set of plain marble stairs that rippled out from the court entrance, that *this* was the keystone, that *this* was where all things had begun in the horrid triumph that was the city of Karesh Syl.

And there at the end of the chamber, as though to reinforce the idea, the man that could only be the Tash himself waited, calm and regal in robes of white and violet, watching them with dark, impassive eyes from his raised throne.

LIII

The sovereign of Karesh Syl, it transpired, was a well-worn man who looked to have seen near twice as many summers as Raz and Syrah put together. He sat in the middle of a trio of high-backed stone seats set atop a large dais whose steps fanned outward, much like the stairs Raz and Syrah now stood atop. On his right, a younger, rather ugly man with an ample stomach barely hidden by his black-and-orange silks sat similarly composed, mirroring his master's calm. The man on the Tash's left, on the other hand, was obviously agitated, his posture rigid beneath his grey satins, his dark hands gripping the arms of his throne so firmly even despite their fair separation Raz could see his arms shaking. On either side of this pair, at the very edge of the top-most steps of the dais, two odd, large clay pots sat, somewhat out of place in the otherwise somber splendor of the marble room. Raz hardly gave these a thought, though, as his attention was rapidly stolen by the more pressing concern along the base of the steps.

There, like a living wall of steel, at least half-a-hundred soldiers stood three-men deep in a curved line along the bottom of the dais, shields raised and locked, swords out to curve overhead in the fashion of the Percian army.

Suddenly, Raz thought he knew where the guards outside the courtroom doors had vanished to.

"Clever," he muttered in annoyance.

Beside him, Syrah nodded. "They knew where we'd end up. I *thought* we should have had more trouble getting here…"

"Makes two of us," Raz answered, heaving Ahna up onto his shoulder.

"Three," Akelo corrected him, stepping up on Raz's other side to survey the scene below them now he was sure the others had control of the door. "Why send their best to be cut down one after the other, when they can just force us to face an army?"

"Why indeed?" Raz grumbled resignedly, eyeing the contingent of soldiers with a twinge of concern.

Managing to shove his worry aside, though, he spoke to Akelo without looking around. "No one gets in or out until our business is done here. Understood?"

Akelo's face was hard as stone. "Not a soul," he promised.

Then, with a single pat on the armor of Raz's arm for luck, the former slave hurried back to assist Karan and the rest of his surviving men.

Raz, in turn, glanced around at Syrah.

"Ready?" he asked her quietly.

All he got was a stiff nod, her one good eye fixed on the three thrones and the men who occupied them on the other side of the room.

Together, they started down the steps toward the court floor.

Raz left Syrah to watch their forward as they descended, his eyes scanning the room, looking for any sign of a trap. Unfortunately the columns hid much from view at any given time, and the air was so thick with a myriad of smells and tastes that he couldn't deduce anything through the sweat and stench of the army before them, the lingering perfume of the gentry that likely crowed these halls later in the day, and—oddly enough—the underlying scent of what might have been vinegar. Wrinkling his snout at this, Raz decided instead to study the soldiers before them, calculating the variables of their approach, wondering if perhaps he could goad or intimidate them into breaking rank, making the fight ahead that much easier. To his disappointment—if not his surprise—not a one among them moved as he and Syrah cleared the last step, walking quickly along the carpeted way between the columns. Behind them, the *clangs* and *bangs* of guards' swords and shields outside against the silver and gold gilding still echoed about the vastness of the chamber as they tried to get in.

Raz had just started to pray to the Sun that the doors would hold when, at the other end of the hall, the Tash was the first to break the quiet.

"Raz i'Syul Arro," he said by way of greeting, though his voice sounded equal parts displeased and strained as he struggled to push himself to his feet. "You have the great honor of being the first of your kind to ever set foot in the halls of my predecessors."

"An honor, is it?" Raz growled in sarcastic reply, glaring up at the old man. "I hope you'll forgive my lack of enthusiasm, Your Highness. I believe my friends and I may see this event far differently."

"Your *Greatness*," the nervous man in grey robes corrected him with a snap as Raz and Syrah reached the halfway point between the door and the dais. "And mind your tongue, beast. It is far below the honor of the Tash to speak to the likes of you, free or not."

"How kind of him." It was Syrah's turn to simper mockingly. "One can only *imagine* the burden such a difficulty must place on His Greatness' tired shoulders."

The Hand who'd spoken scowled at the woman, and looked about ready to retort when his master cut him off with an angry look.

"I hope you'll excuse Naizer," the Tash said, not taking his eyes off the man. "My Second has never known how to play this sort of game well, I'm afraid."

"No games today," Raz said coolly, fixing the Tash with a fiery look. "I imagine you're well aware of the reasons we are here."

"Yes, yes," the Tash said with an impatient wave of his hand. "There aren't too many outcomes one can deduce, given the circumstances." He frowned down at Raz. "That being said, if you truly think taking my head will be as simple a thing as it was to butcher the Mahsadén of Miropa, then you have sorely underestimated the influence of Karesh Syl, Monster."

Raz sneered, he and Syrah stopping when they were about fifteen feet from the line of guards, all of whom were watching the pair of them with equal parts determination and apprehension.

"I don't think you can fairly accuse *me* of underestimation, Your *Greatness*." He twisted the title snidely, making sure the man knew what he thought of it as he scanned the line of soldiers. "I admit, Syrah and I might break a sweat disposing of your men before dealing with you, but we'll manage."

It was a lie, of course. Raz had technically faced worse odds, it was true, and alone even. But on that occasion, he'd managed to limit his opponents to a single avenue of attack, had nearly burned alive in the escape, then almost broken his neck, *then* been shot in the side with a crossbow bolt.

It was not a situation he wanted to repeat.

Still, this time, Syrah stood at his side.

"Ah, yes…" the Tash said slowly, eyes turning to the Priestess, like he was reading Raz's mind. "The sorceress. Don't think I'd forgotten about you, Priestess Brahnt, White Witch of the North."

The name shivered over Raz and Syrah, and he heard her hiss under her breath in either shock or anger. At the same time, that feeling of disquiet returned once again, but he brushed it aside without issue this time. Syrah's name was known far and wide throughout the Northern realm, and the mountain clans of the Saragrias had been calling her 'the Witch' for years before that. It wasn't hard to believe whatever spies Karesh Syl likely had spread across the world had provided the Tash with such information when he'd gone looking for it.

"If you think me a witch, Your Greatness," Syrah seethed, her staff *thunking* against the stone beneath the carpet as she set its point against the ground, "then you can understand why it would seem common sense that only a fool would deliberately seek to goad me."

That got a rise out of the Tash and his Hands. The man on his left— Naizer, he had said, his Second—leapt to his feet with a shriek of outrage. On his right, the other—who must have been the First—lost his composure for a moment, stiffening at Syrah insult.

"Mind yourself, woman," he said evenly, his voice full of menace. "An offense against His Greatness will not be taken lightly here…"

The man settled back into his throne, though, as the Tash raised both hands to silence his Hands.

"A far as 'fools' go," the Tash hissed, his features calm but his eyes boring into Syrah with such vivid irritation Raz thought it might have been the first time in the old man's life *anyone* had seen fit to openly mock him, "I can think of none greater than you, at the moment. My Hands and I have already drawn first blood in this battle, and you don't even realize it. We've stripped you of what few advantages you once had, and you are yet unaware of it." He pointed a bent, crooked finger at the Priestess. "It is unwise to scorn the victor in a fight you don't even know you've lost."

This time, Raz couldn't ignore the feeling as it welled up inside him, his eyes flying over the courtroom around them, looking for the trick, seeking the trap. He cursed himself, peering into the shadows of the far walls, studying the Tash and his Hands, the odd clay pots, the soldiers before them, even the rug beneath their feet. They were too calm, too ready. There was something not right, in this place…

"Syrah," he warned the woman quietly. "Watch your back. They've got something up their sleeves."

Syrah, though, didn't seem to hear him.

"You arrogant shit," she snarled at the Tash, taking a step forward as magic flared unbidden about the hand not holding her staff, rippling and guttering to match her anger. "You insufferable, pathetic, bent little bastard. You hold yourself in such high esteem, hold yourself above all others in your twisted little world, and yet you don't care *in the least* that you only stand so tall because you have climbed atop a mountain of corpses and chained men and women who you've stripped of any ability to pull you down." The magic billowed, engulfing her fingers in a glove of seething fire. "You don't see that you would be *nothing*, not a speck of importance on the face of this world, had you not spent your life dining on the labors and sweat of those beneath you. You are vile. You are weak. You are—"

At that moment, though, the Tash appeared to run out of patience, his wizened face twisting into a mask of pale, pure rage. "*Weak?*" he snarled, interrupting Syrah. "You *dare?* Enough. Enough! It is time to put an end to this madness. You may have sparked rebellion in my city, but we will crush the dissenters as quickly as they stand. Then, when it is done—" he raised a threatening hand "—I will see to it that what shadows remain visit your home atop that mountain in the North, Priestess, as they intended to in the first place."

Shadows, the animal snarled in Raz mind, realizing all at once what he meant. *Shadows!*

But too late. The Tash snapped his fingers once, the sound ringing in an echo through the chambers, and at once a number of fearfully familiar figures, nearly ten in all, stepped out from where they'd been lurking behind the pillars on either side of them to surround Raz and Syrah. Their faces and bodies were swathed in loose, dark wraps, their grey eyes still and dead on the pair of them as their smoke-blackened blades, drawn in gloved hands, shone in the arcane fire dancing about Syrah's fingers.

Shadows! the animal shrieked as the assassins made themselves known. *SHADOWS!*

Raz, though, wasn't looking at the men around them, didn't care that he and Syrah were suddenly trapped. His own eyes were yet fixed on the top of the dais, held fast by the figure who'd stepped out from behind the Tash's own throne. Bedecked in his familiar black leathers, the Percian gazed down at Raz like he was some pest he intended to rid himself of, his white teeth cutting a leer across his dark face, one hand grasped casually about the black leather hilt of the curved saber at his side. He hadn't changed in the year since they'd last met, facing off as Raz dragged Quin Tern through the carnage of the Arena.

Unbidden, the roar built in Raz's throat. Like a memory transposed on the scene around him, he saw a black-haired little girl staring at him with wide, horrified green eyes. He saw the curved steel blade that had been pressed to her throat, met the uncaring gaze of the man who'd held it. Like a ripple from the past, Lueski Koyt's last words reverberated in his ears.

I'll miss you.

"KOROOOOO!"

Raz's howling scream was so sown with rage, it sent a ripple of terror over the faces of the Tash's soldiers like a shockwave. Before he could stop himself, Raz was already moving, charging the short distance left between him and the wall of shields and blades, the animal rising to consume all sense of anything else.

"Raz! Wait!"

Syrah's cry ripped him back into the world, color returning to the scene as he realized his vision had begun to fade into shades of red and black. He stumbled to a halt, talons tearing at the carpet, to stand mere feet away from the soldiers' swords, so close they might have braved striking out at him had they not all recoiled in fear at his sudden rush. Pulled back to his senses, his heart hammering with unbridled hate as he continued to stare up at the figure above, Raz took a single, slow step back, fighting to gain control of himself.

For his part, Azzeki Koro, former Captain-Commander of Azbar's brutal city guard, managed a twisted sneer, like he was disappointed Raz hadn't hurtled head-first into the waiting blades of the sentries.

"I wish I could say it was a pleasure to see you again, Monster," the man said, stepping by the Tash and descending the first few steps toward the courtroom floor as he spoke. "I admit, when I heard you would likely be visiting our great city, I was less than thrilled."

"I'll take that as a compliment," Raz said through grinding teeth, watching the man continue to approach. "I don't know why I'm surprised to find you here, Koro. Of all places, you fit best in a nest of vipers and filth."

Koro shrugged off the insult, stopping three or four steps from the floor so that he still stood well over Raz, twenty feet away. His eyes swept across the scene, taking in Syrah and the assassins she'd spun about to face. "My last employer met an unfortunate end, as you well know. Azbar was not so inclined to maintain its... uh... *hospitality* after Alyssa Rhen took control of the council."

"Quin Tern died a less miserable death than he deserved." Raz spat the man's name out like it was a foul piece of meat. "If Rhen had been sensible, she would have ensured the same fate for you."

"Oh, she might have," Koro said with a smug little nod, drawing his saber slowly from his side. "I was gone long before she could have me snatched up. It was a long journey south, I can tell you. Still, there are some benefits." He swept the sword at the nine men that surrounded them on three sides. "You have more enemies on this end of the world than I thought possible, Monster. The Mahsadën alone are so desperate to have your head, *they* paid *us* just for the right to have these fine gentlemen wait on you to come for His Greatness' life…" He smirked in hard amusement. "You can't imagine what help they've been, planning for this day."

A knot formed in Raz's throat, and he couldn't help but glance briefly around at the Southerners, still and silent while they waited for the signal to lunge. He took another step backward, then another, until he felt Syrah's back against his.

"They knew we'd be coming," he muttered under his breath to the woman, watching as Koro followed his retreat, taking the last few steps to the courtroom floor, where the soldiers split momentarily to let him through. "They knew. Syrah… I'm so sorry."

He felt her press herself against him momentarily.

"All your old enemies in one place," she said with a half-hearted laugh. "We should take this as a compliment, I think."

Raz took a deep breath, drawing comfort from her cheer, as forced as it was.

"Just wait," he muttered jokingly as Koro stopped half-a-dozen feet away, blade held by his side. "Any moment now the corpse of Gûlraht Baoill will come rushing in."

He didn't see it, but he knew the jest had made her smile.

"So…" Raz addressed Koro now. "Only the ten of you?" He scanned the assassins, double-checking his count. "I didn't think you were that much of a fool, Koro."

The Percian smiled, tapping the blade of his saber against his thigh like he was considering Raz's words.

"That depends on many things, doesn't it, Monster?" he asked pensively, like they were carrying on a pleasant philosophical discussion. "I'm not mad enough to think I can beat you single-handedly, don't worry, but I've always thought we'd make for a good match overall. Perhaps you'll be surprised by what ten can do, given a little help."

A little help? Raz repeated to himself worriedly.

Before he could form a question to try and figure out what the man meant, though, a voice called down from above.

"Koro!" the Tash cut in impatiently. "Enough of your banter. I want this finished. *Now!*"

Koro, to Raz's amazement, turned completely away from him, bowing low to his sovereign as he replied with an "Of course, Your Greatness." In that brief instant, Raz thought to lunge forward, to strike the Percian down when his back was turned. He hesitated only for a moment, fearing that the deliberate disinterest in keeping his enemies in view was another one of Koro's ploys.

Instantly, though, Raz regretted his uncertainty, because a second later his reflexes were all that kept him from being skewered through the belly by the man's curved blade.

369

LIV

Azzeki Koro struck with such blinding speed, it took Raz's breath away. He had never seen a human move so fast. Not Ergoin Sass, not Gûlraht Baoill, not even the shades of the Southern assassins now converging on them in the wake of Koro's attack. The Percian was a black streak from where he'd been standing five feet away, his blade nothing more than a flicker. Unable to get his gladius up in time to deflect the blow, Raz jerked back, shoving Syrah with him so that he heard her yelp and almost fall, and even then he felt the ripping burn of the steel catch him a glancing blow across his midriff. In the next second Koro retreated and attacked again, and this time Raz managed to deflect the slash, though only barely. They exchanged a flurry of rapid sword blows, Ahna too heavy and cumbersome in his dominant hand to be of use. As Koro nicked him again, this time across the forearm, Raz made a hard choice.

Dropping the dviassegai, he drew the sagaris from his belt and put the axe to rapid work.

As they fought—Raz occasionally having to block and deflect a blow from the side as the assassins got around Syrah behind him—he was reminded of a realization he'd made almost a year ago now, the first time he had met Azzeki Koro. He remembered the bitter cold of the night, kept at bay by the blazing trough of burning wood the Azbar council had been sitting around. He remembered noting the figure clad all in black at the back of the Chairman's box, looking out over the Arena. He remembered thinking little of the man as Quin Tern had introduced him.

And he remembered reevaluating that judgment when Koro had drawn his blade at the first opportunity, even then nothing more than a subtle shift of darkness and steel in the light of the fire.

Now, Raz saw he had been correct to think the man was more than a common sellsword.

Their blades moved in patterned unison, Koro dislodging and reengaging his saber as quickly as Raz could pull it away from the fight with his axe or parry it with the gladius. Raz could tell that he might have had the upper hand on even footing, but the Southerners kept pressing him from either side, and he couldn't move without leaving Syrah's back exposed. Koro, on the other hand, seemed able to work his sword like the blade was an extension of his own arm, and he took full advantage of his mobility, dodging back and forth and sideways as he struck, sometimes even ducking away to rest a moment as Raz was forced to engage with the Mahsadën's men.

All the while, Raz could hear the ringing of steel behind him and the *whoosh* and *crack* of magic as Syrah took on the rest of the group.

Soon, the world around them was ablaze. White flames snapped over the columns and floor, catching in the fabric of the rug beneath their feet and the banners fluttering overhead in the heat of the spellwork. The room brightened and dimmed all at once, the space around the fight illuminated as

Syrah's magic spread while the shadows along the walls beyond the pillars deepened and twisted. Raz heard the awed gasps of the soldiers—and likely the Tash and his Hands—as he and Koro traded blows once more, and he imagined what the scene must have looked like. He and Syrah, back to back in the center of a broiling battlefield, fending off the dark shapes that were Koro and the Southerners. At one point he heard the shouts of Akelo and the others as well, along with the sound of approaching boots, and he roared for them to get back, to guard the door with their lives.

He couldn't make out the group through the smoke and fire, but knew they had followed his orders when no one interfered with the fight.

Steel rang against steel as gladius and axe and staff met the curved blades of Koro and his men. Syrah's spells snapped and roared, and occasionally Raz would see flashes against the columns that rose up around him, or catch a glimpse of a fiery lash streaking across the field, keeping the assassins at bay. As they turned in a slow circle, Raz saw the Priestess had claimed the first of their victories, noting the unconscious form lying sprawled at the edge of the ring, blade fallen from his hands, the fires that snaked over his body eating at his dark swaths.

Raz himself drew next blood, snagging the hilt of one Southerner's sword in the crook of the sagaris and dragging it past him, driving the blade into the belly of another assassin on his other side even as the gladius whipped crosswise, cleaving the owner's head from his shoulders.

All at once, the ten had become seven.

If he expected Koro or the others to balk as their comrades fell, though, Raz was sorely disappointed. The Percian maintained his assault in a steady stream of blows, stepping away only when the others were in a position to engage, never giving Raz a moment of respite. Though the dark forms flickering in the firelight numbered less now, Raz knew he would tire eventually. It drove him to fight with a savagery that would have made most men pale and run, his sword and axe a violent stream of silvery steel moving about his body. The sagaris caught one assassin's sword at its base, shattering the thinner metal with a screech of breaking. He deflected a downward blow from Koro with a looping parry, transitioning the momentum in a crushing kick that caught the man in the chest, sending him flying four feet into the air and ten back. Two of the Southerners descended on Raz at once following this, refusing to grant him even a moment to breathe. His weapons screamed as they worked independently of each other, engaging a figure each, his tail snaking out in an attempt to sweep their legs out from under them. One leapt over the appendage, jumping back so that Raz couldn't take advantage of the forced movement. The other, though, was slower, his grey eyes too concentrated on managing the battering blows of the gladius. The tail caught him about the ankles, knocking him to the floor with a surprised "Oomph!"

Raz had just raised a foot, was just about to stomp down on the man's neck, when Syrah screamed.

Feeling her slide away from him, Raz whirled around, uncaring that he left his own back exposed to Koro and the others. The Priestess had fallen to her knees, clutching at her leg. A third unconscious form now lay next to her, hand outstretched and clutched around a reddened knife, and with a thrill of fear Raz saw the blood spilling from the long gash across Syrah's thigh, darkening her clothes and splattering the charred remnants of the carpet beneath her feet.

For a blink, the world stopped. Not even the flames around him seemed to move as the cold thundered upward, starting at his feet and rising like boiling water turned to ice. All around Raz, men stood frozen, some in mid-leap as they pounced, others crouched with blades held ready at their sides. He could smell the blood, smell the smoke as cloth and clothing burned, smell the odd lingering scent of vinegar mixed with the sweat and perfume that still clung to the air. All he saw, though, was the split flesh beneath Syrah's free hand, the meat of her leg showing through the fabric of her robes, reddening the white cotton and spilling through her pale fingers.

Then the abyss ripped open, Raz fell, and all was blackness and death as the animal took over with a screaming, chilling roar of rage.

"By the *Twins*," Naizer said, standing beside Ekene, eyes fixed in horrified fascination on the battle below as Raz i'Syul Arro's hair-raising bellow echoed even over the crackling of the fire. "What a *terror*!"

In reply, the Tash said nothing. He, too, had seen the change descend over the atherian as his woman fell, a sudden horrible stillness grabbing hold of him for the briefest instant.

Then the Monster was moving again, and this time when he killed it was with a feral savagery beyond anything Ekene had ever seen even in the wilds of the savannah.

In less than ten seconds, of the five assassins who'd still been left standing, three remained. Arro cut into them like a butcher carving through meat, utterly uncaring of the wounds he took in the process. Koro had regained his feet and was dancing around the creature once more, an impressive sight on his own, snaking between the Southerners in a clear attempt to get to the Priestess, still kneeling with one hand pressed to her mangled leg. Arro, though, was having none of it, and more than once the Third only barely managed to retreat with his life, often a little bloodier than he'd been before the attempt.

Still... Ekene thought to himself, watching the Dragon's axe cave in yet another man's skull, splattering blood and bone and brain matter across the pillars along the left side of the hall. *We expected this.*

"Be ready," he told his Hands. "It will be soon."

At his word, Yseri pushed himself up from his throne on the Tash's other side. Together, the two men hurried over to the great clay pots waiting atop the steps.

They didn't have to wait long. As Koro managed to strike a blow, slashing Arro across the arm, they watched him retreat several steps, allowing the last pair of the Mahsadën's blades—Na'zeem and one of his lieutenants—to engage the Monster. As he did, Koro raised his curved blade straight into the air, the red stain of blood dancing in the firelight as it trickled down the steel.

"NOW!" Ekene shouted.

At once, Yseri and Naizer put a foot each against the body of their pots, shoving them with every ounce of force they could muster. With a grinding screech against the marble of the dais, the great clay things tilted and toppled over, each bouncing once, then twice, then smashing into a dozen pieces to spill their vile contents out over the clean white of the steps.

CRASH!

The mirrored sounds of shattering clay didn't register with Raz for several seconds as he fought, his gladius and sagaris winding a lightning-like pattern about his body as he circled Syrah protectively. Through the fog of battle, he noted the Priestess's head jerk up in alarm at the noise, tears of pain and anger streaking down her left cheek. Raz never saw the stillness that overcame her, then, the horrified twist of her face, but he did hear her choking, wrenching gasp. Alone, even that wasn't enough to pull his attention away from the fight at hand, his mind consumed by black need to kill the three men still ringing them.

Then, though, the overpowering stench of vinegar and flesh crashed over him, pungent even through the flames, peeling away just enough at the animal's control to drag his attention toward the dais.

What he saw there, sprawled across the ivory marble of the tapering stairs, dragged him out of the bloody world so viciously it very nearly cost him his life.

The two bodies were bloated and warped, their skin pallid, like drowned corpses. One was a man's, large and balding, the other was a woman's, dreaded hair tangled and lank, one side of her head shaved. They were both naked, their arms and legs and torsos covered in horrid bruises, like they'd been beaten within an inch of their lives before death. The woman had it far worse, though, and Raz felt his own heart constrict as he took in an all-too familiar pattern of marks around her wrists and legs, the pointed discolorations of rough hands about her breasts and neck.

He knew all too well what such bruises meant.

Despite this, though, it wasn't the injuries that brought Raz to his knees. It wasn't the vulnerability of their nakedness or the swollen condition of the corpses that ripped him from the fight, causing him to lose all sight of the blades lancing for him even as his own weapons faltered.

Rather, it was their faces that ceded Raz's life to the steel of Koro and the assassins. It was the twisted condition of their features, the violent panic frozen eternally there. The man's wide eyes were milky in death, set against the faintest trace of the war paint that had streaked across his brow and mouth. The woman's teeth were bared, lips pulled back in a grimace of horror that combined with her scarred nose to give her face a cadaverous, skull-like impression.

Raz knew what the eternal fear of their features meant. He knew the man and woman had been beaten and tortured to the edge of death, knew the latter had been subjected to other horrors at the hands of her male captors. He knew that then, as their bodies were on the brink of being unable to suffer any more, they had been hauled from whatever squalor they'd been imprisoned in, dragged to the two pots Raz realized suddenly he'd seen before.

They'd kept him and Syrah company, waiting for the pirates to find them, hidden away in the smuggling hatch of the *Sylgid*.

As Koro shouted in victory, seizing on the distraction to leap up and bring his blade arcing around for a final blow, Raz knew that Garht Argoan and Lysa had been drowned in the putrid vinegar of their own trafficked goods.

That was when he heard Syrah gasp in wretched despair, and the magic came alive around him.

LV

Raz's ears popped as the pressure in the room suddenly dropped. There was a deep *whooshing*, like air being funneled through a tunnel, then utter, abrupt quiet that drowned out all sound.

Then, just as his stunned mind understood that Azzeki Koro's blade was inches from taking him between the eyes, a concussive blast shook the very foundations of the room.

BOOM!

The discharge tore over him, hurtling Raz, Koro, and the two remaining assassins head over heels as effortlessly as dead leaves blown about in a fall storm. In the confused tumble and heavy landing some dozen feet away, Raz didn't have a prayer of holding onto his weapons, hearing the sword and axe clatter away across the marble floor behind him. Off to the side, he heard the *thuds* of two bodies landing nearby, as well as a sickening *crunch* of someone striking one of the columns and sliding heavily to the ground. He barely registered any of this, though, and was just clambering to get up when an intense shock of heat crashed over him, tingling across his skin in a solid wave, like the Sun had fallen to earth at their very feet.

Finally managing to stand, Raz stared—along with every other person in the room—at the base of the steps.

Syrah had pulled herself up, leaning on her staff as she limped her way slowly, silently toward the dais, ignoring the blood that seeped like a sash down her right leg. It was from her that the power was rippling forth, a palpable, undulating aura that was hard to look at despite not producing any actual light. The air shimmered about her form, the magic closest to her scorched and churning. About her feet, the carpet burst into white flames with every step she took, approaching the column of soldiers with such utter disinterest she might not have even known they were there.

Which is possible, Raz thought in a panic when he saw that her gaze, cold and still and dead, was fixed on the body of Lysa, sprawled and naked across the right side of the steps.

"Syrah!" Raz roared, started to rush forward only to be rebuffed by the searing heat as she neared the bristling wall of shields and blades. "Syrah! Wait!"

But it was no good. Raz couldn't get within five feet of her before the magic was too much for even *his* hide to bear, and his voice was muffled and dull, like the air around her had thickened and congealed. He could only watch with dread as Syrah took the last few steps toward the soldiers, who were yelling, warning her not to approach any further, their threats shrill with fear.

When their leathers and the wood of their shields started to blister and smoke, though, the center of the group began hollering in pain and alarm as they fell into disarray, splitting to let the Priestess through.

"NO!" the Tash howled from the top of the dais, shrinking back into his throne while his Hands did the same on either side of him. "NO! STOP HER! STOP HER!"

Syrah, though, took about as much notice of the old man as she had the soldiers. She ascended the steps slowly, one after the other, never looking away from the first mate's corpse, like nothing else in the world mattered in that moment. When she reached it, she slipped to her knees, as though unable to keep bearing some great weight that pulled her down, laying her staff gently across the stairs beside her.

Then, with such tender, gentle care it made Raz's heart break to watch, she gathered Lysa's beaten form into her arms, head bowed over the woman's bare bruised chest, white hair spilling over her bloated skin. The Priestess shook with unsuppressed grief, and through the continued screaming of the Tash and the shout of the rallying soldiers, Raz thought he could hear broken, gasping sobs. He watched, frozen and unable to move, as Syrah's pale fingers reached out to trace the black and blue marks where fingers had dug into the first mate's flesh as she'd been held down against her will. Raz could see Syrah reading the patterns like the lines on a page, recreating the story of the horrors in her mind.

It was as he realized this, as he watched Syrah's hand shake and shiver over Lysa's corpse, that all the warmth in the room suddenly vanished.

For one horrifying instant, Raz thought the truth the Priestess saw painted across her friend's bruised body had broken her, had dragged her mind away to a place even the magics couldn't follow. He'd almost started moving, almost started making a mad dash for the woman even as the rest of the room realized the spellwork appeared to have faded, when it came to Raz that the temperature still seemed to be dropping. Indeed, his rush faltered when he started to see his own *breath* in the air before him, the humidity frosting like the courtroom had suddenly been plunged into the depth of a Northern freeze.

With a thrill of terror, he realized that Syrah seemed to be gathering the heat of the early summer morning, her shivering form drawing the energy from the space around her so voraciously, even the Sunlight appeared to warp and bend in her direction.

"SYRAH!" he roared even as his talons carved divots into the marble beneath his feet, screeching him to a halt. "SYRAH! NO! WAIT! YOU CAN'T—!"

His words, though, were drowned by an even more urgent voice.

"THE SPELL FAILS!" the Tash howled from where he had pressed himself as far back in his throne as possible. "NOW, FOOLS! KILL HER NOW!"

The soldiers responded to their master's call without a moment's hesitation. The threat of the heat apparently gone, the men cared little for the growing cold as they roared in unison and charged Syrah, still kneeling with Lysa in her lap, collapsing on her from either side of the stairs. Raz caught a glimpse of triumph gleaming in the eyes of the Tash and his Hands, and he wanted to curse them, to scream at them for their rashness. He wanted to shout to Syrah again, wanted to howl for her, to bring her back from the dark place her mind had receded to. He understood, though, that the Priestess was too far gone to be reached with mere words.

He understood it just as surely as he understood the single, screaming urge every fiber of his being was telling his body to follow as the air began to crackle ominously around the kneeling woman.

RUN.

Raz whirled away from the scene just as the soldiers closed the last dozen feet between them and Syrah, his powerful legs hurtling him away with desperation and madness as he felt the air shimmer around him again. He'd just reached the closest pillar when all the noise vanished from the room once more, like a spell had been cast to swallow all sound for the briefest of moments as calamity gathered itself. He bolted between the two Southern assassins, still struggling to get to their feet, when the pressure in the chamber bottomed out again.

Raz just made it behind the column, just plastered himself against the rounded stone, when he heard Syrah scream, a single shrill note of keen, grief-stricken anguish.

And then the world was fire.

LVI

BOOOOM!

The deafening sound of the eruption struck Raz like a hammer in the back of the head, setting his ears to ringing as the force of it swept over him even through the marble colonnade. It staggered him, blasting him with such an impact that he nearly stumbled out from his place of shelter. In the next moment, the air itself blistered and rippled, seething and warping before his very eyes, and with an earth-shaking *crash* the ivory fire reached him. It billowed around the edges of his pillar, churning like a tornado of flame, washing over the ground around his feet and the ceiling above to engulf the wall he was facing in a lake of flickering white tongues. Raz roared in fear and pain, sliding down the stone to ball himself up, throwing his arms protectively over his head and tucking his wings so tight to his back they hurt. His armor was superheating, searing his scaled skin. The atmosphere was boiling, making it impossible to breathe. He couldn't see, his entire world consisting of nothing but fire and heat and a raging, fathomless power at its center, feeding it all. Nearby, the only thing to penetrate the cacophony of the inferno were the agonized screams of the assassins, who'd been standing in the open not ten feet away when the magics broke free.

Then, just as Raz began to pray to the Moon that he would be allowed to see all those he had loved and lost when She came to claim him too, the fires were ripped away again.

As swiftly as they'd come, the flames receded with a *whoosh* like a tide being dragged violently back to its source. Through the ringing in his head, Raz heard silence take hold of the room once more, but it was a different sort of quiet than the magically-induced one which had preceded the spell-wrought explosions. This time, the stillness was true, as though everything that mattered in the world had been dragged to a halt, everything that stirred ended and silenced.

Raz heaved in a shuddering gasp, hacking and coughing and twisting to fall onto all fours as he inhaled breath after breath of cool air. It tasted like soot and smoke and iron. Eventually, through the thrum of the stillness, the ringing began to fade until Raz's ears had adjusted enough to hear the shuddering *thuds* of what sounded like a battering ram against the outside of the courtroom doors. Next came Akelo and the others shouting to one another, calling back and forth from the other side of the room. "What in the *Sun's name* was that?" one voice demanded, though more were yelling "They're getting through! Hold them! *Hold them!*"

Then, though, Raz made out one last sound.

The broken, wretched gulping of grieving, sorrowful sobs.

Putting a hand on the column for support, Raz finally managed to haul himself to his feet, still retching as his lungs struggled to compensate for the boiling suffocation they'd momentarily been victim to. When he finally managed to steady himself, he took several shaky steps around the pillar, his body feeling weak and cold after the onslaught of the fire.

As the expanse of the courtroom came into view again, what he saw nearly brought Raz right back down to his knees.

For a hundred feet around the steps leading up to the trio of thrones, the once-polished floor was blackened and charred. The only clean marble remaining jutted out in lines from behind the columns where the fire hadn't managed to reach, white against the dark soot, like inverse shadows. The red rug that not a minute before had regally led up to the base of the dais was nothing but an ash stain for half its length, starting again in the center of the room in a twisted, smoldering tatter of crimson threads before continuing cleanly back toward Akelo and the others like nothing was amiss. Similarly, above his head Raz saw the banners that had once hung handsome and proud from the ceiling were shredded and burned, pale flames still clinging here and there to what little white-and-gold fabric remained. The glass crest along the ceiling had half-shattered, shards still breaking off to *clink* or fracture against the floor. Overall, it was a terrifying sight, like witnessing the aftermath of a meteor which had come hurtling through the roof above to crash into the dais steps, reigning devastation in its wake.

And there, at the very center of the chaos, in the blackened ring of splintering marble that was all that remained of the steps where she'd fallen, Syrah still knelt, her pained wails tearing at the air.

It was as he found her that Raz saw, then, the truest horrors of the scene, and he gave a trembling, hissing exhalation of mortified shock.

Of the Tash's soldiers who'd so foolishly charged her, not a one looked to have survived the wildness of the magic. All that remained of those who'd been closest to the Priestess when the power had broken loose were faint traces of shadow in the charring and soot of the stone, like some pitiful barrier had stood in the way of the rage of the fire storm. Further away, smoldering husks of what might once have been men lay scattered across the steps, limbs twisted and scorched, armor and shields almost wholly burned away to leave nothing but the smoke-darkened steel of blades to glimmer here and there throughout the carnage. To his left, Raz didn't have the courage to look around at the two forms nearest to him, the bodies of the Mahsadën's men who'd been caught in the blast. His ears told him that they, too, were dead, but his nose spoke of little more than raw flesh and smoking bone, and he didn't know if he had the stomach for it in the moment.

Instead, with an uncertain breath, Raz began picking his way across the floor, making for Syrah.

His clawed feet slipped as he reached the steps, their surfaces made only smoother by the thin layer of ash settling over the scene. He climbed carefully, his heart breaking a little more each time Syrah wailed and cried, clutching at herself as she knelt in her small crater of broken stone. He saw, as he neared her, that there was nothing left for the Priestess to hold, now. Lysa's body was dust, nothing more than soot that stained the front and arms of the Priestess' robes, discoloring the usual white into a mess of grey and black. With a pang of grief, Raz glanced over to see that Argoan's form, too, was gone, blasted into nothingness by the hellish force Syrah had let loose.

When he reached her, standing over her shoulder, Raz couldn't help but hesitate, acutely aware that some small part of his mind suddenly feared the sobbing woman before him.

Then he dropped to his knees, took Syrah in his arms, and pulled her back into him as she continued to sob in horror and grief.

They stayed like that for longer than they should have, Syrah howling out her misery, shaking violently in Raz's embrace. She didn't fight him, didn't even flinch as he touched her, but he felt as though she only slowly became aware of his presence, moment by moment returning to the plane on which he was there, holding her close. Slowly, after nearly a full minute, Syrah's body began to still, her weeping subduing little by little. Eventually she reached up, grabbing hold of his arms so tightly, it was like she needed something to hold onto.

"No..." the Priestess whispered with anguished desperation between every breath she took. "No... Laor, please... No..."

Finally, after another minute, she stilled completely, lifted her head to look at the shattered glass of the ceiling above, and spoke.

"Raz," she said in a pleading, broken voice. "Raz... What have I done? What have I done?"

He knew there was nothing he could tell her, in that moment. He had all the answers he would have given himself, all the words that would have allowed him to cope with the ruin that surrounded them. She had been defending herself. She had been protecting him. She had been fighting for the freedom of thousands.

None of it would help, though. Raz knew that. Something had broken, some intangible connection between Syrah and the world, one that he couldn't really see but understood as wholly as he understood the woman herself.

Syrah Brahnt, Priestess of Laor, had become a killer. She had broken the cardinal rule of her faith, and done so with such brutality that even Raz had trouble looking around at the corpses that lay, burned to hollow nothingness, around them.

In the end, all he was capable of was holding her tight, doing all he could to let her know without words that he was there, that he shared her pain, and that he would do so until the world itself fell apart around them.

Then a sound reached him, and Raz stiffened, ears twitching as he listened.

After a second, he heard it again.

"Syrah, stay here," he told her quickly, briefly touching his snout to the back of her head.

Then, as she let him pull his arms away, Raz stood and navigated the shattered steps once more, making for the top of the dais.

The sounds came louder as he climbed, and by the time he reached the platform upon which the three thrones stood, Raz had identified its source. In the right and left seats, the bodies of the Hands of Karesh Syl were slumped where they'd been sitting, twisted with their arms over their heads and faces, like they'd hoped the paltry defense of their own flesh would be enough to save them from the magics. Raz gave them a cursory once-over, grimly satisfied that the corpses seemed mostly recognizable in the curled remains of their silks and satins.

Then, with cold, pitiless harshness, his eyes settled on the last form.

The Tash, by some cruel miracle of the Sun, had survived the eruption. He looked—like Raz—to have understood the warning signs of the impending cataclysm, but—*unlike* Raz—hadn't been able to get out of the way in time, his frail body betraying him. Instead, the Tash seemed only to have managed to throw himself to the floor before his throne, perhaps praying that the angle of the steps would protect him.

Unfortunately for him, he'd been only half-right.

Of the old man's white-and-violet robes, little was left, the silks nothing more than discolored scraps that clung in frayed tatters about his ruined body. Much of his mottled skin had been seared away, revealing the charred flesh of muscle along his torso and thighs. Raz wrinkled his snout at the unpleasant smell, watching without so much as a twinge of sympathy as the Tash's raw, blistered chest twitched and heaved while he tried desperately to breathe. More than one of his ribs were visible, as were the bones in his arms and hands, which he too seemed to have brought up to protect his face. There was nothing left that would give the man the right to call himself a "man" anymore, and his dark eyes were wide in fear and agony, fixed on Raz as he shook violently, obviously rapidly falling into shock.

For a long moment, Raz met his gaze impassively, tilting his head to the side to study the Tash with detached disappointment.

"Not half the death you deserved," he muttered, grinding his teeth in annoyance.

That, though, gave him an idea.

"Akelo!" Raz roared, whirling and hurrying back down the stairs, sliding into the shallow crater to stand over Syrah. "On me! Away from the doors! Let them in!"

"*What?*" the old Percian demanded from the far end of the courtroom, his voice echoing between the *crashes* of the battering ram. "But—!"

"*Let them in!*" Raz boomed again, no longer paying attention as he knelt down to take Syrah under the arm, whispering to her softly. "Syrah, I'm sorry. I need you on your feet. Please. We still have to get out of here."

It took a little coaxing, but he got the woman up, helping her to favor her good leg. The moment she stood, Syrah looked around blearily, taking in the blackened corpses scattered about her, and promptly fell on all fours again.

When she was done vomiting, Raz helped her to stand again, guiding her as quickly as he could to the top of the stairs.

By this time, Akelo and the others were joining them, winded from their mad sprint across the chamber. Raz saw once again with a welling sadness that their numbers were not what they were. Aside from Akelo and Karan, of the seventeen he had led into the palace, no more than a dozen looked to have survived the ordeal. He noted, as the men gathered about on the stairs below he and Syrah—every single one of them staring about in horrified fascination at the devastation around them—that Akelo's *kuja* now seemed to number only two, most of the newer recruits were nowhere to be found, and Hur was the only Northerner left among the little army they had been.

Offering up a brief prayer to the Moon that She would see them safely into Her Stars, Raz ordered all to settle in and wait.

It took less than two minutes, without the added mass of the men against the timber, for the gilded doors of the court to give in to the hammering of the ram. After a score more reverberating *booms*, the distant opening cracking a little wider each time, the right door shuddered and split off its bottom hinge, swinging wide. At once, a veritable swarm of soldiers in the white-and-gold armor of the city began vaulting over the splintered wood, pouring into the chamber and flooding down the stairs with a mountainous roar of a hundred voices. Raz's hands tingled with anxious anticipation as they descended in an endless wash to the chamber floor, charging with the courageous desperation of those whose only purpose was to protect the life of a single man. He worried for a brief moment that there would be no stopping the assault, worried that panic and fear for the life of their sovereign would wipe away any sense of danger the soldiers might have.

But, as the first line of men reached the half-way point of the courtroom, they faltered and slowed, their blades and raised shields freezing in shock as they came to a halt at the very edge of the blackened marble left by Syrah's loss of control.

"Steady," Raz said so that only his men could hear as several of them shifted nervously, weapons clenched in tight fists. "No sudden moves."

He waited, then, until the whole of the guard had quit its rush, five score men gaping in open, paralyzed shock at the scene. He gave them a few seconds more, allowing their eyes to sweep over the still-smoking corpses of their former comrades.

Then he spoke sidelong to the woman at his side.

"Syrah," Raz said in as kind a voice as he could manage, "I need you with me. I'll need your help. Can you stand? Can you do it?"

For a second, he worried that the Priestess was going to refuse to answer, or even shake her head. She was still shivering, even as she stood by him, and between the gash in her thigh and the circumstances of their surroundings, he wondered if he wasn't asking too much of her

Then, with a flush of relief, he saw her give a small, almost imperceptible nod.

He squeezed her hand once, and started his descent down the steps, wings extending as he did.

"Your Tash is gone, friends," he spoke to the silence calmly, trusting in the echoes of the room to carry his voice over the packed mob of Percian soldiers. "He and his Hands are no more, along with half-a-hundred of your own number."

In reply, there was a resounding wail of grief and disbelief. Many voices picked up at once, some shouting prayers to the Twins, others hurling denial and slurs his way. In response, Raz swept both hands out at the ruin that surrounded them as he neared the bottom of the steps.

"Look around you. Who is it that you think has fallen? There is no trickery here. You are simply too late. Your city is done for, and there is no reason left for us to fight."

"Liar!" several calls rose shrilly from the ranks of the soldiers, unanimously desperate. "The lizard lies!"

"It is no lie!" Raz snarled in response, and at once the voices died. Reaching the floor once more, he kept walking toward the palace guard, ignoring the nervous inhalations of his own men at his back. "Look upon the seats of your power! Are those the corpses of *my* men, do you think, smoking in the thrones of your Hands? Do you now see what punishment the Dragon brings to your kind? You number many, yes, but so did the fifty men who stood in this room before you, as well as the assassins your sovereign kept hidden up his sleeve."

To make his point, Raz paused to kick a blackened sword over to the front line of the soldiers as he passed it. The dusty blade still gleamed, clattering over the rubble and shattered glass, an edge of curved steel that was very obviously *not* a blade of the Percian army.

"All of that, in addition to the added cruelties your Tash had in store, and where is he?" Raz twisted to point back up the stairs behind him, though he never took his eyes off the soldiers. "Do you see him standing there? Do you hear him screaming for my death? No. You don't." His eyes scanned their ranks. "Would anyone else like to call me a liar, then?"

Unsurprisingly, not a single denial rose.

"I thought not," Raz growled dangerously, coming to a stop right where he wanted, some twenty feet from the base of the steps. "The Tash *is* no more. Believe this. He has fallen, along with any who might take his place. This leaves you with a choice." He stood tall, arms by his sides in loose fists, hoping he cut an impressive figure against the ravaged court. "You can drop your weapons. You can leave this place now. There is nothing left for you to protect here. Do this, and you may yet have a chance to flee Karesh Syl with your families before I raze it and all its vileness to the ground."

He paused, then, meeting as many eyes as he could. With a spark of hope, he saw more than a few faces paling as they absorbed the threat.

"That is your first recourse," Raz continued finally, "and the wisest choice. Your second should be reserved for the mad or foolish among you."

As he spoke, he hooked a foot under the weapon on the ground beside him, half-hidden in the soot where he had left her. "Stay. Stay, and face us. Stay—" he kicked up, and the weapon dragged itself out of the dust and ash, leaping up into his waiting grasp "—and die for a man who is no more."

With a twist, Ahna shrieked and spun in his hands, her dirty blades coming to rest pointing directly at the soldiers as Raz crouched at the ready before them. In the same instant, the faces of the nearest men twisted in fear, and more than one soldier tried to take a step back, colliding with their comrades behind them.

Then, though, Raz saw that hardly any of their dark faces were turned toward him anymore. Instead, they were angled upward, over his shoulder, eyes wide as more prayers to the Sun and Moon were uttered. For a brief moment, Raz was confused, not understanding what had happened. Then, though, he felt the warmth on his back, and noticed the sheen of light against the flats of the soldiers' blades and the pointed steel of their helmets.

Unable to help himself, Raz looked around to see what it was that had so effectively enraptured the palace guard.

Syrah stood at the top of the dais, robes and hair billowing about in the heat of her spells, her one good eye glaring down at the soldiers like some goddess of fire and magic. Along the steps on either side of her, Akelo, Karan, and the others were hurrying away from her, hands up to shield their faces from the light and heat exuding from her form. Raz couldn't blame them. He had expected the Priestess would pick up on the cue, of course, but what he'd hoped for paled in comparison to how fiercely she had risen to the occasion. He'd expected her to summon the spellwork about her hands, or perhaps the lassos he had so often seen.

Instead, though, Syrah had *become* flames.

She stood in a blazing inferno that completely enveloped her body, like the bulb of a flower made of fire, its petals writhing and twisting around her as they shimmered and mirrored the color of the blood that still trailed down her leg like a sash. She was hard to look at, especially for Raz, who had to half-turn his head away in order not to be blinded. The heat she exuded, even from where he stood, was incredible, and he was glad to have moved so far away.

Then Syrah spoke.

"The Dragon has offered you a choice," she said in a hard, cold voice behind which Raz could hear the strain of effort and grief. "He is generous in this." She scanned the ranks of men, then took a single, deliberate step down toward the floor. "*I* am less so. Leave, now, or the White Witch will find reason to leave you as nothing more than charred bones and dust for the winds."

LVII

It didn't take long, after that, for the last of the palace guard to flee. Some dropped their weapons, as instructed, but most were in such a rush to put as much distance between themselves and the 'Witch' that they had no other thought but to run. Initially, some twenty of the bravest and most loyal had stood their ground, but as the other eighty or so turned and bolted, half of those lost their courage.

The others didn't last much longer after Raz began moving toward them, twirling Ahna dramatically about his bloody body like he was itching for the fight.

When the final stragglers were gone, scrambling through the broken frame of the court doors, Raz turned back to the dais just in time to see Syrah's magic flicker and retreat, leaving her oddly bland, her hair and robes settling about her as she fell to one knee with a groan. The men scattered about the room blinked and cursed under their breath as they approached the stairs again, some looking up at the wounded Priestess apprehensively, others still gaping around at the destruction left in her wake.

Tossing Ahna over one shoulder, Raz, too, hurried to the dais, kicking aside helmets and debris as he took the steps three at a time.

"Your leg," he muttered worriedly once he reached the top, kneeling so he could study the wound. It was an ugly thing, maybe an inch deep and four wide, and blood still welled from it even as he watched. "What can I do?"

Syrah grimaced in response. "You?" she asked with forced amusement. "Nothing. Me, however..." She passed a hand over the gash. There was a flash of white, and she hissed in pain.

When she pulled the hand away, the smell of seared hair and skin told Raz the slash had been crudely cauterized.

"I'll do a better job later," Syrah muttered, breathing hard and shutting her good eye in what was probably an attempt to control the ache of the sealed wound. Raz nodded absently, his attention already turned back to her face.

After a moment, he reached up with his free hand to cup her chin gently.

"Are you all right?" he asked her softly.

This time, Syrah *did* flinch at his touch, but didn't draw back, bringing her own hands up to grasp at his as she tilted her cheek into his palm, sighing with what might have been relief.

Then she pulled his fingers away.

"No," the Priestess said with a sad shake of her head. "Not at all. But now isn't the time to dwell on it. Like you said: we still need to get out of here."

Raz watched her a moment more, not missing the fact that she didn't let go of his hand. There was a deep, aching sadness across her porcelain features, but he couldn't tell how much was grief for Lysa and Argoan, and how much was sorrow for the broken vows that lay heavy upon her.

"We'll honor the captain and Lysa the moment we get a chance to," he promised her. "If I'd known this is how it was going to end, I never would have had us set foot on that ship…"

Syrah smiled dolefully, choking out the sort of small laugh one gives when one's heart lies in pieces at their feet. "You didn't want to in the first place…" she said, almost despairingly, her lips tightening as she fought back more tears. "You were the only one who… who…"

"Who thought the *Sylgid* might be a trap," Raz finished firmly. "I hesitated out of self-preservation, not out of concern for Argoan and the crew. If their death is anyone's fault, Syrah, it's mine."

"It is not," Akelo's voice broke in. "That blame rests on neither of you."

Together, Raz and Syrah looked around at him. The old Percian had doffed his helmet respectfully and was standing over the place where Garht Argoan's body had been cast across the stone, frowning down at the faint stain of dust that was all that remained of the corpse. Around him, the rowers from the *Moalas* who had survived the palace assault stood by his side, a few with heads bowed as they prayed. Only Aleem, Esser, and Nudar—the only men left alive from the slaves rescued along the eastern roads—waited at the base of the stairs, not having known the captain or his first mate.

"I recall that the captain's boat was manned only by freed slaves and anyone looking to start life anew," Akelo continued, blinking a tear away as he raised his eyes to Raz and Syrah. "He took us aboard without hesitation, even offered us a place among his crew. I cannot imagine he did not know the risks of offering you passage as he did. He was a brave man. He and his first mate both."

And then, for the first time ever, Raz saw Akelo's face twist into something ugly, a wrath-filled, vengeful grimace as the Percian's gaze moved past him and Syrah and on to the figure still twitching on the floor behind the Priestess.

"That he and his first mate were brought here, though," the old *kuja* thundered, ramming his helmet back over his head, "tells me that there *is* someone responsible for their death." He started ascending the steps, drawing his sword as he did. "If anything, their death was ordered by the only man in Karesh Syl with the power to reach them *so far away.*"

There was a grumbling of angry agreement from the others, but as Akelo neared the top of the dais, Raz moved to block his path, barring him from getting any closer to the fallen Tash.

"Not yet, my friend," he told the old man calmly as Akelo started to snarl in outrage at the interruption. "This is not the place. We may yet need him."

"*Need him?*" the Percian demanded in disbelief, his blade clenched so tightly at his side the blade trembled. "The only thing we need is his *head*, Raz!"

"Agreed," Raz answered with a nod, reaching out to take the man by the shoulder, keeping his tone level, "but the manner by which it is taken, and *where* it is taken, could have great importance."

For a few seconds, Raz feared Akelo would punch him, or at least yell at him to get out of his way. Then, though, the man relaxed, realization dawning across his face.

"The Hands as well?" he asked in a much more composed voice.

Raz smiled in grim relief. "Yes. Even as corpses, they'll be of value."

Akelo nodded, his eyes straying back to the shaking form of the dying Tash, still choking and wheezing at the foot of his throne.

Then he sheathed his sword with a *click* and turned to the others gathered across the steps, shouting orders as he descended once more.

As the men began moving, following the Percian's commands and climbing the dais to collect the Tash and the corpses of his former advisors, Raz caught Karan's eye, motioning the young atherian to join him. She stepped in beside him at once, looking curious as he led her back to where Syrah still knelt.

"Karan, help Syrah," he told the female quietly as he lent the Priestess a hand, pulling her to her feet. "Stay with her. Keep the others away as best you can, at least for the time being."

Karan very clearly found this request odd.

"Keep the others... away?" she asked, confused, blinking between the pair of them.

"Far away."

It was Syrah who spoke, her voice a little steadier, though she still looked worn and miserable. Even as she clung to Raz for support, her free hand was absently tracing the scars of her other wrist, and she gave him a pained, grateful smile which only served to rip at his heart even more.

As he'd feared, Lysa was dragging up old memories.

"I'm sorry, Karan," Syrah continued, turning to the younger atherian, who still looked befuddled. "I'll explain as we walk. It might... It might do me good, to talk about it."

Karan, at last, seemed to deduce some inkling of what was going on, and with a sad drop of her face she nodded at once, accepting Syrah's weight and guiding the limping woman back down the steps. They were halfway to the floor below, Raz already turning to see if he could help the others, when the Priestess stopped them and partially turned to look back up at him.

"Raz," she said uncertainly, her face twisting in what might have been sadness. "My... My staff... Could you...?"

"Absolutely," he answered as her request trailed off, already looking around. He found the weapon gleaming some thirty feet from the crater along the right side of the steps, looking as though it had been blasted away by the explosion like most everything else on their side of the room. Hurrying down the stairs, he extracted it from beneath the charred torso of a soldier that had fallen over it, relieved to find the steel unharmed. Returning to the base of the dais where Syrah and Karan waited, he made to hand it over.

For a long moment, the Priestess stared at the staff, her one eye tracing its length with an odd mix of fondness and misery. Eventually she reached out with her free hand, as though to accept it, but hesitated before her fingers could touch the steel.

"Actually," she said, looking up at him miserably as she retracted her hand. "Could you... Could you hold on to it for me? I'm... a little tired..."

If Raz's heart fell any farther, it was going to be crushed beneath his feet. For a second he stared at her, lost for words, starting to see the true toll the morning's events were having on the woman.

"Of course," he said finally, trying for an encouraging smile as he slid the staff over the shoulder where Ahna already rested, but managing only what he thought must have been a pained grin. "Let me know when you want it back."

Syrah nodded gratefully, relaxing as the patterned steel was pulled away. Then, with a final look at him, she and Karan started the long, slow walk up the courtroom, following Akelo and the others as they hauled the Tash and his Hands in pairs toward the shattered doors of the chamber.

It was as he watched them go, grief welling in Raz's throat, that he noticed the gleam along the far wall of the room.

It took him a moment to recognize the curved shape of the head of his sagaris shining against the ash, but when he did he hurried over, picking up the weapon and blowing it free of soot as he checked it for damage. Finding it intact, he looked around, spotting his gladius a dozen feet away. He made for it, sliding the haft of the axe into its loop on his hip even as he bent to pick up the sword.

It was then that Raz discerned a weak, broken chuckle from his left.

At once, he whirled, snarling instinctively, blade held at the ready. Expecting to be faced with some enemy that had been lying in wait in the smoky shadows of the battle's aftermath, it took him a moment to figure out what he was seeing, his mind playing catch-up to his body.

Finally, Raz realized he was looking into the hard, empty eyes of Azzeki Koro, propped up with his back against a nearby pillar, legs splayed out over the floor and white teeth stained with blood even as he grinned devilishly.

"I guess my gamble didn't pay off?" the Percian wheezed, watching Raz straighten slowly at the sight. "Almost, though. Almost."

Raz said nothing, studying the man's shattered body for a long moment. Koro looked to have avoided the worst of the flames. Only his left arm and leg were seared and smoking, like he'd managed to drag himself across the ground to get behind the column just in time. By the way the limbs dangled, though, along with his other leg, Raz realized that the man appeared to have no control over them. Only his right arm still worked, and then just barely, his hand and fingers loose and useless as the former Captain-Commander of the Azbar guard reached up to awkwardly wipe blood and spittle from his lip.

Koro had broken his neck.

"Na'zeem *told* us to watch out for the woman," the Percian continued with an exasperated sigh as Raz started moving slowly toward him. "He told us. I thought we listened, but I guess not well enough. In the end, I was as blind as all the others."

Raz frowned in disgust, reaching the former assassin and easing himself down to squat before the man.

"Garht Argoan and his first mate," he growled, easing Ahna and Syrah's staff off his shoulder and onto the floor by his feet. "Your idea, I take it? I recall Quin Tern tried something similar. You should have known better..."

Koro shrugged, or tried to, only managing to awkwardly hitch his right shoulder a little.

"It was all about the timing," he said with a huff, so dispassionately they might have been talking about what part of the day was best for a jaunt about the city. "So close. So close." He gave Raz another reddened grin, raising his lame hand again to tap at his forehead with some difficulty. "Almost had you. Right there. Right between the eyes. So close."

"Almost," Raz told him with a slow nod. "But you failed, as cowards tend to do."

Koro's face twisted in anger.

"Coward?" he demanded in a wheezing voice as he struggled to breathe. "*I* met you face-to-face. *I* drew first blood. *I* was nearer than anyone to becoming the slayer of 'the Monster.'"

"No," Raz said with a shake of his head. "You weren't. Another came closer. *Much* closer. And as vile a man as he was, he was anything *but* a coward. He didn't hide in the shadows, waiting for the moment to strike. He didn't strive to use my heart and conscience against me." Raz snorted, bending forward the slightest bit so he was eye-to-eye with the man. "If you're hoping to die with the pride of being the closest, know that you are a distant, *distant* second, and craven to boot."

At that, Koro did his best to lunge, his howl of outrage weak and pathetic as he swung his limp arm at Raz's face.

He didn't even get close to landing the blow before Raz's left hand took him about the mouth, crushing his jaw shut as he slammed his head back against the column behind it.

"No," he hissed into Koro's ear then, baring his fangs and leaning forward to bring them inches from the side of his face. "No. No more surprises. No more daggers in the night. You feel you deserve my respect? Feel you deserve my admiration? The only thing you've ever earned from me is wrath, Azzeki Koro. You've butchered too many of my friends, stood in my way too many times. I should have killed you when you blocked my path in the Arena, should have torn you to pieces then and there."

Raz drew his head back so that his golden eyes could bore into the Percian's. "This is better, though," he hissed hungrily, lifting the gladius he still held bare in his hand and pressing its edge to the man's throat. "There's something I've wanted to do for almost a year now, Koro. Something I *do* feel I owe you."

Then, with slow, deliberate ease, Raz drew the blade sideways, feeling it cut through skin and flesh.

"I wondered what it must have felt like," Raz continued loudly, raising his voice over Koro's muffled scream of pain and terror through the leather of his gauntlet, utterly ignoring the man's flailing right arm as the Percian tried desperately to fight him off. As blood began to flow across the steel of the gladius, Raz laughed. "I wondered what thoughts must have crossed your mind, as a little girl cut her own throat on your blade."

The sword wasn't even halfway along when Raz felt it start to saw through windpipe, and Azzeki Koro's screaming stopped even as his thrashing redoubled

"Is this what you lived for?" Raz asked him, pressing the man's head harder back against the stone. "For the moment where you owned another completely? Where everything they were or could be started to slip through your fingers as they died? Is this what brought you pleasure, what brought you joy?"

The last few inches of steel found bone and, as Raz finished drawing the gladius through the man's neck, Koro's violent struggles began to lessen.

"I can see the appeal," Raz told him with a cold smile, staring into the man's eyes as the light began to fade from them, blood pouring in a sheet from the great wound that now half-severed his neck. "Given the right situation, I can *certainly* see the appeal. I knew a little girl once, too, who might have felt the same…"

LVIII

"Do not be fooled into believing that cutting the head from the snake will put a quick end to the fight. The body will thrash and squirm, struggling to live without the mind. In the end, it will die, but—in the meantime—try not to be crushed in the writhing of its coils…"

—Ergoin Sass

The battle came to a head in the very central plaza of the south-east district, the Sun blazing clean and fearsome to the west in the clear mid-morning sky. It was a good sign, Dulan Yazir hoped, glancing up at Him from atop his destrier, thinking it might be a favorable omen in the fight to come.

That didn't help his nerves, though, as his attention was drawn earthward again by the rumbling of their enemy, innumerable and seething, across the vast expanse of the square.

The slaves had spent the night wreaking havoc across the quarter, chasing residents from their homes, burning down shops and food stores and granaries, and freeing their fellows from the other camps scattered about the sector. With each compound razed their numbers had swollen, until now Dulan and the other generals faced well over fifteen thousand desperate rebels armed with anything they could get their hands on. Most wielded nothing more than bars of wood and iron they ripped from buildings and palisades, but a fair number bore stolen and scavenged swords and shields, a few even looking like they'd learned at some point in their miserable lives how to use them. At his back, Dulan could feel the nervousness rippling throughout their own ranks, cascading like a wave as muttering and prayers spread through the soldiers. The plaza was a massive space, but it wasn't *near* large enough to house either force, much less both of them. The roads and side-streets that webbed out from the square were as packed and churning as the main bodies of the armies, the only clear space in sight being the twenty meters of open ground between the generals and the front line of the mobbing slaves. In every direction, shouting and screaming and the ring of steel were steadily gathering, like the skirmishes that had plagued the evening and early morning when starting up again. It did little to settle Dulan's uneasiness.

Nor—apparently—the other generals'.

"What in the *Sun's name* is going on?" Enaro Sulva, Lord General of the Tash's army, snarled under his breath from atop his speckled charger, the plume of his spiked helmed swaying to and fro as he tried to casually glance left and right. "We should have received orders *an hour ago*! Where are the First's runners?"

"Lost to the outskirts, undoubtedly," Abul Haro, one of the Lord General's two deputies, muttered in response from over his superior's right shoulder, frowning as he looked west. "Those clashes sound like they may be getting out of hand…"

"Agreed," Zale Ima, commander of the south gate, pitched in from off to Dulan's left. "Whatever orders the honored First might have for us may not reach us in time, Sulva. You will have to make a field decision."

The Lord General stiffened at Ima's informal address of him, but said nothing in rebuke. He might outrank the man, but no one ever forgot that the lower general was also the elder brother of the Second Hand, and that alone came with some clout.

Dulan had never liked Ima—the man was a shame to his uniform, taking advantage of his position to openly run a successful smuggling operation in and out of the city—but he couldn't help but admire his gall sometimes…

"So be it," Enaro Sulva growled, tucking his chin as he scanned the mass of slaves ahead of them, some of whom had started to yell and throw stones, bits of bricks or wood, or whatever else they could get their hands on. After a moment, the Lord General reached around his hips and unsheathed his sword, roaring his command as he thrust the weapon into the air.

"DRAW!"

As Dulan and the other generals followed his lead, the lieutenants on foot along the front line of the army behind them echoed the order, and within seconds the hard sound of thousands upon thousands of blades being freed rang about the high walls of the buildings that surrounded them.

Over it all, though, the sounds of fighting to the west still appeared to be growing louder.

"SLAVES OF KARESH SYL!" Sulva boomed, heeling his horse forward several yards as he addressed their enemy. "THIS IS YOUR LAST CHANCE TO SURRENDER! DROP YOUR WEAPONS AND RETURN TO YOUR CAMPS, AND YOU HAVE MY WORD AS LORD GENERAL THAT ALL PUNISHMENTS WILL BE MINIMAL! STAND AND FIGHT, AND WE WILL NOT HESITATE TO SUBDUE YOU BY ANY FORCE NECESSARY!"

The response was instantaneous. If Sulva had hoped for an easy victory, he was sure to be disappointed. At once, the mob of slaves swelled and rippled, roaring and jeering in infuriated unison as they pelted the man with debris, forcing him to drop the reins of his animal in favor of raising his shield overhead. With a curse, he guided the horse around with his knees, still protecting his neck from behind as rocks, heavy iron horseshoes, and even a few vegetables continued to rain down about his shoulders.

"Moon take them all," he raged as he returned to their line, his cheek bleeding from where a projectile looked to have caught him across the face. "Enough is enough. The South's slavers will have a wealthy business these next few months." He reached up and straightened his helmet, then brushed dust and pebbles from his greying beard, glancing nervously westward as he did.

"Time to end this," he said finally, pulling his horse around again and bellowing out once more. "SOLDIERS! READY!"

"SOLDIERS READY!" the generals echoed in unison, looking to their lieutenants, who repeated the command yet again. As the thundering *clunks* of shields being lifted and interlocked vibrated around the square, the Lord General lifted his blade once more.

"SOLDIERS!" he boomed. "MARCH!"

And with that, the Tash's army started forward, a bristling wave of white-and-gold leather, shields, and raised swords splitting around the generals in a steady wave to slowly close the gap between themselves and the gathered slaves.

Before the soldiers even made it halfway across the plaza, though, a voice unlike anything Dulan had ever heard ripped through the thrum of boots on stone and the taunting and shouts of the revolting slaves.

"HOLD!"

The voice was so fierce, so commanding, that a large portion of the front line of the advancing army faltered, almost tripping over one another. In the ensuing confusion, the march slowed, warping as the men along the west edge of the plaza came to a complete standstill, like they were afraid of pressing forward while the rest continuing on uncertainly. As one, Dulan and the other generals turned toward the voice, and with a thrill of fearful awe understood why.

"All Her Stars…" one of the others cursed from Dulan's left, and he couldn't blame them their astonishment.

The Dragon of the North, after all, had himself just stepped out from an alley into the open space between the two armies.

The appearance of Raz i'Syul Arro, the Monster of Karth, rocked the scene of the approaching battle as surely as an earthquake might have rent apart the square. There was a roar of enthusiastic excitement from the slaves, cheers ringing up from their ranks and building until it made Dulan's head hurt. On the other hand, the Tash's soldiers, apparently forgetting their vast number, balked as the beast strode past them, moving so swiftly across the now-mere thirty feet of empty space between the armies that he was in front of the generals before anyone had a chance to shout the alarm. At once the soldiers who stood in the vicinity of the officers' horses yelled and converged, encircling their superiors dutifully with body and shield.

The Dragon, though, made no move to attack.

The atherian had been described to every soldier in the Tash's army a hundred times in the last month or so, but the depiction Dulan had built in his head didn't remotely do the creature justice. He stood an easy seven feet tall, clad in exquisitely crafted steel armor that encased parts of his arms and legs, complete with a pair of plate gauntlets that ended in long metal claws. In one hand he held an odd pair of weapons, a silver staff and the strange, twin-bladed spear the whispers claimed he'd named after a murdered sister. In the other, a long-handled axe Dulan recognized as a sagaris, a common weapon of Perce's eastern pirates. The Dragon seemed to have no distinguishing markings, but his golden eyes were bright against the blackness of his scales, more alive than any Dulan had witnessed among his kind. They smoldered with calm, confident danger, sharp and calculating despite the fact that the beast was on the verge of being pinned in the center of what promised to be a bloody exchange. Then, to his horror, Dulan realized that both armies had stopped , the sheer presence of the Dragon in the center of the plaza apparently enough to press both sides into hesitation.

Maybe it had something to do with the fact that the winged atherian looked a violent mess, hardly a square inch of him—from his clawed feet to the pommel of the straight sword slung across his back—not stained in dark blood, like he'd waged a one-man war to reach them.

With this unnerving thought, Dulan glanced back toward the west alley the beast had emerged from, noting the sudden lack of battle sounds.

That was when Arro started to speak.

"Are you in command of these forces, officer?" he asked impassively, looking up at Enaro Sulva, his voice deep and utterly unflinching.

The Lord General had been gaping at the atherian, taking him in with such utter astonishment the lizard might as well have been some gilded envoy of the Moon herself. He stirred, though, at Arro's words, remembering his place.

"Mind your tongue, creature!" he snapped, a muscle twitching in his cheek as his horse shuffled beneath him. "You speak to the Lord General of the Tash's armies, second only to Yseri Suro, First Hand of His Greatness and—"

"So you *are* in charge," the Dragon cut him off with an irritated curl of his lip, revealing the white fangs beneath. "Excellent. I would have us discuss the terms of your surrender."

That took all the wind out of Sulva's sails, at least for a moment. The man's words choked off, and for a breath he looked utterly lost for words.

Finally, anger got the better of him.

"'OUR SURRENDER?'" he roared indignantly, so enraged his horse half-reared in surprise. "Are you *mad*, lizard? Perhaps, given you're fool enough to stand between us and the swift ruination of this little revolt you've caused." He swept his sword over the Dragon's head, indicating the slaves still lined behind the beast, men and women and children and atherian of all ages and sizes. "I've had enough. You will regret showing your face here. We will crush you beneath our boots, just as we will crush your rebellion. SOLDIERS! MAR—!"

"My men are *at this moment* in the process of assaulting the slave camps in the north- and southwest districts," the Dragon interrupted him yet again, his voice carrying over the plaza like the boom of a massive bell. His eyes swept across the army before him. "If you wonder how many I could possibly have slipped into the city without your notice, it matters little. They have been reinforced by a large majority of the six hundred slaves once kept by the Tash."

Only the clashing of the outskirts could be heard after this announcement. It washed over the generals and their army with such force they were struck dumb, registering the layers of the atherian's claim. The camps in the other districts? If that was true—if Arro's men somehow managed to liberate even two of the three remaining districts—then the Tash's army would be outnumbered five to one at least.

More concerning, though, was the far subtler implication that he had *already* freed the slaves of the palace…

Dulan felt a stone drop into his stomach as he considered that possibility.

"Do not attempt to spread your deceit here, lizard," Sulva finally managed to get out, eyes narrowed through the slots of his half-helm. "We will not fall for your lies so easily."

In response, Arro only looked left toward the alley mouth he had appeared from, waving something forward with his axe. At once a knocking, rumbling sound picked up, like wood on stone.

"I'm no fool, Lord General," the Dragon said without bothering to turn back to the officers. "I would never expect you to believe me without cause."

As he said this, an odd pair of figures appeared from between the buildings, a female atherian with a patch of yellow scales beneath her neck, helping along a hobbling woman Dulan recognized at once. Syrah Brahnt did not bear herself with the calm confidence of the Dragon, though. He had imagined her as a tall, regal figure, standing in flowing white silks that matched her hair, with magic of fire and light twisting in her eyes. *This* woman, though, looked weighed-down and tired, the front and arms of her robes smeared and stained with what might have been soot, her face dirty and one eye covered by a crude swath of black cloth. There was something dangerous in that gaze, though, and she held her head high—with what seemed like great effort—to look the generals in the face.

Still, none of the officers spent more than a few seconds studying her or the young atherian, their attention pulled almost immediately to what followed the pair of them into the square.

A two-wheeled cart, clattering over the cobblestones beneath it, bumped steadily into view.

It was a narrow, dirty thing, hauled by a pair of ragged-looking women in filthy smocks who looked simultaneously utterly terrified and distinctly proud to be present for this unexpected display. The smell that wafted from it almost made Dulan balk, but as it approached any revulsion at the thing was washed away by growing fear. The walls of the cart were deep, but from atop their horses the man had little doubt the other generals, like him, had caught a glimpse of what lay within as it bounced along. By the time the two women brought it to a creaking halt beside where Brahnt and the atherian had come to stand on the Dragon's right, Dulan felt his body growing cold.

When the lizard moved around to the far side of the thing, Dulan found his voice paralyzed, unable to shout out, to stop the man.

"Lord General!" the Dragon called over the quiet of the plaza, dragging Sulva's eyes to him and putting a clawed foot on the wall of the cart as the two slaves scurried out of the way. "Tell me… is this enough proof for you?"

He gave the cart a massive shove, overturning it with a *crash* and allowing its horrid contents to spill over the plaza at the feet of the army of Karesh Syl.

As one, there was a resounding wail of horror and denial from the soldiers.

Among the putrid detritus and rotting food that must have half-filled the bed, a trio of bodies lay partially buried. Two were still and growing rigid as rigor mortis settled into their limbs, their corpses and clothes ravaged by what looked to have been some sort of fire. Still, their faces were mostly recognizable, and Dulan choked as he stared into their dead eyes.

That was nothing, though, compared to when his gaze settled on the shivering, convulsing form of the last man.

"Sun take us," a soldier started muttering nearby. "Sun take us all…"

Dulan, silently, joined in the prayer.

The figure was the least recognizable of the lot but—by some terrible mercy of the Twins—seemed to have survived whatever flame or magic or dragonfire it was that had stolen away the lives of the other two. His face was raw and blistered, the skin of his cheeks bubbling up and peeling away. His torso and arms were little more than wet muscle and charred flesh through which bone gleamed white and black from the terrible oozing wounds. He was gasping as he convulsed, his mouth moving wordlessly, eyes flinching around to settle briefly on the Dragon, then the soldiers, then each of the generals. When the wild stare met his, it took all Dulan had not to vomit over the side of his horse.

How else could one react, after all, upon witnessing the great Tash and His honored Hands dead and dying, strewn among the palace refuse like common filth…?

"No…" Enaro Sulva could be heard to say, his voice breathless and weak. "By Her Stars… No…"

Then, though, a louder, harsher shout rose up abruptly.

"BASTARD! I'LL KILL YOU!"

Before anyone could stop him, Zale Ima howled and heeled his horse forward into an all-out charge, seemingly not even remotely concerned for the soldiers his mount slammed out of the way. He broke through the front line in mere seconds, sword swinging above his head as he rode down the Dragon, who was just stepping back around the upended cart.

"IMA! WAIT!" the Lord General shouted after him desperately, but it was far too late. The man and his horse barreled forward, thundering toward Arro, who watched him come almost lazily, even taking the time to settle his spear and the steel staff against the nearest upturned wheel.

Then Ima was on the beast, his blade striking down as he roared.

"FOR MY BROTHER!"

It was over in a flash of steel and the *thud* of a body against stone.

No one saw the Dragon move. No one saw the axe flick up to trap the wrist of Ima's sword-arm in the crook of its head and pull the blow away and earthward. All they registered was the general bearing down on the lizard in one moment, screaming in grief and hate, and in the next he was unhorsed, dragged from the animal's back with a gasp as his mount continued on, forcing several of the slaves behind Arro to yell and throw themselves out of the way. Ima hit the ground with a sickening *crunch*, his helmet *clanging* hard against the stone. It was in that briefest of instants that people began to shout, voices from the Tash's army yelling in alarm while the rebels howled in triumph.

Then, in a blink, the Dragon dragged the axe still secured around the man's wrist upward, flipped the general over onto his stomach as the man began to scream in pain, and brought a clawed foot down on the back of his neck.

In less than five seconds, Zale Ima, general of the Tash's army, commander of the south gate, lay dead in the dust beside his younger brother.

The Dragon, though, wasn't done.

In two steps he stood over the convulsing form of the Tash, reaching down with his now-free hand to grab the man by the little that was left of what must have once been white-and-purple robes, hauling him from the mess he was half-buried under. He dragged him up the heap and over the bodies of the dead Hands, the old man choking and writhing as he tried vainly to fight through his shock. From the top of the pile Arro took a single great step onto the side of the upturned cart, heaving the Tash up behind him, and pulled the man around so that he settled awkwardly onto his knees between the atherian's clawed feet.

Now raised some four feet above the throng of soldiers and slaves that penned them in, Arro settled the hook of his axe head under the Tash's weeping, blistered throat.

"Listen well, soldiers of Karesh Syl!" the Dragon announced in a carrying roar, not even bothering to look to the generals now as he gazed down on the footmen of the army. "Your city falls, and your sovereign has fallen. Your Tash will die. There is no stopping that now, and over the next few days the slaves you have so diligently oppressed and abused for generations will rise up and repay you all your cruelties twice over. You have a choice to make now, and it is a simple one: live, or die."

"Do not heed him!" Enaro Sulva roared, pointing his sword at the man. "Soldiers of Karesh Syl, it is our duty as sworn protectors of—!"

"Of WHAT?" the Dragon snarled in response, cutting him off so viciously the front line blanched. "Protectors of WHAT, Lord General? Of the borders of your city?" He smirked, raising his eyes to the fading plumes of smoke still lingering over the rooftops that hung over them. "You have already failed there. Protectors of *this* man?" He jerked the axe back a little, causing the Tash to spasm and choke in his grip as the beast's amber eyes continued to scan the army. "He will die regardless of what you might do. Steel is a mercy now, to say the least. No... You are protectors of *nothing*, of *no one*. There is no more left for you to stand for, to die for. It is for this reason, I say, that the choice is simple. Fight here, now, and you may certainly win. The odds are in your favor, I admit. If you do that, none of you will live to see the next Moon rise. What men survive the battle will be nothing more than a pest to be eradicated by the greater will of those you have only ever shown cruelty and contempt towards. You will be hunted, like animals for sport, scattered and disjointed as you and those you care for are hounded and slaughtered."

He grinned grimly, then. "Or... You can take your lives and flee. You can come to the same understanding the palace guard did when I told them there is nothing to die for here, and *much* to live for somewhere else. You have my word I will do all in my power to guarantee you safe passage from the city. You will have the chance to start anew, to leave this place behind with your families and hopes and desires intact before I see it all turned to ash and rubble."

There were several seconds of harsh silence after this, the sounds of fighting echoing overhead like an omen.

Finally, a voice from the middle of the ranks called out.

"What of the nobility?" the soldier asked, lost among his brethren. "What's to become of our lords and ladies?"

Arro had just opened his mouth to answer when Enaro Sulva cut him off.

"ENOUGH!" the Lord General howled in outrage, the outburst from one of his own men apparently the very last straw his nerves could tolerate. "It is not for us to choose how our lives are to end! If we are to die in defense of His Greatness and Karesh Syl, then SO BE IT! I will not stand by while—!"

Shlang!

Once more, Arro moved so fast, most didn't catch the throw. The axe was a blur of silver. It ripped through the air in a rush of wind before taking Sulva between the eyes, splitting the steel and cloth cushioning of his plumed helm like paper. The Lord General's body keeled back, getting hooked for a brief second on the straps of his saddle as blood coursed darkly over the black skin of his nose and cheeks.

Then the straps slipped, and Sulva's corpse fell to the plaza floor with a *thud.*

"I make the same guarantee for your nobility." The Dragon boomed on as though nothing out of sorts had happened, utterly ignoring the shocked expressions on every face before him. "If anything, let us see how they fair among the cruelties of a life without means and wealth."

There was a rumbling of assent at that.

"You may *live*," the Dragon pressed them, still holding tight to the dying Tash. "There is no need to die here, today. Karesh Syl is no more. Before week's end, I will see it burn." He looked around then, almost imploringly. "I would ask you not to force me to bury you and your families among those ruins."

At this, Arro reached down and pulled the Tash up with both hands by the collar of his tattered robes, half-turning as he did. For several seconds he stared into the man's wide eyes, taking him in as though burning the triumph of the moment into his memory.

Finally, he addressed the soldier one last time.

"The choice is yours, now," the Dragon of the North boomed over the silence, never looking away from the Ekene Okonso's terrified face. "Live… or die broken and alone."

And with that, he flung the old man fifteen feet back off the cart, into the waiting mob of freed slaves, who fell on him with howls and roars of glee that were pierced only for the briefest moment by a single horrible scream of pain and fear.

LIX

*"Of one kind, and yet of another,
wings and wind bear him forth.
From chains comes his second birth
and never shall he stand for them.
Child of the Daystar, he will speak the language
and be the speaker of his people.
To leave and then return,
bearing a woman of ice and snow on his arm."*

—Uhsula of the Other Worlds

Raz looked down the sweeping expanse of the hill from atop Gale, feeling the cool caress of the wind whisper through his wings and armor. The breezes of the cooler seasons were calmer here, gentler, he realized. Perce was, in so many ways, a much milder world than the harsh sands of the South.

As the others caught up to him, though, the collective hammer of their horses' hooves thudding over the grasslands, he felt his enthusiasm waver and fade, and he frowned down at the sight far, far below.

The sprawl of the city could not have been more unlike the towering wonder of Karesh Syl, but was no less impressive. It spread, seemingly without pattern or purpose, over the swaying terrain of southern Perce, its broad encircling wall snaking itself into a loop up and down and around the land, cutting the carefully knit buildings within off from the plains that surrounded them. Within the eastern swell of the city a structure rose, familiar in its build, a pattern of geometric structures surrounding fragile petal-like constructions that curved inward toward a central tower.

The Sun, the Moon, and all Her Stars... Raz thought to himself, grimacing as he remembered Akelo explaining to him how the palace of Karesh Syl had been a tribute to the Twins.

"Looks like they've spotted us."

Akelo himself pulled his mount up beside him, then, and Raz glanced around at the man just long enough to take in the now-familiar white-and-gold leathers that had become the *kuja*'s habitual armor. Akelo, though, wasn't looking at him, his eyes somber through the slots of his spiked helm as he, too, took in the city below. Following his gaze, Raz saw that a great gate in the northern façade of the wall had opened, and that a swarm of figures—too far away to distinguish individually—was pouring out of the city to form up in ranks a hundred yards into the plains. Indeed, as he listened, the sound of blowing horns and ringing alarm bells reached his sensitive ears.

"Looks like it," he agreed with a humorless smirk. "Guess we've lost the element of surprise."

On his other side, Syrah chuckled darkly.

"If you think that's ever going to be an advantage we can count on again, I'd reassess a few things."

Raz snorted, turning to eye her for a moment.

Syrah was bedecked in the swath of grey and black silks several of their freed slaves had cobbled together for her from the supplies they'd pilfered from Karesh Syl. Her dark hood was up, but as the cooler seasons had started the Sun had grown kinder, and she'd only rarely been forced to shield her face. It made Raz sad, in a strange way. When the days grew too bright, Syrah had no choice but to don the pale veil the Laorin had gifted her, nearly seven months ago now.

It was the only time she ever touched any of her old things.

"They want to meet us in the open field?" Karan Brightneck asked from Syrah's far side. "That seems foolish…"

Raz smiled at the comment. He'd grown fond of the young atherian over the last several weeks. The female was smart, quick-thinking, and fast on her feet. Best of all, she wasn't human, and she wasn't male. It made her the perfect companion for Syrah, and Raz didn't think he ever saw the two far from each other when the Priestess wasn't with him.

"It's a greeting party," Raz replied, indicating the gathering soldiers below them with a steel claw, drawing parallel lines in the air. "There can't be more than five hundred, and see how they're lining up on either side of the gate? It's a presentation. If you give them a moment… There."

As he said it, one last figure exited the city, this time on horseback. Raz still couldn't distinguish the details of the man's armor or face, but he was fairly sure even Syrah and Akelo on either side of him could make out the massive strip of white cloth, cut into a decorative triangle, waving along atop the spear the rider had thrust skyward in one hand.

Karan cursed in disbelief at the sight, slipping into the guttural tongue of the atherian. The female had been teaching Raz and Syrah the language, and while Raz was having ironic difficulties mastering the enunciations, the Priestess was picking it up with rapid ease, claiming it wasn't so different from the throaty syllables of the Northern wild men.

"A truce?" Karan demanded derisively. "They want a truce?"

"Ultimately, it's possible," Akelo answered her from Raz's left. "For the moment, it's more likely they're looking to simply parley."

"But we're *not* going to parley," Karan said, her confidence in the statement betrayed by the pleading look she gave Raz, who was still watching the antics at the gate below them. "Right? Tell me we're *not* going to offer them terms…"

Raz, for his part, didn't look away from the scene of the city, studying its walls and the lounging drape of lavish buildings that covered the swaying land like a stain across the face of the world. In his mind, he tried to imagine what erecting such a wonder must have cost, what the toll of lives had been to raise such magnificence from nothing but dirt and grass.

He didn't even realize how long he stayed silent, gripping his reins so tight they were on the verge of tearing, when Syrah's hand settled on his arm.

He turned to look at her, taking a steadying breath. She was watching him with her one good eye, the warmth in its rose depths drawing him back to the moment.

"What do you want to do?" she asked him.

For a few seconds, Raz didn't look away from her, taking what strength he could from her gaze. Then, straightening himself in his saddle, he pulled Gale around to face north, looking out over the fields on the other side of the hill.

His breath caught in his throat, as it had every time he'd taken in the scene at his back over the last four weeks of marching.

"Akelo," he said quietly, "send a rider. I have a message for the city."

"Aye," the Percian responded at once, pulling his horse around to peer across the plains. "And what would you have him say?"

For a moment, Raz said nothing, gazing out over the scene before them.

A hundred meters across, almost thirty thousand men and women stood at the ready in a trio of practiced columns each nearly half a mile long. At their head, a thousand cavalry riders Akelo and Cyper had personally picked awaited their orders, seated tall and proud atop the stallions and destriers they'd pillaged from the Tash's own stables. At the rear, some two hundred carts and covered wagons, recovered from the food stores and granaries and the fields around the city, were still trundling along over the uneven surface of the savannah, bearing with them all their supplies. Steel gleamed even in the overcast light of noon, swords and shields and spiked helms pillaged from the barracks and armories after the armies of Karesh Syl had laid down their arms and been routed from the walls. Armor had been salvaged and distributed as evenly as possible, and it had taken Raz some time to get used to seeing the men and women under his command bedecked in the white and gold that had once been the oppressive colors of Karesh Syl.

Now, the sight only filled him with pride and courage.

After all, nearly a third of the city's newly-freed slaves had flocked to the Dragon's banner when word had spread of where Raz i'Syul Arro was marching on next. A banner that now rose at the very apex of the army, hefted in Hur's powerful hands form atop his horse, depicting a human woman with long hair that covered her bare breasts, seeming to fly on leathery wings extending over each of her shoulders.

The emblem, of course, had been painted over the crossed golden spears of a vanquished enemy.

Finally, Raz spoke.

"Tell them there will be no parley," the Dragon growled, lifting his eyes to where the somber glow of the clouds hid the Sun from view. "Tell them they have a choice: free those they've bound in iron, or witness their city crumble to steel and flame."

From among the ranks of the army, several dozen sets of golden eyes watched the top of the hill to the south, studying the forms of Raz i'Syul Arro and his confidants, outlined against the grey sky atop their steeds. It hadn't taken long after the fall of the Tash for the group to form, for the individuals to find one another and gather. As one—and as they often did when the march came to an end—their gazes lingered on 'the Dragon', assessing him, studying him.

Striving to learn from afar what kind of man he was, had been, and might be.

In the center of their midst, one male of about forty summers turned to his older female companion.

"*He must be told*," Urlen whispered in their native tongue. "*The moment approaches, Zal'en.*"

"*No yet*," the female answered with a frown, the greying membranes of her ears twitching as she watched Arro's third-in-command—Akelo Aseni—break off from the others and return to the main force. "*It is not the time.*"

"*When is the time, then?*" a younger female, somewhere in her late score of years, demanded from Zal'en's right. She sounded more desperate than impatient, fingers absently tracing the scars about the wrist of the hand that clutched the hilt of the sword at her side. "*Zal'en, please. He needs to know.*"

"*Not. Yet.*" Zal'en's voice was firm but kind as she looked to the female, giving her an encouraging smile. "*We are far from the sands of the Daystar, young one. I don't know if even Uhsula herself can see us here. It is not our place to speak for the gods. If the First Born wishes Raz i'Syul to know all that he is and could be, He will find a way.*"

"*And yet every hour we wait, more of our kind are stolen away and thrown in chains*," Urlen muttered angrily in response. "*What would you suggest we do, in the meantime?*"

"*In the meantime*," Zal'en answered calmly, eyes lifting once more to the broad form of Raz i'Syul Arro, stoic and powerful atop his great black warhorse, white silk cloak whispering about him in the breeze, "*we fight to ensure our Queen has her heir returned to the world from which he was born.*"

EPILOGUE

"The Monster isn't what you think. If you pull his strings, expect him to bite, not dance."

—Ergoin Sass, to Imaneal Evony

"Karesh Nan has fallen."

The woman's voice, like silk splitting over a sharpened blade, dragged Adrion from sleep so violently he couldn't help but gasp as he awoke. He knew better than to yell, of course, to call for help or summon the guards. All the same, his heart thudded in his chest, his mind reeling to cope with his sudden consciousness. He floundered in his sheets, pushing himself up and back against the carved oak of the headboard with some difficulty, the stump of his left leg a useless reminder of his own weakness. When he managed to sit up, breathing hard as sweat began to cool on his back and arms against the chill of the evening, the man peered about the darkness, searching the corners of the room.

To his surprise, he found Lazura easily enough, seated in a chair by his feet, the paleness of her thin silks distinct against the black of the night. Even in the dark he felt a conflicted knot build in his stomach when he took her in. Her face, beautiful and perfect, was partially lost to the shadows, but the fabrics draped about her frame were of that seductive fragility she'd always been partial to, toeing the edge of indecency but leaving enough for the imagination to wonder at.

The effect it had on the man was disconcerting, given that every other part of his mind was screaming at him to get as far away from the woman as possible.

Then, though, he saw the loose roll of parchment she held in one hand, rolling it back and forth between her fingers, the wax seal broken along the lip of the letter.

"So soon?" he asked her, relieved that he was able to control the fear in his voice, his question coming out even and surprised. "It's hardly been a month since we received word that Karesh Syl had been razed…"

"Our spies inform me it was not a long battle," Lazura said calmly, though there was a tremor in her voice that revealed the fury she was clearly attempting to subdue. "Apparently your cousin has been busy training his men on the march."

Adrion bristled at the subtle jab, but brushed it aside.

"An unfortunate development," he said, annoyed. "*Very* unfortunate, even. But you'll forgive me if I say I don't see why this couldn't wait until morning."

"There's more," Lazura hissed, and the danger in her tone was palpable now, like poison in the air. "It seems you may have to suffer a family reunion soon, Adrion."

At that, Adrion felt his stomach turn over, and he inhaled sharply.

"Here?" he demanded, the word shrill with uncertain trepidation. "The bastard is coming here? You're sure?"

In response, there was a *snap*, then a searing flash of white light that nearly blinded the man as the letter in Lazura's hand erupted into brilliant white flames. All the same, Adrion couldn't find the strength in his arms to raise them to shield himself from the glare. His eyes were transfixed, staring at the spot where the woman's face had been illuminated, visible in the dark for one brief, horrible second.

There, in the lines of what were usually delicate, fragile features that bore well the beauty of her Northern heritage, Adrion saw something unlike anything he had ever borne witness to. A deep, horrifying hunger echoed over the rage etched into the scars about Lazura's right eye, twisting the woman's face into something monstrous, something utterly demonic.

In that moment, in that one, petrifying instant, the sorceress was far, *far* less human than Adrion thought the "Dragon of the North" could ever be.

"I am *sure*," Lazura's voice slithered through the dark of his stolen vision as the letter fell to ashes from her hand, her words as sharp as a viper's bite. "Arro has finished his work in Perce. Over a week ago, his army turned north, fifty thousand strong now."

There was a moment's pause, like the woman wanted the venom in this news to seep, icy and pure, into Adrion's very bones.

"The Monster of Karth, it appears, is coming home."

NOTE FROM THE AUTHOR
[AKA: THE PLIGHT OF THE WRITER]

It seems insane that I find myself yet again at this point, wrapping up As Iron Falls. It is such an incredible feeling to see your characters come to life, and yet the prospect of releasing them out into the world is also terrifying. Release them we must, though, and we do so with the hopes of getting them in front of as many eyes as the world will allow.

It is with this note that I move on to a more personal plea, a cry for assistance from all of you who got to the end of the book and were even just a little bit sad to have to put it down:

Please, *please*, consider rating and reviewing *As Iron Falls* on Amazon or any of your favorite book sites..

Many people don't know that there are thousands of books published every day, most of those in the USA alone. Over the course of a year, a quarter of a million authors will vie for a small place in the massive world of print and publishing. We fight to get even the tiniest traction, fight to climb upward one inch at a time towards the bright light of bestsellers, publishing contracts, and busy book signings.

Thing is, we need all the help we can get.

Your positive input into that world, however small you believe your voice may be, makes the climb just a little bit easier. Rating and reviewing books you enjoy gives your favorite authors a boost upward.

With that all out of the way, thank you so much for picking up *As Iron Falls*. If you'd like to give me feedback directly, have a question about Raz and his adventures, or just want to chat, drop me a message on Twitter or Facebook, or directly at bryce@bryceoconnorbooks.com.

As ever, it has been an honor to entertain you, and I vigorously hope you continue to follow *The Wings of War* series to see what becomes of Raz i'Syul Arro.

Bryce O'Connor
https://www.patreon.com/bryceoconnor

77840522R00236

Made in the USA
Middletown, DE
26 June 2018